TRUE LOVE THE HARD WAY

BY

RAY CARPENTER

This book is a work of fiction. Places, events, and situations in this story are purely fictional. Any resemblance to actual persons, living or dead, is coincidental.

ISBN: 1-4107-6078-2 (e-book)
ISBN: 1-4107-6077-4 (Paperback)
ISBN: 1-4140-2732-X (Dust Jacket)

Library of Congress Control Number: 2003093721

This book is printed on acid free paper.

Printed in the United States of America
Bloomington, IN

1stBooks - rev. 10/30/03

Table of Content

The Texas Tornado

The day was March 28 in the year 2000. It was late afternoon; the sky was eerily dark and ominous. The clouds in the western sky looked very angry. The following is the way I can best remember it.

As I looked up at the sky, it was spitting lightning every few seconds and in every direction I looked. The thunder was deafening; it rolled like timpani drums during the great crescendo of a large symphony orchestra. The big difference was that they were the only instruments being heard over the great, deep whirring sounds of the tornadic winds. The whistling winds made a eerie whirring sound as they blew through the giant oak trees that had stood for over a hundred years.

In the distance, I could hear the sound of heavy rain beating on the rooftops of the buildings and on the parked cars along the streets below. The wind succumbs for just second, that's when I hear the sound of large hail beating on the car tops and on the roofs of the buildings.

Unfortunately, a lot of the buildings had glass siding. You know the kind I mean. If it wasn't blown off the buildings, the hail would beat holes in it.

Cars passed by with all of the windows broken out.

Cars with no drivers lined the streets, while the owners scurried to safety anywhere they could find it.

Downtown Fort Worth was now a nightmare for everyone. The next two hours were unimaginable to the average person and especially bad to anyone who had never seen a Texas tornado. These tornadoes play hell with buildings, cars, and people in their path. The Texas plains were now a disaster for miles around. Fort Worth is in total chaos with the sirens of fire trucks, ambulances, and police vehicles wailing everywhere.

I had earlier ducked into the doorway of a large building that happened to be nearby. It appeared to be my best chance of saving my hide. The wind whistles around the corner of the doorway, whipping the rain into my face with the force of number-two buckshot being fired from a twelve-gauge shotgun.

The stinging hurt so bad that I huddled up in the corner of the doorway in a fetal position with my back to the street hoping to stop the beating I'am taking, also the pain I was feeling.

The next thing I remember hearing was the wailing of the National Weather Storm warning sirens. They are always blown when any type of severe storm or tornado is approaching.

The glass from the sides of the building is falling and being blown into the doorway where I'm hiding. It's getting worse with large pieces of glass paneling that covered the building being blown off. It was falling toward the ground and into the doorway where I'm trying to hide. They keep hitting me in the back and the back of my head. They were being broken into millions of pieces. The wind is blowing them into my face and body, cutting small places in my skin.

Pieces of roofing come next. Large sections of the roofing broke loose, and the decking came down with it. Next come the limbs from trees, hitting the side of the building and splintering into a million pieces.

What the hell! All of a sudden I can't see. I can't be blind. My eyes are feeling no pain; I don't understand what is happening to me. There seemed to be a vacuum all around me. I can hardly breathe. All I can hear is a giant roar. It sounds as though a freight train is coming right over the top of me.

The sky has turned totally black, and large hailstones are hitting me all over and all around the doorway. Damn, now I am getting hit by some of those baseball-sized hailstones. I didn't know how much more of this I can take.

I seemed to hear a voice. I have no idea how long I have been out of it. I hear that voice again and again.

"Wake up, Professor, wake up. Come on, old friend, wake up." I keep hearing this voice again and again, but my eyes just don't want to open. I fight hard to open my eyes to see who is talking to me.

When I am finally able to open my eyes, I see Charley Johnson. Charley is a policeman I had known from a long time back. Charley is a good friend to all the street people. He did his best to see that we didn't get into trouble. He even took us to jail on real cold nights if we didn't have a bed at one of the shelters.

Charley has found me huddled in the doorway and he is trying to get me to wake up so the medics could help.

"Professor, are you all right?"

"Hey, Charley, what the hell happened? What're you doing here?"

"My head feels real funny, Charley, kind of like someone has been beating on it."

"Hey, Charley, what's happened to my arm? It sure does hurt. The last thing I remember was having a few drinks with Cowboy and Bing down at Heritage Park. I was on my way down to Lancaster Street when the wind got real bad, and the rain started to get real heavy. I ducked inside the doorway of this building to get away from it.

What gives, Charley? What happened, fill me in?"

Before anyone could answer, I felt someone picking me up and putting me onto a stretcher and then into an ambulance. Just as the ambulance was about to leave, I heard Charley say, "Professor just be a good guy and do what they tell you to do. I'll come by to see you in a day or two – if you're still in the hospital."

"Thanks, Charley, you're a real good friend."

Things are still real noisy, and it was still raining cats and dogs. I am finally able to open my eyes again. I see an ambulance attendant and two other people who'd been hurt during the storm. I am able to see these people are bleeding beneath the bandages the attendant had applied earlier. They appear to be scratched and bruised all over their heads and bodies.

Right now I begin to wonder about myself. I reach up to feel of my own head. I find that I am bleeding, too. There are bandages on my head and face.

A big gust of wind whipped the ambulance sideways, making it slide down the wet streets. It must have scared the hell out of the driver because I heard him cussing real loud. He finally gets control of the ambulance again, and away we go.

I hear a radio dispatcher asking if the driver knows our ETA. I guess that means the estimated time of arrival. He answers something I couldn't understand.

I feel real faint again so I laid back and lowered my head to keep from passing out again.

Finally, we are at the Tarrant County General Hospital Emergency Entrance. They wheel me in and start to work on my arm. Something had hit my left wrist and broken a bone in it. The nurse tells me I have a black eye and several bruises on my head. There is a large gash on my right leg that will have to be sewn up. They take me down the hall to another room where the work began. I am numb all over, and I don't even feel any pain at all when they sew me up or worked on my face.

The doctor asks if I could feel anything on my right leg where he is sewing.

"Hell, no, Doc, I'm numb all over."

He just laughs. "Professor, you really are something else. At least this time you can talk to me. The last time I worked on you, you were so drunk you didn't know what I was doing and really didn't seem to care."

As he walks off down the hall to another room, he looks back. "Professor, next time find a better place to hide."

As he turnes to leave, I hear him tell the nurse to take me to X- Ray and take a picture of my wrist before they put a cast on it.

As he walks on down the hall and almost out of sight I hear him say again, "See you later, old friend."

After they take the X-rays, they roll me out of the room and into another area where some lady starts asking me questions for the admission chart.

Hell, they know as much about me as I know about myself most of the time. The questions are about such things as my name, age, and information about my family.

I have to start lying a little. You see, I am what the city calls, "one of their street people." What they mean is that I don't really live any place special and didn't have an address to send the bill to.

I live in the parks during the nice weather. I live in the tunnels and overpasses during the rainy weather. Sometimes in bad weather I go to one of the many shelters provided by the Salvation Army, Churches, Red Cross, or other organizations such as the Gospel Lighthouse, or the Bible Sanctuary for God's Family. These are all good people. They are real nice to people like me and my friends.

I tell the lady asking the questions that my name was "Robert Dixon, James Robert Dixon. Professor, James Robert Dixon, to be precise." "I have no home address; I am forty-nine years of age, and I have no idea where any of my relatives are."

That last part wasn't exactly the truth. You see, I originally came from Chicago, Illinois, and I assumed that what family I might have still lives there.

Right now, my head hurts real bad. I am beginning to get a little sick to my stomach. I tell the nurse how bad it hurts and about my nausia.

She talks to the doctor, and he decides it would be best to keep me overnight since I did have a mild concussion. This will give them a chance to look at my leg and change the dressing. They need to put a cast on my wrist before they release me. Even with a mild concussion they have to be careful, so they would just keep me awhile.

Another ambulance arrives with more wounded people. I still didn't know just exactly what had happened. I asked one of the ambulance attendants what kind of storm this had been? He looked at me in total disbelief, as I was off my rocker or something.

"Hell, man, that was the worst tornado I've ever seen."

So that was what that was? First one I'd ever seen. I'd heard they had tornadoes in Texas, and now I really believed it. "So that's what that was?" That was a real Texas Tornado. I'll be damned.

Things are starting to get real hectic around here. More injuries coming in. I started worrying about my friends and what had happened to them.

I had just left Cowboy and Bing at Heritage Park. They were heading for downtown to try to pick up a few coins from people getting off work. Some of us have regulars who slip us a buck every now and then just because they had a soft spot in their hearts — or maybe it is in their heads. I didn't know, but every little bit helped, and we appreciate it.

Our little group is kind of like a small family. My friends and I kind of look out for each other. Everybody had a nickname such as mine. I had once been a very well-respected college professor, but that is another story.

Cowboy used to be a world-class bull and bareback and saddle bronc rider, until he got hurt real bad. He lost his nerve for a spell. By the time he got his nerve back, he wasn't in any condition to try riding again. He had lost his family and everything else from the way I heard it. We never question each other much about our past.

I guess you might say that Bing was the next one. Bing could still sing real well. He said he used to headline some real fancy clubs around the country.

You can tell he used to be real good looking also, and as I said, he could still sing a ballad that would almost hypnotize you. You could hear him sing just one time, and you knew where he got the nickname of Bing. You know...a real crooner with a beautiful, deep-baritone voice. You know, the kind that the ladies really love to hear. Well, maybe it had mellowed just a bit. Now it sounded more like a whiskey baritone – still real good though.

He got to gambling a lot when he was appearing in Las Vegas and lost everything he had and more. He got into debt real bad and had to take off. You know, leave the area for safer parts unknown. He had been living on the street ever since. He said it was a lot safer on the streets in the Dallas-Fort Worth area than it was in Las Vegas.

I guess you could say that Pug just didn't know any better. Pug had once been a world-ranked middleweight contender. Unfortunately, he had one too many fights. Even now, he has real bad horrible headaches from time to time. He was a real good friend to the rest of us. We all palled around together.

Most of the street people knew Pug, and they didn't bother any of his friends. They knew he could still pack a pretty good punch. "He let everyone know not to mess around with his friends, or they would answer to him."

At this point I guess Doc comes next. Doc came in handy when Pug got the headaches. Doc always seemed to be able to get Pug to settle down when he got one of these headaches. He was usually able to give him something that knocked him out for a while.

This generally worked if he wasn't where he could make it to the hospital. He normally went to the hospital to get a shot of some kind and some blood thickener. I think Doc called it Vitamin K. Most of his headaches lasted at least a day or two.

Next came Mabel. Mabel was an ex-carnival worker. When she was younger, she must have been pretty good looking. She said she had been a "hoochie koochie" dancer in one of the side shows.

Later, she gained too much weight for that, so she learned to be a sword swallower and fire eater. She quit that when she caught her hair on fire. She got drunk one night, and the carnival left town without her. She'd been here on the street ever since until she joined our group.

Truth is, Mabel is a real good friend to everyone. She is a real good cook too. She can make our food taste better by using some of the little tricks she picked up in Louisiana from her mother. You know, seasoning and spices.

Sometimes, in the summer, we even get enough money from selling cans and panhandling to get meat. If we get meat, then we steal a few vegetables from the Farmers Market. When we do, she makes shish-k-bobs.

She finds old coat hangers and straightens them out. We make a nice fire down on the lower riverbank where it won't catch anything on fire, and she cooks for us. You know, kind of like a shish-k-bob picnic, living high on the hog.

Last, but certainly not least, is Doc. Doc had been a corpsman in the Army during the Vietnam War. He had made staff sergeant before he was discharged. He attended to a lot of wounded men in many of the battles and he was twice wounded himself. He sure had the scars to prove it.

In one particular battle, he had been credited with saving his lieutenant, a sergeant, and two other soldiers. He bodily carried them about three hundred yards to safety, one at a time. This was done after he had already received a bullet through his left shoulder. After getting them to safety, he applied tourniquets to the soldiers wounds where necessary. After he stopped the bleeding, he applied the antibiotics and bandages to other wounds of the others where they needed more attentio before returning attention to his own shoulder wound.

For these acts of bravery and unselfish heroism he received the Silver Star commendation for bravery. It should have been more, but he really didn't even want to accept that. He said he was just doing his job.

Unfortunately, while this was happening, his wife had found that one of his best buddies back home had become her best buddy. While Doc was in the hospital recovering from his shoulder wound, he received a Dear John letter. She had filed for divorce; and just as soon as it was final, she and his buddy got married and moved to California.

When Doc got home, he just kind of lost it. Thank God they didn't have any children to suffer the consequences of divorce. He went on a binge and never stopped drinking. He was truly one of the nicest, most honest people I had ever met or hope to meet.

He manages to secure antibiotics and a few pain pills from someone. No one ever asks who. When one of us starting to get down with a cold or diarrhea or something, he always seemed to come up with something to help us feel better. We don't ask questions since he doesn't charge anything. This helps a lot since we didn't have anything to pay him with anyway.

We never talked about it to any of the other street people because we were afraid they might blab it out. The authorities might come in and ask questions about where he got the medicine and accuse him of practicing medicine without a license.

He seemed to know more about medicine than a lot of doctors I had gone to see in the old days in Chicago.

Well, they finally finished with the questions. They pushed me down the hall on the way to my room.

"Hey, Pardner, this is real good. I get clean sheets, hot food, and a warm bed plus TV for the night." I ask one of the nurses if I am in time for supper since it was about 7:30 p.m?

She looks at me grins and winks. "Professor, for you I can find something." She looks at me with that real cute grin again and asks, "How about a good hamburger with a side of potato salad and a couple of cartons of milk?"

"Milk, I...well if that's the best you can offer to drink I'll take it, and tonight I won't even complain." She's a real nice lady, this nurse.

After they get me to the room, my head starts hurting real bad. The trauma doctor comes by right after they put me in the room. The doctor asks, "How are you feeling?"

"Hell, Doc, my head wasn't doing too bad till just a little while ago. All of a sudden it started hurting like hell. It hurts real bad up on the side of my head where you sewed it up. Feels like I got a knot coming up there on the side of my head."

The Doc comes over and looks at my head. He shines a little light in my eyes. The Doc lookes me straight in the eye and says, "Professor, I think we had better keep you here for a couple of days. It seems that you may have a worse concussion than we figured. I want to keep you till we see if there is any more pressure building up inside your head. You may have ruptured a blood vessel in your brain when you got hit on the head. You've got a pretty good knot up there. The damage may be something we can't see externally. From the looks of the pressure building up behind your eyes, it's a possibility.

"I'm gonna have the nurses check your blood pressure and respiration during the night about every two or three hours. I know you don't like to be awakened, but if the pressure grows, we don't want you to go into a deep sleep. That could be dangerous."

"Okay, Doc, but you may have to give me coffee to keep me awake."

"No, we don't Professor, we can't give you any kind of stimulant because that would give us a false reading, and we don't want that."

"Okay, you old sawbones, I'll stay awake tonight just to please you."

Doc laughs a little. "Okay, Professor, I appreciate your cooperation. Now be good and do what the nurses tell you to do."

All night long, about every two hours, these nurses keep coming in and checking on me. They make sure I don't go into a deep sleep. My leg is finally beginning to hurt where they sewed it up. I tell the nurses about it. They said they would give me something in the morning just as soon as the doctor comes by to see me.

It's about 7:00 a.m., and here came the doctor. Boy does he look tired and haggard.

"Hell, Doc, I feel a lot better than you look this morning."

He forces a slight grin. "Professor, have you been a good boy? The nurses tell me you did your best to stay awake or just slept lightly all night. Now let me take a look at you."

He fusses around for about five minutes, listening to everything and feeling of everything he didn't listen to. He looks at the bandage on my leg. It is a little bloody, but it is not seeping too badly or anything like that.

"Professor, the nurses tell me that the leg is hurting pretty bad now. It was bruised pretty good where you got that gash in it. It's bound to hurt pretty good for a while. I will have the nurses give you a little something for the pain. What about your arm where it's broken? How's it feeling?"

"Hell, Doc, it don't hurt as bad as my leg. They did a real good job on my arm. It's sore and hurts some, but I feel like it's gonna be okay."

"Do you think you need a pain pill?"

"Doc, I sure do think I could use one if it won't screw up anything inside my head for you."

"That's all right, Professor."

"Nurse, why don't you see if you can't get Professor a pain pill of some kind. Maybe a Tylenol with codeine.

"I'll see you later, Professor. Now you just keep being good to these nurses, or they'll tell on you."

"Okay, Doc, we'll see you later. Now go home and try to get some rest."

How about that doctor? Telling me I was gonna stay here for a couple of days just to be on the safe side.

It was real quiet in the room with no nurses or doctors around. At least I got me a real TV with remote control. Now I could see the news and find out what had happened to the town. I reached for the controls and turned the TV on.

My God, do you see what I see? So that's what hit me last night. That big black cloud covers the whole thirty-four-story building, along with that other big building right next to it.

Oh, hell, look at that church with the roof torn off. There's another picture of that church downtown with their phone center damaged. It just tore the whole front off of that building and left the desk, chairs, and office furniture looking out at an open sky.

The reporter said that the two ladies in the office didn't even get hurt. The whole front of that building was totally ripped away, and they were left standing there. After it hit, they went into the other part of the church. They were saved because they were able to get into the main sanctuary of the church.

My God, what is this? This reporter said the barbershop roof collapsed and let the roof fall in on somebody. Three guys heard someone hollering and the adrenaline started flowing. The three of them went to work grabbing whatever they could. They were finally able to lift the roof up a little and pull the man out.

Oh, my God, that was Cowboy they just pulled out from under that roof. I don't believe it, that little son of a gun isn't even hurt. He's not even scratched. Boy, the good Lord was sure looking out for Cowboy this time.

I was getting pretty sleepy. I felt as though they had slipped me a Mickey. That was all right, though, because I felt like I needed some rest. I would learn more about the storm later.

I felt like I was coming out of a dream because I heard voices – familiar voices. It sounded like Cowboy, Bing, Pug, Mabel, and Doc. I opened my eyes, and there were all five standing around my bed.

How in hell did they get in here? None of them are bandaged. None of them sound hurt. How'd that happen?

I opened my eyes and looked up at them, and they all started laughing. Here I was with a patch on my head, arm in a cast, and my leg with a big bandage on it. "The first thing I want to know, Cowboy, is how in hell did you get out from under that roof?"

"You even got a television. Did you see me on television last night?" "Well, I didn't see you last night, but I sure did see you this morning. You're a big star now. May I have your autograph?"

They all got a big kick at the thought of Cowboy being asked for his autograph. They started telling me what had happened to them.

Cowboy had gone down to see a friend who sweeps out the barbershop when he heard the warnings. The friend, the barber, and a customer had gone running toward the front door when they had heard it coming.

Cowboy had just gone to the restroom over by the front door when the storm hit. Those that had gone outside ran next door to a convenience store. They all ran into the big refrigerator cooler that was used to store its perishable foods, etc. The store was gone, but the big walk-in refrigerator was still intact. Everyone who went inside the refrigerator was safe, but the building was gone.

When Cowboy had started out of the restroom, the storm lifted the roof up and then slammed it down again. Cowboy was pinned right beside one of the big heavy barber chairs. That chair was all that saved Cowboy. There wasn't any way out till the boys from the convenience store came out of the cooler.

After the storm had passed, they heard Cowboy hollering like hell where he was pinned under the fallen roof. Well, believe it or not, these three guys actually raised the corner of that roof enough for Cowboy to crawl far enough for them to get hold of him and pull him out from under the roof.

Bing had stopped to talk to another guy he knew when he heard the sirens go off. He and this other guy had gone into a Salvation Army shelter a few blocks down from town on Lancaster Street.

After they got inside, they found that Pug and Mabel had also heard the sirens. They saw the dark clouds and went running to safety in the same shelter. Thank God they were all safe.

Right now, they sounded like a bunch of magpies quacking all over the place. I finally got a word in when they stopped to take a breath, and I asked them how they knew I was in the hospital.

Bing told me that after the worst of the storm was over, he, Pug, and Mabel were walking down toward town when a patrol car pulled up, and the patrolman had told them that it would be a good idea if they would go back to the shelter and spend the night.

They found Doc down near the stockyards heading back down toward town. He was a little tipsy, but he was just looking for anyone who might need help after a disaster like this.

"You know Doc; he'll help anyone in trouble if he can. This would be like old stuff to him when you consider what he went through during the war in Nam," Bing said.

The officer that stopped to talk to them happened to be Charley, my old buddy from the street division. He had asked if they were friends of Professor's.

"We sure are. Do you know what happened to him?"

"Sure do, he's over at Tarrant County General Hospital, and I hear that he's gonna be all right. You might want to go see him tomorrow if he is still in the hospital."

"Thanks for the information, Charley," we said. "He is one heck of a nice cop."

Pug had had this great idea. "Since we don't have no phone, why can't we just walk over and see if he's still in the hospital? And, sure nuff, you're still here."

"Professor, can we stay around and watch television with you? How long you gonna have to stay here anyway? You know we don't get to watch television much except in store windows."

I couldn't say no to my buddies. "Well, okay, you can stay for a little while, but then you gotta go just in case the Doc comes around again or if the nurses say something. But if that happens, I tell you what you can do, you can come back tonight and watch it with me till nine o'clock. That's when visiting hours are over. That'll give you about three hours of TV if you get here about 5:30 or 6:00.

"Sure is good to see you guys and know that none of you are hurt. You have to admit that was one hell of a windstorm. Lots of hail, I understand. I heard that one of the tornadoes touched down again in a residential neighborhood in Arlington and that no one was hurt, just a lot of damage to homes. Those poor people sure will have a lot of work to do cleaning up.

"Maybe when I get out of here, we can get some work downtown and make a few bucks to buy a drink or two. What do you say?"

I heard a loud okay from everybody on that one.

"Right now, all of you guys get out of here and get back down to the shelter and get a good night's sleep for a change. Do me a favor will you? Stay sober and out of trouble. I'll see you back here tomorrow evening. Now git."

They all left, and I could still hear them talking all the way down the hall. I turned the TV to something I wanted to see, and the next thing I knew, one of the nurses was waking me up at midnight.

"Professor, how's the head? Now if it starts hurting worse, you reach over there and ring that bell because we want you to ring it. We need to know if there are any changes in the pressure in your head."

We made it through the night.

The night nurse came in one more time before leaving for the day. I finally looked up at the clock and my God, it was 6:30 a.m. I teased her and asked her what she was doing waking me up so early. She knew I was teasing because I couldn't keep a straight face.

She had no more than left when the doctor came in making his morning rounds. He was not the same one that had been here last night. This one was kind of grumpy. I guess I would be too, if I had to put up with a lot of people like me.

He checked the bandage on the leg, looked at the stitches, and told the nurse to put a new bandage on it. He said he felt it was all right to take me off the antibiotic drip they had had me on since they put me in the room. He asked me a million questions about my head and how it felt.

I told him that once during the night I woke up and things had seemed a little blurry to me.

"Did you call the nurse and tell her?"

"No, I didn't. I just turned over and went back to sleep."

He seemed a little "P.O.'D" at that, but what could he say? It was too late to do anything about it.

Then, he came over and shined that little flashlight in my eyes again. When you had a headache, that darn thing looked like a floodlight. He frowned; he did a lot of that. He told the nurse that he wanted me to stay in the hospital till tomorrow.

I thought that was just fine since the bed and the food weren't bad compared to what I was used to eating. Besides, I had told the gang they could come back to visit and watch a little TV with me.

Well, what do you know, here comes breakfast: bacon, eggs, and a small box of cereal, with a half-pint carton of whole milk. I like whole milk; it's so creamy. Don't get that very often anymore. There's also some toast with a little thingy ma jig of jelly and some butter to go with it. Damn, this is really eating high on the hog. I'll have to get hurt more often.

About that time I bumped my leg, and I changed my mind real quick about getting hurt again. The nurses came in to see me every so often the rest of the morning.

At about 10:30 a.m. the door opened, and a nice young man came in. He introduced himself as Bobby Hunter. He explained that he was attached to the chaplain's office of the hospital, and he was here to see if he could help me in any way. First thing he did was to ask if I needed anything.

I could answer that, but it wouldn't have been nice because I knew he wouldn't bring me a drink. I couldn't think of anything else right at that time, so I politely said no.

Next he wanted to know if I would like to have some reading material. I thought for a minute and then asked if he might have a *Sports Illustrated*. He said he did, and he would have the young lady on the book and magazine cart come by and let me choose from what she had available.

Next he said, "I wonder if you would like to share a moment of prayer and thanks for the protection you received during the storm yesterday and the help afterwards."

I was sort of stunned, but said, "Sure, I think that would be fine."

We bowed our heads, and he said a real pretty prayer to God, thanking him for letting me and all of the other people in the hospital survive that ferocious storm. He thanked God for letting a lot of other people survive and asked Him to help the families of the people who perished in the storm. He finally said, "Amen.

"If you're still here tomorrow, would it be all right if I come by again?" I started to say, *Hell, yes I've enjoyed the visit,* but I caught myself before it came out, and I politely said, "Sure, I would appreciate that."

The rest of the day went like most days in a hospital. Lunch was good with green beans, some kind of smothered steak, iced tea, and custard of some kind. I couldn't figure out what the flavor of that custard was, that is, if it had a flavor.

I went back to watching TV. Boy, some of those people on TV really had troubles. Hell, I thought I had troubles till I watched them. Hell, I was just a beginner compared to some of them. Something was funny though. They all seemed to be rich because none of them ever seemed to go to work. I wished I could do that. I knew it was just make believe, but they made it seem so real.

I finally found an old John Wayne cowboy movie that I had seen when I was a kid. I really enjoyed seeing it again. It brought back a lot of old memories. I used to take my son and daughter to see those old cowboy movies, but that was another story. I hadn't seen or talked to them in over ten years.

Dinnertime came a little early in the hospital. They brought me some meat loaf, macaroni and cheese, a salad, some ice cream, and iced tea. Hell, this was a real gourmet dinner for me. I dug in; and, just as I was finishing with dinner, here came the doctor again. He checked me out, looked at my bandage on the leg, checked the arm and head, and asked me if I had had any more dizzy spells or blurry vision. I told him the answer was "no" to all of his questions, and he just looked at me and finally smiled. "Professor, I think I can release you tomorrow."

"Great, Doc, thanks a lot."

"Now, Professor, you'll have to come back to have the leg checked and the wrist looked at."

Eventually they would have to take the cast off my wrist, but he figured that would be several weeks. The cast wasn't too bad, though, because they left my fingers sticking out to where I could pick up things with my hand.

The nurse came in and reassured me that I could get released tomorrow. I laughingly asked where I was supposed to go. She looked kind of embarrassed when she realized what she had said. I told her not to worry because I was going to one of the shelters for a few days, at least till my leg healed up.

"That's fine, Professor, just take care of yourself."

Television and The Decision

I heard noise out in the Other hall. Sure enough, it was the gang. They all came in real excited about watching TV. They each got to choose a program. A couple of them agreed on the same program, making it easier to avoid an argument.

At about 6:30 p.m., Doc said, "Hey, how about watching that new program on ABC called 'So You Want to Be a Millionaire?' It comes on at 7:00, Mondays, Wednesdays, and Fridays. I know because I watched it through the front window of Jodfre's Furniture Store the other night. It's really a lot of fun to watch those people try to answer all of those questions."

Mabel piped up, "Bet Professor could answer those questions. Let's just see how many he can answer tonight."

As we watched, Robert Burns, the host of the show got everyone situated in their chairs and then asked a few questions about where they were from and what they did for a living. They generally had someone with them who sat in a chair back by the audience. He talked to them and asked a couple of questions before coming back to the contestant.

Then they started with the questions. The first ones were real corny. You know, like "Who is buried in Grant's Tomb?" The next three were just about as easy.

"Hell," Cowboy declared, "I could have answered the first four questions myself. They weren't all that hard."

Bing laughed at how easy the first four were, but then they got real hard from there on out. The next question was a little harder, but easy for me since it was about President Teddy Roosevelt and the name of his political party. I had studied that in school. The two-thousand-dollar question was about movies. Since I had been a real movie buff when I was young, I knew that answer also. The four-thousand-dollar question was one about locations of certain lakes in the U.S., starting west and going east. I found that to be real easy also.

By now the gang was really getting excited, especially Mabel. The eight-thousand-dollar and the sixteen-thousand were a little unusual, but not really hard. Then came the thirty-two-thousand-dollar question about an older musical comedy star that I had known personally, so that was no problem.

The more I saw these questions, the more I became interested. Then came the sixty-four-thousand-dollar question that was a question about the writer known as O' Henry who happened to be one of my favorite authors when I was young. The contestant finally ran into a hard question about Adolph Hitler. He had already used up his lifelines, so he decided to take the sixty-four thousand dollars and run. It was a smart move on his part. He was given four dates about when Hitler became the Chancellor of Germany. The host of the show then asked him to guess just to see if he might have won the0 one hundred and twenty-five thousand dollars. He would have lost.

Somehow I knew. I was totally surprised at how much I had remembered from my previous life. I must admit that I had read every newspaper I found along the curb or in trash bins or cans, and I read them from cover to cover. I guess there was just something in me that made me want to keep up with the world even if I was trying to leave it behind with my previous life.

By now, Mabel, Cowboy, and Doc were really carrying on. I started trying to quiet them down because I was sure everyone up and down the hall could hear them. I finally got them quiet, and I asked, "What's the entire ruckus about?"

They told me they had a great idea on how to make a lot of money.

"Oh, yeah, and just what would that be?"

They look at each other and smiled. "Professor, we want you to try to get on that program."

"What program?"

"So You Want to Be a Millionaire.'"

Hell, you guys are totally out of your mind. I couldn't get on that program. You have to call somebody back in New York first, and then you have to answer some questions. You have to answer them right, and then if I did answer the questions right, I would have to fly back there to be on the program.

Pug butts in with, "Wait a minute; we can get up enough money for you to call and try to get on the program. It may take a few tries, but we can each take turns calling for you from a pay phone and when one of us gets through, we just hand you the phone, and you take over from there."

Hell, if I did get through and answer the questions, I still have to have an address here for them to send the tickets to for our flight back to New York City. On top of that, I don't have any clothes that would be fit to wear back to something like that. You wouldn't want me to appear on television looking like I do out on the street would you?

Bing chimed in with, "I think we could work that out too. First, you could use the address of the Bible Sanctuary for God's Family down on 7th Street for your address. I know Reverend Lynn would be glad to help out. Cowboy tells everyone he's real nice people."

There is Chrissie's Used Clothes Emporium down on Berry Street where I'm sure you could get the clothes. She would be glad to help out.

Mabel told Professor, "Yeah, she's had a crush on you for a long time, ever since the first time you went in there and talked to her. She has said she sure likes a man with an education; and besides, she thinks you're real cute. I know because she told me so."

"Well, if I do agree to do this, and mind you I don't say I will, there are a few things we have to do first. Taking first things first, we have to get me out of here tomorrow.

Next, we have to get together downtown and see if we can rustle up some work cleaning streets and buildings or anything that might be available. We might be able to find some aluminum that has blown off the buildings that can be sold down at the place that buys aluminum cans and copper and that kind of stuff. There might even be some copper blown off those buildings or some wiring that we can strip and sell. Are you sure you guys want to do that?

Cowboy let it be known that it was about time for us to get real. It's about time we did an honest day's work. This just might be the thing that can help us get off the streets. Most of those other guys have mental problems, but we just love the bottle a little too much. We don't have any bipolar problems like most of those guys. That's why we all stick together and help each other so much. At least we know we aren't off our rocker; we're just drunk most of the time and either too lazy or too drunk to work. That is, of course, if you guys want to get off the streets.

They all let it be known real loud. "We sure do want to get off the street and out of the bottle."

Okay, now let's have a meeting right here and now and vote to decide if we want to get off the streets for good or not. You all know what that means. It means starting to attend AA and helping each other stay off the bottle. All those in favor say, *Yes*.

The *yes* seems to be unanimous. Now this is not going to be easy. Truth is it is going to be hard as hell, since we have all been on the bottle for so long. There are going to be headaches, upset stomachs, seeing things like bugs and snakes for a while; but if you're willing to do this, then I am willing to do my part and try to get on this program. Okay?"

"Okay." Lets do it.

"Now let's get back to how we're going to go about doing this cause it's gonna take a lot of doing. First, let's see a show of hands as to who wants to work hard as everything to make this work. Now, are you all willing to go to work helping clean up the tornado debris to make the money we will need? Everybody seems satisfied with that so what next?"

Bing raised his hand. "If we do this, maybe I could go back to Vegas and pay off some of my debts and become an honest citizen again."

Pug, what's the matter? Do you have some doubts?

"Oh, no, I was just wondering who would get to go back to New York with you if you make the show. I've never been to New York. I was supposed to fly there to Madison Square Garden for my real big fight but my manager screwed things up for me, and I never made it."

Pug, here's what we'll do. If we make the show, maybe we can scratch up enough money for an extra plane ticket back to New York so you can come along. How about it gang, does this sound okay to you?

They all answered with a resounding, "Yes, we would love to get Pug to New York so he can at least see the place, even if he didn't get to fight there."

Well, it's all settled, Pug. If I go, you go.

Mabel let him know there was one condition, and that was that he had to take pictures and bring them back to show where we had been. That was agreed by both Pug and me.

Now Mabel added, "What the hell, Pug, I want you to bring me a present of some kind from New York."

Cowboy tells Pug, "Since I didn't get to ride in the Garden, you have to take real good pictures to bring back to show me what I missed. Look real close so you can tell me all about it. I was supposed to ride in the Garden right after I had won the NRA finals in Cheyenne, but I got all busted up on the next rodeo and lost my nerve, so I never got there."

You got 'em, Cowboy. If Professor makes any money on the show maybe we will just take you down to the Ft. Worth stockyards and buy you a real good-looking Stetson. Maybe we can buy Mabel a new dress or two. Maybe we can get Bing a new CD walkman with some CD's for good listening, and a whole lot of medical things for Doc.

You know, Doc, one of those whatcha ma callit things that hang around your neck to listen to people's insides.

"Hell, Pug, don't you know they call those things a stethoscope?"

Pug said right back, real mad like, "Hell, no, I didn't know that was called a *stetha* whatever you call it. I just knew that's what doctors used to listen to your heart. They used to use one on me before every fight; and hell, no, I'm not mad. I just look that way when I get real upset. You should know that by now."

Okay, it's all set now. When I get out of here tomorrow, we go downtown and see if we can get some work to raise some money. Mabel said, "Professor, you ain't gonna do no heavy work till your leg gets better, and you don't have no dizzy spells.

Mabel, I know you're concerned about my health, but I promise I won't do anything to hurt myself. I just feel that I should do my share. Sometimes Mabel was like a mother hen.

Now you just listen to me Professor, "you'll do your share just as soon as we get enough money for the phone call and get you on that program. For the time being, you're gonna stay close to the Bible Sanctuary. They know all of us, and I'm gonna ask them to keep a real close eye on you and make you behave yourself. They're real good folks down there, and you're gonna mind them, or I'll sick Pug on you."

Okay, Mabel, just don't sick Pug on me. Now let's everybody get back to some serious TV watching, cause here we can choose what we want to watch. When we get to the Bible Sanctuary, they do most of the choosing as to what we watch.

We watched TV till almost 9:30 p.m. when the night doctor and nurse came calling. They walked in, looked around, and the nurse gave out with, "Okay, everyone out for the night."

They all said, "Okay."

Then Mabel started out, "Guess what? Professor is gonna be on TV."

The nurse looked at her in astonishment and asked, "Just how is that gonna happen?"

Mabel told her, "He's gonna be on 'So You Want To Be A Millionaire. I mean he's gonna try to get on the show.

He's gonna be a millionaire..."

The nurse just looked at Mabel and grinned and winked at me. I felt like crawling under the bed. I probably would have if the bed pan hadn't been in the way.

Mabel tried to continue the conversation, but I told her that I would tell the nurse about it later.

Now, you and the boys should go so I can talk to the doctor.

The doctor looked me over, shined the flashlight in my eyes, looked at my leg, and asked if my arm hurt.

No, it doesn't really hurt, and the leg doesn't either, but they sure do itch.

The doctor laughed. "Professor, that's a good sign."

He and the nurse start to walk out of the room when he turned to me and said, "Oh, yes, I'm releasing you tomorrow morning. I'll be here and see you before you go."

Then he really surprised me and asked what was this about my getting on that TV program. I briefly explained what had happened and how we planned to approach it. I told him that I was real apprehensive about the whole thing.

You know what, Professor? I think you really might be able to do it. What size clothes do you wear?

Sorry, Doc, I really don't know. The last time I bought something to wear I think I was about a size forty-four long. My size hasn't changed a lot since then. I have just gotten older.

He looked at me and smiled. "Professor, if you make that show, just let me know because my wife says I have too many suits in my closet anyway. I would be glad to donate a couple for a good cause like that. I also have some nice shirts and ties that I would like to offer you. I think you should really try to get on the show. It would show a lot of other people that you can get off the street if you really want to."

He turned and walked out the door, and I heard him and the nurse talking as they went back down the hall.

I thought to myself for the first time that this really might happen if we worked it just right.

A short time later, a nurse came in to see if there was anything I needed before turning in. "You know, a pain pill or something?"

This time I remembered to ask her something I had never asked before. "What's that doctor's name? He has sewed me up, patched me up, and taken care of me on four or five occasions in past years, and I don't think I ever knew his name."

The nurse replied, "His name is Dr. David Davis. He has been here a long time."

He sure has been good to me and a lot of other people who live on the street. He treats us real well; you know, like we are somebody and not just a bum off the street, even if that's what we really are. He seems to look into our souls for the person who used to occupy this body. There's something very special about him.

The nurse agrees and leaves the room, but before she walked out, she wanted to know if I wanted her to turn the light off.

Sure, that would be fine. I have a night light, and I don't have any IV attached, so I can go to the bathroom instead of that damn bedpan.

She tells me goodnight as she closed the door.

Thanks a lot, I really appreciate everything you folks are doing for me.

Morning comes and so did the breakfast, along with a cup of coffee and some orange juice. Boy, that's the way to start a day. The nurse checks a last time about the bandage on my leg. She looked at the cast on my wrist "Well, it looks like some of the swelling in the hand has gone down. Can you move the fingers a little better today?"

I wiggled the fingers to show her how well they operated. She smiled, which let me know she was real glad I was doing so well. "The doctor will be coming by about 9:30 or 10:00 to sign your release papers from the hospital."

Time went by slowly, and it seemed like ten hours before the doctor got here, but he came in with a cheery, "Good morning."

I started to get up and put on the old clothes I had had been wearing when the storm had hit. The doctor handed me a nice large grocery sack.

Your old clothes were in pretty bad shape after that storm, so I brought you a couple of pair of jeans and a couple of undershirts, shorts and work shirts. I thought that would look better if you're going to go downtown with the gang to try to get some work. I really don't want you to do much work right now, but I figured you could supervise.

Remember now, when you get ready to go back to New York City if you make the show, you come by and let me know. I might have a little surprise for you along with a suit or two. He turned and walked out the door.

"Thanks a million, Doctor Davis."

He turned, looked at me, and smiled because that was the first time I had ever called him by his name. At least now I knew his name.

Nurse Julie came in and told me to get dressed because she was ready to check me out.

I got out of that stupid gown that opened in the back and froze your butt off. I put on a clean pair of shorts, a tee-shirt, the clean shirt, and the clean pair of jeans that Dr. Davis had just left me.

Hell, now I felt like an entirely different person. First of all, I hadn't had a drink for three days now. I never thought I would be able to do that again. In fact, I didn't think the gang had been drinking since the storm either. Man, that was hard to believe.

I started out the door to the room and looked back at the television that had made a big change in my life. I thought it might make a big change in my life and several others also. I sure was going to try.

I walked past the nursing station and guess what? I was really not limping very much. Guess what, I hadn't had a pain pill today either. My wrist wasn't really hurting either. The swelling had gone down quite a bit, and now it was in a sling, and my head didn't hurt, and I could see clearly.

The Bible Sanctuary for God's Family

The elevator took me down to the main floor. The sun was shining brightly; it looked as though it was going to be a real fine day. All of a sudden I heard all this noise and turned to see the gang. Every one of them had come to see me when I got out of the hospital.

They told me they had already been down to the Bible Sanctuary and told them what we were going to try to do. Lynn, the manager of the Bible Sanctuary, thought it was a good thing and said if he could help in any way just to let him know. He said we could stay at the Sanctuary until we got on our feet, and we could use that address in case we did get through to the contest board and make it to New York City. He was familiar with the program and understood that we needed to have an address where I could be contacted if I made it.

I got to the Sanctuary with all of the gang. They told me that I was supposed to stay there the rest of the day while they went downtown to see if they could scrounge up some work to make a few bucks.

Lynn showed me where I would be bunking and told me he would call me before it was time for lunch. He was really an ordained minister, but he preferred to just be called Lynn.

As he turned to walk off, I stopped him to tell him how much I appreciated everything they were doing for us. I wanted him to know how much it would mean to me and the gang if things worked out. He smiled and said he was glad to be of help.

The gang headed out the door without even looking back. They seemed to be in a hurry. I'd never seen them hopped up so much about anything like this before. It was a good sign.

I went to my bunk and sat down. I started thinking about what might possibly happen if I did get on the show.

Will someone from the old neighborhood recognize me? Will my son and daughter see the program and recognize me? I've been gone over ten years now, and the kids were real young when I left. What about my mother and father? Will they see me or hear about it? These were things I had to take into consideration when I thought about appearing on national television.

I had to ask myself if I had been a coward or just weak when I left. I had a wonderful job at the University as a full professor with tenure.

Was I the cause of my wife having affairs? I told myself that maybe I was the cause of one affair by not being home enough. I really was out on lecturing tours quite a bit. I guess I could have understood just one affair, but four or five was just too many.

When my best friend's wife found them in bed together, I just went off the deep end. I guess I had just lost it. I had already run one of her old flings out of town when I had caught them not long after we had been married. Then for her to continue with this type of activity just blew my mind. I guess she thought that just because her parents were wealthy and well known in the society circles, she could do as she pleased, and no one would say anything.

It was hard to keep things like that from the family. I also tried to think of the children's reaction to what I had decided to do. I felt I had a choice of causing a lot of hell with her and getting the children involved, or I felt that maybe it would just be best for everyone if I disappeared for a while. I really knew that I never had any intention of ending up like this.

I had contacted my father the first month I was gone and told him to tell Mother and the children that I was all right and that I would try to stay in touch with them. I just didn't realize how easy it was to fall into a bottle of whiskey and be unable to drink my way out of it. Once you started, it was like people said, it was hard to get that monkey off your back.

I went to St. Louis, Missouri first, and when winter hit, I was looking for a warmer place. I still had a few dollars on me, so I bought a bus ticket to Dallas, Texas. I worked at odd jobs here and there. I even worked as a tutor once, but the bottle took care of that. Later, I got a job at a library where my job was to put the books back in the shelves after they had been returned. Things went fine for a while, and I kept my drinking to just the evening hours, but pretty soon I was unable to contain myself to just evenings. I was let go for coming to work drunk. Well, I wasn't really drunk, but I sure did smell like it.

For a while, I had stayed at an old dilapidated motel out on Highway 121. The motel was primarily being used by prostitutes who rented the rooms by the hour. I finally got to a spot where I was unable to afford even the two dollars a day for the rooms there.

I met Cowboy under a bridge over the Trinity River one night after I had been kicked out of the motel. Cowboy seemed to be a nice enough guy and halfway honest, so we just started hanging out together.

We later met Pug down at the park. Pug decided we were all right, so he joined us. Later, over the next couple of months we met Bing, Mabel, and Doc. Somehow, we all just seemed to trust each other. This trust worked into respect for each other and understanding of each other's very personal problems. We finally just developed into a type of family who looked out for each other's welfare. We didn't ask questions about each other's past, and we really didn't care. What we knew about each other was that each of us had felt at ease talking about the things we wanted them to know. I hadn't talked much about my past to them. They just knew that at one time I had been a college professor and that I had a very extensive vocabulary. They sometimes teased me about it, but they really didn't mean anything by it. They came up with the name Professor as a nickname.

My father owned a plastics manufacturing company, located on the north side of Chicago. He inherited some money from his father who had made a fortune in real estate and had died at the early age of forty-seven. His wife, my grandmother, had died in childbirth when she was in her early forties. They knew she was taking a chance at her age trying to have another child. I heard that she had problems when my father was born, and she almost died. The doctors had told her that she shouldn't have any more children, but she felt she really needed two children.

She said it wasn't fair to raise just one child alone. She insisted on going full term when she found out she was pregnant. She was about eight months along when she somehow developed bleeding, and then blood poison set in and they lost both the mother and baby. This was very devastating to my grandfather. From what I heard, I don't think he ever got over losing her.

When Grandfather died, my father had been about twenty-four years old and a very smart businessman. He got a lot of that knowledge from Father and Grandfather. Plastics were new, and dad could see the handwriting on the wall. He knew that plastics and fiberglass were in the future, so he took the money he had inherited and started a very small plastics company. He hired the best young engineers he could find who knew about plastics and its future.

He then hired some of the best salesmen in the country to sell his product. Father always said that you didn't have to know how to do the job yourself; you just had to hire the best men and engineers who knew how to do the job. After hiring them, you act as a rudder and steer them in the right direction. He had proven his theory: Surround yourself with smart people. He did just that and he had been very successful.

I must confess that I was a little worried about what might happen if I got on the program, but I felt that it would be worth it. It might be just the thing that I needed to get me back on my feet. Maybe I would finally have enough courage to look at myself in the mirror.

It was getting kind of late, and I wondered what had happened to the gang. I hoped they weren't working too hard. Those guys were so excited at the possibility of this thing happening that they were willing to do just about anything to help it along. I sure had some good friends in those guys. They would do just about anything for me, and I would do the same for them.

I finally heard a lot of noise coming in the front door, so I decided they must be back. Sure enough, they were. They were more excited now than they had been this morning.

"Guess what?" Mabel hollered as she walked in. "We have enough money now to start calling the show. Bing wrote the number down the other night. I heard them say to start calling between the hours of 6:00 p.m. and 2:00 a.m. Eastern Standard Time. It's almost 6:00 o'clock now. Why don't we ask Lynn if it's all right for us to use the pay phone in the hall?"

Doc suggested that we get started. "I have heard that some people have had to call for several days before they get through. We better ask Lynn before we tie that phone up for that long a time."

I got up off the bunk, and we all walked to the office to talk to Lynn.

First thing he said was, "I was wondering when you guys were gonna start calling. I think it would be best if we all take turns on the phone. Say thirty minutes at a time. There are seven of us so that means we only have to be on the phone for thirty minutes every three hours and a half." Everyone agreed with Lynn.

"But, how do we pay you?" I asked.

He just smiled and said, "Let's get you on the show first so you can win some money, and then we will all have a big party right here in the Sanctuary. Oh, I forgot to tell you. A friend of mine came out today and installed one of those automatic redial things on my phone. He works for the telephone company, so there was no charge for it. He just says for us to invite him to the party if you win.

"What this thing does," Lynn explained, "is once you dial the number, if it's busy, the phone stays on that number until there is a hang up or a clear line, then it automatically dials into that clear line. With God's help and if we are lucky, we might get through tonight. I know there are a lot of other people that have these automatic dialers, but let's just keep a positive thought. I'll show you how this thing works, and then we'll get started.

"Cowboy, why don't you take the first turn while the rest of us go to the kitchen and eat, then you can be relieved and go to eat."

"That'll be fine Lynn; let's get started."

We went over to the phone, and Lynn explained how simple it was to use. Bing gave him the number, and he looked at Bing with a surprised expression. "Bing, this is an 800 number, and that means the phone call is free."

Everyone looked surprised. Lynn laughed and dialed it and got a busy signal. "Okay, Cowboy, you just keep watching and waiting until it starts dialing the number again automatically. When it starts to dial you come and get Professor in a hurry. That way he can talk to the people who answer the phone. I'm sure they are going to want to ask him a lot of questions before they either accept or deny him as a contestant."

Cowboy sat down in the easy chair beside Lynn's desk. The rest of us went to the kitchen to eat.

Today was a good day because they had pot roast with vegetables in it and a lot of pot roast gravy and biscuits with iced tea. Tonight there must have been about sixty people having dinner at the Sanctuary. It took a lot of meat and vegetables and tea to feed that many people. Most of them were adults, but there were three or four children here tonight. The number of people varied each night and each season.

This summer there won't be half this many staying all night. Since the weather would normally be nice, and the parks are real pleasant during that time of the year. You could lie there, look up at the stars, and dream about better times and better days.

Once in a while, you would get into an area where there were a lot of chiggers. Chiggers were a little red devil of an insect about the size of the point of a pin. Seriously, they really were that small. Boy, did they make you itch. They dig into the hair folicle and really hurt.

We found that a recipe from Doc works pretty well. If you could cut off their supply of oxygen, they will die. Doc managed somehow to get clear fingernail polish which he painted over them. They died due to lack of oxygen, and then you peeled the fingernail polish off after they died.

After we ate, we headed back to the office to see how Cowboy was doing. He was still sitting there waiting on that phone to start dialing again. He said it did dial once, but it had apparently gotten beat out by someone else ahead of us. Now, he was ready to go eat since the bill of fare sure did sound good tonight and he had worked so hard today.

"Oh, yeah, how about the work? What did you do?" I asked.

Bing came in to relieve on the phone. "Okay, Cowboy, I'll take over the phone watch, and you go eat."

Mabel and Doc started talking at the same time about what they had done today.

I finally had to say, "Slow down a little, now let's just have one of you talk at a time."

Bing looked at Mabel and said, "Ladies first."

Mabel started in with how they had gotten the job. She told in detail how she talked the foreman into hiring them. All the time Bing was shaking his head and grinning. Mabel told how she had gotten him to agree to hire all of them at the same time, and he had agreed to find something for me to do once my leg and arm got better.

I told them I could use my fingers to pick up things now. I would just have to take it a little easy with the leg, but the arm didn't hurt much. I went on, "It kind of itches just above the place where the hand connects onto the wrist.

"How much they are paying?"

Mabel said, "They're paying all of the cleanup help $6.50 per hour. Hell, I got enough money today to buy some gloves tomorrow. They pay us at the end of each day. They say they can't always depend on street people showing up the next day, so they would just as soon pay each evening."

We decided to settle everyone down a little and play some dominos while we were waiting on the phone. Some other guys were watching some historical TV program. We had played for about thirty minutes when Cowboy came back into the room licking his lips and making loud smacking sounds with his mouth to show us how much he had enjoyed the dinner.

Just then Lynn's wife, Annie came into the office. She had been back in the kitchen overseeing the supper cooks and the cleanup crew. She was a pretty lady with what used to be coal black hair but was now highlighted with a touch of silver threads that made it even more attractive. She was what some people might consider just a pound or two overweight, but I liked to say that ladies like this were just very beautiful and healthy looking. They reminded me of my mother who had very, very black hair with a swatch of silver gray just above the left eye. She was also just pleasantly not skinny –

just rounded out real nice for a mother and grandmother. Her pale blue eyes would shine like the morning sun when she would smile. She had small dimples on both cheeks that kind of sucked in when she smiled or laughed. She had the most natural deep red rose-colored lips you have ever seen.

I could see her smiling as my dad would walk up the sidewalk from the driveway where he parked the car when he came home in the late afternoon or evening. She seemed to have an uncommon sense about the time he would be coming in, even if he didn't call and tell her.

I guess I was spoiled in my marriage by seeing what I considered the perfect parents with the perfect marriage. When they looked at each other, there was a love in the eyes of each of them that said all that needed to be said between two people. I was sure they said a lot more in private, but what I always admired so much was that they weren't afraid to show their affection for each other at home or in public.

They weren't mushy, but that love was just always there in the way they held hands or kissed when they parted even for a few minutes or hours. It was as if they were saying *I love you* and *I want you to know it just in case you don't make it back.* They always seemed to just touch as they passed each other or stood near each other. I guess I was just spoiled by loving parents such as this, and I guess this was what I had expected my marriage to be. It wasn't.

The finest things to come out of my marriage were my son and my daughter. I sometimes thought the reason I hurt so much inside was that I felt that I had let my children down. I mean, I couldn't live with my wife, so how should I expect my young children to live with her? I knew my parents would help with them, but I sometimes felt like a real coward for not staying. I knew now that if I got a second chance by appearing on this game show, I would make the most of it. I just knew I would. I had too many people depending on me.

The Phone Call

All at once, Bing started hollering and screaming at the top of his lungs as he came running out of the office. "It's ringing; it's ringing," he said and turned to run back into the office.

All of us jumped up from the table at once and started running for the door to the office. In the melee, we turned the domino table over and sent dominos flying every direction. We almost ran over two or three of the people seated near us. I'll bet they thought we were nuts by the way were carrying on.

I got to the door first, sore leg, broken wrist, and all. I reached for and picked up the phone just as someone on the other end said, "Hello. This is 'Who Wants To Be A Millionaire'; are you calling about trying out for the show?"

I almost swallowed my tongue. "Yes, I sure am."

She had a nice soothing voice that seemed to put me at ease, which sure did help. "First, tell me your name."

I almost forgot what my name was, but then I regrouped, and I told her my name.

"Now, sir, what is your occupation?"

I hesitated and said, "I am a retired Professor of Philosophy."

"Oh, sir, that's nice. Now, how old are you?"

I even had to think about that for a minute, and finally I was able to blurt out, "Forty-nine years old. I was born in 1951 in Chicago, Illinois."

"That's fine, Mr., or should I say Professor, Dixon. You just answered my next two questions. Now we have to go through a procedure to select our contestants. This procedure takes several weeks. I hope you will be patient with us."

The young lady asked me a question and gave me four answers to choose one as the correct answer. I answered the first one correctly. She asked me another, again with four answers from which I needed to pick the correct one. This one I answered correctly which led to the third one, which was the same pattern as the previous two. I was lucky, and I answered it correctly also. The young lady congratulated me and said they would be in touch with me again in the near future.

The same young lady called again four more times over the next five weeks. She finally called and said, "I need to ask you questions about various things. We need to know just how well-rounded your knowledge is concerning a lot of different things in our ordinary everyday life, as well as some of the other phases of our educational life."

I thought I had already answered enough questions, but I didn't argue.

She told me most of the questions were pretty easy. "They are of many different subjects. Are you ready?"

I swallowed real hard. "Yes, ma'am, I'm ready."

For the next five minutes, she questioned me about things that were very simple and some things that were not so simple. Hard questions for some people would be like the one about the year of the Normandy Beach landing during World War II and who the general was that ordered the landing? Another of this type was what was the year of the Spanish American War. Another was who was the director who also starred in the movie *The Treasure of Sierra Madre*. Thank goodness I used to be a movie buff. These and many others were asked, and I guess I answered them to her satisfaction.

She told me my name would be put in the pool, and my grade on the answers would be checked against others who had been called. She told me that if I was picked, they would notify me within a few days.

I thanked her, hung up the phone, and we all just stood in dead silence for about a minute. The room erupted with shouts and laughter. I was in a total state of shock. Cowboy, Pug, Mabel, Bing, Doc, Lynn, and Annie were all dancing and hugging each other and hugging me. It seemed they just couldn't stop laughing and grinning. My grin had to be the biggest grin I had had on my face in years.

Then came the hard part – waiting and waiting and more waiting.

My next phone call came about a week later. They asked me more questions. I was just about to give up. The gang was working and wondering if I was ever going to get on that program. It was beginning to be a joke around the Sanctuary, but I figured that I just had to be in there if they called again.

We decided that I needed to stay off the leg for a few more days, anyway, so I decided to hang around the Sanctuary. One excuse was as good as another.

It had been about five or six weeks by this time, and I was beginning to feel real good physically. My broken wrist didn't really hurt any more, and they were going to take the cast off this week.

The next morning, the gang went off to work. I felt kind of bad staying at the Sanctuary and not doing my part. Lynn and Annie let me know real soon that I would be doing my part if I got on the show. I reluctantly agreed with them. I asked if I could do anything else to help around the place.

"I know that I can wash dishes now because the cast is coming off my wrist. I might have trouble sweeping and mopping, but I sure am willing to give it a try. I find that I can grip the handle of the push broom pretty well with my fingers now. I do pretty well for a while."

Annie came over and asked, "Can you look after the place for a while? I want to take Lynn with me to the grocery store to pick up a few things we need. You need to be here anyway in case they call from the show."

"Sure thing, Annie. I'll be glad to answer the phone." The phone rang several times, but it was not the call that I was waiting on.

Annie and Lynn came back from the store. Annie started lunch, and Lynn went to sorting out a large bag of clothing that a lady had brought by as a donation to the Sanctuary. I helped him for a while.

When we were through, I decided to watch TV for a while. The rest of the day went by without a phone call. My nerves were beginning to show wear.

Lunch came and went with no calls for me. I knew the gang should be coming in from work before too long. Lynn started setting out the silverware and dishes for the dinner tonight. I tried to help, but it was getting harder and harder to concentrate on anything but that darn phone in the office.

It rang.

I ran; they wanted to talk to Lynn. I called Lynn to the phone. Then I heard the noise that I had been waiting for. It was the gang.

Mabel ran in the door hollering, "Did you get the call?"

I just looked at her, and she very quietly told the others, "It don't look like he got the call. That's all right, Professor; maybe it'll come tomorrow."

Everyone was talking at the same time, and you could hardly hear yourself think.

Mabel started off by showing me her gloves. "We're nearing the end of the cleanup work, but these things saved my hands today."

Bing told us, "The glass that fell off the building is real rough on your hands."

Pug agreed and added, "The truth is, it's hard on your feet too. You walk on that stuff, and it eventually cuts into the soles of your shoes. We really worked hard today cleaning, picking up glass, and helping pile up the debris so the front-end loaders could pick it up and load the trucks so they could carry it off."

Doc said, "Professor, I really feel good for a change. I really did an honest day's work without having to have a drink. Hell, if this keeps up, I might end up an honest, sober and changed man. Naw, I ain't sure that will happen, but it still feels good to be tired from working hard. I haven't felt like this in years."

Cowboy, Bing, Mabel, and even Pug all agreed with Doc. concerning how well they were feeling.

I had known these guys for several years, and I don't think I had ever seen them all in agreement like this.

Well, the night went by with a group of us watching the Texas Rangers baseball team playing the New York Yankees. Needless to say, they lost. Sometimes I thought the Yankees had a hex over the Rangers.

It was past midnight now, and I still couldn't clear my mind enough to let myself go to sleep. I heard the gang talking till about midnight. I guess they were hopped up too. I figured that as tired as they were, they wouldn't have much trouble going to sleep.

I had no idea just what time I finally dozed off to sleep, but I woke up to the smell of coffee and the noise of chatter in the kitchen. I finally got out of bed and made my way to the kitchen and found a cup of coffee. It seemed that I must have really had a deep sleep because the gang had already left for work. They hadn't wanted to disturb me. They said I needed the rest.

Today went just about like yesterday with me sitting around waiting on that phone call. I was beginning to get discouraged, but I knew I had to put up a good front for all of my friends. I just couldn't let them down.

We had breakfast, swept the floors, and arranged the tables and chairs. We took out the trash so we could start to arrange for the lunch crowd. We had a pretty good crowd for lunch. A lot more of the people who had been staying here were working downtown to pick up a little extra cash. Some of the guys and gals came back here for lunch. It just depended on how close they were working.

The gang was working right downtown, which meant that it would be a long way for them to walk back to the Sanctuary for lunch. They just bought a soft drink and a sandwich and a piece of fruit off the lunch wagon that came around. This made them feel good because they had some money in their pockets to pay for everything.

I watched more TV in the afternoon, but I had a lot of trouble keeping my mind on it. I could never remember having anything bother me like this waiting game we were playing. This was worse than waiting at the hospital for my wife to give birth to our son and daughter.

Funny, how the kids kept coming back into my mind. Maybe this was a sign of some kind. I had heard that sometimes you get a sign that means something like that. I sure hoped so.

The gang came in from work, loud and anxious as ever. They were disappointed when they found that I hadn't received the call yet. They all hurried to the shower rooms and washed up. That was one thing the Sanctuary did have that the gang appreciated. They had a large shower room for men and one for women. They also had lockers with individual keys, so you could keep some clothes in them and not get them stolen.

They finally came out all spic and span with clean clothes and the whole nine yards. It was almost time for dinner.

Lynn came by and wanted to know, "How do you guys feel about having a little prayer to the ole boy upstairs to see if it might help?"

The group all looked at each other, since they weren't really the praying type.

Finally Bing gave a, "Heck, yes. Who knows what will help, and that might just be the thing that does it. I'm willing to give it a try. How about the rest of you?"

Mabel let everyone know she was certainly in favor, which surprised me. Lynn and Annie laughed, and we all knelt down in the office. Lynn offered a real good prayer asking the Lord to help us if it was His intention that we get Professor on the show, and maybe in the meantime it would help the rest of us get some meaning into our lives and help us get our lives straightened out. He was real clear about us getting our lives straightened out. We could sure use some straightening out.

After the prayer, we all went out to the dining room and had dinner, or supper, as a lot of the people called it. Call it what you want, but it sure is good: Swiss steak, mashed potatoes, gravy, green beans, and a salad.

Doc told Cowboy, "Heck, you would have to go to a cafeteria to get a meal like this."

We ate a good meal and then started watching TV again. None of us could really concentrate on it. Every time the phone rang, our hearts did flip flops. This went on till about 9:00 p.m., and everyone was getting ready for bed when the phone rang. That late at night, we knew it was not for me.

Annie answered the phone, then came to the door, and hollered "Professor, it's for you."

I damn near had a heart attack. I stumbled over a couple of other people watching TV on my way to the door.

Annie was grinning from ear to ear, and Lynn was smiling real big when he handed me the receiver.

I mumbled something like, "Hello, this is Professor Dixon." The voice on the other end of the line was the same sweet, clear voice that had asked me all of those questions on each of the other calls. She told me it was good to talk to me again and said she had some good news for me.

I had been chosen to appear on the show in a few weeks. The young lady said the board that selected the contestants had been very impressed with my interviews. She told me that it wasn't very often they got someone with a Doctorate of Philosophy as a contestant.

I explained, "I have been pretty inactive for several years."

She said, "That's all right, but you are the only one who has ever given the right answers to all of the questions we ask on our phone interviews." She added that this had raised quite a few eyebrows. "They're anxious to meet you.

"You know, once you get here and appear on the show, you still have to compete against nine other contestants to get to the seat where you compete for the big prize. We do send airline tickets for you and a friend to come to New York City. We will also send you one thousand dollars for spending money, and we will arrange accommodations at the Downtown Regency Hotel for the both of you. You will be our guest for the entire length of your stay here in town. The airline tickets are round trip, so don't worry about being trapped here in New York City.

"The other thing is that you are obligated to sign a release of rights in order for us to use any video or still pictures of any and all parts of the show in which you will participate. Do you understand and agree to these stipulations and rules? If you do, please stipulate so by saying I do agree to these rules and stipulations. You know that this phone conversation is being recorded and will be used as a part of your file with this company as your agreement, and you do agree that it will be necessary for you to sign a written agreement to the above stated upon your arrival.

"If this is your wish, please state that it is at this time."

I calmly told her, "I do agree to the foregoing requirements, and I will be more than willing to sign an agreement upon my arrival."

The very nice young lady then said, "Professor – I hope you don't mind me calling you by your title – you will be receiving your tickets via a delivery service in Ft. Worth within two days. Your arrival will be anticipated by all connected with the show, and good luck to you."

You should have heard the gang roar. They told everyone in the Sanctuary what was happening, and they gave us another big hand. They kept coming around and patting me on the back, while I kept thinking that this really wasn't my doing. This was basically the idea and the work and the encouragement of the gang. They were the ones that deserved the credit. I had just answered a few very easy questions. Who could have ever asked for any better friends? I couldn't, that was for sure.

Trip Preparations

The next two days went by very slowly. The gang worked, and I stayed at the Sanctuary because I knew that I would have to sign for the tickets.

On the second day, a young man came to the Sanctuary and asked for me. I introduced myself and he handed me an envelope with two tickets on American Airlines to New York City. There was also a check for one thousand dollars with instructions of what I was to do, and where I was to go upon arrival.

I was very nervous as I read the instructions. You would think I had never seen a check for a thousand dollars. He then asked me to sign a receipt for the items I had received. I must admit, it had been quite a few years since I had seen this much money, much less held the check in my hand for that much money. It still seemed like a dream.

Boy it was gonna be hard to go to sleep tonight. I had to plan out all the things I had to do before going to New York. The first thing I had to do was to go and see Dr. Davis. I hoped he had been serious about those suits and shirts and all of that stuff. Getting the clothes from him would be better than having to go over to Chrissie's Used Clothing Emporium. I know she kind of liked me, but I hate her flirting. I guess that would turn some guys on, but not me. Truth was, she was not really that bad looking. The fact of the matter was she was kind of pretty.

Hell, what am I doing? I guess I am just trying to talk myself into going to see her.

I dodn't have time for such stuff. Well, not right now at this time. *Maybe when I get back from New York.* She did look kind of nice when she was all dressed up. *Hell, Professor,* I say to myself, it's time to knock off such thinking as this.

I know it had been a long time since I have been with a woman. I probably wouldn't know how to act if I went out with a woman after all this time. I would most likely get all nervous and flustered. I have an idea that Chrissie would know how to take care of that all right. No, I'm not going to do it before I go to the show. I have to keep my head on straight and just think about the show. Hell, I don't even know that I'll get on the show when I do get there.

There will be nine other people trying to get on the show, and I am sure they would be more aware of current events than I am – well at least for the last fifteen years. I generally read the newspaper when I can find one even if it is a day or two old. I just get my news a little late. The gang has been real nice about finding a newspaper when they are out looking through trash bins and barrels. They generally are real good about bringing them to me so I can read them and try to work the crossword puzzles. It is kind of hard, though, when you don't have a dictionary.

What the hell am I getting so worked up for? She's only a woman. Well, she is a few years younger than I, and she is built pretty darn good. Those dark brown eyes and that dark hair with a touch of gray make her look kind of sophisticated at times.

Damn it, Professor, just stop all this nonsense about Chrissie, and screw your head on right. You are on an adventure that may eventually lead you back to your home and your children and your parents. Just forget about this woman. At least for now. Just keep this in mind, and you'll be all right.

The others were having trouble going to sleep also, especially Pug. Pug actually saw the ticket that are going to allow him to go to Madison Square Garden – the one place he had wanted most to go when he had been fighting. He wouldn't be fighting there, but he would see it, and he will take some pictures to bring back to Cowboy who wanted so badly to qualify and then compete there in the National Rodeo Cowboys Association National Finals. He qualified and then got hurt before he could make the trip.

Life took on some funny turns. It was kind of like my friend Ray said, "Sometimes life do get tedjious, don't it?"

It sounds as though the gang had finally quieted down for the night. Now, if I could only clear this pea brain of mine so I could go to sleep.

The next thing I hear are the noises in the kitchen. It sounds as though some of the people are up, so I decide I should get up and have a shower and shave so I can go and see Dr. Davis. I didn't remember just how good it was to be able to have a shower in the morning to help me wake up. I also realize that I hadn't had a drink now in over seven weeks. My shakes have cleared up, and I don't have a headache. This is a first for me in several years.

I can actually smell and taste the food I am eating over the smell of my breath and the stench of my own body and the clothes on my back.

I find myself asking myself, Just how in hell did I ever let myself get in this condition? How did an educated man let a woman drive him to this? Will my children ever accept me back?

I was truly beginning to understand just how much this chance meant to me. I realize now how much it would mean to so many people who did not even know it was happening. I tell myself, Quit thinking, Professor, and clear your mind; think tomorrow.

The gang has gone to work. They are really enjoying the work. They really enjoye sweating and getting dirty and then coming back to the Sanctuary and getting into the shower. Hell, most of them hadn't averaged a shower or bath once a month during our normal lives, but this is definitely not our normal life. That tornado has sure changed a lot of lives. A lot of these lives are actually a byproduct of the storm.

I finally get my clothes on after I shaved. I stop at the office on my way out to tell Lynn and Annie where I am going in case anyone wants to know.

I walk just about a mile up to the hospital. I walk into the emergency entrance, and a couple of the attendants speak to me as I go by. One had been an attendant the night of the storm. He was real nice and asked how I was feeling. He wanted to know about my arm and my leg. He noticed my head didn't show much sign of bruises now.

I asked if he had seen Dr. Davis.

"Sure have, he's up in his office on the first floor. Do you know how to get up there?"

"Thanks for the help. I know how to get there."

The emergency entrance is kind of like a basement entrance, kind of like a floor and a half. Well, I make my way up to the first floor and ask a nurse where Dr. Davis' office is located.

She points down the hall. "The third door on the left, you can't miss it. Oh, by the way aren't you Professor?"

I was real surprised by the question. I was a little embarrassed, as I answered, "Yes, I am."

"Have you done anything about getting on 'So You Want to Be a Millionaire? Everyone in the hospital is talking about it."

Just as I was about to explain, I see Dr. Davis coming out of his office. I start in the direction of Dr. Davis, but first I turn to the nurse. "Yes, ma'am, I made it, and I'll be going back sometime this coming week."

Dr. Davis sees me about the same time I spot him and he heads my way with a big smile on his face. He sticks out his hand and says, "Well, I hope you have some good news for us. We haven't had this much excitement around here in years."

"We did call, and I did get selected to go back to New York City. They sent the airline tickets plus the money. Everyone is so excited that you would have thought this was happening to them."

"You're a celebrity," said a nurse standing behind me. I turned to see the nurse who had been so kind to me when I had been in the hospital. She is smiling real big. Hell, everyone is smiling.

You would have thought I was a movie star or something. They all wish me well and tell me to keep them informed about which night I get to be on the floor and challenge the other nine contestants for the right to appear in the big seat. I assure them I will.

"Dr. Davis puts his hand on the Professors shoulder; come on in the office we have some talking to do."

We reach his office, and he tells me to have a seat.

"Well, Professor, tell me all about it and how you feel about so much excitement after all these years.

I explain all of the things that had happened. I also tell him about my fears of what might happen. This is the first time I have ever told anyone about my past and my family.

He just looks at me and says, "Professor, this can be the turning point in your life. I have all the faith in the world in you and that you will do the right thing. My wife and I have discussed your situation and we want to help if you will let us.

"I would like for you go down to Sears and ask for Johnny. Johnny is the manager of the men's department, and he is also a good friend of mine. Johnny says for you to come down and pick out a couple of suits and a sport coat with a couple pair of slacks and some shirts and ties. He is giving them to us at their cost. I'm going to pay for them. You can pay me back after you get on your feet if you want to, but it's not going to be expected. We just want to help you get a new start.

"Professor, we just believe in the Golden Rule and the Bible. We are Christians, and we live accordingly.

We feel that anytime we help someone, it comes back ten fold as the Bible says." He laughingly added, "That doesn't mean that you will need to pay us back ten fold. We're sure you will do yourself proud when you get back there."

Oh yes, "do you think that the thousand dollars the show sent for expenses will be enough?"

"I'm sure it will be just fine doctor."

"Professor, you know I'll let you have another four or five hundred if you think that thousand won't be enough for you and your friend."

"Thanks, Dr. Davis, but I'll be just fine."

"Now, Professor, you go on down to Sears and see Johnny."

"Thanks again, Doctor. I'm on my way."

We shake hands, and I go out through the main entrance. I am amazed at the number of people staring at me as I walk out. I think maybe it is because this is the first time they have ever seen me wearing clean clothes and a clean face instead of whiskers. To tell you the truth it is almost embarrassing.

I arrive at the Sears store down on 9th Street. I walked in the front door and see the Men's Department. It's way back at the back of the store. I walk back there acting just as though I belonged in the store.

A nice young man came up to me. "Good morning, may I be of service to you?"

"I'm Professor Dixon, and I am looking for Johnny," I say.

He smiles and says, "I'm Johnny, and I'm glad to meet you, Professor."

We shake hands. It had been a long time since anyone has done that with me. I tell him I don't know much about styles these days and will appreciate his help in making the decisions.

He looks at me and says, "You look like you might be about a 42 long."

"Well, I used to be a 44 long. As you probably know, I haven't bought any clothes in some time."

He just smiles and said, "You look like the conservative type businessman or college professor. I think we should keep it fairly conservative don't you? I would like to suggest a dark blue pin stripe with a light blue shirt and a darker blue tie."

He pulls out a suit that is real pretty. It has very good tailoring. I used to know good clothes, and some of it is beginning to come back to me.

I ask about a second suit.

He thinks that maybe a solid color blue, just a little lighter than the pin stripe, would be a good choice. He suggested that with my complexion and dark hair that would be good.

He walks over to the rack and takes one off. He comes over and asks me to take off the coat I am wearing and try this one on.

"Oh! This feels good. It fits just perfect, you know what I mean, just like a glove."

While I am looking at myself in the mirror, he walks over with a beautiful blue sport coat that has a very subdued check in the pattern. I look at it and my mind wanders back to a coat with a very similar pattern that I used to wear to informal school functions.

Johnny offers suggestions on the shirts and ties to match. Johnny is very helpful, and he has wonderful taste in men's clothing.

I worry about the cost of all of these clothes but he assures me that Dr. Davis is not concerned. He lets me know that Dr. Davis just wants me to look good when I get back to New York and represent Texas.

I laugh and say that's really funny because, "I am originally from Chicago."

He laughs and says, "Well, you're a Texan now. The doctor tells me that I am going to make everyone real proud of me. Know what? I am really beginning to believe him."

We finally get the two suits, a sport coat, two pair of slacks with shirts and ties to match as well as a pair of beautiful black wing-tipped dress shoes. Hell, I am real pretty now if I do say so myself – or at least I will be when I get all "duded" up for the trip and the show.

With my arms full of clothing, I head back to the Sanctuary.

When I arrive, Lynn tells me to follow him; he had something in the office he wants me to see. I follow him into the office where he shows me two new suitcases sitting on the floor beside his desk along with a couple of smaller bags for our personal articles.

"Professor, the gang saved their pay and pooled enough to buy these bags for you guys." He finally admits that he and Annie added a few more dollars.

"Lynn, how can I ever pay you folks back for what you're doing for the gang and me?"

Annie smiles broadly, "Well, you can't carry all of those new clothes to New York City in a paper bag. You have to look the part. You're a professor, and don't you ever forget it."

"Annie, can I hug your neck and shake Lynn's hand. I must admit that I am totally bewildered at how nice people have been to me since we started this. They have even been more friendly after they heard that I had been accepted to participate on the show. The day will come when I will be able to pay you back, and I will do just that. You folks have taken me into your family, and I will never let you down."

It'is time for lunch, and I need to help Lynn and Annie, so I take my new clothes to my locker and lock them up so they won't disappear. I sure would hate to lose them now.

One thing we have to do now is buy Pug a new suit and sport coat and slacks. We will do that tomorrow afternoon after they get home from work. The stores stay open late tomorrow night.

Right now, I need to help carry the dishes back to the kitchen even though I can't wash them. I can help by taking them back to the kitchen. I would help put the food in the refrigerator that wasn't eaten tonight.

After everything is put away and the tables have been straightened up, I find a broom and start to sweep out from under the tables. When I am finished, I ask Annie if it will be all right if I go to lie down for a while. I have walked quite a long way this morning, and I have to admit that I am getting real tired.

She thinks it will be a real good idea for me to forget the afternoon TV and take a good long nap instead. She don't have to say it twice. I am heading for the bed.

The gang comes in after work. They want to see my new clothes. I take them out of the locker and show them off to my friends. Pug seemed a little sullen until I tell him that we are going out tomorrow night after they got back from work to buy him some new clothes to wear back to the Big Apple.

His disappointed look turned into a great big wide smile. "Do you really mean that?"

"I sure do, Pug. Now go get ready for dinner."

"Sure thing, Professor."

They go to clean up and get ready for dinner or supper, whichever you preferred to call it. We all set together and enjoy dinner and discuss what we are going to be doing for the next couple of weeks until we leave for New York.

"Work, Professor, work."

Mabel is real serious. "We intend to make some more money while you are gone just in case you don't hit it big."

"Mabel, wash your mouth out with soap. You know we are going to do good. Only teasing Mabel, only teasing. What would we do without you around here to keep us in line?

"Bing, what do you have to say about that?"

"Professor, I think it is great to have some change in my pocket making a tinkling sound while I walk. I haven't heard that for many years, and I dearly love it."

"Thanks, guys, for pitching in and buying the suitcases and bags for us. Pug thanks you too, don't you, Pug?"

"I sure do, Professor. I really know what kind of friends I have at a time like this."

Bing said, "It's the first time I have had folding money in my wallet in quite a few years. I intend to hang on to all of it I can because I may want to do something else before long."

"Bing, you have really changed. Now you walk straighter with your head held higher."

"Well, Professor, I know I have changed, and I intend to stay with that change."

There has been an amazing transformation in all of the gang. They are sober and clean, and lately they have been real tired at the end of the day.

I had heard that waiting could get tiresome, and now I believed it. These last ten days seemed like two months at the rate it was going. We passed the time by the gang working downtown and me doing a little work around the Sanctuary in order to help pay for the food and lodging. They have even insisted on paying Lynn and Annie some money to help with the cost of their room and board.

Lynn and Annie didn't want to take it, but the gang insist.

The gang has a calendar on the wall, and every day they mark off another day and say, "One less day, Professor. Just one day less."

Pug seems to be having more trouble waiting than I am. I actually beat him last night at dominos. He generally beats almost everyone who comes in here. He just couldn't seem to get his mind on anything except going to New York.

The Flight to New York

The day finally arrives. We are to leave DFW at 11:00 a.m. and arrive in New York City at 5:15 p.m. The instructions say that they will have a limousine at the airport to take us to the Downtown Regency Hotel so we don't have to worry about that.

Then, we have to worry about finding the limousine and its driver. I understand the driver will have a card that he will hold up with my name on it.

Boy, do we look snazzy. Pug and I both have on our sports coats and slacks with new shirts and ties. I don't know how long it has been since I have worn a tie, but I have to admit it feels real good. Pug looks real fine, too. I needed to tie his tie for him because he said he had never ever worn a tie before except to church, and then his mother had tied it for him. Oh, yes, he had gone to church with his mother when he was a young man.

"Come on, guys, we've got to be going."

"Okay, I tell Lynn, we're on our way."

Mabel comes over and gives me a big hug and then gives Pug a big hug and a "Make us all proud, Professor.

"Pug, you look out for him and see that he don't get hurt or mugged or something. I've read a lot of stories about people getting mugged in New York City, so you watch out for him and see he don't get hurt. Pug, did you hear me?"

"Yes, Mabel, I heard you. I'll take care of him."

Cowboy, Bing, and Doc came over and gave both of us big hugs and shake our hands. "Good luck, and hang in there."

I believed I even see a tear in Mabel's eye as we turn to walk out the front door heading for Lynn's car. Annie is standing at the car and gives us both big hugs and a peck on the cheek. "Professor, we're pulling for you. Make us proud. I know you will. I really didn't have to say that because we all know you will. Heck, Professor, you know that Lynn and I will have you and Pug in our prayers."

We arrived at DFW Airport and head straight to Terminal C gate 27 for departure to New York City. The baggage attendant takes our bags and hands us the torn off end of the ticket. "I hope, gentlemen, you enjoy the trip."

I hand him a five-dollar bill for his tip. Man, it has been a long time since I'd been able to do that – I mean tip someone who does something nice for me. He thanks me and tells me we have a straight through flight. It is nice to have a straight through flight. No stops on the way, so it will only take about four or five hours to get there.

As we start to walk off, he hollers over his shoulder, "Have a nice trip."

"Thanks we intend to, don't we, Pug?"

We go inside the terminal stopping at the metal detector. This surprises Pug since he had never been through one of these things before. Matter of fact, he had never been on an airplane either.

He empties his pockets, and then he has to remove his big Texas belt buckle and take all the change out of his pockets before he finally clears the detector. I forget to take the pen and pencil I had received as a going away gift from some of the guys at the Sanctuary from my pocket, and I have to go back around and go through the gate again. Pug gets a big kick out of that.

Lynn didn't come in, he had to get back to the Sanctuary so we wave good-bye to him as he heads back to the car and we head to the check-in counter. We find the counter right by a big sign that said Gate 27. The agent greets us with a smile, looks at our tickets, and tells us that the flight is over sold; and if we would like to wait for a later flight, they will be glad to give us a free flight to be used at a later date. They also promise to get us on another flight behind this one to New York City. We explain that we have to be in New York City on this flight because we have people waiting for us to arrive on this flight. They understand and immediately offer the same thing to the guy standing behind us. He accepts it if they would get him out on the next flight to New York City.

They promise they will, and he still gets a free ticket to be used at a later date. Some deal if you aren't in a hurry.

We have a seat and start to read a paper when a young man comes up to us and asked me if I am Professor Dixon. I admitt that I am and I ask what I can do for him. He explains that he is from the *Fort Worth Morning News* and wonders if I would mind him asking me a few questions about how I got on the program. He tells me that he has heard about it from a nurse at the hospital who worked with Dr. Davis. It seems we had been the whole conversation around the hospital this morning.

"Go ahead and ask me a few questions, and I will answer them if I can."

We talk for a short time, and I answer most of his questions until the public address system announces that they are ready to start the boarding of our flight. We have to leave in a few minutes.

I apologize to the young man and tell him that if we do have a successful trip, I will be happy to talk to him when we got back. I ask his name so I could look him up when we get back. His name was Robert Hitch.

"Well, Robert, we'll see you when we return." If I don't, please call and remind me that we have a date.

"That's a date, Professor."

As he walks off, he turns and gives us the thumbs up sign and says, "Good luck to both of you, and "Pug, I hope you get to see Madison Square Garden."

We walk down the boarding ramp and into the plane where we are greeted by a young lady. I believe they still called them stewardess. I don't know for sure because it had been a long time since I have been on a plane.

She checked our tickets and thanked us. "Your seats are toward the rear of the plane."

We get to the seats, and I place the luggage we had carried on board in the overhead compartment. I ask her if this was the right seat. She checked our tickets and assured me they were the right ones: row 42, seats A and B. I tell Pug that we are in the tourist section.

"Yes, sir, this is where you belong; these are definitely your seats."

"Thank you, young lady."

"Pug boy, they really take care of us, don't they?"

He looks at me and grinns that grin that only Pug has. It is a cross between a six-year-old kid caught with his hand in the cookie jar, and that of a seventy-five year old man stealing a kiss from a good-looking widow woman. In other words, it is difficult to explain, but once you see it, you never forgot it. We sit down and relax.

Pug starts looking around. "Hey, Professor, if I have to go to the bathroom, what do I do?"

I point to the rear of the cabin. "Pug, there is a commode behind that door, but you will have to wait till we are up in the air before you can use it."

"I don't understand, Professor. What happens when we flush the commode? Does it fall on the people down below us on the ground?"

"I'm not real sure, Pug, but I think it has a large tank on the plane that it goes into, and then it's emptied when we land." This answer seems to satisfy him.

Before we reach our seats, I ask if he wouldn't like to sit by the window so he could see out while we were in the air. This really pleased him. He was like a kid with his first real big toy. He has lots of questions, and his eyes are wide open taking in everything around us. I am really glad he got to come with me.

After about thirty minutes all the travelers are in their seats. The seat belt sign comes on. The young ladies walked down the aisle to check and make sure everyone has the seat belts on and fastened properly.

One of the young ladies comes on the intercom and starts her speach by greeting us and then asking us to double check our seat belts. She goes on to explain about overhead oxygen masks and the floatation devices.

Pug looks at me and asks, "Professor, I didn't know we were going to fly over the ocean."

I explained to him that we really weren't going to fly over the ocean, but that the occasion might arise when they should have to divert our flight because of some weather or other thing. If that did happen, we needed to know what to do in case of a crash. This didn't set too well. I now have to assure him that we are going to be just fine.

Just at that time the plane starts to back up to prepare to leave the terminal.

Pug looks at me and with very wide eyes said, "Professor, I didn't know these things could go backward."

I had to laugh a little bit at this one before I explained. I explain that a tractor had now attached itself to the nose wheel of the plane and was pushing us backward and around so we could leave the terminal building. This seemed to satisfy him, and he sighed a big sigh of relief.

Then we were on the cross taxi strips, and I saw him looking real hard out the window. Now he wanted to know what would happen if another plane came down while we were crossing those runways. I assured him they wouldn't.

We finally reach our takeoff runway and are behind about four or five other planes. We sit quietly for about fifteen minutes before the engines rev up and the plane starts to move. I see Pug tighten his grip on the armrest of the seat.

"Okay, Pug, here we go; we'll be airborne in about two or three minutes at the most."

We start to move slowly at first, and then the captain poured the coals to it, and the engines are revved up to full power, and away we go. I see that Pug is real tense now, so I tell him to look out the window and he would be able to see Lake Worth because we are taking off to the west, and then we would circle to the east and head for New York City.

He eases his head over against the window. "Well, I'll be darned. I sure can see the lake. Hell, now I can see another lake down there. As a matter of fact, there are several lakes down there, and I can see Texas Stadium. Boy, everything sure does look different from up here. Hey, Professor, this is great, real great. People and cars down there on the ground look like ants crawling around."

About thirty minutes after we are in the air, the stewardess comes down the aisle and stops at each row of seats and asks if we would like something to drink. Pug looks at me with that questioning look on his face.

"Pug, I think a Coke would be just fine. How about you?"

He gave me a kind of sheepish grin. "Yeah, how about a Coke? Nothing stronger on this trip, right, Professor? We both settle for a Coke, right?" That's right Pug, nothing but a coke.

"Pug, from here on, it's just Coke or some other soft drink."`

"Professor, do we have to pay for it?"

"No, Pug, we don't have to pay because that goes with the ticket, especially if you are just drinking soft drinks."

He just grinns.

In a little while the girls brings our drinks, and I showed him how to fold the tray down from the back of the seat in front of him.

"Boy, this is neat," he says.

We sit quietly, and he continues to look out the window, soaking up everything that is happening. Again I think how happy I am that he got to come along. I just wished the others could have been able to make the trip also. Maybe if I get lucky, we can take them all for a plane ride one of these days.

Quickly we are over Tulsa, Oklahoma. The reason we know where we are is that the captain has just come on the intercom and told us where we were. Here come the two young stewardesses again; only this time they have food trays. They handed out trays to all of the passengers until they got to us.

Pug pulled his head over real close to me and asks, "Is this free too?"

I said, "Yes, Pug, this is free."

The lunch consisted of a pimento cheese sandwich and some potato chips and a pickle. There were a couple of cookies in a small sack on the corner of the tray. Pug ate the sandwich and chips, drank his Coke, and then ate his cookies and looked over at me. He glanced down at my cookies.

"Pug, would you like to have the cookies since I really don't care for this kind of cookies?" The truth was I hadn't even looked to see what kind they were.

"Sure, if you're sure you don't want them."

"I'm really not much of a sweets eater," I said and handed them over to him.

He takes the sack and quickly consumes them.

The flight is going real well. We talk for quite a while about the things we want to do first when we get to New York City. Pug, of course, wants to see Madison Square Garden for sure.

"Pug, we will definitely see the Garden before we go back to Ft. Worth. We have to remember that we also need to purchase a 35 mm camera and some film just as soon as we get there so we can take plenty of pictures to take back and show the gang, Lynn and Annie, and Dr. Davis.

One thing that I really want to do is, I want to take you to a real nice fancy restaurant for dinner."

"I'm not too sure about that, Professor."

"And, I want to take you to a Broadway show while we are here."

Pug isn't too sure about the Broadway play either.

"I saw a stage play one time, and it was just a bunch of people standing around on a stage under a lot of bright lights hollering at each other."

"The actors have to talk loud so the people in the back of the theater can hear them." This seemes to satisfy him.

Just then the captain comes on the intercom and tells everyone to buckle their seat belts. We are approaching rough weather ahead, and he has received permission to climb to a higher altitude to try to get above the rough weather. Nothing to worry about, this is just a precautionary measure. We sit quietly for about fifteen minutes when we feel the plane bounce just a little; then it gets rougher. The captain comes on the intercom again and tells us that this should only last a few minutes and again apologizes for the turbulent weather. "We are almost over the area now, so just have patience."

I look at Pug, and he is almost white. Our seats are at the trailing edge of the wing, so he can see real well.

"Pug, is this bothering you?"

He looks at me rather wide-eyed. "I don't know, but something seems to be bothering me."

I keep talking to him, and then I noticed that he is holding onto the arms of the seat so tightly that his knuckles were white again. Just as I am assuring him that everything is going to be just fine, one of the nice young stewardess comes by and asks if we would like anything.

I assure her that we are in good condition, but if we need anything, we would immediately call her. She looks at Pug and then at me; and just as she starts to leave, she leanes over and reminded me that if Pug got sick, there was a barf bag in the pocket of the seat in front of him.

I asked Pug if he was nauseated.

"Not too much."

I really didn't know just what that meant: a little, a lot, or something in between. "Just in case you do get sick, there is a barf bag in the pocket of the seat in front of you."

He turns to me in total disbelief. "Professor, if you think I am gonna puke in a bag in front of all of these people, you've got another thing coming."

I really had to work hard to keep a straight face on that one.

In just a minute he looks at me; his face is kind of white. "I've been needing to go to the bathroom ever since we left DFW, and I think now is a good time."

I stood up and allowed him to get by. He made a beeline to the lavatory. It was a good thing that no one was ahead of him.

After a few minutes, he comes back. It looks like he has washed his face because his hair was still wet in front. Just as he gets back to the row of seats, and I start to get up, the plane hit an air pocket and dropped about a foot. Thank God Pug had a good hold on the corner of the back of my chair. He darn near fell, but managed to stay on his feet.

"Professor, I think Cowboy could ride this bucking plane a lot better than I can." He grinned that little grin of his so I knew he was doing all right.

He made his way to his seat just as the captain came on the intercom again and said, "Well, folks, I apologize for that last bump, but I think that will be the last one in this area. We have just reached the top of the storm and we are looking down at it now."

With that, Pug pushes his face against the window, "Well, I'll be damned. That's the darndest thing I ever saw. Professor, I can see lightning below us, and look at all of those real dark clouds. Not all of them are dark; some of them are real puffy white."

The captain comes on the intercom again and says, "We lost about fifteen minutes climbing over the storm, but we have a real good tail wind now, and that should take us into New York City on time."

Everyone breathes a sigh of relief.

The stewardess came by and asked if either of us would like to have something to drink now that the plane had stopped bumping and shaking.

Pug asks, "Do you have a Seven-Up?"

The young lady smiles, "I think I can find one for you, and how would you like some salty peanuts to go with that?"

"Lady, that sounds like a great idea." He really likes that suggestion. He is no dummy. He knows how to settle an upset stomach. He's had enough of those. They had not been from riding in an airplane though.

The next time we heard the captain, he is on the intercom saying, "We are now passing just south of Chicago. If you look out the window on the left side of the plane, you may be able to see some of the Great Lakes, at least Lake Michigan."

Pug is really enjoying this. It is about 2:30 p.m. now, and Pug had trouble believing how fast we have been traveling. "Heck, we'll be in New York City by 4:30 p.m. just like the ticket agent said."

"I agree, Pug; we're really moving along."

Pug finally settles back and starts reading one of the magazines from the pocket of the seat in front of him. Just then he reached slowly into the pocket of the seat in front of him where he got the magazine and pulled out the barf bag. He looks at it, then he looked at me.

"You mean I am supposed to puke into that little bag if I get airsick. I don't think I could hit the hole in the top. It would likely land all over me and the guy in the seat in front of me. No, thanks."

Just watching him was a lot of fun. It was nice to see the excitement in his eyes when he saw and heard things he had never experienced before.

Just then the captain came on the intercom again. "Ladies and Gentlemen, we are now approaching J.F.K. International Airport. We should be landing in about fifteen minutes. Please buckle your seat belts and restore your seats to an upright position and put away the tray on the seat in front of you."

The stewardesses came down the aisle checking to make sure everyone was properly buckled up and their seats were in the proper position. We felt the plane bank slightly to the right, and then it straightened up on the approach to the runway.

The captain came on the intercom again. "We have been cleared for landing and are on the last leg of our approach."

A minute later we felt a shudder through the plane. I looke at Pug, and he is gripping the seat again with white knuckles. "What's that, Professor? I can see a part of the wing surface on top come up, and part of the wing below it goes down. Why are they doing that?"

I try my best to explain that the top part of the wing is called a foil, which the pilot raised to slow the plane. "The lower part of the wing that went down is called the flaps, and it also helps slow the plane, but also allows the plane to continue to fly, but at a lower speed until we land. If we were to try to land at the speed the plane would be gliding for a landing without the help of the flaps and foil, we would not be able to stop before running off the end of the runway. You will also hear a different noise when the captain reverses the thrust of the engines after the wheels touch down. This also helps to slow the speed of the plane and make it easier to stop. Just the brakes would not be sufficient to hold a plane of this size with all of this weight."

"Thanks, Professor, but I just wanted to know what the flap and the foil things were. But thanks anyway for that great explanation."

Boy do I ever feel foolish. I guess I had been a teacher and lecturer too long.

We are finally on the ground and slowing down near the end of the runway. We start our trip across the access strips that leads to the terminal.

Pug looks at me, and I knew another question was coming. "How do those other planes landing and taking off know to watch out for us? Looks like they would run into us as we cross the runway."

I assure him. "The tower is talking to everyone and informing them where all of the planes are."

"Wow, what a job!"

I agree. We are almost to the portable ramp that came out from the terminal for us to walk through in case of bad weather or hot weather or whatever.

Just before we are ready to leave the plane, the captain comes over the intercom again and says, "The crew would like to wish Professor Dixon the best of luck on his appearance on the TV show, 'So You Want to Be a Millionaire.'"

With that a lot of people start clapping. Darn, this is embarrassing.

We sat for a while as they made all the connections to the plane. Since we were near the rear, we were among the last to leave the plane.

As we walk into the terminal, we heard a voice over the loud speaker telling us where to pick up our luggage. We head down to the area where we were to pick up the luggage. When we arrived, we found that we had to wait for about fifteen minutes before our luggage started coming in from the plane. We finally found our luggage and headed for the door.

Pug nudges me, "Professor, there's a man over there holding a card with your name on it."

Sure enough there he was just the way they said he would be.

I walk over and introduced myself. He tells me his name is George Sherwood, and he would be our driver during our stay in town.

I introduced him to Pug. Pug is intrigued with his uniform.

George takes a couple of the bags, and Pug took the others. We follow him outside to the car. The car turns out to be a limousine, not a stretch, but one of those nice ones that seated about seven or eight people. George openes the trunk and put our bags inside. He opens the door for us to get inside.

Pug nudges me, "Man, what service."

We pull away from the curb and head downtown. Pug asks George if we could go by the theater on the way to the hotel.

George just smiles at him. "Sure, Mr. Pug, that won't be a problem."

Pug says, "George, I'll make you a deal. I won't call you Mr. George if you don't call me Mr. Pug. Let's just keep it on a first name basis. How about that?"

"Sure thing, Pug, anything you say."

We travel for about forty-five minutes or so until we get to the real downtown part of New York City. We finally pull up in front of a large well-lighted building, and George stops.

Pug looks at the building kind of stunned.

"George, this isn't a theater; this is ABC Television Studios."

"That's right, Pug. The show is taped in this building. The set or stage, if you prefer, is specifically built to handle the show. It is built in an oblong circle seating area so the people in the audience can be close to everything that's going on during the show. They have the cameras set, some on booms and some on rollers on the floor, in order to cover everything that's going on. You'll see tomorrow.

"Now if you don't mind, I'll take you on to the hotel."

We had traveled only about twenty minutes more when we come to the hotel. This traffic was really something. It seemed that everybody spent more time blowing the horn and hollering at each other than they did driving their cars. That was everybody, of course, except George. He sat calmly behind the wheel and did his job.

"Here we are gentlemen, this is it." He pulls to a halt in front of the hotel. As soon as he stops, he pops the lid to the trunk of the car, and the hotel doorman comes to the car and starts lifting our bags from the trunk of the car. George comes around and tells us he would like to pick us up tomorrow morning after breakfast.

He suggests a time of around 9:30 a.m. to pick us up.

We agreed that would be fine.

He smiles, bows slightly, and says, "Have a good evening gentlemen and I will see you in the morning."

Pug runs behind the doorman who is already entering the lobby of the hotel. A young man at the bellman's station comes over to meet the doorman who politely hands over the bags. The new man, a bellman, leads us to the registration desk where we were met by another nice man at the registration desk.

The man at the desk introduced himself and says, "Professor Dixon, we have been expecting you."

How the hell did he know who I was? He introduces himself first, and I didn't even mention my name.

Well, anyway, he says, "It's a pleasure to have you with us. I understand that you are to be a contestant on "So You Want to Be a Millionaire?" We would like to wish you the best in your appearance. We have had others stay with us who have done fairly well, but no millionaires yet. Hope you make it. Now, if you will just fill out the information needed on this registration form, it would be helpful.

"We were given some information about you by the network, but these are just a couple of things they don't know."

I fill out the form and hand it back to him. He thanks me and tells the bellman to take us to our rooms.

We head for the elevator along with a couple of other people. We enter and the bellman punches the button for the twenty-third floor. The elevator stops, the door opens and we exit to the left for a short distance. The bellman opens the door and ushers us inside.

I can't believe it. This is a suite. Pug goes running to both bedrooms and then back to the living room. The bellman has taken our bags to our respective rooms and has hung our clothes up for us. He comes in, hands the key to each of us, and tells us there was ice in the buckets and soft drinks in the small refrigerator if we so desired. "Is there anything else I can do for you before leaving?"

"Young man, what is your name just in case we need something?" I ask.

He introduces himself as Chip Rowan.

Pug says, "Know what, Chip, you're a pretty nice guy for a Yankee."

Chip looks at Pug and grins, "Pug, you aren't too bad for a guy from Texas."

They both laugh, they shake hands and say, "It's nice to make your acquaintance." Friends,,,Friends both men say.

Chip, you have been so nice to us that we would like to continue our acquaintance with you. I guess I sounded a little country with that statement. We don't like having to break in a new friend each time we want something. He smiles, I thank him and hand him a nice tip.

He leaves and Pug comes in. "Professor, can you believe it? We each have a bedroom, and it has a bathroom right there with it? Hell Professor, this is really living high on the hog."

"I have to agree with you, Pug; I have to agree. Pug, why don't we just sit and relax for a while and decide where we want to eat tonight. I don't know any place near here, but I'll bet you Chip Rowan knows some good place to eat."

We hurry up, freshen up, change clothes, and head for the elevator. We arrive in the lobby and look for Chip. He is over at the bell captain's station. We walked over and ask if we could talk to him for just a minute.

"Sure thing," he says and he walks over to discuss our problem.

"Chip, we're looking for a good place to have dinner tonight, and we thought, since you are a native around here, you may know a place."

"Okay, just what kind of food do you want?" Chip asks.

Pug immediately says, "I want a steak. A real good, big, thick steak."

"Hell Pug, I thought that was all you Texas guys ate."

"Tell you the truth, Chip, we couldn't afford one till just recently."

"Pug, you and Professor go two blocks south, look back to the left, and you will see a big sign with a bull made of neon lights. That's the Black Angus restaurant. Go inside and ask for Big Ernie. He and I grew up together over in Queens. Just tell him I sent you and tell him I said to treat you right."

What a nice guy this Chip is.

We head out the front of the hotel, go to the corner, and start south. The light is green, but I almost get run over by a taxi.

An old man standing on the corner looks at me. "Son, you must be from out of town. I can tell you're from out of town by the way you try to walk across the street. Don't go till I do, and we'll get across safely."

I did just what he said, and we made it across to the other side. He turns and says, "Boys, just watch the crowd and do what they do. You'll find that's a good policy when you're in traffic here in the city."

"Thanks, sure appreciate your help."

The Black Angus

We go south for another block. As we approach the intersection, we look back to the left, and there it is – a big neon sign with a bull on it and another sign below the bull saying the Black Angus. We headed for the door.

As we walk in the door, we are met by a young lady who asks how many are in our party. I look around at all of the people sitting and standing, waiting for a table. I think, "Maybe this isn't such a good idea."

I remembered what Chip Rowan had said, so I ask the young lady for Big Ernie. The young lady turns to a big man behind the counter near the cash register. "Ernie, these guys want to see you."

He walks over and then I knew why they called him Big Ernie. He must have been about six feet five inches tall and weighed about three hundred twenty-five pounds or in that neighborhood.

"Hello, I'm Ernie."

I introduce myself and then Pug. I tell him that Chip had said for us to come over for a good steak.

Ernie smiles and asks, "How's ole Chip doing these days?"

I explained that we just met Chip today at the hotel, and that I was in town to be on the TV program.

He laughs. "Well, ole Chip is still helping out when he can by sending me customers. We've been friends for many years."

"Yes, he told us that you guys grew up in the same neighborhood over in Queens."

"He's right, we grew up together. We went to the same schools, played on the same football teams and baseball teams. We even double dated in high school. Good guy that Chip. One of the best friends I ever had."

Ernie then turns to a nice looking waitress. "Pam, see if you can find a booth for these friends of mine." He winks at her and tells her to see that we were treated royally. "They're friends of Chip's."

She smiles politely and says, "Follow me, gentlemen."

As I turn to thank Ernie, I see a lot of scowls on the faces of people who had apparently been waiting some time for a table. I politely apologize and tell the folks "Sorry, I'm new in town and don't know the rules yet." I sincerely do apologize though.

When we arrive at the table, I asked Pam if we shouldn't have waited our turn.

She assures us that any friend of Chip's was always at the head of the line. "He and Ernie go back a long way."

"Thank you, Pam. She hands us a menue. Now Pam, what would you recommend in the way of a steak?"

"Well, we have a real nice sixteen-ounce New York strip, but if you are really hungry, we have one that is a twenty-four ounce rib eye. It's really a big one, and it's delicious. It's a big one, so be sure you're hungry if you order it."

I decide on the sixteen-ounce strip. "And, I would like to have it cooked medium. Pug wants to try the twenty-four-ounce rib eye, cooked medium rare."

"How would you like your potato fixed? Everything Miss, everything but the dishrag. What kind of dressing do you want on your salad? And now, what would you like to drink?"

We tell her we would like iced tea.

Armed with that information, she heads for the kitchen. As she walks off, I think to myself that she is no ordinary little lady. With those blue eyes and blonde hair and that body, she is really something special. She had extremely good manners for a waitress — not that they all don't have good manners, but hers were just extra special. I'd bet she wasn't an inch over five feet, three inches, and she couldn't have weighed more than about 115 pounds. I am not one for guessing the measurements of ladies, but I would have guessed her to be about 35 or 36 top, 21 or 22 waist, and maybe 33 or 34 inch hips. I knew she must have been older than she looked, but this lady was beautiful.

I jokingly tell Pug, "I think I'm in love."

Yeah he says, "I can see why."

We sit and discuss what we thought tomorrow was going to be like. Neither of us could even imagine what was going to happen to me tomorrow. I just know the first thing I have to do is to get off the floor and onto the seat opposite the host of the show.

Just as I was getting nervous thinking about it, Pam comes back with our salad. This gives me a chance to think about something else. I just hadn't thought I would get nervous, especially not this early. Well hell, I'll just eat my salad and calm down.

Pam comes over and asks if we would like something in addition to our tea to drink, like maybe some wine. Big Ernie wanted to send us a bottle of wine.

I explained to her without hesitation that both of us were alcoholics, and we had been on the wagon for over two months now. We feel it would be best to stick to coffee, tea, milk, or water. She understands and goes back to tell Ernie.

Ernie comes over, sticks out his big hand, and says, "Man, I do admire you for sticking with it. I don't think I could, but I want you to know how much I admire you guys for being able to do it."

A couple of minutes later Pam came back with our steaks. Mine is large, and the potato is real big. Pug's steak is gigantic and so is his potato. Someone had slipped some fresh asparagus on the side for us. Boy is that stuff good. It used to be my favorite vegetable.

Pug looks at his steak and a slow grin crosses his face. Those dark brown eyes start to shine and sparkle. You can see immediately that this is a big adventure for him. He starts slowly to pull his steak knife across the meat when he stops about half way through. He looks at me and put the steak knife down, picks up his fork, and actually cuts the meat with his fork. "Never saw a steak in my life that was this tender." Looking me straight in the eye, he tells me, "I have never in my entire life had a steak like this one. I can actually cut this thing with my fork."

He stops talking for a while and settles in to the chore in front of him. The chore of eating a steak about four times the size of his hand, along with the asparagus and potato.

I hadn't even noticed the bread yet. The bread is a kind of miniature loaf that has a sourdough smell and taste, but still contained the smell of fresh yeast bread. "Man, oh, man, this is great bread," I commented.

By now, I have dug into my steak. It was juicy and cooked just right. We eat and talk about the old times in the parks in Ft. Worth and the cookouts down at the river bottom. We finally got back to the realities of the day and finished eating.

Pam came by and asked how we were doing. "Hey, guys, how about some coffee?"

"Yes, thank you."

"How about you, Pug. Want some coffee?"

"That would be real fine if I had a piece of apple pie to go with it."

Pam bends over and whispers into his ear that she has some real great apple pie. "How about a scoop of ice cream to go on the pie?"

He readily agrees to that.

"I'll have a piece of that lemon pie, but no ice cream, please. I'm about to pop right now after eating all of that food. By the way, Pam, who decided on the asparagus for us?"

"Well, sir, I have to plead guilty to that one. You looked like an asparagus kind of guy."

"Well, I want you to know just how much we appreciated it. It just happens to be my favorite vegetable."

You know, I never really noticed before, but Pam is not just a pretty lady, she was just plain beautiful. She had a beautiful face. She seemed to be beautiful inside as well as outside. It was hard to guess her age, but I would say she was maybe in her late thirties or early forties. She has the poise and grace of an older woman, but the body appears much younger. She is beautifully built as the guys would say, and it appears she must work out because she sure didn't have any soft tissue showing.

When she brings the pie back, I look to see if she has a wedding ring on her finger. No ring there on the third finger of her left hand.

We finally get through with the pie, and then we have difficulty in getting up from the booth. "That's some of the best food I've had in years.

"Pam, before we leave town, I would like to come back and have dinner here again. Would you wait on us if we come back?"

"Sure will, fellows, I would be honored."

I explain what I am doing in town and that I would definitely be back to see her. I leave a pretty nice tip for a very pretty and very nice lady. I take the check and head for the cashier to pay the bill.

After paying the bill, we start out the door and we heard a big booming voice behind us. It is Big Ernie who is sticking out that big hand of his to say good-bye. "It's been a pleasure, fellows. Be sure to come back before you leave town."

I assure him we will just do that very thing. I turned to Ernie and asked him if Pam is married or spoken for.

He smiles that big smile and says, "Not to my knowledge. I have never heard of her even dating anyone, but I don't know everything. She has worked for us for about eight years, and I have never heard her mention a boyfriend. Seems to me that she might have been married to a sailor when she was real young. Seems that he was killed in an accident of some kind in the Navy. She's a pretty little thing, isn't she? She doesn't date anyone that I know of. Are you interested?"

"That's right, I just may be. Do you think she might like to take in a Broadway show one night while I am in town?"

"Well, it sure can't hurt to ask. If you don't ask, you'll never know what might happen."

We leave the Black Angus with a full stomach and a good warm feeling inside. We even manage to cross the streets without getting run over on the way back to the hotel.

As we walk in, we see Chip Rowan the Bellman. We tell him what a friendly man his buddy Ernie is and what a good meal we had eaten. We had not expected anything like that when they had told us we were coming to New York City. Everyone had just been super friendly.

"Pug, I hate to admit it, but I'm a little tired, and if it's all right with you, I think I would like to go up to the room and get some rest."

He admits he was pretty tired himself. "Professor, a soft bed sounds pretty good to me."

We headed upstairs for a little R and R.

I decide to read the paper which had been delivered to our room courtesy of the hotel. I like to stay up with current events when possible, and when I am sober enough to read it. I have a feeling all of that is going to be different from here on out. I liked this feeling of being sober and being able to focus my eyes.

My head hasn't hurt in over six weeks, which is a record going back about ten years or more. My God, what have I done to let myself get in that condition? Can I ever straighten up my life and make up for at least part of the damage to my family that I had hurt so badly? All I can do is try real hard and ask forgiveness.

What am I going to say to my mother when I saw her? Mother, I'm sorry I have been missing for the past ten years. I didn't have time to write you a letter. No way, man. When I see my children, what would I say? Something like My, how you've grown in the last ten years. *I would hardly recognize you.* No, I surely couldn't say things like that to the people I have said I loved, and yet I had walked away from them without even telling them why.

I am sure that I was in a drunken stupor when I left. I really don't think I have been consciously sober for any period of time since then when my mind had been thinking about those people who so dearly loved me.

My father was the strong, silent type, the salt of the earth, the man who always knew just what to do regardless of the situation. The man I admired so much. I didn't have the courage to talk to him about my own personal family problems. I guess I just didn't want to admit how weak I had been when trying to handle a personal problem like the one I had.

Now I realize that I should have talked to him. My children had been teenagers. I guess I just didn't give them enough credit for being young adults who would have been able to understand the problem between their mother and me.

I should have talked to everyone and filed for divorce. Now I believed that I loved my wife too much, and just the thought of her making a fool of me by going out and sleeping with other men was just too much for me to handle. I may have been a little too vain also.

Once I had started drinking, I started feeling more sorry for myself instead of getting mad and doing something about it like filing for divorce. I had all of the evidence I could have wanted to get a divorce. I had totally incontrovertible evidence.

I know now that I am just feeling sorry for myself and have also been a coward. If I get another chance with my parents and children, I will certainly make the most of it. Believe it or not I have learned a lot from my friends on the street. They taught me in unbelievable ways that I must be me, and I must stand up for what is right. I believe I could do that now.

I ask myself just what am I doing to myself right now? I was giving myself a lecture about something I couldn't change, at least not tonight. I must make myself realize that my time for making apologies to my family and friends back home would come, and I must be ready. Right now, I had to get some sleep and rest, so I would be able to think about the questions tomorrow.

I hear Pug singing over in the other bedroom. I thought this was the first time I had ever heard him sing since I had known him.

I holler over to him, "Good night, Pug. Now you get a good night's sleep because we have to have breakfast in the morning and be ready when George comes by to pick us up." "Good night, Professor. I'll see you in the morning."

The Arrival of the Big Day

The alarm went off, and I am still in a daze at everything that has happened in the last couple of weeks. I crawl out of bed and head for the shower to see if cold water on my head would help me wake up a little. It had been a long time since I had used a shower like this.

I turn the cold water on and reach for the little lever that transfers the water to the showerhead before I turned the hot water on. Big mistake! That cold water really wakes a guy up when it hits him right on top of the head. I should have turned the hot water on and gotten the temperature of the water right before I reached for that lever. I surely would know better next time.

Thank God they have a hair dryer here in the bathroom.

I smelled coffee.

"Professor, how do you take your coffee? Black, cream, sugar, or cream and sugar. Pug, please make mine with a touch of cream and about a half spoon of sugar.

O.K., They have a coffeepot right here in the room for us. Professor, would you like for me to call down for breakfast, or do you want to go down to the restaurant and eat?"

"Well, Pug, what say we just go down to the restaurant this morning to eat?"

I finish my shower and my coffee. Pug is still drying his hair. He liked the hair dryer, but then he has more hair than I did.

We finally get through with our primping, shaving, and all the other things a guy does to get ready. We are finally dressed, and we head for the door.

We board the elevator with several other people who were very friendly. On the way down we found that one couple was from Iowa. They were here on their honeymoon. We wished them well and congratulated them. By the time we reached the lobby, they seemed like old friends. We walk out into the lobby and look around.

"Man, Professor, this looks a lot bigger in the daylight than it did last night when we checked in."

I glance around the lobby and see the entrance to the restaurant. I nudge Pug, and we head for the entrance to the restaurant. A very nice young lady asks, "How many? Do you want smoking or nonsmoking?"

"Nonsmoking, please."

She leads us to a table by the window. This is nice since we could watch all of the people going to work. This is real interesting. I used to do a lot of people watching in the old days when I had lived in Chicago.

That was another time and another place. A nice young man approached our booth and introduced himself and handed us a menu. I didn't catch his name; on the other hand, he didn't throw it very hard. He was extremely soft spoken or else I needed hearing aids.

"Pug, I think I just want some sausage and eggs with wheat toast and coffee." What about you?

Pug was looking at the menu when he suddenly stopped, looked up, and asks, "Professor, what are eggs Benedict or whatever you call it?"

I explained they were eggs with a small slice of Canadian bacon on toast with a sauce over them.

"Well," he hesitated for a minute, "hell, Professor, are they any good?"

"Pug, I used to enjoy them quite often, and I think you'll enjoy them. If you don't enjoy them, then tomorrow you can order something else. If you don't take chances on things, you never really learn, now do you?"

He seemed embarrassed. "Okay, I think I'll try them today and like you say, if I don't like them, I can order something else tomorrow."

Old "What's His Name" brought us coffee while we waited on breakfast and watched the people on the street. Pug really enjoyed watching the people as they passed by. Our food finally came, and Pug looks at his eggs Benedict, takes a bite, and smiles. I knew that meant he liked them.

He looks at me and says, "Maybe I'll have them again tomorrow."

I couldn't help chuckling a little. He is in a world of his own right now, and he is loving every minute of it.

We finish, paid our check, left the tip, and walked slowly through the lobby looking at everyone and everything as we head for the door to the street out front.

We enjoyed standing outside in the cool brisk morning air with the sun shining between the buildings, making heavy shadow displays here and there on the other buildings and streets.

The noise of the traffic was very different from that in Ft. Worth. What a wonderful day!

We had been outside for about fifteen minutes when we see a limousine come around the corner. Sure enough, it was George. He pulls up to the curb, and the doorman opens the door for us. This time George didn't have to get out of the car. We got in the car to a cheery, "Good morning," from George.

"George, you must have had a good evening after you left us last night in order for you to be so happy this morning."

"Professor, I think I have found the love of my life. Believe it or not we went to high school together. We just happened to meet again last week at a class reunion party, and we got to talking about old times. We had dated a couple of times when we were in high school, but that was when we were freshman and sophomores, and it was with other couples, never anything serious. I found that she has never married, and I have never married. We now live right near each other. She's a real beauty with black hair and black eyes that shine like bright stars on a night when there is no moon. We went out on our first real date last night, and the chemistry was really there. We both admitted it, but we want to take it real slow so we can be sure."

"George, take it slow and be real sure of yourself.

This goes for your young lady also. I speak from experience. But on the other hand, if it is the real thing for both of you, don't lose her; don't let her get away. If you do, you will be sorry for the rest of your life."

After giving my advice, I decide to change the subject. "Boy, this traffic is awful."

"Oh, Professor, this is just about normal for this time of the day. It's worse earlier in the day."

Pug is really taking everything in.

I asked George, "Do you know what happens to us next?"

He tells us he is taking us to the studio where I would be briefed on the program procedures and told how to act. They will take us to the makeup room where they will apply cosmetics to my face so I wouldn't look so pale. "The camera seems to make people look pale, so they put some suntan makeup on you. They go over the lifelines you will be using during the show, etc."

"Well, I guess I'm just about ready, so let's get in there.

Just as I said that, we arrived at the studio entrance. I was met by a young man at the door of the studios who looked something like an usher, but what did I know? He very politely asked my name. I gave him my name, and he looked at a sheet in his hand with a lot of names on it and finally said, "Here you are. They're expecting you."

He lead us into a large room full of people. A man came over and introduced himself. He explained that he was the producer of the show, and that I, along with the other people, would meet the director and the host of the show in just a few minutes. The man told, me to introduce myself to the other contestants. He told Pug there was another group where he belonged, and he took him over and introduced him to the people who had come with the other contestants.

I look back over my shoulder, and it looks as if Pug was doing all right, so I just relaxed and started introducing myself to the people in my group. I found there were people from all over. There were several women, but it seemed that the men outnumbered the women.

We started discussing the type of questions they would ask.

One man said, "Boy, do I have some good lifelines," and he started to tell us about them.

I was a real dummy because I had not thought about people to call if I needed to phone someone. My brain started to run a mile a minute trying to figure out who I would call in case I got stuck on a history question, and who I would call on religion and medical.

Holy cow, I thought, I have a good person in Lynn to call for the religious, and there is Dr. Davis that I can call for a medical question. Who do I call on music?

What's wrong with me? Bing can help me with a musical question.

For sports, I could use Cowboy because he knows a lot about all sports even when he's drunk. Now that he is sober, he should be real smart on sports. I can't use Pug on boxing or sports because he will be my audience guest. On war questions, I can get Doc on the line because he sure knows a lot about the last few wars including World War II.

Well, thank goodness I have that taken care of so I can give them a sensible answer when they ask me about my phone line people. Now, if only my own pea brain doesn't fail me. I don't know a lot about movies except the old ones and westerns in case there is a question on that subject. I wish I had Pam's phone number; she mentioned something about going to a lot of movies. Well, I guess I will just have to work with what I have.

Here came the producer again along with another guy that I assumed was the director of the show. The producer called for our attention and introduced the director and a couple of stagehands. The director first told us that he wanted to welcome us to New York City, ABC, and "So You Want To Be A Millionaire."

"I'm sure most of you know we have a certain amount of rehearsing to do before each show. We try to appear spontaneous; it is only about half spontaneous for you, but wholly spontaneous for the audience. Well, not totally," he said. "We have a light that tells the audience when to applaud and when to be quiet. There is one thing we want you to do for us. We want you to take your time in answering the question, even if you do know the answer before it appears on your screen. Act as if you have to think a little about it, or you might give a short explanation about why you know the answer. This is what puts more suspense in the program. We don't even mind a little pun directed at Mr. Burns, your host of the show. He will play with you on some of the questions and get a little more conversation going for the folks at home.

"Now, most important of all, we need to know something about your past, your occupation, and your marital status. If you are married, we need your wife's or husband's name along with something about where you met and maybe how you proposed to her and how many children you have, and a little something about the family."

Well, a lot of that sure left me out. I didn't know much about my family, and I sure didn't want to discuss my marriage.

We were then assigned to a person who would take down the information. We filled out the first part of the information sheet, but they asked questions and filled in the remainder of the information.

Believe it or not, I actually told them the truth about myself. I told them how I came to call the show for a tryout, and the names of the people that insisted I call, and what had happened since.

You should have seen the face on the interviewer when I told him that just a month ago, I had been a street person. I also told him that as ashamed as I was of it, I would not lie to him about it. "I have been sober for about two months now, and I intend to stay sober. That is, I will stay sober with the Good Lord's help."

He asked about family, and I told him briefly about my family back in Chicago and that I was in hopes of making amends with them now that I was back on my feet. I told him that I was looking forward to finding my children and my parents after I had completed my participation on the show.

He was totally dumfounded that I was so honest with him. I explained that I would have nothing to gain by telling him a lie.

After he recovered from shock, he went over to the director, and they talked for a while. The two of them went over and talked to the producer of the show. Then, the three of them came over toward me, and I could see the puzzled looks on their faces. They were very nice, but very inquisitive. They assured me they didn't want to get too personal, but my story was the first of its kind they had ever encountered while doing the show.

They asked if I would mind answering a few more questions. I told them to go ahead and ask because it was all going to come out sooner or later anyway.

The first question was, "How will you feel about our telling the TV audience about you and how you went about getting on the show and about the people who have helped you?"

"I don't mind at all; but don't embarrass my family by exaggerating any of the story; just stick to the facts."

"Would you be willing to sign a release for us?"

I would if it was written up to my specifications.

They were more than willing to write it the way I wanted it written. The producer and director left, but they assured me they would stick strictly to my instructions.

The interviewer told me that they wanted to get all of us together so they could show us the floor where the contestants competed to get into the main contestant's chair. We were ushered into the area surrounding the two seats where the host and the contestant at the time were seated. There were ten chairs placed in a semi-circle around the floor of the inner part of the studio. We were told to take a seat and to look closely at the board in front of the seat.

Next, they turned the lights on the boards and told us they were now going to show us how it worked when we were competing. They asked us a question simulating what we would be doing when we competed to get into the contestant's seat.

There were four states on the board, and our job was to tell which ones followed each other starting on the west coast and going to the east coast. This, of course, was one of those real easy ones, and everyone got it right.

Now he said, "Let's look at your times. As you can see, there are a couple of real fast times. Now that's what you want to do. Get the answer on the board as soon as possible, but remember that accuracy counts most. It doesn't help if you get done first, unless you have them right."

We got the idea.

"Next," he said, "I am going to take you to the makeup rooms and let you get acquainted with what happens there."

We followed like a bunch of ducks being led to water. We arrived and were greeted by five ladies who explained just what they would want to do when we came in to be on the show.

Next came the big question, "Just when do we appear on the show?"

The young man explained, "Ten of you will be on the first taping today; and if we have time, the other ten will be taped later this afternoon."

He added, "However, this being Friday, we're running behind, and it appears we may have to hold you over till Monday since we don't tape on Saturday or Sunday. We will have you all draw numbers to see who is on the show first and who will be on the show second. This way you can notify anyone you need to notify that you are being held over till Monday's taping. That taping will be on Monday morning."

We all gathered around the young man who had a container in his hand. There were twenty balls inside the container with numbers on them. "If you draw between one and ten, you will be on today's taping, but if you draw between eleven and twenty, you will have free room and board through Monday."

He shook the container and said, "Good luck to all of you; I hope you get what you want."

Each of us reached over, and he poured a ball out into our hands. Most of us looked very cautiously at the number on the ball. I looked at mine; it was number sixteen.

This meant we would stay over the weekend. Well, this won't be too bad because it will give us a chance to see the city and especially Madison Square Garden. We'll have three more nights in that great hotel, I thought.

We all listened intently for more instructions about what we were to do and where we were supposed to be and when we were expected to be there.

Just about that time, the producer came over to the group and said, "Folks, I'm sorry, but ten of you will have to stay over till Monday. But, we can assure you, we will pick up all expenses and even advance you a little money to take care of your weekend of activities. Now will those people with numbers one to ten please come with me, and those people with numbers eleven through twenty may go just as long as you are back here on Monday morning at the same time you were here today.

"Oh, yes, your limousine driver will take you back to the hotel, and he will also be there Monday just as he was this morning. Remember now, he will be there at the same time as today. Please be ready. If you aren't ready, we will have to replace you with another contestant, and I really don't think you would like that."

I find Pug and told him what has happened. A real big grin came across his face, and his eyes light up like a Christmas tree. "You mean we will have all weekend to look around. Professor, do you think we could ride on the subway? I want to see what a worm feels like when he crawls underground. I've never seen one, and I would really like to ride on one if we can."

"Pug, we will definitely ride on a subway." "The first thing tomorrow morning we can go to Madison Square Garden."

"Hell's fire Professor, why don't we go out there today? It's still early."

We said good-bye to the other people and headed for the front door of the studio. And, what do you know, George is standing there. Good old George.

"Well, Professor, I understand you guys will be here for the weekend. I'm glad cause I like you guys. How about me taking you back to the hotel now?" That's fine with us isn't it Pug?

"George, we need you to tell us the best way to get to Madison Square Garden."

"Sure, I can tell you, but why don't you let me take you. I don't have anything else going, and you guys are my responsibility while you are here."

"We don't want you to waste your afternoon with us if you have something else to do."

"No, the limousine has been checked out to me for the weekend and all day Monday if you are still in town."

"George, we wouldn't think of you bothering with us all weekend."

"Why not? All the other people have that option with their drivers."

I look at Pug and ask him, "Well, what do you think, old buddy?"

There went that grin again, and those eyes were signaling yes, yes, yes.

George wanted to know what was so special about the Garden.

"Pug was supposed to have fought there, and his manager screwed things up. Then he got hurt before he could arrange another fight in the Garden." I also told him about Cowboy and how he was supposed to have participated in the National Finals Rodeo quite a few years ago and how he had been hurt so badly while riding a bull that he could no longer participate in the bull riding. "He wants to have some photos of it just for a keepsake. We promised we would bring some pictures home for him."

George said, "Well, come on, let's get going."

I had no idea where we went except that after about thirty or forty minutes, he was slowing down and telling us we were there. He found a place to park. He locks the car, and we got out to look around. The front of it looked just like the pictures we had seen in newsreels, movies, and on TV, except that it looked a lot older now. I had expected something more elaborate I guess.

George said, "Come on, let's go in."

We walked over to the entrance and start inside when we were stopped by a guard. George comes over and talks to him. He explained who we were and why we were there.

The guard came over to Pug. "This young man tells me you were supposed to have fought here several years ago, but something happened and you didn't get to make it. Well, I'll tell you what. You come on in. I see you have a camera, so let's go where you can get some good pictures." He takes Pug in tow and tells him to ask anything he wants to know, and he would see if he could answer the questions.

He starts by telling Pug of the great fights he had seen since working here at the Garden. He told him he was now in his forty-sixth year as a security guard at the Garden. He talked and talked and talked while Pug asked question after question.

Pug was taking pictures all over the place. He finally asks me, "Professor, do you have any more of that film with you? I'm out of film."

I reach in my pocket and handed him a new roll of thirty-six exposures, while he handed me the roll he took out of the camera. "Hey, Professor, I'm getting some pictures for Cowboy too."

The guard looked at me and winked. How lucky we were to find a security guard like this.

We spent the next hour and half just walking, looking, and talking to the security guard. George was enjoying this also because he saw how much it meant to Pug. We were very lucky to have a guy like George assigned to us.

After we had just about exhausted the questions for the security guard and taken two whole roles of film, I suggested we leave. I thanked the guard for his courtesy and offered him a tip for his trouble.

"Hell no he says, it's been my pleasure."

We left the Garden and headed somewhere. I didn't know because I was turned around, and I didn't know which way was which or even if it might be just straight up. I was not only lost, but I hadn't known where we had been ever since we had gotten off the plane. I left it up to George.

I mentioned to George that Pug wanted to ride on the subway, so if he could just drop us off where we could find our way out and back, we would appreciate it.

George looked at me, smiled, and said, "You might find your way out, but you also might have a hell of a time finding your way back. I still have some time left before my date, so why don't I take you guys for a subway ride for an hour or so. I haven't been on the subway in quite a while. I think that would be fun."

"Okay, you don't have to twist our arms; we'll let you, but you have to do something for us. You have to let us treat you and your young lady to a night on the town tomorrow night. How does a Broadway show and dinner sound?"

George was stunned. "Professor, I don't know about that. I'll have to talk to my girlfriend, but for me it sounds real fine."

He finally parks the limousine, and we walk about a block to the entrance of the subway. We went down the stairs, through the tollgate, and into a large railroad station looking place. The big difference is that it was underground, and there were hundreds of people getting on and off the trains.

George hollered, "Follow me, fellows."

Just as he said that, a train coming in stopped right in front of George. We all three basically ran through the door and into the train. Sardines didn't have a thing on these cars full of people. All we needed was just a lot of oil and some salt, and we would have been just like them.

We rode out to someplace called Queens. We got off and walked up the stairs to the surface and looked around.

George tells us, "This is my old stomping ground."

I told him about Chip Rowan, the bellman at the hotel. He remembered a guy named Chip Rowan who was a few years older and who had been one heck of a football player in high school.

I asked him if he had ever heard of a guy named Big Ernie something.

"That must be Big Ernie Hasnah. Is he about six feet, four or five inches tall and probably weighs about three hundred pounds?"

"That sure does sound like the guy. Chip sent us to the Black Angus restaurant and told us to ask for Big Ernie."

"Yep, that's got to be him. From what I've heard, they were inseparable in high school. They grew up together and played football all through grade school and high school. Chip got hurt during the last game of his senior year and was unable to accept a scholarship at Notre Dame University. He got some kind of damage to his hip; and when he got out of the hospital, he found that he just couldn't run the way he used to run. You know, quick cutbacks and hard drives through the line. Yeah, he was that good. He was All State half back in high school, and Ernie was All State tackle.

"When Chris couldn't go to college because of his injury, I heard that Ernie decided to stay here and go to night school at New York City College and go into business with his folks who owned this Black Angus restaurant franchise. I heard Ernie got his degree in Business Administration.

"There was something else too about his feeling guilty for missing the block on the guy that put Chip in the hospital. I understand that Chip did everything he could to get Ernie to go on to college, but he just wouldn't do it. I heard that Chip has had a couple of operations, and now Ernie wants him to go to night school. They say Chip was a real good student in school. You know one of those guys that is a real good student athlete. His folks couldn't afford to send him to college, but now that Ernie is a successful restaurant manager-part owner, he wants to loan Chip the money to go to school because he knows that Chip wouldn't take it as a gift. Those two guys' pictures are still up on the walls of our old high school. They were almost like legends around the school. Everyone who ever went to high school here knows the story.

"Well, it's time to head back to the subway and get back to town."

We walked the three or four blocks back to the subway entrance. We went down through the turnstiles again and back into the crowd. It wasn't so bad going back, because when we came out, there were a lot of folks going home from work. We got back and George told us when we were supposed to get off the train.

We were back where we had started, and we headed up the stairs to fresh air again. Well, it was really not so fresh – not like it was in Texas. I knew that Ft. Worth was badly polluted, but in my opinion it wasn't nearly as bad as New York City. We found the limousine, loaded up and headed back to the hotel.

George pulled up and stopped in front of the hotel and turned to me and wanted to know about him giving me a call in the morning and letting me know about that show and dinner.

"That's fine, George; just give me a call."

"Yeah, that's fine, except I don't know your name except they call you Professor Dixon."

"I'm sorry, George, for not properly introducing myself. My name is James Robert Dixon. I guess that would make it easier for you to find me if you knew my name. Pug's name is not known by many, but I'll tell you what it is if he doesn't mind.

"How about it, Pug, can I tell George?"

"Yeah, go ahead and tell him."

"Okay, his name is Harold Wayne McKenzie. Now you know the reason everyone calls him Pug. He doesn't like either of the names Harold or Wayne. Now he just settles for Pug.

"Now, George, you get out of here and go find that lovely young lady of yours and let me know tomorrow if you would like to take in a show and dinner. Let me know early so I can see about getting tickets for everyone."

"Fine, Professor, have a good evening," George said as he left us.

I turned to Pug. "Pug, are you hungry for another steak?"

"I sure am, Professor, and I think you would like to see that nice lady waitress again."

"Well, that would be nice," I said, and we headed for the Black Angus.

Just as we started down the street from the hotel, Pug noticed that his shoe has come untied. "Wait a minute while I tie my shoe," he calls out.

He had forgotten that he was not back in Cow Town, Texas, and he bends over to tie his shoe. Just as he bends over and has hold of the shoe strings, a young kid came running down the street with a lady right behind him hollering like a banshee. The kid had stolen her purse.

The kid was looking back and running at top speed, and he runs right into the rear bumper of Pug bending over to tie his shoe. Pug flew through the air like a frog on its first big jump and landed on all fours with his head and nose going down first. He was lying on the sidewalk looking like a Texas jackrabbit that had just been run over by an eighteen-wheel diesel truck.

He started to get up. This kid was still stumbling and falling all over himself as well as Pug. When Pug realized what had happened, he grabs the kid. He is mad at getting flattened out on a New York City sidewalk and also because he heard this woman screaming at the top of her voice.

Pug grabbed the kid and held on for dear life. Pug had just gotten to his feet while pulling the kid up at the same time, when the lady came in flailing with both fists at the kid and screaming something about her purse. Pug had picked the purse up at the same time he picked the kid up.

Now the kid was hollering. "I didn't steal her purse, it's this guy that is holding onto me. Hell, can't you see that he is holding your purse."

That was when everyone who had seen this circus act started hollering also. They let the kid know real quick what they saw and that it was he that was carrying the purse when he ran into the man who had stooped over to tie his shoe.

By now the doorman from the hotel had arrived as well as a policeman. The policeman started questioning everyone as to what they had seen.

The doorman comes over and asks, "Professor Dixon, are you all right?"

Yes sir thank you, "I am, but I think my friend might need some alcohol for his skinned elbows and nose."

The doorman explaines to the officer that we are guests at the hotel and that it truly was this young man who had stolen the lady's purse and who had run into my friend.

The policeman took Pug's name. At first when the policeman asked for his name, he just said it was Pug.

That was when the policeman said, "No, sir, I mean your full name for the report."

He politely told him his name was Harold Wayne McKenzie. I told the policeman that this was twice today that he had to give someone his real name.

He and the doorman both laughed. "If you men will come with me, I will see if we can find a little first aid for Mr. McKenzie's elbows."

We walk back to the door of the hotel and enter. There was a small crowd of spectators who were now talking it over among themselves.

We went to this small room where a young lady was seated behind a desk. The doorman told her what had happened.

She looked at Pug and said, "Yes, I can see that you need a little assistance. You look like you have been in a fight with that skinned nose."

I had to laugh at that one also.

Pug grinned and said, "No, ma'am, I just got run over by a young New York Yankee."

Then everyone laughed.

She walked over to a cabinet that appeared to be full of first aid medicine and equipment. She opened the door and took out a bottle of alcohol, "I think this would be better than Betadine since this isn't colored and won't show up so much where I put it on your nose." She took a cotton ball and dampened it with the alcohol and very softly applied it to Pug's nose.

He flinches for just a moment, and then he admitted, "It doesn't really hurt; I was just flinching because it was cold."

"Yeah," we all said.

Next comes both of his elbows. At that time I noticed that his pants were torn threadbare at the knee on the right side where he had apparently hit the concrete when he went down. I suggested that we should go back up to the room so he could change his pants and wash his hands where they also had gotten dirty when he went down. We headed for the room after thanking everyone for being so helpful.

When we got to the room, I told Pug that we had forgotten something real important. He wanted to know what we forgot.

"We haven't called Lynn and Annie and the gang since we got here. We should call them." I go over to the phone and place the call while Pug is washing off his hands and changing his pants. He spent a little time looking at his nose in the mirror.

"Hey, it's been a long time since I had my nose skinned like this. Really, it isn't that bad, just a small place on the bridge of the nose, but it will be noticeable."

Their phone was ringing and when they answered, I heard a voice on the other end of the phone saying, "Bible Sanctuary for God's Family." I recognized it as Annie's.

"Hello, Annie, this is Professor."

There was a little scream on the other end, and then I heard her holler real loud, "Lynn, it's Professor."

Lynn got on the extension and let me know they had been expecting us to call, but he had told the gang there would be a lot of things I would have to take care of before I would have time to call them. Lynn told us the gang was all there in the dining room eating.

I heard Annie hollering out the door to the gang that I was on the phone.

Lynn wanted to know how our flight was and how everything was going in the Big Apple.

Cowboy came on the phone and asked if we got to go to the Garden yet. By now Pug was on the other phone in his room, and he starts telling Cowboy all about the Garden. He tells him all about the Security Guard who had been there so long and how helpful he was in showing him around. "He helped me decide what to take pictures of so you would enjoy them also." Then I could hear them all talking in the background. Lynn was saying, "Just a minute and all of you can have your chance to talk to them."

They all took turns, and they all asked just about the same questions. Pug and I gave them all just about the same answers.

After about fifteen or twenty minutes, I tell them that we will call them every day from now on to let them know what we were doing. I explain to them that we were being kept over till the Monday show. They understood. Pug finally says good-bye and hangs up.

Pug combed his hair and checked himself over; when he was satisfied with what he saw, we headed for the door and the elevator.

We headed out the doors to the street again.

"Please don't bend over to tie your shoe. If your lace come undone, just let it stay that way until you get out by the curb or up by the building. Before you bend over, let me know so I can stand behind you and block anyone who might be running down the street and knocking you down."

It was about 8:00 p.m., and I was beginning to get a little hungry. We walk the couple of blocks to the Black Angus. As we walked in, I see Big Ernie again, and he sees us. He stops talking to the lady at the register and comes over, shakes our hands, and says, "So you guys didn't get enough last night, huh?"

"The truth of the matter Ernie, is that it was so good we just had to come back for more."

"Well now in that case let me see if we can't find you a table. Oh, yeah, there's one over in Pam's area. I hope you don't mind having the same waitress." Then he winks at me.

We walk on over to the same booth we had last night. Pam sees us and smiles as she walks back toward the kitchen. In a minute she comes out with two glasses of water and a very cheery, "Well, hello. I didn't think I would see you again, at least not for a while."

I have to admit to that the cooking – and the company – was so good we just couldn't stay away.

She asks if we wanted anything else to drink. I order tea and Pug orders a Coke.

As she walks off, she says, "I'll get your drinks while you make up your minds about what you want to eat."

In a couple of minutes she comes back with our drinks and wanted to know if we had made up our minds yet.

"I know what I want. I want that sixteen-ounce New York strip, with potato and everything on it. Then, if you have any of that asparagus left in the kitchen, I sure would like some of that again this evening. Tonight I think Pug just wants the strip also with baked potato and a salad with ranch dressing. He thinks that maybe he will be able to eat some more of that dessert if he doesn't get too full eating a big steak."

She writes everything down and walks back toward the kitchen. Pug grins and says "Professor, I think that lady kind of likes you."

"Well, Pug, the feeling is mutual."

We watched the people come and go down the street as we waited for our food. Big Ernie came over to see if everything was all right. I told him about our little trip to Queens with George today and about our conversation.

Ernie's eyes seemed to get kind of watery as he heard about the old days. He looked kind of sad for a moment, and then he said, "You know what, Professor, that kid Chip could have made the pros."

"Yeah, and I understand that you could have made the pros also."

"Naw, not me, I didn't have the discipline that Chip had. I wanted to run around and play too much for me to ever make it in the pros. Chip was dedicated and knew just what he wanted. It really broke my heart when he got that hip busted up."

"What are the chances that Chip will go to night school?"

"They look great right now. I talked to him just the other day, and he is enrolling in NY City College next semester. He wants to study business administration and maybe get his MBA. He says he can keep his job at the hotel while he is going to night school."

"Has he finally agreed to accept some help on his tuition?"

Ernie smiled, "If you mean help, yes, he will let me loan him the money for the tuition, but he insists that he is definitely going to pay me back just as soon as he gets his MBA. Hell, Professor, that kid can go through that school with flying colors. That's why it made me feel so bad to see him as a bellman at a hotel. He's too smart to be doing that."

"Maybe that's where he is smart. He makes good tips, and he isn't indebted to anyone. He also knows that you are behind him in case things get rough, just like the old days on the football field."

Ernie looked kind of sad and said, "Well, I can tell you I'll never let anyone else hurt him again like I did before."

"Now look here, Ernie. You shouldn't blame yourself for what happened to Chip. That was a game, and almost anything can happen in a game like that. If you really think hard and remember the game clearly, I am sure you will find there was some reason why you let this guy get through the line and hit Chip. How many men were coming through your position on that play?"

"Well, they had been doubling up on me for a couple of plays before Chip got hurt."

"So, what you are saying is that they would have two man engage you while another went through the hole between you and the guard."

"Well, yeah, now that I think about it, that's exactly what they were doing to me the couple of plays before Chip got hurt."

"Don't you understand now that they couldn't handle you one on one, so they sent two to handle you so someone else could get by you and get into the backfield and to Chip. It wasn't your fault, Ernie; you did everything you could. You couldn't handle the whole side of the line by yourself. Chip knows this, and I am sure that he understands what happened that night better than you do."

"Professor, you know he has been telling me all these years that it wasn't my fault, and I really didn't believe it. Now I understand that's true. Thanks, Professor."

"Now, Ernie, I want to ask you a question. I know that in most businesses like yours it isn't allowed for employees to date customers. I would like to ask Pam if she would like to go out to dinner and a show tomorrow evening, that is if she doesn't have to work."

"Professor, I'll guarantee you that if she wants to go, she will be off work, and she won't lose any pay either. She needs to go out once in a while. Her husband passed away several years ago, long before she went to work for us. She hasn't been out with anyone since that time. As I think I mentioned on your other visit, I understand that he was killed in an accident on an aircraft carrier while he was in the Navy. I feel it's about time she went out and had some fun. Go ahead and ask her."

Pam came toward our booth with dinner. I was really ready to eat after such an eventful day. I look at my meal, and sure enough there was that asparagus.

Pam was really such a beautiful woman. I had thought she was last night, but now I realized that she was not just a pretty woman physically, but she radiated an inward beauty that I hadn't noticed last night. Her smile just lit up the area when she came near.

Now when she had placed all the food in front of us, she wanted to know if there was anything else that we needed right now.

"No, thank you, Pam, we're doing all right."

We dig in. The steak was cooked to perfection, and the potato was really loaded down with butter, sour cream, cheese, and chives, and – of course – the asparagus on the side. I couldn't forget that.

"Boy what a meal." Pug digs right in and seems to be enjoying everything.

We finally finished our meal. Pam came around with that dessert idea again. After we had eaten dessert last night, I had been so full I was miserable. It was good, but I was miserable.

Pam suggests some dessert and coffee. I asked what kind of cake they had. She started naming off several kinds, and then she came to carrot cake.

"Whoa, that's far enough for me. I love good carrot cake."

"Professor, I promise you it's almost as good as I make."

"How would I know?" I jokingly asked her. "I guess I will just have to take your word for it unless you want to invite me over for some cake and coffee."

She smiles and winks, "Well, maybe you should come over some time."

"Is that an invitation?"

"Could be," she smiled.

Before she could leave, I just had to say, "Whoa, lady, back up, we need to talk for a minute."

She stops, backs up, "Well what is it?"

"I asked Ernie if it would be all right for me to ask you out to dinner and a show tomorrow evening. First thing I would like to know is what is your last name? I know that it's Pam, but Pam what?"

She smiled and said, "Jackson, like Andy Jackson."

"Okay, Ms. Jackson, now I know your name. My name is Dixon. Remember that for me, it's Jim Dixon. There's a young man I would like to ask to bring his date and come along with us and make it a double date. I thought you might feel more comfortable if there were four of us on our first date."

"Oh! You think there might be more than just this one time?"

"I certainly hope so since I would like the opportunity of getting to know you better and for you to know me better than our just being one of your customers here in the restaurant."

She laughs and here comes that smile again. "Ernie got me cornered back in the kitchen a while ago and told me you were going to ask me out. He also said that if I wanted to go, I could have the night off. Well, Mr. Dixon, I would love to spend the evening with you and your friends, but what about your friend here with you? Doesn't he get to come along?"

I was dumbfounded and embarrassed because I had been so stupid. "Well, sure, I would love to have Pug come along. I just wasn't thinking."

"Professor, I have a lady friend who lives next door. Your friend might like to spend the evening with. She's about thirty-five years old and very nice looking but I won't tell you she is any raving beauty. You'll have to judge that for yourself. She is a very nice-looking and nice-acting person. I will assure you that she knows how to act, and she does love Broadway shows. She used to be a dancer a few years back. Honestly, she's real nice. I'll be glad to ask her if she would like to come with us if your friend would like.

"And, Professor, just for my own education, do you mind telling me what your friend's name is. I know you are Professor James Dixon, is there anything else to go with it?"

"Yes, it's James Robert Dixon, and my friend here is Harold Wayne McKenzie."

"Okay, where does the name Professor come in? Are you really a professor?"

"That's a long story, and I really did used to be a college professor." I explained that I would tell her all the gory details at a later time if she still wanted to hear them.

"That's fine; now what about your friend Pug?"

"Pug or Mr. McKenzie used to be a fighter, a world- ranked fighter at one time, but that story will also have to come at a later date with his permission."

O.K. Jim, who are we were going out with. "What's the other couple's name?"

I tell her about George and his limousine. "He has said we will go in it if everyone can go."

By now Pug was really getting into it. "Heck," Pug tells her, "I have never been to a swanky dinner place or a Broadway show. Things will be just fine, and all of us will have a fine time tomorrow evening."

He asks Pam about her friend. Well let's see, first of all her name is Angie and she really is a very pretty lady that I am sure you will like.

"Now Jim says, I have one more big problem. I just have the problem of getting tickets."

I ask for suggestions on which show they would like to see.

"Well, I hear they are about to close *Cats*, and I would like to see it before they close if you don't have something you would like to see more..

"Professor, can I call you something besides Professor? May I call you Jim or Robert or Bob?"

"I'll tell you what, Pam. My mother used to call me Jimmy, so if you would like, why don't you call me Jim or Jimmy, whichever suits you at the time. All my friends used to call me Jim. Maybe after the show tomorrow evening, I'll have a chance to explain a few things to you. I feel you should know a few things about me."

She looked puzzled, but that was just fine with her.

I asked for her address and phone number and tell her that I will call her in the morning just as soon as I talk to George and find out about the tickets.

It's time for us to get out of there and let this lady get back to work. I reached out and take her hand for a minute just to look at her. She really is beautiful.

She looks up at me and as our eyes meet, I can see them smiling like a young lady seeing her first love. Well maybe it isn't her first love but I had a feeling that mine were smiling also. I hadn't been this happy in a long, long time.

We said good-bye and headed for the cashier.

We had just stopped at the cashier and started to pay our check, when Ernie comes over and tells the cashier that this dinner was on the house. That was a pleasant surprise and we really appreciated it.

"Well, Professor he says as he sticks out that very large ham hock of a hand. How do things look for tomorrow night?"

"I owe you a big debt; and if I ever have the opportunity, I will definitely pay it back."

He just smiles, "Be good to her, Professor."

"Jim to you, Ernie. Jim is what my friends call me."

"Okay, Jim it is." Once again he tells me that he appreciated what I pointed out to him tonight about the football game. From now on it will be a lot better since he wouldn't feel so guilty about what had happened to Chip.

After we got outside, Pug looks at me and says, "Professor, we forgot to get our cake and coffee."

"Well, I'll be damned, Pug. We sure did, didn't we?

Well, just which would you rather have, a date with a nice lady tomorrow night or a cup of coffee and a piece of carrot cake tonight?"

"Hell, Professor, that's no choice. I had some carrot cake before we left Fort Worth, and I haven't had a date with a lady, especially a nice lady, in almost fifteen years. Do you know what kind of women hang around fighters? Well, I'll tell you one thing; they certainly aren't as nice as Miss Pam or her friends. That question is a real no- brainer."

"Let's stop at the coffee shop at the hotel and get some carrot cake and coffee."

I couldn't believe it, but I told him that coffee and cake was just fine for a nightcap before retiring.

We reach the hotel in about ten minutes or so, and we head for the coffee shop. It was now about 10:30 p.m. We go into the coffee shop and are ordering our coffee and cake when Chip comes walking in. It seemes that he had been working a little overtime for a friend who had some business to take care of. We invite him over.

We thanked him gain for introducing us to Big Ernie. We also told him about our trip to Queens and the high school. We told him we had heard about him and how he had hurt his hip and had been unable to go on to college.

"Well, that's just a temporary setback. I'm enrolling in New York City College this next semester, and I'm going to major in Business Administration, and then I am going to try to get my MBA."

I told him how much I admired him for going on and getting his education. I also tell him that I was a former college professor, and I understood how much an education could mean to a person.

He wants to minor in Physical Education. That way he might be able to get a coaching job at a high school level, but if he couldn't do that, he would at least have his MBA to fall back on.

I tell him he might think about getting his teaching certification while he is in school to go with his minor in P.E. At least he wouldn't have to run as hard and fast as he had while he had been playing football.

"Thanks Professor, that's what my dad suggested also,".

"Chip, it sounds like you have a pretty smart father."

"Well, he didn't get a lot of education, but he sure does want me to get mine. He has encouraged me ever since I was just a little kid. He tells me he doesn't want me working in some factory for the rest of my life like he has done. I love my father a lot Professor, and I want to be able to help him and my mother have a better life one of these days. I figure if I get an education, I will be able to help them live a better life. I feel I owe them a few things after all they have sacrificed for me over the years."

Pug and I start over to the elevator. I look at Pug, and I see that he seems to be hurting. I ask him about it, and he tells me he has a headache.

Pug has experienced headaches every once in a while since he took a real bad beating in his last fight. The doctors said there was nothing they could do at this time to prevent them. They were similar to a migraine headaches, but sometimes worse. He says he sees flashing lights and stars and black spots before his eyes, but it was the pressure inside of his head and the base of his skull that really hurts most. When these headaches came on, he usually has to go to the emergency room at the hospital where they give him a shot to knock him out for several hours. The headaches generally goes away during his time out, or maybe I should say his long sleep. I was afraid this was one of those times.

I holler at Chip and asked him if there is a doctor in the hotel.

"Yes, there is one, and I will tell him Pug's problem." He goes to the desk. The desk clerk makes a quick phone call. When he hangs up, he says the doctor would be up to our room immediately.

I hurry Pug to the elevator, and we get to the room as fast as possible. After we enter the room, I have Pug lay down while I get some cold, wet towels to put on his head. These seems to help a little while we are waiting on the doctor.

There is a knock on the door from the doctor. I let him in as fast as possible. He hurries to the bedroom where Pug is lying down on the bed. The doctor introduced himself and starts asking questions about Pug's health.

I explain that Pug had been a boxer who had taken quite a beating on his last fight. "Since that time he has real bad headaches from time to time. The fight doctor who examined him said the concussion he received was severe. He stated that upon examination and X rays, they found that he had an aneurysm in an artery in the Circle of Willis area of the brain.

The doctor tells me the Circle of Willis is that area at the base of the brain that splits into four other arteries and furnishes blood to all of the brain. It is also in an area that is almost impossible to reach by surgery.

"It seems that the aneurysm seeps blood sometimes if the blood gets too thin. This is why they have never operated on him to repair the aneurysm. The aneurysm in the Basilar Carotid of the Circle of Willis sometimes leaks blood out into the base of the brain, and the pressure from the collecting blood causes these headaches. The doctors have him on a blood thickener to prevent this from happening, but sometimes he forgets to take his medicine. When he fails to take his medicine, he apparently has some seepage into the brain area, and this causes the headaches. I'm sure that in the excitement of being here in the big city he just forgot to take his medicine."

Fortunately for us, the doctor was very familiar with this problem. He said he used to run into it when he had been working the Emergency Unit at the hospital where he had served his Residency.

He talked to Pug for a few minutes. They seemed to agree on whatever it was the doctor said to him. The doctor went to his bag and removed a syringe. I heard him tell Pug that he was going to give him a shot to relieve the pain.

He was going to order something from the drug store so he could give him an IV injection so it would act more quickly than the medicine he was taking by mouth.

Pug shook his head in agreement.

He gave Pug his first shot and then went immediately to the phone and called the drug store. "Professor, if you don't mind, I will just have a seat and wait for the medicine to get here. It should be here within five minutes."

We sat and chatted about different things. He inquired our reason for being in town.

I explained that I was to appear on the TV program "So You Want to Be a Millionaire."

He thinks this is great. He asks a lot of questions about the show that I couldn't answer since I hadn't gotten that far yet. I explained that we were being held over until Monday for my taping.

There was finally a knock at the door, and it was Chip Rowan, the Bellman. Chip had the medicine for Pug's shot, and it had been charged to the hotel.

The doctor gives Pug the shot in the vein of the right arm. He tells me to let him sleep the night through, but to check on him every once in a while maybe every couple of hours just to be sure he is all right. If he gets worse or has any problems at all during the night, I am to call the front desk, and they will contact him right away. He reminded me that he could be here within ten minutes of the call since he lives here in the hotel.

I thanked him and he left. Before leaving he cautioned me to be sure and check on Pug during the night. I assured him that I would; we said good night.

Chip was still here and just starting out the door. I try to stop him and give him a tip for the help in getting the medicine and the doctor but he would have none of it. He just looked at me real serious like and said, "Not this time, this time it was for a friend."

I check on Pug to make sure he was okay before I turned in for a couple of hours. He seems to be feeling pretty good now and was just about asleep. I go to my bedroom and set the alarm to wake myself in a couple of hours. I finally get settled in and doze off to sleep. It seemed as though it had only been a few minutes when the alarm went off, but it had already been two hours. I go quietly into Pug's room and walk over to the bed. He is still sleeping soundly. I could see his chest rise and fall as he breathed, so I knew he was doing all right. I go back to bed and set the alarm to wake me in another two hours. This continued through the night until 8:00 a.m. the next morning. When I went in he was awake and his eyes look good and clear.

Just then the doctor called and told me he thought it would be best if Pug didn't have any strenuous activities today. He said that maybe this evening if his head was all right, he could go to the dinner and show with us.

Oh, my gosh! I had forgotten to call about tickets. I explained to Pug what the doctor had just told me. That it would be best if he would just loaf today and be a good boy so he could go with us tonight.

The Date

I call the desk to see if they knew anyone who could help me get tickets to the show tonight. "I realize it is very short notice, but I really need six tickets badly."

They didn't know anything right then, but they would see what they could do.

I decided to try a backup plan. I called the TV studio and asked for the producer of the show. Now this was dumb because I realized this was Saturday, and they didn't normally work on Saturday.

They asked who I was. I told them who I was and what my problem was. They asked me to wait a few minutes. They finally came back on the line and said they were sorry, but there was nothing they could do to help me at this late date.

Now I was desperate. I decided to try another angle. I got the phone book and looked up the number of the Black Angus. I called that number and asked if Ernie was there. They told me that he didn't come in until just before the lunch crowd.

I told them who I was, and they said, "Sure, we remember you. We're sure that Ernie wouldn't mind if we gave you his home number."

I quickly called the number and bless ole Ernie's hide, he answers the phone. I quickly tell him who I am and what my problem is.

He very quietly says, "Now, Professor, don't get in a tizzy. I think I may be able to help you. How many tickets do you need?"

I need six Ernie, I need six very badly.

O.K. just stay right where you are, now what is your room number.

The next fifteen minutes were the longest in this old drunk's life. The phone finally rings; it's Ernie Bless his Little Pea Pickin Heart and thank God.

"Good news, Professor, I found six good tickets for tonight. They will be delivered to your room before noon today." It seems he had an old buddy who was in the Concert and Broadway shows ticket business. He just collected a debt owed.

"Ernie, how can I ever repay you?"

"Hey Man, Just Have a good time tonight and see that Pam has a good time." He told me that he learned long ago that happy employees made better employees. He hangs up before I could say anything else.

The next few hours went very slowly. Finally, about 11:00 a.m. there was a knock on the door. What a wonderful sound that was. I opened the door, and sure enough there was a young man who asked, "Are you Professor Dixon?"

"I sure am."

"Well, sir, I have six very good tickets to the Broadway production of *Cats* for tonight." He hands me the tickets along with a bill for them at the same time. I pay him and give him a nice tip for his service.

I heard a voice from the other room asking, "Is that the tickets?"

"Sure thing, man. We're all fixed up. How are you feeling?"

I feel good, but a little weak. "No more head ache now, so we must have caught it just in time to keep it from becoming real bad,".

"Pug, just be a good boy and lay back down and watch television. Can you eat a hamburger and drink a Coke?"

"Sure can," which from Pug means he was feeling better now getting pretty hungry.

I called room service and had them send up a couple of hamburgers, French fries, and a couple of Cokes.

While we are waiting on the food, I call George and tell him I have the tickets. He told his girlfriend who happened to be there, and they were both eager for tonight to get here.

I call Pam to tell her about the tickets also. I also tell her what had happened to Pug. She wants to know if this was going to keep him from going with us tonight.

"The doctor says it will be all right if he doesn't exert himself today, and if he takes it easy tonight."

She is really happy to hear this. I tell her what time George is going to pick us up, so she could figure it would take us about forty-five minutes to get to her place according to George.

"That sounds great Jim. My girl friend and I will be ready when you arrive."

George was right on time. We finally get to meet his lady friend Carol. She really was a knockout. She was a small girl with black hair and eyes that absolutely sparkled when she started to talk. She was very expressive with her hands and eyes. You could tell that she was very crazy about George even though they had just gotten back together.

We headed down 42nd Street to pick up Pam and her friend. George knew this town like the back of his hand and went directly to Pam's address.

Pug and I got out of the limousine and went to the door of the duplex where they lived. I rang the bell, Pam slowly opened the door. Holy Cow, did she look beautiful or what? I couldn't believe this was the lady from the Black Angus. She asks us to step in for a minute while she called her friend who was in the back room.

She very softly said, "Angie, are you ready?" The boys are here.

With that we saw a very beautiful young lady come walking into the room. She had such grace in her stride that she looked to be walking on clouds. She was a blonde with blue eyes, and she stood about five feet, five or six inches tall. I knew it wasn't polite to talk about a woman's measurements, but this girl had to have measurements to knock your eyes out, you know, about 37-25-34. Boy was she, as the boys would say, stacked. She had a beautiful warm and friendly smile.

Pam introduces us. She walks over and shakes hands with both of us. She looks at Pug and says, "Pam told me about you, and she didn't exaggerate. You are very good looking." She look Pug straight in the eye and says, "Your arm, please."

Pug couldn't believe it, but he sure did stick his arm out in a hurry.

On the way out of the door, I heard Angie ask Pug if it was all right for her to call him Harold or Wayne. It seemed that Pam had told Angie Pug's real name, and she preferred either of the names to Pug. She thought Wayne fit him better than Harold. She felt that Harold just didn't seem to fit an ex-prize fighter.

Pug grinned his cute little grin, "Angie, you can call me just about anything you want to call me."

Back at the limousine, I introduce Pam and Angie to George and Carol. After we were all situated, George tells us that he and Carol talked it over, and they had made reservations at a very nice club which has a combo for dinner music down on 42nd Street. He heads that direction. "The restaurant is only a couple of blocks from the theater, so it won't take us long to get there after we have dinner."We pull up to this very nice-looking club called Spencer's Downtown Club. We get out, and for once, George had someone else park the car. We walk in and there were some of the most beautiful chandeliers and fixtures you would find anywhere outside of a palace in Italy or France.

There were beautiful dark blue velvet draperies with matching velvet ropes holding them in place. The tables were a beautiful black with gold trim, and the chairs had black velvet seats with gold beading on the backs and seats of each chair. I hadn't seen this type of establishment since I had left Chicago many years ago.

The maître d' met us with a big smile. Just as soon as George gave him his name, he called the assistant maître d' to take us to our table.

The seating was in a very nice area, not too close to the stage and not too far away. We thoroughly enjoyed the dinner and the dessert. During dinner they had a very good quartet playing some of the old swing big band music. You know, kind of like elevator music. A few people danced.

While we were waiting for our dinner to be served, I asked Pam if she would like to dance, she said she would love to. She told me she hadn't danced in a long time, so I had better watch out for my toes. She was a real fine dancer, very smooth and very easy to dance with.

I noticed that Pug was a little hesitant, but Angie suggested they dance. He reluctantly got up, and they came onto the floor. Guess What? Pug was a darn good dancer. This was something I hadn't counted on.

When you think about it though, most boxers would be good dancers. They are light on their feet and moved easily about the ring. I saw the look of surprise on Angie's face when they started dancing. Since Angie used to be a professional dancer, you could tell she was very smooth and easy to dance with. Pug and Angie made a very cute couple. The way they danced, you'd think they were professionals.

Soon George and Carol joined us on the floor. We danced a couple of dances. When we saw the waiters heading for our table, we also head back. We beat the waiter there so he would know just where each of us had been seated. A fine dinner was had by all. Great food, music and most of all wonderful dinner companions and conversation.

It was just about thirty minutes till the shows starting time. We decided to walk to the theater, then come back here for a nightcap after the show. We quickly added that Pug and I would have our cake or pie and coffee, since neither of us felt it would be wise to have a drink. They all understood.

It felt wonderful to walk the couple of blocks to the theater. We arrive about ten minutes before curtain time. Pug's eyes got real big as he was taking everything in tonight. Angie was right at home here since she used to dance in some of the shows in this very theater when she had been younger. Now she works for a national travel agency. She books travel for people all over the world. She tells us it feels real good to be inside the theater even if she is out front instead of on the stage.

Pam and I really did enjoy the show. It felt so good to be sitting with a lovely young lady and holding her hand. It brought back a lot of memories of years gone by.

I began to wonder again about my family. All of a sudden I realized that I was truly on the road to recovery so I had better get my head screwed back on straight. I looked at Pam and realized that it was nice to have someone else who seemed to care about me and who I was. Unfortunately, she didn't realize just who I was and what I had been for the past ten years. Looking at her made me realize where I am; I suddenly look at the stage; my mind comes back to reality. What a wonderful show, and what great music, what wonderful friends.

On our way back to the club for our nightcap, we talk, laugh, and discuss the show we had just seen. I asked Angie about working on stage plays like this. That started a string of good stories, most of them very funny. She was still telling us stories when we reached the restaurant.

Inside, the maître d' greets us and showed us to a table this time. The restaurant didn't have very many people due to the late hour. We all ordered coffee and cake or pie. This time I went with some cherry pie since I hadn't had any in a long time. I forgot what the rest of the folks had. I was too busy looking at Pam.

I was beginning to get a little worried about Pug and his headache. He said he felt fine, but his eyes told me that he was getting real tired. After we finished our pie and coffee, I suggested that maybe we should call it an evening even though it was still not quite midnight. They all agreed.

We had a lot to talk about on our way home. George took us to Pam's place first. He said they would be glad to wait for us.

"Thanks, we won't be long."

When we got to the door, Pam turned to me, took hold of my right hand with her left one and told me what a wonderful evening she had just experienced. She then reaches up puts her right hand behind my neck and pulled me forward. She gave me a wonderfully warm kiss, definitely not the sisterly kind of kiss. She tells me she hopes she would see me tomorrow. I assured her that she would. I then give her one more wondrfully warm embrace and kiss feeling her body next to mine nearly drove me wild.

By now Pug had said goodnight to Angie who lives next door to Pam. That duplex made it nice since we were both going with girls who lived there.

Pug and I reached the limousine about the same time.

"Okay, guys, I guess you are ready to go to the hotel."

I assured him that we did need to get Pug back to the room so he could get some rest.

Upon arriving at the hotel, we say good night to George and Carol. "It was so nice to meet you, Carol, and we hope to see you again.

"Goodnight, George, and thanks for everything."

"No problem, Professor, we'll see you later."

We went inside, and I asked Pug to tell me the truth now about how he felt. He finally admitted that he was pretty tired and strung out from the excitement this evening.

He grinned kind of sheepishly and said, "You know what, Professor? Angie kissed me goodnight. I thought I would wet my britches. She sure is a nice lady. I hope I get to see her again."

"You will, Pug; you'll get to see her again before we leave because I want to see Pam again. I promised Pam that we would see them tomorrow."

When we got to the room, I made him go right to bed. I was a little worried about my friend, but he assured me he was all right.

Morning came, and I smelled coffee. Pug had already been up and made coffee.

"Hey, Pug, how do you feel?"

Before I could get the words out of my mouth, he says, "Fine, just fine. I will never forget last night. What a wonderful evening that was. That Angie lady is one very special lady."

"Pug, don't tell me you're in love."

"Well, I don't know her that well yet, but I sure hope I get to know her better." I'm sure I need a little more time, but boy oh boy.

After a cup of coffee and a shower, we decided to go down to the restaurant and have some breakfast. After breakfast we go back to the room.

We just get back to the room, when the phone rings. It was Pam.

"I know this may sound a little corny, but Angie and I were getting ready to go to church, and we just wondered if you and Pug or pardon me, Wayne, might like to come over and go with us. If you do, we can fix some lunch when we get back, and then we can spend the rest of the day together."

"You know what, that's the first time I can ever remember a girl asking me to go to church with her."

I turn to Pug and ask, "How do you feel about this latest proposal of going to church with the girls?"

He brightened up real fast. "Sure does sound good to me."

"Well, Pam, Pug, pardon me, I mean Wayne says that's the best proposal he has had all day, and it sure does sound good. It will take us about thirty minutes to get dressed and another fifteen minutes to get over to your house. You better give me your address again, so we will be sure to come to the right house."

She laughed and gave me her address again. "We'll see you in about an hour."

We change clothes right away and head downstairs. The elevator seemed slower than usual today. We get to the front door of the hotel, and the doorman hailes a cab for us. We give him the address and away we go. I hadn't even thought to ask what kind of church we were going to, not that it mattered.

After what seemed like an hour, we arrived at Pam's house. We were greeted by two lovely ladies ready to go to church. It turned out that they were both Catholic, and so was I. I wasn't sure about Pug, but that didn't make any difference now.

Pam had her car in front of the house ready for us to go to church. We loaded in and away we went.

At church, it seemed good to hear a sermon from the pulpit instead of from the street corner or at the Sanctuary. They had communion, and this was also the first time I had attended or participated in a communion in over ten years. You know what? It sure did feel good.

Next thing I know, I might even be going to confession. Pug took communion too, even though he was Protestant. He said that it sure couldn't hurt him. Maybe a little religion would do him some good at a time like this.

After church, we offer to take the girls to lunch, but they said that they already had taken care of lunch. Off we go back to Pam's apartment.

We found that Pam had put a nice plump roast on to cook before we went to church. You know the kind, a good pot roast with all the vegetables cooked in the pan with the roast. When we walked into the house, we could smell that roast all over the house and out on the front porch. Oh, how my mouth started to water! This sure did bring back some good memories of my mother's cooking.

I mentioned this to Pam, and she just smiled and said, "You'll have to tell me about your mother one of these days."

That would be fine, I would enjoy doing that very little thing.

I could see that Pug was really enjoying himself. He was actually helping Angie set the table. He was doing a pretty good job of it. It seemed that I was finding out a few things about Pug that I hadn't known before. Truth is I had never seen him sober this long before.

He told me last night that he was never going back to that old way of life. That sure made me feel good because I told him I was going to follow his lead, and I would never go back to that old way of life either.

It was good to see the way he looked at Angie and the way she looked at him. I knew this was awfully soon, but I really felt they liked each other a lot. Now if he could just tell her all about his past without scaring her away. I had to think about that also when I told Pam, but right now she was ready to take the pot roast out of the oven.

I helped her with the roast because it was real hot and I didn't want her to burn herself. I put the pot on the stove where she could take the roast and vegetables out and put them on a platter. She did this just as if she had done it many times before. When this was done, she took the liquid in the bottom of the pot and made gravy to go with the roast. This lady knew how to cook good old home cooking.

After we finished off most of the roast and vegetables, Pam asked if anyone would like some dessert? How would you like to have a piece of lemon pie and a cup of coffee, she asks? She remembered that I liked lemon pie. I was ready for that slice of pie since lemon was one of my very favorite pies. Pug was also ready, so we all sat and talked and talked some more and had our dessert and coffee.

Pam, I feel it is time to let you and Angie know who you are associating with. They didn't seem surprised in the least, but they were anxious to hear. I started by telling them that I was an alcoholic. They had already guessed that due to last night's conversation about our coffee and cake for a nightcap.

I proceeded to tell them about the events leading up to my being an alcoholic. I explained that I now saw just how weak I had been and how ashamed I was for being so weak. I told them about my ex-wife, my children, and my parents. I told them what I had been doing for the past ten plus years and what had led up to my being on the TV show.

They seemed to accept what I said as being the truth, because as Pam said, "You didn't have to tell us anything." You could have made up a big pretty sounding story if You had wanted to lie. They could accept what I had said, and they say they could accept me for what I am today and not what I had been for the last ten plus years.

Pug was next to come clean and tell his story. He told of his many fights and how his manager was supposed to have him fixed up for a fight at the Garden and how he had failed to do it. He told how he had taken another fight while waiting for the Garden fight to materialize, and how he had been badly hurt in that fight.

It seemed he had filled in as a substitute fighter for a match that had been scheduled, but one of the participants had broken his hand before the fight and had to pull out. They offered Pug a lot of money to fill in on short notice.

Pug was a middleweight who would be fighting a heavier man who was a light heavyweight. Things had gone well for the first five rounds, and then the bigger man finally got in a good solid punch in the sixth round and almost knocked him out. Pug managed to stay on his feet, but in doing so he had taken a very severe beating. It was after that fight that they had found out he had the aneurysm at the base of the brain. The doctors said it could have been there since birth and just recently showed up. On the other hand, there was no telling what caused it and how long it had been there in his head. Since that time, he had had to take medication to keep his blood thick in order to prevent the aneurysm from seeping into his brain and spinal column.

He had started to drink to kill the pain from the seepage of the blood. Later he drank to forget what he had wanted to do so badly, and that was to fight in the Garden. He said he had no family and that the street people had become his family. They looked after him, and he looked after them when they needed his help.

"Well," he said, "I guess I really do have a family, but they don't know where I am or what I am doing."

The girls just sat quietly as we told them our life stories. When we had finished, they just looked at each other and then at us. Pam said, "We have heard all we need to hear."

They liked what we were today, and they would like to help us move forward from this day on and not have to look back at our past.

That was when I explained that if I did win a lot of money, I had to go back to Texas and help some of the people who had helped me over the years. I explained to them that many people had helped me when I was down and out. "Now I feel that if I win some money, it will be my chance to repay them for their kindness to us."

The girls agreed with what we were saying. I had never thought I would ever meet anyone as understanding as these ladies are.

I also explain that I have to go back to Chicago and set things right with my parents and my children if they will listen to me and accept me back into the family.

Pam assured me, "If you tell them what you have told me today, they will be more than ready to accept you back into the family. I have no doubt in my mind that there is still love there, just waiting for you. You absolutely must go back and see your family first and then go back to Texas.

"Now it's our turn to tell you about ourselves," Angie says.

She had been a dancer in Broadway shows for many years. She was actually from Omaha, Nebraska. As a teenager, she had won several dance contests back home in Omaha, so she had wanted to try her luck on Broadway. When she got to Broadway, she found it wasn't exactly what she had thought it was going to be.

After almost four years of dancing on different shows up and down Broadway, she finally married a man who worked on the stage crew as an electrician. She had been very much in love with him, and she thought he loved her also. It turned out that he already had a wife back in Washington. Angie got an annulment as soon as possible after finding out the truth. She had been married to him for two years before she had found out the truth.

She decided that she didn't want anything more to do with the people in show business. What she had to learn later was that all show people were not alike. Everyone had his or her own problems. She went to work for the travel agency where she now worked as an assistant manager of the office. Her mother had passed away recently, and her father now lived with her brother in Omaha. They were all the family she had left.

She would like to go back and see her father before too long because he was getting pretty old, and she wanted to see him while he was still able to be up and around the way he used to be. He had always been a very active person, and she would like to have a nice visit with him while he was still active. She would like to see her brother and sister-in-law and their two children. The children were almost teenagers now. They had been five and seven when she had last seen them. She would like to be able to go and see them this summer.

She said to be honest with us, she really hadn't wanted to go out last night, but Pam had said we were nice men. She had taken the chance that Pam was right. Now she felt that Pam was very right, and she was very glad she hadmade the decision to go. She laughed and said she had never been out with a boxer before, and she really hadn't known just what to expect. She smiled and told Pug she was pleasantly surprised at his dancing prowess. She told him once more how much she enjoyed last night and today.

Then it was time for Pam to tell us about herself. Pam was from Virginia. She had met a young sailor at Norfolk where there were a lot of sailors. They had met at a church canteen for service men. They had dated for about two years before they decided to get married just before he shipped out for a long cruise. They were married, and he had to ship out within a month after the wedding. Her husband had been aboard an aircraft carrier. He had been gone for about five months on the cruise when the accident happened.

While they were on a practice run in the South Pacific, one of the planes that had been out for some time called the carrier and said he was having motor trouble. He was told to return to the ship as soon as possible.

The crew apparently saw him coming, and they were all ready to receive the disabled plane for its landing.

Just as the plane approached the ship, the motor quit, causing him to lose altitude as he approached.

He came into the fantail of the ship where her husband was waiting in fire fighter's gear in case of a crash. The plane had apparently hit right where her husband had been standing. He had been killed instantly. They had brought him back to the states where they buried him in a family cemetery near Norfolk.

She hadn't known at the time of his death that she was pregnant. Pam had become real sick, and at about five and a half months along with her pregnancy, she had a miscarriage. The doctors told her she would never be able to have any more children. She was very disturbed for a long time with losing her husband, and then the miscarriage along with that really hit her hard. She finally decided to go to the big city and see what she could do about getting her head together.

The Black Angus was the first place she applied for a job. Big Ernie was so nice and offered her such good hours and after talking to some of the other girls, she learned they were making real good tips along with the base salary and meals. They also had a real good hospital medical plan, a dental plan, and even an optical plan. They even had a 401K savings plan, and if you wanted to participate, they would match whatever amount you put in the plan. You couldn't ask for a better plan than this. "On top of all of this, they are real fine folks to work for." Now, she said that I was the first man she had been out with since she had come to New York City.

With her personality and her beauty it was hard to believe that some fast-talking guy hadn't enticed her to go out on a date. She admitted that many had tried, but she just hadn't felt that she wanted to date anyone until I came along.

I must admit that things were moving real fast right now, and I needed to let these things soak in.

She had a mother and father and a sister and two brothers in Norfolk. "Well, it's not really in Norfolk; it's in a real small town just outside of Norfolk." She said she would like for me to meet them sometime.

"How about after my attempt at the TV show?"

She smiles and says, "You're serious, aren't you?

"Well, aren't you?"

"I sure am if you are."

"After you are through with the show, let's see what we can work out. I have some time off coming from the restaurant. I don't think Ernie will object to my taking a few days off. Well, I guess that pretty well settles things, doesn't it?"

Things were really moving a lot faster than I had expected. "Pam, I have just one question; what if my family sees me on TV and contacts the station. We have to decide where our priorities are. Is it seeing your family first or seeing mine if they contact me? That's always a possibility you know."

"I think your family is a lot more important at this time since you haven't seen them in such a long time. So many things have happened since you last saw them."

I believed this girl had her priorities straight. I felt that she was almost too good to be true.

"Jim, it's such a beautiful evening and there is a nice park just a couple of blocks down the street. Why don't we go down to the park and take a stroll?"

"That sounds like a great idea. Maybe I can walk off some of that great food I just had for lunch."

"Pug, would you and Angie like to come along for the stroll?" Pam asks just to be friendly I think.

Almost simultaneously they say, "Why don't you guys go ahead. I think you need some time alone together. It seems that you've always had someone with you ever since you met. Pug and I will stay here and visit and get to know each other better while you're gone."

That sounded fine to Jim and Pam. they walk out the front door and down the street holding hands like a couple of teenagers. Well, it was not just teenagers that held hands.

I recalled watching my mother and father walking and holding hands an awful lot of the time when I was been young and even after they were in their middle years before I left home for the unknown. I can remember the smiles on their faces and the way they looked at each other. I guess that was what I'd always wanted. I thought maybe I had what I was looking for when I had married, but it just hadn't worked out that way.

What a beautiful park to take a walk in. The late afternoon breeze was soft around us as them as they walked. They almost stumbled due to looking so closely into each others face. It was as if they wanted to study each other and totally absorb everything possible by just looking at them. This park was so well cared for, with flowers and even some beautifuul roses, Jim even recognizes a couple of them as being the same as some of his mother's roses. There was a Climbing Peace on a trestle and a beautiful pink Queen Elizabeth. What a wonderful place for the children to play without getting hurt. There were strolling or jogging paths all around, which really made it nice. We had headed down one of the paths when she, said, "Jim, I hate to tell you this, but I could get used to having you around real easy. As I told you, Pam says, I haven't dated since my husband died. I haven't had any desire to date. I feel that things between you and me are going real fast, and I honestly think we should really take our time with our relationship. The trouble is that my heart tells me one thing, and my head tells me something else. We really don't know that much about each other yet, and I feel that we should really get to know each other before we go off the deep end making any kind of plans.

"Jim, I know I want you real bad, but I also know that isn't practical, and it could lead to heartaches for both of us. How do you feel about our situation?"

This girl really floored Jim with her honest and straight thinking. "Lady, I think you're something else. I don't think anyone could have said it better. You totally astound me with your logic and good common sense. I know how right you are, and I also know how I feel about you already. I have never felt like this about anyone, not even my wife. You kind of scare me with your good sense and the way you think.

"You see, I've always thought if I ever did find someone again, I would want it to be forever. I know in order for that to happen, I would want to know them totally, and love them the same way, with no reservations and no questions. I feel that with you we can work all of that out in a short time. You are so beautiful that every time I look at you I think I'm dreaming. Never in my wildest dreams did I think someone of your class and stature could learn to love me. But as you said, let's take our time if we can. I say that because I know how hard it is going to be for the both of us."

We sat and talked and talked and talked. We talked about this, and we talked about that, and even more than we realized, we found that we thought the same about almost everything. We must have talked for a couple of hours or more just sitting there on the grassy slope watching the kids play and listening to the birds and smelling that wonder hunysuckle in this beautiful little park in the middle of this great big city.

We decided it was time to head back to the house, and away we went. When we arrived, we found Pug and Angie on the front porch sitting and talking. It was apparent they had been basically doing what Pam and I had been doing for the past couple of hours.

They were sitting holding hands and looking real pleased with themselves. They said they had a good time just talking and wondering about things and what would have happened if they had met years before.

Pug laughed at and said, "I think I know what would have happened. I think Angie wouldn't have had anything to do with a fighter who spent most of his time in a stinking, sweaty old gymnasium somewhere on the wrong side of the tracks. My friends were mostly fighters, and the people that follow the fight game aren't the most savory type people to have as friends.

"I'm glad we waited until now to meet. There's one real problem, and that's the headaches. I think we all realize that eventually I'm going to have to have an operation to try to repair that aneurysm in my brain. That could be a real problem since it is in such a difficult area to operate. I know I will be taking quite a chance by letting them operate, but on the other hand I am taking quite a chance by not letting them operate. If I don't let them operate, the aneurysm could explode, and I could have a severe stroke or die within a few minutes of the rupture of the aneurysm. I'm sure that sometime in the near future I will try to arrange to have the operation done. It seems that now I have a lot more to live for, I want to be alive for a real long time. I will just put all my trust in God and the surgeon who does the operation."

Angie had been real quiet all the time Pug had been talking. Now I could see she had something she wanted to say. She finally said, "If Pug wants to have the operation, I will stand by him all the way. He can recover at my house if he has the operation while he is in New York City."

Now that was quite a proposal. Pug looked completely stupefied. He couldn't believe what he had just heard. "Angie, do you know what you just said. You don't really know me that well."

"Wayne, I feel I know more about you than you know about yourself. You just need someone to bring out your good points, and I think I just may be that person. I'm at least willing to take a chance on you and try to help any way I can."

"Well, Pam, it looks like these guys are working faster than we are."

"Yes, it sure looks like it, doesn't it?" she agreed.

Angie pipes up, "I didn't say we were going to get married; I just said he could stay at my place until he gets on his feet. Then maybe we will talk about marriage possibilities and the future after we take that first big step. You guys just remember that I have a two-bedroom apartment. Besides, if he gets operated on, he won't feel like doing anything for a while, if you get my meaning."

It seemed we had just about touched every base during this day of talking, both Pug and Angie and then Pam and I. I had to admit that we had covered a lot of territory in the last three days.

"If we told people what has happened, I'm sure they wouldn't believe us. This last couple of days would make us sound like a real romance novel. You know what I mean, one of those love story magazines. I always thought those stories were just made up by lonely little ole ladies writing about what they wished would happen to them. Love like this or at least the feelings that I have felt the last few days are something I never believed could have happened to me. It's here; it's happening to me, and I love every minute of it."

Changing the direction of the conversation, I turned to Pug. "Pug, I hate to say this, but it's about time for us to be heading back to the hotel."

"Not yet, boys, there's still some pot roast in there to eat, and Angie and I can't eat it all by ourselves. Besides, who is going to finish off that pie? Let's warm everything in the microwave and eat before you leave. That won't take long."

Off went Pam and Angie to get the food on the table while Pug and I set the plates and silverware on the table. It only took a very few minutes to get everything ready to eat. We had our meat and potatoes so to speak, and then there was just enough pie for each of us to have a slice with a cup of coffee.

When we were finished, I called for a taxi to take us back to the hotel. Pam offered to take us, but we resisted because they had done enough for us today.

Soon the cab came, and we kissed the girls good-bye and headed back to the hotel.

Back at the hotel we saw Chip Rowan who was just getting off work. He spoke and stopped to talk for a minute. He had to be going because he was getting up early to go to the registrar's office at NY City College.

He seemed real anxious to get started back to school and pursue his education. What a nice guy – and smart. He seemed to know just what he wanted out of life.

Pug and I headed for the elevators and went upstairs to our room. We knew I should have a good night's sleep because tomorrow was going to be a long day. We talked for just a while about the girls and what had happened to us in the last few days. It was truly hard to believe.

Pug told me it was gonna be hard for him to go to sleep tonight because he couldn't stop thinking about Angie.

I told him to try hard because that was what I was going to do.

I went to bed and tried as hard as I might, but I just couldn't stop thinking about Pam. I'd never been bothered about anything this way before. The last time I looked at the clock on the nightstand, it was a little after 1:00 a.m. I guess I finally went to sleep because I woke up again to the smell of coffee.

The Big Day at Last

It seemed that Pug had gotten into the habit of waking up early. Thank goodness he had because the coffee helped me to open my eyes. I downed my first cup of coffee and headed for the showers to complete the eye-opening process.

We went downstairs, had breakfast, then we waited for George. Sure enough, George was right on time. We had our usual meeting with "Good morning," and "How's everybody doing this morning."

George told us how much they had enjoyed the evening the other night. "Carol said to wish you good luck for her at the program taping today."

I thought that was real nice of that young lady.

It didn't take long to reach the studio. George got out, came around, and opened the car door for us. "Good luck, Jim. I guess it's all right if I call you Jim, isn't it?"

"That's what all my friends call me, and I certainly count you as one of my very good friends."

In we went, where we were met by one of the assistants who takes us back to the staging area. We get our lecture on what we were going to be doing today.

Well, here we go. They put us all together in a separate area of the studio and gave us a chance to get acquainted.

There were people from almost every walk of life in our little group of ten people. Our group included a doctor, a mailman, a hairdresser, two teachers, an attorney, a youth minister, a mortician, a man who ran a nursery for gardeners, and a kindergarten schoolteacher. We introduced ourselves to each other and had a chance to visit for a while before they came in to talk to us.

The first person was an assistant to the producer along with an assistant to the director of the show.

They explained the workings of the cameras. They explained what they would be doing while we made our selections on the initial questioning for us to get into the chair with the host of the show. Everyone seemed to be very compatible. It might sound unusual, but we found everyone encouraging each other and wishing each other good luck.

We were told to take our time when answering and also to elaborate a little if we would like, but not to do a full dissertation on the answer. "You know, make it interesting. Remember," we were told, "that you are here for two purposes: entertain the audience and make a lot of money."

I kind of liked it the other way; you know make money and then entertain.

"Either way," they said, "let's all have a lot of fun."

"Now remember, if you make the hot seat as they call it, don't get nervous. Remember that you have already had a good time and a nice trip to the Big Apple at our expense, so if you don't hit the million-dollar mark, try to be happy.

"I see that you have all come wearing clothes that will be friendly to the camera."

They had told us not to wear anything too light, especially no white. Subdued colors come off best to the eye of the camera.

Next we were all taken back to the makeup room. This took about thirty minutes with several people working on our makeup.

Finally when we were just about ready, we began to hear a lot of noise out front in the theater. As we walked out to the floor, we saw why. They had an audience waiting for us.

It was about time for the show to begin, so they instructed the audience about applause and the signs and the director who dictated the actions on the floor and stage overall.

We were all asked to take our seats and get ready. Then, we were given the quiet sign, the count down, and the director pointed to the audience and the applause sign as the lights went up.

The host of the show was spotlighted. He made his usual customary remarks to open the show. He turns to the camera and introduces a man who was in the seat when the last show had run out of time. He talked about several things while also asking the man how he had spent the weekend. Then he went into the lifelines, etc. Then he asked the man to go to his seat, and he asks the audience if they were ready. They all scream, "yes," and the show is on the way.

The man was at the $64,000 level and anxious to reach the $125,000 level. His next question was one on the location of four towns' locations on the map, which was northern most, and which of the other three followed going south. A couple of the towns were smaller towns that a lot of folks had never heard of. I thought the towns in question were Seattle, Washington; Boise, Idaho; Golden, Colorado; and San Diego, California. The contestant said he knew that Seattle was northernmost and that San Diego was southernmost, but he wasn't sure about the location of the one in Iowa and the one in Colorado. He and his wife had talked it over during the weekend, and they had decided if he hit a question he wasn't real sure of, he would take the $64,000. Since that was more money than he had ever seen, they could use the money to pay off the mortgage on their home.

Robert, the host, asked him if he was sure that was what he wanted to do, and he says, "Yes."

Robert finally says, "Is that your last answer?"

"It sure is." That's my decision.

"I don't blame you because that's a lot of money, and if you can pay off your home, I think you would be foolish not to do just that."

There applause was loud as he got down from his chair and walked toward the rear of the room where his wife had now arrived from her seat in the audience. They hugged, and he walked off the set a rich man, richer he said than he had ever dreamed of being.

Robert Burns, the host, tells us it was time to get someone else in the hot seat. He tells us to look at our monitors and answer the question by picking in order the movies as they first appeared on the screen from oldest to latest. The movies listed were Gone with the Wind, The Great Train Robbery, The Dirty Dozen, and Stagecoach. We all hurried pushing buttons like crazy. Luckily, I had always been an old movie buff. I lined them up quickly as did everyone else.

First, I knew that The Great Train Robbery was one of the first movies produced. I also knew that The Dirty Dozen was the latest, but the two that had me for a second were Stagecoach and Gone with the Wind, so I said Stagecoach, Gone With the Wind, and The Dirty Dozen.

There were six of us with all of the right answers. Now the time comes into play. Robert says, "We have a winner, and that winner is Professor Jim Dixon from Ft. Worth, Texas."

I couldn't believe I had made it on my first try. I was truly elated, but extremely surprised. I had answered the question in 4.6 seconds.

Robert asks, "You must be a movie buff in order to answer the question that fast since that is one of the fastest times we have had up till now."

By the time he finished saying that I was standing beside the him and was shaking his hand. I must admit that my knees were shaking at the same time. I had had no idea that I would be nervous like this.

He said, "Let's get started, Professor, and see what you can do to make Fort Worth and Texas proud."

He was in his seat, and I was in mine. He tells me to get comfortable, take a deep breath and relax. I tried my best to get comfortable while he was talking about something. I don't think I even heard what he was saying at that point.

"Now he says, for the $100 question."

I must admit that I don't really remember the next four or five questions because they were all very simple questions that anyone could have answered. He finally said, "Now for the $1,000 question."

I don't remember it or the next three questions, because by now we are really getting serious. We are at the $16,000 level, and that to me was real serious money. The $16,000 question was regarding baseball.

He wanted to know who the pitcher was that developed and perfected what was at that time called the blooper ball pitch. The names given were Babe Ruth, Toothpick Simpson, Rip Sewell, or Stan Williams.

I was a big fan of the Pittsburgh Pirates, and I had read about Rip Sewell and how he had developed this pitch when I had just been a kid. I had that one "nailed" as the gang would say. I answer that it was Rip Sewell.

"You are absolutely right. Professor, it was Rip Sewell back in the early 1940's, and you now have $16,000. Rip was quite a pitcher.

"Now we are looking at $32,000. Are you ready for this one?"

I said, "Let's get on with it."

The question will appear on the screen for the $32,000. That question iss to pick the name of the man who was Commander-in-Chief of all of the allied armies in World War II. The names given were General George Patton, General Montgomery, General Ike Eisenhower, or Omar Bradley. "This is an easy one Bob, since my uncle was in that war, and he often spoke of General Ike Eisenhower; and of course, we all know that he later became President Eisenhower."

"You are absolutely right Professor, and you now have $32,000. Now you can't go home with less than the $32,000. Now here comes the $64,000 question to your screen, and it is concerning boxing.

"Pick from the names listed below the name of the last bare-knuckle boxing heavyweight champion. The names are Abe Attel, Benny Leonard, John L. Sullivan, and Georges Carpentier."

"My father was quite a boxer himself when he was young, and he was a great fan of the last great bare-knuckle champion, and that was the Great John L. himself."

Robert looked at me and asked, "Is that your last answer?"

"It sure is Robert, that's my answer and I'm sticking with it."

He looks me straight in the eye and says, "Are you sure?"

"Yes, I am Robert, I am very sure."

"Well, Professor, I hesitate to tell you this, but you now have $64,000. The applause finally dies down and Robert continues. I guess you're ready to go for the $125,000. I hope you make this one, Professor, because it looks like you're on a roll."

"I sure hope so too Robert."

"Here is the question for $125,000. In which part of the Bible do you find the saying, 'Let he who is without sin cast the first stone."

I am given four books of the Bible in which to choose the answer: Ruth, Romans, John, and Matthew. I had to think back to my Sunday School days. I remembered about the lady being stoned by the crowd for committing adultery, but I had trouble remembering what part of the Bible it was from. I decided to use a lifeline and call Lynn.

Robert asks, "Who is Lynn?"

"He's a minister friend of mine back in Ft. Worth, Texas."

Robert laughs and says, "Well, he sure better know this one since he is a minister. The operator will get Lynn on the phone for you."

The phone rings; and when Lynn came on the line, Robert asks, "Is this Lynn?"

"Yes, it is."

"Well, this is Robert Burns on 'So You Want to Be a Millionaire. I have Professor Jim here with me, and he needs your help on a question about the Bible. Jim will come on the line and ask you a question and give you four possible answers, he needs you to help him select the right answer. You have thirty seconds, and it starts now."

I read the question and the answers to Lynn, and without hesitation he told me that was in John, and he gave me the chapter and verse. He told me that it was talked about in another area of the Bible too, but that area was not one of the four answers. I didn't even question him about how sure he was of the answer because I knew how well he knew the Bible.

I only take time to say "Thanks, Lynn, I'll see you soon."

"Good Luck Professor Lynn replies"

I immediately told Robert that it was in John, and I gave him the chapter and verse, and "That's my last answer. I trust Lynn totally with any answer from the Bible."

Robert just looked at me and said, "It must be great to have friends like Lynn to call on in an emergency." He looks straight at me and says, "Professor, you now have $125,000."

The applause was greater after each answer, and with each right answer I kept getting more confidence. "Now, Professor, the next question is for a quarter of a million dollars. Are you ready?"

"I sure am ready; bring it on."

"Now, for $250,000, here is the question. Who of these four men was the inventor of the cotton gin? Was it Thomas Edison, Isaac Walton, Eli Whitney, or Marconi."

Thank God again for little favors. I had a teacher in the third grade who had talked to us a lot about the invention of the cotton gin and the impact it had had on the world we lived in today. "That man who invented the gin was definitely Eli Whitney. He invented the cotton gin."

"Professor, is that your last answer?" Robert repeats the question.

"It sure is my last answer because it's the correct one."

He looks at me and sas, "All right, if that's your last answer, I guess we will have to give you this check for $250,000."

By this time I am about to swallow my tongue. I had thought I might be doing all right, but not this well.

Robert asks me, "Are you ready and prepared for the half-million-dollar question?"

I don't even hesitate; I say, "Let's get it on."

"Okay, Professor."

The question appears on the monitor before me. "The question is who was the fighter pilot during the World War II era that formed and led a group of offbeat missfit pilots called the Black Sheep Squadron? Was it Billy Mitchell, Jimmy Doolittle, Greg Boyington, or Hap Arnold?"

"This I remember from tales my father told about the way the Black Sheep Squadron was formed. Dad also flew during World War II. That was Colonel Greg "Pappy" Boyington."

Robert just looks at me and shakes his head as if I had missed the question. He says, "Well, Professor, YOU just won a half million dollars."

The audience goes so wild and loud I could hardly hear myself, Robert or what is going on. I am having trouble believing this is really happening. It is kind of like I am in a time warp. I am just glad it was happening. I am also thanking God for all these right answers.

Robert asks, "Professor, if you get all of this money, what are you going to do with it?"

"I owe a lot to the people who helped me while I was on the street, and I would like to pay them back." This was the first time either of us had mentioned about my being on the street.

Robert looks me straight in the eye and asks, "Professor, do we have your permission to tell briefly the story of how you came to be on the program?"

I hesitatingly agreed. "Okay, go ahead if you think it might help someone else."

Robert briefly tells everyone that a month ago I had been living on the street, an alcoholic, not knowing where my next meal or dollar was coming from. There was a stunned silence over the audience. It was as if they couldn't believe what they were hearing. He explaines briefly what had happened – about the tornado and my ending up in the hospital and how my friends had gotten me to call in, and how they helped me. I would bet you could have heard a pin drop, and then all of a sudden there was an explosion of applause.

"See, Professor, the people appreciate how you have overcome what you were. You are now truly on the road to recovery. You Professor, are an example of a man who has done like the Phoenix in ancient history. You have risen from the ashes to start your life over. Everyone here at the studio is very proud of you. We know you will continue with your rise back from the gutter that you were in a few months ago. More power to you.

"Now, before we go on to the million-dollar question, I want you to know we are all pulling for you. Now, for the million-dollar question. The studio goes ghostly quiet. You could actually have heard a pin drop on the carpet. It was actually that quiet.

Let's get it under our belts. Here it comes on your monitor. Which one of the following four movie western stars was named Leonard Slye before he became famous in the movies? Was it John Wayne, Roy Rogers, Hoot Gibson, or Tim Holt? Now for a million dollars can you tell me which one of these men was named Leonard Slye?" Robert looked at me and saw the smile I was wearing and says, "I think we may have a winner. Professor, do we have a winner?"

I tried to milk it a little by telling what a cowboy fan I had been when I was a kid. I explained that I had read the life story of Leonard Slye, and how he had grown up back in Ohio. I told about his buying his first guitar and learning how to play the guitar and sing. "He and his family finally moved to California where he formed the Sons of the Pioneers. That's when he changed his name to Roy Rogers and later became known as the King of the Cowboys."

The crowd erupts with applause. I have actually won the million dollars and still had two lifelines left.

Robert says, "This is the first time anyone has ever done this." He looked stunned, and he finally came up with this great big grin and hollered just as loud as he could, "Professor, you have just become another Texas millionaire. You are absolutely correct; it was Roy Rogers." You have won a million dollars and only used one lifeline. That has never been done before and you certainly do deserve our congratulations. The applause continues as the confetti falls from the ceiling.

I am now in another world. All I can think about is the people back in Ft. Worth. Robert is handing me the previously made out check for one million dollars. I jokingly ask him if he could tell me where I could cash it. He isn't sure just where I could cash it at this time, so I asked him if he has a quarter so I could make a phone call back to Texas and another local one.

By this time Pug is almost as happy as I am. He is absolutely jumping up and down with joy. He must have instantly jumped from his chair and started making his way around to where I had been sitting while I was a contestant.

Confetti continues to fall from the ceiling while horns are now going off, and lights are flashing everywhere. Robert finally tells me that one of the assistant directors will show us where to go. We are led to a room where we are told there would be some necessary paper work to sign tonight and we could take care of the rest of it tomorrow morning.

The Celebration

I asked if they had a phone I could use to call my friends back in Ft. Worth. The Assistant Director wants to know if I would like to talk to Lynn again.

"I sure would like that if it can be arranged."

"Professor, it won't be a minute. Why don't you sit at that desk while they're getting in touch with Lynn for you."

I had no more than sat down when the phone rings. I pick it up, and I hear a bunch of voices on the other end of the phone all talking at once. I hear Lynn's voice saying, "Professor, are you there?"

"Yes, Lynn, I'm here, and I just won the million dollars I came here to win."

He turns and tells everybody at the Sanctuary that I have just won a million dollars. There is a big roar going up, and I can hardly hear Lynn. I finally heard him say, "Professor, Annie wants to talk to you."

Annie comes on the line, and she immediately says, "See, we told you that you could do it. We just knew you could. Maybe those prayers we have been saying for you every evening since you have been gone have helped some also. The whole gang has even been joining in on the prayers each night for you guys. We're real proud of you. Now the gang's going crazy wanting to talk to you."

Mabel is the first one to come on the phone, and she screams, "Professor, we love you. Do I really get some new clothes and maybe a trip to Louisiana?"

"Mabel, I'll assure you that you will get some new clothes and a trip to Louisiana."

"Here comes Doc, and he wants to talk to you. Hang in there, and remember we love you."

O.K. Mabel I'll do just that very thing.

Doc came on the line with, "You really made believers out of those Yankees didn't you?"

"I really hadn't thought of it that way, but if you say so, I guess I did. It looks like you're going to get that thing to hang around your neck so you can listen to people's hearts. While I have you on the phone, Doc, I want to tell you real quick that I have an idea I want to run over with you when I get back to Ft. Worth. I think I know of a way for you to start a clinic for the street people with the help of a doctor friend of mine there in Ft. Worth. I think he'll work with us and help us get it started if you will agree to run it. How does that sound?"

"Great, Professor, that sounds just great, and funny you should mention that because that is something I have wanted to do for a long time. Hurry back so we can start thinking about it real strong. Hurry and get back here we're lonesome here without you."

"It will possibly be a couple of weeks before we get back since Pug and I have some business to take care of here in New York City."

He hands the phone to Cowboy.

"Well, Professor, I guess I get my new Stetson."

"Yes, you sure do, and I'm hoping for a couple of other things for you. We will discuss it when I get home. Right now you just help Lynn and Annie all you can and see that the gang stays sober.

"No celebrating with alcohol just because I won. I won in order for all of us to stay sober and away from alcohol from now on. Cowboy, I'm depending on you to help me out on this. I know you can do it. Just watch the others and be sure they don't fall off the wagon. We all have too much at stake here. We've been sober this long, let's just stay sober. Keep the others attending the AA meetings, please."

"I promise, Professor. Bing is here and wants to talk to you."

Bing comes on the phone with, "That's the way to do it, Professor. We all knew you could do it."

"Bing, I'm anxious to talk to you when I get back to Ft. Worth because I have an a plan that I think you might just be interested in helping me with."

"Sure, Professor, anything I can do to help, you know that."

I tell him that I am depending on him to help keep everyone sober. "You know what I am talking about, no alcohol for the celebration. Just keep it to Cokes, tea, and coffee. And, be sure that all the gang keep up with their AA meetings because it's essential to everything we've accomplished up till now."

He agrees they will stay clean. I tell him that it will be a couple of weeks before we get back home due to some personal business that Pug and I needed to take care of here in New York City. Bing, "I need to talk to Lynn again before I go".

"Sure, Professor, just a minute."

I hear him calling Lynn.

"Hello, Professor, Bing says you need to talk to me again."

"Yes, I do Lynn. I want to tell you that it's going to be a couple of weeks before we come back home. In the meantime, I want you to do me a favor and call Dr. David Davis over at the hospital and tell him that I won the money and tell him the show will be on TV the day after tomorrow. They have asked us to stay around a couple of days for publicity, etc. Tell Dr. Davis that I'll call him just as soon as I get back to Ft. Worth. If you happen to run into Charlie Johnson, the policeman, you could tell him the good news also. He might want to watch the show day after tomorrow. You might also want to call the *Star Telegram* and talk to a young reporter named Robert Hitch. Tell him that I won, and I will be glad to talk to him when I get back home. I guess that's just about all from here. I want to thank you again for all the help that you and Annie have been to me and the gang. I intend to repay you for all of your help. Bye for now and keep us in your prayers."

Now it is time to call Pam and let her know what has happened. I look up the number at the Black Angus and dial it.

A man answers the phone, "This is the Black Angus, Ernie speaking."

"Well, how about that? Listen to me Big Ernis, this is your good friend and the newest Texas millionaire speaking."

There is a real loud whoop at the other end of the phone. He is hollering at Pam just as loud as he can, and that's loud, telling her to come to the phone because someone wants to speak to her.

I assume she came running because he no sooner had gotten the words out of his mouth, when she says, "Hello."

Hello Little Darlin, you are now speaking to the newest Texas millionaire. There is a squeal, then laughter, then some other sound that was hard to describe.

"Jimmy, is that for real?"

"It sure is, Hon. I made it all the way. What time do you get off tonight? I want to come by for you."

She turns and asked Ernie what time she can get off tonight.

I hear him hollering, "Hell, you can take off right now if you want to and tell him to get his big butt over here soon as possible."

"Did you hear that Honey?"

"I sure did, and I also heard what you called me. I'll be there just as soon as I sign a couple of papers and find a taxi." She starts telling everyone what's happened before she even gets the phone hung up because I can hear the applause, laughter and screaming.

When I hung up, they have the temporary releases for me to sign, which I did real fast.

They tell me I can wait until tomorrow or the next day to sign everything else since I had to make the decision on just how I want to receive the money, lump sum or monthly for twenty years.

"O.K. Guys, I'll be back sometime tomorrow morning to talk business with you,".

Pug and I go outside and hail a cab. "Take us to the Black Angus restaurant." The cab doors close and away we go. It seemed to take forever to get to the restaurant when in reality it only took about fifteen minutes.

When we arrive, there was Ernie and Pam standing outside by the curb to greet us. Big Ernie was first to the cab and he opens the door for us to get out. He slaps me on the back with that big hand of his and almost knocks me down. I think he is almost as happy as I am with my win.

Standing behind that big guy was that most beautiful perky little blonde who jumps and grabs me around the neck and gives me a big bear hug and then plants a great big kiss on me right in front of everyone.

Lord, oh, Lord, what a feeling this lady puts on me every time I touch her.

Pug was trying his best to stay out of the way for a while. We head into the restaurant. Ernie starts hollering to everyone in the restaurant that he wants them to meet the latest Texas millionaire. proceeds to tell them I had just answered the million-dollar question on "So You Want to Be a Millionaire." By that time everyone is clapping and hollering and just whooping it up in general. They are treating me just as if I was one of their old long, lost friends. Imagine me a transplanted Texan being taken in as a friend by all these Yankees. Great and wonderful folks they really are.

After about ten minutes or so, Pam suggests we go back and sit down. Se had a booth near the back of the restaurant where we could have a little privacy. The three of us walk back and sit down. This was the first time I had had a chance to relax since I had won. I explained to Pam that I had already talked to the folks back home. I seemed to refer to Ft. Worth as my home now since those I considered my closest friends all lived there. "I have explained to them that Pug and I will be here a week or more before we can get back to Texas."

She just smiled, which I knew meant she understood. We talked about the show and what had happened at the show for about thirty minutes. She finally suggests, "Let's get out of here. I have my car at the parking garage just down the street."

"Pug, have you called Angie yet?"

"No, I haven't. I've been so excited with our calls to Texas and coming over here that I haven't had time to call her. I was wondering if I could call from here."

"I'm sure Ernie would let you use his office to call her if you want."

Ernie comes over, and she askes him if Pug could use his office and phone to call Angie. He is more than happy to help him out. They walk back to the office where he unlocks the door and tells him, "Now you can use the phone on the desk to call her, and you can take just as long as you want. You don't have to hurry, if you know what I mean."

He walks out and closes the door behind him. He comes back to the booth again and lets us know that Pug is on the phone talking to Angie. He asks if there is anything else he can do for us, if there is all we had to do was ask.

"Ernie, I'm gonna ask something now. Is there any chance Pam could have a few days off to help me get some things taken care of before we go back to Texas?"

"Professor, that lady has more days off due her than anyone who has ever worked for me. She works for the other girls when they are sick or have family problems, and they all owe her. She hasn't taken any vacation in over two years, at least no more than three days at a time. She's overdue for a vacation. As for her job here, it's up to her when she works. She'll always have a job here anytime she wants it, and we will always work with her to see that she gets some time off. As of now she is off, and I don't want to see her around here for at least a couple of weeks. If she decides she needs longer, she has it. Does that answer your question?"

I couldn't believe it. "Ernie, I can never thank you enough for what you have done for us and for your understanding."

Pug comes from the office and tells us that Angie wants us to come on home so we can all celebrate together. Pam and I agree that's a great idea. Pam goes to the back room to get her purse and things out of her locker. She returns saying, "Let's go see Angie." Away we go.

We walk the block and a half down the street to the parking garage. She takes us up to the second floor of the garage where she always parks because it is close to the elevator, and there is a lot of light. The owners were real good about keeping people out of the garage who didn't belong there. She let us know they hadn't had anyone mugged or robbed there in the past four years, which is some kind of a record in New York City.

We get into the car and head for Pam's home. We were still very excited about the happenings of the last eight hours. Actually, we were almost giddy.

We arrive at Pam's, and Angie is sitting on the porch. Their duplex is one of the old-fashioned looking houses with a porch all the way across the front of the house with a porch swing and a couple of chairs on it.

I love houses with big porches and porch swings and big chairs. Our house back home in Chicago has a porch like that. Funny I should think of that now.

Angie comes running to the car. Just as soon as the doors are open, she grabs Pug and hugs and kisses him. She lets him go and grabs me and hugs me, but kissed me on the cheek and screams how happy she is for us. We all just sit down on the porch and start talking.

The weather is beautiful; the moon and stars are shining. There is a light breeze winding its way through the trees and up onto the porch where we sit. This is an exceptionally beautiful night for all lovers to dream by. I tell them about calling Texas and how happy everyone there seemed to be. I tell them about Annie saying they had been praying for our success every night since we had been gone.

Pam said she thought that was great. She knows of a small church just a few blocks from her house. "Why don't we all go down and give thanks for all we've received. We need to thank the Good Lord for bringing us all together, and then we can also ask for further guidance in the problems facing all of us now and in the future.

"They aren't really problems like most folks have. I feel the four of us will need all the help we can get in order to get our feelings and actions straightened out for the future."

"How about it, are you ready?"

"I think that's a very good idea, says Angie".

We hold hands and start down the street just as they do in storybooks when young folks are in love. The only trouble is that we aren't really that young, but that makes no difference to us. We finally reached the church, and you know what? It feels good to be back attending church as I used to before my life had begun on the streets. This was twice in the last two days we had attended church. Pug also thought this was a great idea.

When we arrive at the church, there are some people coming out of the door so we have to wait a minute. It seems they had a late Christening because the father always works the afternoon till midnight shift, and it is hard for him to get to the church any other time. The priest seems to be very accommodating.

When the family had gone, he turns and greets us while asking if he could be of service. We explain what had happened to us and tell what we were there to do. He seems genuinely touched that we would want to offer thanks for our good fortune. He introduced himself as Father Francis Brockman; then he opens the doors for us and walks inside with us. We introduce ourselves and thank him.

As he turns to leave, he says, "If I can ever be of any help to you, I would consider it a privilege to be of service in any way that I might help."

As he walks off, we all say, "Thank you, Father Brockman, nice to have met you. Pam says, you may see us again in the next few days."

As he walks off, he turns, smiles and says, "Good night folks."

He sure seems like a nice guy, a real down-to-earth guy about our own ages. Sometimes it is easier to talk to someone near our own ages than an older priest or preacher.

Pug says, "You know what? I like that priest. I was raised a Baptist, but that guy is real nice. I don't think I have ever really met a priest before. As a kid I always went to the Baptist Church Sunday School. As I got older, I kind of strayed away from the church. My mother and dad always went to church though. I guess a lot of people stray at one time or other. It feels real good to go to church and talk about God and such things. Boy, have I changed. Angie, see what you do to me? You're making a new man of me."

She laughs and says, "I hope so, but I never knew the old one. I can only look forward from here on."

We finally went inside and found a pew where we wanted to sit. We sat quietly, and then each of us knelt, and we quietly prayed without interrupting each other. I knew what I asked for, and I knew that I thanked the man upstairs for doing such wonderful things for my friends and me. I truly knew that without his help, I could not have accomplished what I had done this evening. When I was through, I really felt good about everything.

I felt better because I also asked for guidance for Pam and me in our relationship. I knew down deep that things were moving really fast between Pam and me. I also knew that I had never felt more sure of anything before in my life. I knew now that I must meet her family and talk to them. I needed for them to know of my past and what I hoped for in the future. I wanted to know how they felt about Pam's being associated with someone like me. I hoped she understood, and I was sure she would.

After several minutes, we all get up from our seats at about the same time and head for the doors of the church. As we walked hand in hand, we all knew that something here was right. It just had to be right for all of us. I felt that all four of us had probably asked for guidance in our feelings for each other and the future of our association.

No one spoke until we were outside.

Pam looked at me and said, "I sure hope my prayers are answered."

I looked into those beautiful blue eyes and told her, "I hope mine are answered also."

Angie smiled and said, "Me too."

Pug finally speaks, "It felt strange praying in a Catholic church, but you know what, it felt real good. I'm not saying I would ever become a Catholic, but it does make you feel good when you're in their church. My Uncle Lewis would have a hissie if he thought I was praying in a Catholic church. You know what? I haven't even thought of Uncle Lewis in the last ten years or more, so why should I think of him now? He's kind of a bigot anyway. He thinks if you aren't a Baptist, you can't get to heaven. He never was known for his brain power anyway. I feel kind of sorry for him.

"Sorry, Professor, I just never told you anything about my family. I'm sure they have all disowned me by now. I should have told you guys all about my family earlier, but I really do feel that the street people have been my family for the past ten years or so. I think I would like to contact them after I get, on my feet real good. I'd like to show them that I didn't turn out quite as bad as they had anticipated.

"I never told you this, but I was a good athlete in high school. I played football, basketball, and baseball, but I liked boxing most of all. I began boxing real young. I had a brother who had boxed professionally when he was young, and he began teaching me when I was about eight or nine years old. I boxed in the CYO boxing tournaments, and then high school and Golden Gloves came next. I was pretty lucky. I won state titles two years in Golden Gloves. I started to college, and in my sophomore year a boxing promoter came to the school and visited with me. He told me he had heard a lot about me, so he was here to see if I would be interested in making some good money.

"I was just a dumb kid, so I said, 'Sure. I would like to make some easy money.' He told me he would train me and manage me and bring me along slow, so I wouldn't get hurt. He figured that after three or four years, he could get me a shot at the middleweight title if I was as good as he had heard.

"Like the dummy I was, I believed him. I left school thinking I would someday return and get my education finished. Well, it didn't work out that way. I started out fine. I had a lot of wins the first year and a half. The next year I was able to get fights with some pretty big names. I won all of them except one. I started all over again with the big name boys and was on my way to the Garden. He had said he had a title fight all wrapped up and that it would just take one more good fight for me to get there.

"A light heavy fight was to have taken place in Los Angeles, but one of the guys had broken his hand a week before the fight, so it was either get a replacement or call off the fight. If they called the fight off, they lost all of the money they spent on training facilities and advertisements. They came to my manager and offered him a good payday for me if I would take the fight on short notice. I was outweighed by about thirteen pounds.

The other guy was a light heavy, and I was only a middleweight. That's a lot of weight to give away to a world-ranked light heavy.

"I finally agreed that I would do it if my manager assured me that the title fight was still on for the Garden. He said, 'Sure it's still on, don't worry."

"To make a long story short, I gave the light heavy a boxing lesson the first five rounds, and in the sixth round he finally got me in a corner and darn near killed me. I couldn't get out of the corner, and he hit like a mule kicking. My corner threw in the towel, but by that time it was too late. I ended up in the hospital, and I've had these severe headaches ever since that night. I just felt that I couldn't go back home after everybody had expected such big things from me. My parents and family took it better than I did. I was embarrassed and hurt mentally by taking such a beating.

I went on a long weekend that lasted over eight years.

"Professor finally helped me believe in myself again, and he helped me see the light where I had gone wrong. My folks don't really care what my record was. I hope they just care for me. I told Professor last night that I would like to contact them again. My home is Moab, Utah. It used to be a nice small town near the Colorado River. My folks are one of the few Baptist families in the town. Most everybody else are Mormons.

"The last time I heard, my mother and father were both still alive as well as was my older brother Neil and a younger sister Elaine. Now that I have my head screwed on straight, I think maybe I can eventually make things right with everyone. I would sure like a chance to try."

We all three just sat and listened to what Pug had said without saying anything and interrupting him. He seemed to feel better after telling us all about it. He grinned sheepishly and asked, "Now does anyone have any questions?"

"Pug, I never asked you any questions about your past before, and I'm not going to start asking now. You're my best friend and have been for the past eight years. If you have something you want me to know, you will tell me."

The girls echoed that the same went for them also. He looked very relieved.

It was now about 1:00 a.m., and we were all tired, but still excited.

Love, the Big Decision

Finally Pam said, "Look guys, it's late and getting later. Angie and I have talked it over, and we have decided it would probably be best if you guys would just spend the night here tonight. I hope you don't get the wrong idea, but we just feel it's time for us to get to know you guys better.

"I admit that I was a little hesitant at first, but then my feelings got in the way. I know how I feel about Jim, and Angie thinks she feels the same about Pug, or should I say Wayne. I think that sounds better if Pug doesn't mind being called by his name."

"Heck, no, I don't mind. In fact, I think it sounds kind of nice. My family always called me Wayne, so from now on, Wayne it is – with all of you guys." "Well maybe not with Professor."

Pam suggested it was time for us to say goodnight to Angie and Wayne. She took my arm, and we walked into her apartment. I must admit that the excitement and anticipation was overwhelming. As we walked into the bedroom, Pam turned to me, those blue eyes shining with love and excitement she asked, "Do you mind if I get into something a lot more comfortable?" She then walked over and very softly kissed me on the lips and said, "Jim, I know this is very sudden for both of us, but I'm sure I am in love with you or I wouldn't be doing this."

The smell of her perfume in my nostrils was about to make my hair stand on end – along with other things. I hadn't even dared to dream of an evening like this for the past ten years.

"Jim, why don't you go ahead and get into bed, and I will be back in a few minutes. I want to freshen up a little. I want you to remember tonight forever."

As she leaves the room she turns the lights down low so there was just a light glow in the room. I undressed and got into bed and waited for her return.

Oh, my God, here she came in one of the most beautiful pale blue nightgowns I have ever seen. You know the kind that seemed to flow softly behind her as she approached the bed. Her hair was soft on her shoulders, and she was absolutely radiant.

She turnes back the covers and slips between the sheets and snuggles over close to me. Her body is touching mine, and I think I am going out of my mind. We reached for each other. We snuggled closer to hold each other. I know I had died and gone to heaven. The nipples of her breast push against my chest, and the touch of her lips softly on mine, then harder and more demanding. I feel her snuggling close to my neck and kissing my ear...I pulled her closer to me, and I feel the cheeks of her bottom. I pulled her closer. The excitement is overwhelming as I kissed the nape of her neck and nibbled on her ear lobe.

We were both in a state of total nervous excitement when I pulled her close and entered her body and we became as one. I knew God must have made her just for me as the rhythm of our bodies, locked in the ritual of love, reached a high crescendo that sent us both shivering with an excitement that I had never ever achieved before.

I kissed her softly and told her how much I loved her and how wonderful making love to her had been.

She told me she had never in her life felt such passion. We held each other close in a state of complete exhaustion. She ran her hands over my body as I did the same to her, feeling every inch of the body of this wonderful lady, that flat stomach, that tight little bottom, and the breasts that would look perfect on a woman half her age. They were so firm and so perfectly shaped. They were so firm, and the nipples were so hard and erect when she was excited and making love.

As we lay there holding each other, I kissed her lips, cheeks, neck, and then I moved down and kissed her firm, tight breast. She began to shiver with excitement, so I moved down to her flat, tight belly and kissed it and the navel while I was feeling the other parts of her body, arousing her.

She seemed to explode with passion and squealed that I had done it again; she had climaxed again.

We lay and held each other for what seemed an eternity, and then she eased her body over on top of my body. She kissed me tenderly and moved her body in rhythm and told me she wanted to make love again, which we did.

After I entered her again, we started very slowly, and then as our kissing and holding and petting increased, so did the sexual stimulation that came between two people who loved the way we did. The sweet smell of her perfume and bath powder just about drove me nuts. Making love to someone so extremely special as this little lady who said she loved me more than anything in this world could not be explained in a way that another person could understand. It was something you had to experience in order to know what I was talking about.

Later we fell asleep in each other's arms and held each other closely, spooning for the rest of the night. If her dreams were anything like mine, she had the most wonderful dreams of her life. I know I did and I was loving it.

The next morning I was awakened by the smell of coffee. I raised my head and saw Pam coming into the bedroom with a cup of coffee. She was wearing the pale blue lacy gown with a very sheer pale blue negligee over it. The blue of the negligee matched the blue of her eyes, and it just made that blonde hair shine that much more. The negligee and the gown didn't really cover everything. Her body was revealed through the beautiful sheer blue material.

"I hope you like the coffee; I used a little cream and a little sugar."

"That's just the way I like it." Damn, she was beautiful, even in the morning before she put on makeup. She had a real nice natural beauty that most women dream of having and never quite make it. She came over and put the coffee down on the night stand, sat on the side of the bed, leaned over, and gave me a real good, good morning kiss.

"My Darling, Pam, I will never be able to tell you how much I enjoyed the night and how good it felt just holding you close when I fell asleep after we made love."

"I agree, Darling, that it was unbelievable. It felt real good being held by you. I think I could get used to that. You know that's the first time I have made love to anyone since my husband was killed. "I have to admit I was a little scared because it had been so long, but once I felt your arms around me, all the fear just vanished. As much as I hate to admit it, pure lust set in for a while. As we lay there and I felt your heart beating next to mine, I knew how love really felt for the first time in many years."

"Pam, if you think you were nervous, how do you think I felt. I haven't made love to a woman in over ten years. I wasn't sure I still remembered how, but when I felt your warm loving body in my arms, the sweet smell of such a beautiful and loving woman, everything I ever knew about making love came back to me – not that I was ever a Don Juan or Casanova."

"Jim, if you did forget anything about making love, it all came back to you last night. No girl could ever ask for a better lover than you."

"Speaking of bodies, do you know that you still have the body of a twenty-year-old girl. How do you stay in such terrific shape? Now that I am speaking of shapes, I don't recall anyone I have ever known with a more beautiful body than you have. I hope I'm not embarrassing you, but I think you should know just how beautiful you are. If I could have conjured up the woman I would think of as the most beautiful woman I have ever seen or known, it would be you, just as you look right now.

"Now that we're over the hurdle of the first time making love together, it should be easier and better in the future."

"Jim, how could it be any better than it was last night. I felt like Cinderella with her Prince Charming and Sir Lancelot all rolled into one."

"Well, now, young lady, you aren't trying to give me the big head are you?"

Like the lady she was, she said, "No, I wouldn't do a thing like that; I just tell the truth."

"Pam, I think it's time for my coffee before it gets cold. Before I drink my coffee, there is something I think you should know. I have fallen in love with you, and it wasn't because of the sex last night; it was because you are such a wonderful and beautiful person inside as well as outside. What I would really like right now is for you to crawl back into this bed, and let's make love again before I have to get up."

"Darling, if that's all you want, I think I can take care of that right now; move over because here I come."

After we were through making love again, I was totally exhausted, but what a wonderful feeling.

"Now, let's get back to our coffee." She smiled as if she didn't know what to say, but I loved hearing it. She took the coffee back into the kitchen and heated it in the microwave for me.

We had coffee and talked and showered – yes, we took a shower together; we took turns washing each other's body, and later we took turns drying each other. Boy did that take restraint. I had never taken a shower or a bath with a woman before.

We got dressed and waited for Pug and Angie to let us know they were awake. Pam decided to make some toast while we were waiting on them.

Just as the toast was ready for buttering, she turned to me and said, "Jim, I have been in love with you from the second time I saw you at the restaurant. You seemed so honest, and it seemed like you wanted to tell me something. Now, that you have told me, I am even more in love with you. I know things are happening awfully fast, but I can't help it, and I don't think you can do anything about it either."

She walked over and put her arms around me and held me close. We kissed as we held each other and agreed that our love was here now, and it always would be here.

After about thirty minutes, we heard a knock on the door. It turned out to be Pug who asked if we would like to go out for breakfast. Angie knew a nice little Tea Room just a couple of blocks down the street where we could have breakfast.

It was a beautiful day for walking, so Pam and I both said, "Why not?"

Angie came out her front door smiling like a lady in love and asking if we were ready to go for breakfast. It was a beautiful morning with the sun shining brightly, the birds singing, and a lot of flowers blooming; and love was in the air. Who could have asked for anything more than this?

We arrived at the Tea Room. It was beautifully decorated as they would have decorated it in *Home and Garden Magazine*. There were a lot of green plants and a trellis with flowers on it near the French doors at the side of the dining room. The sun was shining in from just the right angle to make the organdy curtains seem even more frilly than they really were. They were blue and white with a blue swag tying them back to the windows. It was a wonderful place for lovers to have breakfast.

We ordered more coffee first, and after it was served, we ordered our meal. Pug ordered eggs Benedict. I think he has developed a liking for them cooked that way. Pam and Angie ordered sweet rolls with butter. That sounded real good, so I ordered the same.

I have been sitting here thinking, "*How lucky can a guy be?*

I just won a million dollars so I can help my friends and get myself back in condition to possibly contact my family. I have the most beautiful lady in the world in love with me and I love her."

We talked about the things we were going to do during the coming week. "First thing I have to do today is to go to the studio and finalize the paper work on the winnings. It shouldn't be too long."

After we finished eating, we had a leisurely stroll back to the house enjoying every it every step of the way. I felt that I was in a dream world. I knew however that was not what was happening. I knew it was real. I was glad it was real. It was a feeling I couldn't put my finger on or describe in any way. I just knew it was there, and I loved it.

When we got back to the house, I told Pug to be ready in fifteen minutes, and we would go to the studio to complete the paper work and make my decision on how I wanted to receive the money. "I'm sure I will take it in a lump sum because that way I can get some good things started real soon. If I take the monthly payments, I never would be able to do what I have hoped to do for my friends."

Pam and I talked about the next couple of days. We decided we would just hang around for a couple of days and relax. She suggested that if we wanted to check out of the hotel and come over to their homes, it would be all right.

"What about Angie and her job? Will it be hard for her to get away from the travel agency?"

Pam was sure Angie could get a few days off. She knew that Angie had called her boss early that morning at home and asked if she could have the next few days off. "He told her to go ahead and take the week off since she had more vacation than that coming to her."

"Hey, everybody, how about a picnic somewhere tomorrow? I haven't been on a picnic since I was a kid, and now I feel like a kid again, so how about it?" I asked.

"Sounds good to me, Pam agrees. Angie and I will fix some fried chicken and potato salad, just like the old days. How does that sound to you?"

"Great, Pam, just great."

Quickly, Pug was knocking on the door saying he was ready to go.

"Tell Angie that we are all going on a picnic tomorrow."

He left for a minute, came back, and told Pam that Angie thought that was a great idea.

Pam suggested I use her car, but I said, "No, thanks. I don't have a driver's license, and the other thing is that I would get lost in this town, and you would never find me. Why don't you just call a cab for us?"

She went back into the house to call a cab for us. In just a minute she came back out on the porch. "It'll be here in a few minutes."

We sat on the porch and talked for about ten minutes; then a cab rolled up in front of the house. We kissed the girls good-bye, got into the cab and headed for the studio.

Upon arrival, we were met by one of the assistant producers. The producer and the accounting office manager were expecting us. We went right in, and sure enough, they were expecting us. We all shook hands and dispensed with cheery greetings so we could get down to business. They ask if I had given any thought as to how I wanted to receive the money.

I gave them an emphatic, "Yes. I want the money in a lump sum."

They laid out just what that would be and how much difference it would be if I took the monthly payments. I explained to them that I had an obligation to some friends, and I was going to take care of that obligation, so I had to have the lump sum. They agreed.

Since I didn't have any other income to worry about, and since the IRS man was there to receive his cut, we got things under way. I finally ended up with about $600,000.00 after taxes, due to the way I had it set up in a trust for me to handle for my friends. They agreed to give me a cashier's check for $550,000, and I wanted $50,000 in cash. They worried about my carrying that much money with me. They sent a runner over to the bank to get the $50,000. I told them to get all hundreds to make it easier to carry.

We discussed how we could be contacted in the next few days in the event they needed to find us. I gave them Pam's number, and they agreed if they needed to contact me they would call me there. We sat and talked for a while until the runner came back into the studio with the cash. They had put it into a briefcase that he hands to me and says, "Please count it. I want to be sure it's all there."

Just to make him feel better, I counted it, and it was all there. The briefcase was given to me with the compliments of the studio. I thanked everyone for their help and friendship.

We said, "So long," and Pug and I had headed for the door to leave when the producer says, "Professor, I hope someone from your family calls you. I think that would just about make the story complete."

I thanked him and said, "I would like that also. If they do call, just tell them to call the number I gave you. I may be out of pocket for a while, but if they just keep trying, they will be able to get me." I thank him again, and we are out the door.

We got a taxi and headed for the hotel.

Upon arriving, we saw the doorman who congratulated me on winning the big prize. I thanked him and as we entered, I ran into Chip Rowan again who says, "Hey, Professor, I hear you won the big one. Ernie told me about it. I think that's swell."

We took the elevator ride up to our floor, and into the room we went.

I had started to get my things together when I got to thinking about what would happen if someone called the studio and didn't get the message about the new phone number. I decided I should call the studio and tell them that I had decided to stay at the hotel and if someone called, they could give them both of the numbers. They should be able to catch us at one number or the other. If they didn't catch me, they could leave a message at the hotel, and Pam had a message machine on her phone. "This way we won't miss any messages or phone calls. I think I should call Pam and tell her what I've decided to do."

I called Pam and told her what I had decided and asked if the invitation to spend the nights with her was still available.

"Well, you had better, because if you don't, I just might come up to the hotel and stay with you. But you know we'll have a lot more privacy here, and besides I make a better breakfast than they do at the hotel. I hope you like the waitress here more than the one at the hotel."

"Okay, Darling, I can assure you, that's just what I had in mind to do."

Pug agreed with me if the invitation from Angie still stood.

"The invitation still stands; Angie just told me it did.

It's almost time for lunch."

"Would you ladies like to go out for lunch?" I asked.

"Why don't you boys come back to the house, and we will fix some sandwiches or something here. No need going out when we can spend the time here together and get to know each other better. You know what I mean, just talk and talk and talk."

"That's a great idea, Sweetheart. Let us get some clothes together and get our toothbrushes, and we will be on our way.

"Right now we need to leave some laundry to be done while we are gone."

"Why don't you bring it with you?"

"Pam, I feel it's a little early for you to start doing my laundry."

"That has nothing to do with it. I have a washer and dryer, so why pay someone else to do it when I can do it here while we talk? Tell Pug to bring his also, and I'll do both at the same time. Bring your shirts also because I iron a mean shirt."

"Okay, but..."

"Now don't argue with me. Bring the clothes with you, and we will take care of them for you."

"Okay, I'll bring our dirty laundry along even though I don't think it's exactly the right thing to do."

We gathered our laundry and when that was done, I call the front desk and told them to please take any messages for me. "If it's an emergency, could you please give the caller this other number where I will be for the evening."

They were very gracious and let us know they would be more than happy to give anyone the number if it sounded really important. I thanked them, hung up, and told Pug to get his dirty clothes together. We headed for the door with a valise full of dirty clothes.

We hailed a cab and headed for Pam's house. We arrived in one piece after a perilous ride in a yellow cab. I couldn't see why they called it a yellow cab; it would challenge any other car on the street. This driver had trouble understanding what we said, and we couldn't understand anything he said. I finally wrote the address down on a piece of paper and gave it to him. He looked at it and smiled, shaking his head and taking off. How this guy ever got his driver's license I dodn't know. Like the old saying went, "I think he got his driver's license out of a box of Cornflakes." The next time I get a yellow cab, I am going to look at the driver before I got into the cab.

This sure felt good. It was almost like coming home. You know: a sweet-smelling woman waiting at the door with a kiss and a hug for you. I explained why I had done what I had done at the hotel. Pam understood because if one of my kids or my mother or dad happened to see the show tomorrow night and decide to call, she didn't want me to miss it. This little lady was one great woman. Now I knew for sure that one of the reasons I had fallen in love with her was that she was so understanding.

We go inside, and she has a big pitcher of iced tea.

Pug goes next door to see Angie. I knew he would. In a few minutes, we hear a knock on the door, and sure enough it was Angie and Pug. They came in, sat down, and had a glass of tea with us.

After we got settled and were enjoying our tea, Pam got up from her chair, and went and put our laundry in the washer; then she came back and sat down. I admitted to all that I was a little embarrassed to be bringing our dirty laundry to our lady friends' houses for them to do while we were visiting. They both laughed at that and said that it was no big deal since they both had a washer and dryer, which made it real easy.

After a short while, Pam wanted to know if we would like a sandwich to go with our tea.

"Great, I think that would be just fine," and Pug added, "Sure, why not?"

The girls went into the kitchen to prepare sandwiches, while Pug and I watched television. After a short while, they said, "Okay, boys, sandwiches are ready, are you?"

"Hey, Pug, I'll race you to the kitchen."

Jokingly Pam said, "Okay, boys, no running in the house."

I remembered saying the same thing to my children. It brought back old memories.

We had a seat and Pam says, "I hope you guys like tuna salad sandwiches."

How could she know that it was one of my favorites? "I haven't had tuna sandwiches in long time, but I sure do love them."

After lunch I offer to help clean up the dishes. The girls tell me in no uncertain words they will take care of that.

We men were supposed to go back to watching television. Instead of watching television, we go out to the front porch. The weather is real great, about eighty degrees. It's real nice to just sit on the porch and watch the people. There is a slight breeze, and the smell of flowers from the next door yard permeates the air.

"Professor, this reminds me of back home in Moab. We used to sit on the porch late in the afternoon and speak to all of the people on their way home from working downtown. In a small town like Moab everybody knows everybody else, and that makes it real nice. You know, it's a real close- knit community. Well, at least it used to be ten or fifteen years ago. I hope it still is, however I doubt it because I hear it has really grown. Maybe I can see it before too long."

"Pug, if you want to go back to Moab, I'll see that you get to go. I think you should go back and get things straightened out with your family. That's something I know you look forward to doing."

We talk about the gang and some of the things we were going to do, once we got back to Texas. I know it might take another couple of weeks or more, but we will get back and help those people.

The girls come out to sit on the porch with us.

It is real nice out here listening to the birds and the neighborhood noises. You know, cars, kids playing, lawnmowers mowing the lawn, and music from cars passing by playing their radios so loud you couldn't help but hear it. It reminded me of some areas of Ft. Worth. We sat quietly for a while and enjoyed the afternoon weather.

Pam finally asked, "Why don't we go back inside and see if we can work out some kind of a schedule for the next few days."

Back inside I tell Pam that I want to go to Norfolk and meet her family. "Pam, I ask, do you' think we might be able to fly down there on Wednesday?"

"Well, let me call home and see if they'll be around. Now you know we'll have to have separate bedrooms when we go to my parent's home."

"I was sure that would be the case, and I think that will be just fine. When in Rome, we do what the Romans want us to do, not as we want to do. I feel it would only be fitting. We don't need to embarrass the folks or ourselves as far as that goes. They don't even need to know that we are staying here at the house with you. If it's all right with you, why don't you call them and set things up?

"Pug, this just might give you and Angie some time together and give you a chance to get to know each other better. You might also want to call your folks in Moab and see if you can set up something for the next week or so. Maybe Angie would like to go with you. That's something you can discuss later."

Pam had gone into the bedroom and was on the phone for about ten minutes. She comes back with a big smile on her face. "Well, it's done. They're very anxious to meet you. I told them a little about you, but I am leaving it up to you to tell them everything."

"Okay, Hon, that's just fine with me. I'll lay everything out before them, and they can either accept me or reject me. I hope they will accept me because I'm kind of crazy about their daughter."

She smiles and says she was sure they will accept me. "I have to warn you though; I told them to watch the show tomorrow night so they can see what you look like before they meet you."

After they see me, they may not want to meet me."

"Jim, I'm gonna spank you for saying something like that. I really don't think that will happen. I have a feeling that tomorrow night they will have the whole family there watching the show. I can just hear my brothers trying to help you on some of the answers that you might have trouble with.

"You know what? I don't even know what questions you answered, and if you even needed any help on any of the answers."

"I did have to call Lynn on the question about the Bible."

She really laughed at that one. "I think most of us would have had trouble with questions from the Bible."

"I was right with my answer, but I just wanted assurance from Lynn that I was right. I couldn't afford to lose at that point. I hope this shows your folks that I am just human and nothing more."

Pug pipes up with, "Yeah, he's just human, but a real smart human. Wish I knew half as much as he does."

"Yeah, and I wish I could throw a left jab and a right hook the way you do."

That gives all of us a good laugh. Imagine me throwing a left hook.

"I think it's best if we all just accept what we are, we don't need to be anyone else. What do you say?

"Pam, I need to talk to you. Do you have a bank close by that you do business with?"

"Yes, I do, but why?"

"I need to put most of my cash money in the bank, and I thought you might help me do that."

"Well, big boy, that shouldn't be any problem; we can go down first thing in the morning, and I'll introduce you to the people in the bank. They can take care of that for you. I know a couple of the cashiers and one of the new account executives. I think he is the person we will want to talk to."

"Pug, Jim says, I have something for you."

"Okay, Professor, what is it?"

"You're going to have to go and buy a new wallet. Maybe Angie can go with you and help you pick one out." I handed him some money. "Here are twenty-five, hundred dollar bills for you. Tomorrow I want you and Angie to go downtown, buy that new wallet, and put the money in it."

I turn to Angie, "Next, I want you to buy Pug some more new clothes. Buy a little of all kinds of clothes that he will need to have when he goes back to see his family.

"Pug, let Angie help you pick them out since she hasn't been out of circulation for the last ten or fifteen years like we have been. She will know what's in style and what's not. I'm sure you will need some jeans and sport shirts, etc., if and when you go home to see your folks. If you need more money, just let me know.

"After you guys get that done, we'll talk about the next step in our plans for all of us to get back on the right track again.

"Angie, will you do that for Wayne?"

She smiled and says, "Jim, you know I would be more than happy to help out. Don't worry, I won't let him get anything too old-fashioned."

"Now, I know that twenty-five hundred dollars won't go a long way, but we'll take care of that when the time comes. I'm going to take Pam with me tomorrow morning, and we are going to do the same thing."

"Jim, why don't we go together, Pug asks."

"Pam, how about that, are you willing to help me get a new wardrobe?"

"Jim, I was wishing you would ask. I sure would like that."

"Well, I guess that's taken care of, says Jim."

We spent the rest of the afternoon just enjoying each other's company. I finally asked Pam where the nearest grocery or supermarket store was.

"It's just a little way over to a large grocery where we can find just about anything you want. Just what are you thinking of buying?"

"I would like to go and buy some big fat steaks to cook on that charcoal grill you have out on the deck behind the house. It looks like it hasn't been used in quite a while."

"You're right Hon, it hasn't been used in quite a while. The last time was when one of my brothers and his wife came to visit me over a year ago."

"Well, I see it has a butane tank connected to it. Is there any gas in the tank?"

"There was gas left the last time we used it."

"I'll take your word for it, but I think I had better go and check it just to be sure. Know what? A big baked potato would go good with the steak, and then we could get some vegetables and make a salad to add to the dinner menu. What do you think?"

"We might also want to get some dinner rolls; we already have the tea."

"Sounds like a great idea. Let's go."

Angie and Pug both speak at the same time and say they want to go with us. I take off out back to check the butane and see if we might need to buy some more gas for our little dinner that we are planning.. I found she still had almost a half bottle of gas left so that took care of that.

"No need to worry about the gas problem because there isn't one. Come on now; let's go get the groceries."

Everyone heads for Pam's car.

We all four pile into the car and head for the store. This was the first time I had really noticed, but Pam is a real good driver. Before this I had been so busy looking at her other features I hadn't bothered to look at the traffic.

I have to remember when I get into the store that I hadn't done any shopping for groceries in about ten years, and I know the prices have changed. I am sure they will be a lot higher than when I last shopped.

We arrived at the huge parking lot. Pam found a parking place near the front door, which was definitely not an easy thing to do. She parked, and we headed for the door like a group of high school kids on the first day of summer vacation.

Inside, I grabbed a shopping cart and instinctively headed for the fresh fruits. I found a fresh pineapple, examined it carefully, and put it into the cart. Pineapples had always been one of my favorite fresh fruits. Both girls and Pug just stood and stared at me, and then they started laughing.

"I guess I haven't had a fresh pineapple but once or twice during the ten years I have been on the street. I remember once when Lynn and Annie put some' fresh pineapple in the fruit cups they served to those having lunch at the Sanctuary. I think it was Christmas. I remember that I went back for seconds, which I very seldom ever do. I'm like a magnet drawn to a horseshoe when I get around a fresh pineapple," I felt that I needed to explain my actions.

The next stop was over at the vegetables. I saw a pile of great big beautiful Idaho baking potatoes. I said, "Come on over and help me pick out a couple of potatoes for each of us because we are going to have baked potatoes for the next couple of days."

They picked out the ones they thought they would like with a lot of butter, bacon bits, sour cream, and chives. They all laugh as I grab the handle on the cart and away we went down one aisle and up another.

We finally reach the meat counter. I had forgotten how good those big steaks looked. "I know we had steak at the Black Angus, but you have to remember, this is steak that I'm going to cook."

I tell the girls and Pug to pick out what they think they would like to eat. Pug pickes out a very large New York strip that was about two inches thick. Each of the girls picked out a small fillet mignon. The small fillets looked so good that I decided that was what I would have.

I knew if I took a large steak, I wouldn't have room enough for my pineapple, a salad, and potato. I wanted to be sure and save enough room for the pineapple and possibly some good dessert.

The girls wanted to get a few other little things while we were there. They found some nice small dinner rolls that would just fit in great. When they added the iced tea, they had the perfect dinner for four hungry loving people. We all started laughing when I repeated the previous statement. It had soaked in by that time.

I asked the girls if we should get some Pepto Bismol. They really didn't think we would need it.

We finally reach the checkout counter. It sure did feel good to be able to reach into my pocket and hand the man a hundred-dollar bill to pay for the groceries.

My old wallet was bulging quite a bit, so I tried not to flash it because I didn't know New York people very well yet.

We finally arrived back at the car and headed back to the house. Upon arrival, we hurriedly unloaded all of our new purchases, and I headed for the grill. I lit it and hurried into the house and asked Pam for the steaks, salt, and pepper.

"Slow down, cowboy you're gonna bust a cinch on your saddle the way you're going."

All of a sudden I realized that I was acting like a nerd. I thought it was because this was the first time in a long while that I was doing something like this – something I really enjoyed doing. It felt as though we were doing a family thing. Quality time, you know what I mean. There was a certain togetherness happening among the four of us. We had so much respect and love for each other. It felt as if I had been doing this type of thing for a long time, and yet I knew it had only been a couple of days.

By now Angie and Pam were starting to make the salad and were washing the potatoes and oiling the outside getting them ready to bake. Hold on a minute; they were doing something I hadn't seen before. They had ice cream salt and were rubbing it all over the outside of the potato before they wrapped it in foil and put it into the oven for baking.

When I questioned them, they told me a cook on TV had said that this added flavor to the potato and made it fluffy inside through and through. It was going to take a while to bake a potato this large.

It just now dawned on me that we didn't have any dessert. I mentioned this to Pam, and she said, "Oh, yes, we do. I have a Mrs. Smith's apple pie and a lemon pie in the refrigerator. I figured you two guys might be needing something sweet like that before the weekend was over, and I was right. We'll have something for dessert while we watch the program this evening."

After about twenty-five or thirty minutes, Pam told me she thought I could put the steaks on now. I put Pug's steak on first since it was so thick it would take longer to cook. After about ten minutes, I put the three fillets on so they would all get done about the same time. I walk back into the kitchen, and I see her standing there. She looks so beautiful standing there with that cute little apron around her waist and her beautiful blonde hair surrounding that beautiful, gorgeous face and those blue eyes that totally mesmerized me.

How could this beautiful woman have stayed single all of these years with all of these New York men meeting and talking to her every day in the restaurant where she worked? They must be either blind or the dumbest people on earth. She wouldn't have lasted six months in Texas. They would have been standing in line at her door. Maybe it is the way she said. Maybe she really didn't want to date anyone or go out with anyone. Now I wonder how I could be such a lucky person. I'm sure glad she changed her mind when I came along, but I will admit that the two of us make an unusual couple.

I had really been praying hard that this thing between us would be the real thing. I'd been thinking of all the things I had done in the last ten years, and now I was wondering how God could be so good to me and let me find someone like her. Right now the only thing I could think about was making this little lady happy for the rest of her life, that was if she would let me have the job.

Pug was actually setting the table and helping to get things ready to eat. Angie was at the kitchen sink fixing my pineapple. She had peeled and cored the pineapple, and now she was slicing it. Oh! What's this! She's offering me a bite of pineapple before dinner. I'm in heaven.

"Thanks, Angie, now you're absolutely one of my favorite people," I said.

There was a laugh all around the room with that one.

I saw why Pug liked this lady, she was a real thoughtful person to go along with her beauty. Boy, that pineapple was good. As I have previously stated, it was the best I had tasted in many years. Truth was that it was the only one I had tasted in many years.

It looked as if they were just about ready with the salad, so I had to run back outside and check on the steaks. It was time to turn Pug's steak over since it had been cooking longer than the rest. I checked closely, and it seemed the fillets needed turning also. I felt truly domesticated doing this kind of thing again. I could sure get used to a life like this again.

Pam took the potatoes out of the oven and checked them to see if they were done; they were. Everything was coming together at the same time.

I remembered that my mother used to work so hard at Christmas and Thanksgiving trying to make sure that everything was ready at the same time. That way, she would say, "Nothing gets cold before time to eat." She was right, and she was a master at having everything come ready at the same time. My mother had been a wonderful cook. I had really missed that over the years. Dad used to tease her and tell her that he married her for her cooking, but after I got older, I knew that wasn't the truth. I could tell from the look of love in his eyes every time he looked at my mother. They were the perfect couple. I had always wanted to have a love like theirs, and I thought that I might have, at long last, found it.

Now it was time to get serious about all of that food the ladies had prepared and placed before us this evening. Fond memories kept coming back all through the dinner as I watched the smiles and heard the laughter of a wonderful group of friends that I was a part of. Yes, God had truly blessed me by bringing me to my senses and to where I seemed to belong with a wonderful woman with whom I wouldn't mind spending the rest of my life.

Maybe I'd have the chance to watch my children raise a family of their own and make me a grandfather.

Thank you, God, for bringing me this far.

We ate and ate and ate. I got so full I hurt all over.

Pam wanted to know if we wanted our dessert now or if we should save it till the show was over. Angie suggested we save it until the show was over. "That way we can have our dessert and discuss the show at the same time."

Everyone agreed on after the show, so after the show it would be.

All four of us started taking the dishes up and carrying them to the sink while Pam started putting the leftovers into the refrigerator. We finally got everything to the dishwasher just as Pam put the last of the leftovers into the refrigerator.

We adjourned to the living room. Pam and I took the love seat, and Pug and Angie took the couch. This made a real nice cozy way to spend the evening watching "So You Want to Be a Millionaire," featuring me as one of its contestants. The show came on at 9:00 p.m. here in New York and that, of course, made it come on at 8:00 p.m. in the Chicago area and Texas.

"Well, here it is, at long last I get to see how I look and sound on television," I commented.

It was amazing how quiet everyone became as the show came on.

Robert Burns came into the spotlight and introduced the guy who was on just before me.

They went through the thing about his deciding to stop and take the money instead of continuing on to the next question. He decided to take the money and run.

Now came the time deciding who got to take the chair again. "Guess what?" I said. "Hey, folks, I won it again."

Everyone laughed at that one, and so did I. I felt if I couldn't laugh at myself, then others would have trouble laughing with me.

We started out with the simple silly questions they asked for the first four or five steps in the program. Everyone was answering the questions the same way I did, and they were all laughing and saying they could have done as well as I did on those questions. I agreed.

They finally get to the harder questions.

The $16,000 question was the baseball question about Rip Sewell's blooper ball pitch. The gang had no idea which ballplayer it was that started the blooper ball pitch. They all got a kick out of the story.

Next came the $32,000 question about the Commander-in-Chief of the Allied Forces during World War II. Everyone knew the answer to that one. Now came the $64,000 question, which was about boxing. Well, Pug knew that answer real quick. I had expected him to know that answer.

Now for the $125,000 question. It was the one about the Bible and in what book the story about the woman being stoned was. Both of the girls knew the answer to that one. That didn't surprise me.

Now came the $250,000 question, which was "Who invented the cotton gin?" I thought every kid who had ever taken a history lesson would know that one. All four of us knew the answer to that one.

Now, for a real hard question, the question about the Black Sheep Squadron and who the leader was. I was the only one of the four to know that answer. It seemed they didn't watch TV much because there had been a television show on the air for a lot of years about the Black Sheep Squadron.

Finally, there was the million-dollar question, the one about the cowboy named Leonard Slye who changed his name and became a great cowboy movie star. I was the only one to know it was Roy Rogers. The reason I knew it was because I had been such a western movie buff when I had been a kid and also because I had read his life story.

By now we were all celebrating again just as we had the other night. Now it was time for a commercial announcement to take up some time and to pay for the progam sponcers.

Pam says, "we won, now It's time for dessert." She gets up, and she and Angie adjourned to the kitchen to get the pie and coffee. They had to heat the apple pie for Pug. They had everything ready, and they come back into the living room with a tray, which they set on the coffee table. We prepared to dig in just as soon as the commercial announcement was over.

My Family

Just as they set the tray down, the phone rings. Pam looks at me. The others look at me and say, "Maybe this could be the call you have hoped for."

Pam answered the phone. "It is one of the boys from the studio saying they had a call from Chicago, someone saying they needed to get in touch with you."

I get on the phone, and he tells me, "We gave them this number, and they should be calling in just a few minutes. I hope that's O.K. with you Professor. I wanted to call and to tell you while they are talking to Robert on another line here at the studio."

He says, "Good luck, Professor," and hangs up.

I was just about to sit back down when the phone rings again. Pam looks at me and says, "You answer it."

I answer the phone with a simple "Hello."

I heard a voice from the past. "Jimmy, is that really you?" It was my mother's voice.

"Yes, Mother, it's me; this is really Jimmy."

She began to cry. I had to wait for her to get control of her nerves before she said anything more. Finally, she said, "I can't believe it's really you. We saw you on television and heard the host of the show say what you had been doing for the past ten years. Your father told us you had called once after you left, but we never heard anything more. We didn't know if you were dead or alive."

I know, Mother, I know, and I apologize for having done such a bad and stupid thing to my family. I just went off the deep end, and I will explain it all when I see you. I think I'm on the road to recovery with the help of some friends.

"How are my children, and how is Dad?"

"Son, your father passed away about a year after you left. He had a heart attack and died right there in the office where he spent most of his years building the business."

"We didn't know till now how to get in touch with you to tell you. We needed you here to help run the business. We have been lucky to have the employees we have because they have taken over and run the business just as if you or your father were still here in the office."

"Your children are almost grown now. Your daughter is a beautiful young lady, and your son is a big six foot, three-inch, good-looking man of about 225 pounds. You'll be so proud of both of them. They have both graduated from high school and college, but we can talk more about that when we see you."

"Mother, how is your health? How have you been doing without Dad to look after you?"

She laughs and says, "You mean how am I doing without someone for me to look after don't you? You know how your father and I were. We looked after each other. I have to admit it gets mighty lonesome not having someone to take care of since the children have grown up."

"Jimmy, when are we going to see you?"

"Real soon, Mother. Maybe in a couple of weeks or so. I have to make a trip to Norfolk with a friend, and then I will be coming to Chicago."

"That's fine, son, we're just anxious to see you. You know you are a very rich man now."

"Yes, Mother I know, I just won a million dollars, but that money has to go to help some people in Texas who helped me when I was down and out."

She says, "No, I don't mean that. I mean the money you have here. Your father willed everything to you when he died. He made the stipulation that the trust fund and you take care of the children and me. What I'm saying, Jimmy, is that not counting the Plastics Manufacturing Co., you are worth about a hundred and fifty million dollars or more.

"It seemed that your father had faith in you and invested a lot of the net profits from the company in stocks and growth funds in addition to the profits of his own business which is now your business. The money he invested for you in the stock growth fund has grown into that amount according to our financial accountant.

"The Plastics Manufacturing Co. is worth about $700,000,000 to $800,000,000 dollars. The value fluctuates depending on the stock market. Several analysts have put the value at more than a billion dollars. We don't really know what the gross value is. At least that's what the Board of Directors turned down on an offer to buy it last year. It may be worth more now with the new government contracts we just landed."

"Mother, it sounds like you have been staying on top of everything from the way you talk."

"Jimmy, I sit in on the Board of Directors' meetings. They voted me a place on the Board after your father died. I have to stay up with what's going on. I hope you will be able to come home and take over for me since it's all in your name."

"Mother, I'll promise you that I will be there within the next two or three weeks. Do you mind if I bring along a very special lady that I have met and think a lot of? I want you to meet her."

"Lordy, no, I don't mind if you bring her with you. Are you getting married again?"

"Right now, Mother, it's just a little early to say about that, but I want your approval before I do anything this time. I remember you weren't very fond of my first wife. It seemed that you were a lot smarter about women than I was. I wish I had listened to you. I know you never told me not to marry her. You just kept saying, 'Be sure it's what you want to do."

"I guess it was what I wanted to do at the time, but it was a bad mistake. It took a lot of good years out of my life and the lives of my family, but I'm sure

I have it on the right track now. Mother, did the kids see the show? Do they know about me yet?"

"Yes, they do. Johnny called me before the show was over, and Jennifer called right after he did. I told them I would contact the studio and try to find out how to get in touch with you. I told them that just as soon as I found out anything, I would call and fill them in on everything. Now I can tell them that their father will be home in a couple of weeks or so.

"You say you have to go to Virginia? Is this on business or pleasure?"

"Mother, I think you could call it a little bit of both. This lady I told you about has a family there near Norfolk, and I would like to meet them and have them meet me since I may become one of the family.

"She would like that also. I have already promised her that we will go to see them tomorrow or the next day. We will probably stay two or three days with them and then come back here before coming to Chicago. I promise I will stay in touch with you at all times, so you will know just when we will be coming home.

"Oh, yes, I have a friend from Texas with me that I would like for you to meet, but he may be going on a quick trip to Omaha, Nebraska, while we are in Norfolk. I'm not sure just yet, but he may be coming with us to Chicago. He also has a lady friend that I am sure you'll like. Do you think you could find rooms for all of us at your house?

If I remember right, it should still have seven bedrooms."

"That's right, son your memory is still good, and we can certainly accommodate four more people. Oh, yes, Oscar, our man who takes care of everything, is still with me and taking care of me and driving me everywhere I have to go so I don't get into trouble with the traffic.

He says to tell you hello for him. He looks just about the same as he did when you were here except for a few more gray hairs.

"We are all so excited about the possibility of seeing you, and now it is becoming a reality. Your father would be very proud of you for hanging in there and not ever giving up on your life. I'm anxious to meet the young lady you told me about. You haven't told me her name yet. I need to know that."

"Mother, her name is Pam, Pam Jackson, and I'm sure you'll love her."

"Well, is she there with you now? If she is, I would like to talk to her if that's all right with you?"

"Mother, I think that's a great idea."

I turn to Pam. "My mother would like to speak to you."

Pam looks stunned. She comes over, takesthe phone, and says, "Hello, Mrs. Dixon, this is Pam."

Pam's heart was beating so hard at this point that we could almost hear it pumping. You could see her blouse rise and fall with each breath. We could only hear one side of the conversation, which went something like this.

"Yes, I've heard a lot about you also. I'm looking forward to meeting you and Johnny and Jennifer. From the conversation I just heard, I assume that Mr. Dixon has passed away. I'm sorry, and I hope there is something we can do to help. Oh, don't worry, I'll keep him on the straight and narrow. No, I don't drink anything but an occasional glass of wine. No, I agree with you that he probably could, but we don't want to take any chance right now. It's too soon to know. Yes, I'm sure we will have a good visit with my parents while we're in Norfolk. I'm looking forward to meeting you real soon. Yes, I sure do, Mrs. Dixon. We'll see you in a week or so. Thank you so very much for asking to talk to me. I have really enjoyed it. Tell Johnny and Jennifer that I'm looking forward to meeting them also. Yes, ma'am,

I'm sure of my feelings for Jim. We'll see you all in about a week or ten days. Yes, ma'am, I sure will."

Pam hangs the phone up. She turnes and looks at me, "Know what, she says? I like your mother, and we're only going to spend a couple of days with my folks, and then we're definitely coming back here, regroup, pack, and head for Chicago. Your mother and your children want to see you, so we're going to see them. Your mother insists that I come with you, and with your permission I'm going to do that very thing. I really want to meet her. She seems so nice."

After Pam was finished telling of her conversation, I asked everyone to sit down. "You're going to need to be seated when I tell you what Mother told me. I have a surprise for all of you. I know that I just won a million dollars, but I have something even better. Mother has told me that my father passed away about a year after I left. That, of course, is the bad news because no man ever had a better father than I had. The thing is, my father left me a very large business worth millions of dollars, and it is mine just to come home and start working.

"The next information has to stay in this room, and we are not to tell anyone else what I am about to tell you. Is this all agreed? Okay then, here's the news. My father invested money in my name from the time I was very young until the day he died. It seems that those investments are now worth about a hundred and fifty million dollars or more."

I look at Pam, and she has turned as white as a ghost. It scared the hell out of me. I grabb her and ask her if she was all right. She finally starts coming around. She almost fainted; her eyes were starting to turn back in her head. I was scared to death she might really go totally out. Her face is finally beginning to get some color back into it.

Angie comse running in with a wet towel to put on her head or let her wash her face, whichever would do the most good.

She looks at me again and asks, "Did you say a hundred and fifty million dollars?"

"Yes, that's what my mother says the accountant says it's worth."

"This is awful. Now everybody will think I'm after you only because of your money. This scares me to death, Jim. I never knew anyone before with more than ten or twenty thousand dollars in the bank. I don't know if I can live with this."

"Wait a minute lady, you told me that you loved me and wanted to spend the rest of our life together before you knew that I had a cent. You thought I was going to Texas to give away all of the money I had won, and you still wanted to go with me. This money shouldn't change the way you love me. It better not, or I will give it all away."

When I realized what I had just said, I felt like fainting myself. That meant I loved this woman so much in the few days that I had known her that I was willing to give away a king's ransom in order to keep her love. "Pam, if this is going to come between us, I really mean it, I'll give it to my children or the employees of the plant or someone who really needs it before I will lose your love. You mean so much more to me than money ever could that I would give it all up just to keep you."

By now Pug and Angie are looking totally dumfounded.

"Pam, I mean every word I've said. If this money means losing your love, then to hell with it. I can make a living like any other man if I need to."

Pug is still holding Angie's hand and looking as if he doesn't know what to say. He finally says, "Professor, is this going to change the way we feel about each other or the way you feel about the gang back in Ft. Worth?"

"Hell No, Pug, hell, no, this isn't going to change my feelings about any of you. You'll always be my best friend. It just means that I can help a lot more people than I had figured on helping. This means that I'll have enough money to help people and also make sure my family never has to want for anything the rest of their lives."

Pam was beginning to feel a little better now, and I think it was beginning to soak in that we were going to be rich – richer than either of us ever figured.

"Jim, I won't know how to act if we get married and have all that money. I like working for a living."

"I assure you, lady, you will be able to work all you want to after we are married. How about that pie and coffee that started this whole thing?"

"That's fine except I think I should warm your coffee since it's probably cold now."

Pug lamented, "I wish I wasn't a teetotaller; I sure could use a drink about now. Hey, Professor, do you mean that all this time I have been buddies with a man who is worth a hundred and fifty million dollars?"

"That's what my mother tells me, and I have never known her to lie. Now we can do all the things for our friends back in Ft. Worth that we want to do. This means I can help Doc set up that store-front clinic for homeless people, and maybe I can get Cowboy about sixty acres and some rodeo stock for breeding to go on it – something he can make a living doing.

"Now I can help Bing pay off his debt to the Mafia and quit hiding from them. One thing for sure is that I want to help Mabel get back to Louisiana and find her daughter that she hasn't seen in a lot of years.

"Now, my friend, what would you like to have?" I expected him to say he wanted something simple, and he really did.

He simply said that he would like to have some kind of business where he and Angie could work together and just make a decent living.

Who could argue with that? The thing he really wanted was to get his head operated on, and then see if Angie would marry him.

"I'll bet we can take care of the operation for you, but you'll have to convince Angie to marry you, I can't do that."

The coffee was finally hot, and the girls return with coffee and pie. I really enjoyed the coffee and lemon pie. Pam knew just the right buttons to push, but right now I didn't think she was interested in pushing any buttons. She was still in a state of shock. We enjoyed our coffee and pie and talked. Pam wanted to know if I ever had any idea of what my father had been doing for me.

"Once when I was about fifteen or sixteen years old, he said something about my being able to do what I wanted to do after I got out of college, and that I wouldn't ever have to worry about finances. I never really thought too much about it at the time. Now I know what he was talking about. He was talking about that stock growth portfolio he was investing in for me. I do know he was also investing in a growth portfolio for each of my children that is similar to what he had done for me. I never had any idea just how much money my father made or how much money he had.

"He started Dixon Plastics Manufacturing Co. on a shoestring when he was young. When my grandfather died, Dad took his inheritance and invested it in this plastics manufacturing business when plastics was pretty new to the public. I guess he saw the handwriting on the wall and decided to take a chance on plastics, so he started his company.

"When I graduated from college, I just wanted to be a teacher. Dad never asked me to come into the business. He just said that he wanted me to do what I wanted to do, and if teaching was what would make me happy, then I should teach. I started teaching and lecturing and never looked back.

"I know now that I should have talked to him more and asked if he had any suggestions as to what line of work I should pursue. Now I know that he would have just told me to be happy and teach others to do the same. That's the kind of person he was. I had no idea he would leave the business to me in his will. I guess I just figured that after I left, he would leave the business to Johnny. Now I have to go home and start figuring out what I am going to do for the rest of my life. I hope Pam likes Chicago."

She looks at me, "I think I could learn to love any place where I live if it's with you. I don't have to be in the society circles, do I?"

"No, my Darling Pam, you won't have to do that. My mother will help you and answer any questions you might have about her friends and some of my old friends. I'm not sure which ones will welcome me back and which ones won't have anything to do with me after what I have done."

We were all still in a state of shock when the phone rings again. Pam answers it, "Jim, it's for you. I think you'll want to take this call also."

I answer the phone. A very nice, deep baritone voice on the other end said, "Dad?"

I am stunned and I ask, "Johnny, is that you?"

"It sure is, Dad," came this very grown-up voice on the other end. We're all real excited about your coming to see us. Jennifer and I would like to plan a party of some sort for you if you don't mind?"

"Son, if you don't mind, just let me come home first and let us spend some time together. I know you and your sister and grandmother have a million questions, and so have I.

"Son, you sure do sound grown up now. Your grandmother tells me that you are over six foot, three inches tall, and that you weigh somewhere around 225 pounds."

"She's mighty close with those figures."

"I hope you are a singer since you have such a beautiful baritone voice. I remember when it was changing, and you did a lot of squeaking, and your voice was breaking once in a while."

"Yeah, Dad, I remember that too, but that was some time ago." Then he asks how my health is and how I am feeling.

I assur him that I wam feeling fine and staying sober.

"Well, you should be after just winning a million dollars. I heard you on the show, and I admire you for what you want to do, and I admire you for picking yourself up and coming back to life as you once knew it.

"Dad, Jennifer and I want you to know that there have never been any hard feelings toward you for leaving when you did. We knew what Mother was doing. We were young, but we understood more than you think we did. I don't think Grandmother told you, but our mother died about two years after you left. I hate to say this, but she and one of her boy friends both died of an overdose of heroin. We found out that she had been using it for a long time. One of our friends told us after she died. He had known of her heroin use for the last three or four years before you left, and then it just got worse after you left. She had filed for divorce from you and died before it was final. She had some life insurance that neither of us kids knew about. It was a pretty large policy. After her death we found that she had named Jennifer and me as co-beneficiaries. We can tell you about all of that stuff when you get home.

"Grandmother tells me that you're bringing a real nice lady home with you. I think that's great, and so does Jennifer. We think it's about time you had a little happiness. Maybe with your new lady as our stepmother, we can be a family again – that is if she thinks she can put up with. a couple of spoiled kids in their early twenties."

"Johnny, I think you and Jennifer are going to love this lady just as I do. She doesn't have any children of her own, but she loves all children. She lost her only baby prematurely and was unable to have any more children after that. The doctors told her she could never have any more children. She is beautiful inside and out, and I hope you will give her a chance."

"We will, and we are looking forward to you both coming home. Jennifer says she wants to just wait until you get here so she can hug your neck and talk to you in person. She's real nervous and anxious for you to come home.

"Well, Dad, I'm sure you have a lot of things to do before you come home, so I'll let you go for now. You and your lady, Pam, have a good time in Norfolk visiting her family. I'm sure they're real anxious for your visit.

"Love you, Dad, and we'll see you soon. Jennifer sends her love. Bye for now."

I hang up the phone a happy man.

It looks as though I am going to be getting a big part of my life back together real soon. I tell Pam, Angie, and Pug about my conversation with my son.

Pam laughed. "Boy, what a beautiful baritone voice that boy has. He must be some kind of a young man."

The Shopping Trip

"Well, gang I think it's about time to call it an evening. Pam and I have a lot of getting ready to go shopping before leaving Wednesday. Pug, if you need some more money to make a trip back to Omaha, let me know. Remember, we're all going shopping first thing tomorrow morning."

This sounded fine to them.

They walked out the door after saying good night to Pam and me. They had to walk all the way over to the other side of the duplex that the girls lived in.

Now it was just Pam and I. She looked at me a while before she spoke. "Well, I guess I should ask Angie to get us plane tickets to Norfolk for the day after tomorrow. Does that sound about right, Darling?"

"That sounds just right as far as I'm concerned. My kids wanted to have a party for us upon our arrival, but I told Johnny that I think we should wait a couple of days so we can get to know each other pretty well before we have a party. Besides I wanted to talk to them about whom they were going to invite. There are some people I would just rather not have at the party. They are some of my wife's old friends.

"I haven't mentioned it yet, but I should tell you that my wife died a couple of years after I left, from an overdose of heroin. It seems that she had become a heavy user of heroin even before I left, according to some of Johnny's friends. They only told him after she was dead. They were afraid they would upset him if they told him while she was alive, so they just kept their mouths shut. I think the kids took it pretty well. It seems they were aware of her behavior even before I was. Kids are real smart, and we just don't give them enough credit for being smart.

"Pam, I sure hope your folks like me because I want you to be my wife so badly I can hardly stand it."

She walked over and put her arms around me and held me real tight; she kisses me gently and looks up into my eyes. "Thanks, Hon, I needed that."

"Pam, I love you so much that it's scary."

"Yes, Jim, I know that feeling, and I want you to know that I love you just as much as you love me. I want more than anything in this wide world to be your wife for the rest of our lives."

She looks up into my eyes and asks, "Jim, will you marry me?"

I was stunned, totally stunned. "Wait a minute; I'm the one who is supposed to propose."

"Mr. Dixon, that's right most of the time, but this time I just decided that it was time I told you how much I really love you. I figure if I ask you to marry me, you're too much of a gentleman to say no."

I look into her eyes and see that she is serious, very serious. "Yes, oh, hell, yes, I'll marry you, and just as soon as possible."

I think for just a minute, and then I asked her if it would be all right if we wait until we get to Chicago to get married. "I would like to have my children and my mother with us at a small, quiet wedding in our home in Chicago."

"That's a wonderful idea, I like that idea very much."

I apologize to her because I hadn't happened to think that maybe her folks would like to be at our wedding also. I assure her that if they would like to be there, "I'll be more than happy to fly them to Chicago so we can make it a real family affair. How does that sound?"

"Now that's just another reason why I love you so much, you're always so thoughtful of other people. I'm sure we can work something out with my folks."

"When I say your folks, I mean your brothers and their wives and your sister and her husband and their families if they have children. Let's just make this a big, big family affair. If we are going to be a family, let's make it a real family. I'm sure my mother and the children would love to do it that way.

"We've never had a wedding in our house, and I assure you that it's big enough to have a wedding and a reception both right there in the house."

She looked at me quizzically. "You told me the house was large, but just how large is it?"

"Well, let's see; there are seven bedrooms and nine baths in the main house, three bedrooms and three baths in the guest house, and the apartment over the garage has two bedrooms with two baths. The servant's quarters are on the rear of the lot near the house with a walkway between their house and the main house. I guess you could say there are actually twelve bedrooms available and fourteen bathrooms with four half baths. I don't know what the footage of the main house is, but I think it's about 15,000 square feet. I just don't know for sure. I think we can all be comfortable there.

"I hope Pug and Angie can make it back for our wedding because we need a best man and a bridesmaid."

Pam readily agreed. "Jim, Darling, you never told me anything about your folks and this big house before. Why not?"

"Well, Darling, I just didn't want you to think that I was bragging, and I sure didn't want to scare you away."

"What do you mean scare me away? I probably would never have gone out with you in the first place if I had known about it. It would have scared me to death. I'm pretty darn scared right now. I find out that you aren't just the nice teacher that I met who has picked himself up off the streets. You know, like that mythical Greek bird the Phoenix that burned, then arose from the ashes to regain its rightful place in the world. That's what I should call you, Mr. Phoenix. You just the same as burned when you became a derelict street person, and now you have arisen to reclaim your rightful place in this world. I doubt if my folks will ever believe it.

"Do we have to tell them everything all at once? Can't we just tell them a little bit at a time? You know just a little bit at a time. What do you say, Hon? Think we could do it that way? Maybe not tell them the size of the house until they get to Chicago, and then maybe after we're married, we could kind of slip the bank account figures to them a little bit at a time."

"We can just tell them that my father left me well fixed for the rest of our lives. We don't have to tell them how much money I really have. Sweetheart, I'll promise you one thing, and that is that your folks will never have to work another day in their lives, and they will have a nice place to live and plenty of money to live on. We might be able to help your brothers and sister get their own business or something a little later on. What do you think? I'm really not trying to bribe you because it was you who asked me to marry you, and I said, 'Yes, just as soon as we can.'"

"I think that we had better get together with Angie and Pug and see how they are coming along with their plans."

We went next door and rang the bell. Pug comes to the door and invites us in. Angie comes walking in with a smile on her face.

"Well, it looks like you guys are happy. Pam and I were just wondering how you were coming along with your plans to go to Omaha."

"I just talked to my brother and my father and asked them if it would be all right if we came to visit them for a few days. They were tickled to death. I told them about Professor, and they said they saw him on TV the other night. They had trouble believing he was a friend. Pug took a little more explaining than Professor did, but they seemed satisfied and excited about our coming to see them."

"Guess, what happened to me? Pam has asked me to marry her, and I said yes."

They both gave out a big whoop and a hug and congratulations.

I explain to them that we were going to be married in Chicago at my folks' home, and we would like them to be our bridesmaid and best man.

They burst out laughing. I really didn't think it was that funny, but they continued to laugh.

After the laughter had died down a little, I ask them, "What's so funny?"

Angie had just asked Pug to marry her, and he had said yes also.

I was totally dumfounded. How could this have happened to the both of us? I had thought we were the aggressive half of the species, not the females. I loved the way it happened anyway.

"Would you consider flying to Omaha and then back to Chicago. After the wedding, you could go on to Moab, Utah, and see Pug's folks. Hell, what am I thinking about?"

I look at Pam and she was looking at me and asked, "Are you thinking what I am thinking? I'll bet a dollar we are both thinking of the same thing. Double wedding?"

"That's what I had in mind."

"Angie, how would you and Pug like to go to Omaha and visit your brother and his family and your father and then bring them back to Chicago for the weddings?"

She had to stop and think for a minute. "Well, if my father's health is where he can fly, that sounds great."

"I'm sure we'll have plenty of room for everyone, and I'll have Mother hire a little more domestic help while we're there.

"How about it Pug, what do you say?"

"Everything is happening so fast that my head's in a whirl. Don't worry, it's not a headache; it's just that it's all happening so fast that it's hard to think."

After a little thinking, he says with a big smile on his face, "Well, why not? I wanted you to be my best man, and Angie wanted Pam to be her maid of honor, so I guess you and I can be each other's best man, and the girls can be their maids of honor. If it's necessary, Pam's mother can be one bridesmaid and my mother can be the other. Pam's father can give her away. My son could be a best man for me, and Angie's brother could be best man for Pug if her father wants to give her away. We can work that out when we get to Chicago.

"After the weddings, Pug and Angie can go to Utah, and Pam and I will go to Texas, and then we can meet you there after your visit in Moab. How does this sound?"

Pug takes my arm and pulls me over to the side of the room and says, "Professor, this is going to cost a lot of money." He is as serious as he can be.

"Pug, as of now you're on my payroll as my executive assistant. I'll give you another five thousand this afternoon to help with the expenses to carry you through the wedding, and I'll pay for the airline tickets for all of us. We'll need to have Angie go to the office tomorrow afternoon after we do our shopping and get on the phone and arrange for all of our tickets – yours and Angie's to Omaha, then back to Chicago, then to Denver, and a commuter flight on to Moab. After that, on to Texas a week or so later. This will give you guys time to visit with both families and for you to get reacquainted with your family. She'll need to get tickets for Pam and me to go to Norfolk, then back here, and then on to Chicago. We will arrange our own tickets from Chicago to Texas because I'm not sure just how long it will take to get everything settled in the business. There may be some people I will have to meet and some papers I will have to sign while I'm in Chicago, and I have no idea how long that will take, so let's just plan on meeting in Texas in two or three weeks after the weddings.

"Pug, please don't worry about the money because you now have a job starting at two thousand dollars a week. I hope that will be satisfactory, and I'll advance you another five thousand or so just to be safe. When you get to Texas, you'll start earning your money. You'll help me finalize all of the plans we have for all of our friends. You'll be my leg man and do a lot of running around to get these things done. How does that sound to you?"

"It sounds great if I can have my wife with me," Pug said.

"Pug, you know I have been thinking about that. If Angie is one of these ladies who just has to work, how do you think Angie would like to have her own travel agency? It might be in Texas, Chicago, or even Moab, or Omaha. I will tell you this; I'm pretty sure that after we get everything rolling in Texas, Pam and I will almost surely have to move back to Chicago. My mother is getting on in years, and the business is there, and I should be there to look after it. I figure you might be able to help me by flying back and forth to wherever you are needed if necessary. You could help Angie in the travel agency when you aren't busy for me.

"I know that I would like to have you with me. You're the best and closest friend I have ever had, and I would really like it if you guys came back to Chicago with us. I know that Pam would love to have Angie close by. They're such close friends it would be hard to separate them. Good friends are hard to come by, and you two are very special to us. How do you think Angie will feel about this?"

"Well, first off, I have to say thank you for the job. Is that anything like a bodyguard?"

"No, it's not like a bodyguard; it's like having my best friend working side by side with me. I know I can trust you, and it would take a long time to know anyone else and be able to trust him the way I trust you. I would trust you with my life. Now does that answer your question?"

"Yep, that answers my question. Just thought I'd ask," he said, giving me that very special grin of his.

I did swear that sometimes he was like a teenage kid. But the more I was with him, the more I found out about him. Now that he had sobered up for a while, I found that he was really a very well-read person. He knew a lot about history and even economics. When we were drunk, we had never talked about anything except where to get the money for the next drink. This boy knew a lot about Religion, American and Ancient History also, which really blew my mind.

One day, recently, when we had started talking about the Bible, he started quoting scriptures and passages from the Bible. I'd be he was a darn good student in high school and college before he left to be a professional boxer. I found that he was real sharp in math also.

It was amazing just what a bottle of whiskey could do to a man. No, I should have said it was amazing what a man could do to himself if he had a bottle of whiskey and no self-esteem. Now that I looked back, I knew that it was a lack of self-esteem that had caused me to do what I had done. I was sure that I had felt it was my fault that my wife had been doing what she did. I thought I couldn't hold on to my woman and offer her enough to keep her from running around. Now I knew that was not the case at all. She had always had her way. Being married and tied down to a couple of young kids just hadn't fit her style. She had been an only child in a very wealthy family. They had always let her have her way to do anything she wanted to do. Being a PTA mother just had not been her cup of tea.

Pug's Call Home

"Pug, I have a favor to ask of you."

"Sure, anything you want, what is it?"

"I want you to go into the bedroom and use that phone and call Moab, Utah, and get the phone number of your parents or your brother and call them right now and tell them what is going on. Tell them about yourself and about Angie and that you want to come home and see them. See what they say. Tell them about Pam and me, and tell them that we want to meet them. I want you to let them know that if they want to come to the wedding, we'll send them airline tickets so they can come. I've been thinking about this thing, and it doesn't come up right. You haven't talked to them, and they don't know you're getting married, and dammit to hell, they just might want to see their youngest son get married. If they do, we will be more than happy to send for them. They can be at the wedding, and then they can fly back to Moab with you after the wedding, and you guys can spend a few days with them back at your home. How does that sound?"

He had kind of a puzzled look on his face. "You mean you'd do that for me? You've never met my family. They're just plain common folks. They wouldn't know how to act with all the fancy frills and stuff that'll be at the wedding and at your house."

"Pug, we aren't snobs, we're just people who worked hard, got lucky, and made a lot of money. Now your family is just as welcome as anyone else in this world to come to the wedding and stay a couple of days with us. Now you go and call them and tell them just what I said or I'm gonna see how good a boxer you really are. Scares hell out of you don't it?"

"Well, all right, but if they come, I hope they won't embarrass you."

"Pug, you get your butt in there and call your folks. If they'll come, we'll have Angie make the arrangements. I think it would be nice to give your folks and Angie's folks a chance to meet and get to know each other since they're going to be related. Now *go*."

He heads into the bedroom. I hear him on the phone getting the number, and then I closed the door so he could have some privacy. He talked for about twenty minutes and then came out of the bedroom with a great big smile on his face.

He says, "They're real anxious to come to the wedding. I told them all about it, and they said they would love it, but they wanted to be sure it wouldn't be any extra work for your mother and family with them coming in like this. I explained to them that it would be just fine.

"I told them all about Angie and how wonderful and beautiful she is and how much I love her. I had to answer a million questions about where I'd been since I'd been gone. I told them I had a new job as your executive assistant.

Dad said, 'Son, that sounds kind of high fallutin to me.' I assured him that it wasn't anything except working with my best friend doing things he needed to have done. You know, all kinds of things. 'Hell, I don't know just what all it will entail myself. I'll learn real soon though. I'm really looking forward to working with Professor.'

"Mother wanted to know what to wear. I told her I was sending her some money for some new clothes for the wedding. I told her to take the money and go to a nice dress shop and ask them what would be proper to wear." They'll show you and explain it all to you so you won't be embarrassed." I let her know that as far as I am concerned, she could never embarrass me.

"I'm sure she and Angie are going to be real good friends. I know Dad will like her because he really likes a pretty woman, and Angie sure is that.

"My brother said he couldn't get off work, so he would just wait and meet Angie when we get to Moab. Neil is a wonderful guy with a good sense of humor. His wife is real nice too.

"Angie will like my little sister Elaine. She is real pretty. At least, she was the last time I saw her. She wasn't there, but Mother said she couldn't come because she has a three-year-old baby girl, and she is expecting another. It would be hard for her to make it, so we'll see her when we get to Moab. It doesn't seem possible that my little sister is a mother."

Angie came in, and he basically told her just what he had told me.

I tell Angie to make arrangements for Pug's parents to fly in for the wedding. I tell Pug that maybe he should slip a little extra money in the envelope for his father in case he would like to have a new suit to wear to his son's wedding.

"Remember, Pug, this is the first, last, and only wedding you will ever have."

Angie looks at me and says, "Jim, that's for sure. He's not going to get away from me because he has said he would marry me, and that means forever, and when I say forever, I really mean it. Good, bad, or otherwise – he is stuck with me once he says I do."

Angie adds that she would take care of the transportation and see that the tickets are delivered in plenty of time for them to make the wedding.

"I'm real anxious to meet Wayne's family. I just hope they like me."

"Honey, they couldn't help but like you. They'll love you just like I do. You just wait and see."

Angie goes back to the kitchen to see what Pam is doing.

"Hey, it's time to get the girls into this conversation so we can decide what we're going to do. We need to get some rest tonight so we can go shopping early in the morning, and then we have to get ready to leave by day after tomorrow.

Pam and Angie came into the room from the kitchen. "Well, we have it all worked out. Angie is going to the office tomorrow afternoon and order all of the airline tickets for everyone. After we have our visits, we'll meet in Ft. Worth. How does that sound?"

"Honey, I couldn't have said it any better myself, could I Pug?"

Pug just grinned and said, "I don't believe you could."

"Now that that's settled, shall we get some rest so we can go shopping in the morning?"

The girls agree.

"Why don't I call Mother and tell her to arrange for a display of wedding gowns when we get to Chicago so you girls won't have to go out to the store. They'll bring them to the house and put on a wedding dress style show for you right there. You'll be able to select what you want, and they will arrange to tailor it if needed, and you can probably get it back in one day. That'll speed up the wedding. Pug and I will arrange for proper attire at a shop not far from our house in a nice shopping center, that is if it is still there."

"Don't tell me we are going to wear tails."

"Mr. Wayne McKenzie, we sure are. We're going to do this thing up right."

He looks down at the floor and says, "I've never had a tux or anything like that on before, but if you are going to do it, so will I."

"I will, and you will. We all will, and we'll all enjoy every minute of it. Now let's say goodnight."

I go out Angie's front door and into Pam's front door. Inside the door, Pam turnes to me, put her arms around my neck, and gave me a great big hug. "Jim, I love you so much it hurts. I think being Mrs. James Dixon is going to be wonderful." She gives me another big wonderful kiss that turned up my toes.

"Honey, you had better watch what you're doing because it could lead to other things."

She smileds and said, "Well, I sure hope so."

We turned off the lights in the living room and kitchen and headed for the bedroom.

"This is just like our honeymoon only better if it could be better." As I said before it would and did lead to other things. There was no describing the feeling inside our minds and bodies and the love that was between us on this wonderful night. I felt that all future nights would be like this until we were very, very old.

After the lovemaking, we spooned, and what a wonderful feeling it was just holding her body close to mine and feeling the warmth of the woman I loved more than life itself, lying here beside me. I felt sorry for the people in this world who had never known this feeling. It was a feeling that words could not describe or express.

I woke up again to the smell of coffee. I look up, and here comes this beautiful angel into my bedroom with a smile that lights up the world for me. She comes over, hands me my coffee, gave me a wonderful kiss, and says, "Good morning, Darling."

Man, what a way to wake up in the morning. She tells me we had better have some breakfast so we could get ready to go shopping.

"We have a lot to do today. Angie has to go to the office after we finish shopping and make arrangements for our tickets."

I would rather have made love again this morning, but I did as she suggested. I got out of bed, showered, and got ready to eat a bite. She had my favorite breakfast, sausage and eggs over easy with biscuits and jelly. She really knew how to push my buttons.

While I was eating, she went in, showered, and did her cosmetics. She really didn't need very much in the way of cosmetics. I sometimes thought she was just covering up beauty with those cosmetics. I knew I was prejudiced, but I was a good judge of beauty also.

Just as I was finishing with my breakfast and second cup of coffee, I hear Pug and Angie at the front door. I holler for them to come on in which they do. They are all ready to go. Angie sure did look pretty this morning. Pug was a very lucky fellow.

Pam came walking out of the bedroom. "Is everybody ready? The stores are open, so why don't we go shopping?"

Out the door we go and down the street to a very large shopping mall. We go from one store to another buying what we needed. We wanted to be sure we had enough to last for quite a few days. Pug and I would pick something, and the girls would see it and say, "Don't you think you should look at something else? That is kind of old-fashioned."

After taking their advice a couple of times, we began to look at other men in the stores, and we saw what they meant. We were a little behind the times. We ended up listening to the suggestions from the girls and trying to stay in style even though we weren't too happy with the way some of those styles looked on us. I guess if we were going to be old married men, we would have to learn to take advice from the girls until we are been back in the swing of things long enough to know for ourselves.

It was lunch time, so we stop for a sandwich before heading back home. With the shopping over, Pam suggests we take Angie to her office. We dropped Angie off at the office. She says she'll call for us to pick her up when she gets the travel arrangements made.

We had to stop and pick up a couple more suitcases or traveling bags, as I believed they were called in these days vernacular. Pug and I both bought another bag to take care of the clothes we had bought today.

We arrive home and go inside. We start getting things ready to travel. I start by cutting the tags off my newly purchased items. Boy, how the styles and prices had changed. I was sure I would get used to it after a while. Pam was busy getting her clothes sorted and deciding just what else she might need to take with her. This had been going on for about three hours when the phone ring. It was Angie; she is ready to come home so she can start getting her clothes together for the trip.

"Jim, why don't you go pick her up? The keys are on the coffee table."

"Sorry, Hon, I can't do that. I don't want to get off on the wrong foot with the New York police. You forget that I don't have a current driver's license."

"Sorry Jim, I forgot about that. No, problem, I'll run over and pick her up while you go ahead with your packing."

She was back within twenty minutes. She had chicken and potato salad with hot fried pies for each of us for dinner. That was a good idea because I dearly loved chicken, potato salad, and fried pies. I remembered the fried pies my mother had made when I was a little boy.

She made some of the best chocolate pies I had ever tasted. She had also made fried lemon pies, which were my very favorite. These sure brought back old memories. When you added iced tea, you really had a meal.

After the meal was over, we were all full of good food, and we were tired. I asked Angie if she had taken care of everything.

"I sure did," she says. "Pam, I suggest you park your car in long-term parking and leave it there till you get back. I figured you would like to have a day to do some laundry and whatever shopping you might want to do before you go to see Jim's folks in Chicago.

"Am I right, Jim?"

"Angie, I think you're a wonderful and thoughtful travel agent. You seem to think of everything."

"We have tickets to Omaha, leaving tomorrow morning at 8:45 a.m., so that means we can ride to the airport with you. We'll come from Omaha back to Chicago."

"After the weddings, Wayne and I will go back to Moab with his mother and father. I figure we should stay at least a week with his folks and give him time to get reacquainted with them. It'll give me a chance to get to know them and them a chance to know me. There'll be so much going on before and right after the wedding that we really won't have the chance to get to know each other very well. That's why we need the time with them in Moab.

"We will need time to just sit and talk and answer questions. We might want to ask a few questions ourselves. That'll also give me a chance to meet his brother and sister and their families. I am really looking forward to getting to know everyone."

"All the tickets are arranged, so what's next?"

The Banker

I ask Pam what time her bank closed.

"It stays open until 7:00 p.m. why"

I saw that it was about 4:45 p.m. so I asked, "Would you take me to your bank, so I can take care of this cashier's check. I don't like to be carrying it around with me."

She understood. "Sure, I'll take you. It's only about a five-minute drive to the bank."

She parked, and we went inside. She spoke to a man at one of the desks at the front, and he told her to see the man seated at the desk behind him. We go back to the man at the big desk. He stood when we approached. It was apparent that he knew Pam. He greeted us; we shook hands as Pam introduced us. His name was Mr. Rogers. He was vice- president of the bank. He invited us to be seated and asked what he could do for us.

I explained to him that I had a cashier's check for five hundred and fifty thousand dollars that I wanted to leave with him for safekeeping until I got to Chicago and set up my new checking account.

He looked at Pam quizzically. "You apparently know this gentleman."

"Yes, I do. In fact, we're going to be married very soon. He just won a million dollars on the TV show 'So You Want to Be a Millionaire' and this is part of the winnings."

I handed him the check. He looked at it and said "Well, I'll be darned. I saw that show the other night, and I didn't recognize you. I even remember the question you won the money on. It was about an old western movie star that I was just crazy about as a kid. I even bought a Roy Rogers guitar when I was about twelve years old. I guess I figured since my name was Rogers, we must be related until I read his life story and learned that

Leonard Slye was his real name. I laughed when you answered that question because I had already answered it. I told my wife that I had just won a million dollars. Well, Professor, it's a pleasure to know you.

"You say you want me to hold this check here until you get set up in Chicago. Is that your hometown? I mean before you were on the street. I'm sorry, I didn't mean to embarrass you. I just was referring to what they told the audience on the show." Mr. Rogers, that don't embarrass me. It's people who don't understand it can happen to anyone that embarrasses me.

"Mr. Rogers, my father was the founder and owner of Dixon Plastics Manufacturing Co. in Chicago. He passed away a few years back, and I inherited the company. If I remember correctly, we have a branch office here in New York. I'm not sure just how much business it does, but I am sure your bank could use a little shot in the arm from a company the size of ours. What do you think?"

Mr. Rogers almost fell over the desk. "Professor, we can certainly accommodate you on such a trivial matter as holding this check a week or so until you get back to Chicago. I'll give you a receipt and put it securely in the vault. You just have your bank in Chicago call me when you're ready to transfer it, and I'll take care of it for you. No charge for the transaction."

"Mr. Rogers, I can assure you that within the next six months you will be getting a new customer, and that customer will be the branch office of Dixon Plastics."

"Pam, how in the world did you ever meet this interesting man?"

She just smiles, "Oh, we met through mutual friends."

"Well, congratulations on your coming wedding. Please let us know the time and date; we would like to send a card or something appropriate."

I signed the check, took his receipt, and thanked him for his courtesy. We left the bank and headed back to the house. Pam had this kind of smirk on her face. I started laughing. "Okay now, tell me just what is so funny." "That guy has been a real horse's rear end to me on a couple of occasions. He sure got friendly when he found out who you were. He sure does want that account. Are you really going to give him some business?"

"Pam, there is one thing I learned from my father at an early age. If you tell a man you are going to do something, you do it. You never go back on your word. Dad always said that any man is only as good as his word. It doesn't have to be written down on a piece of paper to be a contract; just a hand shake is good enough. I told that man I would change our account over to his bank, and I will see that at least a good part of it is changed over to him. I may not change it all over, but I'll keep my word. That's one thing you're going to find out about me. I never break my word.

"Just like I gave my word to those people in Texas that I would come back there and help them if I won some money, and I am sure as hell going to do just that. I know you would be disappointed in me if I didn't.

"Right? I would hope that you would be because I would be disappointed in myself if I didn't."

She just smiles and says, "That's my man. Things like that just make me love you that much more."

She starts laughing. "Know what, Jim. Now that I am getting to know you better, I think I could love you even if you didn't have any money." Then she really started laughing – and so did I.

"Well, you little Imp, I do have the money, and you're just gonna have to learn to live with it. I'm gonna get even with you for that remark."

We arrived back at the house and found that Angie had made sandwiches, tea, and leftover potato salad for dinner.

"That's fine with me. I'm not really that hungry anyway. It's only been a couple of hours since we ate. I pass on the sandwiches and salad."

Pam is telling Angie about Mr. Rogers at the bank.

Angie asks, "You mean that old stuffed shirt?"

"Well, I wish you could have seen him when he found out who Jim was. It was even better when he saw that check for five hundred and fifty thousand dollars. When Jim told him that he was the owner of Dixon Plastics, he almost fainted. Jim told him that since he was helping him out on this matter, he would transfer some of his bank business over to him from the branch office here in New York. I thought the guy was going to offer to shine Jim's shoes. You know how stuck up he has been with us about our little accounts. My little savings account didn't mean much to them, but now that he knows Jim and I are getting married, he couldn't be nicer."

"I'm sorry, girls, but you shouldn't be too hard on Mr. Rogers, he's just a hard-hearted businessman. I needed something, and he had it. I had to trade something for something. It's that simple in the business world. I just couldn't be carrying that cashier's check around in my pocket. This way, I know the money is safe. Not only that, I know where I can get money real quick in case of an emergency.

"Okay Pam, what more do you have to pack?"

She had almost everything packed except her cosmetic bag which she would finish packing in the morning.

"Okay, I'll take my shower tonight and shave in the morning while you are getting your shower."

"That sounds like a good plan."Angie and Pug said they were going back over to Angie's apartment to finish their packing. They would see us in the morning early, and we should be at the airport about an hour before the plane left.

Angie said, "Our flight leaves at 8:45 a.m., so we should be there about 7:30 a.m."

"That should work out well for us since we leave at 9:05 a.m.. This will give us time to get checked in without hurrying."

We all agreed and said goodnight.

The Future In Laws

Morning came early. I smelled the coffee again, and I looked at my watch. First thing I asked, "How long will it take us to get to the airport?"

"If we're lucky, we can get there in about an hour and a half at this time of the day."

"What time is it now?"

"It's a little past 5:00 a.m.; I hope you don't mind. We should leave here around 6:00 o'clock. Now drink your coffee and shave so we can get ready."

The phone rings. Pam answers, "Yes, we're up. With any luck we should be able to leave about 6:00. Will you guys be ready? That sounds good, so let's plan on leaving at that time."

I still had cobwebs in my eyes as I drank my coffee and shaved. It was a little disconcerting to have that beautiful woman standing stark naked in the shower next to me. What made it worse was that I could see her silhouette as plain as day in the steamy glass door.

"Sorry, Professor," I said aloud, "you just don't have time for any lovemaking this morning. That'll have to wait till later, but it sure doesn't hurt to look while you're waiting."

Maybe I'd better keep my mind on shaving before I cut my throat. Looking at her could make a man do something like that if he couldn't get to her. Oh, well, our day would come.

Pam finishes her shower, I finish my shaving, and we get dressed. This was the fastest I had moved in a long time.

We were just finishing our second cup of coffee when the doorbell rings. Pam hollered, "Come on in the door's open."

They came in with bags sitting on the porch. We knew that was our cue.

We rinsed our cups, set them on the drain board and said, "We're ready let's go." We grabbed our bags and everyone headed out the front door. Pam had brought the car around before she had awakened me.

We loaded our luggage and pile in, and Pam heads for the airport. Boy the traffic is heavy this morning. I began to think we would never get there, but all of a sudden the traffic cleared up a little, and we were really on our way. Pam was just about right. We headed into the airport long-term parking at just a few minutes after 7:00 a.m. This gave us plenty of time to get to the luggage area and check our bags.

We got inside the terminal and said our good-byes. We hugged, shook hands, kissed, and all of that stuff. They headed to their departure gate, and we head to our gate. We had time to go to the little coffee shop inside and have a sweet roll and another cup of coffee while we were waiting.

The time passes quickly, and we head for the departure gate with our tickets in hand.

They call for boarding, and we head for the gate attendant. A nice friendly young lady looks at our tickets and says, "Have a nice trip."

We walk down the covered ramp to the plane entrance where we are met by another nice lady who looks at our tickets again and tells us, "You are in first class, which is up front to your left."

We go left and find our seats. We had been seated for about twenty-five minutes before they came on the intercom and ask us to please buckle our seat belts and bring our seats to an upright position. We do this, and the plane starts backing out. I knew it wouldn't be long now before take off.

After about five minutes, we feel the pilot push the throttle, and next comes the thrust of the engines. We were off. I mean it was literally just that fast once he throws the throttle forward. We were really on our way to meet Pam's family.

All of a sudden I was nervous. "Pam, Honey, you're not going to believe this, but I am getting real nervous."

She just laughed at me. "Jim, you're going to be just fine."

The flight to Norfolk wasn't that long. They brought us coffee, which I sure didn't need. I had been to the bathroom twice already. They also brought us a couple of cookies to go with the coffee. I could have had orange juice, but I decided what the hell, I might just go ahead and get loaded up with caffeine. I already had the shakes so a little more caffene wasn't going to make much difference.

I couldn't believe it, but the captain is on the intercom again saying we are going to arrive in Norfolk within the next fifteen minutes. The young lady came on the intercom right after the captain and asked us to please fasten our seat belts.

My stomach was getting real queasy. This was stupid. What did I have to be nervous about? Right!

Let's be honest, I chided myself; I have a lot of things to be nervous about. They may not like me; I may not like them. We may not like each other. Hey, man, this is just plain stupid being so nervous. Pam will be there with me, so what can happen?

The plane banks slightly and heads straight into the airport landing strip. We touch down and head for the terminal. *Well,* I told myself, *here we go.*

I looked at Pam and saw her smiling face, and all of my fears seem to vanish. She seems real excited, so I figured I might as well be excited about seeing the folks too.

The plane stops, and everyone starts to unbuckle. We are among the first to leave the plane. As we start up the covered ramp, I turned to Pam and asked, "Do I look all right? I want to make a good first impression."

She just laughs, "Honey, you look just fine."

We see daylight at the end of the little tunnel. I hear someone hollering real loud, "Pam, Pam, Pam, over here Pam, over here."

She grabs my arm and starts pulling and steering me over to this small group of people who are waving and talking. She hugs her mother and father, turns to the rest of the gang that had met us for just a second and then she, turn back to her parents. Dad, Mother, she says, this is my Jim, the man I told you about on the phone the other night." She then introduces me to her sister Louise and one of her brothers, Tommy.

I asked about the other brother.

They say, "He couldn't get off work, but he'll be over with his wife this evening for dinner."

I asked her brother where his wife is.

He says, "She is home taking care of the kids." They have two little boys, ages one and three.

I agreed that boys that age could really keep a lady busy. Then I began feeling kind of funny because everyone was looking at me. "Pam, I think I had better go over and get our luggage." Her brother Tommy went with me. We headed for the baggage area.

Tommy says, "Jim, don't let us get to you. We're just plain people, and we love our family. We also love our big sister. I understand that you're going to be a part of the family real soon, so don't worry about anything. What you have to understand is that Pam is the mainstay of this family. She is the one that everyone depends on in a crisis. She always has been, and I guess she always will be. You know, there is generally one in every family."

Changing the subject, he said, "We saw you on TV the other night, and you did real good."

"Yeah, but part of that was luck, Tommy, especially getting up into the main chair with Robert Burns. I only won the right to go to the seat by a couple of seconds."

"Yes, but you did make it, and you did real fine once you got up there. If I remember, you only used one of your lifelines.

"Jim, it's none of my business, but what did you do before...well you know...before you got on the street?"

"Oh, that, I thought Pam probably told you. I was a professor of psychology at a university in Chicago. Please, Tommy, don't hold that against me. I think my teaching days are over."

"Jim, I think teaching is a great profession. I just wish I had enough education to be a teacher. I think it would be great." Truth is, I always thought I would make a good teacher because I love kids so much.

"Tommy, you're not just saying that to make me feel good are you?"

"Oh, no. I would like to have more education, but I had to go to work right out of high school."

"Tommy, how old are you?"

"I'm twenty-eight, why?"

"Tommy, you can still get your education if you really want it."

"I wish that was true, but I couldn't make a living and go to night school at the same time with this family of mine."

"Tommy, let's you and I talk more later. I have a plan. How about it?"

He looked kind of stunned, but said, "Sure, if you know a way I could do that, I would sure be interested."

I see our luggage coming down the ramp. We reach for the bags, show our ticket stubs, and head out the door to meet the rest of the family. They were just outside the door still talking up a storm. "Okay, Tommy, where do we go from here?"

He hollers at the group and says, "Let's go."

They all head our way, and we head out the side door toward the short-term parking area. We walk over to a Chevy Suburban. Then I knew how everyone got here and how everyone was going to get home. We put our bags behind the back seat, and everyone got inside.

By now Tommy was behind the steering wheel. "If everyone is ready, we're going home. We should get there just in time for lunch."

Mrs. Jackson said, "Sure, Tommy, what are we going to eat?"

He laughs and says, "Don't worry, Mother; I didn't tell you, but Lorene and her mother are going to have everything ready when we get home. Lorene's mother called and wanted to know if she could do anything to help, so Lorene told her she could help take care of the kids and also figure out something for lunch. I'm sure they'll have everything ready when we get home."

Pam laughs and said, "Sounds like Tommy is up to his old tricks, taking care of things."

Mr. Jackson wanted to know how long we were going to be able to stay.

"Dad, we can only stay a few days since Jim has to get to Chicago and see his folks and check on the business."

He looked surprised and asked, "What business? I didn't know Jim was in business."

Pam looks at me, and I looked at her and she said, "Okay, Jim, what do I do now?"

"Well, you might as well go ahead and tell them because you're going to have to tell them sooner or later."

All of a sudden they are all sitting on the edge of their seats, and I was being stared at.

"Mother, Dad, we hadn't really planned to tell you about Jim's financial situation at this time, but I guess it's just as good a time as any. You'll find out anyway when you come to Chicago for the wedding. It's really no secret."

Mr. Jackson says, "All right, young lady, whatever it is, you may as well spit it out. It can't be all that bad. We all know that Jim was on the street for several years, now what?"

"Well, after Jim left home and went on the street, his father passed away."

"Okay, his father passed away, a lot of people pass away." Mr. Jackson seemed a little impatient that it was taking so long to hear what Pam had to say.

"Jim's last name is Dixon, as in Dixon Plastics Manufacturing Co. When Jim's father passed away, he left the company to Jim. Jim just found out about it the other night when he talked to his mother."

Pam's mother looks at her and says, "You mean that your Jim is the owner of the Dixon Plastics Manufacturing Co.?"

Pam very quietly says, "Yes, Mother, he is."

You could have heard a pin drop in that Suburban. "You mean *the* 'Dixon Plastics Co.?"

"Yes, sir, Mr. Jackson. My father started the business and when he died, he left the business to me with the provision that I take care of my mother and my two children for the rest of their lives. Now you see why it's more important than ever that I stay on the right side of the bottle. I'll never take another drink until I know that I have really conquered it. I really don't think the drink was my weakness. I think my willpower and my lack of self-confidence was my weakness, and with Pam's help, I don't think I will ever be bothered with that problem again.

"You see, I was a college professor before I fell off the deep end and landed on the street. Now that I know what led me to do it, I feel I can control the problem without much trouble in the future. I feel that your daughter is the answer to all of my problems. With her help, we have a long and beautiful future ahead of us."

Things were real quiet for a few miles, and then Mrs. Jackson speaks up. "Jim, it's just going to take us a while to get used to the thought of having a rich man in our family. We've never been anything but poor working-class people."

"Mrs. Jackson, my father was just a poor working man who took a little bit of money left to him by his father and invested it. He worked sixteen to eighteen hours a day when he first started this business. We never had a lot of time together when I was a kid, but when we were together, we enjoyed every minute of it. We had a special relationship when I was growing up. I can say the same for my relationship with my mother. They never gave me anything but my food and clothing. If I wanted something, my father would arrange for me to work at the plant doing everything from sweeping the floors to loading the trucks after I got old enough to do that type of work. I worked for my first ten-speed bicycle. I worked for my first car. I'll admit though that he paid my way through college. He wanted me to get a good education, and he was willing for me to spend my time studying instead of working.

"When I told him that I wanted to become a teacher, he just said for me to study hard and be the best teacher that I could. He said he wanted me to be the best that I could be in whatever endeavor I chose. I had decided a long time ago that I wanted to become a teacher. He never tried to get me to follow his footsteps in the business. He did say if I ever wanted to come into the business, it would be there for me.

"I feel that now is the time since I have a young son that might want to come into the business, and I would like to be there for him, if and when he does decide to come into the plastics business. He's a good young man, and I want to make up to him for what I haven't done during the last ten years. I owe it to him and my daughter.

"Their mother passed away a couple of years after I left, and my mother has raised them for me. Unfortunately, I didn't know their mother had passed away. Now I feel that Pam can take their mother's place.

Their mother was never there for them when they needed her anyway. Pam is near the age their mother would have been, so I really think she and my daughter will get along famously. I know my mother will love her just the way she would if she had a daughter of her own. Pam is such a level-headed woman in everything I have seen her handle so far."

We arrive at their home, a nice clean, well-cared for home that showed the type of people who lived there. It was a nice medium-sized bungalow that appeared to be a three- or four-bedroom house. There was a double garage in the rear of the house with a fenced backyard. This place was a real homey looking place. You know what I mean, it had that kind of lived-in look. It was a place any family would be proud of.

Tommy pulls to the curb and parks. We all start climbing out of the suburban, when the front door of the house opens, and a young lady came running out. She was hollering Pam's name. This I found out was Lorene, Tommy's wife. Lorene's mother was right behind carrying one baby, and one was walking beside her. She also grabs Pam and gives her a big hug.

When things had calmed down a little, Pam introduces me to the ladies. Next, came the little ones. The little boy, who was walking, headed straight for Aunt Pam. She picks him up, hugs, and kissed him, and then she takes the baby in her arms and holds her and looks at her so very lovingly. Pam introduces me to the babies who were named Larry and Steven. You could see by the way she looked at the little ones that she would have made a wonderful mother. It was sad that she would never have that chance. I just hoped that someday we would have grandchildren to love and for us to take care of for our children. She would be a *wonderful* grandmother.

Everyone was finally inside, and we are told to put our bags into the back two bedrooms. I took them back with Tommy leading the way. He sayys, "Jim, this is

Mother's idea; she's a little old-fashioned. If it was up to me, you guys would share the same bedroom, but I'm not in charge."

"Tommy, you're my kind of man, but I respect and understand your mother's wishes. I totally agree with her that it wouldn't be appropriate for us to share a bedroom in their house before we're married. We can wait a couple of weeks or so. There's plenty of time for that after we're married," I added.

We went back to the living room and had a seat. Just then, Pam comes back into the room. She sits down beside me, takes my hand in hers, and says, "Now, we'll answer all of your questions. I know there must be hundreds of them, maybe millions but we will do our best to answer all of them. I feel like a school teacher saying, 'Now raise your hand if you have a question. I don't think that will be necessary, but who goes first?"

Mother asks, "Have you set a date for the wedding?"

"No, Mother, we haven't. We have to wait until we get to Chicago and see what Jim's mother and daughter have on their calendar. They're going to arrange to have some wedding dresses brought to the house and modeled for Angie and me to pick from. I understand she wants to buy them for both Angie and me. I've heard of things like that happening, but I never thought that I would be so privileged as to be able to select a wedding gown that way. The truth is I had never thought of getting married again until Jim came along and swept me off my feet. I've talked to his mother on the phone, and she seems awfully nice and helpful, but she does not want to take over the wedding plans because she says they belong to the four of us. She wants to help any way she can, but that is only at our request."

Dad asks Pam, "Whose idea was it to take our whole family to Chicago for the wedding?"

She looked at Jim and said, "Daddy, that was Jim's idea. He wants Angie's family and Wayne or, Pug, as he is called, to ask his family to come also. Jim has offered to pay for all of the transportation for everyone."

"Mr. Jackson, can I call you something like maybe your first name if you don't mind? I feel kind of awkward referring to you as Mr. Jackson."

He laughs and says, "Sure, Jim, I'd like that a lot better. My name is Art, and Mother's name is Nora. Feel free to call us by our names."

"Well, Art, I hope you don't get the wrong idea when I offer to pay for the expenses, but I want this to be a family affair. The guests will be primarily family, and that's the way we would like it. I think the girls feel the same way. With just the families, there'll be quite a few people.

I hope you won't hold it against me for having a little money so I can do these things. I promise you it won't be a habit if that's what you're worried about. I really don't just throw money around. I only put money where people need and deserve it, like some of my friends in Ft. Worth that have stood by me all of these years —through thick and thin. They have proved to me what real friends are. We'll talk a little more later about some other things I have in mind. I would like your input if you don't mind. I would love to pick your brain on a couple of things."

"Well, I don't know if I can be of any help, but you can ask; and if I'm capable of helping you, I sure will be glad to do my best."

Art ask, "What about sleeping facilities? Can we stay at a hotel or motel while we're there so we won't be a bother?"

"No sir Art, you can't. What I mean, Art, is that we actually have about twelve bedrooms available at our home including the ones over the garages and the guest house on the back of the property."

He smiles and says, "Well, that ought to take care of the families. I hope there is something we can do while we're there to help earn our keep."

"Art, that will all be taken care of. Nora, you can help the girls pick out their bridal outfits and anything else they might need help doing. I know Angie's mother recently passed away, so it will be just her father and brother and his family. Pug or, Wayne, as we now call him, will have his family, which consists of his father, sister, and brother Neil and his family. The housing won't be a problem. We expect Tommy, Jerry, Louise, and their families if they can make it. We hope to go out on the town one evening after the wedding. We'll go to some nice club that has a show and good food. I doubt if the food will be as good as that at the Black Angus, but we'll try.

"I'm sure you've eaten at the Black Angus when you've come to visit Pam. I'll always hold a place near and dear to my heart for the Black Angus and big Ernie Hasnah. They helped me find Pam."

Pam and I continued to sit and answer questions for a few minutes more, and then Lorene announces, "If anyone is hungry, we have some sandwiches and other things in the kitchen."

Tommy and Art give me that *come on* look, which said they would like to have a sandwich, so I joined them. "A sandwich sounds great."

Nora says, "Art loves his iced tea. Would you like to have tea also?"

"I sure would. Well, at least we have one good thing in common. You can't beat iced tea for a drink in the summer."

Art and Nora just looked at each other and smile.

Pam tells her mother and the others, "It won't do any good to offer him a beer because he'll just thank you for the offer and refuse the drink. He's at least, for the time being, totally committed to being a teetotaller. Nothing stronger than tea and Cokes for him, at least for the time being that is. Maybe later, after he's sure just what made him an alcoholic, he might try to have a social drink once in a while, but he just doesn't want to get back on the bottle, and he feels this is the best way to do it. I intend to help him do things the way he wants to do them."

"That's my girl," says Art. "Hang in there and help your man when he needs help, Honey. That's what your mother has always done for me. Without her behind me, I would have been in trouble many times.

"Jim, I hope you know that Pam generally means exactly what she says. She never has been known to mince words. She doesn't change her mind very easy either."

After lunch everyone adjourns to the patio at the rear of the house. The weather is great, only about eighty degrees with just a light breeze. We walked out to the patio, and I was absolutely taken in by the beautiful backyard. There were roses, mums, peonies, and other flowers blooming in very well-manicured flower beds. The grass was neatly edged up to the curbs enclosing the flower beds. I was really taken in by the flow of colors in the beds around the yard. There was a little windmill in the northeast corner of the yard.

I ask about the windmill and was told by Art that it was for the grandchildren. They loved to watch it go round and round. Art had painted flowers on each blade of the fan on the windmill. This made a beautiful collage of colors for the children when it was turning, and then when it stopped, it had beautiful colored flowers for them to see. I could see why they would love it.

This was a house filled with love. It reminded me of the love that had been in our home when I had been growing up. There had been very little dissension in our home. There had always been so much love between my parents, and that love had been passed on to me. I had always known there was more than enough love to go around.

I guess that was one thing that had hurt me so bad when my wife had started playing around. She didn't seem to have any love left – for me or the children. She seemed to forget how to show her affection for our family. I couldn't remember ever hearing her tell the children that she loved them. I didn't remember her telling me that she loved me either unless she wanted something. I guess I had just been too weak and too used to family love to handle it.

Now that I know what was going on, I think I can handle it. I feel that Pam and I will have more than enough love to go around to the children and grandchildren. I knew how Pam felt about children. Since she couldn't have children, she just seemed to love them that much more. I wondered how she would feel about Johnny and Jennifer and any grandchildren they might present us with in the future. Now I have no doubts in my mind whatever.

When I start thinking of such things, I realize just how much I love Pam. I know it has only been a short time, but everything seems so right. It seems that we had known each other for years instead of days.

We passed the afternoon just visiting and answering questions. I felt by now that Art and Nora knew quite a bit about me. They also knew what I hoped to be able to do in the future, what my plans were for Pam and me and the rest of the family. This also gave me a chance to talk a little more to Tommy about that education he wanted to have so badly.

While his dad and wife were with us, I put a question to him that surprised all of them. I could tell it surprised them by the way they all reacted to it. I asked Tommy if he would go to college if he could and still make a living for his family.

He said, "Sure, I would love to go to college, but that's impossible."

Just about that time Pam came back out to the patio.

"Tommy, I want to make you a proposition. If I pay you to go to college, will you go to work for us here in Norfolk at our plant when you graduate?"

He had a quizzical look on his face. "What do you mean?"

"Tommy, I mean that I will be willing to pay you to go to college locally if you will get either an engineering degree, preferably a chemical engineering degree, or a business administration degree. I feel that I can pay you $75,000 a year for four years if you will give me your word that you will go to work for us at our plant here in Norfolk when you graduate."

He looks at Lorene and says, "Well, I guess I would be a fool to say no to a proposition like that."

I ask Lorene what she thought of the idea. She smiles and says, "It sounds too good to be true."

"Tommy, I'll even make it better than that. If you will go ahead and get your MBA or your Masters Degree in chemical engineering, I will pay for that time also. You should be able to do that in five or six years. Your pay will be the same as if you were working for us. You'll have the same benefits such as hospitalization, etc.

"Art, how do you and Nora feel about this? I want the entire family to voice their opinions. I don't want you to think that I am trying to buy your love or respect. The boys will work hard, and they will earn every penny they get by showing me some good grades.

"When I first talked to Tommy, he said he would have liked to go to college, but he couldn't go to school and make a living for his family. All I am asking is that he work for us when he is through with college. He would only be 33 or 34 years old when he graduates. He'll have a job at the plant the day he receives his diploma.

"Tommy, this isn't going to be a free ride. You'll be treated just like any other employee, and you will have to earn any raises in pay or position you may get. Does that sound reasonable to you? This also means that you can go to school twelve months a year if you want to. If you don't want to go to school all year, you can work at the plant during the summer."

Pam walks over and put her arm around my shoulder, "Jim, you didn't tell me you were going to do this."

"Honey, I didn't know I was going to do it until I met Tommy and found that he was very sincere about wanting an education. Anyone who wants an education that badly is someone I *can* and *want* to help. After I meet Jerry, I might offer him the same thing. It depends on how he and his wife feel about this type of commitment."

Tommy comes right back at me with, "Jim, you just might have another employee in Jerry. He and I have just recently talked about going to night school and pursuing more education. I'm sure he would be more than enthusiastic about a proposition such as yours."

"Tommy, do you know where our plant is here in Norfolk?"

"Sure, I know right where it is. I go by there all the time. It's only about a mile or so north of here. Have you ever seen it, Jim?"

"I haven't seen it in a long time. I remember coming with my father many years ago when I was in college. You see, Dad would have liked me to come into the business, but I wanted to be a teacher. I felt a calling to teach. Now I feel it's time for me to do what my father always wanted me to do, and that's to come into the plastics business."

The conversation starts flying among Art, Nora, Pam, Lorene, and Tommy. Before long I look at my watch and realize we have been visiting and drinking tea for almost four hours.

Suddenly Pam jumps up and says, "That's the front door." She heads for the front of the house as fast as she can go. I hear a squealing and a lot of chatter and laughter. I hear adults and children. Pam comes back into the house with her arms around a man on her left and a girl on her right, preceded by two other children. I stand up to greet more members of my future family.

Pam introduced Jerry and his wife Betty, and their children Shawn and R. J. They are all clinging to Pam as if she were the Matriarch of the family. Everybody is talking at the same time, while I am just standing and listening.

Suddenly someone says, "Jim, we're sorry, we didn't mean to cut you out, but it's been quite a while since we've seen Pam, and we have dozens of questions for her."

Louise asked Pam, "Is it true that you and Jim are going to be married?"

"Yes, it's true, and Jim has said that if you and Ralph and the kids would like to come to the wedding, he would be glad to pay for your transportation and expenses. How about it?"

"I'll have to talk to Ralph to see if he can get off work. If he can get off work, we would love to come."

Believe it or not, the door bell rang again, and it was Ralph and Louise's children. Once again they all started talking at the same time.

Finally Tommy told everyone to hold on for just a minute. "Jerry, you're not going to believe what Jim has to offer us." He went on to tell Jerry that he could go to school on a salary if he just promised to go to work for the Dixon Plastics Mfg. Co. upon graduation. "The other thing is that you should get a degree in either engineering or Business Administration; and if you want to go ahead and get your Masters in Business Administration, you'll be allowed to do that."

Jerry turned, looked me right straight in the eye, and said, "Jim, is he telling it straight? You're willing to pay us to go to college and get an education if we just promise to go to work for your company?"

"That's right, Jerry; all I need is your word. Now don't think this is all goody goody on my part. I'll be able to write off your expenses since I'll have you on the company payroll as employees. When you guys are through and go to work full time, you'll be eligible for stock options and retirement benefits and an investment program where you put in a part of your salary, and we will match it. You don't have to give me an answer right away, but when you do decide, just let me know."

"Hell, man, we don't have to think over a proposition like that."

"Jerry, you know that you will be treated just like any other employee once you go to work. Just because you will be my brothers-in-law won't cut any special mustard. I just want you both to be aware of that."

They both looked at each other and simultaneously said, "Jim, you've got a deal."

I turned to Louise and said, "Louise, I'm not forgetting Ralph. If he's interested, I'm sure we can work out a similar deal. We always need good, dedicated employees. People we can trust. Good men never have been that easy to find when it comes to hard work."

"I think Ralph would be very interested."

I asked Ralph if he was interested.

"Sure," he said, "it's just that I'm more inclined to be the salesman type employee."

"That's just fine; you can get a degree in engineering. That would make you more knowledgeable of the material and what goes into the manufacturing of it. That knowledge would, of course, make you a better salesman if that's what you're interested in. With knowledge of the product like that and a good personality, you could make a lot of money. You will have plenty of time to think about it."

Nora told everyone it was almost time for dinner.

We had been talking for several hours, and time had really flown by. Pam came over, hugged my neck, kissed me on the cheek, and said, "Jim, you absolutely amaze me. I never expected you to do anything like this for my family."

"Pam, I'm not just thinking of your family; I am thinking of three good employees for the company. People I can trust. People I can depend on.

"I think your mother needs you in the kitchen to help with dinner," I said, changing the subject.

She gave me another hug and kiss on the cheek and headed for the kitchen. The girls all went in to help in the kitchen while the children and men continued to sit on the patio drinking tea and talking.

Ralph finally asked, "Do you really own Dixon Plastics Mfg. Co., and are you really willing to do this for us guys?"

"That's right, Ralph; I inherited the company from my father; and since you guys are going to be family real soon and you seem to be interested in getting an education, I'd like to help. As they've told you, there's one stipulation involved. You have to agree to go to work for the company when you graduate. I will also help you get your masters in engineering or you can get an MBA if that is what you would prefer. All you have to do is agree, and you'll each receive $75,000 per year with medical and all of the other side benefits."

The girls called us in to dinner. As we walked into the kitchen, Ralph comes over and put his hand on my shoulder, and says, "I've heard of sugar daddies, but you beat anything I have ever seen. You aren't only nice to Pam, but you're great to her family too."

"Ralph, just don't disappoint me, and everything will be fine."

"Jim, I'll work my tush off to do what you expect from me, and I'm sure Tommy and Jerry will do the same."

"Sounds good to me. Well, boys let's go and eat."

I didn't know who had done all of this work, but there was enough ham and trimmings, potato salad, coleslaw, green beans, corn on the cob, and I didn't know what else. Next, there was pie and cake for dessert. Believe it or not, there was a lemon pie. Somebody had been talking to her mother before we had arrived. I didn't mind though.

If you'd seen pictures by Norman Rockwell of people at Thanksgiving and Christmas dinners, well that would tell you what we were looking at. I would swear these people sure did know how to cook and feed. I ate so much I thought that I would pop before I got through with the pie and coffee.

After dinner we adjourned to the living room where we talked, talked, and talked. They asked questions about my life on the street and my friends in Ft. Worth that I wanted to go back and help. Once, Pam asked them to talk about something else because she was sure I was tired of talking about those days.

I told them, "I'm not the least bit tired of talking about those people because those people acted as my family for almost ten years. They looked after me, and I looked after them. I'm not ashamed of my friends back in Ft. Worth."

At about 11:00 p.m. someone looked at me and said, "Jim, you look awfully tired. If you'd like to go to bed and get a good night's sleep, none of us would object. We know that you've been under a lot of strain the past couple of weeks."

Nora tells me, "We have a lot of girl talk to do since we haven't seen each other in quite a while. If you're tired, don't feel embarrassed about going to bed before we do. We will try our best not to be too loud."

"Ladies, that was a wonderful dinner," I said. I went over and kissed Pam goodnight. The men said goodnight, and I headed for the bedroom. I really was tired tonight, so I appreciated the chance to get some rest.

I got to bed, and I doubt my head did anything more than hit the pillow before I was asleep.

The next thing I heard was someone knocking on the door and asking how I would like to have a cup of coffee.

I gave out a very positive, "Yes," because I recognized Pam's voice.

She came in the door looking absolutely radiant, such a beautiful woman and to think that she was all mine. I sat up in bed as she started to hand me the coffee. She asked, "What'll you give me for it?"

"My best offer right now is a Yankee dime."

"Great, I'll settle for that," she said, and she bent down so I could give her a great big good morning kiss. That was when I held her real close and told her how much I missed her last night. Damn, that woman smelled so wonderful every time I held her that I had to admit my mind began to wander. I told her how much I loved her, and I wished we were alone.

"Well, big boy, you're not the only one who was lonesome last night. I could get used to having you in my bed real easy. In fact, I'm already getting used to having you there." She looked around to be sure that her mother wasn't listening. She gave me another kiss and told me that breakfast would be ready in a few minutes.

I ask, "Will I have time for a quick shower?"

"Yes, if you hurry."

I gulped down my coffee and head for the shower. I take a real fast shower, shaved, and got dressed in about ten minutes or less. I couldn't remember doing all that so quickly before. After I showered and dressed, I headed for the kitchen.

Boy, the smell in the kitchen was wonderful. It brought back memories of when I had been a kid at home. I smelled sausage, and then I saw the eggs on the plate just as Nora took a big pan of biscuits out of the oven.

Art was already at the table with his cup of coffee waiting on the rest of breakfast. He nodded to me to come on over and sit down beside him. Pam offered to warm up our coffee at about the same time. Everyone sat down, and we had a wonderful family breakfast with gossip and everything.

I am beginning to realize just what a wonderful family this is. They treat me as if I had been a member of the family for a long time.

Art surprised me by saying that he had never known anyone so willing to help someone else get an education as I had been with the boys.

I explained to Art that I'd always felt that education was the best way to get ahead in this world. "I feel that if a person has the ability to help others get an education and doesn't do it, he is missing one of the most wonderful feelings he could ever have. The boys seem to want to get ahead; and as I've said before, it's not easy to get well- educated, loyal employees. I feel that if I help the boys get their education, they'll be very special employees."

Pam chimed in that she agreed with me a hundred percent. She tells her dad that she also agreed with my wanting to help my friends in Texas. I really enjoyed the gabfest we had here with the folks. I really liked them, and I hoped they liked me.

Pam asked if I would like to do anything special while I was here in the Norfolk area.

"Nothing special, except that I might like to drop by our office while I'm in the area."

"That's fine. I asked because I would just like for you to meet some more of the family while we're here."

"That would be fine, Hon I'd like to meet all of them."

On the morning of day three, Pam asks, "Would you like to go to the plant today and visit the officers there?"

"I think today would be a good day for that."

"Jim," Art offered, "I'll be more than happy to act as your chauffeur if you would like."

"Art, I think that's a great idea."

After breakfast, Art and I headed for our branch operation here on the outskirts of Norfolk. Art was a good driver, and I was glad because I hadn't driven much over the past ten years. "This is a beautiful area of the country. I had forgotten just how pretty the area around Norfolk is. I was only here with my father when I was a young man, but I did remember what the countryside looked like, and it's still just as pretty as I remembered," I told Art.

The Norfolk Branch Manager

We arrived at the plant which had grown quite a bit since I had been here with my father. This was going to be quite a surprise to the plant manager when I walk in and tell him who I am.

We parked in the visitor's area and headed for the front door. We walk in and are met by a very nice young lady who introduces herself and asked if she could be of help.

I introduced myself as Jim Dixon and explained that I would like to see the manager. She picks up the phone on her desk and said, "Mr. Wells, there is a Mr. Jim Dixon here to see you." She hung up the phone and tells us that Mr. Wells would be with us in just a minute and asks us to have a seat.

In just a minute, I heard a door down the hall leading off the lobby open, a man comes walking down the hall toward the lobby.

The man comes into the lobby, walks right over to us, and introduces himself. "I'm Frank Wells, and you must be Jim Dixon."

"Yes, sir, that's right, and this is Mr. Art Jackson, a friend of mine."

"Jim, you don't remember me, but you and I met years ago when you were just a young man still in college. You were on a trip here with your father. I was just a plant foreman at the time. We knew you might be coming by because your mother called and said you might be in the Norfolk area. She said that if she knew you as well as she thought she did, she was pretty sure you just might want to come by the plant since you're the new owner. We were all very sorry to lose your father. He was the kind of boss and owner that everyone likes to work for.

"Since his death, your mother has been sitting on the Board of Directors, and she's a very special lady as she has proved so many times. She's hired personnel to fill vacated jobs over the years that have all worked out great. She's a great judge of people. She has stated on several occasions that she believed you would be back someday, and she was right. We're all very glad to have you here to help your mother and the business since you grew up in the business and know what it's all about.

"By the way, Jim, how does it feel to be the winner of that 'So You Want to Be a Millionaire' program? Did they really give you a million dollars for knowing the answers to those questions?"

"Frank, they gave me a million dollars, but it wasn't really a million dollars after Uncle Sam took his cut out of it. But, it wasn't too bad when you stop and think about it.

"Frank, can you tell me if you have a scholarship program being sponsored by the firm here in Norfolk?"

"No, we sure don't at this time. We used to sponsor kids in high school and give scholarships, but somehow it just went by the wayside."

"Frank, how about bringing it up at your next Board or business meeting and see how they would feel about reinstating it. I'm very much in favor of sponsoring scholarships and helping young people get a good education. I think a plant this size could sponsor at least two kids a year. That would give you eight kids to sponsor at the end of four years. What I mean by a scholarship is that you help these kids through college for four years if they keep their grades up. If we cut some here and there, I'll bet you can find a way to do that. If you have trouble doing that, maybe I could help you from the general fund. That would mean you give two new scholarships each year and continue to help those other students who continue in college and get good passing grades. How do you feel about that?

"Frank, what I'm talking about is maybe about $30,000.00 per student, per year. That would mean that the end of four years an output of $240,000 per year, and we can write off at least fifty percent or more of it. I'm not sure of the tax codes now, but we might be able to write it all off. See what you can do and let me know. I'll be in the Chicago office in a couple of months, and you can contact me there.

"In the meantime, I'm getting married to Art's daughter. We're going to be busy in Texas for about a month getting a few things going there, but if you need to talk to me, you can call my mother, and she'll know where I am and how to contact me."

Frank agrees that he thinks this plant could work out a scholarship program that would meet with our approval. Frank says, "As soon as we have it worked out, we'll submit it to you for approval."

"Frank, you know what I would like, so I'll just leave it in your hands. No need to contact me. I trust your decision. Dad trusted you, so I know I can also.

"Frank, it was nice meeting you again after all these years. Now could you show us around the plant before I have to leave?"

Frank was more than happy to show us around the plant and introduce us to the department heads.

"Now I'd like to meet some of the other employees besides just department heads. I feel it's the worker as well as the department head that makes a business what it is."

He introduces Art and me to several of the people who were working in the production area. I asked him to introduce me to the maintenance men and the custodians. He calls a couple of men over and introduced us to them. They were the custodians. I was glad to meet them, and I explained that my father had made me start by sweeping floors and keeping the place clean, and that I considered the way a plant looked inside and out as very important to the community and to the morale of the employees.

The maintenance men were next. We had a nice visit with them. These men were very well versed in the engineering and maintenance of the production machinery. These were the backbone of every plant, regardless of what was being produced.

After meeting these folks, I told Frank that I had to go now since my lady had some plans for this afternoon. Art and I thank him and head for the car.

As we get into the car, Art says, "Jim, you're really serious about this education thing aren't you?"

"Sure I am, that's not just the future of our company, but it's the future of our country. If our kids are not educated, we're in trouble."

He just smiles and says he couldn't agree more. We head for the house, and by this time it is nearing lunch time.

When we arrived back at the house, we find what we had expected. Lunch. These ladies were really on the ball.

As I walked in, I could see a question in Pam's eyes. "Jim, I have a favor to ask of you."

"Okay, what's the favor?"

"Well, there are a few of my old high school girl friends and their husbands who would like to meet you, so they've planned a little get-acquainted party after dinner this evening."

"That's just fine with me, if you want to go see your friends, I don't see why we shouldn't. I'm going to ask you to go and meet some friends of mine, so why shouldn't I meet your friends?"

"See, Mother, I told you he wouldn't object. That's why I love him so much. He always thinks about the other person before thinking of himself. We can have dinner here and then run over to Margie's house and visit with all of the old gang."

Art and I sit around and talk until the girls are ready with lunch. The food was great, as usual.

I tell Pam, "I need to make some phone calls after lunch and let the gang in Texas know what's going on and when we hope to get back to Ft. Worth. I also need to talk to Mother and let her know about when we'll be in Chicago and what our plans are."

"Jim, why don't you go into the bedroom and use that phone; that way you'll have some privacy."

I go back to the bedroom and call Texas. I phon the Sanctuary first, and Lynn answers. I visited with him a while, and he fills me in on all of the activities of the gang. "They're still working on the damage done by the tornado."

That surprised me, but it also really made me feel good. He tells me they are staying sober and away from the bottle, and that made me feel even better. I had to admit I had been a little worried after I left because I was afraid the work would slow down and they would go back to the bottle. Maybe they really were going to remain sober. I couldn't think of anything that would please me more than for them to keep their word.

"Lynn, I'm getting married in about a week. Pug and I are both getting married. We're having a double wedding at my mother's home in Chicago. I know this sounds awfully quick, but I couldn't be more sure of anything in my life, and Pug feels the same way about his lady. You'll meet them when we get back to Ft. Worth. I'm sure you'll love both of these ladies just as we do.

"I want to talk to you about helping with the Sanctuary's finances. I'd like to set up a trust fund for the Sanctuary, which would give you an income for a long time. Just the interest on the account should take care of a big share of your expenses.

"I also want to try to help Doc get a storefront clinic set up. I think I can get Dr. Davis to help us with it.

"I have plans for the rest of the guys also. I'm looking forward to coming back and getting these things started. Tell Annie and the gang that I called and that I'll see them in a couple of weeks. Thanks, Lynn, for all of your help and your prayers. I really need them in times like these."

Then, I called my mother. She was surprised that I called while I was at Pam's home with her folks. I explain, "We're going to be there in about five days, and Pug and Angie will also be coming to Chicago. We're all looking forward to being with my family. We're also looking forward to the weddings."

"Jim, I have the shop all lined up to bring the wedding dresses out for selection by the girls. I have hired more help for the household chores when you get here.

"We're really looking forward to meeting Pam's, Angie's, and Pug's families. This should be a wonderful time for all of us. It's going to be so good to have you home for a few days with your children."

"Mother, this is not going to be for just a few days. Well, it will be for this time, but I intend to come back home permanently after I get things going in Texas.

I want to go to work with you in the business. I feel that if I go to work in the company, maybe Johnny will want to come into the business. I think that would be the capper for me to see him in the business also. I just want you and Pam to become close friends and for the kids to love her as I do.

"Mother, she's a very loving person, and I just can't wait until the kids are married and have some grandchildren for us to love and fawn over and spoil. It'll be fun to spoil them and then send them home.

"No, Mother, I'm only kidding. I just wanted to call and let you know where we are with our plans. We're going back to New York day after tomorrow. After we wash our clothes and rest a day or two, we intend to head to Chicago. We'll let you know when we'll arrive so someone can meet us at the airport."

"Jim, there will definitely be someone to meet you. There'll probably be all three of us if you don't mind," Mother added.

"Mother, I would be disappointed if you three weren't there.

"Mother, can you do me a favor and send me a cashier's check to the office here? I have put the check for my winnings in the bank to hold for me, and I need a little cash.

"Can you call Frank Wells and ask him if he can manage to get me another twenty thousand dollars in cash. I would sure appreciate it. Have him call me when he has it, and I'll go by and pick it up. I appreciate your calling him for me. Thank you, Mother. I love you, and I'll see you soon."

I hang up and head back to the den where the rest of the folks are. Pam greets me with a big hug and asked, "Is your mother all right?"

"She is expecting us, and she is anxiously awaiting our arrival. Mother assures me there will be at least three people there to meet us and take us home when we arrive."

Nora asked if I would like a glass of tea.

"Of course, I want some tea," I said jokingly. "Nora, that mother of mine is really looking forward to meeting you and the family. I tell you, Nora, this is really going to be something big in my mother's life.

"Pam, Mother has already contacted the store about bringing the dresses to the house."

Pam explained to Nora what Mother was doing concerning the dresses. Nora couldn't get over Mother's having a store come to the house with wedding dresses for the girls to choose from. She thought that was great.

We all continued to talk about everything from the stock market to religion. Nora was happy to find out that I had been raised in the Catholic religion. She always worried when people of different faiths married.

"Nora, Pug and Angie are of different faiths, but I don't think that will make one bit of difference." She hoped they were both broad minded.

I reassured her. "They are or else they wouldn't have gotten this far."

"Jim, I think you're probably right about that."

I walk over and hug her neck, which surprised everyone.

"Nora, I think you're going to like Pug."

Pam couldn't believe what she had just seen. "Jim, when did this start?"

"Oh, I took a liking to this lady when I first saw her. I hope it's all right with you and Art if I hug my mother-in-law's neck once in a while."

They both laugh and give me an okay.

"Now, back to our conversation. I know you have met Angie, and I understand you like her. Pug is really easy to get to know. Heck, Nora, if you like me, I know you'll like Pug."

Art just laughs and says, "Nora, you know you're just talking. You'll like everyone you always do. She's just talking, Jim. She's real loving and easy going, just like her daughters."

"I kind of thought that or else I wouldn't have risked hugging her neck. She might have slapped me, but I thought I would take that chance anyway."

Pam's Friends

After a few hours Pam comes over and suggests, "Jim, you might want to get ready to go over to Margie's if you need to change into something more comfortable. They're all going to be comfortable, so you really don't need a suit and tie unless you would feel more comfortable that way."

"No way, Hon. I think it'll be a good idea to change into a sport shirt and slacks or something like that." I head for the bedroom and return in about ten minutes without the tie and suit. I have a sport shirt, slacks, and sport coat on. Real comfortable outfit.

"Now you look more comfortable, Darling. You look like the Jim I love most."

"You sure do look less formal, Jim, and I agree with Pam, you do look more comfortable," Nora comments.

"Thank you, Nora."

"Daddy, do you mind if we borrow your car for a while to go over to Margie's house?"

"Sounds like the good old days when you wanted to borrow the car to go over to Margie's house."

We all got a laugh out of that. I asked Art if that used to be a problem.

"Only when I needed the car.

"Pam, the keys are in the car. You guys go ahead and tell Margie and Bill that I said hello."

Pam informs me that Margie married her high school sweetheart. They had been sweethearts from junior high school. "I don't think they ever dated anyone else. They fell in love, and it looks like it's going to last forever.

"Let's go, Jim. You drive. I'm sorry, Honey, I forgot. I'll drive till you get your license."

We arrived at Margie's house, and there are about a dozen cars parked on the street near the house.

"Pam, just what's going on?" I ask.

She assures me she don't know.

"Really, Hon, I didn't expect so many people to be here."

"Well, Jim, you may as well get ready, so let's go in."

When we reach the door, it flung open like an automatic door opener was handling it. There they stood at least twenty or more people in the living room. One of them started yelling and grabbed Pam around the neck, squealing all the time. Another seven or eight people flocked to the door, and we couldn't even get in. They were overflowing out onto the porch now, all of them talking, laughing, and squealing.

I had just kind of stepped back, when a real nice-looking, big man came over, took me by the arm, and said, "Hi, you must be Jim. I'm Bill."

"Thank God, Bill. I didn't know just what was happening for a minute."

"Jim, you must be kind of dumbfounded by all the fuss and ruckus. Let's sneak past the girls and go back to the den where we can meet the other guys and get something to drink."

As we headed by Pam and Margie, Pam looks up at me, and I wave as we walked by. She just laughs and continues to answer questions. When we reach the den, Bill introduced me to all of the guys who are standing around.

Bill asks if he could get me a beer. I started to say no, when he said, "Man, I'm sorry. I forgot."

"No need to apologize. I'm used to it by now," I say.

I turn to the guys and say, "Fellows, I'd like to have a beer with you, but you see I'm an alcoholic, and I'd prefer a diet Coke right now if you don't mind."

You know what happened then? Every one of them came over, shook my hand, and said they admired me for being able to stay away from the bottle. A couple of them said they thought they should learn how to do it. Sometimes it seems to get hold of them.

"I tell you what, boys. The only way to do it is to add up the plus side and the minus side. If the plus side outweighs the minus side, then go ahead and have a drink. If the minus outweighs the plus, then put the drink down and realize just how much your life and family mean to you and appreciate it. It's not easy to do. Some need the help of AA, but some can do it by themselves.

"I did it by myself after I got hurt in the storm and ended up in the hospital for four days without a drink. After the four days, I realized that I really didn't need the bottle, I had just thought I did. I'm sure most of you know the rest of the story."

"You mean the program and your winning the million dollars?"

"Yeah, that's part of it. After the program I heard from my family and found that I had missed my father's death and funeral. That made me more resolute than ever to stay sober."

They understood and admired me for it.

One of the boys said, "Jim, I don't mean to be nosy, but how did you meet Pam?"

I told the story; and when I had finished, I asked why he wanted to know.

He says, "I'll tell you something you probably don't know. Your girl friend was voted Most Popular Girl in High School our senior year. She was also voted the most beautiful girl that same year. She was the head cheerleader for three years in high school and chosen the School Sweetheart two years in a row. No one had ever done that before, and no one has ever done that since. I'll bet she never told you anything about that, did she?"

I was totally dumfounded because I knew she was beautiful, and I knew that she had a perky personality that would have made her popular. "I can see why she was chosen the School Sweetheart. I'm just astounded that she never once mentioned any of that to me," I responded.

Bill asked, "Did she also tell you that she was the Valedictorian of her graduating class? She had several scholarship offers, but she got married instead. She chose marriage instead of college. When her husband was killed, she just went into a shell for a long time. That's when she lost the baby, and after that she decided she needed a change, so she moved to New York City.

"Man, oh, man, Jim, you've got yourself one hell of a woman. Most of the guys in this room have been in love with her at one time or another."

Pam and Margie come into the den, trailed by the rest of the girls. "Well, Jim, I see that Bill introduced you to the guys. As you may be aware by now, we were all very close in high school. We were kind of like a gang that did things together – except for Margie and Bill. They always paired up from the seventh grade on through high school," Pam informed me.

Pam started introducing me to the rest of the ladies. I generally prided myself with having a very good memory, but my mind was totally boggled trying to remember all of those names.

I finally said, "*Hold up, everybody!* If you'll just have patience with me, I'm sure that before the evening is over, I'll get your names straight, but for right now, just please bear with me in case I call you by the wrong name."

This brought a big hoot from the crowd. "Don't worry, we know who you are and that's what counts."

One of the girls wanted to know, "Just how in the world did you ever get Pam to say "yes"? She hasn't so much as had a date in the past six or seven years or maybe longer."

"Well, maybe I'm a good salesman."

One of the guys says, "Yeah, I hear that you sell a lot of plastics."

"No, I don't sell it, we have people who do the selling. I haven't been around for the past ten years. I'm sure you all know that I was on the street all of that time. I'm not proud of it, but I feel that in some ways it has made me smarter and stronger. I know what I did wrong, and now I feel I can prevent that from ever happening again, especially if I have Pam to help me."

Another guy wants to know if I really own the Dixon Plastics Manufacturing Co.

"Let's put it this way Buddy, my father left it to me when he died. I inherited it. I was just a lowly college professor before I went on the street. I had always had a feeling that I wanted to be a teacher, so my father encouraged me to do that even though he wanted me to be in the business with him. My mother told me he always felt that I would eventually come into the business, and you know what? He was right, I am going into the business, but I have a lot of things I need to do first before I get too involved with the business.

Another of the guys asks, "How in the world did you manage to answer all of those questions? We were watching you, and I flunked out at about $4,000.00."

"Well, I've always been blessed with a good memory. I read a lot as a kid and in college. I had always watched the news on TV even as a very young kid, and I remembered what I saw and heard. I guess I was just lucky. I used to discuss a lot of things like that with my father. He always encouraged me to pay attention and to ask questions. If he didn't know the answer to a question I might ask, he would go and find the answer and then come back and give me the information I was looking for. He was very special that way. We didn't have a lot of time together, but what time we did have was always very special time for me."

Bill says, "Jim, he sounds like a real great father." I have to admit "Bill, I always thought he was very special."

One of the girls says, "Jim, you still haven't told us how you met Pam and got her to go out with you."

I told the story again.

They couldn't believe their ears. One of the girls looks straight at me and says, "You mean you met her at the restaurant, and she agreed to go out with you?"

"Well, it wasn't exactly like that. I became friends with her boss who was a friend to another man I had become friends with, and he kind of helped me convince her,

"Now hold on, big boy," Pam said, "by that time I had already decided that one way or another you were going to ask me for a date. I don't know how I would have managed it if you hadn't asked, but I would have found a way, even if I had to ask you. I wasn't about to let you get away. Even before I knew who you were, I had made up my mind that you were going to be mine. The girls will tell you that I have always been one who makes up her mind to do something and then does it."

There were a lot of "yea's" from the girls, which I assume meant they agreed with what she had just said.

"Girls, I told you about him, and now that you've met him, can you blame me?"

"Hell, Pam, you're embarrassing me."

"The truth will out every time," she says as she hugged my neck and kissed me on the cheek. The truth is that I asked him to marry me, and he said yes."

"Oh, man, what a woman I have on my hands. Pam, why didn't you tell me about your high school days?"

She laughed and says, "I didn't want to run you off. I have a favor to ask."

"Well, okay, ask and if I can do it, you know I will."

"Can we invite the gang to Chicago some weekend after we get settled?"

I look around, wink at Bill and very slowly I say, "Well, I guess we could put up with them for one weekend." Now I was the one who was laughing.

"Sure, Honey, we can have all of them up for the weekend. I think that would be a lot of fun. We'll need to buy out some club so we can have it all to ourselves" I added.

Bill looks at me with an embarrassed look on his face, "Jim, we don't want to put you in a compromising position. You know what I mean."

"Bill, I can always drink Coke, and Pam can drink anything she wants to drink. That would be just fine with me."

Pam lets them know, "If Jim drinks Coke, then I drink Coke."

For the next three or four hours we just visited, got acquainted, and had a lot of fun. These were some real fine friends, and they all really did care a lot about Pam. This was real easy to see from the way they looked at her and talked to her. These were real friends, not just sunny weather friends. I was very happy that Pam had such friends.

As the evening went on, they started leaving one by one, or I should say one couple at a time. Most had to get up and go to work the next day. Some of the girls were school teachers, and they had to prepare for their classes the next day.

As they leave, Pam and I say good-bye and let them know how good it was to see them and how glad I was to have met Pam's special friends. I reminded all of them that we had a date in Chicago after Pam and I got settled into our own home.

Finally, it is just Bill, Margie, Pam, and I left. We sit and have a cup of coffee and visit some more. I really liked these people. They were just good, honest-working people. They were so sincere about their love for Pam. This made a big impression on me. This wasn't fair-weather friendship, but the real thing. I wished I had had friends like this. I might have again some day.

I remembered the names of several people who used to be my real friends. I was looking forward to that again. At least, I hoped that some of them would still remember me and have something to do with me after what I had done.

Pam was ready to go home, so she suggested that we head for the door. We say goodnight to these fine people and head for the car. They follow us all the way to the car holding our hands, and saying good-bye. We told them it wouldn't be good-bye for long since they were coming to Chicago as soon as we were settled. They agreed that they were coming to visit us.

Pam and Margie were hugging and saying good-bye, while Bill and I were shaking hands and doing the same. Pam hugged Bill's neck and kissed him, and I was surprised when Margie came over and hugged my neck and kissed me and told me to be good to Pam because she deserved some happiness. I assured her that I would love her and take good care of her. She told me she felt that I would do just that, and she appreciated it.

We head for Pam's home. When we arrive, the folks were still awake. They wanted to talk about all of the old gang and find out how everyone was doing. We visited for a while, and then we realized it was past midnight. I had wondered why we were getting a little sleepy.

We talked a while longer, and then I had to excuse myself. I apologized, but I was very tired after the day I had had, so I gave Pam a little good night kiss, and headed for the bedroom. I got into bed, and again I doubted if my head had any more than hit the pillow before I was asleep.

Morning came, and I was awakened again by the same sweet voice that had been waking me up for a few days now, along with the smell of coffee. I was really getting used to this good morning coffee and the good morning kiss that accompanied it. What a way to wake up!

Pam said breakfast was almost ready, so I hurried with the coffee. I showered and got dressed quickly because I could smell those great biscuits that Nora makes to go with the sausage, eggs, jelly and jams. I thought I was getting spoiled, and I liked it.

Everybody says, "Good morning," as I walk into the kitchen.

"Well, what's up today I ask?"

Nora tells me that she thinks it was about time for me to meet some of my future relatives. I had figured this was coming up soon.

"If you don't mind, we still have some of Pam's aunts and uncles that want to meet you. They would like for us to come over to her Aunt Jodie's for lunch. The rest of the local family will be there. They seem real anxious to see what kind of a man Pam has finally found. They had just about given up on her ever getting married again.

"Jim, to tell you the truth, Art and I had just about given up also."

My answer to that was, "Nora, I'm sure glad she waited for me to come along. I want to tell you and Art something. I love your daughter more than life itself. I love her more than I have ever dreamed of loving anyone. I can promise you that she will never want for love or attention.

"I'm real anxious for her to meet my children and for them to get to know her. I'm positive they will love her just as much as I do.

"I feel the same thing will happen when she and Mother meet. They both have a lot of the same ideas on life. I am real anxious for you folks to meet Mother. I want you to know that just because my mother has money doesn't mean that she is one of the rich-acting people. She prefers to be in the kitchen cooking lunch or dinner and looking forward to a family get-together. We may have money, but we try not to act like it.

Ray Carpenter

"When I was teaching, I lived on exactly what I made as a teacher. I never accepted money from my father for any of my personal needs. I figured that if I couldn't make it, I would just do without. I was a grown man with a good education, and that should have been enough for me to be able to make a living for my family."

The Tale to Art and Nora

"I am going to tell you something in strict confidence with your assurance that you will never relate it to anyone, not even to the other members of the family until Pam or I say you can. What do you say?"

They both agreed they would respect our wishes and keep what I was about to tell them a secret until we told them they could reveal it, that was if we ever told them they could reveal it.

Their word was good for me, and I looked at Pam, and she said, "Jim, I didn't think you were going to tell them yet."

"Honey, I think I know your parents well enough by now to know that they won't say anything."

"This is your decision, so do whatever you want to do," Pam said.

"Pam, I feel they should know."

She just smiles and says, "That's fine with me."

"Art, Nora, I don't exactly know how to tell you this, but your daughter is marrying a man that has a trust fund of over one hundred and fifty million dollars."

They just looked at each other, then at me, and then they say, "Jim, we knew you were wealthy, but we had no idea it was that much."

"Well, that's not the worst part of it. You see, since I inherited the business, that means that I will be in control of a business worth between seven hundred and eight hundred and fifty million dollars. Some say it may be worth over a billion dollars. To be honest with you, I have trouble even figuring out how many zeros come after each number. I can't even begin to fathom how much money that is.

"I want you to know now that from now on you folks will never have to want for anything, and I won't hear any argument from either of you. I know you're very independent people, but now you're part of my family, and I insist on taking care of my family."

"Jim, we don't really need anything. We have all we need right now. We have a small retirement income plus some social security, and our home is paid for, and we don't owe anybody anything. We've never lived on credit cards, so our debts are just about nil."

"Nora, haven't you ever wanted to take a cruise or go on a trip to Europe for a couple of weeks?"

"Well," she admitted, "I have dreamed of it, but I never got my hopes up because I knew we would never be able to do it and keep our savings for needed things after Art retired."

"Nora, would you mind letting me do some of those things for you. It would make me very happy to do this for you folks."

Art looked stunned, but he said, "Hell, I don't know what to say."

"Just say that you'll let us do these things for you. Pam will have a lot of problems getting used to not having to want for anything. This doesn't mean that we are going to spend money lavishly – no limousine or fancy jet airplanes. We'll just keep what the company has at this time.

"Art, I may call on you to help me do some of the things I want to do in Texas. I think you could help a lot with what I want to do. I don't know if Pam has told you, but I want to establish a storefront clinic for the homeless in the Ft. Worth area. My friend Doc has wanted this for years, and now I can help him establish it with the help of a doctor friend of mine in Ft. Worth.

"I also want to help Cowboy get a few acres out at the edge of town with a few head of good rodeo stock of horses and some bucking bull stock. I feel if I do this, he can take it over and make it a paying proposition since he is so familiar with rodeo animals. Maybe he can breed some good bulls for rodeos. I figure you can help me find the right small ranch or farm to start with.

"Next, there's Bing. I'm going to help him pay off his debts to the Mafia boys from Las Vegas. After that, we'll see if we can find him a small nightclub to put him into and let him run it. When he makes enough money to pay me back for the money I used to pay his debts off, I'll give him the club, which should start him on the road to a good life.

"Last is Mabel who has a daughter somewhere in Louisiana. I would like to find that daughter so they can get reacquainted. After that I would like to set her up in a small town café where she can really display her talents as a cook. She's a real good cook, and she should be able to make a go of that.

"Now, I'm sure you are wondering just why I want to do these things. Well, the real reason is, for the past ten years they have been my family. Mabel has cooked many meals down in the riverbed for us. Cowboy always was good at finding clothing or other things that one of the six of us might need. He really hung in there to help all of us. Bing always kept us entertained, and he was real good at raising a few bucks when one of us needed it. And there is Doc. Doc would always manage somehow to get antibiotics for us when we got sick or had a sore throat or cut ourselves. He always had salves for us when we cut or scraped ourselves. He not only took care of the six of us, but he also took care of a lot of the other guys and gals. Now you can see why I need to do something for them."

"Well, Jim, I must say that you really believe in taking care of your friends and family. I sure admire you for your attitude. Not many men would want to do that. I think I'm finally beginning to see why my Pam fell for you."

"Art, thank goodness that Pam didn't know any of this before we fell in love. We fell in love with each other without any of this being known. I didn't even know I was worth a nickel when Pam and I fell in love. We found out about the money after we had fallen in love.

"My mother called me after I had won the million-dollar prize on the show. I fell in love with Pam the first time that I saw her."

Pam says, "Dad, I knew I was in love with Jim on the first date we had. I tried to fight it, but it wasn't any use. I knew he was what I wanted, and I decided I was going to have him. The truth is, I asked him to marry me.

"When we found out about all that money, the money almost caused me to back away from him. After he and I talked, and he told me of his plans – even before he talked to his mother, I knew he was a good man. Then when his mother called and we both talked to her, I almost backed out again. His mother is such a sweet lady that I decided she knew her son better than I did, and I was going to take the chance because I loved him so much. I just didn't know if I could handle being that rich.

"After we talked and made our plans, I knew that he was the man I wanted to spend the rest of my life with. I also made up my mind that I wasn't going to act like a rich person. I don't intend to let it change me. I know that will be hard to do, but I sure am going to work at staying the same little old country girl. I hope you and Mother understand."

"Pam," her mother says, "I think you made a good decision. I think you have a good man here. Daddy and I promise you we will keep your secret."

Turning to me, she says, "As far as anyone is concerned, you are just a good man, who just happens to be wealthy, and Pam is marrying you. They don't need to know anything more than that you're one of the family that owns Dixon Manufacturing Co. There is no way you can keep that a secret. Your friends already know that, and that is all they need to know. Nothing else is any of their business. Believe me we can keep a secret real well."

"That's right, Jim, they really can, and I can promise you that if they say they will, horses couldn't drag it out of them," Pam added.

"Folks, I'm gonna love this family. What am I saying? I do love this family.

"Now, what about lunch and the family this afternoon, is there anything I should do or know before we go over there? Do you have any uncles that I should be aware of or look out for? I know most families have an uncle or aunt that can ask a lot of questions or try to embarrass you. Do you have any of those? I used to have an uncle Cliff that thought it was funny to embarrass members of the families when they brought new friends around."

"Well," Pam looked at me and kind of stuttered for a moment, and then she said, "Well, there is Uncle Oscar."

Nora starts laughing and says, "Jim, we don't even have an Uncle Oscar. She is just pulling your leg. I really don't think there are any of the family that will give you a bad time. I think they will be in total awe of you. They have never met anyone with more than five hundred dollars in his pocket. I think they will just want to look at you to see what you look like. None of them ever thought that Pam would get married, especially to a good-looking millionaire."

"Thank you, Nora. That's the first time I have been called handsome or good looking by anyone in a long, long time."

"Jim, it shouldn't take your mother-in-law to tell you that, you should look in the mirror. Here you are, six feet, two inches or more, dark wavy hair, about one hundred ninety pounds. What size suit do you wear?"

"I wear a 44 tall or long or whatever they call it now."

Everybody was laughing now including me. I must have sounded pretty dumb.

"Well, just look at me and then look at that little blonde doll standing over there and wonder just how I ever got her."

"Well, you did; now don't fight it because you can't win."

We fiddled around the house for the next three plus hours until Nora told us she thought it was about time to head out to Aunt Jodie's. We all head for the door.

On our way to Aunt Jodie's, Art said, "This is going to make my heart feel real good."

Nora said, "Now, Art, none of that."

I ask, "What's going on?"

Pam says "Well, Mother, you might as well tell him."

"Well, Uncle Edgar, Aunt Jodie's husband, has been bragging for years about their daughter marrying a doctor. He rubs it into everyone in the family that his daughter married better than anyone in the family has ever married before. I know it isn't nice, but you see they don't know that you are wealthy yet. They just know that you were on the show and won a million dollars. They know nothing else about you."

Art said, "Jim, I hate to ask you this, but will it be all right if I tell them that you and your family own Dixon Plastics Co?"

I look at Pam and she says, "Don't look at me; that's your decision."

"Hell, Art, why not? If it'll take him down a peg or two, then take him down a peg or two. I don't mind just this once."

He starts laughing. "Well, I'll bet Edgar won't believe it even after we tell him."

Now I was beginning to think that I was going to enjoy this. I knew that wasn't nice, but from what they had said about good old Uncle Edgar, I thought he deserved a little put down, and if Art could do it, then more power to him.

After a ride of about fifteen minutes across town, we came to a nice little neighborhood about the same as the one where Art and Nora lived. We turned into a driveway where there were about seven or eight cars lining the street. It looked as though they had left the driveway for the guest of honor.

Hell, now I felt kind of mean toward Uncle Edgar. I have known some people like him.

We stop, and everyone started getting out of the car when the front door opens, and several ladies and kids come out heading straight toward the car.

Hell, I thought, *maybe I should just stay in the car. What the heck though, I can put up with it if Pam and her parents can.*

Aunt Jodie is the first to reach the car. She grabs Pam and says, "Oh, Pam, I'm so excited about meeting your young man."

Young man, hell, I am almost as old as she is, I thought.

Anyway, Pam says, "Aunt Jodie, I want you to meet Jim Dixon.

"Jim, this is my Aunt Jodie."

She looks at me and says, "Well now, Pam, you got a real pretty one this time."

I felt like hitting her, but Pam just grinns and says, "Yes, Aunt Jodie. I don't think I would exactly call a six foot, two-inch, two-hundred-pound man pretty. I prefer to think of him as handsome, worldly, and wise looking."

I thought Pam took some of the wind out of Aunt Jodie's sails.

Pam patiently introduces me to the other aunts and children. The men are in the backyard where they have set up picnic tables under some beautiful trees. The weather was great with the soft breeze and the sun shining with the temperature in the mid to high seventies. As we go out the backdoor to the yard the men all looked my way. I felt like a gold fish in a bowl.

I contained myself when this guy walked over and introduced himself as Uncle Edgar. I tell him what a pleasure it is to finally meet him. "I've heard a lot of good things about you."

He looked pleased with that little white lie. He turns and starts introducing me to the rest of the men. When he came to this small, nondescript looking little guy, he proudly pushed out his chest and says, "This is my son-in-law, Roger. Roger is a doctor you know."

"Well, no, I didn't know, but I am sure glad to meet you, Roger. What kind of doctor are you?"

"I'm an MD; I'm a proctology specialist."

"Well, I am sure that is an interesting field," I commented politely.

Uncle Edgar started laughing and said, "Yeah, at least he gets to the bottom of things."

I could see how much this hurt Roger, so I turned to Roger. "I have to say that I really admire medical doctors because it takes such dedication and so many years of work to get your credentials. I don't think I could ever be that disciplined."

He kind of smiled, and I could tell this had made him feel a little better after having heard Edgar's crude and rude remarks.

I thought I had a friend in Roger.

He asks what kind of work I was in.

"I used to be a college professor. I was a philosophy instructor."

He tells me how much he enjoyed his philosophy course in college.

Art steps up and enters the conversation again. "Jim's not teaching any longer."

Edgar says, "I understand that you just won a million dollars on a TV show."

"That's right, Edgar."

Edgar comes back with, "Well, I understand that you had been on the street for some time before you got on the program. How did you make out on the street for that long?"

Art is waiting for that one and he explains it. "He really didn't have much trouble. But if he had needed anything, he could have called his father or mother, and they would have taken care of his needs."

Edgar inquires, "Just what does his father do?"

"Well, his father is dead now, but before he died,

he owned the Dixon Plastics Manufacturing Co. When he died, Jim inherited the business."

Dead silence fell over the crowd.

Edgar says, "You mean to tell me that Jim owns the Dixon Plastics Co?"

"Yes, he sure does, Edgar."

You would have thought Edgar swallowed a rat from the expression on his face.

Edgar asks Art, "Do you mean that Jim owns the Dixon plant in Norfolk?"

"Yes, he does, Edgar, we were out there yesterday and spent some time with Frank Wells and some of the other people."

Edgar swallowed real hard, "Well, hell, he's my boss."

"Art, you didn't tell me that Edgar was employed at the Plastics Co."

"Well, Edgar, we need all the good people we can get. What department are you in?"

"I'm in production. I run one of the burners and shapers."

"Well, I'm glad to know that. I'll tell Frank to keep an eye on you. As I said, we need all of the GOOD help we can get. How long have you been working for us?"

"Twenty-two years Sir."

"Well, it looks like you'll be getting ready for retirement one of these days."

Edgar says, "I hope not too soon."

I turn to some of the others including Roger who gives me a wink and walks off with me. Like I said, I thought I had a friend in Roger.

After a while, Pam comes out to the yard and comes over and takes hold of my arm and kind of hugs me as she turns to Uncle Edgar, she says, "Well, Uncle Edgar, what do you think of my Jim?"

Uncle Edgar couldn't find enough superlatives to say what he wanted to say. As we turned to go over and talk to some other people, I asked Pam, "Why didn't you tell me your uncle was an employee?"

She just laughs and says, "If I had, it wouldn't have been half as good or funny."

"Pam, I really like Roger."

"I do too, and I'm sorry that Uncle Edgar gives him such a bad time about his specialty."

I laughed and suggested, "Honey, maybe he will give Uncle Edgar a discount. He will need one as often as he makes an ass out of himself."

Pam hit me on the shoulder real hard and said, "Baby, that wasn't nice."

"No, it may not be nice, but it sure is honest."

For the rest of the afternoon, I really enjoyed meeting her family. One of Art's brothers was a real funny guy. He knew stories about everything. The nice thing was that he knew how to tell them. His name was Jarred. He was such a nice person that I could have spent the whole afternoon talking to him. He was telling some fishing stories that reminded me of the times I had gone fishing with my father. I'll bet Jarred would have been a hoot to go fishing with.

I asked him if he would like to come to Chicago and go fishing with me after we got settled.

"Are you sure you want me?"

"Jarred, who do you think I want to go fishing with, Rupert Murdock! I'm just people, and I want you and your family to remember that. I want you to treat me just as you would any other member of this family. Money does not make a man. Please remember that. We put our pants on one leg at a time just like you do. We enjoy sausage, biscuits, and eggs for breakfast and an occasional hamburger and milkshake just like everyone else. If I wasn't that way, Pam would never have had anything to do with me. She's really a great down-to-earth girl."

"I know, we think the world of her. We're sure glad she has found a good man. We've been worried about her up there in New York City by herself."

"Uncle Jarred, that girl can take care of herself. I can vouch for that. Jarred, I just hope you and the rest of the family will accept me for what I am and not what you think I am worth financially. "If you'll help me with that, I will sure appreciate it."

"After the way you handled Edgar, you made a lot of friends."

"I just hope I didn't upset anyone. Jarred, I like that Roger.. How do you feel about him?"

"I like the guy, too, but Edgar is continually putting him down."

"Well, maybe I can help out a little on that since he's one of our employees."

The ladies come to tell us that lunch is ready. They had tea glasses for those who wanted tea, and Coke and beer for those who would rather have that.

These people sure did know how to feed. I'd bet I'd gained five pounds since I have been here.

After lunch we just sat in the shade and visited. I had to answer a lot of questions as usual, but they were really not that digging type of questions that I sometimes faced.

At about 3:00 p.m. everybody started saying good-bye and going home. I guess they had seen all they wanted to see and asked all the questions they wanted to ask. Pretty soon it was only Aunt Jodie, Uncle Edgar, Art, Nora, Pam, and I.

Art came over and asked, "Are you ready to go?"

"I'm ready when you are."

Pam came over, put her arm around my neck and shoulder and said, "Hon, you look a little tired, how about us going home and getting some rest?"

That sounded real fine to me. I looked over, and Art and Nora were headed for the door, so Pam and I fell in right behind them and headed for the car. We said good-bye to Aunt Jodie and Uncle Edgar, got in the car, and headed for home.

On the way home Art told me he liked the way I had handled Edgar. "I thought he was going to swallow his tongue when he found out he worked for you. I loved the way you handled him when he introduced you to Roger. You know, Jim, Roger is really a good guy, but he just doesn't know how to handle Edgar, but I think you gave him some ideas tonight."

"Art, I have a favor to ask of you. Would you consider helping me with my work in Texas once in a while as an advisor?" I know I have asked you before, but I am real serious about this. I will need you.

"What kind of advisor?"

"There'll be times when Pug and I will need help. I'll need you to be there to give me answers and suggestions on these things that I want to do when I get back into the swing of things."

"Sure, Jim, I'll be glad to do that."

"I would like to pay you for helping me with my work," I said quietly.

Art let me know right away that he wouldn't take any money for helping me.

"Wouldn't you want to get paid for your work?" I asked.

"Hell, no. I'll be doing this for my son-in-law, not for money."

"Well, we don't work that way, Art."

He laughs and says, "I'll be right there when you need me."

"I know that, Art, but I would appreciate it if you would let me pay you something for what you are doing. I pay everyone else, and we can certainly afford it."

"Well, you sure as hell aren't going to pay me. I won't take it. If I do something for my daughter and her husband, I don't intend to take any money for it."

Pam told me that "Daddy will be there to help you, but don't insult him by offering him money for his work."

"Well, can I at least pay you for your expenses?" I asked.

"That you can do, but that's all. Remember that."

"Okay, I'll remember that, and I'll remember that this is a hard-headed family."

Everyone chuckled at that.

"Art, does that mean you will help me in Texas?"

"Just give me the plane ticket and tell me where and what time you want me there."

When we arrived back at the house, I realized I am really getting tired. We walk into the house, and Pam says, "Honey, you look tired. Why don't you go back and take a nap. I'll call you before dinner if you don't wake up."

I didn't argue with her on that suggestion, and I headed for the room. I pull off my shoes and lay down on the bed, and that was the last thing I remembered until I heard Pam saying, "Wake up, Honey. Frank Wells called and asked if you could come by the office before it closes and pick up a letter he has for you."

"Oh, yeah, that letter. Ask Art if he can run me out to the plant real quick."

She left for a minute and came back into the bedroom. Daddy's ready as soon as you are. You guys hurry back because we're going to have dinner before too long."

She went to the kitchen to help her mother as I freshened up and washed my face with some good cool water to get the sleep out of my eyes and headed for the kitchen where Art was waiting. We made it to the plant just before closing.

Frank met me with a big, thick envelope. He handed it to me and told me if I needed more before I left to let him know.

I tell him, "We're leaving in the morning and I really appreciate all of your help, Frank. I won't forget this."

When we got back to the house, the girls were sitting around the table.

Art says, "Nora, get this young man a glass of tea, he's been running."

She heads to the cabinet and comes back with a large glass of iced tea for the both of us. Great refreshment.

"Jim, I understand that you need to be getting back so you can go to see your mother and children. I can certainly understand that. You go on back so you can see your family. I know that Pam's anxious to meet them. We'll have plenty of catching up to do later. You and I will have a lot of time to really get to know each other when we get involved in the programs down in Texas that you want to start. I'm looking forward to helping you any way I can."

"Art, you and I are going to get along just fine. Pam has already contacted the airlines, and we have a flight out of here in the morning at 9:15 a.m. That will get us into New York City before noon. That will give us time to do some washing and get some cleaning done if necessary."

"It looks as if you've taken care of things."

"Nora, now you seen why this girl's going to be so much help to me. She anticipates what needs to be done, and she does it. I have a feeling she is going to be able to take over my activities schedule and keep track of them and keep me where I am supposed to be when I am supposed to be there. She should be an office manager, but I just want her to manage me. That may sound selfish, but I really need her. Who else can have the love of their life as their manager? I've got it made."

"It sounds like you guys are just made for each other, and that's not just because I'm her mother talking."

We look at each other and agree, "That's right, Mother."

She laughs and tells us to get busy eating. "Jim, I hadn't thought of you calling me mother, but you call us just whatever makes you feel good. Truth is I kind of like it."

After dinner we just sat around and enjoyed each other's company. We talked about the future and what we feel it might be. We were all very optimistic about the future for all of us. It was great to have a family that we could talk to and relate to. They were so easy to talk to about things. If you wanted advice, they would give it, and if you didn't, they kept their mouth shut. That made for a great family feeling.

We finally went to bed at about midnight. We talked so long we didn't realize how late it was.

We got a good night's sleep, and again I was awakened by the smell of coffee, along with a good morning kiss from my favorite lady. I had to hurry and shower and shave and get ready to have breakfast. After breakfast, I packed in a hurry because Pam had already packed her bags, and they were sitting by the front door. I finally got mine ready, and by that time, Art had the car ready to go. Nora and Pam were waiting at the front door.

We arrived at the airport just in time to check in and get on the plane. We had our hugs and handshakes over with, and then Nora came over and gave me a real big bear hug, then a kiss, and said, "Jim, it's great to have you as a part of this family."

Art, who was standing behind her, said, "That's right, Jim that goes for me too. I hope you don't mind if I slip sometimes and call you son."

"Art, I don't mind that at all I consider that the highest compliment I could get if you and Nora look at me in that way."

Nora kissed me on the cheek again and says, "Be sure to take care of our little girl."

I assure her that I would certainly do that.

Pam nudges me. "Come on, Hon. We had better hurry."

She turned and waved to her mother and dad and said good-bye again.

We were finally on the plane and on our way back to New York City to pursue our new life together. We were undoubtedly two of the happiest people in the world right then.

The ride to New York City didn't seem to take very long. We arrived at the airport, got our bags, went to get the car, and headed home.

We arrived home, and boy did it look good. We parked and took our bags inside. Pam went in first, and I followed carrying everything. As I stepped in the door, she grabbed me and put a great big kiss on me and said, "I've been wanting to do that ever since we left. Do you think we really need to bother with washing and cleaning right now, or can we have a little time to ourselves?"

"Honey, the cleaning can wait. Let's play honeymoon."

We did, and what a preview for a honeymoon it was. Every time I held her like this and we made love, I realized even more just how much this lady meant to me. When I was holding her body so close to mine, I didn't want to turn her loose. I wanted to keep holding her, but I knew that wasn't practical. It still didn't keep from wanting to hold onto her. Our lovemaking was something the poets had written about for centuries.

About three o'clock p.m., we decided it was time to start doing some planning as to what we were going to take and what we were not going to take. That was easy for me. I was going to take everything I had because it really wasn't that much. Pam had to pick and choose. I told her to just take the things she liked the most, and anything else she might need, she could buy.

I thought it was about time to get her used to having some money in her purse. I took her over to where my suit was hanging and reached inside the coat pocket. I took my wallet out and took ten one hundred dollar bills and handed them to her.

She looked real surprised and asked, "What's this for?"

"Pam, I don't ever want you to be broke again. I want you to always keep several hundred dollar bills tucked away somewhere just in case you need them. You don't need to let people know they are there, but you never know when youmight need some extra money."

"Jim, I don't want all your money."

"Pam, this is not all of my money, and I want you to have money to buy things when you get to Chicago. If you need more for clothes or anything else, you just write a check or pay cash, but I don't want you to ever want for anything again in your lifetime.

"Just as soon as we get to Chicago, I want to set up a checking account for you in your own name so you will always have plenty of money handy. I'll start a checking account when we get to Chicago, and I want you to be able to sign on it also."

She began to cry a little. "Jim, I'm not used to this, and it's going to take a little getting used to. I never had anyone treat me like this.

Chicago, at Last

"Dry your eyes Little Darlin' because I have a suggestion. How about us going down to the Black Angus for dinner tonight to see Ernie and the gang before we head for Chicago?"

She squealed with delight and said, "You know what, I was just thinking the same thing."

We worked hard getting everything ready to leave in the morning. Pam called the airlines and changed our reservations to tomorrow. She finished calling and turned to me and said, "We can leave about 11:00 a.m. tomorrow and be in Chicago about 2:00 p.m. their time. How does that sound to you?"

"That's fine. It's about 5:30 P.M. now, so why don't we head downtown."

We lock everything up, and she tells me to drive again before she thinks. Sure will be when you get your drivers license. "I sure will be glad to get you to Chicago so you can get your driver's license."

"Honey, I think I'll be just about as happy about that as you will. I think we will need to get Pug a license also."

"That's right, he hasn't been driving for a long time either has he?"

We arrive at the parking garage, leave the car, and walked down the street to the Black Angus. As we walked in, Ernie spotts us and comes running over. He picks Pam up like a rag doll and twirls around with her. He plants a kiss on her cheek and says, "Boy, what a wonderful surprise. We've been talking about you guys all week."

He turns and to those who hadn't already seen what was going on up front, hollers, "Hey, look who's here."

All the girls come running up to see Pam, even a couple of the cooks in the kitchen come running out for a quick hug and then they head back to take care of the food.

They all wanted to know what our plans were.

"Well, first I want to tell you that Jim and I are getting married next week in Chicago at his mother's home."

Now the squealing coming from the girls really gets loud. They all start asking when we decided. "How did I ask her? What did I say when I asked her to marry me?"

She looks kind of embarrassed and says, "You know what, he didn't ask me, I asked him. Now don't get the wrong idea I asked him before I knew he had any money. I knew that second night when he came in here that he was the man I wanted for my husband. He helped a lot because it seems that he wanted me too. It was what you might call a Mutual Admiration Society.

"We've been home, and he has met my family, and now I am going with him to Chicago where we are going to be married. After the wedding, we will go on to Texas to take care of his business there.

Ernie wanted to know about Pug.

"Well, it seems that he and Angie are going to be married also. It's going to be a double wedding."

By now Pam is telling the girls about Mother having the store bring the wedding dresses out to the house for them to pick out their dresses instead of their having to go to the store. They all giggle and talk about how lucky she is.

I asked Ernie what he had heard from Chip Rowan.

"He's doing fine and is going to submit his application to the New York City University right away."

I briefly told him about my father's passing away and that I was eventually going to take over the management of the company. He was surprised, but pleased for me.

I tell him that I would like to do something for Chip. "Ernie, I want you to make me a promise."

"Sure, Professor."

"I want you to promise me that if Chip needs any kind of financial assistance while he is pursuing his education, you'll let me know. I'll send whatever you need in the way of money to make sure that fine young man gets his MBA."

Ernie was silent for a minute, and then he says, "Professor, I don't know what to say, but I can assure you that if I can't take care of his needs or if he needs money for anything, I'll sure let you know."

"There is one other thing, Ernie. I'd like to offer Chip a job with our New York plant when he gets his MBA, that is if you don't want him for your business. I'll probably be able to use him somewhere else if he would like to move, but I just figured he might want to stay close to home. I know how close he is to his family. I'm glad he has a good friend like you. I'll stay in touch with you anyway because I sure don't want to lose your friendship. Good friends are hard to come by."

"I agree, Prof., that I do.

"I guess you know that you are getting just about the greatest little lady in the world," he added changing the subject.

"Ernie, I agree that I am one lucky guy. Will you come to visit us when we get settled in Chicago?"

"Professor, I sure would like that. I don't know much about Chicago, but I would love to visit."

I was getting hungry, so I finally got Pam back to the booth where we liked to sit. The booth we liked best was at the back of the restaurant where the girls could come by and talk on their way to and from the kitchen.

As we start back to the booth, a couple of the girls come over and ask Pam if it was all right for them to kiss the groom.

"Well, she says with a grin, he isn't a groom yet, but since you won't be at the wedding, I think that would be just fine."

They all laugh, and I got a couple of kisses. Before long, I got a couple more kisses when the other girls came over and said, "We missed out, so it's our turn to kiss the groom." They each gave me a kiss.

One of the cooks was looking out at all of this, and he said, "I ain't gonna kiss Professor, but I sure am going to kiss Pam before she goes off and gets married." He laughs and tells me he really wanted to marry her, but his wife would have objected.

She laughs and says, "Now, Tim, you know that Mary is one of my favorite people. I wouldn't think of taking you away from her even if I could, and I know I couldn't."

"You're sure right there, Pam. We've been married over thirty years, and I'm kind of used to her. I sure do want to wish you guys the best in your married life. I hope you'll be as happy as Mary and I have been all these years.

"Professor, all you have to do is just keep saying, "Yes, dear. That works every time."

"Okay, Tim, I'll try to remember that."

Pam tells me that Tim is one of her favorite people. "His wife is one of the sweetest people you'll ever meet. I just love both of them to death. They're just like family for me."

I finally got one of the girls over to the booth to take an order instead of just talk. Pam ordered a small prime rib, baked potato, green beans, and salad. I ordered a small fillet steak, medium with a baked potato. And then I asked, "Do you have any asparagus?"

"Not today, Professor. I think you ate the last asparagus we had."

"Well, bring me some baked squash if you have it to go with the potato and steak and a small dinner salad."

She smiled and said, "It's on its way."

She gave the order to Tim, and he started immediately to put our dinner together. Before long she brought the food. We ate and talked to everyone as they came and went from the kitchen.

When we were finished with dinner, we asked the girl for a check.

"No way. Ernie threatened to break my arm if I gave you a check."

We left her a nice tip. Pam told her to share with the rest of the girls. She agreed that she would. When she looked down at the hundred dollar bill that Pam had left, I thought she was going to cry. She called the other girls over to show them.

As we were starting to say good-bye to Ernie, they all came running up to the front and grabbed Pam and hugged her and told her how much they loved her and how much they were going to miss her.

Ernie gave me a big bear hug. "Professor, good luck to you guys, and you take care of my little lady."

He looked at Pam, and she came over to hug and kiss him. That was when I saw tears rolling down that big old teddy bear's cheeks. "Hell, Professor, I can't help it; we all love her. Pam, if you ever want a job again or need a recommendation, you just call me. I'll fix you up, but I really don't think that will ever be necessary.

"We love you guys; now get out of here before we all start bawling and ruin my business."

We left laughing with tears running down our cheeks also. What a wonderful bunch of friends!

We walked back to the garage, got the car, and headed for home. "Yes, I said home. That little duplex feels like home to me. Pam, why don't we just see if we can buy that little house where you live so we can always have a place to stay when we come to New York City. I'll always love that little place. We don't need a big place to stay when we come to town. I want that house because it was the first time and place where I knew you really loved me. It was the first place we made love. What do you say?"

"Jim, you're so sentimental, and I love you for it. I'll call in the morning before we leave and see if it's for sale. If it is, I'll tell them to write up the paper work and send it to your mother's house. If the price is agreeable, we'll send them a check for it. Is that what you want?"

"It sure is, Darling; that's just exactly what I want."

We reached the garage, got the car, and headed for home.

Upon arriving, we both just stood in the street and looked at that little old house. "Jim, I know this little old duplex isn't much, but it'll always mean an awful lot to me."

I agreed totally. I grabbed her by the arm, and in we went like a couple of high school kids, giggling and all. What a wonderful feeling it was to love someone the way I loved this little lady.

When we got inside, I remembered I had to get my clothes packed except for what I was going to wear. I would pack my electric shaver and toiletries I needed after I take my shower and shave in the morning.

Pam was busy packing the bags she was taking. I remembered that since we were going to take a cab to the airport, she should put the car into the garage tonight so we wouldn't have that to do in the morning. She pitched me the keys and told me I could at least drive the car around to the alley and put it in the garage.

I hesitatingly took the keys and went out the front door. I got into the car, put the key into the ignition, and started it. That was the first time I had started a car in ten years. I drove around to the garage, punched the electronic door opener, and drove in.

Guess what, I didn't even hit the door going in, and I didn't run through the end of the garage and into the storage room. My first driving lesson in ten years, and I passed it. Maybe I'd be able to get my license in

Chicago. I locked the garage doors and went inside, real pleased with myself.

"Pam, I made it without scratching your cute little car."

She laughed, "Maybe you are on the road to getting your license after all."

She was real busy getting everything together, trying to decide what she might need and what she should leave here. "Hon, does your mother object to slacks or pants for ladies?"

"Pam, Mother wears them herself – quite often. At least she did when I last saw her. I don't think she wears them to the company Board meetings, but she used to wear them quite a lot. Take yours with you, especially those tan ones that fit real tight. They show off your cute little ass."

Believe it or not, she was actually blushing.

"If you need more dresses, we'll get them for you. I think it would be fun for you and Mother to go shopping together.

She smiles and continues with what she was doing. We finally got to bed, but it was hard to go to sleep. The anxiety of getting to see my mother and my children tomorrow kept me thinking of all kinds of things. I just couldn't get my mind to clear up.

We were lying there in bed all snuggled up spoon fashion, when I asked, "Honey, are you as nervous as I am?"

"Yes, I am possibly even more nervous. I've never met these people, and here I am coming into their lives with their prized possession, their son and father. I'm going to be an outsider who has to win their confidence and love. Yes, I'm scared, I am real scared but as long as you are there beside me, I know everything will be all right."

The last time I looked at the clock it was past midnight. Having Pam so close to me and being able to hold onto her helped me feel better and more secure.

Just holding her gave me more peace of mind. God, how I loved this little lady.

Next thing I know, I smell coffee. I rise up on one elbow, and there she was with coffee. I got my coffee and a good morning kiss that got my attention and opened both eyes. Damn, that lady was beautiful, and as I'd said a hundred dozen times before, she is mine, all mine.

After coffee, a shower, and a shave, she had breakfast ready. After breakfast she told me she needed to take some perishable items over to our next door neighbor. "She's an elderly lady who lives alone and on a fixed income. She's a real sweet lady, and she can use these things. They'll just go to waste if we leave them here in the refrigerator. You haven't met her yet so why don't you go over with me and meet her?"

"I think that's a good idea, Hon."

We pack up the meat, eggs, bread, etc., put them into a bag, and head over to her house. She opens the door and is smiling when she sees us. She is a real sweet little old lady about seventy-five years old I would guess. Pam huggs her and tells her we have some things for her that would go bad while we are gone.

Pam remembers to introduce me. "Mrs. White, this is Jim Dixon, my fiancé. We're going to Chicago to his mother's, and I don't want to leave these things in the refrigerator."

"Pam, I've seen you come and go a couple of times, and I wondered who that handsome man was with you." She looks at me again and says, "You sure do look familiar."

"Mrs. White, you may have seen me on television. Do you watch the TV show 'So You Want to Be a Millionaire'?"

"I sure do." She looks at me a little closer and says, "You're the professor who was on the show that won all that money, aren't you?"

"Yes, ma'am, I am. I'm the guy."

"I was pulling for you all the time."

"Mrs. White, Jim is also the owner of the Dixon Plastics Manufacturing Co. I didn't know that until after we were in love and had decided to get married." She hurriedly tells Mrs. White the whole story, which she really seemed to enjoy.

She told Pam that it sounded just like a story out of a romance novel. "Jim, you know you're a very lucky man. Pam is one of my very favorite people in this whole world. I sure will hate to see you leave. You keep the neighborhood happy with your perpetual smile and happy greetings."

"Mrs. white, we're going to try to buy the duplex, so we will have a place to stay when we come to New York City. We will still be your neighbors when we come to town."

She smiles when she hears that. "That's wonderful, Pam. That way I won't be losing you completely."

She asks about Angie. "She's such a dear girl."

Pam tells her, "Angie is getting married also, and her new husband will be working for Jim. They aren't sure just yet where they will live, but they'll always have the duplex to stay in when they come to town also."

Mrs. White really liked the sound of that.

I nudge Pam. "We had better get to moving so we can get to the airport early enough to check everything in."

She agreed, and we say good-bye to Mrs. White and head for the door.

Mrs. White wished us good luck and added, "May you have a happy marriage. I just know you will."

We thank her and go back to the house.

Pam looks at her watch and reaches for the phone. She calls for a taxi to take us to the airport. Pam hurriedly calls a friend of hers that is in the real estate business and tells her to offer the owners of the duplex a bid on the house. She tells her we want to buy it if it was for sale. "We're more than willing to offer a real fair price, but we won't be gouged on it."

Her friend said she would be more than happy to make the offer and wanted to know where she could get in touch with us when she gets an answer. Pam gave her Mother's address and phone number and tells her she could call us there when she gets an answer. The lady apparently asked Pam about the rumor that she was getting married. Pam had to start telling her the story. After a short while, the horn honked at the curb, so Pam had to hurridly say good-bye.

We picked up our bags and went out the front door being sure to lock it securely. The driver helped us with our bags and put them into the trunk of the car. "Take us to the United Airlines gate twenty-seven at the airport please."

He says he was familiar with the area, so away we went. He sure did know the way because he made it in about half the time it took us to go out there.

We arrive, he helps us with the bags and gives them to the curb check-in agent. I pay him, and he was gone. It really did happen that fast, believe it or not in New York City.

Since our bags were already checked in at curb side, we headed for the check-in counter inside to make sure we had our seats.

I check with the agent, and she assures me that our tickets are just fine and our boarding pass seating was correct. I looked at the boarding pass, and I happened to notice that we were in the business section. I mentioned this to Pam.

"Yes, but they were almost $150.00 cheaper, and it's such a short flight I just couldn't see spending that extra money."

Boy, I was going to have to watch myself with this little lady because I have a feeling she is going to be watching her pocketbook and mine.

She laughed and says, "Just because you have money, no need to waste it."

You know something Hon, "You're right."

We finally get on board, and we don't have to wait long this time before they were backing out and heading for the runway.

Away we go to Chicago, and I was really getting nervous. I look at Pam, and she is looking as calm as a cucumber. I knew she must be churning inside at the thought of meeting my mother and the kids.

Here came the nice lady asking if we would like to have something to drink. "I could use a good cold diet Coke," I said, "Pam would like one also."

When she turns to look at me, I could see love in her eyes. "Jim, Hon, I'm really looking forward to meeting your family. I just hope they will like me."

"Pam, you know they will like you. There's no question about that."

We drank our Cokes and talked about small things such as the man at the bank and what we were going to do when we get to Texas. It didn't seem any time until the pilot comee on the intercom and says, "Folks, we are nearing the Great Lakes, which means we should be in Chicago within the next thirty minutes. The weather is clear, and the temperature at the present time is 82 degrees with a slight north wind."

Before long the stewardess comes by and asks us to put our seats into an upright position and replace the tray to its original position. I couldn't believe it, but I looked out the window, and I could see the skyline of Chicago in the distance.

The Family Reunion

"Pam, I can see the outline of the downtown buildings in Chicago."

"Jim, do I look all right? Is my lipstick on straight? Is my hair all right?"

"Pam, you look wonderful. Honey, don't worry about it."

The plane starts to bank and start its descent toward the runway. The next thing I hear is the squeal of the tires hitting the runway and the reverse thrust of the engines.

Now I was really beginning to get butterflies. I think Pam was getting a few butterflies also. We had slowed down and are on our way to the terminal gate. This all seemed to be happening in slow motion as we approached the building. Once we stopped, everything started to move a little faster.

Since we were in tourist class, we were toward the last to leave the plane. The anticipation was killing me. We finally got out of our seats and headed for the ramp to the terminal.

By the time we got to the terminal, there were a lot of people ahead of us being greeted by their families. I saw Mother, and she saw me. She was waving and crying at the same time. I saw Johnny who towered over her. Damn, he was good looking. Next to him was his little sister, except she wasn't little any more. She was a beautiful young lady with raven black hair and dark eyes. They said she had gotten those qualities from my grandmother whom I had never known.

I grabbed Pam by the arm, and we head up the end of the ramp in the direction of Mother and the kids. I arrive first and grab Mother, giving her a great big hug and kiss.

Standing next to her was Jennifer who grabs hold of my neck and hung on with all of her might. Along with the big hug, she gave me a big kiss and says, "Daddy, it's so good to see you and have you home."

With all the noise I couldn't hear what Mother was saying as she stepped past me toward Pam.

Then I was hugging that little boy of mine, who was standing there looking me eyeball to eyeball. Mother was right, he is big and good looking, with that black wavy hair and blue eyes. He got the blue eyes from his mother.

I turned to look behind me, and Mother was hugging Pam and talking up a storm. As I turned around to see what was going on, I feel an arm on my right and another on my left.

Jennifer says, "Daddy, you're not ever going to get away from us again."

"I'll second that," said Johnny.

We stepp back to where Mother and Pam are talking.

"Jim, this lady is more beautiful than you said. She is so sweet I can see why you fell in love with her."

"Pam, I see that you have met Mother, now I'd like to introduce you to the rest of the family.

"Jennifer, this is Pam, your future stepmother."

Jennifer hugs Pam and says, "I won't think of you as stepmother. From now on, you are just going to be Mother."

"Johnny, I want you to meet Pam."

He steps over and put a big hug on her and kisses her on the cheek and says, "Welcome to the family. If you don't mind, I think I'll just put a second to what Jenny said and call you Mother."

Then Pam started crying, "Jim, they're precious. I know that's something you would normally say about small children, but these children are just wonderful. I know we're going to get along famously."

My mother was hanging onto Pam, and you could tell that she had fallen in love with her already. We all just stood there hugging each other and looking at each other.

It didn't seem possible that these kids could be this grown up. Now that I think of it, Johnny is twenty-four, and Jennifer is twenty-two years old. Wow, where des time go when you are in a bottle?

I asked Johnny, "Which way to the baggage center Big Fellow?"

He leads the way with Pam following, and Mother holding an arm on one side and Jennifer holding the other one. It was just as though they had known each other for a long time.

We finally arrived at the baggage area, find our baggage, and head for the door.

Johnny says, "Dad, do you want to drive?"

Pam starts laughing, and she finally tells Johnny that I didn't have a driver's license. She suggest that maybe he can help me get one just as soon as we get settled in.

Maybe he can take me down tomorrow and get me a license, I say.

"Dad, I'm sorry. I just didn't think. I guess you really didn't do much driving all that time did you? Maybe you will have some time to tell us all about it later."

We head for the short-term parking and find the car. We put our bags into the trunk, and Johnny drives out of the airport and heads for home. What a wonderful sound, *home*.

Things were beginning to look familiar. I saw buildings I remembered and street names that rang a bell. After about a forty-five-minute drive, I see a familiar driveway just ahead of us, and Johnny turns in. We drive up the circular drive in front of the house.

Just as we stop the car, the door opens, and Oscar comes out. "Mister Jim, it's wonderful to have you home again. We have certainly missed you. I hope this time, you are home to stay."

"Oscar, I'll be here for a while, and then I have to go to Texas, but I will be back to stay after that. I will have to make some trips, but from now on, Chicago is going to be my home. You will have to run me off if you want to get rid of me. No way Mister Jim, now way.

"Pam, I would like to introduce you to Oscar. Oscar has taken care of this household for over thirty-five years. He came here and helped straighten me out as a teenager. I have always appreciated his guidance when Dad wasn't around. Oscar and I had a lot of man-to-man talks when I was growing up and when Dad would be out of town on business. I knew I could always go to Oscar and get good advice."

Johnny agreed, "I don't know what I would have done if it hadn't been for Oscar to help me keep my head screwed on right. He kept me on the straight and narrow."

"Oscar, you must be a very special and good friend to this family," Pam says.

"Miss Pam, I like to think so."

"Oscar, would you do me a favor and not call me Miss Pam. Please just call me Pam. I think that would be best if you don't mind."

He looks at Mrs. Dixon. She smiles and says, "Oscar, just do what the lady asks you to do, you don't have to look at me."

Johnny and Jennifer start laughing, and Jennifer says, "Oscar, I think we all have some things to learn about Pam. I love the way this lady thinks."

The front door was opened to go in, but first Pam steps back and looks at the house. "Jim, you told me it was big, but you didn't tell me it was a castle. Where is the moat? What if I get lost, do I just holler for Oscar?"

"Oscar or Julia," says Johnny. "She works here with us also."

"Mother, does Julia still work for you?"

"Yes, she does Jimmy she's been with me for over thirty years also."

"Honey, Julia is one of the best cooks you have ever seen. Wait until you taste her lemon pie. Does she still make those great lemon pies?"

"Dad, they're still just as good as they always were. How do you think I was able to grow so tall and big it was because of those lemon pies?"

"Now, I finally know where his love for lemon pies comes from. That was one of the first things I found out about this big guy after we met was that he loves his lemon pie."

"Honey, Mother makes a mean lemon pie herself. I think she gave Julia the recipe for the ones she makes, right Mother?"

"Right, Jim. I gave her that recipe when she first came to work for us, and she has continued to use it all of these years. However, I think she has done something to improve on it."

By this time we were in the vestibule. Pam was still looking around at the entry, when Julia walked in. She walks straight over and hugs Pam, and then she turns to me and says, "Welcome home, Mr. Jim."

"Julia, I want to introduce you to Pam, you will get to know her because she is the lady I am marrying next week right here in this house."

"Hello, Julia, Pam says. Before you say anything, I would like for you to just call me Pam."

"Nothing fancy about this lady is there, Mister Jim? She's a perky little thing, isn't she? Awfully pretty too. I think Pam and I are going to be real good friends."

"I sure hope so Julia because from what I have heard, you can give me a few cooking lessons," Pam said.

"Mister Jim, does she always say what she thinks?" Julia asks.

"I have to say that she does, Julia; she always has with me, so I guess she does the same with everyone. Does that bother you?"

"Oh, no I like that because I always know just where I stand."

Now that that is taken care of, we go on inside, and Oscar took our bags to our rooms. Oscar took my bags upstairs and asked Pam to follow him to her room.

When they get to her room, Oscar turns to Pam and says, "Pam, I have a feeling you're going to add some sunshine to this old house. We're sure glad to have you with us."

"Thank you, Oscar, that means a lot to me. You see, I come from a working-class family, and I've worked all of my life. It's going to take a lot of getting used to around here. I'm not used to having a lot of money and living in a big house, so if you and Julia will bear with me until I get used to things, I would appreciate it a lot."

"Don't worry, Pam, and you remember that if either of us can do anything for you, please feel free to ask. We like your spunk. You'll find that Mrs. Dixon is a wonderful lady. She has a lot of spunk too. Sometimes she seems like a saint to us. I have never known anyone so understanding and loving to her family. Having Jim back is a big step toward getting things back to normal.

"Jim was always a lot like his father. He loved his family so much that when things went wrong, and he couldn't correct them, he didn't know how to cope with it. That woman of his drove him to the streets. It wasn't his fault. No kinder or more gentle man has lived than Jim and his daddy. They were two of a kind when it came to the love of their family. You'll find that out more and more, the longer you live around here, and not to embarrass you, Miss, but I hope that's a long time.

"Now, if you will excuse me, I need to take Jim's things to his old room," Oscar said.

"Pam, come here," Jim calls from down the hall.

Pam follows Oscar down to the room and walks inside.

"Here is Jim with all of the pictures of him and the children when they were small," Oscar says.

"Would you look at this, Mother left the room just like it was when I was here before I want on the street."

"Jim," Oscar says, "your mother wouldn't let us touch anything except to clean it. She always said you would be back. She was right, and it sure is good to have you here. May I hang your clothes up for you?"

"No thanks, Oscar, I would like to do that myself.

"Pam, I want you to look in this closet. It's just like it was when I left. I had moved the kids and myself back home before I left. The kids have rooms just down the hall. Can you believe this? I have a closet full of ten-year-old suits. Some of them haven't changed so much, especially the sports coats and shirts," I said and I started hanging up my clothes.

"Jim, if you don't mind, I need to go back and hang up my own clothes."

"That's fine, Hon, I'll be there just as soon as I get mine hung up."

Pam heads back down to her room to straighten up her clothes before they get wrinkled. She opens the closet doors, and she can't believe her eyes. This closet was almost as large as her bedroom at the duplex. She just stads there looking for a while, then she starts laughing and hanging up her wardrobe.

When I walk in, she says, "Honey, I could get lost in this closet and never be found again."

I laugh and tell her that I would come hunting if that happened.

"Jim, when I walked in that front door and saw that twelve-foot ceiling with those carved beams everywhere, I thought I was in a cathedral. Then, when we walked into the waiting room or whatever you call it, I saw the library off to the left and the music room on the right. A little further down is the beautiful dining room. That dining room must seat thirty people. I began to get scared. I don't know what to do in a place like this."

"First off, Honey, the dining room doesn't seat thirty people; it only seats twenty-eight when totally full. I've never seen it totally full of people. My father just liked to have these things because he said it was expected of him when he entertained government officials and dignitaries from overseas firms. That's one of the ways he built the business."

"Will I ever have to entertain dignitaries?" Pam asked.

"I'm not sure just yet what we will have to do. Don't worry though, we'll have Mother and the kids to help us if we do. The kids were raised in this kind of thing, and they know how to handle people like that. You'll be just fine, and you'll be the bell of the ball.

"Speaking of that, have you seen the ballroom?"

"You are kidding, aren't you?"

"No, I'm not, Darling; I really mean it. Let's go down and look at it and the rest of the place because we'll be living here until we can get things in Texas going and then get a place of our own."

"What if your mother wants us to live here with her? What'll you do?"

"I will tell her that the decision will be between you and her and the kids. I won't enter into it unless you can't decide on your own.

"Come on now, let's go down and see Mother and the kids and the rest of the house."

Down the winding stairs we go. Pam looks at me and says, "I feel just like Alice in Wonderland."

We headed for the kitchen where Mother and the rest of the folks were. I had forgotten just how large the kitchen was.

"Jim, this kitchen is larger than my whole house."

"Well, not quite, Honey. Your house is a little larger than this."

"Jim, I don't know if I want to marry you if I have to learn to live like this. I love you more than life itself, but this is a little much."

Mrs. Dixon laughs and says, "Honey, don't you worry about it. You don't have to do anything you don't want to do. Why don't you come with me and I'll show you around the place. And by the way Mrs. Dixon sounds very stuffy, so why don't you call me Roxanne, or Roxie like my friends do?"

"Do you really mean that? You want me to call you Roxie? How about me calling you Roxanne when others are around and Roxie when it's just you and me. You know what I mean, Roxie when we are at home, and Roxanne when we are out in the public or with a group. Would that be all right?"

"Honey, I think you've got it.

"Jim, I love this lady she is going to be just fine. I love a good short name like Pam. That makes it easier."

"Well, my name is Pamela Jean. I haven't even told Jim what my name is."

"I heard that Pamela Jean, says Jim."

"That's all right, Honey I like that name just fine."

The kids were standing around enjoying all of this. We start out the door toward the back and Pam turns to Jennifer. "Do they call you Jennifer or Jenny?"

"My friends call me Jenny."

"Jenny it is then. So, Jenny, aren't you coming with us?" Pam asks.

The three girls walked out the backdoor into the magnificent yard. "This house and garden must sit on at least ten acres," Pam says.

I was right behind them so I add, "No, Honey, I hate to tell you this, but it's almost thirteen acres. There are a couple of peach trees, oak, birch, sugar maple, and several others that I'm not familiar with. I did see a couple of apple trees and a pear tree near the rear of the property."

Roxie tells Pam that the building over there is the guest house. "It isn't used that much anymore, so I'm really glad to have some people coming to stay in it for a few days. I'm really looking forward to meeting all of the families."

"Mercy, mercy, Jim, I don't know what Mother and Daddy are going to say when they see this place."

"I hope they say 'hello' first, and then 'how's about a glass of iced tea after that."

By now everyone is laughing at Pam for being so nervous.

Roxie tells Pam, "When I married Jim's father, I had just come to town to work like you were doing in New York City. I was a waitress in a small diner, and I was looking for a job as a secretary. My father was a very poor farmer. I worked in the diner to make money to go to secretarial school.

"Jim's father came in one day, and we fell in love just before Jim's grandfather passed away. Jim's father, John, had been working for his own father in the real estate business. John didn't have any money to even buy an engagement ring when we became engaged. He got me a job with the real estate company as a secretary and I loaned him enough money on my second paycheck to buy me a small diamond engagement ring. "It's this one right here that I am wearing right now." She showed Pam a real cute little diamond ring on the third finger of her left hand that was right in back of a beautiful diamond, ruby, and sapphire wedding band. "You know what, Pam, I'm more proud of that little ring than I am of the big one. The little ring is what started the whole thing.

"When John started the plastics company, I went to work in his office as his office manager, and that's where I worked for the first seven years. We finally got our first real big government contract, and that's the day I quit and came home to raise Jimmy. I haven't always been Roxanne. Most all of my young life I was just plain Roxie, John Dixon's wife.

"Now you are going to be going through just part of what I went through, with this difference. You're going to have Jim, Roxie, Johnny, and Jenny in your corner all the way. If you have questions or problems, we'll be there for you, and don't you ever forget it. We'll be right there behind you all the way."

"Roxie, I have to admit that makes me feel a whole lot better. Roxanne is some kind of a lady."

She goes over and takes Pam's arm and says, "Let's take a look at the yard."

Pam said, "I must admit this yard looks more like a park than a yard. This is the most beautifully manicured grass that I have seen in years. All of the flower beds are full of color at this time of the year."

"Pam, I understand that your father has a beautiful yard. Jim told me. I hope he likes ours, and maybe he will be able to give me some suggestions when he gets here."

"Roxie, I don't think my father would know where to start in a yard like this. He will love it, but he will be in total awe of this yard. He'll love your roses and peonies as well as your mums and dahlias. I think dahlias are one of his favorites."

Roxie turns to me and says, "Why don't we go into the house and have a cup of coffee so we can visit. I think I would like to get to know my future daughter a little better. I have a feeling we are going to be very special friends."

Jennifer thought that was a great idea because she wanted to have some time with Pam also.

Pam was surprised at this, but she accepted it the way she accepted most things. "That sounds fine with me, so come on, Jim, let's go in. I can spend some time in this beautiful yard later. I have a feeling I'll be spending quite a bit of time in this yard. I love it out here."

Inside the kitchen Roxie tells Julia to make a big pot of coffee because we had a lot of talking to do. "Now let's talk about the wedding plans. Just what do you and Angie have in mind? Who all will be here, and how soon do you want the wedding to happen?"

Pam answers her with, "Well, Roxie, Angie and I had figured they should be here tomorrow or the day after. We had talked about having the wedding on Saturday if that's all right with you."

"Let's see now; today is Tuesday. If they get in on Wednesday, we can have the dress showing on Thursday. That'll give us Friday for taking care of any alterations that need to be done. In the meantime Jenny can call and make the arrangements for the flowers. I can also arrange for the music and food with Julia's help. She seems almost as happy as I am that Jim is finally finding happiness.

"Jim, have you and Pam decided on a minister? We can get one from our church if you would like, but if you have someone else in mind, I think you should contact him and arrange the time."

"Pam, do you remember Father Brockman from that little church in New York City?" I asked.

"Yes, I do."

"Do you think he will remember me if I call him? How would you like to have him marry us?"

"He knows all four of us. That would be great if he can come. Why don't you call and ask him?"

"Okay, what's the name of the little church where we met him."

"His church is St. Baranbus, and it's on 128th. St. I'm sure information can give you the phone number."

"What time Saturday do you want to get married?"

Roxie asks me, "Don't you think you should find out what time the priest can make it before you set the time?"

"Mother, you always were so practical."

Johnny and Jennifer tell me this sounds like old times hearing us spar with each other. "We love it," they said at the same time.

"If you folks will excuse me, I'll go to the study and call to see if I can get in touch with Father Brockman."

Roxie asks Pam, "What kind of flowers do you and Angie like, and what color of dresses do you think you would like to have?"

"Roxie, we talked about that before we left on our trip and since we both wear blue a lot, what do you think of a very light blue silk with an overlay of lace that's just a little lighter shade of blue."

"Sounds wonderful, Pam, but are both of you blonde and blue-eyed?"

"Yes, we are, and we are just about the same size. She is about an inch and a half taller than I am. She's also a little better endowed than I am, she has a great body. She used to be a Broadway dancer so you can judge from that approximately the way she looks. She's still in great condition and works out all the time," Pam explains.

"Man, oh, man," Johnny said, "you mean to tell me we're going to have two beautiful blondes in this house for a while?"

Jenny tells him, "Don't go getting any ideas, right Mother? I hope you don't mind me calling you that now, but it feels so right that I feel good calling you that."

"I don't mind, Jenny, and you can call me Mother any time you want to. I consider that the highest compliment I could have," Pam said.

"What about me, Pam, can I call you Mother also?" Johnny asked.

"Jenny," Johnny asks, "can't you just see the eyes on some of my friends when I introduce them to my mother? Their eyes are going to bug out on sticks. I'll have the most beautiful mother of all of them."

"Johnny, you can call me Mother," Pam says "but don't carry it too far. I don't want you to embarrass me in front of your friends."

"I wouldn't do that for anything, but we sure will be glad to have you for our mother."

Jenny told Pam, "It's sure going to be great to have someone that I can talk to about, well you know, woman things.

"Grandmother, I don't mean that the wrong way, but you're a lot older and look at things differently than someone Pam's age looks at them."

Pam turned to Roxie and says, "Roxie, I sure don't want to take your place with these young folks, but I think you know what they're talking about."

"Pam, I don't mind in the least, and I am not going to be jealous. I'm just happy that you're here to be a friend and mother to Jenny, and Jim's here to be the same for Johnny. They've needed this for a long time. Now I'll have all four of you."

I came walking back into the room and I tell them I have just talked to Father Brockman. "At first he was hesitant about coming to Chicago, but I assured him that he would not have any getting around by himself to do. He said we seemed like such nice couples, and he would enjoy the trip and getting to know us better. I told him about it being a double wedding, and I also told him we were trying to buy the duplex, so we would have a place to stay when we go to New York City. I also assured him that he could stay with us here at the house, and just to make it easier for him, I'll have a prayer rail in his room. He thought that was a good idea. He said he's never had anyone do that for him before. I assured him that I would personally meet him at the airport.

"He will be here Friday afternoon. I told him that we would arrange his passage from here. All he'll have to do is go to the airport. I'm having his plane tickets delivered to the parsonage at St. Barnabus Church for him. Now all we have to do is set the time on Saturday.

"Pam, do you have the phone number of Angie's folks? If you do, why don't you call her and make sure the time would be all right with her and Pug."

"That's a real good idea. Jim, can you show me where the study and phone are?" Pam asked.

"Come on," Jenny says, "I'll show you, I think it's time for you to get used to this big old house so you can find your way around it."

Jenny and Pam go into the hall and a couple of doors down to a beautiful room full of bookshelves and furniture that is elegant. The chairs are all covered in soft leather, and the tables are dark mahogany with beautifully carved legs and cove edging. There is even a ladder that ran on a track up near the ceiling that people could use to find the books up high. The ceiling was about twelve feet high.

Jenny tells Pam that the phone is over on the desk. What a desk, it must have been about nine or ten feet long and about four feet wide with beautiful light tan leather inlay on the top.

Pam sat down in a chair by the desk to phone Angie. "This chair feels like it is made of glove leather. Boy this is going to take some getting used to, but like Roxie said, I should learn without too much trouble, right Jenny?

Pam dials the number, and a man's voice answers. She asked if Angie is there, and she could hear plainly when he turned and says, "Angie, it's for you."

The next voice on the phone was Angie's.

"Well, lady, are you ready to get married?" Pam asks.

Angie squealed on the other end of the line. "Is that really you, Pam? I have been thinking about you all day. How are you guys doing, and how was your trip home?"

"They were all fine, and we're doing fine," Pam says. "Now, I have a question to ask you. Do you and Wayne think you can make it back to Chicago tomorrow?"

"You aren't going to believe this, Pam, but Wayne and I have already changed our tickets so we can come back tomorrow. What's the hurry anyway, not that it makes any difference?"

"Well, I find that they can have the gowns here Thursday for us to choose from, and then that gives us Friday to have any alterations they need to do. Guess what? Jim called Father Brockman and asked him if he would fly to Chicago and marry us. He has agreed. Really, he has agreed to come and marry us. He seemed to like us, at least he said he did. Isn't that a great surprise?" Pam asked.

"Oh, yes."

Pam added, "I haven't told you, but Jim wants to buy the duplex so we will always have a place to stay when we come to New York City. I know it's nothing fancy, but we have a warm feeling toward that little old house, and I'm sure you and Wayne do also. It'll be kept for either of us that needs it, or maybe all four of us will want to go back once in a while," Pam suggests.

"Pam, that guy of yours just keeps on surprising me with the nice things he keeps doing. My folks are real excited about coming to the wedding."

"Angie, you're not going to believe this house. It sits on almost thirteen acres near the heart of Chicago, and the house itself has over fifteen thousand square feet in it. Some of the ceilings are about twelve feet high, and most of them are at least ten feet high. Just wait until you see this kitchen and all of the velvet drapes and the carved wood staircase," Pam rattles on excitedly.

"Pam, now you have me wanting to come to Chicago today, but I won't."

"Angie, tell me how Wayne's getting along with your brother and his family and also with your father."

"My father just loves him. They talk about a lot of things that I never heard of, but they really have a lot more in common than I would have ever dreamed. My brother and Mary Lou and the children love him too. He's so good with the children. I couldn't believe it, but he is having a ball with them, and they're in his lap every time he sits down. It's real evident that he loves children, and they love him.

"Pam, do you think it's too late for me to have a baby?" Angie asked wistfully.

"Angie, I think that would be wonderful. If you want a family, then go right ahead and have one. How does Wayne feel about it?"

"Well, we haven't exactly talked about it, but I think he would like to have children."

"I suggest that you talk to him about it just as soon as you are married. You should start trying if that's what the both of you want. I think that would be wonderful because that way I could be grandmother or aunt to your children as well as those of Johnny or Jenny.

"What time are you going to arrive in Chicago tomorrow?" Pam asks. "We want to meet you. I'm so glad Wayne and your dad get along so well. That makes everything a lot better, doesn't it? Are your brother and Mary Lou and the children going to be able to come to the wedding along with your father?"

"Pam, I think they will all get to come if that's all right with the folks."

"Angie, we can almost put up a full company of soldiers in this house. You just won't believe it. I know I told you that, but it's true. You've got to see it in order to believe it.

"Oh, yes, you're going to love Jim's mother. She is so down to earth. Can you believe it, she used to be a waitress too. That was before she and Jim's father married.

"How have Wayne's headaches been doing? Any more headaches? I hope not, so you had better see that he keeps taking his medicine."

"Don't worry about that. I make sure he takes his medicine. I know there'll be a lot of excitement this weekend with the weddings and all."

"Oh, yes, Angie, I almost forgot to ask what color dress you think you want? Do we want the same color? I think that would look real pretty if we did."

"Pam, I think that would be wonderful if we have dresses just alike, don't you? How about light blue? How does that sound to you?"

"Honey, you will never believe this, but that's the very thing I was thinking. I told Roxie that since we're both blonde and blue-eyed, I thought a soft blue silk with a lace over it that's a little lighter blue than the silk would be real pretty. How does that sound to you?"

"That sounds great. Can we get some blue shoes to go with it?"

"No problem, they're going to bring some shoe samples with the gowns.

"Angie, I know you have a lot of things to do in order to leave tomorrow," Pam says, changing the direction of the conversation.

"Pam, we're looking forward to meeting everyone."

"Angie, we'll pick you and your family up at the airport tomorrow. What time did you say you were arriving? Two fifteen p.m. sounds fine, and we will be there waiting."

"Are they going to make it on time?" Jenny asks.

"Sure thing, Hon, they're going to be here tomorrow right after lunch, 2:15 to be precise.

"Jenny, maybe you would like to go to the airport with us to pick them up."

"Daddy can take the limousine because it will carry eight people comfortably," Jenny says.

"Jenny that sounds like a real good idea. Let's go tell him what you and I have planned for him tomorrow."

"Daddy, guess what Pam and I have planned for you tomorrow?"

Pam starts laughing. Then Jenny was laughing, and pretty soon everyone was laughing.

"Okay, girls, I can already see what I'm going to be in for. It's going to be you two against poor little ole me. Just what have you got planned for me tomorrow?" I ask.

"Well daddy, we thought that maybe you could take the limousine and go pick Pug and Angie and the family up at the airport."

"Oh, no you don't. Johnny can drive because I don't have a driver's license yet," I reminded them.

"Oh, Daddy, Jenny said, "can't you go down to the bureau first thing in the morning and get your license? They won't be in until after lunch. Can't you go down first thing in the morning please?"

"Pam, see what I'm going to be putting up with from now on? There's no way I'm going to be able to stay ahead of the both of you.

"Johnny, can you run your old father down to the bureau first thing in the morning?"

"Well, Dad, if you can't say *no* to those ladies, I guess I'll have to do that or go to the airport myself. I think we should go down early in the morning, so why don't we go down and be there when they open up? You know, after all these years you're going to have to take a driving test. Do you think you can pass it?" Johnny asks, all the while laughing.

"Well, son, I don't know, but I do know that I'm going to give it one heck of a try."

"Pam," Johnny asks, "does Dad ever use foul language anymore?"

"No, Johnny, I don't think I have ever heard him say anything worse than *hell* or *damn it*."

"Well dad, when I was a kid, that was one thing I noticed about you. You never had to use foul language to get your point across. I'm proud of you for sticking to it. I would have thought that you might have started using some pretty rough language on the streets."

"Son, I found out that I kind of got their attention when I didn't use rough language. They respected me for it even if they were street people. Most of them didn't know any other way to talk, but some of them even toned their language down when they were around me for a while. They found that it wasn't necessary in order to get their point across. I like to think that I just might have been a good influence in their lives."

"Okay, so now it's settled. I'll try to get my license first thing in the morning. If I do get it, then Pam and Jenny can go to the airport with me to pick up Angie and Pug and Angie's family.

"Now, let's get down to the real serious discussion about the wedding.

"Mother, we need you in here. Pam would like to discuss things with you and Jenny about the music and the flowers. We need to talk to the Father at the church to see if there is anything else that Father Brockman might need such as alter boys or whatever. Heck, I don't know what they'll need for a home wedding like this.

"Johnny, can we come back by the church in the morning and talk to the priest at St. Matthews? I hope you know him personally."

"Dad, you know him. Father Brady is still there, and he'll remember you."

"Yeah, I'm sure he will. After that's taken care of, we can come back here for lunch and then on to the airport. As soon as Pug gets here, we need to go to the tux shop and arrange for tuxes for both of us and our best men.

"Johnny," "I do hope you'll be your father's best man."

"Great, Dad, I would love to. I was hoping you would ask me."

"Jennifer," Pam asks, "will you be my maid of honor?"

Jennifer squealed really loudly when she was asked. "Pam, I would love nothing better. Thank you, thank you for asking me."

"I think Angie will probably ask her sister-in-law if she comes. If not, she may ask Pug's sister or mother to be her maid of honor."

"Remember now, Pam reminds everyone that we have to have corsages and boutonnieres made up for everyone."

"Jim, Roxie says, I just wish your father could be here to see you and how happy you are right now and to meet Pam."

Johnny agreed. "Grandmother, I could just see Granddaddy's eyes light up when he looks at them together and sees the love there. Ours is finally going to be the family that I've always dreamed of."

"Roxie, do you mind if Jim shows me around the house so I won't get lost? I've seen some of it, but there is still a lot I have never seen," Pam asks.

Roxie laughs and says, "I think that would be a good idea. It's about time one of us does. We seem to keep getting interrupted each time we try."

I take Pam's arm and leave the kitchen with her. As we walked out, we heard Julia ask Roxie what we would like to have for dinner.

"Julia, why don't you surprise us."

I usher Pam down the hall through the corridors and passed room after room, and as I passed each of them, I referred to them by name.

"Jim, are you telling me all of these rooms have names?"

"They sure do, Honey otherwise you wouldn't know where everyone was. This big room right down here is going to be our bridal suite, and the next one will be for Pug and Angie."

We walk into the rooms and Pam can't believe how large they are. She walks to the bath and looks through the door and just stands there for a minute. Jim, there's a sunken bathtub in here. It looks like a small swimming pool."

"I know, I've had a few baths in that tub over the years. After my wife and I split up, I stayed here in this room for quite a while. I hope you like it."

"Like it? Jim, I love it. I have never slept in a four-poster bed before. Now I'm looking at a four-poster king-sized bed that we're going to spend our wedding night in."

"Pam, would you rather we go to a hotel or some other place instead of staying here?"

"No, Jim, I would rather stay here. I love this house and the people in it. We had our honeymoon in New York City, so we can stay here with the family until we have to leave for Texas, which won't be that long. I just hope Pug and Angie feel as we do."

"When we get back, we can help them find a place as well as us finding a place of our own," I suggested.

"Jim, we have so much to look forward to, and thank goodness Roxie and the kids are a big part of it. I love your family."

"Pam, they love you too, and it's not just my family any longer it's our family. Those kids have never acted this way about anything or anyone in their life before. They are both so smitten with you."

"Jim, I hope I never let them down. Now, can you please show me the rest of the house, or do I have to call for another tour guide?"

"Okay, Baby, let's go."

The next half hour was spent going into and out of the other rooms that we had missed up till now.

Pam finally asks, "Where do Oscar and Julia live?"

"Julia and Oscar have a room in the servant's quarters. The servant's quarters are actually a three-unit apartment house. You know a triplex. Each has their own entrance separate away from the others, so they have some privacy. Dad felt that would be better when he built them. Before that they lived in the garage apartment. It also has two entrances, two kitchens, two baths, and a nice living room. The guest-house has two entrances and three bedrooms and three baths and two kitchens, with large living rooms. Basically, one is a one-bedroom apartment, and the other is a two-bedroom apartment. Now, my dear, do you have any more questions?"

"No, my dear, let's go back to the kitchen and see what everyone else is doing."

As we walked into the kitchen, Johnny jokingly says, "Grandmother, are we dressing for dinner this evening?"

Pam turned to me and said, "*Dressing?"*

I start laughing. "Honey, Johnny has a sense of humor. Don't worry about that we only do that on alternate Tuesdays, Thursdays, and Saturdays, and then on Sunday if we have guests."

Roxie was looking at her son like she could hit him. "Jimmy, you shouldn't tell Pam something like that. We do not dress for dinner on all of those nights, we just dress on Mondays, Wednesdays, and Saturdays. Sunday if we have guests."

Johnny and Jenny and Julia just can't hold it any longer as they all burst out laughing.

Roxie finally looks at Pam and said, "Pam, Honey, I hope you can get used to this sense of humor around here. Jim's father had a sense of humor that took a little getting used to, and I guess it has rubbed off on everyone else around here."

Pam had a relieved look on her face. She turned and hit me on the shoulder just as hard as she could.

"Hey, lady, I'm not the only one in on this, Johnny was in on it as well as Mother, so go hit them."

"You started it. Just because I'm a little ole country girl, you don't have to treat me like one and scare me half to death. You just wait, Roxie will show me the ropes, and how to dress when the time comes, and how to act when the high fallutin come around here. Won't you, Roxie?"

"Yes, I will, Pam, and I won't let them tease you any more, at least not very often."

By now Pam was smiling. "Well, now Jim, see there, your mother's going to help me. She doesn't want you to be ashamed of me. Remember, she is going to be the one introducing me as her daughter-in-law. Now tell me, Sir James, are you going to battle both your mother and me?"

"Hell, no, Honey, I know what that would mean, and that would be suicide."

"Anyone hungry for hamburgers?" Julia hollers. "How about some good old American hamburgers tonight with cheese if you want, along with some pickles, tomatoes, onions, mustard, and ketchup or mayonnaise?"

Everyone seemed to speak up at the same time with a real loud, "Yes, that sounds wonderful."

"Jim, Roxie says, it's been a long time since you made hamburgers, how about it?"

"Yeah, Dad, how about it?"

Jenny agreed that if I would cook the hamburgers, she would run to the store and get the buns.

"Jenny, that'll be great; I have the ground meat. I bought some this morning thinking we might do just this very thing. You remember, just the way we used to do it," Roxie says.

"Pam," Jenny asks, "how about you going to the store with me if you aren't too tired?"

"Great idea, young lady, let's go."

Johnny suggests they check the cold drinks before they go. "We drank a lot of them the other night, and we might need some more."

They go to the cupboard to check the soft drinks, and sure enough, they were short of drinks.

"Johnny, we'll just get some of everything.

"Dad, Jenny asks, do you still like root beer?"

"Yes, I do, Honey; that's the only kind of beer I'm drinking these days."

"Sounds good to me. How about you, Johnny? Do you want anything special?"

"Root beer or Coke sounds great to me. Do you need me to go along with you and carry the sacks?"

"Yeah, you'd like that wouldn't you? This is going to be girl talk so you stay here."

Pam and Jenny head out the backdoor to her car. Jenny is leading the way when they came to a little old 1957 MG. She tells Pam to get in.

"Where?" Pam laughingly asks. "I'm sorry, Honey, but I just didn't expect you to be driving a car this old."

"This was Daddy's pride and joy before he left. He bought it in pretty bad shape and fixed it up all by himself. He took so much pride in this little old car I just couldn't stand the thought of getting rid of it."

Pam smiled, "Now, if you'd been driving a pickup, I would have really been shocked."

"No, I don't drive the pickup; Johnny drives that. That's how I got the MG. I wanted the pickup, but Johnny is tall, and he had trouble fitting into the MG. He drives a 1973 Chevy Fleetside. It's another of Daddy's pride and joys. He bought it new and treated it like it was gold. He wouldn't let anyone other than Granddaddy drive it. They both had a thing about old vehicles. Granddaddy even had an old J3, 1943 Piper Cub out at the airport that he bought and fixed up before Daddy left.

"Did Daddy tell you that he's a pilot? I should say he used to fly. I'll bet he never even mentioned that did he? No wonder though, he never talked a lot about the things he knows how to do.

"Granddaddy flew during World War II, so when he came back home, he kept it up. He used to take us up in his other plane once in a while. The company had a Beechcraft King Air. It seated six people plus the pilot and co-pilot. They sold it after he died, and now I think they have some kind of corporate jet. I never have been up in it. I guess Daddy will have to get his pilot's license renewed too."

"Jenny, I'm learning all kinds of good things about your father. The only thing he ever told me when we met was that he used to be a college professor, and that he went on a lost weekend and never got up out of the bottle for the next ten years. I'm sure that if he had told me about all of these things, I would have turned him off real quick as a blow hard. You know, a braggart," Pam commented.

"I know what you mean. A lot of guys come on to me with that kind of attitude because they think I have money. I really hate that. Why can't they just like me for what I am?"

Jenny pulls into the parking space near the front of the bakery. "I'll be back in a jiffy," she says, and she was too. It sure didn't take her long to go into the bakery and get the buns and come back. She had two sacks in her hands. She tells Pam that she had gotten some sweet rolls for breakfast. "We might want something before Julia gets up, so we can heat these up in the microwave with a little butter and a cup of coffee. What do you say?"

"Sounds good to me," Pam agreed.

Pam almost said, *I'm used to serving your father his coffee in bed,* but she didn't. She caught herself just as it was about to come out.

"Pam," Jenny asked, "you really do love Daddy, don't you? I can see it in your eyes every time you look at him. I wish we could have had that kind of love in our family when we were kids growing up."

"Jenny Honey, I fell in love with your father the second time I saw him. I told my parents that I knew it was awfully sudden, but I just knew that he was the man I wanted to spend the rest of my life with. I was impressed with him the first time I saw him, but the second time I knew for sure he was going to be my man one way or another. I don't know what I would have done if he hadn't asked me out. Thank goodness he did ask me out.

"But, I didn't know I was going to get a bonus of a wonderful mother-in-law and two wonderful children who already seem like they are my own. I know that sounds kind of crazy, but I'm just looking forward to you and Johnny helping me catch up on the things I have missed out on during your teenage years. I just wish I had been here to help raise you guys."

"Pam, since you love children so much, how come you never had a family – if I'm not getting too nosy."

"Jenny, I was married when I was young. I was married to a young sailor who was killed in an accident on an aircraft carrier. After he was killed, I found out that I was pregnant. I don't know just what happened, but I had a miscarriage. After the miscarriage the doctor told me that I wouldn't be able to have any more children. I guess it just got the best of me because that's when I went to New York City. I worked there as a waitress, and that's where I met your father."

"Pam, can we spend the night together tonight? I just want to talk to you and learn everything I can about you. You seem to be a blessing from heaven sent to us, and I want to know everything I can about you. I want to know where you came from, what you like, the things we have in common. You know what I am talking about, don't you?"

"I sure do, Honey, and yes we can spend the night talking all night if you want to."

"Do you think Daddy will ever believe this? I used to want to have an evening just to talk with Mother, but she always had some place to go and someone to see."

"Jenny, don't you think it would be best if you could just try to remember the good things about your mother instead of the bad times? I'm sure you had some good memories with her, and those are the times and things you want to remember. In time you'll just remember those good times and forget the bad times. It's a lot better to have good memories than bad memories.

"That's what I have done about my life before I met your father. I had some bad times, but I just try to put them out of my mind and not let them make me feel sorry for myself or be mad at anyone. I just thank God that I had those good times.

"I had a wonderful mother and father growing up. They were always there for me, so I consider myself extremely lucky. I married a wonderful young man, and we had five months of a wonderful marriage. He is no longer alive, and I have to move on. I'm thankful for the good memories I had from that marriage. From now on I'm going to be there for you and Johnny, if you'll have me."

"Pam, please don't worry about that, you've already been accepted by everyone. I heard Julia telling Grandmother today how much she liked you, and Oscar gave that a big amen. Oscar and Julia are good judges of people. They see right through a phony, and you're no phony."

They quit talking as they come to the driveway, and in they go with the buns and sweet rolls.

When they come in, Pam tells me that she had just had a ride in my little old MG. I turned my head quickly as if someone had pinched me.

"Pam, are you telling me they still have my old MG?" I ask.

"Yes, sir, and I got to ride in it. Jenny has taken that as her car, and Johnny has taken your old pickup as his car. Can you imagine that when they could have a new car if they wanted one. This should tell you something about how much your children think of you. Now you need to tell me about that old J3 Piper Cub at the airport. Why didn't you tell me that you flew?"

"Well, I didn't want to scare you off. I was afraid all of that would be a little too much."

"Seems to me that you're going to have to get your pilot's license reinstated as well as your driver's license. I want you to take me flying," Pam requested.

Jenny gave the buns to Julia as she had begun putting the hamburgers together. She put the meat on the buns and let everyone apply their mustard, mayonnaise, or ketchup and the vegetables they wanted.

Pam didn't know what seasoning they put in the meat, but it sure was good. "I don't think I've ever eaten hamburger meat seasoned like this," she said.

Pam asks Julia what she put in it, and Julia said don't ask me, ask Jim he don't even tell me. That's an old family secret."

"I learned it from my father, and I'll pass it on to Johnny, and he can get us some grandsons to pass it on to."

"Dad, you're counting your grandsons before they're hatched aren't you?"

"Well, maybe I am, but you and Jenny had better get busy and get us some grandchildren to spoil.

"Jenny," I asked, "how about it? Do you have a boy friend? I mean a steady one that you really like."

"Yes, I have one, but you may not like him. He's a young man that likes to work with his hands. He started an antique restoration business, and he's really good at it. Some of my friends think I'm nuts because they say he will never amount to anything.

"I remember what you said about Granddaddy, and him wanting you to do what would make you happy. You wanted to be a teacher, so he encouraged you to do that. I encourage Randy to do what he wants to do for a living and to be the best in Chicago or in Illinois as far as that goes. I want him to do what makes him happy, and if he's happy, I think I'll be happy. I don't have to have a lot of money to be happy."

Pam looked at me and said, "Jim, I remember hearing you say exactly what Jenny just said. Your father wanted you to be happy. Now we want Jenny to be happy, and if Randy wants to be an antique restorer, then let him be one. I would bet that a person who was real good at restoring and preserving antiques could make very good money. He might even be able to get some other young men to work for him. He could teach others the trade, and by doing this he could grow. I think I would like to meet this young man, Jenny. How about it? Are you going to bring him over, so we can meet him? I hope you intend to invite him to the wedding. You are, aren't you?

"Johnny, how do you like this young man?"

"Pam, Randy is a real swell guy. I really like him, and we get along real well. We both like to play golf and go to baseball and football games. We double date quite often."

Pam asks Johnny, "Do you have a steady?"

"Well, not exactly. I have a girl I have gone with for a long time off and on, but her parents don't really care for me. They think I am a spoiled little rich boy. I'm doing my best to prove to them that I'm not. They know I work at the plant, but they think that I probably have a real soft job. The truth is that Grandmother has got them making me learn the business from the bottom up. I started in sweeping floors right after I graduated from college. I don't know many college graduates that started out that way. They graduated me on to the loading docks, and that's really hard work isn't it, Dad?

"I heard that you worked sweeping floors and on the loading docks. I heard you made it upstairs just before you graduated from college and then came back to work there while you got your Masters.

"Granddaddy told me that he wanted to give you money so you wouldn't have to work so hard, but you turned it down. He said the only thing you allowed him to do was pay your tuition, books, and supplies. Is that right?"

"Well, not exactly, because every once in a while he would slip an extra hundred in my shirt pocket just to help me over the humps.

"I'm proud of you, son, for being willing to work the way you are. Now can we stop talking about working because my hamburger's getting soggy."

We were having a great time tonight with the process of getting to know each other better.

After dinner we sat around and drank a cup of coffee and talked. Julia was such a great cook, and she made the best dessert you ever tasted. She brought out a cherry cheesecake for dessert. Everyone was going to have to go on a diet after the wedding if we keep eating this way.

Before we knew it, it was 11:00 p.m. and we were all tired.

Jenny told me that she was going to spend the night with Pam so they could do a lot of girl talk.

"Well, how about that? You guys are getting real chummy, aren't you? I think that's great, Honey you guys just talk all you want to, but don't wake me up because I'm tired and need to get a good night's sleep so I can get up early tomorrow morning and get my driver's license."

I told everyone goodnight, went over to Jenny and kissed her and then my mother and then Pam. I looked at Johnny and told him, "All you get is a great big hug, son, I don't feel like kissing boys tonight. Not that I wouldn't kiss you, it's just that tonight you have to settle for a big bear hug."

"That's fine with me, Dad I'll settle for a hug."

I headed for the bedroom upstairs.

Pam gave Johnny and Roxie a hug and a kiss on the cheek and said goodnight to them. She and Jenny headed up the stairs. She turned to Johnny and told him to be sure to wake his daddy in the morning.

"Okay, I'll see that he gets there."

"Don't wake us up too early because we may talk half the night."

Roxie said, "Goodnight. Enjoy yourselves and leave the rest to Julia and me."

"Okay, Grandmother, goodnight all."

It was 6:00 a.m., and there was a knock on my door. I raised my head, and a voice from the hall was saying, "Dad, it's time to get up. We have to go to the Bureau and get your driver's license. They open at 7:30 a.m., and we want to be first in line. Julia has coffee ready, so get your shower and get ready to go."

Johnny headed back downstairs where Julia had the sweet rolls in the oven to warm them up. Johnny got a cup of coffee, while Julia fixed him a sweet roll with a little butter on it.

"You know, Johnny, that little sister of yours has some real good ideas once in a while. Johnny, when you get through with your coffee, why don't you take a tray with coffee up to them."

"Julia, do you really think I should at this time of the morning?"

"Johnny, I think they would like to say good morning to your daddy before he leaves for the morning. Now what do you think?"

"Julia, I think you are a real sharp lady. I'll do that very thing."

Julia got a tray and a couple of cups and saucers, along with a creamer and sugar bowl. "Now if you would like to take these up the ladies, I think they would appreciate it."

Johnny took the tray and was on his way up to the girl's room when he ran into me at the head of the stairs. I looked at the tray and then looked at Johnny and asked, "How about letting me take that to the girls?"

"Fine with me, Dad, I can go back and finish my coffee. You better hurry while the sweet rolls are warm."

I knocked on the door, and there didn't seem to be any response from inside, so I knocked a little harder and louder. Finally, I heard a, "Hello, who's there."

It's me Darling, Jim." "May I come in, are you decent?" I walk in with tray in hand and walked straight over to the coffee table, set it down, poured two cups of coffee, and then I asked, "Would madam prefer one lump or two?"

By now Pam was sitting up in bed, and Jenny had uncovered her head and asked, "What time is it?"

"Six fifteen, madam, would you like for me to draw your bath?"

By now both of the girls were wide awake and laughing.

Pam wanted to know, "Do we always get service like this?"

"Not by a long shot," I bellowed. "I just wanted you to have a memorable first morning awakening." Then I bent over and kissed each of the ladies, turned, and headed for the door with a, "Top of the morning to you, ladies; I'll see you later. I'm off to get my driver's license."

Pam asks Jenny, "Has your father always been like this?"

"Does he bring you coffee in bed, Pam?" Jenny looked at Pam and said, "Well, I thought maybe you could tell me?"

Pam just looked at Jenny.

"Mother, I don't mean to be forward, but I should hope that you and Daddy have slept together. I can see the love in your eyes when you look at each other, and it would be a crime if you weren't making love also. I know it looks better to the folks if you have separate bedrooms until you are married. I guess you have to keep up the moral front. I admire you and Daddy for doing that."

"Jenny, you're quite a young lady. If I had been able to have a daughter, I would have wanted one exactly like you. I could ask nothing more than to have two children like you and Johnny, and now I'll have that love along with your father's. No woman could ask for more. Now my coffee is getting cold, so how about us going downstairs and having some breakfast before we shower?"

"Great, let's go."

They both run for the door like a couple of teenagers. They run laughing down the staircase and into the kitchen.

Julia turns and started laughing with them. "What a great sound! It's been a long time since we heard laughter like that in this old house."

From the kitchen door they heard a very loud, "How about a cup of coffee?"

They all turned, and there stood Roxie posing in the doorway like a Marlene Dietrich pose from one of her movies. Everyone really started laughing then.

"Roxie, I think we can find an extra cup of coffee around here. We also have some very good sweet rolls that some nice young lady brought by yesterday evening and left for us to use in just of these very circumstances. Would you ladies like one? You can have butter or no butter. You apply that yourself."

Everyone milled about the kitchen getting their own coffee and rolls. They all sit down, visited, and had their coffee and sweet rolls.

The Wedding Plans

"Jenny," Roxie asked, do you know what kind of flowers you are going to order?"

"Grandmother, I wanted to talk to Pam about it as well as Angie when she gets here. What do you think about some orange blossoms, lilies, orchids, and maybe some roses?"

Pam says, "I know it's my wedding, and I'm sure that roses, orchids, and lilies would be nice, and I've heard of orange blossoms for weddings. I don't think I've ever seen any orange blossoms. I'm sure we'll like whatever you think would look best. You have to remember Angie and I are just plain people. Would you please just use your own judgment on those things?"

"Jenny, why don't you just call the florist we generally use and have them come out. That way you can show them the area where the wedding will take place and let them decide what to use."

"Good idea, Grandmother, I'll call them when they open."

"The dresses will be here tomorrow morning about 9:00 a.m. that way we can get that taken care of in case there have to be any alterations," Roxie added.

Just then the phone rings, and Julia answers it. "Pam, it's for you; it's Angie."

Angie says, "Pam, my sister-in-law won't be able to come since one of the babies is sick and she can't bring him. She will have to stay home, but we will all get together later if that's all right."

"Angie, I'm real sorry we won't get to meet her and see the children, but we will meet your father and brother won't we?"

"Oh, yes, you couldn't keep my daddy away now that I am going to marry Wayne. He really likes that guy.

They have become real buddies. We will see you at 2:15 this afternoon."

Pam hung up the phone and turned toward Roxie.

"Roxie, Angie's sister-in-law won't be able to come because one of the children is sick, but her father and brother will be here."

They all sat back down to their coffee and discussion, and the phone rings again. Julia answers the phone again, and again she calls Pam to the phone. "It's your mother."

"Mother, is everything all right?" Pam asked nervously.

"Pam, the families have decided not to come and bring the children. They figure they will be too much trouble, but they do want Tommy and Jerry to come with your father and me. They think it would be better if they didn't try to bring the kids on the airplane because they're afraid of how much trouble they would be on the plane and also at the wedding."

This really upsets Pam, but she understands and says, "Tell them we'll get together real soon. Give everyone a big hug, and tell them I love them. We'll meet you and Dad and the boys at the airport. That's right we'll be there at 5:00 p.m. We won't miss you. I know Daddy is kind of worried, but we will be there."

Pam came back to the table looking kind of down in the mouth.

Roxie says, "Okay, little Darlin', tell us what the problem is now."

"My sisters-in-law feel that the children would be too much trouble with the wedding and all. They say they would love to come and visit us after we are married. Mother, Dad, and the boys are coming and will be here tomorrow afternoon at 5:00 p.m.

"Also, I forgot to tell you that Pug talked to his folks, and it seems that just his mother, father, and brother will be the only ones to come from his family. Elaine is pregnant, and the doctor doesn't want her to come because delivery time is close at hand. Her husband doesn't want to leave her at a time like this.

"We had better stop and see how many bedrooms we have and how many will be taken up."

"Well, Pam, your family will have two bedrooms. Angie's family will need two, Father Brockman will need one.

"Pam, will your brothers sleep together?"

Pam said, "They always did when they were growing up. We only had a four-bedroom house, and with the girls wanting a bedroom each, the boys had to room together. They didn't always like it, but they accepted it. That takes care of twelve bedrooms."

"Well, we at least know how we are going to sleep. If we need more rooms, Jenny and Pam can spend another night together, and Jim and Johnny can spend the night together. That would ease up two more bedrooms so we don't have anything to worry about." This was Roxie's explanation of how to handle things if the room situation got too tight.

They all agreed that it looked like everyone was going to have a place to sleep.

Jenny looked at her grandmother and asked, "How about the music?

"Pam, do you and Angie have any favorite songs you want at your wedding?"

"I don't know about Angie, but I have always thought that I would like the song "More" sung at my wedding if I ever got married again."

"Pam, I think that's a beautiful song, now when Angie gets here, we can ask her if she has a favorite. I have already arranged for the organist and vocalist. The vocalist can sing just about anything you would ever want to hear. That takes care of the flowers and music, and Father Brockman will be here Friday afternoon. The guys need to go and be fitted for their tuxes as soon as Pug or, Wayne, that is, gets here."

Pam and Jenny decided it was time to go upstairs and get their showers and straighten up the room.

That was all right with Pam and Jenny, but Roxie had hired someone to do that. "They'll be here in a few minutes to start cleaning house. You get your showers and forget about straightening up the room. That will be taken care of by Marilyn, the new maid that has been hired to assist Julia," Roxie said.

Pam agreed, "Julia can probably use the help for the next few days."

"Julia won't be the only one getting some assistance; Oscar will have a helper for the next couple of weeks also. That should make it easier for everyone."

The girls went upstairs to shower while Roxie and Julia continued with their plans for the day.

After a couple of hours there was a lot of noise at the front door as Johnny and I got home.

"Hey, guess what? Dad got his driver's license, and he drove home. Now I guess his next step is to get checked out in his plane and get his pilot's license again. Maybe he can even learn to fly the new company jet."

"Johnny, I think you had better just let me get used to driving first before I start flying."

"Okay, Dad, but I have thought about taking lessons on the jet myself."

"This is one time I agree with you one hundred per cent. Maybe we can both take lessons at the same time. That would be fun."

I ran up the stairs hollering at the top of my lungs so Pam would be sure and hear me. "Honey, I got my driver's license." I repeated myself three or four times before she and Jenny both came out of the bedroom. Pam was just wrapped in a big towel.

"Jim, are you all right? I thought something drastic had happened when I heard the noise."

"Well, it is drastic; they gave me my driver's license. That means you no longer have to drive me everywhere." I grabbed Pam and swung her around, and she almost lost her towel. When I finally put her down, she was grabbing real hard to get hold of the towel and hold it in the proper places to keep from exposing everything.

She finally caught her breath and told me that she thought I had been shot or something. "Now if you will just put me down, I need to get back into the bedroom and get dressed."

"Killjoy. Sometimes you're a real killjoy," I said, and I winked at Jenny who was laughing loudly by this time.

Pam hit the floor and ran for the bedroom.

I hollered, "Honey, I'll see you later."

She said, "Not like this you won't."

I ran back downstairs to my mother and grabbed her and kissed her and said, "Mother, do I feel good or what?

I feel like a new man; I got my license. What do you think?"

"I think you're mad, young man; I think you're mad, but I love that look in your eye.

"Johnny, don't you have a friend that is a professional photographer?"

"Sure do, Grandmother; he's real good too."

"Does he do weddings?"

"Sure he does, he is especially good at that."

"Well Honey, Roxie suggests, why don't you go and call this friend and tell him to come over and let's make some plans on the pictures we want him to take.

"That sounds great, Grandmother he's a nice guy you'll like him."

"Johnny, I don't have to like him if he is a real good photographer. Just kidding, Johnny. I think I met him with you at a party one night. He seems nice, so go call him and set things up, please."

I walked into the room as they were finishing their discussion and ask Mother for some advice.

"Okay, if I can," she agreed.

"I would like to call Pam's old boss and invite him to the wedding but I don't want Pam to know he's coming. Would you help me do this, and what do you think about it?"

"From what you have told me about him, I think that would be a great idea. You know we don't have any more bedrooms left."

"Oh no, we don't want him to stay here. If he did that, she would know he was here. I thought he could stay at a hotel and come in just before the wedding. If you won't say anything to her about it, I think I'll go to the study and call and ask him to come."

Roxie let me know she or Julia wouldn't say anything, so I headed for the study to make the call. In a while I came back to the kitchen. Pam and Jenny were there helping make the decisions of what to have for lunch. I offered a suggestion which they liked, "Sandwiches and tea."

Julia seemed to like the idea herself. She headed for the refrigerator to check and see if they had something to make sandwiches out of. She found nothing in the refrigerator and could only find a couple of large cans of tuna in the pantry. She turned to the gang and asked if that would be all right.

"Julia, that sounds fine to us."

After lunch, everyone was sitting around talking when Pam suggested to me that we should be getting ready to go to the airport and pick up the McKenzies and the O'Neills.

"Pick up who? Who are they? Oh, you mean Pug and Angie and their family. You're right; the time is getting close, so let's go I'll drive."

Johnny and Jenny wanted to know if they could come along. "We can take the limousine. It seats eight comfortably, and you might get lost if you drive, Daddy."

"How about that, Pam? Now they think I might get lost. Okay, Johnny, you drive, and, Jenny, you and Pam can sit in the back and act like we're your chauffeurs. I'll ask Oscar if we can borrow his cap."

Roxie was getting a big kick out of this. She laughed and told us to get out of here. She asked Jenny if she had contacted the florist and Johnny if he had contacted the photographer, and both gave a resounding, "Yes, they are contacted and ready."

Jenny told Roxie, "The florist will be here at 4:00 p.m."

Johnny said, "My friend will be here first thing in the morning."

"No good, Johnny. You call your friend and tell him that you guys have to go for a fitting first thing in the morning. Ask him if he can come out this evening. Everyone will be here this evening, including Angie and Wayne."

"Okay, Grandmother, I'll take care of it. I'm sure he'll be able to make it."

"Now you guys better get out of here and go to meet Wayne and Angie."

The traffic was not too bad this time of the day, so Johnny made good time going to the airport. We arrive at exactly 2:00 p.m., park the limo, and head for the terminal gate where they were to come in.

We just barely get there when people start coming in from the plane. It seemes that the plane had experienced a tailwind and had come in early. Here they come up the ramp. They see the gang waiting on them.

Angie screamee and comes running to Pam. She grabs Pam around the neck and hugs her, while reaching over for me. Pug was right behind her with his hand stuck out to me. Just as soon as Angie was through with her hug, Pug grabbed Pam and gave her a big hug too.

"Pug, Angie, I would like you to meet my children."

"Children Jim, these aren't children these are a couple of beautiful young folks," Angie said.

"Pam, they're beautiful young adults aren't they?"

"Yes, they are, Angie, and they're two of the finest young people you will ever meet."

Angie hugs Jenny and then Johnny. Pug shook Johnny's hand and hugged Jenny and told me what a beautiful family I had. Angie had totally forgotten about her father and brother who were standing behind them.

"Oh, my God, I almost forgot about Papa and Darryl." She finally introduces her father and brother to everyone.

"Wayne," Johnny said, "if you'll give me your claim checks, maybe Darryl and I can go and get your luggage while everyone else talks.

"How about it, Darryl?"

"Sounds like a deal, Johnny, let's go."

They headed down to the baggage area while the rest of us talked, and talk we did. In a few minutes Johnny and Darryl came back. "Okay, everyone follow us, and we'll get you out of here." We went to the limousine which was parked in the VIP parking area. Everyone got into the car, and we headed for home.

We got back home and started up the driveway.

Angie looked at Pam. Her eyes were big as saucers when she saw our home.

"I told you. It's big isn't it? Just wait till you get inside."

Johnny parked in front of the house, and Oscar came out to open the doors of the car with Julia standing behind him and Roxie looking on.

We all got out of the car and Pam started introducing everyone. "Roxie, this is Angie.

"Angie this is my mother-in-law. Well she's my mother-in-law to be Saturday."

Roxie turned to Pam and winked, "She really is a beauty, isn't she? Just like you said, she's well built too."

This embarrassed Angie who looked at Pam and wanted to know what she had been telling these folks.

Mr. O'Neill was just looking around. When things slowed down, he shook hands with Roxie and Oscar, and then he shook Julia's hand. "I'm not sure just what to do next, so why don't you folks lead the way and let me follow along with Darryl."

By now Darryl had met everyone. We walked to the door, followed by Oscar and Johnny with the luggage.

Roxie offered a solution, "Why don't we let the men put your luggage in your rooms? In the meantime, we girls can go back to the kitchen and have a cool glass of iced tea. When the men get here we can have a cool glass of tea waiting for them.

"How would you like that, Mr. O'Neill?"

It seemed that Mr. O'Neill liked tea as much as the rest of us.

We all settled down in the kitchen for a while. Julia seemed to enjoy having a group to wait on. She wouldn't let Pam or Roxie help at all. She just said, "Sit down and visit."

Pam and Angie were going over the flowers with Jenny, and Roxie asked about the music selections.

Angie said, "I like all music just as long as it doesn't sound like a funeral."

Roxie told her what Pam had chosen, and she liked that very much. She asked Roxie, "Would it be all right to end the wedding with the Lord's Prayer?"

Pam agreed "That would be just great with me. How about you, Roxie?"

Roxie agreed, but let them know it was their choice because it wasn't she who was getting married. "Not ever again," she said.

After everyone had calmed down, Johnny offered to show all of the guests to their rooms. That was fine with them, so off they went.

Pam and Angie were looking around at the size of this house, while Darryl and his father did a little looking on their own.

Darryl said to his dad, "This kind of reminds me of the county courthouse back in Omaha."

"Well, yes, but it's a little nicer than the courthouse," Mr. O'Neill agreed.

Everyone got situated and came back down to the study for a get-acquainted session.

Mr. O'Neill and Darryl asked if it was all right if they looked around the grounds. I thought they just wanted to go outside and get some fresh air. Darryl, Mr. O'Neill, and I went outside to take a little walk.

Outside Mr. O'Neill asked me to call him Sid. "That's my name," he said. "I would feel a little more comfortable if everyone would just call me Sid."

Darryl agreed that all of his friends called him by his given name back home, and he would feel more comfortable if we could do that for him also.

"That's fine with me, and I'll tell the rest of the folks to just call you Sid," if that's allright with you?

He grinned and thanked me. He started walking toward the back of the place where the trees were. He said that he loved trees and the outside. Darryl was enjoying the outside also, when we heard a voice from behind us. It was Pug.

I asked Darryl, "How do you feel about Pug as a future brother-in-law?"

"I really like that guy. He seems to really love Angie, and that's a big thing."

Sid told me that he and Wayne got along real well. "I like to fish, and it seems that Wayne used to do a lot of fishing on the Colorado River near Moab when he was a kid."

"Wayne wants to take me home with him some time so he can take me fishing down on the Colorado. I think I would like that," Sid admitted.

We all roamed around the yard for quite a while just looking at the flowers and trees. Darryl was real quiet, but Sid asked me if I did any of the work in the yard.

"Sid, I used to when I was a kid, but Mother has a full-time gardener now who takes care of everything."

After about thirty minutes, we all went back inside to see what was happening. Darryl thought he would like to go up to his room for a while and straighten things out and maybe lie down for a while.

The girls were still talking up a storm. I went over to the girls and told them they had to go and pick out some wedding rings. This was the first time anyone had thought about that.

"Since we have the time this afternoon, I suggest we go to the jewelry store and do some looking. We can get the engagement rings later if we don't find something we like. I assume you girls want to have a double-ring ceremony?"

They agreed they wanted a double-ring ceremony, so we realized that we had better get on the ball.

"Sid, we need to go, so we'll leave you here with Roxie and Johnny and Jenny while we go to the store."

We went back to the house and told them where we were going.

Roxie wanted to know if we had thought about the marriage license.

"Mother, yes I have, and just as soon as the girls are through picking out their dresses in the morning, we're going to the marriage license bureau to get the license."

We all headed for Roxie's car since there wasn't enough room in the MG or the pickup for all four of us. Roxie pitched me the keys and said, "Be careful, and we'll see you after awhile."

We arrived at the jewelry store of a man who used to be a friend of mine. As we walked in the door, my old friend spotted me and came out from behind the counter with a hand extended. I shook his hand and said, "Hello, Byron, I haven't seen you in a long time."

"Yes, it has been a long time, but I saw you on television, and I couldn't believe what I saw. You looked good on television answering all of those questions."

"Byron, I want to introduce you to my fiancé Pam Jackson, and our friends Angie O'Neill and Wayne McKenzie. We're having a double wedding at Mother's house on Saturday afternoon, and we need some wedding rings for a double-ring ceremony."

Byron called his wife over. She works in the store with him. He told her about the wedding and asked her to show the girls some wedding bands, and he would show Wayne and me some men's rings at the same time.

Pam said, "I think we should all look at the same ones since we would like to have matching bands."

"Smart girl," Byron said. He went behind the counter and came up with a large tray of beautiful wedding bands. We looked at several of them.

Angie said, "I like this pattern."

Pam looked at her choice, and she seemed to like that pattern too, but she said, "I also like the ones just above them, which are a little different pattern."

We all looked at the rings, and we agreed with the girls on the rings they had chosen. Byron told us he was glad we didn't choose the same ones. "Each of them is a double set, and we only have one set of each pattern."

"Byron," I suggested, "why don't you wrap them up?"

Next I started looking at some beautiful rings that I thought would be nice for an engagement ring. Pam and Angie came over and started looking them over with me to see if they could find one they liked. Sure enough, Pam found one she was absolutely crazy about. She showed it to Angie.

I was really fascinated with it too. I said, "Try it on."

She did and it just fit. Just to tease her, I told her that she and Angie should try on the wedding bands to see if they would fit. They both tried them on, and they did fit just fine.

Wayne and I tried ours on, and mine was a little large, but Wayne's ring fit fine.

"Jim, you can bring the ring in to have it sized after the wedding if you would like," Byron suggested.

"Byron, is there any way you can size it for me in time for the wedding Saturday afternoon? I may be heading for Texas soon after the wedding."

"Well, old friend, just for you, I think I can get that done in time for the wedding. I'll deliver it myself no later than Saturday morning." He measured my finger and let me know it wouldn't be a problem. He would have it ready.

I asked Angie if she had found a ring she liked. She and Pam had both found rings they would love to have for engagement rings. I walked over to Byron and quietly asked, "How much are they?"

Byron quietly said, "One ring is $16,000, and the other is $19,500."

"Byron, just send me a bill for them to Mother's address along with the wedding rings, and I will put a check in the mail for them." I walked back over to the girls and asked if they fit.

They each tried them on and said, "Yes, they fit just perfect."

I looked at Wayne and said, "Now it looks like we're officially engaged."

We each kissed our girlfriends and said, "Now it's really official, we are engaged."

Wayne looked at me and told me that he couldn't afford a ring like that. He was kind of embarrassed.

I said, "The price of the ring is your signing bonus for going to work for me. We'll take that out of your first year's bonus. Now let's not hear any more about it."

Angie came over and hugged my neck and kissed me on the cheek. Pam did better than that. She gave me a long and loving kiss and told me how much she loved it. Pug came over and shook my hand and put a big hug on me. He looked at me and said, "Jim, no man could have a better friend."

"Pug, we've been through a lot together, and now we're going to have a lot more to go through."

We all headed for the car to go home.

When we reached the house, we went running in and the girls were hollering for Roxie and Jenny and Julia to come and look at their rings. Everyone was talking about the rings and buzzing around until I asked, "What's for dinner?"

Everyone started laughing, and Roxie came over and put her arm around Pug's and my neck and kissed us on the cheeks and said, "Boys, I'm proud of you. You really did well this time. I love the rings. Now if you can only get the marriage license as easily."

"Don't worry, Mother, we'll head straight down town in the morning after the girls choose their wedding dresses. Now, Mother, what are we forgetting?"

Roxie looked me straight in the eye and asked, "Do you eat cake these days, son?"

"Mother, dear Mother, you are a genius, a true gem of the first class. I assumed you had ordered the cake or cakes."

"Yes, I did my darlin son, and guess what? I also ordered the champagne and white wine and a little red wine for those that would rather have the dark stuff. I also ordered some diet Cokes and Seven-Up and root beer for you. You might want to tempt yourself at a time like this, but I didn't want to be the one to tempt you. That's your decision. They will both be here in case you would like to have a drink of champagne at your wedding. If you do, I can assure you, that Pam and I will see that you don't get intoxicated. If you do, we will put you in a room and lock the door for three or four days and feed you hospital food because that is apparently what happened when you got off the bottle.

"Jim, I do not intend to ever let you get on the bottle again."

"Mother, that's the best news I have had in years, thank you."

Pam gave a big amen to that one. Pug agreed that he might try one drink for such a special occasion.

Sid was standing by and heard what Pug had said. He told Roxie, "If anyone needs any help with Wayne, I'll be right here."

Darryl had been real quiet up till now, but he told his dad, "If you need any help, I'll be right there to help you. Now that Angie has hooked him, we don't want him to get away."

We all had a laugh at that one. Everyone was in such a wonderful mood.

Johnny came in and told his grandmother that his buddy the photographer was here to talk about the pictures.

They went into the other room. In just a minute they called Angie, Wayne, Pam, and me into the room in order to be sure we were getting all of the shots that we would normally take plus anything else we might want. "You know what I mean, unusual shots since this is a double wedding."

We went over what was to be done, and we were all satisfied that the young man would do a good job.

Johnny agreed that everything was fine, and then he said that he needed to be getting over to St. Matthew's Church to get the rest of the equipment that was needed for the wedding. He turned to Darryl and asked if he would like to go with him.

When Darryl found they were going to take the pickup, he was surprised. "Do you drive a pickup, Johnny?" he asked unbelievably.

"Sure do, it's one that Dad bought back in 1973, and he has had it ever since. After he left and I reached legal age, I took it for my own. That seems to be just fine with Dad now." Johnny also told him about Jenny's MG. He was real interested to know that Johnny's dad had had a hobby such as that.

As they drove over to St. Matthews Church, Johnny also told him about that little old J3 Piper Cub out at the airport. Now Darryl was really interested. It seems that he has been taking flying lessons in Omaha.

He told Johnny he had been flying a Cessna 172 for most of his lessons. "And guess what, Johnny? There is an old J3 Piper Cub out at the airport where I'm taking my lessons and I've heard a lot of tales about it. I went over and checked it out the other day and I wondered how it would be to fly a plane using a stick instead of a wheel."

Johnny said, "I'm going to take lessons real soon, so I can fly it."

These young men seemed to hit it off real well. They were near the same age and seemed to have some of the same interests. They arrived at St. Matthews to pick up the additional things needed for the wedding. They found that Father Brady was still there, and he remembered Johnny from the times when he had been an alter boy. He appeared glad to see Johnny again and asked about his father. Johnny told him about the wedding and Father Brockman from New York City.

Father Brady told Johnny that he had met Father Brockman a couple of times at church functions. He spoke highly of him and wanted to know if he was the one that was going to handle the wedding.

"Yes, sir, Father. Dad, his friend, and the ladies knew Father Brockman in New York City. The ladies attended his church in New York, and they introduced Dad and Wayne to him. He wasn't their regular pastor, but the four of them became well acquainted with him and felt a real kindred spirit to him."

Father Brady told them that was easy to understand. He took the boys to the storeroom where the articles they would need had been set aside. The boys loaded them, thanked Father Brady, and headed for home.

On the way home, they talked about doing something for the folks as sort of a wedding present. Johnny explained to Darryl that he and Jenny had talked about reserving the bridal suites at the Hilton Hotel since they had two suites available. "How do you feel about that?"

"Well, I think that would be great, but how were you going to afford that?"

"We have that all worked out. We will just have the hotel bill the company for the rent on the rooms."

Darryl couldn't believe they would do that.

"Oh, yeah, they'll do that because we reserve rooms for a lot of our company's customers when they come to town. They're used to doing that.

"We won't tell Dad and the others about it until just at the time of the wedding. What do you think, Darryl?"

"Gosh, Johnny, I just wish I had thought of something like that."

"Darryl, just how do you feel about Pug or, Wayne, whichever they call him?"

"Johnny, I was a little skeptical at first but after I met him and had a couple of days with him, I really liked him. One of the things I like best about him is the way he treats Angie. You can tell he really loves her and will take care of her. I understand that he's working for your dad as some sort of assistant."

"Yeah, Dad is going to do a lot of things in Texas after the wedding, and he needs Wayne to go and help him. When he gets back to Chicago, he'll be Dad's executive assistant on all of Dad's business dealings.

Dad has big plans for Wayne. He thinks he has a world of talent. He may arrange for him to go back to college and take a few courses that he might need to have for this type of business. I think this will be great for both of them because they know they can totally trust each other."

The gate to the house was just ahead. They turned in, park, and start unloading the items needed for the wedding. After they get the unloading done, Johnny parks the pickup, and they go inside to the kitchen.

Johnny looks at Julia, and before he could say anything, Julia asked if he would like to have something to drink.

He laughs and says, "Julia, you read my mind, don't you."

"Yes, I do, and I have been doing that ever since you were born, young man." She got each of them a large glass of iced tea with a slice of lemon. "This should cool you off. The rest of the folks are in the study if you are wondering where they are."

"Thanks, Julia, we'll head that way and see what is happening."

When Johnny and Darryl enter the study, they find us having a good visit discussing the wedding, and what we are going to do after the wedding.

Johnny looked at Jenny and winked. This was a go-ahead signal for her to call and reserve the two bridal suites at the Hilton. She excused herself and was gone for a while. When she came back, she gave him a thumbs up which meant it was all taken care of. Both Johnny and Darryl smiled and gave her big thumbs up so she knew they understood.

The rest of the evening was kind of boring. We ate a very nice dinner, and we finally got everyone to bed so we would all be ready for tomorrow.

Thursday morning came early, and we prospective brides and grooms had a very fast breakfast. Then we headed for the license bureau, hoping to be first in line to get our licenses so we could get back before the dresses arrived. We had planned to do it afterward, but after talking it over last night, we had decided to give it a try this way.

"If we are a few minutes late, they won't take the dresses back. This is going to be too good a sale for them to be too picky about the time," I said.

We finished our coffee and headed for Roxie's car. She laughingly tells me, "You're going to have to buy yourself a car."

"Okay, Mother, I'll do that, but in the meantime will you call our accountants and have them set up bank accounts in my name for about $30,000 and one in Pam's name for about $25,000. We'll try to get over to the bank right after lunch and sign the signature cards."

Roxie agrees to take care of it for us, and we left for the license bureau.

We arrived at the bureau about ten minutes before 8:00 a.m., and it opened at 8:00 a.m. sharp. We were second and third in line. There were three clerks to handle the business, so all three of us couples were, you might say, first in line.

We answered questions, signed papers, gave the clerks money, and were on our away.

The whole transaction had taken fewer than twenty minutes, and we were on our way home.

We arrive at home, and I call Johnny to tell him that if he was through with his breakfast, maybe he would like to run down to the bank and get the signature cards for Pam and me to sign.

"Take Darryl with you. When you get back with the cards, Pam and I can sign them, and then you and Darryl can take them back.

"By the time you get that done, it should be near noon, and then after lunch you can take Pug and Angie to the airport to pick up Pug's mother and father and his brother Neil."

"Great, Dad, that sounds like a good plan."

As soon as they got through with their coffee, they headed for the bank. They were back within thirty minutes with the cards.

"Dad, Mr. Crane wants you to stop by just as soon as you have time. He would love to see you again. From what he said, you two used to be pretty good friends."

"That's right, son we were good friends, but I wasn't sure he would remember me."

"Remember you? He was tickled silly to know that you were back home and doing real well. He really wants to see you. He said something about you and he used to do a little flying together."

"Yeah, we took lessons together, and then later we used to fly that little old J3 around the area and out over the lake. He's one of the guys I had hoped wouldn't give up on me."

"Give up on you? He didn't seem like the kind of guy to give up on a friend. Were you guys classmates in college? He said something about you guys having classes together."

"Yes, we were, Johnny. We were friends even before your mother and I married. I guess Chris and I have been friends for about thirty years or so."

"Well, Dad, he wants to see you as soon as possible, and he really means it."

"That's nice news from an old friend, and I will get by to see him as soon as possible. I have to have him transfer a check from a New York City bank to his bank as soon as possible."

Just then the door bell rang. Oscar answers it and comes back into the room with the manager of the wedding dress store, and the models were following him.

Johnny nudgs Darryl. "You know what, Darryl, some of those models aren't too skinny. Most models are real skinny, but these are pretty well built."

The models walk by and smile at the boys, which seemed to be making things worse.

Roxie greeted them warmly and led them into the ballroom area where the showing was to take place. Pam and Angie followed them into the room, and the boys try to come in behind them.

Roxie tells them, "No, no, not now, boys. You have to wait till the wedding to see the dresses with the girls in them."

She closed the door, and the girls went about choosing their dresses.

The manager of the store knew they wanted something in light blue, so he showed them several different styles in light blue with lace over them. All of a sudden, one of the models came in with a gorgeous gown of light blue silk with a softer blue lace overlaying the silk. Both girls spoke at the same time. "That's the dress. That's just got to be the dress."

The store manager looked at Roxie and asked if that was the one they wanted. "It's funny, but we just have two of them in stock. They are both size eight."

With this Roxie told the girls to please go with the models and try the dresses on just in case they needed any altering.

In just a few minutes both girls came back into the room wearing the beautiful gowns. There was only one problem with them and that was very easy to fix. They were a little large in the waist and a little tight in the bust. "Angie's will need a little more letting out in the bust area, and Pam's will be just about right except for the waist."

The manager assured the girls they would be ready tomorrow before noon. This tickled the girls to death because these were the very dresses they had both dreamed of being married in.

They looked at Roxie and asked, "Roxie, are you sure you want to spend this kind of money on us?"

"Girls, I can spend whatever I want to on you. It's the last wedding you're going to have, so you can have whatever your little ole hearts desire. Please, don't even think of looking at the price tag. That is the least of our worries right now. If those are the dresses you want, those are the dresses you are going to have."

They returned to the room to have the fittings done. The store even sent the tailor with them. Roxie told the manager to just send her a bill for the dresses. He seemed real pleased with that, so pleased in fact that she finally had to ask him the price even though it wasn't a factor in buying them. He explained that they were only $6,500 each. She just smiled and walked off saying how pretty they were.

Things rocked on till lunch time when Julia came through the house letting us all know that lunch was being served in the dining room. Julia and Marilyn, the new maid, had everything ready and on the table. Today she was serving sautéed chicken breast with some sort of a wine cream sauce with a side of asparagus and a small baked potato with a slice of lemon pie for dessert.

When Pam saw this, she couldn't believe it. "Now I see why Jim is so spoiled. He's gone for ten years, and the first good lunch after he gets home he has his favorite, asparagus with lemon pie for dessert."

Julia smiles and tells everyone, "Jim has liked asparagus ever since he was a little kid. He and his father used to grow it in a small garden on the back of the property. They also grew tomatoes and small new red potatoes, along with squash and green beans. They had a regular little farm back there. The patch is still there. Oscar has kept the weeds out of it just in case Jim came back. He knew how much Jim enjoyed gardening with his father."

Pam looked at me. "Now I know where the desire for asparagus comes from," she said. She told everybody about her adding it to my dinner the first time she had waited on me.

Roxie said, "That had to be a good sign. She knew you even before she knew you, if that makes any sense."

"That's an oxymoron if I ever heard one."

"That has to be a sign of some kind that you two were meant for each other."

Pug thanked me for liking asparagus because that had led not only to Pam and me getting together, but also to him and Angie getting together.

Pug said, "Angie, I guess that's kismet."

Now we were all looking at Pug.

"Well, I read it in a book on one of my off days. I've read one or two love stories, whether you believe it or not. They turned out to be pretty good books. You know what, I even read *Romeo and Juliet*.

We were all laughing now because I believed that Pug was blushing.

"Well, you guys, just stop to think about it. If Pam hadn't brought Jim that asparagus, I wouldn't be marrying Angie on Saturday, and that would be awful."

By now we were all laughing hysterically. Pug looked at all of us laughing, and he finally started laughing as well.

We all finally settled down to the task at hand, that of eating. When I really thought about it, I realized that it wasn't a task at all to eat the food that Julia cooked. She was a wonderful cook.

Finally I couldn't stand the suspense, so I just had to ask Pam and Angie if they had found the dresses they liked.

Both said *yes* at the same time. They looked at each other and smiled. They looked at Roxie and told her how much they appreciated what she had done.

She just said, "Don't think about it, just enjoy it."

After lunch, Johnny and Darryl took the signature cards back to Mr. Crane at the bank. While they were there, they told Mr. Crane that I had a cashier's check at a bank in New York City for the winnings on the TV show. Johnny told him also that the bank was holding it until I notified them to forward the money on to my bank in Chicago.

"Johnny, just have your dad call me, and I should be able to take care of it over the phone. I will need the name of the man he dealt with and the name of the bank."

"I'll have Dad call you and give you the information so it can be taken care of. This should make him happy because it can be taken care of without too much trouble."

By the time the boys got back to the house, it was time for them to go to the airport and meet Pug's family.

As soon as they got home, they got Pug and Angie into the limousine and headed for the airport. They barely made it in time to meet the plane. Pug's family was standing at the head of the ramp waiting on them.

Wayne saw them and hollered, "There they are."

Angie saw a lady's hand start to wave. She and a couple of men with her came running toward Wayne. The lady grabbed Wayne and held on for dear life. The older man got in on the hugging also, while the younger man walked over to Angie and said, "Hi, I'm Neil, and you must be Angie."

"I sure am." She hugged him and said, "I'm glad to finally meet you. Wayne has told me a lot about his brother."

He wasn't quite as tall as Wayne, but he favored him a lot. He had the big broad shoulders and that boyish grin that seemed to be an unmistakable family trait.

When his father finally let go of Wayne and turned to look at Angie, she saw that he had that same unmistakable smile on his face that the two boys seemed to wear constantly.

He stepped over and said, "I'm Jake, Wayne's dad."

Angie grabs hold and gives him a big hug and a kiss on the cheek and says, "It is so good to finally meet you." Wayne has told me a lot about you. I hear you like to fish. Well I do too and maybe we will get a chance to do some fishing and talking together. How about it?

Mrs. McKenzie finally released Wayne and looks at Angie. She smiles and says "Wayne, she is prettier than you said. Your Angie is not just pretty, she is beautiful.

"Angie, I'm so glad to finally meet you. You are even more beautiful than Wayne said you were." She hugs Angie and tells her how glad she is that she is going to become a member of the family.

Wayne tells his mother, "You know I wouldn't lie to you about her. She's the best thing that has ever happened to me. She has helped me stay on the straight and narrow and away from the bottle."

Neil told Pug that was something in itself little brother. "She must be a great influence on you."

"Now, Mother, Jake says you know how you are." "When Wayne was young, his mother thought he couldn't do anything wrong. She was a little bit prejudiced."

Angie smiles and reaches over for Wayne who told his mother that they hoped someday to give her another grandchild or two.

Wayne's mother just smiles and says, "Angie, please, just call me June. You can call me June or whatever you want to call me, and remember that Daddy is Jake. You can choose what ever you want to call us."

Wayne was going to introduce Neil, but he said, "Yeah, we already met."

"Hey, brother, it sure is good to see you." He walked over and hugged Wayne and held on for a long time. When he let go, he said, "I sure do love you, brother, and I sure have missed you. Don't you ever lose touch with us again."

"Angie, Neil says 'don't you guys ever lose touch with us again. There is no way we are ever going to lose touch with you guys again."

She reaches over and puts her arm around his neck. Now there were tears on all of their cheeks, even Wayne's and Neil's. As soon as everyone had dried his or her eyes, Wayne introduced them to Johnny and Darryl.

"We're real glad to meet you boys, and we're anxious to meet Jim and the rest of the family too."

Johnny, Darryl, and Neil took the baggage checks and headed for the baggage area to get their luggage. They were back in just a few minutes with the luggage and suggested everyone head for the car. When Jake saw the car, he said, "I have never ridden in a limousine, and I didn't think I would unless it was for a funeral."

"This sure isn't a funeral, this is going to be one of the happiest days of our lives."

Everyone got into the car. The boys put the luggage in the trunk of the car and away they went.

On the way home Wayne told them they were going to be surprised at this little house where they were all staying. They talked about a lot of things on the way home – everything from the time Wayne was a baby to the time he went off to college.

They approached the driveway and turned in. Jake asked, "Where is the house?"

Angie said, "It's just past this circular driveway."

As they made the circle, there the house was in all its splendor if you could call it that.

They sat quietly until Oscar opens the doors of the car for them to get out. Wayne introduces them to Oscar and tells them that Oscar has been with the Dixon family about thirty-five years.

Jake smiles and said, "Oscar, do you think this job is going to be steady?"

Oscar just smiled and with a pleasure to meet you, he asks if he could help them. They reach the front door and when Oscar opened it, there Roxie was with Pam. I am trying to stand discretely behind.

Wayne introduces everyone, and I invite them inside to the study. I ask if anyone would like something to drink.

"Jake suggests, why don't we go to our rooms and hang up our clothes before we settle down to a drink?"

Roxie said, "That would be fine, and after you are finished, why don't you come back down and have some iced tea. There just might be a piece of Jim's lemon pie left if you are hungry."

They were asked to follow Oscar upstairs. He showed them to their rooms and took the bags inside for them. He asked if he might be of assistance. He opened up the closet doors for them and excused himself after he showed them the bathroom.

Wayne stayed with his mother and dad to talk while they were putting up their clothes.

His mother was fascinated with this big house. "I have seen houses like these in movies, but Wayne, I never thought I would be spending the night in one."

"Mother, I think you'll find these are some of the finest people you will ever meet. I think I told you that I'll be working with Jim as his executive assistant, both in his personal projects, as well as in the plastics company. He's a very special friend. We have looked out for each other through thick and thin, good times and bad times, for the past ten years. He's like a brother to me. I would trust him with my life. I have never known him to lie to anyone about anything.

"You're going to like Pam also. She and Angie are almost like sisters. They have lived next door to each other in a duplex for several years. Neither of them ever dated anyone so they spent a lot of time together. When Jim came along, Pam fell for him, and he fell for her right off. It was something to see. When we started out on a double date, Pam asked Angie to be my date. Well, I fell head over heels for her, and apparently she fell in love with me. It seemed like love at first sight for all four of us. I know you are going to love her family too. You'll get to know them in the next couple of days."

After they had finished with hanging up their clothes, they headed back downstairs. When they entered the study, Oscar came in and told them the rest of the family was back in the family room. "They would like for you to join them."

They followed him to the family room where everyone already had something cool to drink. Sid got up and offered Mrs. McKenzie his chair and suggested that he go over with the other boys.

She thanks him and asked if his wife is here.

"I'm sorry; I thought you might have known. My wife passed away a couple of years ago."

"Oh, I'm so sorry, I didn't know. I guess Wayne just forgot to tell us. We had so much on our minds when we talked the other day. As you know, we have a lot of catching up to do. I hope we'll have a chance to get caught up on everything after the wedding."

"Mother, Wayne asks, do you think you could put up with Angie and me for a few days after the wedding?" "We would like to come back to Moab with you guys and spend a few days if that's all right."

"Jake, do you think we could put up with these young folks for a few days after the wedding?"

Jake looks real stern. "Well, I guess if we pushed ourselves real hard, I'd bet we could make it work. Hell, yes, we can put up with them for a few days. Angie said something about fishing, well that will give me a chance to give her a fishing lesson. Wayne says look out Pop, she might give you a fishing lesson instead. That would also give Angie a chance to meet Elaine and her baby. Maybe she will have her new one by that time. Boy, are we going to enjoy having you around for a while. Maybe we can get Neil and go down on the Colorado fishing one day and referee the fishing tournament between Angie and me. How about that Angie, are you game? How does that sound, Wayne?"

Jake, Angie says, that's a challenge I can't refuse.

"Like old times, Dad, like old times, and I would love it.

"You know, that might not be a bad idea. Let's just see if she knows how to fish as good as she says she does, but if she catches more than us men, we won't let her go with us any more."

Angie hollered across the room and said, "Hey, I heard that. It looks like we have a fishing contest on for the Colorado River."

Jake tells Wayne, "You know what, I think she means it."

"I sure do, Jake," came the answer from across the room.

Now there were several others getting into the conversation, and it was getting a little rowdy. You know, about who could catch the most and biggest fish. "I guess they'll just have to wait until next week, and we'll find out.

"Jim," Jake said turning to me, "You and Pam are invited to come along."

"Well, thanks, Jake, but Pam and I have a few things we need to take care of here at home before we go to Texas. We'll take care of things here, and then we will meet Pug and Angie in Texas to get a few things under way there. I want to get moving on them as soon as possible because they are real important to those people in Texas.

"I hope we can take you up on that invitation to go fishing one of these days before too long if it is still open. How about it? I don't think I've ever seen the headwaters of the Colorado, and I think that would be real interesting."

"You're always welcome to come see us, and I'll guarantee you that you'll enjoy it."

"Thanks Jake, I would call that an invitation I can't afford to turn down.

"Right now, I think that Neil, Johnny, Wayne and I need to get down to the tuxedo shop and get fitted for the wedding. How about it, boys, are you ready?"

Everyone was ready, and we all headed for the front door. We were gone for about two hours when we came barging in the front door like a bunch of high school boys after a football game. I was teasing Wayne about looking like a penguin in that tux and tails. We were laughing at each other about trying to sit down and how to handle the tails when we sat down.

Neil had the answer, "We just don't sit down. Everyone stands up until after the wedding and the reception so if you have flat feet, you had better get some arch supports for your shoes. Your feet are going to hurt before Saturday is over."

Pam and Angie chimed in with, "Would you rather stand in high heels?"

"Well, no I really don't think I would like that. Besides, it would look funny."

"Okay, Neil, you and Johnny can stop complaining now."

Roxie asks the girls if they had thought about maybe getting blue dresses similar to their wedding dresses for their maids of honor.

"No, we haven't."

"Why don't you let me call the shop and see if they might have some dresses for Jenny and June. I assume Angie wants Mrs. McKenzie to be her matron of honor."

Angie spoke up and said, "June, I would be honored if you would be my maid of honor."

"Well, how about a matron of honor, at my age I feel more matronly than maidenly. Angie, I consider your request the highest honor I could possibly receive since your mother or sister couldn't be here to help you."

Angie came over and hugged June and thanked her for being so kind.

Roxie went to the phone and called the shop to see if they could accommodate her. She hung the phone up and called Oscar over. She asked him if he would be so kind as to drive the ladies over to the shop for a fitting.

The ladies got up and headed for the front door.

June turned to Jenny and asked, "Does your grandmother always gets things done this quickly?"

"After you get to know Grandmother, you will learn that she works fast when she needs to."

By now Oscar had the car at the front door with the doors opened for the ladies. They headed for the wedding dress shop.

After about an hour, they were back home just as it was getting dusk.

When they came in, Roxie asked, "Did everything go all right?"

"We couldn't have been treated any nicer. They'll have the dresses ready tomorrow afternoon late, and they will deliver them with the wedding gowns."

Jenny tells her grandmother that she asked about the price, and the lady just said, "Your grandmother told me to just add them to the bill. I have no idea what they cost."

"That's all right, they'll send us a bill at the end of the month, and I'll take care of it."

Julia comes in and announces, "Dinner is on the table."

"It seems that all we have done is eat and run around since we got here," remarks Neil. "Don't get me wrong, I love it. That way I get to see the city."

By the time dinner was over everyone was getting a little weary, so we all adjourned to the study and just visited and chatted. This gave us a chance to get better acquainted. Everyone seemed to love it. We visited for two to three hours without a word from the television. It seemed almost impossible these days to just sit and visit with each other without that one-eyed monster being turned on and interrupting things every few minutes.

Someone mentioned something about the Cubs playing baseball tonight, but not one of us even mentioned turning the TV on so we could watch it. Around 10:30 p.m. several of us in the group were getting sleepy so we excused ourselves and headed for the bedrooms. Before long there was no one left except the young folks.

Johnny asked Jenny, Darryl, and Neil if they would like to go out on the patio behind the den and sit for a while. It was really a nice night, so they all decided that would be nice. They decided to take a beer and go out and sit and chat for a while. This was the first time anyone had had an alcoholic beverage since I had gotten home.

I saw them walk out with beer in hand, but I said, "Hey guys, that's just fine with me. I don't think I'll have one just yet."

Then a funny thing happened. Pam and Angie asked the young folks if it would be all right if we joined them on the patio.

"Hey, ladies, that would be great."

We all settled down in our chairs, and Darryl asks me if I would tell him about my hobby of old cars and planes. This tickled me because I hadn't had a chance to talk about these things in years.

First I told them about the MG and how I bought it and worked on it at night in my garage for a couple of years. I said, "When I bought the pickup, it was a beauty, and I just fell in love with it. Only my father and I ever drove it. I used to wash it at least once a week and polish it once a month along with the MG. As far as the J3 is concerned, I bought it after it was crashed in a landing. It wasn't hurt very bad."

Darryl asked, "Is it true that you can fly it standing still in a strong headwind?"

"It sure is, Darryl, and you can fly it without stalling out at between twenty-eight to thirty-five miles per hour if you have your tabs set just right. Maybe you can come to see us after we get everything settled in Texas. By then you should have your license, and I will let you fly it. I will fly backseat though. When I got it, all I had to do was replace the propeller, put new in steering cables, then we covered it with new fabric. Once this was done, I had to get it checked out with the FAA inspector."

Darryl wanted to know, "Is there a lot of difference in flying a stick compared to a wheel?"

"Darryl, I can show you how to fly it in thirty minutes of flying, and you'll be flying it like a pro in a couple of hours. I think Johnny wants to fly it also. The motor will have to be checked out since it has been sitting for so long," I explained.

Johnny piped up. "No, it hasn't been sitting all that time, Dad. I asked a friend of mine who works at the airport to take it up once in a while just to be sure to keep it in good shape in case you came back. Now you're back, and that little Cub is flying ready."

"Thanks, Johnny, not just for keeping the plane flying ready for me, but for having enough faith in me to think that I would return.

"Pam, it looks like the kids have been taking care of everything pretty well since I've been gone doesn't it?"

"It sure does, Honey. Looks like they have thought of almost everything."

"Johnny is interested in getting his pilot's license so he should be flying by the time Darryl gets his license. Maybe I'll have the privilege of teaching both of them to fly that little plane. It's not like any other type of flying."

Jenny looks at me and asks if I am getting nervous yet?"

"Well, not just yet, but I'm sure that by Saturday morning, I'll be real nervous."

Pam says, "I'm not really nervous, just anxious. Anxious to get it over with so we can go forward with Jim's plans."

Angie and Wayne both agreed they are a little nervous and overwhelmed with all that had happened and all that would be happening in the next couple of days.

Pam remembered that her folks would be in tomorrow morning. "Jim, we want to be sure to pick them up.

"Jenny, has Julia ordered the cakes yet?"

"Yes, she has, Mother she ordered them the day Daddy and Pam got here. She ordered two cakes. One cake has your names, and one has the names of Wayne and Angie on it. She's a very thoughtful lady."

"This is such a beautiful night it's too bad there has to be mosquitoes. It seems the mosquitoes are plentiful this year and they have come to this house hungry. I hear that they are attracted to dark clothing, and if you will look around, almost all of us have on dark clothing. What say we go back inside the house for now?" I asked.

There was a mass exodus for the door. Inside was a lot better without the bugs. We all agreed that we liked fewer bugs, and by now we had decided it was time to get some rest because tomorrow there was going to be a lot of work to do.

Johnny said, "Dad, you forgot to tell everyone that we are going to have the reception in the backyard Saturday, and the people will be here in the morning to start hanging lights and spraying for mosquitoes. They claim they can get rid of the mosquitoes by spraying all of the trees, shrubs, and removing any standing water they find in the backyard area tomorrow. We certainly hope they can get rid of them. If they don't, there are going to be a lot of people standing around scratching.

"Oh, yes, they're going to wait until Saturday morning to bring the chairs and everything else."

"I wasn't aware all of this was going to be taking place. I thought it was just going to be a small reception inside the house."

"Grandmother thought it should be a little larger so she invited a couple of other people. None that you wouldn't want to be here. Just a few of the people from the company office that have known you since you were young. They are all people you like and who like you."

"Well, how about everyone going to bed now and getting some rest," I suggested.

We all parted with a "goodnight," and "I'll see you in the morning."

Morning came early, and we all went down for breakfast. Pug came in to find a very pleasant surprise. It appeared that someone had told Julia that Pug had a preference for eggs Benedict. She liked to surprise people with things like that. She had prepared eggs Benedict for everyone, along with good, crispy hash brown potatoes. She knew how much I loved good, crispy hash brown potatoes.

"This is much better than you would find at a restaurant," I said. "Put all this with the great coffee Julia makes, and the biscuits that are made by her own hands, and this is just plain old good eating.

"First question on the agenda is what time do the Jacksons get in?" I asked.

"They will arrive at a little after 10:00 a.m., Hon, on United Airlines."

Johnny asked, "Who's going to go with you to pick them up?"

"I feel that Pam and I should go," I said.

"Can I go along also?" Jenny asks. "I'm anxious to meet Pam's family."

I was okay with that request. "There should be enough room in the limousine. That gives Johnny a chance to play chauffeur again. He likes doing that."

The doorbell rang, and it was the men wanting to start putting up the lights in the backyard. They needed

Roxie or someone to show them where we wanted the lights and how any of them would be needed.

Roxie went out the door and took them to the backyard near the patio and showed them just where and how she wanted everything done.

She came back inside after a few minutes and asked for another cup of coffee. "I need something strong, after trying to get through to those people. They're supposed to be professionals, and you just can't seem to make them understand what you want done. I guess good help is hard to get these days."

Johnny needed to go upstairs and get ready to go pick up Pam's family. Pam and I agree and head upstairs to get ready also.

In about twenty minutes, Johnny went out to get the limousine. In just a couple of minutes he opened the front door and hollers for Pam and me to come on. "It's time to get going."

Jenny came running as well as Pam and me. We came in a hurry, and all of a sudden we were gone.

We arrived at the airport just in the nick of time.

The loudspeakers announced the arrival of the flight from Norfolk on gate seventeen.

"Well, what do you know? We're in the right spot this time, and we don't have to go walking a long way to get to the gate," I said.

A few minutes later the doors to the tunnel from the plane open, and a few people start out. In just a little while there were other people coming up the ramp, and it was getting crowded. Suddenly, I saw a hand waving above the heads of the other people. I recognized Art and Nora, and behind them came Tommy and Jerry. You would think they hadn't seen Pam and me in years the way we were hollering at each other. We finally touched and next came the usual hugging. Johnny and Jenny just stepped back for a couple of minutes until Pam and I and her parents had all said hello.

Johnny walked around to Tommy and Jerry and introduced himself. He called Jenny over and introduced her to the boys. The boys seemed real glad to meet them. They told Johnny and Jenny they had heard quite a bit about them from their dad, but he had been referring to them as children.

Tommy said, "As far as I can see, there aren't any children around here. There are a couple of young adults here as far as I can see."

By this time the hugging was over with us older folks who turn to Johnny and Jenny.

Pam introduces them to her parents.

Nora came over and hugged both of them. "I was expecting children," she said, "not a handsome young man and a beautiful young lady."

Art agreed, "They're not what I expected, but a lot better." Art said, "Pam, you have a beautiful ready-made family. I just know that everyone is going to be real happy. We think a lot of your father and admire him a lot for what he is doing."

Jenny says "Everyone in the family is happy with what Dad has done in the last couple of months."

Johnny asks for their baggage checks so that he and the boys could go and recover their luggage. Tommy and Jerry were anxious to go with Johnny to get the luggage. They found the baggage area easily. They had to wait a while before the luggage started coming down the ramp.

Tommy and Jerry started trying to find their bags. They finally saw a couple of bags, which Tommy identified. They took them off the turntable and set them down beside Johnny while they searched for the others.

At long last they finally had all of the bags. Everybody grabbed a couple of bags and headed for the door check station. Everything checked out, and they headed back to the folks. Upon arriving, they asked us to follow them to the car.

We got to the limousine and put the luggage into the trunk. We all get situated and away we go. The boys were busy looking at the town until Johnny started turning into the driveway.

Tommy looks at him and asks, "Is this the place?"

Johnny assured him, "This is the place."

Tommy turns to Jerry and shakes his head. "Man, oh, man, what a hacienda. This is really something."

Johnny stops at the door, and Oscar approaches and opens the car doors for them. As each of the newcomers left the car, he introduces himself. Oscar greeted each one to the Dixon home in his own personal way.

"Johnny, do you and the boys need any help with the luggage?"

"No thanks, Oscar, we have everything under control."

Oscar headed for the door at about the same time it opened. Out came Roxie and the other folks. I rushed around to introduce everyone to my mother. Wayne and Angie's folks needed introducing as well as Angie.

Nora said, "Yes, we have met Angie, but we're very pleased to meet her family." Nora started to say, "Mrs. Dixon," when Roxie stopped her.

"My name is Roxanne, and most all of my friends just call me Roxie."

Nora looked at her and then looked at Pam and told her that Roxie seemed just as nice as she said she was.

Art was busy shaking hands with Sid, Darryl, Jake, June, and Neil. He turned to me and said, "I think I finally got everyone straight. I sure hope so – you know, who belongs to whom and if I don't have it just right as to who belongs to whom, I will before long. I sound like I'm repeating myself don't I?"

Everyone is invited inside by Roxie who leads the way. Once inside she offers to show them to their rooms. "You might want to hang up your clothing as soon as possible to prevent any more wrinkling than necessary."

She showed them the way, and once inside the room she pointed out the closets and the bathroom.

"If you need anything, I'll be glad to see you are supplied with whatever it might be. I will suggest that as soon as you are through putting your clothes away, you might want to come downstairs to the study where we will have some good cold iced tea for you. Jim said you liked iced tea just about as much as our family does. If you want something else, we will get it for you."

Everyone thanked her and starts hanging up clothes.

It wasn't long before the newcomers were all assembled in the study for their tea while they got better acquainted.

We all visited for a couple of hours before Julia came in to announce lunch was being served in the dining room. Julia and Marilyn had prepared some real fancy salads and sandwiches for lunch. Everyone had a seat, and the talk was so heavy we could hardly hear ourselves think.

After a while, I told Johnny I needed for him to go to the airport just one more time. Johnny didn't know anyone else was coming in. I informed him that Father Brockman was coming in about 2:00 p.m., and I would like for him to drive and that Wayne and I would go along to meet him. That was fine with Johnny.

After everyone finished lunch, we adjourned to the patio where Art told me he would like to see the yard. I showed him around for a while, and then Johnny took over while I made some phone calls.

I called Big Ernie to be sure he was going to be able to make it. Ernie assured me that he would be here about thirty minutes before the wedding. "A heard of wild horses couldn't keep me from being there, but I don't want to give it away too soon."

I told him to go ahead and come to the house about 2:00 or 2:30 p.m. because Pam and Angie would start getting dressed about that time, and he might be able to see them just a few minutes before the wedding started.

"That will be fine because I will be arriving at noon."

I thought that would be just fine and told him I was looking forward to seeing him again. I also told him that Johnny would pick him up at the airport.

"Johnny will have a sign with your name on it when you get off the plane."

We said good-bye and that we would see each other tomorrow.

Tommy and Jerry headed for their rooms in the apartment above the garage. They thought the apartment was real cool. Neil had the other room above the garage, so this gave all of the boys an outside entrance if they needed it. The boys said they would like to lie down for a while. I guess they weren't used to all of this excitement.

The rest of the afternoon went by without incident.

Dinner was called, and everyone showed up at the right time. Julia by now felt that she was running a large restaurant. There were a lot of people here to feed three squares a day. Somehow she didn't seem to mind. She just smiled and went about her work.

I said, "One thing we all have to remember is that Julia is no spring chicken any longer. She works very hard for a woman her age. She watches over Johnny and Jenny as if they were her own grandchildren. She has certainly helped raise them."

After a fine dinner of beef stroganoff along with all the trimmings, she offered up a cherry cheesecake. That was something no one turned down. She had all of us adjourn to the study for our dessert. She and Marilyn served everyone dessert, and we all seemed to thoroughly enjoy every crumb of it. At least there was a lot of praise for her culinary arts ability in the dessert form.

She thanked us all for our kind words and cleaned up the dishes and took them to the kitchen to be washed. Thank goodness Roxie had hired extra help to take care of such chores.

It didn't take long before most all of the folks, including me, were heading for the bedrooms and a good night's sleep.

Morning came early once more, and the smell of coffee filled the house. I once again took coffee to Pam and Jenny in their room. I let them know this was the next-to-the-last time I would be serving their coffee in their room. "Sunday it's my turn to be served coffee in bed."

They asked, "Does that mean you're going to bring us coffee again tomorrow morning?"

"Well, I just don't know right now, we'll see how today goes before I say one way or another." I went dancing merrily out of the room after kissing both of them good morning. I turned and told Pam that she must remember that Sunday morning I wasn't going to come to her room and kiss her good morning. "I'll just turn over and kiss you good morning."

"Is that a promise?"

"You bet it is, and I keep my word."

As I started down the stairs, I heard voices below getting their morning coffee to start their motors running. Julia made a mean cup of coffee.

I strolled into the kitchen when I was met by and looking up at my young son.

"Well, Dad, would you care to join us in an eye-awakening cup of coffee?"

"Why not, I like to live dangerously."

Johnny quipped to Darryl and Neil that I was not generally like this. "There must be something in the wind, or maybe it's the water."

Art, Chris, and Nora all got a big kick out of Johnny.

"Could be, he sure does act like it, doesn't he?"

Julia announced that she had prepared sausage, eggs, biscuits, and all kinds of jellies and jams with orange juice, apple juice, or grapefruit juice. If anyone would like a waffle, she had also prepared waffle batter for those who would like one. She also had warm maple syrup and some melted butter to go on them. As anyone could see, no one went away from Julia's kitchen hungry.

We all seemed to have our own little things to do today, so we started our chores soon after breakfast.

I told Wayne not to forget that we had to pick up Father Brockman later this morning.

Wayne remembered it so he said, "I'm ready when you are, just holler when you're ready Dad."

Roxie, Julia, Pam, and Angie all had things to do for tomorrow.

Roxie asked, "Jenny, have you arranged for the vocalist and the music?"

She had.

The photographer had assured Johnny that he would be here on time to get pictures before, during, and after the wedding. Julia assured everyone that the cakes were coming along nicely and would be ready.

Roxie told all the parents to just make themselves at home and if they needed or wanted anything at all, "Just holler real loud."

By this time Sid, Jake and Art were becoming old friends, and seeing this Johnny asked them if they liked to shoot pool.

They all three said, "Yes, we sure do."

"Okay, gentlemen, follow me right this way to the Dixon billiard hall and poolroom." He led them toward the back of the house down a short hall to a large room with a billiard table, a snooker table, and a pocket pool table. "Gentlemen, you may choose your weapons and enjoy yourselves. If you will notice on the wall to the right is a cold drink dispenser with several different bottled soft drinks for you as well as a nice assortment of cue sticks. Just push the button, and they dispense themselves. I hope this will help you pass the time while we are out running around."

As he started to leave, in walked Darryl, Neil, Tommy, and Jerry. Tommy piped up with, "Man, what a room. This room is almost as big as my whole house."

"Tommy, if you guys would like to play some pool, just pick up a cue, and I will see you later.

"Darryl, I thought that a little while before noon you might like to go out to the airport and get a closer look at that J3 Piper Cub that Dad keeps out there. How about it? would you like that?"

"Man, would I? You know I would.

"How about you guys? You want to go?"

Everyone was real enthused about going out to the airport and seeing that little plane and possibly a chance to see the corporate jet since it was kept in a hanger real close by.

Johnny said, "Well, come on, let's go while they are finishing their breakfast."

They headed for the door to go to the airport.

I was reaching for my second cup of coffee when I turned to Nora and said, "You know something? I almost married the wrong girl."

"What do you mean you almost married the wrong girl? Are you talking about our daughter?"

I gave her and Pam a glance and winked at Roxie. "Yes, I'm talking about your Pam. You see, when we went to get our marriage license, they asked our names. I gave them my name, and then I heard this voice I was familiar with saying 'My name is Pamela Jean Rogers.' I turned to see who was speaking. Then she asked the clerk which name she was supposed to use. Her married name was Pam Rogers. I had never heard that before. Then I was listening to my future wife deal me a blow I had never even thought of. I asked her what was going on when it dawned on me that Rogers was the name of her deceased husband. Next she was throwing me another curve when she asked the clerk which name to use when she said, 'After my husband died, I took back my maiden name legally. We had only been married about five and a half months when he was killed. When I moved to New York City, I felt more at ease using Pam Jackson, so I legally changed my name back to Jackson.'"

Pam's mother asked Pam if this was true.

"Yes, it is, Mother. I just never got around to telling you because I wasn't sure you would understand. You see I felt that since we had no children to be affected by my taking my maiden name back, I would just feel more comfortable with it. I already had my social security card and driver's license and life insurance in my name. I had never changed any of those things, so I just thought it would be easier to just leave things in my maiden name. That is when I legally changed it back to Jackson."

Now I grinned and winked at Nora and said, "Now I wish you would tell me just who I'm going to marry tomorrow anyway. I can't marry two women at once."

Pam was beginning to get into the swing of things, and she responded with, "Who do you think you are marrying, and how many men get to marry two girls at once and sleep with both of them at one time?"

"Pam," Nora said scolding her daughter, "that just doesn't sound right for you to talk like that."

"Well, Mother, Jim started it now let's just see how much he can take."

By this time everyone was laughing hysterically.

I yelled out to everyone that I got the best of the deal. "Pug, you only get one wife," and I ran out the door toward the car.

The boys were leaving at the same time to go to the airport, and things kind of cooled down a little. Since Wayne and I would go to the airport to pick up Father Brockman, the boys were heading out to the airport to look at that old J3 Piper Cub.

The rest of the morning moved very quickly with everything seeming to come together just like a jigsaw puzzle. The boys came back from the airport, and as usual they were hungry. Julia fixed them some sandwiches and a beer, and they seemed very happy with that.

Art, Sid, and Jake were still playing pool when Julia asked them if they were interested in lunch. They all seemed real interested in a couple of sandwiches and iced tea. Julia had a way of taming these wild men with food. She was a real wonder in the kitchen.

The ladies came in later and ate. They started discussing tomorrow and the wedding.

About 1:30 p.m., Pam and Angie came in. They asked Wayne and me if they could go to the airport with us to pick up Father Brockman.

We all thought this would be a great idea since we had all met him. Out we went to the limousine and headed for the airport just talking up a storm about what was going to happen tomorrow. We finally arrived and found that we had about a thirty-minute wait. The plane was on time. It seemed the four of us were just a little bit eager and, therefore we arrived early.

We decided to go have a Coke while we were waiting on the plane to come in. We found a booth and got our Cokes and started talking again without paying any attention to the time. The next thing we heard over the loudspeaker was the arrival of the plane from New York City at gate seventeen.

Father Brockman's Arrival

We were quite a distance away from gate seventeen. The four of us went running down through the terminal like a group of kids playing tag because the girls were reaching their hands forward, and we guys were trying to pull them a little faster than they could run.

Finally, Wayne saw gate seventeen and started yelling that we had made it, and he abruptly stopped with the girls running into him.

The reason he had stopped was that a very large man in a black suit with a round white collar was standing right in front of him.

Father Brockman said, "Wayne, isn't it?"

With this, all five of us started laughing very hard.

"Father Brockman is as funny as any priest I have ever known," I told everyone later.

Father Brockman now said, "Let's see if I can still remember everyone's name. You my dear are Pam, you are Angie, and the big one is Jim. Am I right so far? And I am supposed to marry the four of you tomorrow at 4:00 p.m.? Is that right? That's fine; I just wanted to be sure I was at the right airport in the right town.

"Now, let's find my baggage, and then if you will lead the way, I will follow."

I led the way to the baggage area where we found his baggage, and then we went to the limousine.

Father Brockman looked at it very seriously and asked, "Which one of us gets to drive? I have never driven a limousine."

I pitched him the keys and said, "I will tell you which way to go," and we all started laughing and talking. I sat up front with Father Brockman and chatted with him and directed him to our home.

Father jokingly said, "You know what, Jim, this drives so easy maybe I will buy one and change occupations. I hear the tips are good."

Just before we arrived at the house, I told him to be looking for a driveway with a large arch over it and a house sitting a ways back from the road. Father spotted it, and just to be sure he asked, "Jim, is this the right place?"

I directed him into the drive and around the circular drive to the front door. Just as he was about to stop, Oscar came out of the front door. He reached the car just as it stopped. As it stopped, he opened the back door for the ladies and Wayne to get out, then he looked at me with a quizzical look on his face and asked, "Jim, who is driving?"

By that time, the door on the driver's side had opened, and this rather large man got out from behind the steering wheel. He came around the car and stuck his hand out and said, "You must be Oscar."

This totally threw Oscar, he wasn't expecting this. He stuttered and stammered and said, "Yes, sir, I'm Oscar."

"Well, Oscar, I'm Father Francis Brockman, and I'm glad to meet you."

By now Roxie had reached the door, and Father Brockman looked at her, turned to me and said, "Jim, don't tell me this lovely lady is your mother. She is much too young for that."

"Okay, then I won't tell you.

"Mother, if it's all right I would like to introduce you to Father Francis Brockman from New York City. He says that he has met Father Brady and likes him very much and that you look too young to be my mother."

"Well, that's nice that he does since he has been our priest for the past thirty-five years. We love Father Brady very much and I really am your mother even at a young age as I was when you were born.

"Father Brockman, I have heard some good things about you from the folks you are about to marry. They didn't tell me the most important part of it though."

"Oh, what could that be, my dear lady?"

"Well, it appears to me that you are somewhat of a prankster yourself, and that being the case, you will fit in just fine.

"Oscar, would you please take Father Brockman's luggage up to his room while we take him in to meet the rest of the guests?

"Father, if you will come with me to the study, I will introduce you to some of the folks. The others are somewhere nearby, but with everyone's help, we will eventually find all of them."

We reached the study, and Roxie introduces him to the ladies there. As we passed the kitchen, she speaks to Julia and introduces her to Father, and then she tells him that if there was anything in particular that he would like for dinner or breakfast, "Just tell Julia, and she will be sure to have it available for you."

He stopped dead in his tracks and turns to everyone there and asks, "Is everyone treated this way, or is this something special for the clergy?"

We all assured him that it was special just for the clergy, and then we laughed.

Nora says, "She has done this for everyone, and we just can't believe what a wonderful lady she is."

"Believe it," I echoed, "but don't give her the big head we will never be able to live with her."

Father Brockman turned to Nora with a smile and said, "Dear Lady, I can see that I am going to love this family. You have a sense of humor, and you seem to put up with me and my weird sense of humor. If I get too obnoxious, just tell me to shut up, and I will probably just walk off and pout for a while, but I will get over it."

Everyone was having a good time now, and we all agreed that if he got too obnoxious, we would be sure to tell him.

I admitted, "This is going to be an eventful Saturday."

Father Brockman asked if someone could run him over to see Father Brady later. Johnny agreed that he would be more than glad to run him over to say hello.

Father Brockman admitted that he didn't want to just say hello. He admitted he would like to go for mass and meditation if that wouldn't take too long.

Johnny agreed that he would be glad to take him regardless of how long it took.

Father looked at me and said, "You have a real fine son here."

I agreed that Johnny was a very special boy.

Julia came into the room and told everyone, "Dinner will be promptly at 6:00 p.m."

Father asked, "What will happen if I am a little late?" Julia grinned and said, "For you, Father, I guess I could put a small plate aside. Father, do you think you could make it on time if I change the time to 7:00 p.m.?"

He gave a great big, broad smile on his face and winked at her and said, "Julia, just for that I will say a special prayer for you."

"Thank you, Father. We'll see you promptly at 7:00 p.m. and don't forget that little special prayer. I need all the help I can get."

I offered to show Father his room after he had had a glass of good cold iced tea.

He looked at Art and asked, "Did I hear the click of billiard balls down the hall when I came in?"

"You sure did, and they have a very nice billiard room. Would you like to play a game or two?"

"Well,. not today, but how about tomorrow morning while we're passing time waiting on the wedding to start?"

"Sounds good. Sid and I will be there to try to give you a little competition."

The joshing back and forth and the banter kept up for another hour or so. Father Brockman finally asked Johnny if he would like to run him over to St. Matthews so he could have a visit with Father Brady and then have mass and meditation.

Johnny was happy to oblige, and he asked the boys if they would like to go. They thought that would be nice. They could talk over what they had seen today at the airport.

Darryl was totally fascinated by that little Cub sitting out there in the hanger. "Johnny, I want to get started with lessons as soon as I get home so I can come back and fly that little kite. I want to try some loops, stalls, and spins in that little old Cub. I want to see how slow I can fly it without stalling. There are just a lot of questions I want to answer, and the only way I can answer them is to be able to fly the plane myself."

The boys all loaded into the limousine along with Father Brockman and headed for St. Matthews Church. When they arrived, Johnny took Father Brockman to the living quarters of Father Brady. They knock, and Father Brady's housekeeper opens the door.

When Father Brockman introduces himself, he is invited in, and she calls Father Brady.

With that Johnny tells Father Brockman they would be back about 6:30 to pick him up because they didn't want to keep Julia waiting when it came to dinner.

"You're right, Johnny, keeping her waiting would not be the thing to do."

The boys drove off to a nearby lounge where they could have a beer and talk. Time passed fast, and they finally noticed that it was almost 6:30 p.m. They paid their check and headed for the car.

When they reached the church, it was just 6:30 p.m. Father Brockman was waiting on the steps talking to

Father Brady. When they saw the boys drive up, they both waved and came walking to the car.

Father Brady said, "Hello, Johnny. Isn't it nice to have your daddy back?"

Johnny agrees it sure is nice to have him home. This time for good.

"Father Brady, are you coming to the wedding tomorrow?"

Father Brady looked kind of surprised and said, "I haven't received an invitation."

"Well, Father, they really didn't send out any invitations since it happened so quick and it is supposed to be a small wedding, but I know Dad would love to have you there. I'm sure this has just been an oversight on the part of Grandmother and Dad. They have been doing so many things trying to get everything lined up and taken care of in time.

"It would be too bad if our own parish priest didn't at least attend. Please come and be with us tomorrow at 4:00 p.m. We will be expecting you. Now that Dad is back, you will be seeing a lot of the family once he gets everything started that he wants to get going down in Texas."

"Johnny, tell your folks that I'll be there, but you be sure to tell him you invited me, so he won't think I'm a gate crasher. I would love to see Jim again, especially on such a wonderful occasion. Tell your grandmother hello for me and that I will see them tomorrow."

By now everyone was in the car, and away they go back to the house.

As they went walking in, they were met by Julia face to face with, "It's about time you got here. We almost started without you. At least the food didn't get cold."

Julia announced, "Now that everyone is here, we can have our dinner."

I showed everyone where Julia wanted them to be seated. After everyone was seated, Marilyn and Julia were ready to serve the meal.

I asked Father Brockman if he would please bless the dinner for us on this wonderful evening before the marriages of the four of us tomorrow afternoon.

Father Brockman asked everyone to join hands while he offered the blessing. He offered a beautiful prayer, asking for special blessings on the home that had offered him such hospitality and the people therein. Next he asked a special blessing on us four people being married tomorrow and for our futures and the futures of our families and all of those whose lives would be touched. He asked that we be watched over in all of our undertakings and to give us good health in order that we might fulfill our purposes here on this earth. He concluded with, "Please, God, show them their real purpose on this earth and help them in every way you can that they might fulfill their desires to help others less fortunate than they are."

Everyone concluded with an "Amen."

He turns to Julia and smilingly says, "Julia, I'm through, are you ready?"

We were all laughing because this took Julia by surprise. She took it like a real trooper though. She and Marilyn started serving the most delicious looking prime rib I had ever seen with all the trimmings. This included asparagus for me and, of course, anyone else who might want some because she had made plenty for everyone.

"Jim, do you really like that stuff?"

"I sure do, Father, it's one of my favorite vegetables."

With that, Father Brockman started laughing. "Jim, well, what do you know, it's mine also."

Father Brockman had one of the best senses of humor that I had seen in a long time. He kept all of us on our toes.

The evening went on with Art, Sid, and Jake trading barbs with Father Brockman, and we all seemed to really enjoy listening to them.

The dinner was a great success, and everyone was complimenting Julia for her supreme culinary arts. She blushed slightly and said, "I couldn't have done it without the help of everyone, especially Marilyn and Oscar."

It seemed they had even conned him into helping them with some of the shopping chores for the dinner.

We all adjourned to the study and music room for our dessert. Julia entered the room with, "Attention please, you have a choice of cherry cheesecake or two-crust lemon pie."

Then she had the other kitchen help assisting her in serving the coffee and dessert. The time seemed to fly tonight when everyone was having so much fun.

Before long it was getting to be bedtime and one couple after another were excusing themselves and going to bed. The boys had gone outside to get some fresh air because Roxie did not allow any smoking in her house.

A couple of the older ones still smoked. They were being pushed by their wives to forego the cigarettes at least for a few days while they were at Roxie's house. They were really trying. They had only had a couple of cigarettes today. The ladies said, "That's a start, but not good enough." They wanted them to stop smoking totally.

After the smoke, it seemed that everyone was ready to retire. The boys headed for the guest house. We others headed to our rooms and said good night.

The sun came up early this time of the year. The birds were singing outside the kitchen window. There was the smell of coffee coming from the kitchen. There were a couple of people already eating. I had been up a while, and now I was heading for the girls' bedroom with their coffee. I knocked on their door and entered with the tray in hand and the smell of coffee in the air.

They both raised their heads and moaned, "Oh, no, not so early." By this time I was busy preparing each cup just the way the girls liked it. I reached over and kissed each of them as I handed their coffee to them and told them that today was the last day. "Tomorrow it will be a different story."

They both started laughing and said, "Well, I hope so."

By now I was on my way to the door and said, "Farewell, ladies, I will see both of you downstairs soon because you know how Julia hates waiting for someone to come to eat when she has it all prepared."

As I started out the door, I saw Father Brockman coming out of his room. Father told me how much he appreciated my getting the things he needed from the church for him. I suggested we go downstairs and have some breakfast and more coffee."

Father asked, "What do you mean more coffee? You didn't bring any to my room. I feel slighted."

We were almost to the kitchen when he asked, "What is that I smell? Is that sausage? It sure smells like it."

As we walked in, Julia told me she had fixed my favorite breakfast this morning since it was my last day as a single man. "From now on, it will be up to Pam to take care of you."

Father asked Julia if he might have a cup of coffee and some of those sausages and biscuits. She told him he could have them, but asked if he would like some eggs to go with them.

"Well, yes, if it's not too much trouble."

"Well, it is, but if you will say a special prayer for me, I think maybe I could find a couple more eggs around the kitchen somehow. How do you like them cooked?"

"Over easy please, if you don't mind."

She said, "I don't mind because I'm not eating them."

He got a chuckle out of her sharp comebacks. She told us to have a seat and said that everything would be brought in to us. We sat down to have our coffee, and by now others were starting to come down the stairs looking for the coffeepot. Before long there was a good-sized group at the table in the dining room. The boys were up and had come in from the guesthouse. Conversation was really picking up during breakfast.

The doorbell rang, and Oscar answered it. He came back to the dining room. "Mrs. Dixon, the men are here to complete the backyard decorations."

Roxie went to the door. She led them to the backyard to show them what she wanted and where she wanted it. The bunting needed to be put around the tables, and the ribbons had to be strung just right. She hung around for a while to make sure they did it the way she wanted it done.

After a while, she was back inside chattering about how little those people knew about setting up a yard for a wedding when it was supposed to be their business.

"Grandmother," Johnny suggested, "why don't you sit down and have some more coffee and breakfast, and you'll feel better."

She smiled because she realized just how she had been sounding. She sat down and asked Julia for some fresh coffee and a couple of eggs scrambled soft and some wheat toast with sausage please.

After the men not in the wedding party were through with their breakfast, they asked Father Brockman if he had time for a little pocket billiards.

With a sly smile he said, "Sure, I'm ready if you will see yourself clear to take it easy on an elderly fat priest."

They all retired to the pool room. As they walked down the hall, Art told Sid they had better watch this guy because he seemed too anxious.

The rest of us folks headed in other directions as soon as we were through with breakfast. Soon the doorbell rang, and it was the dresses. They asked if the ladies would please try them on before they left, just to be sure the alterations were correct. All four of the ladies headed for their rooms to try on their dresses.

Within the next fifteen minutes the doorbell rang again, and it was the man from the tux shop. He also requested that the men try their coats and pants on to be sure they all fit properly. After all of the fitting was done the ladies from the wedding shop and the men from the tux shop left about the same time. Things were beginning to take shape for a wedding. We all went about our duties getting ready for the wedding again. Before we realized it, it was almost lunch time again.

I called Johnny and told him I needed to talk to him. Johnny came over, and I asked him if he would mind running out to the airport and picking up a friend. "You should be back in plenty of time to get dressed for the wedding."

"Sure, Dad, I'll be glad to go to the airport."

"Take a piece of cardboard and write the name Mr.

Hasnah on it, and take it with you." I told Johnny about Big Ernie and gave him a description of the man. I suggested that maybe the boys would like to go with him.

Johnny called Darryl, Neil, Tommy, and Jerry over and told them to keep it quiet, but, "We're going to the airport to pick up Pam's old boss from New York City. Pam isn't aware that he is coming for the wedding."

I gave him the gate and time of arrival. Johnny found a piece of cardboard and wrote the name Ernie Hasnah on it, and they headed for the limousine.

"That old limousine is really getting a workout these last few days."

Just as the boys headed out the door, Pam saw them and asked where they were going. They told her that they were going on an errand for Julia. Johnny told Neil to run in real quick and tell Julia that if Pam asked, the boys were going on an errand for her to the store. She agreed and Neil again headed for the front door and the limousine.

They arrived at the airport and parked in plenty of time. They got to the gate, and after about a twenty minute wait, they heard the arrival announced. They went to the arrival gate of the flight that Ernie was coming in on.

As the passengers were disembarking from the plane and coming up the ramp, Johnny nudged Darryl and said, "I'll bet you a dollar that's Big Ernie. Look at the size of that man. He reminds me of a saying that a guy who used to work for us had. When he saw a real big man, he would always say, 'He is too big for a man and not quite big enough for a jackass." This man was real big.

As he reached the crowd, Johnny held up the sign with his name on it. He came walking over and introduced himself to Johnny. He said, "Hi, I'm Ernie Hasnah."

Johnny introduced himself, and then he introduced Neil and Darryl, Tommy and Jerry.

Ernie looked at Tommy and Jerry and asked, "Don't I know you guys?"

"You sure do, Ernie; we're Pam's brothers."

"Well, at least I know I'm not losing my mind. I thought you guys looked real familiar. How do we get out of here?"

"Ernie, if you'll give the boys your baggage check, they will go and get your bags, and then they can meet us at the car."

"Gladly," he said, as he handed Tommy the claim checks.

Johnny told Ernie to follow him, and they would head for the car.

When they reached the limousine, Ernie looked at it and smiled. "Well, there's nothing like going in style.

"Johnny, is your dad nervous about the wedding this afternoon?"

"Yes, he is a little. He tries to act like he isn't nervous, but you can tell by the way he acts that he is. I know Pam is a little jumpy as well as Angie and Wayne."

When they look up, here come the boys with his luggage. They pitch it in the trunk of the car and away they go.

Ernie was very excited about being here for the wedding of such a good friend as Pam. He thought a lot of that "Little Lady" as he called her. "She is like an older sister to me," he says, "because she would listen to my troubles, and she was someone I could talk to without feeling self-conscious about it."

Everyone agreed that she was a very special lady.

"Ernie, Jenny is already calling her Mother, which is a real good sign. They have been spending the nights together since Dad and Pam got home."

"That's great because Pam needed someone like her to look after. She'll be a wonderful mother to you kids if you will just let her. One thing for sure is that she will always stand behind you, and you will always know where she stands. You would never be able to find a better person and your dad could never find a better wife. She is like family, and I was real happy when your dad called and asked me to come to the wedding."

By now they were nearing the turn-in, so they slowed down a bit. Ernie looked at the entryway and asked, "Here? Is this where you live?"

"Yes, it is, Ernie; the grandparents built it about forty-five years ago. I think it was built about 1951 or 52. I just know it's been here for a long time."

They drive up the circular drive, and again as if by magic, Oscar was there to open the doors. "He must have a sixth sense about when a car is arriving."

Johnny laughed and said, "No sixth sense, there's a sensor and video camera on the gate that tells him who and what has just come through the gate."

Oscar opened the car door for Ernie and greeted him.

He said, "You must be Mr. Hasnah. Mister Jim told me Johnny had gone to pick you up. We want to welcome you to the Dixon home. My name is Oscar, and if there is anything you need while you are here, please feel free to call me. I will see if I can take care of it for you."

"Thank you, Oscar. It's nice to know you, and if I need anything, I'll appreciate your help."

The door opened, and there stood Roxie. She walked over, stuck her hand out and said, "I'm Jim's mother, Roxie, and you must be Ernie."

Ernie looked at her and said, "Are you sure you aren't his sister? You certainly don't look old enough to be his mother."

"Johnny, I think I'm gonna like this man; he knows just the right thing to say." A priest said something like that just the other day.

They walked in, and Wayne and I came hurrying over to greet him. We were very glad he was able to make it. We both gave Ernie a big hug and handshake and told him how glad we were that he was here.

"Ernie, how about surprising the girls?" I led the way up the stairs to Pam's room and knocked on the door.

She hollered for whoever it was to come on in because she was decent.

We opened the door and sent Ernie in first. From inside the room came a squeal that could be heard all over the house. She ran over and grabbed him around the neck and hugged him real tight, and then she stepped back to look at him, and then she hugged him again.

By now I had stepped inside the door, and she looked at me and said, "Jim, I'm gonna kill you. Why didn't you tell me Ernie was coming to the wedding? I could wring your neck, but I love you for getting him here. Ernie is such a good and dear friend. I feel better just having him here for the wedding."

She walked over and hugged my neck and kissed me on the cheek and looked up with those big loving blue eyes and said, "Jim, I love you so much you'll never know."

Hearing all of the noise, Angie came running into the room and saw Ernie. She stopped dead in her tracks. "How did you get here?"

Ernie looked at her and reached out his arms, and she came over and gave him a great big hug and told him how happy she was that he was here.

"Pam, all of the guys and girls at the Black Angus send their best to you and wish you girls all the happiness in the world."

Pam really appreciated hearing from them. Finally she had to excuse herself. "I hate to run you off, but if I am going to be ready for the wedding, you had better get out of here right now so I can get my makeup on and get dressed."

We all said good-bye for the time being and headed downstairs.

Roxie again greeted Ernie. "Now I know why they call you Big Ernie. You really are a big man.

"Johnny, would you please show Ernie to one of the rooms above the garage, so he can hang up his clothes. When you are through, come on back to the kitchen, and we'll tell you the schedule from here on for the afternoon and evening."

Johnny picked up his bags, and they were gone through the backdoor. They were back in a few minutes. Ernie came into the dining area where he was introduced to those in the room. Finally, he was taken to the kitchen and introduced to those in the kitchen.

The time was growing short, and we men were told to go and get dressed. We all went in different directions. Time went by swiftly and before long all of us men came back into the study, dressed up either in tuxedos or suits and ties.

The Wedding

Roxie asked Father Brockman if he would like to take the men to the ballroom and give them instructions on what he wanted them to do. Father Brockman was more than willing. They headed back to the ballroom. Once inside, he started giving instructions to Wayne, Darryl, Johnny, and me. He told Roxie that as soon as he was through with us, he would talk to the maid of honor and the matron of honor just as soon as they were dressed.

Roxie said, "I will check with the ladies, and just as soon as they are dressed, I will bring them in."

Father went over most everything with us this morning while everyone else was busy, but there were a couple of details he still needed to talk to us about. After a few minutes, Roxie came back with June and Jenny. We talked to Father Brockman a few minutes, and then we were all set.

The organist and vocalist were here already. The photographer had been here for over an hour taking a few shots here and there, and now he was going to take some shots of the ladies getting ready for the wedding. He had the men come into the ballroom where he got a few pictures of us. Everything in the ballroom was ready, the lights were set just perfect to show off the brides and grooms as we all took our vows.

Guests were beginning to come early in hopes of visiting with me before the wedding. Many of them just wanted to have a drink with me before the wedding. I had dressed early and had come down to meet and greet some of the guests. Many, I felt, had just come to see what I looked like after all those years on the street. They were in for a big surprise because I thought that I looked just fine. In fact, I looked real good, considering what I had been through. I was very fit and healthy looking.

Roxanne was greeting guests at the door along with me. She looked beautiful for a lady her age – not that she was old; she was only seventy-two, but she acted and looked like a lady twenty years younger. She definitely did not look old enough to have a son who was forty-nine years old. She carried herself with a lot of pride, which said a lot for her. I didn't know how she did it, but she had fewer wrinkles than most women half her age. She must work out to keep her body in such good condition.

She seemed to be enjoying the looks I was getting from some of the people that came in. She leaned over and told me, "I don't know what they expected, but they sure do seem surprised. It tickles me to death to see them so surprised."

She hugged me and told me how proud she was of me and how happy she was that this day had arrived. She said, "Thank you for bringing Pam to our home and making her a part of this family."

"Thanks, Mother, I'm glad you approve," was about all I could say right now.

Wayne came down, and we introduced everyone to him. Johnny and Neil came in all handsome in their tuxedos. When Art and Sid found out they were to give their daughters' hands in marriage, they had to go to the tux shop and get fitted out in a tux also. These men came in kind of looking at each other, and pretty self-conscious about how they looked. They were also dressed in tuxedos and beautiful black shining shoes. Boy did they look sharp.

By now I was introducing all of them to the guests that were coming in.

I walked over to my mother and asked just how many people she had invited.

"Not many, Jimmy, not many, but you will find some of your old friends here tonight. I'm hoping you won't mind too much. Several of your old high school buddies that you played football with wanted to get together and talk over old times with you. I told them this wouldn't be too good a time, but they could come to the wedding, and maybe you guys could arrange a get-together after you get back from Texas. There were a couple of your friends from college who called and wanted to see you, so I invited them also."

The ballroom was beginning to fill up when Father Brady came to the door. Roxie greeted him and told him how glad they were that he had been able to make it. "Johnny told me he had invited you."

About the same time, Father Brockman came over and asked Wayne and me if he could see us.

"Jim, I understand that you, Pam, Wayne, and Angie have written your vows and that you would like to give them instead of the normal ones used in the Catholic ceremony."

"That's right, Father, is that all right with you?" I asked. "Father, I hate those stuffy old wedding vows that have been used for centuries. I like a little change once in a while."

"Now you realize that Father Brady is from the old school, and he may frown on it a bit, but since I'm officiating at this wedding, let's do it your way. Maybe I can learn something new. Do you have them memorized?"

"Yes, sir, we sure do."

"Okay, but remember that I don't want you to get all mixed up during those vows and say something that might be misunderstood."

Wayne agreed that doing something like that would be very embarrassing.

"We'll watch it real close, and I will inform the girls that it is all right to say our own vows."

Father Brockman said, "I don't think that would be wise since you aren't supposed to see your bride in her wedding dress before the wedding."

I turned to Johnny and asked if he would run up to the girls' rooms and tell them it was all right for them to use their own vows. Johnny hurried up to their rooms and tells them.

Just as he started down the stairs, he heard the organist start playing. Roxie, Wayne, and I left the reception work to Oscar who was extremely good at the job. Time sure did fly by. Ernie came in all dressed up fit to kill. He sure did look nice. We suggested that maybe we should find him a good old Chicago girl to take back to New York City.

Ernie said, "No thanks," when we made the offer.

After a couple of songs on the organ, everyone began to be seated. The ushers were waiting in the rear where they had been seating the guests. The ushers were all friends of Johnny's who asked to participate, a nice gesture on their part.

Everyone was seated, and the ushers took Mrs. Jackson and Roxie to their places in the front row. Next they led Tommy and Jerry to their seats. Wayne and I, along with Sid, Art, Johnny, and Neil took our places. The matron of honor and the maid of honor took their places.

It seemed they played a dozen more songs before they started the song for the girls to come down the aisle. You know the one, "Here Comes the Bride," except in this case, it was here come the brides. This was one of the most beautiful sights you could have ever hoped to see. Two beautiful blonde brides in matching blue dresses coming down the aisle with those long trains behind them and the veils over their faces. It was so quiet you could have heard a pin drop on the carpet. Only the music broke the silence.

As the ladies reached the altar, Father Brockman stepped forward and asked, "Who gives Pamela Jean Jackson's hand in marriage to Mr. James Robert Dixon?"

Art stepped forward and said, "Her mother and I give her hand in marriage to Mr. Dixon."

Father Brockman next asked, "Who gives Angela O'Neill's hand in marriage to Mr. Harold Wayne McKenzie."

Sid stepped forward and said, "I her father, give her hand in marriage to Mr. McKenzie."

Both of the fathers stepped back to the aisle where the rest of the families were seated, and they sat down in the seats reserved for them.

Father Brockman blessed both couples and turned to the congregation.

"Today our wedding is going to be just a little different from most Catholic weddings. I met and became acquainted with these young folks when they visited my church in New York City. The ladies had attended our church, and they brought their boyfriends – who happened to be from out of town – to church one evening. It was there I met and became fond of them. I was very honored when they called and asked if I would come to Chicago and marry the four of them. To me this was quite an honor.

"Today these young people will also give their own vows in their own words. Some of you may say that's not the Catholic way. I ask you what would be more honest than to write or say your own vows to the one you love most in this world.

"After the vows, I will continue with the accepted Catholic ritual and blessings afterwards. I want you all to know what is happening as we do it."

He turned to me. "Jim, do you love Pamela, and are you ready to share your vows with her?"

"Yes, Father, I do love her, and I am ready to share my vows with her," I answered.

"I do take you Pamela as my lawfully wedded wife. I promise to hold you unto myself and myself only from this day forward. I will be there in sickness and health, poverty and wealth. I swear that my soul shall be your soul to have and hold for the rest of our lives. I will protect you with my very life if necessary for as long as we both shall live. You will never have reason to doubt my love for you because it will always be there. My home shall be your home, and my family your family. My children shall be your children for the rest of our lives. I ask that you take me and all that I have to offer in return for your love. These things I pledge to you with all my heart and soul, so help me God."

Father Brockman turned to Pam and asks, "Pam, are you ready to give Jim your vows of love?"

"Yes, I am, Father.

"My Darling Jim, I, Pamela Jackson, take you James Dixon to be my lawfully wedded husband. I promise to hold myself only unto you for the rest of my life forsaking all others from this day forward, to be there for you in sickness and health, poverty and wealth. I swear to you that my soul shall be your soul to have and to hold for the rest of our lives. You will never have reason to doubt my love because it will always be there for you. I can not imagine living the rest of my life without you there by my side. I feel that God brought you to me for a purpose, and that purpose was that I might be your wife, and that we might be able to share this life of bliss as husband and wife for as long as we both may live. I will keep and protect you unto myself, and I will give up my life if necessary in order to protect you. My home shall be your home, and my family shall be your family your children shall be my children just as if I had given birth to them, and it is this love that will make our family a family of love for the rest of our days. I ask that you take me and all the love I have to offer in return for your love and devotion from this day forward, so help me God."

Father Brockman turned to Wayne and asked, "Wayne, are you ready to recite your vows to Angie?"

"I am, Father.

"I, Wayne McKenzie, do take you Angie O'Neill to be my lawfully wedded wife from this day forward, you shall never have need to question my love for you because I will always be there to protect you. I will hold myself only unto you for the rest of my life. I swear that our souls shall be as one from this day forward. We will take care of each other in sickness and health, poverty and wealth. I will protect you with my very life because without you, there would be no life for me. My home shall be your home and my family your family for the rest of our lives. I promise to always love and care for you, as our love grows with each passing day. These things I pledge to you, my darling Angie, for the rest of our lives, so help me God."

Father Brockman now asks, "Angie, are you ready to make your pledge to Wayne in your own words?"

Angie says, "I am Father.

"I, Angie O'Neill, do take you Wayne McKenzie to be my lawfully wedded husband, to have and to hold from this day forward. I will keep you and help you in every way I can for the rest of our lives. Our love is strong enough to carry us through any turmoil that we may be confronted with. I will be with you and love you through sickness and health, poverty and wealth. I cannot begin to fathom the depth of my love for you, or what my life would be without you. We shall always be there for each other to comfort in time of sorrow and to share the laughter in the time of happiness. I cannot imagine what my life would have been if I had not found you and your love to keep me strong and proud. Your love is more than I had ever dreamed of, but now that I have it, I do pledge to make you happy every day of our lives. My home and my family shall always be your home and family, and your family shall from this day forward be my family. These things no one can take from us. I pledge my love to you and you only, from this day forward, so help me God."

Father Brockman blesses us as couples and has us kneel for prayer. After prayer we arise. He asks the best men if they had the rings. They did, and they hand the rings to each of us.

Father Brockman says, "Repeat after me and place the ring on your lady's finger.

"With this ring I thee wed."

We both placed the rings on our wives' fingers and recited the words, "With this ring I thee wed."

Father Brockman asked the matron of honor and the maid of honor if they had the ladies' rings. They handed the rings to the ladies who placed the rings on the fingers of us grooms and recited, "With this ring I thee wed."

Having done this, Father Brockman said, "I now pronounce you husbands and wives. Now, gentlemen, you may each kiss your bride."

After Wayne and I lifted the veils and kissed our brides, Father Brockman instructs us to turn to the audience.

"At this time it gives me great pleasure to introduce to you, Mr. and Mrs. Wayne McKenzie and Mr. and Mrs. Jim Dixon."

Everyone applauds.

"Ladies and gentlemen, I have been asked to tell you that the reception will be held in the backyard just as soon as the brides and grooms have time to get out there."

We couples walked up the aisle side by side. Smiles were everywhere. The matron of honor and the maid of honor exited with their respective best men, followed by the family members.

Once outside of the ballroom, Jenny grabs Pam and squealed," Now you really are my mother." She gave her a big bear hug and kiss.

Johnny was next. He said, "Well, Mother, you can't get away from us now. You're stuck with the job."

They both hugged me and told me how happy they are that I have brought such a wonderful lady into their lives.

Roxie stepped in and said, "I always wanted a daughter, and now I truly feel that I have one. You're a blessing to this household, Darling. We all love you so much."

By now Sid and Darryl were hugging Angie and shaking Wayne's hand vigorously. Jake, June, and Neil were busy hugging Angie and shaking Wayne's hand. Tommy, Jerry, Nora, and Art had all gathered around Pam and me and were talking up a storm.

Johnny took me aside. "Dad, we have reserved two honeymoon suites at the Hilton for you guys, and that's a lot better than staying here."

Big Ernie came over and picked Pam up like a rag doll and told me that he just had to kiss the bride.

Pam said, "Well, what are you waiting for?" She planted a big one on him.

You wouldn't believe it, but Ernie had tears in his eyes. He said, "Now don't get any ideas, I'm just real happy, and when I'm real happy, I cry. You know you have my favorite Little Lady here. Jim, you could look the world over, and you couldn't find a better one than she is."

"You're right, Ernie, that's for sure."

"Johnny," Ernie asked, "would you and the boys like to take me to the hotel a little later?"

"No, way, big buddy," I said, "you're staying here tonight and longer if you would like. We have plenty of room, and we wouldn't think of having you go to a hotel. Tonight there will be three more empty rooms. Besides, if you go to a hotel you would have to eat that old café cooking, and this way you can have a good breakfast prepared by Julia. How about that?"

"Well, okay, if you're sure you have room."

"Ernie, just look around you, man, don't you think we have room for you?"

We all headed for the backyard where we formed the reception line. Mother had said there would be thirty or forty people here. It turned out that there must have been at least a hundred and twenty-five or thirty people here.

After about fifteen minutes, the photographer came over and asked us if we would please come over and cut the cake in order for him to get some more pictures.

We cut the cake and fed each other a piece of it, and then we drank a toast proposed by Big Ernie.

"First, I'm Pam's ex-boss from New York City, and I feel that in addition to her father, I also gave her away today." He asked, "Would everyone join me in a toast to the newlyweds? It's my pleasure to toast four of the most wonderful people I have ever had the privilege of knowing. May the Lord bless them and assist them in all of their endeavors in the future which I know are many. Here's to two of the happiest couples on this earth; we pray for God to look down on and bless them for the rest of their lives."

Everyone took a sip of their champagne, including Wayne and me. There were several other toasts during the next thirty minutes. We tried to sneak away unnoticed to go upstairs and change clothes preparing to leave for the hotel.

One of my old high school buddies came over and congratulated me, as did several of my other old friends from high school. They also congratulated Pam.

Comp, one of my closest friends in high school told me they all wished the very best for my wife and me and it had been a pleasure to meet her. Everyone agreed that I gota real beautiful lady.

"Jim, we've have been talking things over and have just been wondering if we could all get together after you get back from your trip to Texas. We know you're going to be busy, but maybe some evening we could all have a dinner together somewhere."

"Comp, that would be a great idea, but why not have it here at the house when we get back?" I asked. I then took this opportunity to introduce Pam to each of the guys and his wife, and I even told her what position each one played on the football team.

Comp, as he had always been known, was actually George Compton, one of my best friends ever since way back in grade school. He was surprised that I wanted to have it here at my home.

"Why not?" I asked. "We have the room and the yard and the help. Comp, give me your phone number, and I'll call you just as soon as we get back from Texas. That's all settled then, just as soon as I get back, I'll call you, and we'll round up the rest of the gang and their wives and meet for dinner here at our house."

They all agreed and excused themselves because there were others waiting to shake hands with us brides and grooms.

"Pam, I think it was real nice that the gang was invited to the wedding. It sure is good to see my old friends."

Before Comp left, he told me that my mother had called him when she found out I was alive and in good health. She called him again when she found that I was going to be married here. That was nice of Mother to be so thoughtful.

Just as my buddies left a couple of other folks came over to say hello. They were from my college days. One was another professor who gave me a big hug and told me everyone had been all worried about me and had prayed for me after I had disappeared. "Now that you are back and with your beautiful bride, you seem to be in good health and happy. We are all so very thankful."

I introduced Pam to them. "The big one is Professor Robert Reeder and his wife Marilyn. Pam, Bob and I used to share the same part of the building when we were teaching. Our classrooms were side by side, and we spent a lot of time together. Bob was one of the few people that knew what I was going through all of those years. Bob stood by me through everything and tried to help the best he could. Bob had no idea that I would go off and get lost on the street scene."

I told Bobby and Marilyn that Pam and I would like to get together for an evening when we got settled back in Chicago.

We all agreed to meet and get to know each other better. Bobby said, "Your mother has our number, and you can call when you get back. When you guys get back, we can make arrangements to spend that evening together."

"Bob, I have a lot to do in Texas, but just as soon as we get back, you will be hearing from us, I promise."

I turned to Wayne and Angie and suggested they come with me. I grabbed Pam by the arm, and away we went heading upstairs to change clothes and pack an overnight bag.

"Johnny told me he would honk three times when he gets out front. That way we can sneak out without anyone knowing we're leaving."

We changed our clothes, packed a small bag, and went downstairs. We set the bags behind the door so no one would notice them. We casually walked back to the reception area where the photographer took a few more pictures.

Big Ernie was having a ball talking to the guests and telling stories about his favorite Little Lady. Wayne and Angie were visiting with their folks again while the boys stood behind them smiling. They knew what was going on and what was about to happen next.

After about thirty minutes, Tommy came into the room with a good-sized cardboard box and set it in the corner of the room closest to the driveway.

Pam, Wayne, Angie, and I had begun to edge our way toward the front door trying not to be too noticeable. Johnny honked the horn, so we hurried to the front door and got our bags.

What we didn't plan on was for anyone else knowing what was happening. The boys did know however, because Johnny and Jenny had told them.

Tommy went running out the door to the driveway, while Jerry, Darryl, and Neil told everyone to hurry out the side door and beat us to the front door. Everyone went scurrying out the door and up the driveway to the front of the house. Tommy was standing at the front of the house handing out rice packets to everyone.

When we newlyweds came out the front door, we got a big surprise. We were showered with rice. Everyone had at least two or three packets of rice. By the time we newlyweds got into the limousine, it looked as though there had been a rice truck unloaded on the drive and front yard. Everyone was hollering and wishing us happiness, and some of the ladies were even crying.

We did manage to get into the car without getting hurt, and away we went.

The Wedding Night

The kids had not told anyone where we were going to stay, however, because it had been their agreement from the time they had started planning this little surprise. Now we newlyweds were laughing at the thought of the kids surprising us with the rice shower. Those kids were really something else. It was hard to explain to other people how much we loved all of them.

I thanked Johnny and told him to thank the other boys and Jenny when he got back home.

We finally arrived at the Hilton and were greeted with the red carpet laid out especially for newlyweds. We couples certainly had not expected this. We were ushered into the hotel and straight to the elevator, which took us up to the penthouse where there were two bridal suites.

Pam and I took the one on the right; Wayne and Angie took the one on the left. I reached over and picked Pam up and said, "Honey, this is going to be done right. I am carrying you over the threshold, my darling wife."

I turned and saw Pug picking Angie up in his arms, and as he pushed the door open, they turned to Pam and me and said, "Good night to all."

When we walked in, we could hardly believe our eyes.

Flowers were everywhere, with champagne on ice as well as some soft drinks and caviar, a large bowl of fruit, and other snacks on the bar in the living room.

The bridal suites had all been done in a soft blue. The girls could hardly believe it. The last thing to be heard in the entryway was, "We'll see you in the morning for breakfast."

It was best to leave the evening activities to your own imagination. Most of you have been there and done that. Since we had already had our wedding night a few weeks ago, this was strictly a rerun.

The love we four people had for each other was the kind of love that poets write about. Our love was so strong and so deep that words were totally insufficient when trying to describe it. Our actions were the only things that could sufficiently describe our love for each other.

Sunday morning we all slept late after a long, wonderful night of lovemaking, holding each other, and dreaming of the future together. We stayed in bed until almost 10:00 a.m. What a wonderful feeling to just lie there and hold each other and talk and nuzzle and snuggle together.

I finally reached for the phone to call Wayne and Angie to see if they were awake yet. Angie told me they were awake and had been waiting to call us.

"Pam, they're awake." I returned to the phone and asked, "Where do you want to have breakfast, in our rooms or down in the dining room?"

Pam suggested we have breakfast in our rooms. She said, "Jim, we can have them bring the breakfast to our room for the four of us. Find out what they want, and we'll order for all of us."

Angie checked with Wayne and told me what both of them would have. "We will be over just as soon as Wayne finishes his shower I have already had mine."

I thought that would be good since we hadn't showered yet. This would give us time to get ready. I told Pam she could run in and have her shower first if she would like. That way she would have more time to put her makeup on and fix her hair.

She smiled and said, "Honey, why don't we just take our showers together? That's a real large shower stall, plenty large enough for the both of us."

"What a great idea, Darling. Sweetheart, I had thought about it, but didn't know just how you would feel about it."

Both of us hurried to see who was going to be first in the shower. We stood in the shower for a long time just holding each other and caressing each other as we had never done before.

"Jim, this is the first time I have ever showered with a man."

"Well, Darling, it's my first time to shower with a woman, but you can bet your bottom dollar it won't be the last time."

We spent a lot of time rubbing soap over each other's body and caressing it while we were lathering the soap. This made the shower last longer than usual, but it also made it much better and much more interesting.

Pam laughed and suggested we get out and dry off before Wayne and Angie came over. We hurried, taking turns drying each other instead of drying ourselves. This, of course, took a little longer than usual, but we both eventually got dried off.

We dressed quickly, and Pam was putting on her makeup, and I had just finished dressing when there was a knock at the door. There stood Mr. and Mrs. Wayne McKenzie waiting to be invited in.

I did just that I invited them in and said, "The breakfast isn't here yet because I just now called down to order it. I was inadvertently detained by a beautiful blonde lady that spent the night in my bed."

"Jim, we know the feeling, and it took a little longer to get dressed this morning than usual. Wonder why?"

We turned on some beautiful music and sat down to talk about the evening and the wedding. It seemed that everything had worked out so perfectly that no one could complain.

Then we started to talk about when Wayne and Angie were going to Utah, and when Pam and I were going to Texas. I felt it would take me about four or five days to get things straightened out here in Chicago before I went to Ft. Worth.

"Jim, we would like to have about five to seven days in Moab with my family if that would be all right."

"That's just fine with me." I said, "Wayne, we will meet you in Ft. Worth."

I said, "Do you think that you and Angie could stay a couple more days in Chicago so we could go to the plant and check on some work things, and then maybe by Wednesday we can all four leave the same day?"

"That sounds good."

There was a knock on the door. When I opened the door, the steward rolled a cart full of food into the room. There was everything anyone could ask for on that cart. It had what we ordered and a lot more. There were flowers for both of the ladies and a corsage for them to wear when we left to go back home.

The steward congratulated us and asked if there was anything else he could do for us before he left. I started to sign for the food, but the steward told me the breakfast was a gift from the hotel to all of their couples who stayed in the bridal suites.

We all thanked him, and I slipped him a twenty dollar bill and closed the door behind him. We sat down to breakfast and had fun talking about the previous day.

Each of us commented on what a wonderful wedding it had been. As we were sitting there looking at each other, I looked at Wayne and said, "Well, old buddy, do you realize what has just happened to us? I'm talking about you and me. *We have just FOUND TRUE LOVE THE HARD WAY, and we have gone from the gutter to the penthouse.*

We all looked at each other, and Wayne gave a toast. "To men who were lost and have found new life, and most of all THEY HAVE FOUND LOVE THE HARD WAY, and they have literally clawed their way from the gutter to the penthouse. To men who have found the love of their life and to the women who helped them make this great transition."

We all toasted Wayne for such a wonderful and truthful toast to the four of us. After breakfast, I decided I should call home and check on Father Brockman and Big Ernie.

I called home, and Johnny answered the phone with a question. "When are you guys coming home? Should I take Father Brockman to the airport before you get here, or do you want him to wait so you can talk to him before he leaves? He has a flight time just after lunch, but it can be changed if you aren't going to be here before he leaves."

I turned to the others and asked if they would be willing to go home before lunch so we could say good-bye to Father Brockman and Ernie. "That would seem to be the proper thing to do."

We finished our coffee, get dressed, and prepared to go home. The girls put on their corsages and packed their bags. We boys were ready when the girls were. We called the front desk and told them to have the bill ready, and we would take care of it on the way out. The desk clerk told me they had been instructed to send a bill to the company, and they would take care of it. "It won't be necessary to stop by the desk to check out. It has been a pleasure to have you stay with us, and we hope you enjoyed your stay."

We headed downstairs, and the doorman called a taxi for us. It only took a short time to get home. As we arrived, we were met by the boys and Big Ernie. He acted as the doorman and opened the taxi door, bowed from the waist, and asked for our luggage. He was really a big ham, but what a wonderful friend. The boys had really enjoyed him and some of his tales of football games.

Father Brockman came in and greeted everyone. He told us how much he enjoyed his visit with the family. He let us know how much he enjoyed the beautiful wedding, not because he was in it, but because of the vows we each wrote and recited. He admitted they were the best he had ever heard. He told us that Father Brady even liked them. Now that was something when Father Brady liked something that wasn't strictly by the book. "I think you guys might bring him around after all. Just hang in there because he is really a great guy when you get to know him. He just comes from the old school."

Roxie came in and grabbed the girls and hugged them. After she had finished hugging the girls, she turned to Wayne and me and gave each of us a big hug and told us how happy she was for everybody. By now all of the families were there. Julia came in and told us that lunch would be served in just about an hour, "so don't anyone run off."

Wayne sat down with his mother and father. He told them that if it was all right with them, he and Angie would wait until Wednesday to go to Moab. He explained that I wanted him to go to the company headquarters and meet the officers and workers at the home office. He also explained that I wanted him to pick up some forms for reporting his expenses, etc., while he was on the road and sign other forms necessary for the office such as Social Security number and other vital information.

They understood and asked if that would be all right with Roxie. Roxie assured them they could stay as long as they would like.

Art and Nora asked Pam if it would be all right if they went home tomorrow. "Art has some things he wants to take care of just in case Jim needs him to help in Ft. Worth."

Pam asked me, and I said, "Sure why not? We can get together in Norfolk or in Ft. Worth, or you guys can come back to see us any time you feel like it."

"Jim, we can get a flight out in the morning and be home before noon, and that would give Art time to take care of some of the things he needs to do."

"Everything is set then. Johnny and Neil can take you to the airport," I said.

Jenny came in, and when she saw us, she came running over and grabbed Pam around the neck and hung on for a minute. She finally let go and stepped back a step and asked Roxie if she didn't think she had the prettiest mother in the whole world.

"Yes, Honey, you sure do, and I have the prettiest daughter."

I looked at them and told Father Brockman, "I wish I had my boots on because it's getting a little deep around here."

Everyone, even Big Ernie, laughed at that one.

Ernie asked Johnny if he and the boys could take him to the airport with Father Brockman after they had lunch. It seemed they could get the same flight back to New York City. The boys thought that would work just fine.

Everyone visited for a while, and Julia came and issued a call to lunch. Everyone headed for the dining room where Marilyn and Julia had set a very nice lunch as usual.

After lunch Father and Big Ernie went to their rooms and returned with their bags. They suggested they head for the airport so they wouldn't miss their plane. I told Ernie to be sure and say hello to Chip Rowan for me, and I reminded Ernie of our conversation before we had left to come to Chicago. Ernie let me know that he wouldn't forget.

Johnny brought the limousine around, and everyone was ready to go. We all said our good-byes, and the girls gave Big Ernie a kiss and told him they would see him when they got to New York. "That shouldn't be too long."

We thanked Father Brockman, and I slipped a check for $500 into his pocket as they left for the airport. I assured Father Brockman we would see him again when we came to town.

The rest of the afternoon was spent just wasting the time and visiting. We had a wonderfully relaxing dinner. Pam and I were to spend our first night in our home. At least that was what Roxie and the kids hoped.

They got Pam and me cornered and asked us if we would consider making the family home our home. Roxie told Pam, "It would be wonderful to have the entire family together. You can have any part of the house you want to live in. Just pick your rooms and tell us what you want us to do.

We want you here that badly."

I looked at Pam, and she looked at me. "Pam, Honey, would you like some time to think about it?"

"Jim, dear, I couldn't think of a better place or better way to spend the rest of my life than here with my new family."

Jenny squealed, and Roxie look relieved.

"Roxie, I know I am being selfish because by doing this I won't have to pick out new furniture, drapes, and carpet. It's all done in such wonderful taste that I couldn't and wouldn't want to change a thing unless the entire family decides to do it."

As of right here and now, Roxie told us that she was the happiest person in the world. It appeared she was not the only happy person here.

Time passed until bedtime. The boys got back a long time ago and were in the back room playing pool. Everyone had had a busy day, so we all chose to make it an early evening.

Monday morning came with the usual good smell of coffee, and I realized that Pam was coming in the door with my coffee. She came over, set the coffee down on the night table, and gave me a good morning kiss. "Jim, Hon, it is my turn to start bringing you coffee in bed, at least when I can."

I hurried to get ready and go down to breakfast where I found Wayne and Angie were already there. We all sat down to eat breakfast.

When it was over, I told Art, Nora, Tommy, and Jerry that I hated to leave, but that Wayne and I needed to get to the plant.

"Tommy and Jerry, I hope you won't forget about your agreement to go to school. Tell Ralph also, and all of you be sure to set things up, and I will have the office call and get the information they need for the bookkeeping department."

"Jim, we are all really thrilled at the thought of being able to go to college. We will get together and set things up and make arrangements to tell our employers what we are going to do. As soon as we find out when the next semester begins, we will call the office and inform them of the date."

I kissed Nora and shook Art's and the boys' hands. Wayne and I kissed our wives good-bye, and I checked with Jenny to make sure that she could get everyone to the airport all right.

"Don't worry, Daddy; I can do it for you."

I asked Johnny to bring the limousine around and drive us to the plant for our meeting. Johnny came around in a few minutes. Wayne and I met him out front. We got into the limousine and headed for the plant and our meetings with the plant management.

The Plant Meeting

Just as Johnny turned onto the street, I asked him if the Lincoln Mercury dealership over on West Shore Blvd. was still in business.

"They sure are, and they're still owned by Mr. Jim Robertson."

"Good. Johnny, take us over there."

"Okay, Dad, we're on our way."

We arrived at the dealership, and I got out of the car. Johnny and Wayne walked into the showroom with me.

I asked a salesman if Mr. Robertson was still there.

"Yes, sir, if you will have a seat, I will tell Mr. Robertson that he has a customer who wishes to see him." The salesman disappeared. As he did, Wayne asked me, "Just what's going on?" "Nothing in particular, he's just an old friend."

Mr. Robertson and the salesman came walking back into the showroom and over to me. As we stood up, Mr. Robertson looked at me and said, "Well, I'll be damned. Jim, you're back from the dead.

"Son, I've wondered so many times about you and worried about you after your father died. Son, I'm awfully glad to see you. How's Roxie taking all of this?"

"Just fine, Mr. Robertson, just fine. You'd never believe it, but I got married yesterday at Mother's house. She has even asked us to stay on and live with her."

"You said "yes" I hope, didn't you?"

"I sure did, and I intend to take over the business just as soon as I get some things straightened out in Texas."

"What's this I hear about you winning a million dollars on some TV show?"

"That's right, Mr. R., I got lucky. That's one of the reasons I have to go back to Texas. When I get back, we'll have lunch, and I'll tell you all about it. Oh, by the way, this is a friend of mine that will be working with me, and we need a car for him. You remember my son Johnny don't you?"

"Johnny has grown so much, Jim, that he is as big as you are. Maybe even better looking."

"Now for business, I need a Continental for my wife and a Town Car for myself and one for Wayne here. I want my wife's car to be a light powder blue with a soft blue leather interior. What color car do you want, Wayne?"

"Hell, Jim, I never thought about what color car I wanted. Can I just have a Continental or a Mercury Marquis instead of a Town Car? I won't know how to act driving a car like that."

"Sure, Wayne, you can have whatever you want.

"Mr. R., we don't need these today because we will be gone for a few weeks starting Wednesday. If you can just order them and have them here when we get back from Texas, I would appreciate it. I want my car to be white with white interior.

"What color do you want and what do you want, Wayne? Tell the man."

Wayne finally says, "I would like to have the Mercury Marquis. I think I would like the powder blue also since that's my wife's favorite color."

"Speaking of wives, Mr. R., make that two powder blue Continentals. We need one for Wayne's wife also."

"Jim, when you get back from Texas, they will be in your driveway waiting for you. Call from Texas just before you leave so I won't have them in the dust and sun for very long."

"We'll call you just before we leave."

"Johnny, how about you? Would you like to have a new car since your old man hasn't bought you anything in a long time?"

"Not if you will let me keep the pickup and maybe use your car once in a while to go out on dates."

"Son, you can have the pickup, but I think you should have a car of your own for taking your girlfriend out on a date."

I told Mr. R. to get together with Johnny and fix him up with a car.

"Jim, Johnny and I will get together and take care of that little problem.

"Johnny, why don't you come by one day this week, and we will get you all fixed up?"

Johnny smiled and said, "SUV's are nice. I really think that if I get a car, it will be an SUV."

I was ready to leave. I said, "Mr. Robertson, it's sure nice to see you again."

"Same here, Jim, you look great."

"Well, okay, Mr. Robertson, if Johnny wants an SUV, fix him up with one. It seems like old times except that Dad isn't here. Dad brought me in here the first time I ever set foot in this dealership. I don't think Dad ever bought a car from any other dealer in all of those years."

"Jim, that dad of yours was a very special person and a very special friend. We played a lot of golf together over the years, and we attended a lot of masses at St. Matthews with Father Brady over those years.

"Sure do miss him, Jim.

"Well, let me get started on this order for you. Tell me, Jim, do you want everything on them?"

"Sure do, Mr. R., we sure do. Radio, tape, and CD player, separate air controls, and all that good stuff.

"I hate to run now, but we have to be going. I need to get out to the plant. Talk to you later when we get back from Texas."

Mr. Robertson waved good-bye as we left the showroom.

Back in the car and on our way, Johnny said, "Dad, you didn't have to do that."

"I know, but I wanted to. Don't tell the girls about this, though, because I want to surprise them when we get back from Texas.

"Do you think Jenny would like a new car?"

"Not if she is going to lose the M.G."

A Visit to the Home Office

It took about forty-five minutes to get to the plant. As Johnny started to park in the front parking area, he happened to notice a new sign on one of the parking places. It read, "Reserved for Jim Dixon."

Johnny pulls over and parks in the space.

"Dad, did you read the sign?"

"Sure did, son; I'm really surprised to see it."

"We went to the entry, and surprise, surprise, we were met by the entire office staff and officers of the company. It seemed that Roxie had called and told them we were on our way out to the office.

The next two hours were spent shaking hands and introducing Wayne to everyone while renewing old acquaintances. What a pleasant surprise. I also learned that my mother and the Board of Directors had voted to transfer Frank Wells to the home office as the new general manager of the home office and plant. I certainly hadn't expected that.

"Wayne, I'm really beginning to feel at home again."

Wayne was just about overwhelmed with all of this attention.

One of the officers said that he understood that he was going to be my personal assistant in all of the operations of the company.

"If that's what Jim wants Pug says, that's what I'll do. I admit that I have a lot to learn."

The day went by fast with meetings of one kind or another. Wayne was beginning to see that this was going to be a full-time job just keeping up with me. I was on the go all day with just about a half hour out for lunch in the cafeteria with the workers, some of whom I had known since I had been a teenager.

The day was over, and we finally headed for home. Johnny had gotten tired just following the two of us around to all of the meetings. He finally ended up in the lounge sipping on a Coke and waiting for us to get ready to go home.

Finally, we were on our way home. Traffic was heavy, so it took a little over an hour to get home. When we arrived, we were met with a cold Coke in hand. We were told that if we wanted a beer there was one in the refrigerator but we said, "Not now. Let's wait a while. We made it through the wedding and the champagne, so let's just coast for a while."

I went into the library with Pam and Angie; Wayne followed with Coke in hand. We all had a seat and relaxed. I told Pam that she and Angie might want to poke around Chicago tomorrow and see if they could find a travel agency somewhere that Angie might like to have if they stayed in Chicago.

"Wait a minute, Jim," Angie said, "I can't let you do that."

"Would you like to stay in Chicago with Pam?" I asked.

"I sure would, but I don't know about letting you buy me a business."

"Angie, you know that I'm not buying you a business. I'm just investing in you, and you will be expected to pay me back in time. Nothing around here is free. You'll work, and you'll build your business, and you'll make money, and then you will pay me back. I'll finance you with a no–interest loan and no due date for the payoff. We'll talk more about all of this after we get back from Texas.

"Pam, did your parents and the boys make their flight, and did everyone have a good time?"

"Everything was just fine, Hon, and they made their flight. They said to tell you that Art would see you in Ft. Worth."

"That's just fine, Honey; that's great."

Tuesday went just about the same as Monday with meetings, signing contracts, etc. and Wayne getting together with the personnel department. Wayne was finally remembering a few names and how to get around the plant. He seemed to feel a little more at ease today and not so much of an outsider. It would all take time.

At the end of the day, we went home and had dinner with the folks. Sid and Darryl tell Wayne they are leaving first thing in the morning. They could go to the airport with Wayne and Angie and the McKenzie family.

I tell them that "Pam and I will leave a little closer to noon. We'll let Johnny take you to the airport, and then he can come back to get us."

I asked Pam if she and Angie had found anything interesting today in the way of travel bureau offices for sale.

They admitted they had looked at about four or five, but none of them seemed interested in selling. None was really what Angie thought would be a good business either. "We'll look some more when we get back from Texas."

Roxie moaned.

"Do you know how quiet it's going to be around here when everyone leaves?"

Jenny hugs her grandmother's neck. "Grandmother, remember you still have me and Johnny."

I added, "It won't take long to take care of things in Texas."

Roxie seemed a little better after we assured her that all of us would be back home in a month or so – this time to stay.

Everyone was pretty tired after a full day of running, so we went to bed early. We all knew that tomorrow was going to be a busy one.

Pam and I had to pack tonight. Wayne and Angie said they had to pack also, but they weren't sure just what to pack.

"I suggest that because we aren't sure just how long we will be in Ft. Worth possibly a month or so you might want to think of it from that point of view. I hope it won't take that long, but you can never tell. It might take longer."

I added, "I just happened to think about something else that I should do today. The summers get real hot in Texas, so I was thinking about getting Lynn and Annie to help us set up a large air-conditioned building for the homeless and other people who don't have air conditioning. This would be a good place where they could come to play dominos, checkers, cards, and watch TV. We could put in two or three TV's, and that would give everyone a better chance of watching what they want to watch and still stay out of the heat.

"I'll bet they will help us arrange it if we can get the money to set it up, and I know we can do that. I might even get our plant in Dallas to subsidize it.

"Who knows, maybe the city of Ft. Worth would help us do something like that for their homeless citizens. We could write most of it off as a public relations program. What do you guys think?"

Pug admitted there had been many a day he sure would have liked to have a place to get in out of the heat.

"Just as soon as we get to Ft. Worth, we can get together with Lynn and Annie and take it from there."

I called Lynn and told him we would be arriving after lunch tomorrow. "There is no need to meet us because we need to get a rental car to use while we're there. Tell everyone that we'll see them tomorrow afternoon."

The Return to Texas

The night went quickly and the alarm awakened all of us newlyweds at 6:00 a.m. No coffee in bed this morning. We all went downstairs to have breakfast together. It appeared that we had all packed our bags and were ready to go. Pug, Angie, and the McKenzies were ready as well as the O'Neill family just soon as they finished breakfast. Everyone seemed anxious to be on the way.

Pug was anxious to get home and see his sister and her baby as well as to meet her husband, whom he had never met. He was anxious to see how much the old hometown had grown. He wanted to go fishing with his father on the Colorado River the way they had done when he had been a kid with the exception that he wants Angie to go with them this time.

Everyone was outside, Johnny loaded them just as soon as they said good-bye to Roxie and the help. They had taken quite a liking to Oscar and Julia and Marilyn. They said good-bye temporarily to Pam and me. It seemed they had all had a good time during the past few days.

Johnny hollers, "All aboard," and away they went.

"Dad, I'll be back in time to take you guys to the airport."

"Johnny, wait just a minute, would you like to go to Texas with us?"

"Are you serious? You know I would love to go to Texas with you."

"Well son, if you get back here in a hurry and pack a bag, I just might take you with us."

Johnny was so excited he almost hit the gate as he drove out onto the street.

The rest of us went back into the house. I told my mother that I was going to take Johnny to Texas with me. "I think it would be good for him to see the way his daddy lived for all of those years. I want him to meet the folks at the Sanctuary, the doctor, and the policeman who helped us so many times. I want Johnny to understand what it was like to be on the streets.

"Jenny, I'm sorry that I can't take both of you, but I think you should stay here with your grandmother."

"Dad, I understand, but you owe me one at some future date."

"I promise you that just the three of us, meaning Pam, you, and me, will take a trip somewhere."

O.K. Daddy I'll remember. Then she turned to Pam, "Mother, you heard what he promised, and you have to help me make him keep his promise."

"I agree, Honey we'll make him keep his promise.".

We were all busy until Johnny got back from the airport. Just as soon as he parked in front of the house, he came running in, and up to his room he went. You never saw anyone pack so fast in all of your life. I was sure he was going to have to have everything pressed once we got to Ft. Worth.

He came running down the stairs with a bag and suit cover for his suits and sports coats. He came running into the kitchen where we were having one last cup of coffee before we left. He hugged and kissed his grandmother and his little sister. He looks at all of us and suggestes that it was time to get loaded to go to the airport. He forgot to ask who was gonna drive.

"Oh, heck, where is Oscar? Can he please drive us to the airport?" asked a very frazzled Johnny.

We all burst out laughing as Oscar walked in looking very calm about everything and asked, "Is everyone ready to go?"

Johnny looked at him and then at us, and then he realized we had it planned all the time. We just had to have a little fun out of him once in a while.

I asked, "Johnny, do you need any money to take with you?" "Dadgummit, Dad, I forgot all about that. I don't have but about fifty dollars in my pocket."

"We still have enough time to stop by the bank and pick up some money. We can go through the drive-in window. I need a few bucks myself."

We all got into the car after saying our good-byes, and Oscar headed for the bank. That didn't take very long. Johnny asked for a couple of thousand, and I asked for ten thousand just to be on the safe side. This was done quickly, and we headed for the airport. Johnny was really anxious.

We arrived at the airport almost an hour before departure time. Johnny looked real funny and says, "Dad, I don't have a ticket. I forgot all about the ticket in my excitement." He was almost crying he was so disgusted with himself.

I put my arm around his neck and said, "Well, maybe this will work. It has your name on it. I hate to tell you this, but I have been planning on taking you with me ever since we got here. I would never have had it any other way."

I wish you could have seen the look on Johnny's face when he saw those tickets. Johnny, I picked the tickets up the other day when Wayne and I came to the airport to get Father Brockman.

Johnny looked like he could hit me. He turned to Pam and told her, "This is just the start, you are going to have a lifetime of such things as this."

Pam laughed, "Well, I hope so. I'm looking forward to it."

Johnny laughed also, "Yeah, me too." Johnny told Pam, "It sure is good to have Dad back home so we can do things together."

I assured him we were going to be doing a lot of things together. "You, big boy," I said to Johnny, "are going to learn to run that plastics company. You are going to follow Pug and me around for a long time, and you are going to learn everything there is about plastics so that you can take care of me in my old age."

"Is that a challenge, Dad? If it is, I'm gonna take you up on it."

The time finally arrived for us to board the plane and find our seats. This time we didn't have long to wait before takeoff. After a short while we were told we were now passing over the Kansas City area and would be nearing Oklahoma City before very long. Sure enough, it wasn't long before we were over Kansas City.

"Johnny, it won't be long now before we reach DFW," I told him.

By now Johnny was sitting on the edge of his seat. He had no idea what to expect from Texas or Texans. He acted as though it was some foreign country.

Sure enough before long, the captain comes onto the intercom and says, "Folks, we will be arriving at DFW within the next twenty minutes."

We fastened our seat belts and placed our seats upright and get ready to land.

In just a short time the plane banked and headed down toward the runway to land. We heard and felt the tires hit the runway with a screech. This told us, "We are in Texas, pardner."

We had a short stay on the access runway to the terminal. The plane finally stopped, and Johnny was jumping up.

"Johnny, just sit a minute and take your time, and take your turn heading for the door," I suggested trying to slow him down a bit.

He didn't really want to, but he did what I asked him to do.

Finally, it was our turn to get up and leave the plane. No one was there to meet us this time.

Johnny took the claims checks and headed for the baggage area. Pam and I followed.

"Jim, have you ever seen Johnny this excited before?" Pam asked me.

"Never in my life have I ever seen that boy so excited – not even at Christmas time."

Johnny got the baggage quickly and was back dragging a couple of them. I took the ones he was dragging, and we headed for the auto rental desk. I gave the clerk my name and asked if they had my car ready for me.

The clerk thumbed through some papers and pulled out a couple of sheets. He said, "Everything is ready if you will just sign on the bottom line. A Lincoln Town Car is outside in the third row. It's a light blue one, license number 1LTM66. Have a good visit while you're here."

"Thank you, young man we're here on business, but we'll try to have fun also."

We walked out to the car and sure enough there it was, a soft powder blue. What a coincidence!

"Jim, what a beautiful car. That would be just my favorite if I had one."

"Well," I said, let's get loaded and get out of here. Johnny, do you want to drive?"

"Sure Dad, I'd love to drive if you'll just show me where to go."

"Okay, let's go."

We left the airport and headed for Ft. Worth and 7th Street. We went down through town and looked at the big buildings that had been damaged by the tornado.

As we neared downtown, I told Johnny to pull over at that big building just ahead for a minute.

Johnny pulled over to the curb and stopped. He looked at the curb and told me that this was a no-parking zone due to construction.

"That's all right Johnny. See that doorway there at the front of the building. That's where I was when the tornado hit. I was hunkered up in that doorway in a fetal position trying to keep from being killed."

I started to open the door and get out when Johnny said, "Uh, oh, Dad, here comes a cop."

I looked up, saw who it was and went walking back to where the policeman was. I hugged him and shook his hand and brought him up to the car. "Charley, I want you to meet my wife, Pam. We have been married all of five days. I also want to introduce you to my son, Johnny."

"Professor, you really are lucky, and it's great to see you, especially with your wife and son."

"I have another child back in Chicago Charley. My daughter's back there with my mother. We all got together after I was on the TV show."

"Yeah, that's right, Professor you won a million dollars, didn't you?"

"I sure did Charley, and I need some help from you while I am in town. I'll be here for about a month. When do you have a day off?"

"Well, Professor, I'm off tomorrow morning if that will be of any help."

"Good deal Charley, meet us at the Sanctuary tomorrow morning about 9:30 a.m. for coffee, and we'll start making plans."

"Okay, Professor, what ever you say I'll be there."

Johnny looked at me in wonderment. "Just how did you become such good friends with the police while you were on the street?"

"Long story, Johnny. You'll learn more tomorrow. Now, take me to the Tarrant County General Hospital. You drive, and I will tell you where to turn."

We drove for another ten minutes, then I tell Johnny that the big building just ahead was the hospital. We drive up to the front and park.

We were lucky to find a parking place because most of the time they were all taken. "Pam, I want you and Johnny to come inside with me."

We go inside the hospital which was very busy as usual. I went to the admitting desk and had been standing for a second or two when the lady at the admitting desk got up and came around the desk. The lady hugged me and shook hands with me. We talked for a minute, and then I motioned to Pam and Johnny to come over. I introduced them to the lady.

She said, "I am real proud of Professor for what he has done. It's the talk of everyone at the hospital. Looking at Pam and Johnny, she says, "I've checked Professor in many times over the last ten years, and he never gave anyone any problems. I had heard through the grapevine that he had married."

"Yes, we're married, and now we are back to see the old gang and get them set up and off the streets." I thanked her for all she had done and then I asked, "Is Dr. Davis is here?"

"He sure is. Let me call him for you.

"Dr. Davis, Professor and his family are here."

Dr. Davis told her to have me come on down to Emergency Receiving.

She asks, "Professor, I'm sure you know the way, don't you?"

"I sure do."

We took the elevator down to Emergency Receiving and exited toward the Emergency Room. Just as we walked out of the door there were about ten or twelve people standing there who started clapping when I stepped out.

"My Lord, what's all of this?"

Dr. Davis steps out and says, "They all wanted to say hello. Professor you're quite a celebrity here at the hospital." "Dr. Davis, I would like to introduce you to my wife and son."

"Well Professor, I heard that you were married, but no one said you married such a beautiful lady. Professor I don't mean to embarrass you or your wife, but your wife is absolutely gorgeous, and your son is a very handsome young man."

Everyone started asking questions, and I was trying to answer them the best I could. I finally asked Dr. Davis if he could meet with me and a few other people over at the Sanctuary tomorrow morning at 9:30 a.m. "Dr. Davis, it's for a good purpose."

"I will consider meeting with you if you will quit calling me Dr. Davis and just call me David."

"Bring your wife if you would like, she might have some good ideas that we could use."

Sounds like a good idea Professor, I'll change my shift and bring my wife and be at the meeting."

We all shook hands and headed back to the car.

"Well, Johnny, the next stop is the Sanctuary."

Johnny couldn't believe that I knew all of these important people.

Johnny, they're just people like you and me. If you treat them the way people should be treated, they'll be your friends too."

Johnny, Pam adds, "I think we have a lot to learn about the man they call Professor."

Most everyone here in the area knows me by that name.

I had Johnny turn on 7th Street, and we had gone about a quarter mile when I tell him, "Pull over to that building with the big cross on it."

Johnny pulls over and stops.

When we get out, I asked them to follow me. I tell Johnny to lock the car. You will find out why later."

We walk into the room, and Annie saw me first. She squealed, hollered, and came running. She grabbed me around the neck and hollered for Lynn. "Professor's here, Lynn Professor's here."

Lynn comes out of the office in a hurry and heads straight for us.

By now I was introducing Pam and Johnny to Annie. Lynn grabbed my hand and started pumping it madly. I introduce him to Pam and Johnny. I started looking around. As I am shaking his hand I am wondering where they are. "Professor, are you looking for the gang?"

Yes, I am. Are they around?

"Not right now, Professor they are working."

"Do you mean they're still working on the cleanup?" I asked.

"Part of them are and part of them have other jobs now. Mabel is cooking in a restaurant. You'll be proud of them and they're all staying sober. No one has had a drink since you left. At least none that I have heard of and I think if they did someone would have told me. They said if you could do it they could do it too.

"Professor, where is Pug?"

"Lynn, you know that he is married also, and he will be here in about a week.

"Lynn, I hope it's all right with you, but I have asked Charley Johnson and Dr. Davis to come here in the morning at 9:30 a.m. for a meeting with us."

Plans for Texas

Let's find a cup of coffee, and I'll fill you in.

We all went over to one of the tables with benches where the people eat their meals.

"My father-in-law will be here later in the week to help us also. I have everything in my mind that I want to do, but I will sure need your help."

"Professor, you have my help, and you know that's on anything you want to do."

"Lynn, I would like to set up a trust fund for the Sanctuary and let the money be invested by someone reputable and honest. The profits from the trust fund will go to help you fund the Sanctuary expenses just as long as you want to run it. When you're gone, and if the Sanctuary closes, the money will revert to my account that I am setting up to help other people in other endeavors such as these. All endeavors will be non profit. That way I could help some other organization similar to your Sanctuary."

"I can't believe it Professor. Annie, did you hear what Professor wants to do?"

"I sure did Lynn, and I can't believe it either."

I tell them what I have had on my mind for some time. I would like to set up a trust fund in the amount of something close to a million dollars."

Now they really couldn't believe it.

"I need to talk to Dr. Davis and Charley Johnson to help me find the people I need to help us. We need a stockbroker and a good, honest attorney-at-law."

Lynn laughed at that statement. "Just where do you expect to find an honest attorney?"

Well, I'm sure Dr. Davis can help me.

Next thing I want to do is to find a good private detective who's good at finding people. You see, I want to find Mabel's daughter. If I can get them back together, I would be very happy.

Lynn, you must have a new cook because this coffee is almost drinkable. Do you happen to have any iced tea around here?

Annie headed for the kitchen with a quick, "Coming right up, Professor. Does anyone else want a glass of iced tea? That is one thing we do have around here, Professor."

I got used to drinking tea when I was visiting Pam's family in Norfolk.

Pam and Johnny were taking all of this in without saying a word.

Finally Annie's curiosity got the better of her. "Professor, I have two questions for you."

Okay, Annie, ask away.

"Just how in the world did you get such a beautiful wife and handsome son? The next thing is, please tell me all about how you met and how you ever got her to say 'yes.'"

I was laughing by now, and finally I told Annie, The truth of the matter is that Pam asked me to marry her before she knew I had a nickel.

Now Annie was really in disbelief. "You mean to tell me that beautiful lady asked you to marry her when she thought you were a street person?"

Pam spoke up to set the record straight so they wouldn't think she was totally crazy. "We met at a restaurant where I worked. The only thing I knew about him was that he was in town to be on the TV Show. He told me after a couple of days that he used to be a college professor. But he only told me that after I asked him. I guess he didn't want to scare me off. He was so nice and courteous, and I could tell he was well educated. I could also tell that his mother had made him learn good manners when he was growing up. All of this plus his good looks, made me fall in love with him."

"Johnny how do you feel about having such a good looking dad and beautiful stepmother?" "As far as I'm concerned, she isn't my stepmother. My sister and I look at her as our mother not our stepmother, and that's the way it always will be."

Annie was shocked and looked at me. "Boy this lady must have made quite an impact on the entire family."

"Annie, my mother calls her daughter now so I guess it runs in the family."

Lynn looked at Annie, and she looked at him, and Annie said, "Pam, I hope we can call you our very good friend."

Pam was quite taken with their honesty about their feelings for me. Pam could see they went real deep, and that they really did care about me. This made points with her and Johnny.

We talked for some time until we heard a great big whoop from the door, and in came Bing, Cowboy, and Doc. They all ran over to me and grabbed me and hugged me. It was like a high school reunion.

They all stopped suddenly and looked at Pam and Johnny. Bing, who acted as spokesman for the group, turned to me and wanted to know who the lovely lady was.

"Professor," Bing asked, "could this young man possibly be your son? If that's the case, you not only won a million dollars, but a beautiful family also."

I introduced Pam to the boys, and then I introduced Johnny.

Johnny said, "I sure have heard a lot about you, and I have been real anxious to meet you."

"Boy, what a handsome son," was heard from the group somewhere behind me.

By now, others were coming in from work and off the streets. I looked at Pam and Johnny and said, "Well, it's about time to get to work. Annie, do you have a couple of extra aprons?"

"I always have a spare apron somewhere near.

Lynn said, "Annie, you can't do that to these folks."

I stopped him and let him know that I wanted Pam and Johnny to know what kind of a life I had had for ten years.

We were led to the kitchen where we were given aprons. We spent the next two hours setting tables, cleaning tables, and pouring coffee and tea for everyone who came in for dinner.

"Annie, I think they're finally getting the idea of what it was like to have to come in and take handouts."

Johnny finally came over and put his arm around my neck, looked me in the eyes, and said, "Dad, I'm beginning to get the picture."

"Johnny, you haven't seen anything yet, but you will."

After dinner I told Annie and Lynn I needed to use the phone so I could call and get a room over at the hotel.

"Professor you know where it is in the office."

I went into the office and made the call. I came out in a few minutes and told them, We have rooms over at the Ft. Worth Cowtown Hotel, which is only a few blocks away. It's an old hotel with a lot of history; dignitaries generally stay there.

I had learned a lot of the history of Ft. Worth while I had lived here even if I had been drunk most of the time.

I said, "Lynn, Annie, we need to get on over to the hotel so we can get unpacked and get a good night's sleep."

We went back to the car, which by now had a large group of people looking at it and wondering just who it belonged to. Some of them recognized me and said hello. Several told me that they were proud of me for winning that million dollars. I let them that I would see them later.

Johnny slipped into the driver's seat and we headed for the hotel.

The hotel was a totally different world from the place we had just left. There was a doorman, bellhops, and a beautiful interior to the lobby.

"Jim, it's hard to believe the two worlds exist so close to each other."

That's the problem Honey they do exist, and I want to help ease the pain of those people we just left.

She slipped her arm around my neck and told me that she was sure I would do just that. She was also sure they would appreciate it. You know what? Lynn and Annie are wonderful people. I can see why you care so much for them. How long have they been doing this?

Pam, I know this is going to be hard to believe, but they have been doing it ever since they got out of Seminary. Both of them are ordained ministers. It's hard to find people like them."

By now we had registered and were in the elevator on our way to our rooms. We walked in and found it was all western motif.

Johnny just stood there a few minutes before he spoke. "Did Roy Rogers decorate these rooms?"

"No, but you remember that he helped me win a million dollars?"

"That's right Dad I had completely forgotten about that. He must have really been a good guy if he helped you do that.

I was a great fan of his when I was growing up Johnny and it paid off.

Pam agreed that it sure had paid off – and big.

Dad, if it's all right with you guys, I'm going to go to my room and take a shower and hit the sack.

No, problem, son. I think that's what Pam and I will be doing real soon.

Pam agreed, "I am tired from working the dinner at the Sanctuary. That's worse than a Saturday night at the Black Angus. The tips weren't as good either but the satisfaction was wonderful. I could see the gratitude on the faces of the people.

Jim, I was surprised to find that they had facilities for both men and women with showers and dormitories for both men and women. They have a lot of time and money invested in that place.

When they started, it was just a small diner with a kitchen. They have built it up over the years to what is now. They are well thought of by Community Chest and other organizations that help the needy. The city even figures money in its budget to donate to the Sanctuary, I told her.

It was getting late, and we had all had our showers, and we were trying to prepare mentally for tomorrow.

As we crawled into bed we snuggled up together, and Pam said, "Jim, with a heart as big as yours, I understand one of the main reasons I love you so much. You are always thinking of the other person. Now kiss me goodnight and go to sleep. I'm really tired tonight. No headache, I'm just tired. Goodnight, Love..."

Morning came early as usual in Texas.

The first thing I hear this morning was someone knocking on my door. It was Johnny saying that it was time for us to get up and that he was hungry and wanted some breakfast.

I nudged Pam and asked her if we had a coffeepot in our room.

Oh, yeah there is one over on that stand by the dresser."

"Johnny give us just a minute and then come on in. We will have a cup of coffee, and then we will all go down and have breakfast together.

Pam and I got dressed, and we all had a cup of coffee and headed downstairs to the dining room.

I looked at the clock in the hotel and saw that it was only 7:30 a.m. "Damn, Johnny, I didn't know you were such an early morning person."

Well, Dad, I just didn't want us to be late for your meeting. I wasn't sure just how long it would take us to get fed here at this restaurant.

We went on into the restaurant and had a seat. We had a nice waitress who took our order and brought more coffee. It didn't take long to have breakfast here, so we ended up with plenty of time before the meeting.

That's great, Dad now we can go downtown and look at some more of the damage that tornado did when it hurt you.

Now I see method in your madness. Since Pam already has her eyes open, her makeup on, and her hair fixed, I don't have an excuse for not showing you around.

They brought the car around and we headed downtown to see the other damage. As we went downtown, I showed him the other buildings that had been damaged along with the church that had been badly damaged and the barber shop where Cowboy had been trapped for a while. I told him to drive us down by the river so I could show him where I had spent most of my nights when the weather had been nice.

We did a lot of sleeping under the stars during the periods of good weather. If there was a lot of dew, we would sometimes find a roof to sleep under like the roof of the farmers' market. They would generally ask us to leave real early in the morning because the farmers got there early to open up their stalls to sell their fruit and vegetables. Sometimes we would sleep under the bridge nearby. Sometimes we would have a light weight plastic sheet to cover with. The bridge was always a good place to be during the rain if the wind wasn't blowing too hard. Sometimes we just slept under a large piece of cardboard.

When the weather was bad, we would go to one of the several places open to the street people. The Sanctuary run by Lynn and Annie is by far the nicest of all of them. They feed better also. They also have showers for the men and women as you saw yesterday. They are always full during the winter months and the spring rains.

As long as you do what they ask, you're always welcome. They do not allow troublemakers of any kind. You start trouble, and you are out of there.

I finally looked at my watch and told Johnny to head for the Sanctuary because it was almost 9:00 a.m. and I needed to be there first so I could get a schedule made out.

We arrived at the Sanctuary and went inside. Lynn had cleaned up the office to use as a meeting place for us. We no sooner had gotten inside than in came Charley Johnson, and right after him came Dr. Davis and Mrs. Davis. Doc, Bing, Cowboy, and Mabel came in immediately after.

Mabel came running over and hugged my neck and went on about how proud she was of what I had done and how happy she was to see me.

I finally got a word in and introduced her to Pam, Johnny, and Mrs. Davis.

Professor, I couldn't believe it when I heard you had gotten married.

I asked everyone to please have a seat. I made sure everyone knew everyone else. I started by telling them of my plans to set up a trust fund for the Sanctuary. I asked Dr. Davis if he knew of a good, honest attorney and a good, honest stockbroker.

David assured me that he knew an attorney who handled things for the hospital who was very good and very honest. He also knew a stockbroker who handled his own personal stock portfolio, and he was very honest and trustworthy.

Good David. I hope you don't mind my calling you David since we are going to be working so closely on these things."

Dr. Davis says, Not at all. I would prefer it that way, Professor, or do you want us to call you Jim? If all of you will remember that I am David and my wife is Nancy, we will try to reciprocate. It appears we are all going to be in this thing together, so we had better be on a first- name basis.

Everyone agreed.

We will set the trust fund up in order for the Sanctuary to receive all of the profits for its needs in running this business of helping street people. If for some unknown reason, they ever become defunct, the money reverts to our corporation in order that it might be channeled into another such venture to help the homeless.

David said, "I am sure they can set that up without too much trouble."

When all of the necessary papers are set up, we will meet again and go over them and sign the papers.

Next on the agenda is for Doc.

Doc, I want Dr. Davis, I'm sorry I mean David and Charley to help us in setting up a storefront clinic for the homeless and street people. I'm thinking that in this endeavor Nancy might be of help to us. My point is that some of her friends might be the wives of men who own property that might be good for this program. If we have trouble finding the right place, we can always use the help of women. Maybe they can influence their husbands to help us out.

You have to remember that we need a woman's touch because there are women out there on the street as well as men. As you can see, I will stoop to anything to accomplish my goals.

Again, I will put up the money in the same way as with the Sanctuary, and Doc will run the clinic with the medical direction of Dr. Davis. I need Charley to help us find a location also.

"Charley, do you have any locations in mind that we might be able to rent or buy?"

Not right of the top of my head, Professor, but give me a few days, and I will find something, then I will get together with Doc and David and Nancy and make sure it's what they need in the way of space and location. There are some other policemen who will want to help out on this type of program too.

Professor, I think the city council would like to know what you are doing. Do you mind if I tell a friend of mine who is a councilman?

Not if he doesn't interfere and want to run things. This is going to be Doc's baby since he has taken care of so many of us for the past ten years or more with no money and no facilities. We want no politics and no interference. We would however, like to have the city's blessing. I plan to spend another million or more on this little baby also.

David, do you think you can get the attorney and the broker to work up the same type of agreement for this little project?

Sure do, Professor, I'm sure they would be glad to do it. When they hear what you are doing, I am pretty sure they might want to do the work gratis.

David, I'm not asking for charity on this, but if they want to help us, that will be great. You know I will be more than glad to pay them for their work. I just have to know they are honest.

No problem, Jim, they are honest, and I don't think they will want to charge you for doing something like this.

Next on the list came Cowboy. Cowboy, I have a question for you. If you had, let's say maybe sixty to a hundred plus acres of good grazing land with a couple of barns, sheds, and pens along with a few acres to raise hay, could you breed and raise rodeo stock if you had the proper breeding stock to start with?

Hell, yes, Professor, that would be easy.

I'm sorry, Lynn, I didn't mean to cuss.

If you feel you can do that, my father-in-law will be here later in the week. When he gets here, I want you, he, and Johnny to search Tarrant, Denton, and

Dallas counties and anywhere else near here for just what I have described. I'm willing to spend the money for the breeding stock and the property to get you started.

Now remember, Cowboy, I'm not giving you anything.

I'm getting you started. Once you get started and get on your feet and you're making money, you will be expected to pay the money back to the foundation. You will not be charged any interest on the money. You will only pay back the exact dollars spent to get you started. Is that agreeable with you?

"It sure is Professor I'll make it pay, you just watch and see what I can do with that livestock. Rodeo stock is the one thing I do know.

Okay, Cowboy, then just as soon as my father-in-law gets here, let's get going. He should be here this weekend. That means you guys can go ahead and start looking around tomorrow.

Johnny, I want you to go to one of the car rental places and rent a pickup – no, wait a minute, that would be too crowded for the three of you. Why don't you see if you can rent an SUV for you guys to run around in and see what you can find?

Now for Mabel. Charley, who is the best private investigator you know?

"Well, there is Jimmy Green. He is one of the best and most honest in this part of the country."

If he is as good as you say, then he is the guy I'm looking for.

Mabel, where do you think your daughter might be? What area of Louisiana could she be living in right now if you had a guess?

Well, Professor, I would say somewhere near the Many or Leesville area near the Texas eastern border near the Toledo Bend area.

Charley, let's get this Jimmy Green together with Mabel. I want that young lady found for her mother. I want them to have a reunion.

In the meantime Mabel, you Pam and I are going to make a trip down to the Many and Leesville area to see if we can find you a small café or restaurant. We are going to do you like everyone else. We will buy the business and let you run it. You will have operating money for no more than five years by which time you should be able to make it a paying proposition. You will then pay the corporation the money they invested in your business with no interest charged. You will be able to pay it back with small monthly payments until it's all paid back. That way we can take the money used to help you and help someone else.

By the way, Mabel, which town do you think we should start in, Many or Leesville?

I can assure all of you sitting here that I will see to it that when my wife and I are no longer alive, my son and daughter will run the foundation. This will make the money help a lot of people for a long time.

Pug is working for me as my personal assistant. He is now a married man, so that takes care of him.

Bing you're next. Bing, can you contact the men you owe money to in Las Vegas?

"Well, Professor, I'm not for sure. Why would you want to do that?

Because, Bing, I want to pay them off if I have enough money and get you out of trouble and into a small club or showplace of your own. You know a nightclub of some type. How much do you owe these guys anyway?

Well, Professor, years ago it was about eighty thousand dollars without the interest.

Do you think they would take a hundred thousand and call off the hounds?

I don't know, but I guess we could try.

Charley, do you think you would like to take a little vacation and go to Las Vegas to deliver some money for us. The trip and expenses are all on me. What do you say?"

Well, Professor, "I do have quite a bit of overtime on the books that I need to do something with. I think I would love a trip to Las Vegas."

Charley, if you can take care of that, I sure would appreciate it.

Now for Charley Johnson. I want to do something in your name. I want to donate five hundred thousand dollars to the Police Widows and Orphans' Fund and another hundred thousand to the Police Officers' Retirement Fund.

David, do you think you can get the attorney to take care of this for me?

"Sure, Professor. I hate to ask you this, but didn't you only win a million dollars before taxes. That would normally only leave you about six hundred and fifty thousand dollars. I don't mean to be nosy, but you sure are spending a lot of money."

David, Nancy, Charley, and friends, let me just tell you one thing. When I was a baby, my father started a stock growth fund for me. Each year he took a part of the profits from Dixon Plastics Co. and invested it in my name. My father died a year after I left. That stock continued to grow until it is now worth well over one hundred and fifty million dollars. I can afford to do what I have talked about today and lots more.

You see, I also own Dixon Plastics Manufacturing Co. My father left it to me in his will. I want to leave it to my son and daughter, but I still have money enough to do these things that I have proposed today. With your help I will accomplish my goal and repay a few people for the kindness they showed me during my ten years on the street.

Can we meet back here next Monday and see how things are progressing?

Everyone seemed to be in accord that we would see each other next Monday.

Oh yes, David, here is a check for five hundred thousand dollars to buy some new emergency room equipment for the hospital. We'll talk about more money later if it's needed. I still owe you for the suits you bought me so I could go back to New York City."

"Forget it Jim, that's on the house."

"By the way," Nancy asked, "would you and your family consider having dinner with my husband and I one evening this week?"

Pam, what do you say Honey do you have any plans?

No, I haven't any plans and I would consider it a pleasure to have dinner with your family.

Nancy says, "Sorry, Pam, unfortunately we have been unable to have children.

"I understand, so no need to apologize at least your wife and I have one thing in common. You see Nancy, I'm unable to have any children also. I lost one and after that the doctors told me I would be unable to have any more children.

Nancy, if you will just call and leave a message at the hotel if you can't catch us here, we will get back to you. We are in room 525."

After a while the meeting is about to break up. Charley comes over and wants to know where he and Jimmy Green could get in touch with Mabel in the morning.

Mabel quickly says, "I'll be working, and you can come by there to see me. My boss won't mind he is a nice guy."

They all had their jobs, so they start to leave.

Bing asks, "Professor, do you want me to try to contact the guys in Las Vegas to see what can be worked out?"

Sure do Bing, "Let's do it together. Come by the hotel this afternoon and we will see if we can make contact."

By now Lynn and Annie were getting ready for the lunch crowd.

I ask Johnny and Pam if they wanted to work the lunch crowd. Pam thought it would be best if I would show them around the Dallas - Ft. Worth area. I wanted to go by the Dallas branch office for a few minutes. We decided to ride around and show Pam and Johnny the area along with a stop at the branch office in Dallas.

"Well, it's not really Dallas, it's really on the west side of Dallas near Grand Prairie. They just have a Dallas mailing address."

Dad Johnny says, "I don't really care just where it is located. Let's just stop by for a few minutes. Right now, let's ride around a while and let these people do their work. We will get back together with them later."

I thank everyone for coming to the meeting, and we leave with everyone else telling Lynn and Annie we would be back later.

We drive around for quite a while. I show Pam and Johnny some more of the areas where I used to hang around. I even stopped and said hello to some of the other people I knew who were also on the street. I slipped a couple of them a few bucks to help them through the next couple of days.

I found myself on the way to Grand Prairie to take alook at the plant there. We stop to have a bite of lunch on the way. Good chicken fried steak, french fries and good ole country gravy and biscuits.

After lunch we drive the few blocks to the plant where we park and gp inside. I introduce myself to the receptionist and told her that I would like to see the plant manager.

The young lady asks us to have a seat. She get's on the intercom and says, "Mr. Kountz, Mr. Jim Dixon is in the lobby and would like to see you."

Mr. Kountz comes out and introduces himself. "Jim, I talked to your mother this morning and she told me that you would probably stop by to see the plant since you and your family were going to be in the area."

Mr. Kountz was a very congenial man who seemed to know what he was doing. You could tell that he was all company which is good. He was delighted to meet Pam and

Johnny and asked us if we would like to go with him and let him introduce us to the members of the office staff and sales personnel. "We have very nice people and a very nice office.

We were just about to have a board meeting, Jim. Would you and your wife and son like to sit in for a few minutes until we're through?

"We would love the opportunity to meet with them for just a few minutes."

After their business was over, they ask me if I have anything to say. I tell them that I am very partial to programs where the company sponsores scholarship programs for high school kids. I ask if they have such a program. They like the plant in Norfolk used to have one but they no longer sponsor these programs.

This is one of my favorite things for the company to do and I hope you will try to find a way to renew the program. I would like to see a program similar to the one Norfolk has instituted. Maybe you could contact the Norfolk plant and speak to Frank Wells. See if you can do something similar to what they are doing." I'm sorry, I forget that Mr. Wells is being transferred to the home office in Chicago. Give him about a month or so to get settled in and then contact him. He will be more than happy to explain what he did in Norfolk.

Mr. Kountz assured me, "We will contact Frank and have him send the particulars on their program so we can study it to see about instituting it here in the Dallas - Grand Prairie - Arlington - Ft. Worth area."

They adjourned the meeting, and Mr. Kountz took us on a tour of the plant and introduces us to people in the production and maintenance departments. I always seemed to be interested in the little men in the work areas of the plant. I believed they are the real backbone of the company. For a college professor I surprised a lot of people with my business knowledge. Most of that I got from my father while I was young.

Pam and Johnny just stood back and listened.

Johnny was learning a lot about me. He learned I really knew people and how to handle them to get what I wanted. I was never a bully. I was always the congenial boss who solicited their help and understanding in getting things done. I like to make them feel they are the most important persons in the room when I talk to them. I make them feel that each one I was speaking to was the only person to whom I was speaking in a large crowd. In short, I made them feel very worthy of my attention.

What Johnny didn't realize was that this was something I had learned from my father. I had also learned that if the people in a company who have less significant jobs feel left out, then they wouldn't be as interested in getting the jobs done right and on time. They needed to be recognized, as well as those in the front offices. Everyone has to feel important and needed.

We visited all departments before deciding we must get back to Ft. Worth. We said good-bye to everyone and headed back to Ft. Worth.

As we were driving west on Interstate 30, we pass the new Ballpark in Arlington of the Texas Rangers.

Johnny looked at me and said, "The Rangers are playing at home for the next few days. Do you think you might like to see them play, Dad?

How about you, Pam? Have you ever seen a big league baseball game?

Pam smiled and looked at me.

By this time I was smiling also. Johnny, I ask, would you like to go to the game tonight?

Would I? Oh, man, would I? I want to see Pudge Rodriguez in action. Dad, do you know that he is batting over 360 and already has 24 home runs and 72 RBI's this season? His average is fourth in the American League, and he is tied for second in home runs. He is leading all catchers in all of these categories. Man, Dad, I would be on top of the world if I could get his autograph.

Johnny, what happened to the Cubs and the White Sox?

They're all right, Dad, but that Pudge is something else. There's just no one like him, and what about Rafael Palmero? He's the best first baseman around, and he has almost 500 lifetime home runs during his career and he has another three or four years before retirement.

It sounds like you know quite a bit about this Texas team.

What do you say Pam? Would you like to go to a baseball game?

Great, boys, just show me the way and tell me when.

"How about tonight since we are in the area? We could go and have dinner at their club, and then watch the game before we go home. We can even go through their museum before we eat if we are too early.

As Pam looked at me, she said, I could eat a little something if you are hungry also.

We both agreed we were a little hungry, so we made an exit on the next off ramp and headed back toward the ballpark.

Who are they playing tonight, Johnny?

Dad, they're playing the White Sox.

Well, I say as I let out a great big whoopee, how about one for the home team?

Pam says, "Just wait and see Big Boy, just wait and see."

I reminded them that Bing was coming by the hotel so we could try to call Las Vegas and try to contact the men he owed the money to. We can do that and then come back in time for the game. Don't worry, Johnny, we will come back tonight and watch Pudge catch a few innings and hit a few balls. Does that sound all right?

It sure does, Dad that sounds great.

If that sounds all right to you guys, let's head for the hotel.

We arrived at the hotel and went straight to our rooms because Bing should have been getting here anytime now. We watch the television news for a short time, and then there was a knock on the door.

Johnny opens the door, and sure enough it is Bing.

Once inside he asks, "Jim, are you sure you want to go through with this plan of yours?"

I assured him that I wanted to go through with the plan. I asked Bing for the names of the people so I could call information and get a phone number where we could call these men.

Bing gave me the names of the two main guys who used to run the loan operation. Bing said, "Jim, these guys aren't really very nice people."

Okay Bing, but let's just take one step at a time and see what happens. How long ago did you borrow the money, and exactly how much did you borrow? I don't mean including interest I mean just exactly how much money did you borrow?

"To be best of my recollection, Jim, I think it was $85,000."

Bing, just how long ago was it that you borrowed this money?

"Well, now, let's see; I think it was eleven years ago that I borrowed the money."

Tell me the name of the establishments they hung around most of the time. I need that just in case I can't get them at their office or home.

"Well, Professor, there's a little strip-club-type lounge on the strip where they used to hang out, it was called the Bamboo Club. A lot of their crowd hung out there."

I pick up the telephone and dial the area code for Las Vegas. I asked Information for the phone listing of Jimmy Dale or Buck Roberts. There was a pause in the conversation between me and the operator.

All right, operator, how about the Bamboo Club on the strip?

The operator apparently had no trouble finding that number. I told her to go ahead and dial it for me if she didn't mind.

The phone rang a couple of times, a man answers and I ask, "Does either Jimmy Dale or Buck Roberts happen to be there?"

The man on the other end of the line asks, "Who is calling?"

I told him who I was and that "It's about possibly paying off a little debt I owe them."

There was a long wait when another man's voice came on the phone. "Who did you say you were?"

"I tell him again who I am. I just want to speak to either Jimmy or Buck."

"Well, that might be a little hard to do at this time."

"Why?" I asked.

"Well, you see, Jimmy got snuffed about four years ago by some guy who found out that Jimmy was playing around with his wife. He had a beautiful funeral. They put him in a solid walnut casket with beautiful white roses on the top of it for a casket piece. Can you imagine giving white roses to a little creep like that?

"Now Buck, that's a different story. Year before last he got picked up by the Feds for charging exorbitant interest rates on his loans and now he is serving thirty years for that and something else they got him on. If you owed them anything, you can forget about it because the Feds got all of the books and all of their paperwork.

"They put it in the archives, and a lot of people here in Vegas are real happy. A lot of people owed them a lot of money, but the Feds canceled all of that. I hope you owed them a lot. They really weren't that nice." The man on the phone said, "Have a good evening; I know I am because I owed them over fifty grand."

I turned to Bing and said, "Well, it looks like we have some real heavy problems on our hands."

Bing looked totally devastated. "Jim, what can we do now?"

We can start looking for a club to buy for you, I answer.

Bing almost swallows his tongue. Jim, what are you talking about?

Well, to make a long story short, they are no longer in business. Jimmy is dead, and Buck is in prison for the next twenty or thirty years, and the Feds got all of their books and paperwork. What I'm saying Bing, is that you are clear to go forward in your life.

Bing grabs me and hugs me. Jim, if it hadn't been for you, I would never have known they were dead and in jail. I would have probably kept running the rest of my life. How will I ever be able to repay you?

You might make a success of the club when we find you one. Now, how about you going to the Rangers and White Sox baseball game with us tonight. We can celebrate with a Coke and a hot dog. Johnny wants to go to the game real bad. How about you? Do you want to go?"

Bing looked at Pam and then at me and Johnny and said, "What the hell, I haven't seen a baseball game in fifteen years, and I would love to go.

We headed out the door and to the ballpark in Arlington. We finally found a parking place and headed for the ticket booth. I got the tickets and we all went inside for our first glimpse of the ballpark in Arlington. We were surprised at the architecture of the ballpark. It was a cross between the older ballparks and the newer parks. Something old and something new. There was a beautiful museum, as well as a couple of fine restaurants.

We found our seats along the front row of the first base line. The ball players were already on the field. Johnny was looking for Pudge Rodrigues whom he couldn't seem to find. He turned to a man in the next seat and asks if there was something wrong with Pudge.

Haven't you heard that Pudge broke a thumb the other night and will be out for the rest of the year?

This really threw Johnny a curve. He had been looking forward to getting his autograph. The guy says, "You're in luck tonight because Pudge is here with his family, right up above us in a box. I've seen a couple of people go up to see and speak with him and get his autograph."

Dad, I'm going to go up and see if I can get Pudge's autograph.

Johnny takes off up the stairs, and in a few minutes we saw him standing beside the box where Pudge and his family were seated. We could see him talking and laughing and shaking hands with the folks in the box. In a few minutes he shook hands with Pudge's left hand.

In just a little while Johnny came trotting down the stairs back to our seats. Pam and I saw that he had a piece of paper in his hand. It was a program.

"Dad, Pam I got to visit with Pudge and I even got his autograph on this program. I even told him to give us a call when he comes to Chicago to play the Sox. He asked me for my phone number and said he would try to give me a call when he comes to town. He sure is a nice young man, extremely polite and well mannered. He probably gets bothered a lot by people like me, and yet he is still polite and thoughtful."

He showed the program where he signed it next to a picture of himself in the program. With Pug's autograph this had truly been made a blue letter day for Johnny. "Johnny's day."

He turnes to Pam and asked if she had been to a ball game before. "You know what I mean, Pam, a real professional ball game?"

Do you mean a game where Frank Thomas was hitting for the Sox, or if Sirotka was pitching and Charles Johnson catching. Would you believe it if I told you that Thomas is hitting .336 this year or that Ordonez is still hitting above .300? Johnny, how do you feel about Johnny Oats splitting time on first between Raffiel Palmero and this young kid Catallanero? You know he is pretty good with the bat but he isn't quite as good at scooping up the low throws as Palmero is. Did you know that Palmero just hit his four hundred ninety something career homerun?

Dad, do you hear this woman? She sounds like a sportscaster.

Pam, where did you learn all this about baseball?

Well, Johnny, if you must know, I grew up in a house full of men and it was either join in on the fun, or get left out. Everyone in our house turned out to be Chicago fans. I used to study statistics when I was in grade school. Daddy would get all of us kids together and see which one knew the most about the Sox team.

"You may not believe this but my sister Louise knows more about baseball than I do. She is a lot more knowledgeable about football and hockey than I will ever be.

I even played some softball in high school. I was a pitcher. I had an ERA of 2.87 my senior year with a batting average of .347 for the season.

Johnny couldn't get over it. He had a new mother who was not only the most beautiful woman he had ever seen but she knew sports as well. What next?

I was just sitting there taking this all in. I turned to Bing and asked, "Well, what do you think of my little lady now?"

Damndest thing I ever saw. The two just don't go together. I see it, and I hear it, but it's still hard to believe.

The game began, and it turned out to be a pitchers' duel. There were no scores for the first five innings. The Sox pitcher began to get tired, and Kapler got a double with Lamb following up with a homerun giving them a two-run lead. This continued until the ninth inning.

They took Kenny Rogers out and called for Wetland to pitch the ninth inning. He did well on the first couple of batters and then Singleton the center fielder got a hit. This put the tying run at bat. Johnson came up next, and you know what kind of a bull this big man is. Johnson hit the ball to center field, and Kapler was playing him deep. He made a run for the fence, and the ball was high and about to go over the wall when Kapler gave a mighty jump that took him just above the lip on the top of the fence. When he came down, he had the ball in his glove and the crowd went wild. Kapler had without a doubt won the game for the Rangers. He was also chosen the player of the game and that last leap he made had made him the owner of the "Play of the Game."

Bill Jones the announcer of the game for TV went completely nuts. We knew this because we could see him and Tom Grieve jumping around like a couple of high school kids up there in that booth. The TV crew even turned the cameras on them because they were having so much fun.

Well the game was over so I wanted to know who was ready to head for the hotel.

Everyone seemed to be ready. We finally got to the car and out of the parking lot. On the way into town, Bing asks me to drop him off at the Sanctuary please. He was still staying there and would be until he got started on his new career. We dropped him off at the Sanctuary and went straight to the hotel.

When we arrived at our rooms, I asked Pam, "Would you call your father and see if he can come in over the weekend? Tell him to let us know when he is arriving, and we will be there to pick him up. We need him to help find a place for Cowboy to get settled into. I know it's late, but call him anyway I don't think he will mind.

If he can make it, tell him to pay for the tickets and we will reimburse him on his monthly expense account.

Johnny was still with us. He turned and asked, Dad, just how big a place do you want to find for Cowboy?

Well, Johnny, it depends on what you find. Why don't you and Art look around the area when he gets here? Charley and David both mentioned something about some good grazing land between here and Denison where Lake Texoma is located. Another area they mentioned was something down near Lake Granbury. The last place they mentioned was some good pasture land between Kaufman and Athens. This should give you guys plenty of running around to do.

"Johnny, I want you to go with me first thing in the morning, and we'll rent you guys an SUV of some kind to run around in. Cowboy will be available around Wednesday or Thursday. He can go with you to look at what you and Art have already looked at. He'll need to see which one has the best grazing and the best barns. He'll need a house on it good enough to live in until he gets things moving. We will have to supply him with some living money until he starts to turn a few dollars. Let's set up a checking account for him when the three of you find a place that he thinks will do the job."

"Dad, you never did tell me how many acres you are really thinking about."

"Well, Johnny, I feel that you and Art, along with Cowboy, can decide that. I feel it should be somewhere between sixty and a hundred or more acres with good water. That water is going to be very essential along with some pretty good barns at least good enough for us to fix up to do the job for him."

Okay, Dad, I see where you're going with this, and I'll try to work with Art and find something suitable before Cowboy gets here next week.

Now if you and Pam don't mind, I'll say goodnight and get some sleep. I kind of like this thing of getting up early.

Pam calls her dad and asks him about coming to Texas. She tells me that he would be here tomorrow afternoon. Do you think it would be all right if Mother comes along with Dad so she can get an idea of what Texas and Texans are all about? She wants to meet all of your friends also. I told her I was sure it would be all right with you. I hope I didn't make a mistake."

"Honey, I think that would be just fine. I would like for your folks to meet everyone and see Ft. Worth and this area of Texas.

Now, if you don't mind, I think we should get some rest also because I have a feeling that tomorrow Johnny is going to want to do some running around. I have a feeling that we had better be rested up for that. That boy is getting more excited every minute.

We retired to get some rest for the new day tomorrow.

The phone rang about 7:00 a.m. it was Saturday morning. Art asked, "Did I wake you up? Oh, heck, Jim, I forgot that you are late risers. We will be arriving at 2:45 this afternoon on United Airlines if it is on time. You know how they have been running lately. Nora is sure excited about getting to come to Texas."

"Art, can you hold on just a second? Your daughter wants to talk to her mother."

Pam came on the phone and asks, "Mother, are you packed? Jim thinks it's a great idea for you to come with Dad. No, he really doesn't mind. I think he really wants to introduce you to Texas. No really Mother, he really doesn't mind and he will be glad to see you and show you around and introduce you to his friends. All right Mother, we will see you at 2:45 this afternoon on United Flight 212 from Norfolk by way of Chicago. Don't worry Mother we will be there. Jim hasn't missed an arrival since I met him. See you later this afternoon.

Pam looks at me and says, "You're spoiling my mother."

I just laugh and say, "Yes, and isn't it fun?

By now Johnny was up and had his shower and was knocking on the door. Hey sleepyheads let's go and get some breakfast.

Johnny, go and make some coffee while we have a quick shower and we will be ready real soon to go down to the coffee shop."

It was getting to where I was real fast on getting that shower and quick shave and Pam was really getting fast at putting on her makeup.

Coffee's ready. Pam, I have yours already for you, and Dad I am fixing yours. I have already fixed mine. Joke Dad, just a joke. I really don't have mine yet.

Johnny gave Pam and me our coffee to drink while we were getting ready. Like I said, it didn't take as long to get ready as it used to.

After breakfast Johnny wanted to go to an auto rental company. We adjourned to the lobby as our car was being brought around, and then it was off to the auto rental office out on the airport highway. We were met by a very nice young man who wanted to show us something very expensive, but he was told right away that we wanted to rent an SUV for about a month or six weeks. I looked at the ones they had and I decided that instead of an SUV I would rather have a Chevy Suburban. The Suburban was larger and a better ride and we might have to take several people with us, so we decided the Suburban would be better for our needs.

Johnny looked real hard at the Ford Bronco, but he finally agreed that if everyone wanted to go to look at property, it would be better to have the Suburban.

Could you believe that Johnny accepted a nice dark blue one? He followed us back to the hotel where we left my rented car, and we all went in Johnny's Suburban.

The first place we wanted to go was to the Sanctuary. We arrived and went in to find everyone busy cleaning up from the Saturday morning breakfast. Lynn and Annie seemed surprised to see us. We found that Cowboy, Bing, and Doc were still at the Sanctuary. Mabel had gone to work so she could be off this evening. Her boss had switched her shift in order for her to have the evening off.

"Annie, Pam's parents are coming in this afternoon, and she would like to bring them by to meet you guys."

"That would be just fine."

Lynn, do you know where a cellular phone rental is located? I feel that Johnny and I both need mobile phones while we are out hunting properties.

Lynn gave me an address and we headed for the mobile phone office. Upon arrival we go in and tell the people what we wanted. The man seemed a little skeptical when I told him that I wanted ten phones with consecutive numbers if possible. This proved to be quite a problem but he finally came up with all ten numbers in consecutive order.

I want the best phones you have with a thousand or fifteen hundred minutes a month including long distance with no roaming and no long-distance charges. I will pay for the first three months in advance.

The man was surprised to have this happen since most people didn't have the money to pay that much in advance.

The man finally programmed the phones and assigned names to numbers for me. He assured me they were all activated, but I tried each one of them just to be sure. I paid the man cash, signed the lease agreements, and we left.

I handed one of the phones to Johnny. I made sure it was the one with the consecutive number next to mine and Pam's.

Pam said that she had been wanting a phone for some time but she hadn't felt she could afford one.

I explained that the rest went to Art and the gang, including Angie. This way we can all stay in touch with each other.

With that we headed back to the Sanctuary, where the gang was. When we arrived, we found that the gang was still there, so we called them into Lynn's office. Once we were in the room, Johnny put the box of phones on the table and opened it. I started taking them out one by one, and Pam started reading off a name and a number for each of them.

I handed each of them a phone as Pam read each name. They had trouble believing what was happening. They took the phone and look at it and then they look at each other.

Cowboy wanted to know, "What do we need these for?"

These may be pretty important before too long. They are going to be our link to each other. In the next few days and weeks, we will need to stay in touch, and this is the way of doing it. Now, I want all of you to go tomorrow and get your drivers' licenses. You may need them before too long. Right now, I am going to give each of you a thousand dollars, and I want you to be looking around for a place to live. If you want to live together, that will be fine, but I want you to move out of the Sanctuary so Lynn will be able to make room for others. If you need a little more money for deposits, etc., just let me know, and I will get it to you. You no longer need to be looked after.

Next week, after you have found a place to live, Pam and Nora will help you buy what you need to make it a home. Why don't you all go to a movie or something, but just please be good and stay sober.

Doc looked a little hurt, and said, "Professor we have stayed sober till now so don't worry about us. We intend to do that very little thing. If I feel the urge to have a drink, I'll call you on this telephone you just gave me."

Jim, Pam scolded, I don't think you have a thing in the world to worry about because they really mean it. You can tell by the way they talk and act.

"That's right," said Bing, "you can count on us."

We have some things to do this afternoon, so we will be running for now, but if anyone needs me for any reason, just call, no matter what time it is – day or night. Does everyone understand? You all have all of our numbers, and don't loose the card with them on it.

They all gave a big, "Yes, we sure do, Professor."

Pam, Johnny, and I said, "Good-bye for now. We'll see you later."

We headed back to the hotel to make some phone calls before lunch and the time to go and get Art and Nora. Instead of taking it easy, I reached for the phone as soon as we arrived back at the room. I was calling Dr. Davis to let him know what we were doing and to ask if he and Nancy would like to have dinner somewhere tonight with Pam, Johnny, Pam's mother and father, and me. I thought that possibly David would know a nice restaurant where the five of us could have a quiet dinner and become better acquainted.

Jim, it just happens that we don't have anything special on for tonight, and we would love to have dinner with the family. What kind of food does everyone like so we will know what to recommend?

"David, it may sound funny, but everyone still likes to have a steak pretty often.

That's fine, and I know just the place.

Do you mind riding in a Suburban? That way we can all go in one car. If we all go in the Suburban, we can pick you up if you will just give me an address. That way you can give directions to the restaurant.

That sounds fine. Nancy and I will be ready about 7:30 p.m., if that's all right with you? If that sounds all right, I'll call and make reservations for about 8:00 p.m."

We all agreed, and I got off the phone.

Pam couldn't believe what was happening. He was picking up the phone again. I looked at Pam and asked her if she had the phone number of Mr. and Mrs. McKenzie in Moab, Utah.

Pam started laughing and handed me her address book. She said, "Look it up under the "Mc" section of the book."

I just grinned and started fumbling through her personal phone book for the number. Pam was great at keeping the phone numbers of everyone right at her fingertips just in case anyone needed us. Pug had given her the number of his parents' home before they had left just in case I needed to talk to him.

I dialed the number, it rang a few times. A man answered.

"Jake, is that you?" I asked.

"Sure is, who's calling?"

It's Jim you know, Professor.

Hell, Jim, I know who you are, you don't have to draw me a picture. Are you guys having fun in Texas? I guess you want to speak to Wayne.

Well, Jake, that would be nice if he isn't busy.

"Naw, we're just sitting here chewing the fat about the fishing trip we went on yesterday. You know what? That Angie caught more fish than any of us men. She got a twenty-seven-pound catfish out of that Colorado River. She and June are in the kitchen cooking part of it for supper. Wish you were here to help us eat it and listen to her brag. Well here comes Wayne. Nice talking to you, Jim.

Wayne got on the phone and once again told me I wouldn't believe what that gal had caught yesterday. "Biggest darn catfish that's been caught around here in a couple of years."

Pug, you be sure to bring some pictures with you. I just wanted to call and see how your visit is going. Has your sister had her baby yet?

She hasn't had the baby yet, but it sure does look like it won't be too long now.

Well, I just wondered, and I thought maybe you would be able to come to Texas as soon as she has the baby.

Jim, we don't have to wait till the baby's born to come to Texas. We have really been having some quality time together. I have seen a lot of my old friends, and it's wonderful, but I have been wondering about the gang. How are they doing?

Wayne, you wouldn't believe it. Mabel has a real good job as a cook in a nice restaurant, and she is loving it. The rest of the gang are real excited about our plans for everyone.

"How's Angie doing?"

"Well, you won't believe it, but she asked me this morning when we were leaving for Texas. Now that I am back home and the folks know that I can come back any time I want, I think it makes it a lot better for everyone. I'm not lost to them anymore. I'm real anxious to get back with the gang to see what we can do for them. Would it be all right if Angie and I come to Texas on Tuesday?"

If that's all right with your folks, it's all right with us. We'll reserve rooms for you here at the Ft. Worth Cowtown Hotel where we are staying if that is all right with you.

Sure is, Jim, and we sure do appreciate it. Now give me a phone number where I can call you as soon as we know our arrival time.

I gave him the number of the mobile phone and told him to call anytime he wanted to. I told Pug that everything seemed to be going real well here in Ft. Worth. We will be looking forward to your arrival. Good-bye for now.

Pam asked Johnny and me if we were getting hungry. We thought it would be a good idea to go ahead and eat so we would be able to go to the airport early and not miss Art and Nora. We decided to go to the lunchroom and have a nice leisurely lunch.

After lunch we walked around the neighborhood of the hotel for a while and talked to some of the people who lived here in Ft. Worth. I noticed that it was getting close to time to pick up the Jackson family so I suggested to everyone that we head for the hotel to get the car and go to the airport.

The Jacksons' Arrival

We arrived at the airport with plenty of time to spare before the plane arrived. We stopped and had a cup of yogurt with some nuts on top for dessert since we hadn't had any dessert with our lunch. We had just gotten through with our dessert when the announcement came over the P.A. system that the plane was arriving at gate twenty-three, which was right near where we were standing. We went to the gate and waited.

Before long Art and Nora came up the ramp. Pam ran to meet them and welcomed them to Texas. Johnny got their claims stubs and headed for the baggage room to get their luggage. We all met him on the street and made our way to the Suburban. Everyone was talking fast and furious all the way to the hotel.

Upon arrival, Art and Nora were shown to their rooms. After they were settled, I told them that I had arranged for dinner this evening with Dr. Davis and his wife, Nancy. They were excited at getting to meet some of my friends.

We visited and talked for a while, and then I explained to Art what had been going on and what I was going to be doing for the next few days with Johnny.

Jim, that sounds just fine. Since I grew up on a farm as a kid, I will brag a little and tell you that I know good soil when I see it. I think I might be of some help finding Cowboy a good place.

Pam told her mother and dad that she would like for them to meet Lynn and Annie at the Sanctuary. They admitted they had been wanting to meet them just because of the things I had told them earlier.

Pam suggested we go by the Sanctuary on the way to meeting Dr. Davis and his wife. This sounded good to everyone, so we loaded back into the Suburban and headed for the Sanctuary. We arrived at the Sanctuary. Johnny locked the car, and we all went inside. Johnny was learning.

Lynn and Annie were surprised to see us, but pleasantly surprised and happy to meet Pam's mother and father. We had a nice visit and were able to see just how they fed the people for supper. There were quite a few today with it being Saturday. Nora was very impressed with the way they handled such a chore.

"Annie, I was a little skeptical when Jim told me how many people you take care of at each meal." Nora even mentioned that she would like to come back and help a couple of days or so while she was in town since the men would all be out running around.

This tickled Annie and she said, "Nora, you would be more than welcome; the more the merrier."

Nora looked at Pam and suggested that she might help also. Pam agreed that she would be more than happy to help.

Everyone had a good visit, and then I reminded them that it was getting close to time to meet David and Nancy for dinner. We followed the directions closely and found Dr. Davis' house without any problems. I went to the door to make sure it was the right house.

Sure enough David answered the door and invited us in for a few minutes before leaving for the restaurant. Art and Nora were introduced to David and Nancy.

David asked, "Would anyone like to have a drink?" Then he looked at me and apologized for asking.

I laughed and asked, "Do you have a glass of tea or a Coke?"

That was fine. The rest of the family had a cocktail before leaving for the restaurant. We arrived and found that it was a well-known steak house by the name of the Cattleman's Restaurant.

We had a fine dinner with a lot of good conversation. Most of the conversation concerned the work I wanted to do for my friends and the street people. The evening did what it was meant to do. It got everyone better acquainted.

After a couple of hours we headed back to David and Nancy's home. After another hour of good talk and learning more about each other, Pam and I suggested we head back to the hotel. We felt that Art and Nora must be tired after such a fast and hectic day.

We said good-bye and went back to the hotel. Johnny was beginning to learn his way around town so he didn't need any guidance back to the hotel.

No one needed to be persuaded to go to bed. It seemed that everyone was tired, and tomorrow we wanted to show Art and Nora around the town.

Sunday morning dawned with a bright sun shining in the window because we had forgotten to pull the shade last night.

Since we were awake, we made a pot of coffee to help us open our eyes. We finally called Art and Nora to see if they would like some coffee. It turned out that Art and Nora had been up for quite a while, after all it was almost 8:00 a.m.

We decided to call Johnny and wake him up. The call found Johnny had already been up for some time and had made coffee also. He had already had his shower to help him wake up, and now he was ready to go downstairs and have breakfast. Pam and I told Johnny and Art and Nora that we would be ready in fifteen minutes. We showered in a hurry, and Pam put on her makeup, and I shaved. We got dressed and looked at our watches and saw that we had actually done all of this within the fifteen minutes allowed to us by our family.

We all went downstairs for breakfast.

The rest of the day was spent by my showing everyone around the Ft. Worth area. I showed them where I used to sleep and where I would eat. I explained it all in detail to them. I asked them if they would like to go to the Sanctuary and attend church with Lynn and

Annie before we continued our guided tour of the town. They thought that would be a good thing to do.

We went to the Sanctuary and attended church services with the gang since they had started attending church services all the time now. They even attended Wednesday evening services when they aren't working. This sure did make me feel good since I was the one who had finally gotten everyone to working and being straightened out. Well, I had done it with the help of Lynn and Annie.

When services were over, Lynn invited us to stay and have lunch with them.

I explained, Pam's mother and father want to see as much of the area as they can. Johnny wants to see the Ft. Worth stockyards and some longhorn cattle.

Art let's me know that he would be interested in that also.

Pam said, "Nora, we can do some shopping while the boys are looking at the cattle."

Johnny asks, Dad, do you know what size hat Cowboy wears?

I was very surprised at this and asked, Why do you want to know?

Well, Dad, you told me when you were in Chicago that you had promised Cowboy a new hat if you won the million dollars. What color does he like?"

Well, Johnny, I'm not sure of the color, but I do know that he wears a size seven and a quarter, and you can guess at the color. Johnny, are you really going to buy Cowboy a new hat?

Well, Dad, I sure am, and I am going to buy one for myself.

Johnny, if you going to buy a hat, maybe you should buy some Levis or Lee jeans and a western shirt or two.

How about a pair of Luccesi cowboy boots?"

That's a great idea, son.

Art, how about you? Would you like to have a good pair of cowboy boots and a hat?

Why not, Jim. If I'm going to be out looking at farms and cattle property and livestock, I guess we had better look the part.

Why don't you get pre-washed jeans so they won't look new? That way they won't know you are greenhorns, Pam suggests.

Nora laughs and says, "That's my girl, always thinking."

This time she is using her head real well, I told her father. Don't you agree?

Art and Johnny both agreed, so we all headed into the Western Boot and Clothing store.

We found that they had two beautiful types of hats. One brand was Stetson, and then there was the Texas brand made over in Dallas, well Garland to be exact, named Resistol. They were both very fine hats, so it was really a toss up as to which one we wanted.

We went inside the store and were met by a man wearing boots, jeans, western shirt, and western hat. He was extremely polite and asked if he could be of any service to us.

We explained that we needed jeans, boots, and the works including a good hat. He suggested that we get pre-washed jeans to make them look worn and then he suggested that certain types of shirts had that look also, so maybe we could match them up.

Art and Johnny tried on the jeans and found what seemed to fit pretty well. With the help of Pam and Nora they found shirts to go with the jeans. They bought three pairs of jeans and three shirts each that way they would have a change of clothes.

Next they told the young man they would like to look at some boots. He asked them if they had a preference of color or brand.

Art asks, "What would you suggest?

Well, if you don't want them to know you're a tenderfoot, I would suggest black or brown. If you want to appear successful, then I would say you need a pair of ostrich skin or lizard."

Johnny spoke up and said, "I think I might like to have the lizard skin in a dark brown or black."

Art seemed to think that would work out for him also.

Now the young man asked, Do you have a particular brand in mind?

Johnny said, Someone mentioned the name of Luccesi.

I could see dollar signs in the young man's eyes when Johnny told him that. He said, They are one of the better brands of cowboy boots, but they are a little more expensive than most.

He had them sit down, and he checked the size of the shoes Art and Johnny were wearing and went to the back room. He came out with a pair of brown lizard boots and handed them to Johnny, and he handed a pair of black ones to Art. They already had their shoes off, so they each started to put the boots on.

If you don't wear boots, you have to understand that there's a knack to putting them on. They each worked for a while, and then the young man came over and offered them a little talcum powder to help them slip on easier. Sure enough, they slipped on easily after he put the powder in them. They each put on both boots and stand up. Johnny was already six feet, three inches tall, so with the boots on he was almost six feet, five inches tall.

Pam walked up to him, looked up at his chin, and asks, "How's the weather up there, pardner?

Everyone just about fell down laughing including the young clerk.

Art stood up and looked around at everyone and took a step or two. "Damn, these things feel good. They fit just like gloves. By the way, young man, how much are these boots?"

"They're just $749.00, sir. But with those boots, all you have to do if the soles and heels wear out is send them back to the factory or a dealer and they will send them in for you. They will replace the soles and heels – at no charge."

Young man," Art said as he looked him dead in the eye, "You wouldn't pull an old man's leg would you?

Oh, no, sir, I wouldn't do that. That's their policy.

Art sat back down and looked at me. "Hell, Jim, I could buy a suit, shirt, shoes, and everything for $750.00."

I agreed but told Art, You can't send them back to be repaired free. Let me do this for you and Johnny. I would like to buy the boots and hats for you guys. You buy your britches and shirts.

Johnny, how do you feel about a deal like that?

Dad, if you're serious, I'm going to take you up on it.

Now to the hats. Johnny spotted a black one that he had really taken a liking to. He asked the young man if he had it in size seven and three eighths."

The young man assured him that he did have it in his size. What kind of crown do you want in it?

What do you mean by what kind of crown?

The young man showed him several pictures of different ways to arrange the crown of the hat.

Johnny looked at them and then he asked Art what he liked. Art told him that he once had a hat with a cattleman's crease in it.

The clerk said, "The cattleman's crease is the most popular especially for older men."

Art said, Then I want a Silverbelly with a cattleman's crease.

The young man brought out this beautiful silver gray hat in Art's size. He walked over to the steam table and started to crease it. He worked it with the hands of an older more experienced salesperson.

Art asked, "How long have you been doing this?"

"Oh! I grew up in this store my father owns it. I love working with these hats and shaping them."

We could tell he really enjoyed what he was doing by just watching the way he would hold the hat up look at it, then brush it, and then steam it some more. He finally had Art's hat ready. He handed it to Art.

Art put it on, and the young man said, Turn and look in the mirror behind you and see what you think of the hat. He added, Check to see if it fits all right too.

Art looked at himself, and then turned to Pam and Nora. Well, what do you think, ladies?

They both seemed real pleased with the transformation of their husband and father.

The young man took the black hat over to the steam table and asked Johnny if he had decided what kind of crease he wanted in his hat.

Well, I kind of like the one that Roy Rogers used to wear on his hat.

The young man suggested, They really don't wear that much anymore. How about a George Straight type of crown and crease?

Yeah, that sounds good, let's do that. I like George's looks in those commercials that he does. Do mine that way.

The young man deftly moved the hat over the steam. He shaped it and held it up to look at, then he brushed it and held it over the steam again. He finally finished constructing the crown and handed it to Johnny.

It was still warm from the steam when Johnny eased it down on his head. He turned to look at himself in the mirror. He heard a couple of whistles behind him. It was Pam and Nora.

Boy, what a hunk! Nora said.

Pam laughed and told her mother that she had actually seen Johnny blush for the first time.

Johnny liked it and told them that it felt real good. You know he said, "just right."

They went over to the counter to pick up the bill for the boots and hats. The young man said, Well, now, let's see that's $749.00 each for two pair of boots and $275.00 each for two hats. He turned to me and asked, What about the jeans and shirts?

Oh, hell, go ahead and put them on it too.

The young man figured for a minute and then rang up the sale. He turned to me and said, That will be $2641.30, including tax.

That's just fine, young man. I hope you will accept an out-of-town check.

Yes, sir, if you have identification.

I was real proud because now I could show the young man a driver's license from Chicago as identification. I wrote the check.

The young man thanked us all and invited us back before we left town.

Johnny stopped suddenly. He looked at me and asked, What about Cowboy's hat?

I turned right around and went back into the store. They all waited on the sidewalk and looked in the windows of the stores next door until I came back out carrying a large hatbox with the Stetson name on it.

Okay, I said, we have Cowboy's hat now, so let's go see those longhorns.

The rest of the day was spent just riding around and visiting the areas that I used to call home. You know, places like under the Lancaster Street Bridge, or down at the Farmers Market, or over in the riverbed when it was dry.

Art and Nora found all of this hard to believe since they had never known me when I had lived that way.

We finally got tired and stopped for a hamburger and a Coke. After eating, we headed for the hotel for a good night's rest since we had a really busy week ahead of us.

Fine Tuning the Programs

Monday morning we had breakfast and headed for the Sanctuary where we met the gang except for Mabel who had already gone to work.

Nora had decided she would like to sleep in this morning and get some much-needed rest. She said, Art, would you please have Pam call me around noon and let me know what is going on?

We were all sure proud of that lady and the way she had changed.

Bing and I told the gang what we had found out about the guys in Las Vegas. Doc told Bing he was real happy for him, and all of the gang chimed in with their congratulations also.

That means he won't have to be looking over his shoulder any longer, and he can live like a normal man I said.

Cowboy, you go with Johnny and Art and start looking at farms and ranches. Johnny has several areas where he has leads on land for sale.

Johnny, Art and Cowboy headed for the Suburban. I asked them, Where are you going first?

Johnny said, I thought about going southwest to the Granbury area. If that isn't what we want, we might go on over east toward Cleburne and then maybe over to the east side of Dallas towards Kaufman and Athens. I hear there are some real fine small ranches and farms over there. They say there is a lot of good grazing, and some of the places have pretty good houses and barns.

Johnny, be sure and keep track of what you spend on food, gas, and other things so we can write off the expenses.

After they left, I turned to Pam and said, I think Johnny is growing up in a hurry, and this should help him. He's learning responsibility by handling a chore such as finding and buying the place for Cowboy.

Okay, now, let's concentrate on a place for a storefront clinic. Charley said he would be looking over the weekend, and he is supposed to be here before too long. David will be making some phone calls this morning to get someone to draw up the paperwork and to contact someone in the city government about getting a permit and finding out just what we will have to do to go about qualifying for such a program.

Pam, I need to talk to Jimmy Green the private investigator. I want to tell him where to get started looking for Mabel's daughter.

I had just finished saying that when the door to the Sanctuary opened. A nice mild-mannered, good-looking, middle-aged man about six foot plus came in. He apologized for interrupting and then he asked if one of the men happened to be Jim Dixon.

I introduced myself.

The man said, Hello, I'm Jimmy Green.

That's funny because we were just talking about you. I introduced him to everyone and then I told him what I would like for him to do.

Jimmy agreed that he could do what I wanted. He asked if it was possible to meet with Mabel.

It sure is.

I asked Cowboy to go with the detective to where Mabel was and let him talk to her and get whatever information he might need.

Just then Johnny came running in the front door and handed Cowboy a big hatbox. He said, Daddy bought this for you yesterday. Then he turned and ran back out the door.

Cowboy quickly opened the box, and there it was, a brand new, silver gray, Silverbelly Stetson hat that was just his size. He slowly looked it all over and carefully put it on his head. He turns to Lynn and asked if he had a mirror so he could see how it looked.

Cowboy, there is one just inside the door at the back of the room.

Cowboy walked back and opened the door, stood there, and very carefully moved it one way and then another on his head until he got it just right. He walked over to me and grabbed me around the neck and held on tight and told me how much he appreciated it.

I reached into my wallet and handed him eight one hundred-dollar bills. I turned to Jimmy and asked him if he would mind stopping by the Western Wear store down by the stockyards to let Cowboy go in and get himself a good pair of boots. Jimmy winked at me and told me that he guessed he could spare the time.

As they walked out, Cowboy turned to me and said, Professor, I'm not going to let you down. I'll never do that to you.

I smiled and said, Get out of here and take Jimmy to see Mabel.

They left just as David, Nancy, and Charley come in the door.

Things seem to be working just like clockwork this morning.

We all exchanged pleasantries.

David said, "Jim, I have talked to a friend of mine who is on the City Council about Doc and his storefront clinic. My friend thinks this is a terrific idea. He just wants to be sure that once it's set up, there will be money to keep it going."

"After we discussed it and I explained how the corporation would be set up and endowed, he was all for it. He will do everything he can to expedite it if we find the property in a suitable location."

Charley tells us that he went looking around over the weekend. I think I found a good spot that would be accessible to most street people." Charley asks Doc, David, Nancy, and Pam if they would like to go look at it.

"I contacted the realtor who handles it this morning before coming over, and he has agreed to be there around 10:00 this morning if that's agreeable with everyone."

I say, "Let's go on over and be sure it has everything you'll need, like plenty of room to make small examining rooms, etc., and an X-ray machine."

David stopped dead in his tracks and turned and looked at me. "What do you mean, X-ray machine?"

"Well, David, you do need an X-ray machine if you are going to be treating broken bones and such. You know a lot of those people will come to Doc that would never go to the hospital with a broken arm or foot or some other smaller type of sprain or break. I just thought I would have you find us a machine, and I would pay for it."

"What are you going to do next, Jim?"

I don't know right now and probably won't know until you guys get it working and find that you need something else. That's when you will tell me, and we will have a Board of Directors meeting and decide if we can get it.

"By the way, David, you, Doc, and Charley are going to be on the Board of Directors, aren't you?"

"Well, I guess so, if you want us to be."

"Well, that's what I would like, and if you can get someone from the City Council on the Board, I would sure like that also. Think you can arrange that?"

"Hell, Jim, I can sure give it a good try.

"Oh, yes! Jim, I forgot to tell you, but I have been talking to some of the guys at the hospital, and a couple of doctors and several of the interns want to help out as well. Several of the nurses have offered to work on some of their days off if it will be of help. I told them I was sure we would be able to work out a schedule where they would all be welcome.

"Oh yes! I talked to a couple of pharmaceutical salesmen who think they can get their companies to donate a lot of samples as well as some drugs you will need, which are not just samples. This will be a big public relations thing for them, and they can write it off as a charitable gift. It seems that everyone wants to get into the act. Maybe we can get some store like Sears or similar stores to donate the linens."

I looked at David and laughed and turned to Nancy and asked, "Does your husband always get into things like this so gung ho?"

Jim, he has never been this enthused about any program before in his life, at least not since I have known him. Jim, you have to understand David. Once he starts something and gets his teeth sunk into it real well, he just doesn't let go until everything is done and done right. He won't stand for second best.

Well Bing, what do you say we all go over to meet this real estate man? I am anxious to see this place they have found for a possible clinic.

I asked Lynn and Annie if they would like to go, but they had to take a rain check.

Everyone, including Bing, loaded into the cars and followed Charley and Doc. They lead us down to a building on Weatherford Street near the intersection with Henderson Street. There near the corner was a nice-looking building that must have had at least a hundred-foot frontage on Weatherford Street. This was a nice brick veneer building with part of the street side of the building having brick veneer and large plate glass windows on each side of a door.

Upon closer scrutiny of the front of the building, we found there were actually two doors. This would be good.

We parked and walked over to look at the building. The real estate man was there waiting. Charley introduced all of us, and we walked into the building, which the man had already opened up.

"The building," he said, "has very good air-conditioning units, four of them. The interior is divided into four sections with partitions, and each section has its own air-conditioning unit on the roof. There are two heating units that are ducted into all of the areas. This building," he said, "is one hundred feet wide by one hundred and twenty-seven feet deep. This should do the job as it was explained to me by Charley.

"Charley, I'm not sure who is heading this project up, but the owner of this property would like to meet him. After I told her what you wanted it for, she said she wanted to meet the man who was heading up the project and have him explain it to her. I have no explanation for this request, but that is one of the provisions of leasing or selling it to you."

David, would you and Nancy like to go with us to meet this lady?

We sure would, Professor.

Doc, you might just as well come along also because this was your idea.

I turned to the realtor and asked him if he could call on his mobile phone and ask the lady if she could see us this morning.

Mrs. Hattie McKinney

The realtor pulled the phone from his belt and dialed a number. He talked to the lady for just a couple of minutes. He turned and said, "She didn't expect to meet everyone, but since you are all here, she says to come on out to her house."

We got into our cars and followed the realtor out to an area just north of Camp Bowie Drive to an older part of Ft. Worth where there were some big beautiful homes. We pulled into the drive of one of these big, beautiful homes and stop. The realtor got out and rang the doorbell.

The door opened, and there stood a beautiful little old lady who must have been in her eighties if she was a day old. She was extremely well groomed, and every silver hair on her head was just perfect, as well as were her cosmetics. She couldn't have been more than five feet, two inches if that, and weighed maybe one hundred and five or ten pounds.

She looked at the crowd and with not so much as a hello said, "Since you're here, you might just as well come on in."

We followed the little lady, and the realtor closed the door after the last one had entered. We followed her into a very large study with a lot of beautiful leather chairs. She told us to have a seat.

Everyone took a chair and she then turned to the realtor and said, "Okay Buck, just which one of these guys is the one that is heading this thing up?"

"Well ma'am, Mr. Dixon or maybe I should say Professor Dixon and his wife are the ones who are financing the program. This young man known as Doc is the one who has had this dream ever since he got back from Vietnam. He was a medic in the army and he feels that this is something he just has to do."

"Okay, I can understand that but what has this Professor got to do with it? Where does he come in?"

"Well, ma'am, he was a street person for about ten years here in the Ft. Worth area, and he wants to do something for the street people and the town."

"What do you mean he was a street person, and now he wants to finance this thing? What did he do, win a million dollars?"

"Well, yes ma'am, he did do just that. He won a million dollars on the TV program "So You Want to Be a Millionaire."

Hattie looked at me and asked, "You say you won a million dollars on that TV show? I watch it all the time young man; when did you win the money?"

"Well, ma'am...by the way, I would feel much more comfortable calling you something besides ma'am. I could call you by your name if I knew it."

"Hell young man, that's no secret my name's Hattie McKinney. Now tell me just where you're gonna get the money to pull off such a thing as you're planning.

Well, Mrs. McKinney, I was on the street for ten years. The reasons I will tell you later when I get to know you better. I will just tell you that my folks started and own the Dixon Plastics Manufacturing Co. My father died and left the business to me, and now I am worth close to a billion dollars including the trust fund my father set up for me when I was born. Now I want to give something back to the people who were my family for the ten years that I lived in a bottle and on the street.

Now I'm sober, I am married again and I have a nice family of a wife, mother, son, and daughter. This young blonde lady is my wife Pam, the man on the right is Dr. David Davis of Tarrant County General Hospital, and next to him is his wife Nancy. They are all trying to help in this endeavor.

Who's that big guy over there?

That, Mrs. McKinney, is Charley Johnson, a policeman for the city of Ft. Worth.

Hell, she grinned "you didn't have to bring the cops along I was gonna sell if I liked you and what I've seen so far I like."

She turns to Pam and asks, "Honey, does this guy of yours do what he says he is gonna do or is it all talk?"

Pam looked her straight in the eye and tells her, "If Jim says he is going to do something, he always does it. He is ready to set up a million-dollar trust fund to take care of this program and if more is needed he will furnish that also. After all these people took care of him for ten years without knowing who he was and how much money he had and now he wants to take care of them."

She turned to me and said, "I like your wife's spunk.

"Now I have a question for you. Can you stay sober?"

"I sure can, ma'am."

"Hell, I wish you'd quit calling me ma'am it makes me feel old. I ain't but eighty-three, so don't go making me feel like an old lady.

Doc, you say this is your idea?

"Yes, Mrs. McKinney, it was my idea. I would like to be able to take care of them better than I have been in the past."

She looked him in the eye and said, "You mean to tell me you have been taking care of these people without any facilities?"

"Well, I did the best I could with the medicines I could scrounge."

"Well, son, you're not going to have to scrounge any more because I am donating that building to the program, and I am going to add another half million dollars to what Professor put up to start this thing. Now how does that set in your belly button? My old man died and left me with all this money and property, and I will never be able to spend or use it. I don't have any children, just some greedy ass-kissing nieces and nephews. I hate ass kissers, don't you?

Professor, I like this Doc's spunk. I like you and Pam for thinking of others.

"My old man found oil on some ranch land we owned out near Odessa, many years ago. The money he made on those oil and gas wells was invested in good things and, Professor, I've got damn near as much money as you have. You say you have a son and daughter? Are they spoiled? Do they get everything they want?"

No, ma'am, they sure don't. Johnny has started working his way up in the company by sweeping floors while he was attending college. My daughter works also. They both have their degrees and will help me and their grandmother in the business."

"Professor, you haven't said much about this lovely wife of yours. What does she do?"

"Well, Mrs. McKinney, she is just getting broken in. We have only been married about two weeks. She also agreed to marry me before she knew I had anything. She just thought I was an ex-drunk who used to be a college professor."

"Well, big boy, she must have seen something in you that I think I am beginning to see, and I just met you.

"Okay, you got your building; now what else can I do?

"Professor, why haven't you introduced me to that good-looking guy over there that hasn't said a word up till now."

"Well, Hattie, that's Bing. That's not his real name, but he sure sings like Old Bing Crosby. He used to be a vocalist and entertainer. I'm thinking about finding him a small nightclub to run and make a success out him again. Don't happen to know one for sale do you?"

"Professor, I don't know of one just off the top of my head, but I have a lot of friends, and I'll ask some of them. If he can sing as well as you say, he ain't gonna have any trouble. Being able to sing and being as good looking as he is, if he knows anything about business,

he'll make a success. Wish I was thirty-five years younger; I'd give him a real working over."

Bing blushed for the first time in a long time, and he bowed and graciously thanked Hattie for those kind words.

Hell, Professor, he has manners too, don't he?

Now what else can I do for you and Pam?

Well, ma'am, I'm not sure just now, but one thing I do want you to do is meet my mother and daughter. I am going to have them fly out this week, so they can meet you. You and my mother will get along famously. Mother started out as a waitress, and so did my wife."

"Hell, Professor, I started out behind a soda fountain in Midland. My husband was just the son of a farmer and rancher with a place between Midland and Odessa. He used to come into the drugstore and drink milkshakes till he would almost get sick before he finally asked me for a date. I was wondering what was taking so long cause I really took a shine to him right away, dirty hands and all.

"We got married when he was only twenty-one, and I was eighteen years old and had just graduated from high school. He worked hard and went to college and got a degree when times were awful hard. His father died and left him the farm. He took care of his mother till she died.

"Right after she died, a man came to the house one day and asked him if he would agree to let them drill a well on his property. There had been a couple of other wells hit in the area, so he said "Sure" why not? You can guess the rest of the story. They hit several oil wells and then a gas well that led into several more.

Before you knew what was happening, we had so many wells on the property, we had to move to town to get room to spit. We finally moved from Midland to Ft. Worth, and he started investing in things. He just kept making money till it killed him.

"He would worry about money. Hell, I never cared one iota about the money as long as we had each other.

"Professor, I can tell you son, he was one hell of a man.

I'm sure he was Hattie, do you mind if I call you Hattie, it seems to fit better.

Now, let's you and me and that little cutie wife of yours do some good with our money now before I die. What do you say?

"Buck, come over here," she told the realtor. "I want you to draw up a deed to that property and have it turned over to whatever the name of this corporation is."

"Mrs. McKinney, we don't have a name for this program yet, but I just thought of one. With yours and Doc's permission we will name the clinic the "Hattie McKinney People's Clinic." How does that sound Hattie? How does that sound to you Doc. Hattie I hope you won't mind us using your name."

"Hell, no, I won't mind; I think that's kind of nice, the Hattie McKinney People's Clinic."

"Hey, Doc, what do you say? I kind of figured they'd name it after you but not after me. I hope you don't mind me stealing some of your thunder."

"No ma'am, I sure don't mind. I get my kicks just watching people like you and Professor do all these good things, and then my being able to take care of my friends without them having to worry about the money."

Well, everyone, how about a drink to cement the deal?

Hattie, I quit drinking a while back, but for this occasion, I will have a drink with you and everyone here involved in it.

Hattie says Professor I have the solution. She brings out the booze and we all salute the new Hattie McKinney People's Clinic.

The realtor looked at Hattie alarmingly and said, "You're serious about this thing, aren't you?

"I sure as hell am, and if you're worried about your damn commission, forget about it. I'll pay your damn commission only I want to tell you that since you have acted the way you have, I can promise you this will be the last damn piece of property you will ever sell for me, you selfish bastard. It wouldn't hurt you to make a donation to a program like this. You might just sleep better at night knowing you have helped someone less fortunate than yourself.

"Now, get to hell out of here, and I'll send you your check. I hope you'll stuff it where the sun don't shine, now get out."

The realtor very sheepishly turned and left the house.

I looked at Hattie and told her she might have been a little rough on the guy.

She popped right back with, "That selfish bastard will get you your deed to the property, and I'll send him his commission check. Now let's have just one more sip of a toast before you leave."

I look at Pam, and she looks at me, and she said, "Well, what the heck; let's have just one more little one.

"Hattie, can I call you when Mother and Jennifer get here? I want them to meet you, and I want you to meet them. I really think you will like them."

"Professor, I will be hurt if you don't call me when they get here. Will your mother take a nip with me when she gets here?"

"Mother will be glad to have a nip with you. She'll be proud to have a couple of nips with you after she sees what you have done for her favorite son."

"Professor, you didn't tell me you had a brother."

"Hattie, I don't have a brother that's why I am my mother's favorite son."

"Oh hell Pam, get this guy out of here before I steal him away from you."

Pam and I both walk over and gave Hattie a big hug and tell her how much we appreciated her and what she had done and what a pleasure it is to meet a person like her. They are few and far between these days.

Doc walked over nervously, and he really didn't know whether to shake her hand or hug her. She took care of that. She said, "Doc get your butt over here and give me a big hug. You're gonna see a lot of me around that place before it's all done. I'm no kid, but there are a lot of things I can still do to help out around a place like that and I need something to do. I'm tired of just sitting here on my butt and not accomplishing anything. Maybe I can finally become useful if you'll let me."

"Don't worry Hattie, because we'll take advantage of your offer just as soon as we start the remodeling inside."

Doc gave her a great big hug and kissed her on the cheek then he turned and headed for the door.

David and Nancy both gave her a hug and told her how much they appreciated her.

Next came Charley. After he gave her a hug, she said, "Hell I've never been hugged by a policeman before. I always wondered what it would feel like. You know what? I kind of like it. How about you, Charley?"

Charley looks at her and told her that after hugging her, he just might go home and throw rocks at his wife. Everyone laughed. With that, we all left in a wonderful and jovial mood.

It was hard to believe what had happened within the last hour. As we started out the door, Hattie asked Bing if he was going to be around the clinic. He told her he'd be there until they found him a place and he could start fixing it up himself.

"Okay, pretty boy, just don't you forget about old Hattie."

We all said good-bye and headed for the cars.

I teased, "Bing, you better watch yourself. I think Hattie has a crush on you."

Bing just grinned and got into the car without saying a word. We were all still stunned at what that little lady had done for our program.

We arrived back at the Sanctuary before noon. Pam decided she should call her mother and see if she'needed to be picked up.

Her mother answered the phone and told Pam how much she had enjoyed sleeping in this morning. She said she had just been a little tired.

Mother, do you feel up to going shopping this afternoon?

Nora said, "Just wait, and we will all have dinner together.

They talked a while longer, and Pam hung up the phone.

Everyone had decided to have lunch at the Sanctuary today. Pam and Nancy decided to help serve. This pleased Annie because she felt she was really getting to know these ladies.

We had a nice lunch, and the girls helped clean up while we men did some planning.

Just as we were about to leave and go looking for a place for Bing, the phone rang. Lynn answered and turned to Bing. "Bing, it's a lady, and she wants to talk to you.

Bing had a real funny look on his face, but he answered the phone anyway. He seemed to be just listening for a while and then he said, "Yes, ma'am, I can do that, I think."

He turned to me and asked if I could take him back by Hattie's house.

Sure Bing, that that can be arranged. How soon do you want to go?

I guess right now. Let me ask her when she wants to see me. He returned to his conversation on the phone with Hattie. He tells her good-bye and says they will see her real soon.

I looked a little stunned, but I asked Bing just what was going on.

"Well, it seems that Hattie has called a few friends, and one of them has come up with a place that used to be a nightclub out on Camp Bowie which is supposed to be a pretty good area for a club. She wants us to go look at it and meet her friend there."

Pam looked at me, and we both looked at Bing, and asked, "What are we waiting for?"

David and Nancy said they had something else they needed to do, so they would talk to us later this evening.

We all headed in different directions. Pam, Bing, and I headed for Hattie's house. Upon arrival, we found her standing on the front porch with her purse in her hand ready to go. She came on out to the street where the car was instead of waiting for us to come up to the porch for her.

"Let's go and see what this guy has, and if it's as good as he told me it was. If it isn't, he's gonna regret it."

Bing and I both told her at the same time, "Please, don't make the man mad because if this one isn't right, he might find or know of another place."

She laughs and says, "Oh, hell, I ain't gonna hurt his feelings. He knows me, and I know him. We know how each other operate. I learned a lot from that old man of mine."

Pam asked Hattie, "Why do you always refer to your deceased husband as that old man?"

Well, Honey, she said, "that's the way most of his employees and friends used to refer to him. They loved him dearly, and that was their way of showing affection for him. I guess it just kind of rubbed off on me over the years."

"Pam Honey, I'll tell you this there never was a better man alive than that old man of mine. He always had his hand in his pocket to help anyone in need and a few who weren't really that much in need. You see Hon, I don't call him that as a put down, I call him that for just the opposite reason. He was a very dear person to me, that's why I never married again. No man could measure up to him.

"Now that that's settled, let's get out of here and over to the building and see if it's as nice as that old boy said it was."

We all load into the car, and away we go to see about the building that Hattie's friend had found for Bing.

Upon arrival at the given address, we see an elderly man waiting at the front of the building. He was right about one thing. This location should be great for a club such as the one that Bing had in mind.

The man was a real dapper looking older gentleman. When we started getting out of the car, he ran over to open the door for Hattie.

She turned to Pam and said, "I told you he was a real gentleman, didn't I? Not too bad looking either for an old man."

Hattie turns to the group and says, "I would like to introduce all of you to Wayne. His name is Wayne Gregory, and he knows just about every building in these parts of town.

"Wayne, I want you to meet Pam Dixon and her husband Jim or Professor is what most folks call him, whichever you choose to call him will be just fine. That good-looking dude over there is Bing. He's the one that wants to open a small club in this area. What do you think?"

"Well, this little club did real well until the owner came down with cancer, and he just let it run down till his family finally had to close it." "I have a key to the place, and the power has been turned on so you can see what it looks like inside."

We all anxiously entered the building with a lot of anticipation. We weren't disappointed. This place looked as though it had a lot of possibilities.

Bing turned to me and said, "I like what I see so far. Now let's look at the kitchen and the stage area and the electronics for the stage."

We went to the kitchen first and found that it was large for a building this size, with plenty of room for the cooks and kitchen help. We saw there were still three great refrigerators and two good-sized freezers. There was also a great "Kiddee" fire extinguisher system over the cooking and deep-fry areas, "Kiddee" is one of the top names in fire extinguishing systems and there are several heads hanging conveniently around the kitchen.

Meanwhile, Hattie and Pam were inspecting the bathrooms and the ladies' powder rooms. They all met behind the L-shaped bar. Next came the counting of the tables and chairs and their conditions. Some would need some work like refinishing and upholstering, but overall they were in good condition.

Bing said, "Professor it looks pretty darn good. It will take a lot of work, but I'm not afraid of hard work. I know some guys who will be more than glad to help me. We do need to check the parking lot and see just how much parking is available. That's real important, you know."

We walked out the back of the building, and there was a nice large parking lot that could accommodate about sixty cars. The surface was good except for a couple of cracks and a small pot hole in the pavement.

Wayne, who had come out behind us said, "That shouldn't be any problem I have a friend who can take care of that for practically nothing. He owes me a favor or two."

Wayne informs Bing, "Just seeing what you have accomplished in the last couple of months is an inspiration for a lot of people and I am one of them. If a man can do what you have done, then he can do just about anything he sets his mind to do."

Back inside, the girls have sat down at a table, and they invited us boys to sit down with them. When we were all seated, Hattie turned to Bing and asks, "Just what type of club do you have in mind?"

"Hattie, I hope you won't laugh when I tell you what I have in mind for the club. I want a swinging years club with our waitresses wearing poodle skirts and saddle shoes, with that beehive hairdo, and I want the waiters and the musicians to have on zoot suits with wide bright ties and those kind of flat hats with the broad brims that they wore back in the very early 40's.

"I also want to have a couple working who are good dancers. They can give lessons in jitterbugging and swing dancing to those young folks who want to learn to dance the swing and the New Yorker, which are types of jitterbugging.

"Maybe we can get a whole new thing started just by giving lessons early in the evening to those people who want to learn how to do the dance. I believe in it enough to want to give it a try. The parking lot attendants can wear saddle shoes and cords with light-colored letter jackets just like those worn back when they were all the rage."

Hattie tells Bing, "I think it's a real good idea."

Pam said, "I would really like to learn to jitterbug," and she turns to me and asks me if I knew how.

"Well, I used to do a little swing and jitterbugging when I was young. It was on the way out, but I did learn to dance it. I think that would be fun."

Wayne chimes in with, "Hell, I used to be real good back in my High School days. I have a daughter right here in town that loves to jitterbug. She and I still dance once in a while when we are out with a group just to show off. Hell, I'm not but seventy-five, and that's not too old to dance up a storm. Professor says that if Wayne Gregory can start back to Jitterbugging so can I.

"Bing, you open this place, and I can guarantee you that me and my daughter and her husband and a lot of our friends will be steady customers if your food is any good. What do you want to specialize in?" "Well, Wayne, I think that since we are in cattle country, we should serve good steaks along with a smattering of seafood. Of course, you always have to have a real good hamburger and a short selection of sandwiches and about three very good salads."

"Bing," Pam said, "if you need some help in setting up the kitchen help and the waiters and waitresses, I would be more than happy to help. After all, I have almost ten years' experience with one of the best steak houses in New York City."

"That's right, Bing," I agree." "Pam has a lot of experience in that type of work, and since she is offering, you should take her up on it."

Hattie says "I don't know how to do some of those things, but I can sure bring in the customers. If they don't come," she said, "I will call in their loans. Well, not really, but I will let them know they owe me a favor."

I look at Wayne and tell him, "If this is what Bing wants, you might as well contact the owner and see what his asking price for the property is."

Wayne looks at me and says, "Ask her yourself."

"Hattie, don't you remember anything? This is your property."

"What are you talking about, Wayne? I don't remember buying a nightclub." "You didn't. Your old man bought this little club way back when, and you have been collecting rent on it all of these years. Your business manager has been collecting and putting the money into the bank for many, many years. You wrote this property off thirty years ago."

Hattie walked over to Bing and reached up and put her arm around his neck and tells him "Bing it looks like you have a new partner.

"Bing, you just cut me in for five percent of the net income on this place, and I will give you a fifty-year lease on the property at a dollar a year. How does that sound to you?"

Bing looked at Pam, Wayne, and me and says, "Folks it looks like I have a new partner in the nightclub business. Hattie wanted to know, "Partner", just what are we going to name the club?"

Bing suggested that they name it the Swinging Years Club.

Hattie liked that name and agrees. "The Swinging Years Club it is."

I tell Pam, "We had better hurry to the airport to pick up my mother and daughter since they will be arriving by the time we get there."

Hattie says, "Go ahead and take off I will see that Bing gets back to the Sanctuary."

Charley Johnson speakes up and tells Hattie that if she had something else she needed to do, he would be glad to take Bing back to the Sanctuary.

Hattie just smiled and said, "Charley, why don't you just mind your own business. I don't get to go for a ride with a good-looking crooner very often, so buzz off."

We all started laughing, and we all headed for our cars.

Jim, Pam said while hurrying me, "have you forgotten that your mother and daughter are coming in this afternoon, and it's almost time for their plane to arrive?

I admit that I kept getting sidetracked. "Mother called me over the weekend to let me know that they didn't like being left behind so they decided they would both come to Ft. Worth and see just what I had been doing all those years. I said "Pam, you know how Mother is once she makes up her mind, and she has made up her mind to come to Texas, so let's go pick her up before I get sidetracked again."

We head for the airport and hope we will get there in time to greet Roxie and Jenny.

On the way to the airport we discuss the way things are coming along so well. We reached the airport with plenty of time to sit and talk for a minute before the plane came rolling in. We had been trying to decide just what to show my mother and when to show it to her.

Sure enough, up the ramp came Roxie and Jenny smiling from ear to ear when they sees us. We were real happy to see each other so soon again. Roxie was very happy about being able to come to Texas and see just where I had spent my time and where we were going and what we were doing now.

We got the luggage and head back to the hotel where I had made reservations for them. We arrive, check them in, and go to the rooms, which thank goodness, are on the same floor as Pam's and mine, as well as Johnny's.

Roxie asks about Johnny and what he is doing. She was surprised to find that Johnny and Cowboy were already out looking at property. Roxie says, "Jim, it looks like you don't let any grass grow under your feet."

Jennifer hangs onto Pam, and she wasn't about to let go of her for a long time. Every time they got through doing something, she went right back to holding onto Pam. It appeared that she was very serious about taking Pam as her mother, and she wasn't about to let her get away.

Roxie punched me on the side and motioned to Jenny and Pam. I just smiled and told my mother that I was happy that Jenny finally had someone to look up to.

We talked and talked and talked. Roxie and Jenny wanted to know what was happening and how things were rolling along.

Pam and I were busy telling them everything that had happened, especially about Hattie McKinney. Roxie was getting a big kick out of the story about Hattie and the clinic and the club. "I have heard about the eccentric Texans she says, and it looks like Hattie might just be the real thing. I'm anxious to meet her."

Just then, there is a knock on the door, and it is Johnny. He and Art had come home and they had dropped Cowboy off at the Sanctuary. Johnny came in and was surprised to find his grandmother and sister here in Texas. He had forgotten that I had talked to them and suggested that they both come to Ft. Worth and see what I was doing. I also wanted them to meet some of my friends and I, of course, wanted my friends to meet them. I was very proud of my mother and daughter.

We all relaxed for a while. Johnny told us what he and Art and Cowboy had seen today. They had looked at a place near Grandbury, which was nice. They then had gone by a place near Cleburne and a place near Waxahachie. All three of the places were nice and had plenty of room for what Cowboy wanted to do. They also had good barns, but two of them did not have a house on the acreage. This would mean that they would have to build a house to live in or put a mobil home on it.

"Tomorrow we want to go to the area near Red River. There is a nice area near Texoma Lake. And, we have a lead on a place near Sherman which has acreage, barns, and good fences, as well as a nice, small three bedroom, brick-veneer frame house with a nice yard. This place, we were told, is on a good blacktop county road that makes it very accessible even in bad weather. It is only about five miles out of the town of Sherman very near the Red River. We are going up to Sherman first thing tomorrow.

"Right now though, how about going to get something to eat?"

Art agrees with that idea. We all head for the dining room where everyone has a wonderful meal. Roxie heard something coming out of the mouth of Johnny that she never thought she would hear. He was suggesting that we all go to bed early so they could get an early start tomorrow in their search. He really seemed to be enjoying all of this.

"Johnny," Roxie said, "I think you look cute in your boots Levis and cowboy hat."

This was one of those times that Johnny actually blushed a little. His grandmother got a big kick out of that.

Roxie and Jenny spent the rest of the evening telling all the things that had happened since Pam, Johnny, and I had left to come to Texas. She told us how many wedding presents we had received since we had left. "Pam will enjoy unwrapping the presents," she predicted. Jenny offers help, "I will be more than glad to help."

I knew that was coming when you mentioned the unwrapping of gifts because I know my daughter. At Christmas she would always want to help everyone else unwrap their presents. She would tear hers open real fast when she was little, and then she would want to help everyone else open theirs, and I can see she hasn't changed.

"Johnny, I think you're right about hitting the sack early tonight because Pug and Angie will be coming in tomorrow, and we will need to pick them up."

"Hey everyone, I'm not a killjoy but Dad agrees with me."

We all adjourned to our rooms to get ready for a good night's sleep after a full day of activities.

As we were getting ready for bed, Pam asks me if I ever thought things would fall into place as they had. "I thought it would take two or three months to do what we have accomplished today."

"Pam, That Hattie is something else isn't she?"

Pam agrees and added, "It seems that she is really into helping on all of the projects you are wanting to do. What about all of those people she knows who will be able to help out on some of the projects? I think she is going to be a great asset to your plans."

With that we say goodnight and turn the lights off.

The next day it was breakfast as usual, then we all headed our separate directions.

Johnny, Art, and Cowboy headed for Sherman to see what they could find out about the lead they had received yesterday about the place near Red River.

Pam and Nora, along with Roxie and Jenny, were going to call Nancy and see if she would like to spend the day with them just running around and maybe doing some shopping. They thought that Roxie, Jenny, and Nora should get a good view of what the Ft. Worth and Dallas area had to offer.

I head for the Sanctuary where I was to meet with Charley Johnson and Lynn. Later I would meet with the attorney Dr. Davis had told us about. We needed to start getting the paperwork put together on the nightclub property and the storefront clinic.

Attorney Bill Bartlett

I reached the Sanctuary just as Dr. Davis and another man were parking. I got out of the car and walked over to greet them.

"Jim, I want you to meet my friend William Bartlett or Bill for short to his friends. I think Bill is one of the best attorneys in the area of Corporate work. Bill is known by all the City Council, and he may just be a great asset when we start filing for permits and licenses."

Bill seemed like an amiable sort of guy who carried himself as if he knew what he was doing. He had a certain air of confidence along with a soft but very authoritative voice about him that made you believe in what he was saying.

"Jim, Bill is very excited about the work he has been asked to do for the corporations. He figures he can be of some help in ways other than just drawing up the paperwork for the projects."

Bill seemed to fit right into our whole group as though he had known us always. It was a real stroke of luck that Dr. Davis knew a man like this.

We all had a seat and David introduced Bill to the rest of the team. I started by telling Bill about each project and how we want it handled.

First, there is the storefront clinic. The nightclub papers as well as the clinic papers need to be drawn up with Hattie McKinney.

David and I spoke at the same time. David I say, you go ahead and tell Bill what we have in mind. He told Bill we believed he was going to like Hattie. Just then the door opened, and in came Charley Johnson.

David introduced Charley to Bill. "Bill, Charley is one guy who may be of help to you when you get ready to apply for the needed permits and licenses."

Annie came in and asked if anyone would care for a cup of coffee. As usual everyone wanted coffee. She brought the cups and the fixings to the table along with spoons for those who wanted cream and sugar or artificial sweetener. I got the coffeepot and filled the cups for the other people.

Once I had my coffee just the way I wanted it, I again addressed Bill. "Bill, we're going to need someone to draw up the papers on the ranch for Cowboy when the boys find it. It looks like they're closing in on a place up near Red River just a short distance from Sherman. They are looking for a place with enough acreage to raise rodeo stock, and they need the barns and feed storage. The barns will be used, of course, for the mares when they are ready to foal. We are hoping it will have at least a small house that is livable for Cowboy.

"One other thing, Bill, is that we are trying to find the daughter of a lady that was with us through the years. When we find her daughter, there may be some papers needed at that time. One other thing is that we are going to put her in the restaurant business over in Louisiana if that is what she chooses after she finds her daughter. The exact town will be dependent on where we find her daughter and what they decide on. We will try to set her up in a town close to where her daughter has been raised.

"The last three things I want you to do are to set up a trust fund for the Sanctuary here. I think we will start with five hundred thousand. The next thing is a donation to the policeman's retirement and widow's fund. We will start with a donation of five hundred thousand there. The last thing we need to do is find out what it will cost to buy and totally outfit a most modern ambulance available for the hospital. After that you can set up a trust fund to pay for the services to help take care of those homeless who are brought into the hospital.

"Oh, yes! I almost forgot one very important thing. Charley, I want to find a large warehouse-type building that can be heated and air-conditioned. I want a place for the street people to come in during the summer and stay cool while playing dominos or pool. We also want plenty of chairs and tables and at least four or five big-screen televisions. I want everyone to be able to watch television if they want to. I want them welcome in the winter when it gets cold outside.

"Bill, can you set up about seven hundred fifty thousand to keep a place like this running after we find it and outfit it. I want Coke and candy machines, and I want them to sell at no profit. Charge just what we pay for the things we put in them. We will work the other stuff out later.

"Charley, do you think you can get some help to run a place like this from the police auxiliary women?"

"Jim," Charley said, "I am sure they will be happy to help run a place like that."

Bill was just sitting back all this time taking notes on everything that I was saying. He finally spoke after I was finished. "Jim, I think I can take care of all of those things without too much trouble. David told me that you had a lot of money, and it's a darn good thing you do the way you are spreading it around. I must tell you that I do admire you, and I do see where you are coming from since you spent ten years with these people. David didn't tell you, but I have been intending to retire for a couple of years now, and this will give me a chance to do that."

"What do you mean retire? I have just given you enough work to handle most law offices at least six months."

"Well, Jim, what I mean is that I can just do this work for you and your corporation without any interruptions from anyone else. This means I can devote full time to this project if you will forgive me for calling it that. I really have no intention of charging you for this work. I just want to be useful in my old age. I feel that everyone should do something for their fellow man before they die, and this just may be my last chance."

"Hell, Bill, you don't look much older than me or maybe David or Charley."

"Well, Jim, that just goes to show you what good, clean living will do for you. I am a good, wholesome seventy-four years old."

Charley was sitting there with his mouth wide open.

"Close your mouth, Charley you're liable to catch some flies."

"Well hell David, Bill doesn't look as old as I do, and I am only fifty-four. I'll be ready for retirement from the police department next year."

"Charley, my good buddy, you've got a job with me the day you retire if you want it. I'll put you to work with one of the companies as long as you want to work. You can work here in the Metroplex area, or you can bring your family and come to Chicago or New York or Norfolk, maybe even the California plant, but you have a good paying job as long as you want to work."

Charley couldn't believe what he had just heard. "Do you really mean that, Jim?"

"Sure do, Charley, and don't you ever forget it. Now let's get down to business."

I got on the phone and called Hattie McKinney to see if she could come over or if she wanted Bill, David, Doc, and Bing to come over to her house.

"Jim, if it isn't too much trouble, I would like for you to come over to my house. I think we will have a little more peace and quiet here rather than having all of the people coming and going that they will have at the Sanctuary."

We all head for the door and pile into David's car and head over to see Hattie.

Lynn, would you like to ride to the airport and pick up Pug and Angie.

Thanks, but no thanks, because I have to do some shopping and pick up some things for the lunch crowd. I'll see you when you folks get back.

As I walked toward the door, Annie came over and hugged my neck and told me how proud they were of me for doing these things for the people who had been my friends for the past ten years.

I blushed all the way down to my shoe tops, and then I turned to Lynn and told him to come and get this woman of his before I get any more embarrassed. With that I headed out of the door and to the car.

I arrived at the airport with plenty of time to spare.

Robert Hitch, a Man of His Word

I stopped to have a cup of coffee, and while I was sipping on the coffee, I remembered Robert Hitch, the young newspaper reporter I had promised to do an interview with when I got back. I took my phone off my belt and called information for the number of the Ft. Worth newspaper. I called the number and asked to speak to Robert Hitch.

Whoever answered the phone turned and hollered real loud at Robert. He finally answered the phone. "This is Bob, what can I do for you?"

"Well, Bob, this is Jim Dixon."

"Do you mean Professor, is this really Professor?"

"It sure is Bob, and I owe you an apology for not calling you just as soon as I got back to town, but I wanted to get everything started before I called you. This way you will have a better story to write."

"Professor, does this mean you are ready ,to be interviewed?"

"It sure does. How about this afternoon at the Bible Sanctuary down on Seventh Street? Do you know where it is?" I asked.

"Lord, yes, Professor, I know it real well. What time do you want to meet?"

"How about 2:30 to 3:00 p.m., if that's all right with you."

"All right, it sure is all right with me. I'll be there with bells on, Professor. I'll see you there he said, and he hung up."

The announcement was just coming over the loudspeaker that the plane with Pug and Angie on it was coming to the gate. I walked down to meet and greet them. After a short while, the passengers start coming up the ramp and heading for the baggage room.

All of a sudden I saw Pug, and here he came dragging Angie by one hand while she waved with the other. I met them at the door of the ramp. Both of them gave me a big hug. It seemed as though we hadn't seen each other in years.

I stepped back and looked at them. "I can't see anything different except that you look like an old married couple now."

Angie thought that was a compliment.

We head for the baggage room to get their baggage. While we are waiting, I tell them about the things that have happened since we arrived back in Ft. Worth. I also told them that Roxie and Jenny were here as well as Art and Nora. "This just makes our family complete now that you guys are here." I kind of grinned as I told them that I had really missed them and that I was sure glad to see them here.

We finally located their baggage and we headed for the car. We arrived at the hotel just before noon and by the time Pug and Angie got checked in and put their luggage in their room, it was time to eat.

We headed for the lunchroom, and I told Angie that she should have been here this morning so she could have gone shopping and looking around with the girls. I was sure we would all be doing a lot of shopping and looking for the next couple of weeks.

After lunch we had just started to the Sanctuary, when Angie asked, "Jim, will you take me by the buildings where you and Pug were when the tornado hit?"

I was more than glad to take her by the barbershop where Cowboy had almost lost his life, but had been pulled out by some of the guys who had been at the barbershop before the tornado hit. Pug even showed her the barber chair that had saved Cowboy's life. It was sitting on the vacant lot behind what used to be the barbershop.

Next, I took her by the large thirty-four-story office building and showed her how I had been curled up on the steps that leads into the doorway of the building when the storm had hit.

"The building still has most of the windows boarded up. I understand that someone has bought it and is going to try to restore it. That will sure be a job, but I guess that it could be done if a person had enough money."

We drove on and headed for the Bible Sanctuary. "Angie, these are the most wonderful people you will ever meet. These people took all of us in and took care of us while we were getting over the tornado and off the bottle. Believe it or not, everyone of the gang is still off the bottle, and it looks like they are going to be able to stay off the bottle."

Just as I said this, we turned the corner at the Sanctuary, and I drive up to the front door.

We all get out of the caar and head for the front door, it opens and there are Annie and Lynn. Annie sticks her hand out to shake hands with Angie, but Angie reaches over and pulls her forward and gives her a great big hug. She did the same thing to Lynn, and then she tells them that that was just a little bit of her appreciation for what they had done for Pug when he had really needed the help. I believed they were both in total shock from the straight forward thanks from this little old girl from Nebraska.

"You will never know how much it means to me that you were so good to my husband in a time of his life that he needed it most. They just don't make people like you guys very often who really care for their fellow man the way you do. I will never forget you, and if I can ever be of help in any way, just ask me."

Annie looks at me and winks as she asked, "Do you really mean that?"

"I sure do," replied Angie.

"Well, Honey, I was just getting ready to clean up the tables and kitchen after our lunch time meal. How about a little help?"

"You got it," Angie winked at me and then asks where the aprons are. They walked back to the kitchen just talking like a couple of kids.

Lynn looked at Pug and said, "It sure looks like you got yourself one fine woman there."

Pug agrees and tells Lynn, "She is beginning to make a real man out of me." Can you believe that when we went fishing with my dad and brother, she caught the biggest fish? She is willing to try anything, and on top of that she is a darn good cook."

"Mighty good looking also," said Lynn.

Pug heartily agreed.

Pug, Lynn, and I went into Lynn's office to discuss the events that had happened since Pam and I had been back in town. I told Pug about Bill and how he was going to do every bit of the legal work free.

"It seems that everywhere I have turned for help it has been there and much more than I had ever imagined. Just wait till you meet Hattie McKinney, Pug she is a real fine lady. Just a little rough on the edges, but what a wonderful person with a heart of gold. You'll love her just the way everyone else does.

"Pug, do you need anything?"

Pug knew what I meant and told me him that he was in good condition, but that if he came up short, he would let me know.

I told him not to forget to turn in his expense account.

Pug just smiled and said, "Okay."

We must have talked for over an hour before the girls came back from the kitchen just a chatting away as if they had known each other all of their lives. They told us men that they had the kitchen all taken care of and all of the dining room tables ready for the dinner crowd. Angie seemed real excited with all that was going on.

We heard the front door open and turned to see Bob Hitch, the reporter, coming in. Bob came in and shook hands with Pug and me. I introduced him to the rest of the people.

Bob wanted to know if I was ready to give him the full story on everything that had happened since he had been hurt during the tornado and the trip to the television show as well as my meeting a beautiful lady and marrying her. He also wanted to know about Pug and Angie since they also fit into this very nice story.

We talked about the tornado and my hospital stay and the calls to the show and then the trip. I told him all about the way the show had been conducted and how I had met Pam and how she had introduced Angie to Pug. We told the entire story to Bob, and the more we talked, the more he wanted to know.

Then we came to what was happening in Ft. Worth and the area. We talked about the clinic, the nightclub, the ranch, the Sanctuary, the building for the street people to spend time in during the summer heat and the winter cold weather, as well as the hospital and the policeman's fund.

Bob wanted to know about all of it. I told him that I would rather not have all of that in the newspapers.

That was the point at which Bob explained his idea to me. "If you will let me put the whole story in the paper, there might be other people who would like to help in various ways. Some may just want to help at the clinic or at the Sanctuary. Some may want to work at the warehouse where all of the TV's and pool tables and domino tables will be. You never know what can happen from a story like this in the paper. We will run it on the front page in the Sunday edition."

I looked at him in total disbelief and asked, Are you sure you want to run it on the front page of the paper?

"Sure do," Bob tells me. "This is a very special human interest story. With your permission I would like to have pictures of you and your family and Pug and his wife Angie and maybe the doctor and the lawyer, as well as the policeman. That Mrs. McKinney sounds like she might just be a story all by herself. We need pictures of Doc, Bing, Cowboy, and Mabel as well as everyone else. Who knows, maybe someone will know Mabel's daughter and call Mabel and help your private eye in finding her. We will play up the part about the Bible Sanctuary with pictures of the place and all the good they do for the homeless and needy in our society. How about it? Will you let me do this little bit to help?"

I looked at him with a sly grin and said, "Well, okay."

"Professor, you know it's doing me a great big favor, and it might help a lot of other people also. Let me give it a try. It might even get more donations to the hospital and policemen's funds."

"Oh, all right," I tell him, if you really think it will help. If that's the way you want it and if you really think it will do some good, you might just as well go ahead, but remember Bob, if you are selling me a bill of goods, you know it will come back to bite you in the butt, don't you?"

"Jim, I am very aware of what would happen if I was not above board and honest with this, but I assure you I am doing what I think is best for everyone. I admit that I am doing what is best for me too, but I am trying to help you guys also."

"Well, okay," I responded, "I promised you I would give you the story, and a promise is a promise, and I don't break a promise."

The next week was spent arranging appointments and taking pictures. Bob was very good about bringing everything to me for my approval before he tagged it for the story release. Not only did I read it, but I also had the person who was featured in the story read it and discuss it with David, Bill Bartlett, and me. The reason for Bill Bartlett's being involved was that he could be sure it was legally acceptable for release, and that it did not open any doors for a lawsuit.

Bartlett seemed to think of everything concerning the corporation and the program for each person and his or her future plans. As everyone watched and listened to him, we knew why he was such a successful attorney-at-law. What was even nicer now was to think that he was working with us and for us pro bono. (For those who don't speak Latin, this I am told means "Free Gratis, No Charge.") This just showed us what a wonderful person this Bill Bartlett guy was. Not many men would do this for someone they had never met before. It seemed that Pam and I had met a lot of people with big hearts since I had started this program.

As I previously stated, Bob Hitch had been spending all of his time with this story. He had even brought the Chief Editor and the Publisher out to meet these unusual people. It turned out that the Editor and Publisher were totally in favor of the story and was behind Bob one hundred percent.

It seemed that some of the people at City Hall had heard of the program and they have contacted me to offer their support any way they could. They had even offered to expedite the permits and licenses needed for the clinic, the nightclub, and to do whatever they could to be of service.

During the week Hattie McKinney had been working on transferring the properties for the clinic and the nightclub. She had even elicited the help of some of her friends to help in any way they could. Some had even offered money to pay for the machines and instruments and basic medicines necessary for the clinic.

We already had an X-ray machine on order that should be here in about two weeks. The examining room equipment had already been bought and paid for. The holdup now was on the interior renovation work being done. Believe it or not there had already been street people stopping by and asking when it would be ready to receive patients.

Doc was really surprised and happy about the way people had received it. Dr. Davis was there almost every day to check with Doc. He had also brought the names of several nurses who were willing to work on their days off in the clinic. The health department had come by several times to help us make sure that what we were doing was within their guidelines. They were assisting every way possible to make sure Doc was abiding by the rules and laws regarding medical clinics. Doc had never believed there were this many wonderful, caring people in this world.

In the meantime the hospital had ordered the fanciest and most completely outfitted ambulance in the whole state of Texas. This was what I had told them to do, and Doc was overseeing it and approving everything.

This is going to take some time for the manufacturer to put this ambulance together. When they are finally able to deliver it, it will be the state of the art in ambulances, I told everyone.

Bill Bartlett had already drawn up the papers for my donation to the Police Retirement and Widows Pension Fund. That would be finalized within the next two weeks.

The nightclub was being remodeled, and new kitchen equipment that was needed had been ordered and would be delivered on the day the remodeling was done. This meant we would have the kitchen ready within the month.

Bing had already put a band together. He had found a bunch of older musicians who played in one of the local Shrine bands. They were absolutely crazy about the chance of playing in a swing band again. Most all of them had played with big bands in their younger years. They could build the most beautiful word pictures of the days when they had played with the large swing bands. Some of them had played with people like Harry James, Tommy or Jimmy Dorsey, Stan Kenton and his jazz band,

and one had even played with Glenn Miller before he had joined the armed forces and become a soldier.

These men could and would have a ball doing arrangements that they had played back in the late 1930's and early-to-middle 1940's. They even had men standing in the wing just waiting for someone to ask them to sub. If someone got sick or couldn't make it for some reason there was always someone waiting to sit in. The nice part of this was that there were a lot of younger musicians in the Shrine who had been playing with these older guys for several years, and they knew all of the music and arrangements that the older men knew. This way if they lost some of the older men, there would always be younger musicians to fill in. They had about three times as many musicians as they needed. They had even talked about taking turns playing, so they could all have the fun of being part of a big band again. Most of them didn't care about getting paid, they just wanted to play with the group.

Since they were all good friends, and most were members of the local Shrine, they felt as though they were all brothers in the Shrine and in the world of music.

Bing felt this had taken care of his band problems, especially since there were several of them who would make vocal arrangements so Bing could sing. All of these fine musicians were very anxious for the day to come when they could walk out onto the bandstand and start to swing again and watch some of the old timers do a little jitterbugging and hope that maybe some of the young people would want to learn how to jitterbug and swing dance also. This in itself gave Bob a whole story just about the musicians and the club.

A Ranch for Cowboy

Some of us had gotten together to talk over some business, and we had started with a discussion of Cowboy's ranch.

"Cowboy, Art, and Johnny have finally found a place that looks to be what they have been looking for. The place is a hundred and twenty acres just north and west of Sherman. It is very near to the Red River and Lake Texoma. This place has a nice barn for the mares when they foal, and it is nicely fenced in. The place also has a nice large corral for use with the bucking stock when checking them out to see if they buck hard enough to qualify them as good rodeo stock," I said.

I added, "There is also a nice frame-brick veneer house in very good condition. The house is just the right size for Cowboy to have as his home.

"One of the men in Sherman told him about Don Gay who used to own the Mesquite Rodeo, and he also raised rodeo stock. They said he might be able to contact Don or his father, Neal, and see if they can tell him where he can get some rodeo breeding stock. They seem to know almost everyone in the rodeo industry, and they should know where he can contact rodeo stock-breeders. They all seem to have breeding stock available to sell to someone who wants to start raising bucking stock. It appears that they are going to get Bill Bartlett to draw up the papers of sale this coming week.

Cowboy and the owner have agreed upon a price, so now it is just a matter of closing the sale since I have given my consent to buy. I have told them that the price is fine with me.

The next thing is to find Mabel's daughter. Jimmy Green told me the other day that he already has a couple of leads, which he and one of his men are following up on. They say it looks promising. We all hope they are able to find something before too long."

I turn to the rest of the people at the table and tell them, "Charley Johnson called and said that he just ran into an old friend he has known for about thirty years or more. It seems that he has just left a job as a chef at Brennan's Restaurant in New Orleans and is wanting to find a place for himself in the Dallas-Ft. Worth area. He said when he told him about the new place that Bing is going to open he wants to talk to Bing about a job as a chef for him.

Charley said that he can vouch for this guy's being a master chef. If he wasn't, he would not have been able to work for Brennan's since they are one of the finest restaurants in the country. If Bing can see him, Charley will be glad to arrange a meeting between the two of them.

"Things are coming along real fine over at the storefront clinic. They have it almost finished as far as the partitions and the rooms. They have a lot of it already painted, and the girls have been helping Doc pick out furniture for the waiting room and curtains for the windows and pictures for the walls and carpeting. They have been having a ball helping him get everything fixed up to start receiving patients.

"There are three other doctors besides Dr. Davis who have offered to help him so he will be legal in everything he does. He already has a long list of nurses who want to help out on their days off. It is absolutely amazing at the way people want to help when they see something like this that is going to be of help to people.

"There are tables and chairs for the examining rooms in boxes in a couple of the rooms. There's no doubt that this will be a great place for the homeless and street people to come when they have medical needs."

Charley said, I have found the perfect warehouse for the place to get the people off the streets in the summer and winter. After the owner found out what it was for, he said he will give us a long-term lease on it for a dollar a year if we will agree in writing to take care of any maintenance on the building, and if we will also carry an insurance policy covering the value of the building. It seems that he has quite a bit of property in Fort Worth, and he had written this property off tax wise several years ago. He feels it would be safer with someone in it than it is just standing idle. I assured him that we could work that out. Is that all right with you, Professor?

"Yes, that's just fine," I said.

I called Doc, David, Charley, Cowboy, and Mabel together to see if they could meet with me tomorrow at the Sanctuary. I still had to call Bill Bartlett, Hattie McKinney, and Jimmy Green to see if they could make it. I also called Pam to see if she, Jenny, Roxie, Nora, and Nancy could make the meeting.

I had Pug call and see just when we could rent a meeting room downstairs at the hotel that would hold all of us.

While Pug was calling the hotel, I called the Sanctuary to see if Lynn could meet with us at the hotel. I had told everyone that either Pug or I would get back to them with the time of the meeting. We would try to make it at a time that would be satisfactory to everyone and fit into their schedules.

When I got off the phone, Pug turned to me and asked, "Is 2:00 p.m. tomorrow agreeable?"

"Pug, that is fine with me. Would you mind calling all of the other people back and determining if it will be all right with them. If it is, then would you please call the hotel back to confirm the time?"

Pug was finally beginning to understand what my executive assistant really did. He made sure that all of the details were worked out so there were no foul ups.

Pug was really getting the hang of it. If you listened to him talking on the telephone, you would think he had been doing this all of his life. He was a great diplomat at getting things done. He seemed to have a real knack for handling people. I think that he even surprises himself.

After about an hour Pug told me that everything had been arranged for tomorrow afternoon at 2:00 p.m. at the hotel in the Lariat Room on the second floor. He also reminded me that tonight was the night that I had promised to take Pam, my mother, daughter, mother-in-law, father-in-law, and my son out to dinner.

I reminded him that he and Angie were coming along also, and that Dr. Davis and his wife were coming along.

That's just fine, "I arranged a private room for us over at the Texas Cattleman's Restaurant tonight at 7:30 p.m. where they serve some of the best steaks in this whole cotton picking area. Remember Jim, that you have all of your family here, and you sure don't want to forget anyone."

I look at Pug, laugh, and tell him that he is really catching on.

"Jim, don't you think that it would be nice to have Doc, Cowboy, Bing, and Mabel there also so they could all have a chance to talk about all the great things that are happening to them."

I thought that would be a great idea. Pug, that sounds "Pug, why don't you call Hattie and see if we can send a car for her. I think she should be there also. What do you think?"

"I think that's great, boss."

"Pug, do you know that's the first time you have ever called me boss?"

"I never thought about it, Professor."

"Well, Pug, do me a favor and don't ever call me boss again. We work together. Okay?"

"Okay, Boss."

I absolutely fell out with laughter on hearing that.

"Sorry, Professor."

After that was all taken care of, we looked at each other as if to ask what we had forgotten. Pug said, "Well, Jim, we have forgotten about a menu, but I think it would be better if we were all allowed to order our own meals tonight." He smiles and says, "Some people may be getting tired of steak and potatoes.

"Boss," he says – "Oh, hell, I'm sorry; it won't happen again, I promise. I know that's what you will want, but some of us might like some shrimp of something else. What do you think?"

"I think that that you are really beginning to be quite a diplomat."

With this we were interrupted by Bill Bartlett who knocked on the door. Pug let him in. He had a briefcase with him and a smile on his face.

"Jim, I have some great news for you. I have finally finished the papers on the nightclub and they just need Bing's signature. I also have the papers drawn up on the ranch, and they have been signed by the seller, and now all the papers need are Cowboy's and your signatures and for you to give me a check made out to the seller."

Things were really coming together faster than we had ever imagined they would. Bill asks if I have heard anything from Jimmy Green or his men concerning Mabel.

"It seems that everyone here has really taken a liking to Mabel. She may be rough around the edges, but since she has remained sober, she has become a favorite of everyone. For one thing they feel sorry for her and her trying to find her daughter. Another thing that has endeared her to them is her outlook on life at this time. She always seems to be so up and very positive that Jimmy Green and his men will find her daughter. Everyone keeps patting her on the back and telling her that they will find that little girl one day real soon."

I ask Bill if he and his wife would like to join us tonight for dinner down at the Texas Cattleman's Restaurant about 7:30 p.m.

Bill thought for a minute, and then he said, "Well, if we won't be intruding, I think that will be a great idea. I would like for you to meet my wife since she has heard so much about all of you folks."

Bill, before you go, let me give you a check for the ranch so you can finalize the deal tomorrow morning.

Fine thing, Jim. That way we can get this one over and done with, and then Cowboy can start deciding what he wants to do to his house. You know what I mean, furniture and curtains and kitchen things. Hell, Jim, you know what I mean.

I turn to Pug, "Pug, call them and tell them to set two more plates on the table for tonight. Before you do that, why don't you call Charley Johnson and see if he and his wife can join us. If they can, you can add another two plates to the table for them also."

Johnny and Art came walking in with Cowboy just as Bill was about to leave. Bill stopped Cowboy and told him that he needed his signature on the papers for the ranch because he had the check for the ranch in his hands and "As of tomorrow morning, the ranch will be yours."

You could have heard Cowboy and Johnny all over the whole hotel. Art grabbed Cowboy around the neck and gave him a great big hug and tells him how happy he is that he had his ranch.

"Cowboy, maybe now we can get to work on the barn and fences that need fixing and maybe put a little paint on the house if you think it needs it. I know you want the barn and sheds fixed first, but remember that you have to have a place to stay while we are doing this work. I haven't been this excited about anything since I was a young man and left the farm. I'm really looking forward to getting my hands dirty and working up a sweat."

He turns to Johnny and lets him know that he is going to be working up a sweat also. Johnny just laughes and lets him know that it wouldn't be the first time he had worked up a sweat.

Everyone was almost giddy by now.

Pug called Bing and told him that Bill had the papers for him to sign, and that he was coming by the club in about an hour or less to have him sign the final papers on the place. He also told him about Charley Johnson and his friend who was a chef.

This was great news for Bing because the man he hired the other day, came in drunk and Bing had fired him before they got started. He told Pug that he hoped that Charley's friend wasn't a drinker.

There was dead silence on Bing's end of the phone for a minute. You heard what I said, that sounds funny as hell coming out of me, don't it? Well, I mean it, I won't have any drunks working for me because I know from experience what that can do to a person, and I won't have any of that around my club."

Pug laughed and tells him about tonight and that he might want him to pick Hattie up.

You see, by now each of the guys had a car. They got to pick it out. I don't mean a Cadillac or Lincoln. Bing and Doc each took a new Ford Sedan, and Mabel took a small Pontiac, while Cowboy took a Chevy Suburban. This way they weren't dependent on taxis or public transportation.

Pug said, "I will talk to Hattie, and if she can make it tonight, I will call you back, and if you don't mind, I would like for you to pick her up."

Within the next hour Pug had everything lined up for the dinner tonight and for the meeting tomorrow. Pug was really getting proficient.

Just as Bill was leaving, in came the girls from a shopping spree. Pam, Roxie, Jenny, Nora, and Nancy had been out all morning, they had had lunch, and then they had done a little more shopping and home they had come. Just as soon as Nancy heard about tonight she told everyone she had to run so she could get ready for tonight because David would be home before too long, and they would talk, and then if she wasn't ready, they just might be late, and she didn't like being late for anything.

When Pam was told about the ranch deal now being finalized tomorrow morning, she asked Cowboy if he would like some help furnishing the house. Cowboy admitted that he knew very little about furnishing a house and he would sure welcome the help.

"Mother," Jenny asked, "why don't we help him out and see if we can at least outfit the kitchen and living room. You know, cooking utensils, flatware, and that type of thing."

Cowboy looked at them and in complete astonishment asks, "What are you talking about? Jenny, I would like a leather couch and chair for the living room. How about a TV of some kind, and maybe a whatcha ma callit, you know that thing that plays tapes and those new things called CDs or something. I like music to sit and listen to when I am tired. I always have. Well, don't look so surprised a cowboy can like music just the same as anyone else."

"Okay," Jenny said, "now how about your bedroom? What do you want in it?"

Hell, I don't know I guess I just want a bed and a closet to put my clothes on a hanger and hang 'em in it. Is that what you mean?

"Well, not exactly, Cowboy. You will need a dresser and a couple of chest of drawers and maybe a nightstand on each side of your bed and a TV for the top of one of the chests in case you want to watch TV after you go to bed."

Jenny, you know what I need better than I do. You mean after a hard day's work, you come home, have some supper, and then go lay down and watch TV? Jenny, you sure do make this sound great. I just hope I don't get lazy.

I assured him that he wouldn't get lazy because he would be too busy with the cattle to get lazy. Tired, maybe once in a while, but never lazy. Cowboy, you will be having so much fun with the new stock and taking care of them that you won't spend very much time inside the house.

Cowboy agreed, Professor is right. I would sure appreciate it if you ladies could help me out. I sure would like to keep it simple because I will be doing the cooking and the cleaning and the taking care of the housè as well as taking care of the cattle and keeping the place up.

Nora assured him that they would keep it simple. We will just get you a washer and dryer and show you how to use them. We will get you a dishwasher if they don't have one there already and that will help with the kitchen cleanup. We'll see if we can find you a nice small microwave oven to heat some of your meals. That will help a little with your cooking problems. They have some real good frozen meals now if you don't want to cook. This way you can fix a real good meal in just a few minutes. We can get you an automatic coffeepot that has a timer. It will turn itself on in the morning, and all you have to do is prepare it the night before. That way when you get up, you will have the coffee there waiting for you when you get out of bed."

Hell, what will I have to do if I have all of those gadgets. Just get me a can opener, a frying pan and a refrigerator, and I will be in hog's heaven."

Pam told him that they wouldn't go that sparingly, but they would try not to overdo it.

Well, if you ladies don't mind doing that for me, I sure will appreciate it.

Cowboy, we will go up to the ranch day after tomorrow and look it over. By that time, the title and everything will be taken care of, and we can get started on the inside while you, Johnny and Art get started on the outside. Remember that we can't do it tomorrow because I understand we have a meeting tomorrow afternoon at 2:00 p.m. is that right?

"That's right, Hon," I tell her. "I want to bring everyone up-to-date on what we have accomplished up to now. It seems that things are really coming together. I haven't seen you to tell you about Charley Johnson's friend who is a chef and who's looking for a job. He used to be a chef at Brennan's Restaurant in New Orleans, and he quit because he wanted to come back to Texas. It looks like he might be just the right man for the job with Bing in his club. Keep your fingers crossed. Charley will tell us more about him tonight."

"Jim, just how many are going to be there for our little dinner tonight?"

Well, Honey, I'm not sure, but the last time Pug counted, I think there were something like twenty people or so going to be there. Don't worry though I didn't order for everyone like I did the last time. I decided that it would be good if everyone ordered their own dinner tonight, didn't we Pug?

Pug just grinned and agreed.

Well," Pam said, if that's all you have invited, I guess it will be all right. Did you invite Hattie McKinney?"

"Yes, dear, I invited Hattie, and Bing's going to pick her up."

We all relaxed for a while and then began getting showered and dressed to go over to the restaurant. Those of us who lived at the hotel were all ready to go about 7:15, which should give us plenty of time to get over to the restaurant.

We arrived at the restaurant and found that Cowboy, Doc, and Mabel were already there. They were sitting in the room having a glass of tea while they wait for the rest of the party to arrive. It wasn't long before Dr. Davis and Nancy came in, and right behind them came Bing and Hattie McKinney.

When Hattie saw everyone, she very loudly said, "You know what, Honey, I haven't seen this many people in one place since my old man's funeral. Hell, I don't mean anything by that Hon, you know I loved that old man like no woman ever loved a man before. He just keeps jumping back into my head and my conversation.

Hell Pam, do you see who's escorting me tonight? Ain't he pretty? If I was just about thirty years younger, I would give him fits. Well, I at least have a lot of memories.

Don't worry, Bing, I ain't gonna bother you tonight, at least not till after we leave here.

By now Bing was red as a beet and blushing all over himself. Also by now everyone was laughing up a storm.

Charley Johnson and his wife came in the door. Charley introduced his wife Mildred to everyone and walked around shaking everyone's hand.

Once again everyone's eyes were on the door as Bill Bartlett and his wife came in. Bill then proceeded to introduce his wife Mary Ellen to everyone in the room. Mary Ellen was a very stunning statuesque lady who carried herself with a regal bearing. She shook hands with everyone and politely repeated their names as they were introduced.

As the evening progressed, I realized what Mary Ellen had been doing when she repeated their names. She was memorizing them. During the evening when she talked to someone, she addressed him or her by the correct name, a feat which astounded some of those present since it was the first time she had met them. I watched the expressions on their faces as they visited.

After realizing what she had done and was capable of doing, I decided to have a little fun with it. I offered a toast to everyone present and thanked them for all of the great work they had done and for their participation. Next, I asked Mary Ellen if she would offer a little toast and name each person seated at the table. I winked at Mary Ellen when I asked her to do this to let her know that I was aware of her prowess in this type of undertaking.

As Mary Ellen toasted each one of them, she told them not only their names, but also what they were here for and what the future held for them. She told Cowboy about his being hurt, and then she told Pug about his last fight.

She told Mabel about her looking for her daughter and Bing about his problem with the Las Vegas gamblers. It seemed that Bill had told her about all of these people before they had come. When she came to Charley, she told him what he did and how long he had been on the police force. She continued through everyone seated at the table.

She then told them this was something she had learned to do when she had been just a very young lady. She had started by paying attention and repeating peoples names and occupations, and before long she had been able to remember the names of up to a hundred people in a room, and this was only after having met them for the first time. She had some kind of a photographic memory.

Everyone got a big kick out of it. She turned out to be one of the most gregarious people you would ever want to know. She just bubbled when she talked, and when she talked, she made you feel that you were the only person in the world that she was paying any attention to. To put it mildly, she turned out to be just one of the nicest, most down-to-earth people you would ever want to know. She was really the delight of the evening. Pam and Jenny were fascinated with her as were Roxie and Nora.

During the evening we did manage to hear from each of the recipients on how they felt about what was happening to them. It was unbelievable to hear these people tell their stories and how they had gotten to where they were when they met me.

It was clear to see that the bonding of us six people was something extraordinary. We were more like family than just friends. You could tell that our feelings for each other were deep and sincere.

I told everyone about the ranch and the club and the clinic and how much progress we had made in getting them ready to become active businesses.

We all assured Mabel that she was going to be the next one. "Jimmy Green is going to find your daughter, and then we will find you a restaurant near her so you can be together."

Everyone applauded when I told her that I was sure we would find her.

I asked everyone if they had been contacted, and if they had talked to Bob Hitch. It seemed that he had contacted everyone and had already taken pictures.

Cowboy told me that Hitch was just waiting for them to take possession of the ranch so he could come up and get some pictures of the place.

Doc told me that Bob had been at the clinic three or four times with photographers taking pictures.

Bing said that he had been out at the club twice this last week and had taken pictures. Hitch had told him he would be back for the grand opening and that he wanted to get a picture of some of the people doing a little jitterbugging. "He thinks this will bring a lot of folks out to see the place out of curiosity if nothing else. He thinks the 1940's and 50's theme is a good idea because a lot of people are beginning to go back to that type of music."

Bing says, "Just as soon as they find Mabel's girl, Bob wants to get pictures of them also to complete his story about the street person who became a rich benefactor to his old friends. I really think that young reporter has a good heart, and he is trying to help all of us at the same time he gets a good, heart-warming story about a lot of good people who take friendship seriously."

The evening went smoothly, and everyone had a good meal with lot of good conversation and fellowship, which was what this was all about. This dinner had given all of us participants a chance to get to know each other on a personal basis, as well as on a business basis. This was the way people got things done.

It's much easier, I said, to work with those people whom you know personally and trust. This is why the friendship of these people means so much to me and my family.

A Word from Roxie

Roxie stood and asked if she might have a minute or two to say something that she had been wanting to say ever since she had come to Texas. Everyone got real quiet, and she started to speak.

"Friends, I want you all to know how much it means to Jim's children and me to know you. You see, I didn't know for so many years whether or not Jim was dead or alive. I wondered where he was and what he was doing and how he was surviving if he was alive.

"Well, now we know how he survived. It was friends like you that kept him alive. Friends who looked out for him when he was sick or needed help. The policemen such as Charley Johnson apparently went so far over and above their duty to see that Jim and his friends didn't freeze in the winter and looked after them in the very hot Texas summers. There were people like Dr. Davis and his staff at the hospital that took care of them when they were real sick or hurt and needed their attention. Doc did the best he could for them with what he had. We will never forget that it was when they had broken bones or pneumonia or extreme cases of the flu that Dr. Davis and the others at the hospital stepped in and saw to it that they were taken care of.

"There were those people, two who are not here this evening, that I want to mention even though they aren't here. They are Lynn and Annie at the Bible Sanctuary. They never take a day off, not even Sundays, to get rest. They are there looking out for the homeless and street people every day of the year. They are always wondering where the money is coming from to pay the bills and feed the people for the coming month. I don't know how they do it, but they always seem to be able to put food on the table for everyone that comes into the Sanctuary. I have decided that I am going to add to the gift that Jim and Pam have given to the Sanctuary by two hundred and fifty thousand dollars. This will be added to the trust fund that Jim has set up for them. I don't ever want to see them scrounging for money to buy food or bedding for the cots where the people sleep. In addition to this, I want to add another two hundred thousand to the Police Retirement and Widows and Orphans Fund.

"Now that I have Jim back, along with his wonderful and lovely wife, I know that he will take care of me regardless of what might happen. This means that I don't really need all the money his father left me, so I want to do something useful with it. This is just one way I feel I would be doing the most good for right now. Thank you all for being Jim's friends, and I hope that you will become our family friends also.

"When I say our, I mean Johnny and Jenny, as well as myself. I know you will definitely be friends with Pam. Who could ever not be her friend? I used to think that Jim would make a good salesman, and now I know he became one when he sold her on the idea of marrying him.

"I guess I have just about said enough for now, so I will sit down. Thank you for letting me speak."

Roxie sat down, and there was silence for just a moment, and then everyone started to applaud, and then they all stood up and applauded her.

Now it was Roxie who didn't know just what to do. Tears started to run down her cheeks, and she tucked her head as if she didn't know what to do.

When the applause died down, David Davis stood and offered a toast to the lady of the evening, Roxie Dixon.

Everyone picked up their glasses and turned to Roxie, and in unison said, "To Roxie who raised a wonderful son."

By now there were a few more wet eyes in the crowd.

After everyone had taken his or her seat, I rose and said, Thank you Mother for saying what I feel in my heart. Now before I get all fuzzy and teary-eyed myself, I want to remind all of you that we have a meeting tomorrow at the hotel at 2:00 p.m. in the Lariat Room. Bring your facts and figures with you, and we will have Jimmy Green and Lynn and possibly Annie with some surprises for some of you, so be sure to be there and on time.

"Does anyone else have anything to offer before we call it an evening?"

No one had anything more to say, so we all began to stand and go to get our coats and prepare to leave. Most came by and gave Roxie a hug and told her how they felt about her and her family, and how thankful they were that they had been asked to become a part of what I was trying to accomplish.

Within fifteen minutes the room was clear, and there was nothing left but the sound of the busboys cleaning up the dishes and straightening up the room.

After we were back at the hotel, we all congregated in our apartment to say goodnight. I looked at everyone and asked if they had enjoyed the night.

Art and Nora were especially complimentary on the evening. "Jim, we can see now why you want to help them so much." She added, "The friends you have are not high society, but they are even better. They have proved themselves to be real true friends in good and bad times."

After about ten minutes everyone had gone to their rooms, and all was quiet. Pam came over and put her arms around my neck and told me that she learned something new about me almost every day.

"Everything I learn," she said, "just makes me love you that much more. It's impossible to show or tell you how much I love you, but I will keep trying."

I just laughed. "We, Honey, are just getting started, and we have a long, wonderful life ahead of us."

I changed the subject and asked, "Pam, do you mind Jenny hanging onto you all the time?"

Lord no, Jenny is the child I never had. She is just like my own and even maybe a little more so. That child is so starved for motherly affection, I just want to cry. I will never let her want for the love of a mother, not even one more day of her life.

Pam, now you know why I love you so much. It looks like we may have a mutual admiration society here; what do you think?

Husband Dear, I think it's bedtime because morning is going to come early tomorrow We headed for the bedroom, and the last thing heard was,"Goodnight, darling.

Sure enough, morning did come early, and Johnny was knocking on the door to see if anyone was ready to go to breakfast.

Johnny, why don't you go and get Art, Pug, and Cowboy. By that time I'll be ready, and I'll meet you in the restaurant. I suggested we let the girls sleep in for a while.

Johnny left, and I shaved quickly since I had already had my shower. I dressed, went over to the bed, and told Pam to go back to sleep if she wanted to, and I would see her and the other ladies later in the morning.

She kissed me good-bye. As I left, she turned over and went back to sleep.

I headed for the restaurant where I met the boys. We had breakfast and discussed the ranch. Cowboy told me about Pam and Jenny and Nora offering to fix up his house for him.

"That's a great idea, Cowboy. Just keep a close watch on them, or you will find pink frilly curtains and soft cuddly pillows on the couch."

Cowboy looked disturbed at that. "Jim, do you really think they would do that to me?"

"No, Cowboy, I'm sure they'll do it the way you want it done."

Pug came walking in just as we were getting ready to order. Good morning, fellows, he said, and with that he sat down and ordered without even looking at the menu.

That's what I like," I said as I winked at Johnny, a man who knows what he wants and sets out to get it.

Tell me, Pug, how did Angie like the dinner last night?

She was very complimentary, especially about Roxie's speech. She is really fond of that lady in case you didn't know it.

I'm glad because Mother is very fond of her. I continued with, I hope you realize that she considers you guys as part of our family now. I hope you don't mind. I guess that means that I'm kind of like your big brother. How does that sound?

Well, I don't know about that, but I will think it over.

Everyone laughed.

While we're waiting, I want to tell Cowboy that Bill is going to have all of the papers ready and filed today, and he will also deliver the check to the seller this morning, and he will be back here this afternoon for the meeting.

He is also completing and filing the papers on the club and the clinic. Let's not say anything about it before this afternoon to Doc or Bing. I would like for it to be kind of a surprise.

Charley also told me that Bill is drawing up the papers on the storage building that we are going to convert for lounging.

Charley is also bringing his friend the chef and will introduce him to Bing this afternoon. If that works out, it will mean that Bing will be ready to open in about ten days to two weeks because he already has the band lined up, as well as the dancers and instructors. The costumes will be ready this week including the zoot suits. The poodle skirts and sweaters for the girls are already done, and they are just waiting to find out what size the waitresses will be, and then they will get their saddle oxfords. The maître d' will even have the flat black or brown hats like they wore back in the early 1940's, along with the long chain that all of them wore. He will look like he just stepped out of the early forties. Some of the girls will wear the beehive wigs that we are having made for them.

We want it to look like the patrons have stepped back in time. We will even have a large Wurlitzer jukebox to play music when the band is not playing. Some of you guys are too young to remember those days, but I'm sure you will get a big kick out of it.

And, Dr. Davis is going to have a big surprise for Doc this afternoon. We'll wait for this afternoon before I tell you about that.

"Cowboy," I asked, "have you contacted Mr. Gay to find out if he has any stock to sell, and if he doesn't, maybe he can line you up with someone who does have. By the way, Cowboy, did you ever meet Don Gay when you were in the rodeos?"

"Well," Cowboy admitted, "I did meet Donnie once when he was first starting to ride bulls. He was a real nice kid. I got hurt right after that. I did see him ride a few times after that before I lost everything. He was something to watch when he rode. He was like glue on the back of those bulls. What made him so different was that at first he did it because he truly loved to do it. He was smart enough to see that this could be his future. I don't mean just riding bulls, but putting on rodeos and breeding stock, so he and his father started a good string of rodeo stock, and they started the Mesquite Rodeo which is known all over the world now. It just shows you what a young man can do when he uses his head. He even flew his own plane between rodeos so he could compete in more rodeos than some of the other guys could. That took a lot of smarts, and he was smart.

"I'll call him right away now that I have the place to put the stock. I will see if he remembers me, and if he does, it might help me get a foot in the door. I have heard that they have sold the Mesquite Rodeo, but I am sure they can tell me how to find Mr. Gay if he isn't there. I have heard that he hangs around there a lot of the time."

The morning went fast and furiously. The ladies were out on the town again. This time they were looking for furniture for Cowboy's house. They were determined to fix his home up really nice in case he found some nice young lady and wanted to get married. He consistently said that he didn't have any desire to get married, but you know how it is when the love bug bites you. Besides, this would give the girls something new to put into their sights and work on.

They had helped Bing get some of the interior decorating done for the club, but most of the ideas have come from Hattie McKinney. She was old enough to remember the zoot suiters. Her husband had never worn one because he had basically been just a good old cowboy who had a knack for making money. Hattie might sound rough and uneducated, but we didn't ever sell that lady short. She was a voracious reader of everything from *Time Magazine* to encyclopedias. She had a mind like a steel trap, and you'd better not say anything around her that you didn't want her to remember. She might not say anything about it for six months to a year, and then all of a sudden she would bring it up for you to explain.

She was a great help to Bing, and she was treating him like a son even though she loved to embarrass him.

Since she had never had any children, Bing had better look out, she just might want to adopt him.

All kidding aside, that Bing really liked this lady, and he admitted that she had been a lot of help to him. He felt that she would probably be a lot of help in the future.

Right after this, the ladies came in from lunch. They all met at a restaurant they had started frequenting recently. They liked the food and the privacy of their booths so they could talk and discuss everything that was going on. You can believe that they knew what was going on, and they were aware of everything that happened and was said. When they were together, they totally dissected each and every one of the happenings.

Now that they were back, we saw that they even had Nancy, Hattie, Nora, Pam, Jenny, and even Mary Ellen along so she could see just what this was all about. It seemed they were here ready to attend the meeting and get their two cents' worth in on all of these things they heard might be going to happen. They felt very strongly about being of service in any way they could. They didn't seem to care what it was or how much work it was just as long as they could be doing something constructive.

Up till now, the only thing they had been doing was shopping and learning the city and where the stores were. Now they wanted to be of some benefit in some way to the program. It looked as though they would raise cane if they weren't asked to do something today.

Well, here it was – almost 2:00 p.m., and everyone was heading for the Lariat Room downstairs in the hotel. Some arrived to find that several were already there.

Bing and Mabel were sitting over in one corner, waiting on everyone to arrive. In another corner we found Lynn and Annie, along with Doc and a couple of the nurses from the hospital that he had invited since they were offering their help at the clinic.

This Meeting Will Come to Order.

I looked around and saw that most everyone was here with the exception of Bill Bartlett and Cowboy. I walked to the head of the long table that had been set up for this meeting and used a water glass as a gavel to knock on the table and get their attention.

Everyone walked over to the table and took a seat. A waiter finished filling the glasses with water for everyone and excused himself. I asked if anyone wanted anything to drink other than water. I got no response.

I proceeded to speak. I first wanted to know if everyone knew each other. I introduced Bill and Mary Ellen because Lynn and Annie had not met them. I couldn't remember if Hattie had met them or not. Hattie assured me that she had not met them, but that she had sure heard a lot of good things about them.

With this, I asked Dr. Davis to introduce the young man he had brought with him.

Dr. Davis had the young man stand, and he introduced Dr. Bill Bates. He first told everyone not to mistake him for the ex-Cowboy football player Bill Bates who was now a coach with the team. This Bill Bates was about twice the size of the football player. He later stated that he went to college on a basketball scholarship. He was about 6'7", and he now weighed about 275 lbs. He still looked like he could have been a tackle for the Cowboys.

David told everyone that Dr. Bates was a specialist in the care and physical maintenance of the body, especially the body of people who do not eat properly and who have to put up with the elements of the weather. To be politically correct, he said that Dr. Bates had spent the last seven years studying and taking care of street people and indigents in three different large metropolitan areas before coming to Texas. He happened to hear about the clinic during a board meeting at the hospital with David. He cornered David and told him that he would feel honored if Doc would consider letting him help at the clinic during his off time. He would volunteer to help almost every hour he was off duty.

I asked, Dr. Bates, "What will your wife think about a pledge such as this?"

"Professor – I hear that's what some folks call you – well so far, no young lady has cornered me, and I am still single. The hours would not be a problem especially if Doc could find a cot for me to get a little rest on once in a while in the evenings."

Doc assured him that he could arrange that.

Next, I asked Doc to introduce the young lady he had brought to the meeting. Doc stood and introduced his guest, "Ms Linda Haygood. Linda has been an emergency room nurse for the past nine years. She is extremely well qualified, and she has offered to help out at the clinic as much as possible. She, like Dr. Bates, is not married, so she doesn't have to worry what her non-existent husband will have to say. She has already been helping me arrange my pharmacy room and has helped me with the 'do's and don'ts' of the pharmacy as far as what has to be kept in the refrigerator and those narcotics that have to be kept under lock and key. She even showed me how to set up the record-keeping system for the State Medical Board."

Doc said, "It's a lot different from the record keeping of the Army, especially when you are at the front line with bullets flying all around you.

"Linda," Doc says, "I want to thank you for the help you have given us so far."

"Doc," she assured him, "I will be helping every time I have a few minutes or few hours away from work. My family does not live in the Ft. Worth area, so I would enjoy something to do in my spare time."

Doc smiles, "I don't know if she is just pulling my leg or not, but most nurses in ER just want to go home and flop when they get off duty. I sure will appreciate all the help I can get from you and your friends."

Everyone greets these people and lets them know how much they would appreciate their help.

Now we would like our good Policeman Friend Charley Johnson to introduce the friend he brought. Charley stood and asked his friend to stand also. Charley introduces him, "This is Shawn Griggers who has just moved back to the Ft. Worth area from New Orleans to take care of his elderly mother and father. His folks are in poor health, and he felt that he was the most likely one of the family to come back home and take care of them."

Charley adds, "Shawn was a chef at Brennan's Restaurant in New Orleans when he decided he should come back to take care of the family."

Shawn stands, "I am married, and my wife and I have a daughter who will be attending TCU, starting in next year's spring semester. It seems that she has applied at TCU and has been accepted. This is another reason we are moving back to the area."

Shawn, "Do you have anything else to say?"

Shawn looks at Bing and asks, "Could we get together after the meeting because I'm looking for a job, and I understand that you are looking for a chef. Maybe we can work something out."

Bing smiles and says, "It'll be a pleasure to visit with you right after the meeting."

The door opened, and in came Bill Bartlett and Cowboy. They each had a grin across their face that they just couldn't wipe off.

I invited Cowboy to have a seat. I asked Bill to join me at the head of the table, which he did.

Just as Bill was about to take his seat, the door opened again, and in came Jimmy Green and a very nice-looking young lady, they are quickly seated near the rear of the room.

I continue, Today is really a red-letter day for this group. We have finally come up with a name for the six of us who always hung around together and who took care of each other. "From now on, we are going to be known as the "Odd Squad." We are five men and one lady.

We became more like family when we met than most families do. We felt for each other. When one was happy, it made the rest of us feel happy. We looked out for each other, and we protected each other. When one hurt, we all hurt, and we tried to ease the pain of that person hurting. We all knew in the back of our minds that better times were in the offing. We knew that we would not be on the street always. We didn't know how, but we knew there was a better place somewhere ahead and that with the help of God we would someday find it.

That may sound funny coming from a person who spent ten years on the street, but we did believe in God. We all believed in God, and most of us pray occasionally. We didn't like to let the others know it, but I think each of us knew the others were praying from time to time.

"People like Lynn and Annie helped us keep the faith that we needed to get through each long day. They fed us, gave us beds to sleep in when we needed them, and even helped us get clothing, especially warm clothing for the winter.

"People like Charley Johnson would help us by putting us in jail for a night or two if he knew bad weather was coming, and we might freeze outside. He even got other officers and jailers to help him by saying that we had been arrested for vagrancy or some other trumped-up charge, but they kept us warm and safe. We knew that their Captains and Chiefs knew what they were doing because the cells might be empty. Then, when a cold front with rain, snow, or ice would come through, all of a sudden the cells were full of street people arrested and brought in for vagrancy or something else. None of us ever had to pay any fines. They just let us out when the weather got better. They can never know how many lives they have saved by doing things such as this.

"Well, tonight I have a few surprises for some of you. As most of you know, my mother Roxie made a sizable contribution to both the Bible Sanctuary and the Policeman's Retirement Fund and the Widows and Orphans Fund. Today each one of those groups is going to receive the trust fund papers and the bank books to show how much money they now have in trust for them. The interest from this day forward will go to each of those funds as long as they exist.

"Next, I am glad to tell you that Dr. David Davis has received word that the hospital will be receiving within the next thirty days, one of the most modernly equipped ambulances in the whole United States. It will have a cardiac care section right in the ambulance with everything needed to take care of a heart patient until he reaches the emergency room. It will also have direct radio and cell phone communications of the latest type anywhere. It will have the ability to send the EEG and EKG directly to the hospital emergency room while it is moving. There isn't anything available for emergency vehicles that this unit won't have. Just think of how many lives can be saved with a unit like this.

"I want to tell Dr. Davis that my mother and I have talked it over, and the next thing on the agenda is going to be the latest model Bell Jet Helicopter equipped with all of the very latest emergency equipment to be used in emergency situations.

"The other day we observed a four-car collision on the interstate that had seven critically injured people. Unfortunately, they only had so much room in the helicopter that came for them. They had to do the best they could for the victims until another helicopter came in from Dallas to help. This took an additional fifteen to twenty minutes.

This meant that some of these lives might have been saved if they had had two helicopters. The outcome was that three of the seven people died. They might have been saved if we had just had more doctors and nurses at the scene earlier.

"Well, this will help alleviate things like this from happening in the future. It won't save everyone, but if it saves just one life, it will be more than worth it. I have learned what life really means since I have sobered up and am now married, and my wife and I are back with my mother and children. I don't want to see this happen if we can prevent it, and we are going to do what we can to prevent it.

"Now let's get to the clinic. Doc, will you come up here for just a minute?"

Doc gets up from his chair and walks slowly up to the front of the room.

"Doc, I think that Bill has something for you."

Bill stands and starts fumbling through papers as if he was having trouble finding what he was looking for. He finally said, "Oh, yeah! Here it is; I knew I had it somewhere." He pulled out this long, legal-sized document and hands it to Doc.

"Doc, I understand that you have always had a dream of having a place like the clinic so you could help your friends who still remain on the street and the indigent people of the area."

"You're right Bill, this has been my dream ever since I got to Texas and saw the condition of some of the street people."

"Well, Doc, you now have one. Here are the papers saying that you are now the CEO of the Hattie McKinney People's Clinic located in Ft. Worth, Texas, and with the help of people like Charley Johnson and Dr. David Davis, along with Hattie McKinney pulling a few strings with the Texas State Medical Licensing Board and the Ft. Worth City Council and the Zoning Commission and the County Medical Boards, they have given me a neat package to give to you. It says that you are the CEO, and Dr. David Davis is the President of the Corporation. Your Board of Directors are as follows: Your Board members are Jim, Roxie, Hattie, Pam, Charley, and me, Bill Bartlett. We will go into further details later and answer any questions you might have.

"This means that you are legally ready to open the doors just as soon as you get the work done on the inside and you and Dr. Davis decide you can start receiving patients.

"There will also be some company representatives from drug companies contacting you to help you get the needed medicines and supplies needed to open your Clinic. This means you have what you needed to make the dream come true.

"Now, what do you have to say?"

Doc just stood there for some time, and then a few tears came to his eyes. He wipes them timidly, not wanting anyone to know that it was making him cry. "Oh Hell! I didn't know I was gonna cry when it came true, but I can't help it."

We all start clapping and stand to show how proud we are of him and what he had done to get his dream.

We finally sat down, and Doc started to say something, then he had to stop. It seemed that he had a frog in his throat.

When Doc got himself under control he continued. "One thing I can promise you is that from this day forward, you will never smell liquor on my breath. I drank enough for a lifetime in the last eight or ten years, and I know what it can do to a person. From now on, no drinking. I won't have anyone work for me who has a drinking problem either. I haven't had a drop since the tornado and I feel that since Jim has enough faith in me to help me do this, the least I can do is not let him and the other people down. The best way I know of doing that is to stay sober and work hard. Thank you for everything you have done for me and for the people who need help on the streets. Thank you again."

Doc walks around the table to where Hattie was sitting. He bends over and kisses her on the cheek and tells her that he would never be able to thank her or repay her for what she had done.

She reaches up and hugs his neck. "Doc, you are the one that will be doing the work. I just want to come and help out once in a while."

"Hattie, you will be welcome anytime you want to come and help or just visit with us." Just having you around will be a pleasure and you will always be welcome. With that Doc walks slowly back to his chair.

When he arrives at his chair, Linda stands and gives him a great big hug and kisses him on the cheek. "Doc, I am so proud of you for hanging in there and doing what you have done."

They both sit down, and I continue. I guess I should just let Bill continue since he has the briefcase open.

Bill stands again and pulls out some more papers. Before I continue, I forgot to tell Doc but Hattie has also included a deed to the property in that batch of papers I just gave you.

With that everyone applauds again. Hattie even wipes a few tears from her eyes and tells Bill, "Oh, hell, just get on with the business at hand before we all start bawling. What I did wasn't much, and besides he needed the property, and I didn't."

"Well, now I need to have Bing come up here since I have something for him also."

Bing jumps up and heads for the head table.

Bill looks at Bing and smiles, Bing I understand that it has been a dream of yours for many years to have a little nightclub of your own.

That's true; it sure has been my biggest dream of all.

Well, Bing, it looks like you just may have your wish tonight also. I have here in my hands a couple of licenses. One is from the State Board of Liquor Control. This gives you permission to sell beer, wine, and mixed drinks in your new establishment. The papers from the proper city and county offices and boards are also in this portfolio. You are properly licensed, and you too can open your doors just as soon as you are through with the remodeling. You also have a license to sell food in a place that serves mixed drinks, so you have no problem that I can see except to have a cook who can make you some money.

You know what, Bing. I think you may have found that man this evening also. I certainly hope so, and I don't think Charley would lead you down a blind alley about something that serious. I understand that you have the band ready, and the dancers are raring to go, so just be sure to let everyone here know when the opening will be.

You will need to get together with Jim tomorrow since he has a bankbook for both you and Doc. I am sure you guys will be glad to receive them. I do have another couple of papers for you to sign, but that's all.

Bill turns to me and asks if he should tell Bing about the property. Bing looked kind of concerned when I said, "Well, you might just as well tell him about the property now because he will find out sooner or later."

By now Bing seemed to be a little concerned with the tone of the conversation and asked if there was something wrong.

"Well," Bill said, "that depends on your interpretation of what wrong means. What I am trying to tell you Bing, is that there is also a deed to the property in the papers you hold in your hand. You own the property free and clear. There will be no mortgage and no rent to pay. Hattie has also given you the property where your club sits. She is still going to be your partner for one percent of the business. She says this is so she can say she is an owner of a night club. Everyone applauds and laughs when they hear this. Hattie says, I always wanted to own a night club and now I'm a partner in one. That's close enough.

With that and without saying a word, Bing walks around the table to where Hattie was sitting. He takes hold of the back of her chair and tells her to stand up. She reluctantly does, and when she is standing, he reaches over and gives her a great big bear hug and planted a big kiss squarely on her lips. When he lets' go, she almost falls back down into the chair.

She finally gets her breath and says, "Hell, Bing if I had known you was gonna do this, I would have given it to you a month ago."

With that the crowd absolutely burst out with laughter, and by now Hattie and Bing were both really blushing which was something that I was sure Hattie very seldom did. She might make the other person blush, but not her; she just didn't normally blush.

When the laughter had settled down, Bing bent over and kissed her on top of the head. "Hattie, I love you; I really do love you. Will you please adopt me?" With that he went back to his chair. She says I sure will big boy.

Bill looks at me with a quizzical look. I tell him, "Go ahead, Cowboy is next.

"Cowboy, will you come up here please?" Bill asks.

Cowboy gets up and goes to the head of the table.

"Cowboy, your part for this evening is not such a secret since you have been with me all morning. Folks, Cowboy and I spent the morning delivering papers, signing papers, and delivering the check for his ranch up near Sherman. This was the first time I had actually seen the ranch. This ranch is beautiful. I really mean that; it's just plain beautiful. It sits on the top of a knoll that overlooks a small valley near the Red River. In fact he said,"you can see the river from his front porch even though it's about a quarter mile away. There is a nice barn and a couple of sheds and a very nice little three- bedroom brick veneer white house, with, believe it or not, a picket fence around the front yard.

"The house faces east so you can sit on the front porch in the morning and drink your coffee while you watch the sun rise. There is a small, screened porch on the rear where you can watch the sun set in the evening.

"There are beautiful trees and a spring out just past the barn that furnishes water for the stock all year long. There are a couple of Red Bud trees, along with a large Magnolia tree in the front yard. There are two beautiful Red Oak trees to the rear of the house. Best of all there are flower beds and several rose bushes that you will have to learn to take care of. You can open the window to the kitchen and smell the big red rose bush on the inside of the house. The Realtor told me it was called a Mr. Lincoln. It sure has a beautiful perfume which I'm sure you will like. It's right beneath the window. There are even some beautiful dark blue Iris in one of the beds.

Whoever lived there before has left a hummingbird feeder still hanging under the eaves of the house near the kitchen window so you can watch them feed while you have your meals.

The water is very nice and sweet. We had a drink from the spring this morning when we were up there. That's something I may have forgotten to mention. There is a beautiful spring near the knoll just west of the house. A neighbor told me that it had been there as long as he could remember, and he never remembers it going dry. This is great for watering the cattle and horses."

Bill looks out at all of us and says, "I am envious of Cowboy. I told you there are trees in the backyard. They are perfect for putting up a hammock, but Cowboy wants a swing out there instead of a hammock. I think Cowboy is going to be very happy there.

"There is also a nice tack room in case he ever gets married and his wife runs him out of the house. If that happens, he can sleep in the tack room."

Bill turns back to Cowboy and says, "Seriously Cowboy, you have the key to the place in your pocket, and now I am giving you the deed to the property. Unfortunately, you will have to pay for it after you get your stock-breeding program in full swing and start making some money, but until then, as the papers will tell you, you don't have to pay anything back. Jim was going to charge you twenty-five percent interest, but I talked him out of it."

Everyone laughs and applauds, and Cowboy swallows real hard and then thanks me and everyone there for having faith in him.

When Cowboy sat down, Bill turned to Roxie. "I think you have something to tell Cowboy."

Roxie rises and tells Cowboy that since they had helped the others so much, she would like to have the privilege of outfitting his home. I mean outfitting it properly with bedroom sets in all three bedrooms including linens, towels, and all such that is needed. The kitchen needs a new stove, refrigerator, tables, and anything else that might be needed along with dishes and cooking utensils. You will need a dining room table and hutch, etc., and you and I have talked about the living room. You want leather in your living room and that's exactly what we will put there. The girls and I want to fill your pantry also if you will just tell us what you want in it, and last but not least is the laundry room. I noticed you had a nice one with all of the connections needed for a good washer and dryer."

By now Cowboy was totally bewildered. He just kind of looked down at the floor, and then up at her. He told her, "I don't know how I will ever repay you and the rest of the ladies."

She looks straight at him and says, "Come here and give me a big hug young man; I don't want Hattie getting all the loving around here tonight I might get jealous."

Cowboy walks slowly around to Roxie's chair and reaches over and gives her a great big hug, and then he kisses her on the cheek, so she, in turn, kisses him on the cheek.

"Cowboy, you remember that you are a member of the family also." Roxie sits back down in her chair and Cowboy goes back to his chair as everyone applauds loudly. Everyone was really getting excited by now.

Bill sits down, and I get up to address the group. I want to have Pug come up here for just a minute. I want everyone to know about Pug and his job and how much help he has been ever since we left Chicago.

When Pug gets to the head table, I look at Angie and say "Angie, I think you had better come up here also."

Angie looked totally bewildered by this, but she got up and came to the head table. "Pug and Angie, you aren't going into business or starting anything where you need help to get on your feet. Pug just has a job with me. Pam and I feel that you need something, something to help you feel that you have a home – something to make you know that you are a vital part of this group – something that you will want to come home to at the end of a day or at the end of a trip somewhere. You know what I'm saying.

"Well, we want you to know that we have made a family decision and when I say that, I really mean a family decision. It took all of us – Pam, Roxie, Jenny, and Johnny, as well as myself, to decide upon this action that we took. I hope you won't be mad at us when we tell you what it was.

"Before we left Chicago, Pam noticed that the property adjoining our home at the rear of our lot in Chicago was up for sale. It was an estate sale, so she sneaked out with Roxie and Jenny one day to check on it.

It turned out that Mr. Cantrell, the elderly man who had lived there for so many years, had died of a heart attack. He only had one daughter who had passed away several years ago. The daughter had a son who lives in California. Pam had the realtor contact the son, and she made an offer on the property. They accepted it.

"Now I have to tell you, it's an older house, but a very good house, and it is only on a half-acre lot. The house has four bedrooms and has about 4500 square feet of space. We want to know if you think you could put up with us as neighbors if we gave this house to you?

I look at Pam, and I think this is the first time I have ever seen Angie totally speechless.

"Pug, can you say anything?"

"Well, Jim, Angie and I can only say that this is totally unbelievable. You know how we feel about you and your family. We had decided to make Chicago our home while we were in Omaha, but I don't think we could really accept something like this as a gift."

"Well, if you don't accept it, we just never know what kind of neighbors we might get. We might get some beatniks or some other kind of undesirables in there. You have to accept it.

How about it, Angie? If he won't accept it will you? If you accept it, I know he will move in with you, and we'll do it that way. What do you say?

Angie looked at Pug, and he looked at her, and they both at the same time say that they guess they will take it under those conditions.

"Jim," Angie asks, "will it be okay if we put a gate between your backyard and ours?"

By now everyone is laughing and having a big time out of everything. Bill hands Pug and Angie the papers on the house, along with the keys. We all hug and Pug and Angie go back to their chairs still shaking their heads in total disbelief.

I try to continue. Now, we must top off the afternoon with the best of all things.

"Jimmy Green, will you please stand and introduce the young lady with you.

Jimmy stands and says, "Folks, at this time I would like for everyone to meet Miss Amber Russell."

Everyone was just politely giving her a hand, when all of a sudden there is a scream from a chair near the front. It is Mabel screaming. She has jumped up from her chair, and she is just as white as a ghost. When she is finally stand up, she looks as though she was going to faint.

There is another scream from the end of the table where Jimmy Green and Amber Russell are.

This time the scream is from Amber Russell who is hollering "Mother, Mother, is that really you?"

They had both pushed their chairs back and the chairs have fallen onto the floor. They are trying to get to each other without crawling over the people around them. They almost fall over the backs of the chairs lying on the floor as they try to reach each other.

When they finally reached each other they hug and hug and push each other back and just look again and then hugged and kissed again and again.

By now there was not a dry eye in the house. Amber wouldn't let go of her mother, and Mabel wouldn't let go of her daughter. Every little while they would just push each other back to get a better look at each other, and then they were hugging again.

I finally have to say, "Just in case you aren't aware of what's going on, Mabel and her daughter haven't seen each other in almost ten years."

"Mabel, I want you to know that I have made arrangements for you and your daughter to stay at the hotel this evening, and for a few days if you would like so that you will have some time to just sit and talk and plan for the future. We found Amber in Mt. Pleasant,

Louisiana, and we told her about you. Amber is still single, and she has no commitments to hurry her back home.

"Our next chore is to find Mabel a restaurant in either Mt. Pleasant or Many or one of the towns in that area if that is where you want to live. If you want to stay in Texas, we will arrange for that also. Right now you need a few days together to get re-acquainted after all these years.

"Mabel, I tell her, we have already contacted your boss and told him about the reunion and he agreed that you can have as long as you need to get to know your daughter. He said, Don't worry about your job; it'll be here when you guys get acquainted."

By now everyone was buzzing about the afternoon and all of the things that has happened.

Now there were several groups talking instead of listening to me so I banged my water glass on the table three or four times to get their attention and I speak real loud. "Folks, this concludes the meeting."

With that announcement everyone continued to do their own thing which they were doing by this time anyway.

Pam came around to where I was standing and suggested we go over and meet Mabel's daughter. As we walk around the table, we are met face to face with Mabel and her daughter Amber. Mabel reaches over for my hand and pulled me close to her and says, "Professor, I want you and Pam to meet my daughter Amber."

I reached out to shake hands with her. She reaches out to me; she pulls me real close, looks up, and then she hugs my neck. When she was finally able to speak without crying, she tells me how much it means to have her mother back again.

"Professor, do you know that this is the nicest thing anyone has ever done for me in my whole life?" She says that she has prayed every night for the past eight or nine years that she would find her mother again.

I suggest we go over and sit down for a while so we can talk. When we are seated, I begin by telling Amber what a wonderful mother she has. "Amber, you must remember that anyone can at sometime in their life lose their perspective. Your mother made a mistake by missing the train that left carrying the carnival where she was working. Her biggest mistake was to lose hope in getting out of town and back home. She apparently felt defeated and took a few drinks, which led to a few more, and the next thing she knew, she had been on the street for several years. It was fortunate for her that she became acquainted with our group.

You see, we had made a pact that we would look out for each other regardless of what happened and we did just that. It wasn't always great living the way we lived but the six of us always knew we had each other to look out for us.

Your mother is a wonderful cook. She is not only a wonderful cook, but she always kept a needle and thread around so she could sew up our clothes when we needed the repair of a rip in our shirts or pants. She was really a mainstay for us men.

We can talk further about all of the things later. I'm sure you'll want to hear about them one day before long.

Professor, have you really arranged for a room for us at the hotel for the next few days? I think I have room at my apartment for Amber to stay with me.

Mabel, you can do whichever you want to do. If you stay here, all you need to do is sign the bills at the restaurant for your food and anything else you might want.

"Amber, your mother has a new car now, and you folks can go anywhere you want to go and do whatever you want to do." With that I will leave you to get better acquainted.

Amber looks at her mother and asks, Why don't we just go to your apartment, and that way we can stay up as late as we want and sleep in when we want to. If you don't mind, Mr. Dixon, I would like to have some of my mother's good cooking that I remember from when I was a very young child. I remember the brownies she used to make with pecans in them and the omelets and pancakes she used to make for me when I was real young.

"Mama," she asks, "can you still make those pancakes like you used to? I just want us to be together where it's nice and quiet. I just want us to be able to talk and talk. You can tell me all about what's going on now and what has happened since the tornado. From what I hear from Mr. Green, you guys have accomplished a lot since that time. He tells me that you and the rest of the gang have absolutely and totally quit drinking. He tells me also that apparently the rest of the gang has stopped drinking too; I think that's wonderful.

Mother," Amber asks, "why don't we just go to your apartment? I think I would like that better than staying in this hotel. I'm just not used to the idea of staying in a big hotel like this.

That's just fine with me, Amber. I'll tell Professor that we have decided not to stay here.

They find Pam and I and say goodnight and leave.

Pam and I are busy saying goodnight to all of the other people. We go over and had a brief conversation with Dr. Bates and thanked him for coming today.

The next stop is over to Bing, Charley, and Charley's friend, Shawn Griggers. It seemed that Shawn was apparently quite adept at cooking all types of food. It looked as if Bing had found his chef, and Shawn had found a job that would keep him in Texas.

Pam and I agree that it look as if this had been a very good afternoon for everyone.

Bing come over to say good-bye. He told us that he was taking Hattie home since she was a little tired and felt that she needed some rest.

Pug and Angie were over in the corner visiting with Dr. Davis and the new doctor, Bill Bates. Pam and I wander over to join in the conversation.

PUG'S WORST FEARS

We started to say good-bye when I noticed that Pug was twisting and turning his head from side to side, and then back and forth. This scared me and I hurry on over to Pug.

"Pug," I ask, are you all right?"

Pug looks at me kind of funny. "Professor, my head is hurting real bad. This is the worst headache I have had in years. My left arm is tingling and my neck is beginning to get real stiff."

I hurriedly tell Dr. Davis and Dr. Bates about Pug's problem with the aneurysm. It seems that Dr. Bates had seen this problem before in Chicago.

Bill tells Pam to call 911 and get an ambulance here immediately.

Dr. Davis then takes the phone and calls the hospital to tell them they are coming in with a patient who needs to be put into the intensive care unit right away. "I don't want there to be any delays of any kind in admitting with any kind of paperwork. This man has to go straight through to intensive care, and they better be set up to receive him when he gets there. The paperwork can wait. I will take personal responsibility for this patient."

The ambulance arrives in about five minutes, and they take Pug and Angie to the emergency receiving at the hospital. Sure enough there is no paperwork for them to worry about.

Pug is admitted, and they get him all settled into the intensive care unit. Once he is settled in, they give him the kind of shot that he normally got to thicken the blood to prevent the leaking. They finally get him stabilized enough to take him to the operating room long enough to do a spinal tap.

After about an hour, Dr. Davis comes to the waiting room where we are waiting.

His news is bad news. It seems the blood in the spine was more than they had expected it to be. They felt they could stabilize him for a day or two, but they are afraid they might have to operate sooner than that.

"If he continues to lose blood, we may have to do the surgery as soon as possible."

This was what we had been fearing for the past few years.

Dr. Davis tells Angie that he has never done this type of operation himself but he has assisted in one operation of this type. He does know one of the best surgeons in the country who does this type of surgery and he is in Houston. He asks if Angie would like to have him call and see if this doctor could come up and consult or possibly do the operation. His name is Dr. Richard Schug. He is one of the best in the country, and that's what you're going to need for this type of operation.

Angie agrees that's exactly what she wanted. She tells Dr. Davis she wanted the best that could be had.

"I agreed with her and told David to contact Dr. Schug as soon as possible and see if he would be available to come to Dallas. "Tell him we'll reimburse him for any and all expenses he might incur for anytransportation and expenses."

David got on the phone immediately and called Houston where Dr. Schug worked. He wasn't there, but when David explained the problem and who was calling, the operator gave him Dr. Schug's home phone number.

David immediately called his home and Mrs. Schug answered the phone. When she heard David was the one who was calling, she immediately called the doctor to the phone.

"David, it's good to talk to you again," Dr. Schug said.

"Dick, I have a problem in Ft. Worth, and I need your help. A good friend of mine has an aneurysm in the Circle of Willis area of the brain. It is actually in the Basilary artery. It's a bad one that is leaking quite a bit, and it looks like this young man needs surgery to correct the problem, and you're the only person I know who has done this operation successfully. I'm hoping you will be able to come to our rescue.

We have thickened his blood which has slowed the seepage to some extent, but we can't get it to quit seeping. The bubble in the artery is large, and it appears to be very thin, and there is a serious possibility of a total rupture, and you know what that would mean. What about it old friend? Can we count on you?"

There was a short silence on the other end of the phone. David heard Dick tell his wife to pack a suitcase for him and that he might be gone several days. She said she would have it ready within thirty minutes.

Dick says, "David, there is a Southwest Airlines plane leaving Houston for Dallas about every hour. I will call just as soon as I find out what time my plane leaves Houston and the time of arrival at Love Field Airport in Dallas."

Southwest has the most frequent flights, and it goes into Dallas, so you will have to meet me there and drive me to Ft. Worth to the hospital.

Dick, call and let me know your arrival time and I'll be there. I turn to Angie, "Angie, Dr. Schug will be coming just as soon as he can pack a bag and catch a plane, which should be within the hour. There is a good chance that he will be at the hospital within four to five hours at the latest."

"Angie, Jim I'll start digging out all of the information they have from past visits to the hospital by Pug. There are records from all the visits over the years that Dr. Schug might want to look at when deciding just what he wants to do. He'll want to see X-rays to help determine the progression of the aneurysm over the past four or five years."

Pam and I talk to Angie and remind her that she knew he had this condition when they had married.

She knew there had been a possibility of something like this happening but she just hadn't expected it to happen this soon.

David assures her. "Dr. Schug is definitely the one I would want to operate on me if I was the one who had the aneurysm instead of Pug.

She lets them know that she was aware of everything they were saying. "I agree with you. You just don't know how appreciative I am that we have a doctor who is experienced in this type of surgery.

Pam and Angie go over to the waiting area in Intensive Care. Within twenty minutes there is a phone call from Dr. Schug to David.

David comes to the girls just as soon as he hangs up the phone and tells them, "Dick will be leaving Houston Intercontinental Airport within two hours, and he will be at Love Field in Dallas by 8:00 p.m. Dick has given us the flight number and gate where he is to arrive. This is the quickest flight to the area, and we can pick him up in Dallas, and it won't take much more time to get to the hospital."

The girls want to know if they can visit Pug.

They tell Angie she can go in for just a few minutes, but "Try not to excite him because that might raise his blood pressure and that would be bad."

"I will be careful in what I say, I promise."

Pam suggest that she should wait for Angie in the waiting room. Just tell him that we are pulling for him."

Angie is shown to the room by a nurse. As she goes in, she could see that Pug was sedated to keep from increasing his blood pressure. He appeared to be sleepy.

She goes over to the bed, kisses him, and asks how he is feeling.

"My headache is better he replies, but it seems that I'm losing the feeling on my right side. My arm and hand are tingling now."

"David," she tells him, "has contacted a doctor friend of his in Houston who has done this particular type of surgery in case you need it. David and Dr. Bates both say that this is the man they would want to operate on them if they needed this type of operation.

This seemed to make him feel better. "Angie Hon, I've known this was going to happen sooner or later. I had just hoped it would be later. I guess if it's going to happen, I would rather it happened here in Ft. Worth where I know the doctors.

"Honey, I really don't worry about the operation because I know I have the best doctors, and all of my friends are praying for me. That should count for an awful lot, don't you think? I just want to get it over with so we can have a normal life and start us a family.

"Well, how about that?"

Angie's smile seemed to really cheer him up. "You hurry up and get well, and we will just do that very little thing. We are going to have a couple of those little fellows or girls as the case may be."

"How about one of each?"

"That would be fine Honey; that would be just fine. I really don't care if they are girls or boys just as long as they are healthy."

He seemed to be real tired now so she encourages him to just lay back and relax. She encourages him to get as much rest as he can. "You're going to need all of your strength if they do operate. Just go to sleep Hon and I'll be right here if you need me.

He relaxes and lays his head back. Within a couple of minutes he seems to be sleeping. The nurse pokes her head in the door and very quietly tells Angie, "It's good that he is sleeping."

As she walks out, Pug opens his eyes just momentarily and says, "I heard that."

Angie just smils and tells him, "Just go back to sleep Darling, and if you wake up or need anything, I will be right here to take care of it.

The doctor had told her she could stay with him as long as he wasn't having to be worked on. You know, like more X-rays or CAT scans.

Everyone was real nice to the families here. They felt the patient did better with the family being around him or her as much as possible.

The next three or four hours went by slowly for Angie because Pug was sleeping most of the time. One time she did come out to tell Pam what was happening. Pam was standing by in the waiting room. Just in case something happened, she wanted to be near her best friend so she could be of some comfort and help to her. These girls were like sisters. They loved each other dearly.

Angie went back to the room with Pug so he wouldn't wake up without anyone there. By this time Pam and I had contacted all of the other members of the gang. Soon they started coming in the door wanting to know about Pug, asking all kinds of questions.

Mabel and Amber were two of the first ones there. Right behind them came Cowboy and Doc who had brought Linda, the nurse with him. Next came Bing who had brought Hattie. He had been at her house dropping her off when his mobile phone had rung. When he told Hattie what had happened, she insisted that he bring her along to the hospital with him even though she was pretty tired. Art and Nora had come down to the hospital with Pam and me when we brought Pug in the ambulance. Lynn and Annie had called twice to see if anything was new on his condition.

It seemed that almost everyone who was at the meeting was either here or had called. Bill Bartlett and

Mary Ellen had called, as well as the new chef, Shawn Griggers.

As Pam was starting to read one of the magazines, she heard David and me come in with Dr. Schug. They just said hello and headed straight for the desk to get Pug's chart and go over it to see if anything had changed since they had gone to the airport to pick up Dr. Schug.

Dr. Bates had stayed here just in case Pug had gotten worse.

After a quick consultation with Dr. Bates, they adjourned to a private room with all of his charts to decide what they were going to have to do. After about thirty minutes, they emerged from the room with very serious expressions on their face.

They immediately headed for Pug's room where they wanted to talk to him and Angie.

"Wayne, the aneurysm has developed another small bubble on the side of the aneurysm, and it looks as if it could rupture at any time. We feel that the only thing left for us to do is to go ahead and operate. We feel that if the bubble ruptures, you could possibly die before we could get inside to stop it since it is in one of the most difficult areas just below the actual brain itself to reach." They explained everything to Pug and Angie.

"Angie," Pug said, "I can't and probably won't make it in this condition, so I say let's get started, the sooner the better."

"Wayne, be aware that your chances of surviving this kind of operation are about fifty percent."

"Yes, I know; Dr. Bates has already filled me in on the possibilities. I realize that, but I feel that if there is a fifty-fifty chance then I'll make it.

"Dr. Schug, I had several fights where I was the underdog and I've always come out on top. I don't expect it to be any different this time. Besides I have a lot of people pulling for me and praying for me and I feel that counts a lot."

Dr. Schug asks "Angie, how do you feel about the operation?"

"I feel sure that Pug knows what he's doing, and if he says to operate, then let's operate. I think that God is going to see us through this crises because we are going to have a lot of good years ahead of us, and he isn't going to take those away from us."

Dick turns to David and Bill. "It looks like we have ourselves a fighter, so let's get ready and take care of this right away."

"Angie, you should understand that this operation could take from five to seven or more hours. This is an extremely delicate operation."

He turns to Pug. "Pug, when you wake up, you will have a bad headache, but probably not any worse than the one you have right now. You also know that you're not going to have that good-looking head of hair for a couple of months."

That's allright Doctor, I can stand that if the headaches go away. "Let's get going, doctor; I'm ready if you are."

As they turn to leave the room they say, "We'll see you in a few minutes. The nurses will be in to prep you in just a few minutes.

"Angie, if you don't mind, it would be best if you could wait in the waiting room with Pam and the others until we get him prepped. After he is prepped, you can come in and stay with him until we are ready to take him to the operating room."

She kisses Pug good-bye and tells him she will see you in a few minutes after you are prepped.

As soon as Angie reaches the waiting room she meets Pam and the rest of those who had arrived. "Jim, Angie asks, will you call Pug's mother and dad and tell them what's happening? she asks.

I leave the room immediately to go where I would have more quiet when I talked to them. I pass the door to the hospital chapel as I am on my way out. I decided that this would be a good time to go inside and talk to God about Pug and offer a prayer for a successful operation and complete recovery. I go into the chapel and there is no one else in the chapel at this time. I walk to the front of the chapel where there is a kneeling rail.

I slowly kneel and start talking to God. "God, I'm not asking anything for myself tonight. I'm asking you to help Wayne through this terrible operation he is facing tonight. I know, Lord, that he like me, has not always been what you wanted us to be when we were born, but I think you know that we have learned from our mistakes, and we have taken a new route in our life.

"As you know Lord, we are both married now, and Wayne and Angie want so badly to have a family. He has become a good Christian since he met Angie, and he will continue to live a life that you will be proud of. If you can just help him make it through this operation tonight, I am sure you will never be sorry for helping him. I know that he will never do anything to make you ashamed of him in the future. He is really a changed person who wants to be a family man and raise a family the way that would make you proud of him. I'm sure he will raise his family the way you would want him to raise his children.

"If he makes it through this night, we will all promise that we will make you proud of us, and we will do what we can to further your teachings in every way we can. Please Lord, place your hand on this fine young man and see that he makes it through this terrible time in his life. If you do this, I promise you he will never let you down, and I will never let you down again as long as I live.

"Thanks Lord, for letting me talk to you for just a little while."

I arose and turned to go out the door when I see that Pam and Angie had been standing in the rear door listening to my little talk with God. They each came to me and put their arms around me, and we just hold each other for a long while.

Finally, I release my hold, and with tears running down my cheeks, I tell the girls what I had just asked God for and what I had promised if Pug made it through this operation.

They both told me that they heard, and they would certainly see to it that all of us would keep my promise to God.

I released my hold on them and told them that I had to go and call Pug's parents now. The girls want a few minutes in the chapel by themselves, and then they will go back to the waiting room where they will be in case I need them.

Just as they arrive back at the waiting room, the nurse came in and told Angie she could come back to the room until they were ready for surgery. When they take him to surgery, she will have to come back to the waiting room. She understood, thanked the nurse and headed for the room.

I found a nurse who showed me an office where I could have some privacy when I call Pug's parents to tell them. I close the door and dialed the phone. After about three rings there is an answer on the other end of the line.

I ask, "Is this the McKenzie residence?"

Mr. McKenzie heard my voice and quickly recognized it and tells me that I am speaking to Jake. He immediately sensed that something is wrong. "Jim," he asked, "what has happened to Wayne? Is he all right?"

I tell Jake the story and what had happened to Pug. I ask Jake if he and June would like to come to Ft. Worth. "If you do, I'll have plane tickets waiting at the airport at Moab first thing tomorrow morning."

Jim, we appreciate your help, but we can take care of it from here faster than you can and we appreciate the offer. June and I will be on the next available flight, which will probably be sometime before noon tomorrow. We will call you just as soon as we get our arrival time, so someone can meet us at the airport.

Do you have a mobile phone, Jim?

I give him my mobile number because that would be the easiest and fastest way to reach me or Pam. Jake assures me that he will call just as soon as he gets the reservations.

After I had completed my call to Jake and June, I decide that it would be a good thing to call Sid, Angie's father. I look in my little black book and find the number which I immediately call. Angie's brother Darryl answers the phone.

I tell him who I am and then I proceeded to tell him about Pug's problem. "Darryl, it might be nice if Sid could come and be with Angie at a time like this."

Darryl agreed, but said, "Dad fell just this morning and cracked a bone in his left ankle. The doctor says it's a pretty bad break, and it will be a while before he can be out and about." Darryl adds, "Jim, it will be almost a month before he will be able to walk with a cane.

"Please let Angie know that Dad is doing as well as can be expected. Jim, Dad's a tough old nu, and he knows that just as soon as he is able to be on that ankle, he will certainly want to come and be with her. You know Jim, Dad really took a liking to that young man. I know he's going to be upset when he hears about this."

"Okay Darryl, but you tell him that just as soon as he feels he can make the trip, I want you to call me, and there will be a plane ticket waiting for him at the Omaha airport. Promise you will do that for me. I want to take care of this for your dad.

"We are very fortunate that one of my doctor friends here in Ft. Worth happens to have a doctor friend in Houston who is one of the very few doctors who have successfully done this operation. He has agreed to come to Ft. Worth and do the operation and stay as long as necessary to make sure Pug gets the best of care.

"Darryl, it happens that I'm extremely fond of your father, and I want to do anything I can to help him. Please give him our love and let him know that we are thinking of him and that we will let you know how Pug is progressing. We will call you every day to let you know both the good and the bad, but we hope there is no bad news."

"Thanks Jim, I don't know what we would do without you and your family. Tell Pam and the children and your mother hello for us. I'll see that Dad gets there just as soon as he is able, and I appreciate your calling us and letting us know what is going on. We will appreciate your calls on his progress in the future. Good-bye, Jim."

I head back to the waiting room where I find Pam, Angie, and the rest of the gang. By now they are all there waiting to find out what is going to happen.

Just as we were all about to settle down, Dr. Schug comes into the room with Dr. Davis. They outlined the operation for the friends and family since everyone is so closely involved with each other. They explain the procedure, and the difficulties of the operation again because of the location of the aneurysm and the fact that it now had another small bubble or aneurysm on itself, which makes it more likely to burst before they could reach it.

The doctors are very good about explaining everything to us and telling us how long the operation could take and what the chances of succeeding were going to be.

Dr. Schug and Dr. Davis leave to go back to Pug's room and talk to Angie before taking Pug to surgery. Now she can fully understood what they are up against and that she has to be strong and have a lot of faith in God and the doctors who would be doing the operation. She knows that Dr. Schug is one of the best brain surgeons in this part of the country. She is glad that Dr. Davis knew him and was able to get him to come to Ft. Worth. The nurse tells the doctors they are ready in the operating room and are just waiting on them.

Now the hard part. The waiting begis with everyone in the room sitting and looking at each other. Every once in a while someone would get up and go for a cup of coffee or a soft drink or something. Some tried reading, but they couldn't seem to concentrate. The time went so slowly that it seemed that it would never be time for the operation to be completed.

Then, after about four hours, the door opened, and in came Dr. Schug. Everyone's heart stopped beating for a moment because he wasn't supposed to be here. The operation was supposed to take five to seven hours. Dr. Schug had a strained look on his face. Dr. Davis came in right behind him. Dr. Schug spoke first.

"Angie, we had to stop the operation for a while because Wayne's blood pressure has dropped so low. We have to stop the operation while we try to raise his blood pressure. They are giving him whole blood to try and get his pressure back high enough for him to withstand the trauma he is going through. His body, even as strong as he is, can not stand this kind of trauma if the blood pressure gets too low. We could lose him, and we just don't want to take that chance. The blood pressure is down to about eighty-seven over forty-five, which is dangerously low. We are doing the very best we can, and we still think we can get it back up high enough to do the operation. We will send a nurse out to let you know when we are able to start the operation again."

They turned and walked back through the swinging doors toward the operating rooms. The swinging of the doors give a sound of bumping and rubbing together and a little squeaking sound that made me shudder inside as they walked back through them and down the extremely quiet hall. It made my stomach queasy when I started to wonder just what was happening inside that operating room.

Once again everyone was back to reading our magazines and drinking coffee and Cokes, but it is hard for us to concentrate on what we are doing. We seem to take turns looking at the clock or asking each other what time it is and how long it has been since they had been here telling us about his blood pressure.

We stare at the floor, and then at each other. From time to time we leave one by one, and in a short while we are back from the direction of the Chapel. Most of the time we are wiping the tears from our eyes as we come back to the waiting room.

Now there is almost dead silence in the waiting room. We didn't even hear the rustle of the paper when we turn the pages of the magazines we are reading or the scraping sound of our moving the toes of our shoes back and forth on the waiting room floor. The silence is deafening.

Just then a nurse comes through the swinging doors and tells me that Dr. Davis has asked her to tell us that the blood pressure was up high enough for them to resume the operation.

Once again time was creeping *oh, so slowly* as we waited for some kind of word from the operating room or from someone from the team of surgeons. I look up at the clock and realize it had been almost eight and a half hours since they had started the operation. I am really getting worried, but I realize I have to keep up a good front for Angie's sake. She looks at me and asks what I thought was happening.

True to my word, I tell her that since it has taken this long, it must be a good sign that everything has gotten better. "His blood pressure has come back up to where they have been able to continue the operation. That is why they have taken so long.

"Angie, you have to remember that they held up the operation for quite a while waiting on his blood pressure to come back up." I must say that "It's a good sign that they are still working."

I talk to them, and I try to smile to show that I really mean it. They seemed to settle down for a while.

After another hour or more of watching the swinging doors, finally in came Dr. Schug and Dr. Davis and Dr. Bates. I figured when I saw all three of them, something must be wrong.

But, I figured wrong this time because Dr. Schug walks over and puts his arm around Angie and tells her that they had completed the operation, and it appears to be successful. He also admonishes her that an operation of this type could throw you a curve once in while.

He told everyone that it would take another twenty-four hours before they knew for sure just what was going to happen. They were hoping that there was no swelling to the brain where the operation had taken place. They would have to monitor it for the next few days.

"But, if he makes it through the next seventy-two hours, he will have a very good chance of making it." Dr. Schug assured us, "He is a very strong young man, and if anyone can make it, he should be able to do it."

My phone rang and it was Pug's dad calling to let me know what time they would arrive tomorrow so someone could pick them up. "We will leave Moab around noon and then change planes in Denver, and then we will catch a flight to DFW on United and be in there at 4:15 p.m."

I assured Jake that I would be at the airport to meet him and June. I let him know that I would make arrangements for them to stay at the hotel where all the rest of the folks are staying.

They sure seemed to appreciate my taking care of these things for them because they wouldn't have known where to stay or who to call to make reservations.

"Jake, Pug is doing as well as can be expected. Angie is hanging in there and won't leave the hospital for fear that something might happen, and she wouldn't be here."

The next two days went by slowly. Angie had absolutely refused to leave the hospital until she was sure that Wayne was over the crises period. The hospital had been kind enough to her to allow her to stay in one of the doctor's lounges at night. She was allowed into the room with Wayne for a few minutes about every four hours. Pam stayed busy bringing her clean clothes and making sure she had been eating and not just living on coffee. Pam had been with her most all night the first two nights, but since there was no place for her to sleep, she finally went home for a couple of hours each night.

The Odd Squad and I had been coming and going all day and night checking on the condition of Wayne or Pug as we called him. I guessed it would take us a while to get used to calling him by his name instead of Pug. We all loved him so much, and we were afraid that something might happen to him. Angie had been able to shower in the doctor's lounge, which helped her feel a lot better. Dr. Davis and Dr. Bates had come by earlier to tell Angie that there had been no change in Wayne's condition. They were a little concerned because they had expected him to regain consciousness by now.

As we were talking to Angie, Dr. Schug came back into the room. He told her that their worst fears had come to them. His brain had swollen and was causing pressure which was one of the reasons he had not regained consciousness yet. They let Angie know that this was not really an unexpected happening.

"This happens quite often when doctors do brain surgery. We are working on reducing the swelling, and we should know later today if we are able to accomplish the reduction. If we can get some reduction in the swelling by tonight, there is a possibility that he will come around within the next twenty-four hours.

I came in just as the doctors were about to leave. They explained the problem again so I would know what we were facing.

Once again the waiting continued. The gang came in from time to time for the next twenty-four hours. They would stay a couple of hours and leave. It seemed that another member of the Odd Squad came in to give his support to Angie. It seemed they had really taken to Angie. She was like one of the family now.

As I was about to leave, Pam came over and told me that she was going to stay with Angie for a while longer. She wanted me to come back for her around ten or eleven this evening.

While we were talking, Lynn and Annie came in to see how everything was going. They told Angie that everyone at the Sanctuary had held a prayer service for Pug last night, and they would hold another tonight and the next night and every night until he was out of the woods. This really surprised Angie, but I explained to her that the people at the Sanctuary loved that young man.

"He has helped many, many of them when they needed help the most. He has also taken up for them when they have been threatened by bullies. He just would not put up with that kind of behavior from anyone."

The waiting room had become hard to get around in due to so many people coming to see about Pug. The phone was going constantly.

I turned to leave and ran right into Robert Hitch, the young reporter for the Ft. Worth newspaper. I was very surprised to see him.

Bob explained that someone had called the paper and asked for him. They had asked him if he was aware that Pug was in the hospital. They had told him that he had to have brain surgery, and that a specialist had needed to be called in from Houston to do the operation. Bob was here to find out what had actually happened.

"Bob, if you will hang around just a minute, we will get one of the doctors to explain the operation and the prognosis."

I left for just a few minutes, and then returned with Dr. Dick Schug. Dr. Schug was very nice about explaining the problem and the type of surgery they had to do. He explained the problems they were currently facing and how they were treating it. He told Bob that the prognosis was good.

"It's not unusual to have some swelling after this type of operation." He felt that Pug would be awake and talking within the next twelve to twenty-four hours.

Bob visited with Angie for a few minutes before he left to get the story into the paper before the deadline.

The next day there was a very nice story about Pug, or Wayne, in the newspaper. They referred to him by both names so everyone would know who they were talking about. Bob even ran a picture of him in the paper with the article.

This resulted in more phone calls, and now the hospital was even beginning to get many cards and letters addressed to him. This was surprising, but they felt that Lynn and Annie might have had something to do with this. Anything to cheer Pug and Angie up.

There had been quite a few floral arrangements sent, but since he was temporarily in Intensive Care, they would have to wait to put them into the room. He was not allowed to have the floral tributes in Intensive Care.

Bob called Annie to see if she had read the story in the paper this morning. She had a good, long conversation with Bob and thanked him for being so thoughtful.

Time still seemed to stand still while everyone was waiting. The night came and went as did his many friends and acquaintances.

Pam stayed the night with Angie and slept in a chair on the lounge, while Angie slept on the couch. At about six o'clock Dr. Schug and Dr. Bates came into the room with big smiles on their faces. When Angie saw this she knew that there was good news coming her way.

"Good news Angie, Wayne has opened his eyes and complained that he has a headache. This is what we were wanting to hear and see.

"Angie, you can go in and see him now, but don't stay too long because he really does need to get some rest after what he has just been through."

There was a great sigh of relief from all of the gang in the waiting room. A couple of them walked quietly down to the chapel. They went into the chapel and quietly offered thanks to God for having brought Pug out of his sleep and allowing him to open his eyes to those around him. This they said would enable the doctors to further treat him and make him well again.

They silently arose and walked out of the chapel and back to the waiting room. Mabel and Amber came in just as everyone was smiling and laughing and giving high fives to each other. They wanted to know what was going on. When they were told that Pug had opened his eyes, they gave each other a high five, and Mabel said, "Thanks, Lord, for these great blessings."

With that she heard several "Amens" from the group. This just showed that they really had changed, and it appeared that all of them intended to stay changed.

After about fifteen minutes, Angie came back from Pug's room. "Hey gang! He is very coherent, and he asked about every one of you. He wants all of you to know that you aren't rid of him yet, and that he will be back on his feet before very long. There were a few other things that he said to me that were kind of personal, so I won't pass those on to you, but you get the idea."

Wayne was back to stay, and he was hale and hardy.

"Angie," "that's the best news we have had in a long time. Now everyone can start planning for the future, and as we all know, Pug is a great big part of that future."

Mr. and Mrs. McKenzie are hugging each other, and now they come over to Angie. They all hug and talk about the wonderful turnabout in his condition.

Jake and June have really been at wits end since they had been here. The last two days of waiting had absolutely worn them out. Now they could relax a little and not worry quite as much.

They tell everyone, "We know he isn't totally out of the woods yet, but at least we can see the light."

Everyone agrees and breathes a sigh of relief.

Jake immediately got on my phone and called home to let Neil and Elaine, his brother and sister, know that he was conscious and that the prognosis looked good. We could hear a squeal on the other end of the phone from his sister Elaine.

"Be sure and give him our love, Elaine says, and when he is able, maybe you can give him a hug from us. Neil wants him to come home to recuperate, and that way they can go fishing again."

Neil came on the phone and said, "This time, we won't let Angie catch the biggest fish. The next time one of us will catch that big one."

When Jake told Angie what Neil had said, she got a big laugh out of it. It was about time that someone around here had something to laugh about.

The next two weeks went by slowly as Angie and the McKenzies spent most of their time at the hospital. At least now Angie was able to go back to the hotel and get a good night's rest, and she could relax in a tub of warm water for a while. This girl had really been a rock through all of this. She was so consistent in her actions and her moods. She was there when she was allowed to be with him, and when she wasn't allowed in the room with him, she was generally in the waiting room.

Today she had picked up the Ft. Worth paper, and there on the second section of the paper, she saw a small article that stated, "Mr. Wayne (Pug) McKenzie is now off the critical list at the Tarrant Co. General Hospital and is expected to be out of the hospital within another week or two."

She called Bob Hitch to thank him for being so kind to Wayne and the rest of the group.

Angie, I have become very fond of all of the group, and I will do anything I can do to help them.

I was busy now helping Doc and David and the nurses over at the clinic. It looked as if they would be able to open up for business this coming week. They planned a big blowout for the opening. The mayor would be there, along with several Councilmen and other dignitaries. Dr. Davis and Dr. Bates had both agreed to be there. Dr. Schug might be there, but that depended on how Pug was doing. So far he was doing just great.

Bing had been working hard over at the club, and Mabel and Amber had been helping out a lot with the kitchen work. They had been working along with Shawn Griggers the new chef. They had even been talking about the possibilities of having Mabel work with Shawn in the kitchen and letting Amber work with them as a kind of apprentice. This had been mentioned, and they all three thought that it might work out real fine since they all got along so well.

Shawn was surprised at Mabel's expertise around the kitchen. He had even learned a couple of things from her, and she had learned a lot from him. This could turn out to be one of the best kitchens in Ft. Worth when they were through.

Bing had arranged for press releases, and Bob Hitch had offered to write a cover story for the opening. They were planning on having the band along with a jitterbug contest the night of the opening. This would be great if they could get some pictures of the dancers on television. Bob Hitch knew a couple of guys over at one of the TV stations, and he had offers to get them to come over with their cameras.

Cowboy had started to move some of his belongings up to the ranch now that Pug was getting better. He had made some contacts and had gotten some leads on some breeding stock for rodeo cattle. He had even gotten a couple of leads on some bucking horses. He was going to try to make some purchases soon. He had already ordered feed to be brought out to the ranch and put into the barns. He had also bought himself a new saddle, bridle and halter, and a couple of ropes to put in his tack room. He had even bought some saddle soap and oil that he would need in the future.

Roxie and Jenny had started picking out furniture for him. They had already delivered his washer and dryer so he could do his laundry. Oh, yes, they installed a stove, refrigerator, and kitchen table with chairs so he had a place to eat. Right now he was sleeping on a fold-up bed in the bedroom without any furniture. The furniture would be there later this week along with the furniture for the living room and the other bedroom. He would make an office out of the third bedroom. The dining room furniture would be delivered a little later.

Before anyone knew it, it begins look like a home. He already had his hammock up in the backyard. He also had a small TV to watch. He didn't know it, but Roxie had ordered him one of those big 50-inch TV's for the living room. Man would he be surprised when they delivered that thing. He would feel as though he was sitting inside of his own movie studio. She also ordered a twenty seven inch for the bedroom.

He didn't know it yet, but Roxie had decided to surprise him by giving all of this furniture to him as a present. She said she would refer to it as an early Christmas present. I could just see his eyes when he heard this.

Johnny and Art had been busy helping first one and then the other with their chores. They had helped Cowboy with some of his repairs around the barn, and then they went out and repaired some of his fences. Cowboy just couldn't get over how nice everyone was to him. He just didn't seem to realize that he was nice to everyone else, and now some of it was coming back to him for all the things he had done for others in the past.

It was getting late in the day, so everyone headed back to the hotel. We wanted to change and clean up a bit before we went to the hospital to see about Pug. After showering, shaving, and having dinner, we headed for the hospital where we found Mabel and Amber in the waiting room.

It had gotten to the point now where every time Amber saw Pam and me, she had to have a hug. She looked to us as family, and I guess to her we were the family she had never had or at least had never known.

As we were standing there talking, Bing and Hattie, along with Doc and Linda, came through the door to the waiting room.

As we greeted each other, Dr. Davis and Dr. Bates came ambling through the doors and greet everyone. Dr. Davis told us that he had some real good news.

Just as he was about to speak, Pam interrupted him with a question. "Where is Angie?"

"Well, Pam, that's what I was about to tell you guys. Pug is in a private room upstairs now and he can have all the visitors he can handle. His swelling in the brain has gone back down to normal. He appears to have no after effects from the operation, and he is up in a wheelchair a good bit of the time now. We've had him up most of the day today.

He and Angie are waiting for you guys right now. If you will follow me we will go up to his room right now. We would however ask that you don't stay too long since he has had a pretty busy day while you guys have all been out playing.

That brought a big, "Ho, ho, ho, and a "Yeah, we sure were playing."

Roxie asked him if he had anything for a sore back.

Cowboy and Johnny told him to just look at these blisters on their hands.

Art laughs and tells them they are just sissies, and that he didn't have any blisters on his hands.

Johnny turns and lets me know that they had only had one pair of gloves and they had felt sorry for the old man, so they had given them to him to keep him from crying.

With that, Art hits Johnny on the shoulder and tells him that he didn't have to tell the truth every time.

The elevator was stopping at the fifth floor, and we all disembarked. We followed Dr. Davis and Dr. Bates down the hall. Cowboy nudged Johnny in the ribs and held his hands about four feet apart while he was walking behind Dr. Bates, indicating the width of Dr. Bates' shoulders.

Johnny told Cowboy, "You had better be nice, or I will sic Dr. Bates on you."

With that Dr. Bates turns around laughing and tells Cowboy, "Don't worry because I haven't bulldogged a steer since I was a freshman in college."

With that Cowboy stopped dead in his tracks. "Dr. Bates, do you mean to tell me that you really did some bulldogging when you were young?"

"Sure did, Cowboy. I worked one summer for an uncle on his ranch out in New Mexico, and we did some of that just for fun and to see what it was like to jump off that horse running at full speed and grab that steer. The first time I did that it scared the hell out of me.

"Now, let's go and see Pug, and then you and I can talk more later about my summer as a cowboy."

Everyone continued toward the room. When we walked in, we found Pug sitting there in a wheelchair. He had a smile on his face from ear to ear. Angie was standing right behind him.

Bing let out with a whoop and then a, "Well, I'll be dammed. You really are in a wheelchair."

Bing turned to the doctors and asked, "Does this mean that he will be well enough to come to the opening of the nightclub when we open it next week?"

Dr. Davis looks at Dr. Bates, and they both speak at the same time. "I don't think that will be a problem if he doesn't get too excited. He will have to be in his wheelchair if that is all right with you guys. He won't be allowed to do any jitterbugging.

"How do you feel about that, Wayne?"

Pug looks at Angie and asks, "Are you busy next week? I would like to have a date with you and take you out to a nice nightclub."

That cute little grin comes on Angie's face and then, "Well, I guess that could be arranged if you are a good boy between now and then."

With that everyone wanted to know when the opening was going to be.

Hattie spoke up and said, "It will be next Saturday evening. It seems that the band is ready along with the dancers. They have already arranged for the publicity in the papers, and Bob Hitch has arranged for a camera crew from one of the television stations to be there. They think they can get it on TV, and that should give them a real good send off.

"With that done, Bob will also put a large article in the Saturday's edition, telling all about the club and the owners and what they will be trying to do for the community's entertainment industry by bringing back the 1950's theme.

"Now that Pug is going to be able to attend the opening, everything is going to be just great. This means that all of the gang will be able to be there.

"Bing," Hattie asks, "would you mind if the Mayor and his wife and a few of the City Council members were to show up?"

"Hattie darling, just what have you done, and what would give you the idea that the Mayor and some of the City Council members might show up?"

"Bing Honey, since I'm a big donor to most all of their races for their positions on the Council and the Mayor in his race for that office, I just thought if I called them and told them about the opening of the club, they just might want to attend." Publicity you know.

Bing looked totally startled at this little bit of information. Upon hearing it from Hattie, he wanted to know just how they had found out about it.

"Well," she grinned, I just happened to call all of their offices yesterday, and since I am one of the very minor partners in this little venture, I just happened to tell them that they should be at the opening to show the public that they are backing and helping some of the people of this fair city get ahead. Not only that, but they might also want a little help with their finances since the next election is coming up later this year."

"Hattie," Bing scolded: "That's just like threatening them if they don't show up."

"Hell, no, Bing," Hattie yells right back, "it ain't like that at all. I didn't threaten them if they didn't show up; I just told them that their campaign fund might be a little short when election time comes around. Most of these guys knew my man, and they know that I do business the same way he did. You scratch my back, and I'll scratch yours.

"Don't worry, Honey, they will be there with all of their finery on, and they will be some of the most outspoken people attending when the TV camera lights come around their way. You just wait and see."

By now all of us in the room had big grins on our faces, even Bing. "Hattie McKinney, I wish you were forty years younger or I was forty years older." "Hattie, will you adopt me?"

With that, the room literally whooped and hollered.

By now Pug is really enjoying everything that is going on. The doctors look at each other and smile.

The doctors tell the gang, "This laughter is the best medicine in the world for Pug, and it will help him get well quicker. He doesn't need to be worrying about anything right now, and from the looks of things, I don't think he will be worried."

"Angie," Dr. Davis asks, "do you think you will be able to control this young man when he gets to go home?"

"I sure will doctor, and if I can't control him, I bet I know where I can get some help."

Everyone is having a good time now. It is just what we needed, and it was just like the old gang used to be. Johnny, Art and June were all are really smiling. They are right in the middle of it which makes it that much more wonderful. Speaking of Wonderful, "what a wonderful ending to a wonderful day."

Everyone stayed for another thirty minutes or so and then we all began to leave.

The doctor suggested, "We should let Pug or, Wayne if you prefer, get more rest so he will be in condition for the Saturday night fling."

Before we all got away, Doc turned to Hattie and asked her if she happened to invite the Mayor and City Council to the opening of The Clinic next Monday morning.

"Doc Honey, I will have all of them there as well as a couple of State Representatives and several County Commissioners. They all love to be there when cameras of any kind start turning, or the flood lights go on.

"There will, of course, be a cutting of the ribbon for the clinic opening. Bob Hitch has assured us that he will be there with a good cameraman, and he will put a real good article in the paper about The New Storefront

Clinic for the street and underprivileged people of the community. Naming it the Hattie McKinney People's Clinic doesn't hurt one bit either."

Hattie is known by every important person in Fort Worth, and they will all be there. They don't want to hurt Hattie's feelings.

This was one of the best things to come along in years for the street people. There are many people who have children and are living in shelters; many of them can't afford any type of medical attention. This would give them a place to go, as well as the street people. Everyone left knowing that between Hattie and Dr. Davis, everything had been well taken care of.

With seven days to go before the opening of the club, and nine before the opening of the clinic, everyone had much to do. We all adjourned to the waiting room at the hospital, and I finally got their attention.

I asked them if they could meet me at the hotel on Monday for lunch after the grand opening of the clinic.

"I'll try to get the Lariat Room for us to have lunch in. I'll also try to get Bill and Mary Ellen to come, as well as Charley Johnson and his wife. I don't want to forget about Wayne Gregory and his wife Fay Jean. These people are the salt of the earth. They are always helping people who need help. Wayne knows most all of the property in Tarrant County, at least all of the good property.

"Doc, you and Linda be sure and be there and bring any of the other girls who want to help."

I turn to Mabel and Amber and ask, "Can you be there?"

Before they spoke, I knew the answer.

"Yes they say, we will be there."

"With God's help, we will see you and anyone you might think of on Monday for lunch at the hotel. It looks like things are really coming to a head now. Time has really flown by, but on Monday with everyone there at the meeting, we can discuss just how far we have come, and how much more there is to do."

The weekend was spent just resting. Angie's father, Sid, was pushing it a little but he said he is finally able to walk well enough to make the trip. He made the trip and arrived a week ago yesterday. His ankle was still hurting a little when he got here. He had been moving around a little too much since arriving in town. After the trip he had been on his feet too much, or he would have been with the rest of us tonight. He needed the rest, so Angie had insisted he stay at the hotel this afternoon and tonight.

Morning came, and we had a family breakfast with Art, June, Roxie, Jenny, Johnny, Pam, Angie, her father Sid, and me. Sid had been with Angie most of the time since arriving, either at the hospital or at the hotel.

Angie had finally agreed to leave Wayne at night the last few days since he had been doing very well according to Dr. Schug.

Sid was finally seeing just how things were done in the big city. It seemed that he was bewildered from time to time with all of the money that had been flying around. He did take a couple of days to go with Cowboy and Johnny and Art. They made a fine quartet.

Art and Sid had been giving Johnny a real good lesson in what a great thing country living could be. Johnny had really taken to this country thing. The truth was that these men had just taken a real liking to this young man and wanted to help him learn anything and everything he could about country living and their way of life.

Just because a man has a college degree didn't mean that he knows all about life. Living or working on a farm or ranch for a while is a whole other education in itself.

After breakfast everyone decided to, just as the kids would say, "hang out." Some of them were going to the mall, and some were going over to the park while

Cowboy, Art, and Sid were going over to the stockyards to look around. They asked me if I was interested in going with them.

I declined this time, but let them know that I would take them up on it one day real soon.

Angie as expected, headed for the hospital just as soon as breakfast was over. Now that most of the pressure was over concerning Wayne's operation, she just seemed to want to spend as much time with him as possible. He kept trying to get her to take more time off and do things with the other women, but she just wouldn't do it.

He worries, that you will get tired of being around me all the time."

She lets him know real quick and real loud, "I will never get tired of being around you or with you for the rest of my life.

He laughs real loud, "Darling," "If I didn't know better, I might get the idea that you are in love with me."

"Well if you don't know by now, Mr. McKenzie, you will never know, now will you?"

They spent the rest of the morning just being together, which was the most important thing in their lives right now after what they have just been through.

Wayne Honey, "Do you realize that we have been in Texas almost eight weeks?"

My Darling Wife, "You may remember it, but I don't remember all of that time since I was out of it for almost two weeks. I mean between the initial hurting, the operation, and the recovery time, along with the little setback from the swelling of the brain, I lost a couple of weeks somewhere, but it looks as if I am finally on the real road to recovery and I have you right here beside me."

Pug's Recovery

As we sat and talked, Dr. Schug came in with a nurse. Dr. Schug had a big smile on his face, and Angie knew immediately that it meant good news.

"Well" he says, young man I think it's time for you to try your legs. You have been in that bed for a long time, and I'm afraid your legs may be getting weak, so we feel we had better get you started walking today – if you are going to be able to dance next Saturday night."

"Doctor", Wayne asks, "are you serious? Do you really mean that I am going to get to try my legs out this morning?"

"You sure are, Wayne; you can start right now with the help of the nurse and me.

"Nurse, will you lock the wheels on this wheelchair so it won't roll either way?"

"Okay, the wheels are locked," Doctor.

"Now Angie, if you want to stand behind the chair just for moral support, let Nurse Little take one side, and I will take the other side, and let's see what happens.

"Is everyone in place?

"Well, come on Wayne, let us help you and let's see if you can stand."

Wayne starts to stand, and the chair shifts just a little. He started to reach back for the chair, and Dr. Schug said, "Don't do that. Nurse Little and I will hold your arms if you need help, and Angie is behind the chair, so it isn't going anywhere."

Slowly he continues to try to rise, slowly and deliberately. The others could see a little strain in his neck muscles as he moved slowly to a standing position. The veins in his neck stood out a little as he finally reached his full height.

He stood there for just a moment looking down at the floor, then slowly, turning his head from one side to the other, he looked at Dr. Schug and then at Nurse Little.

"Hey," he declares, "I'm standing. I'm standing on my own two feet."

Dr. Schug questions him. "Do you have any dizziness or equilibrium problems?"

"No sir, doctor. I feel just fine, a little weak, but just fine. Well, that's not the real truth. Hell, I feel wonderful, but pretty dogone weak."

"Well," Wayne,"do you think you can take a few steps?"

"Just turn me loose Doctor and let me see just how much strength I have lost in my legs."

Dr. Schug and Nurse Little released their hold on his arms very slowly but they aere still touching him with hands just under his armpits. You know, just in case he starts to quiver or go limp.

Wayne takes the first step very cautiously; he takws another, and then another. These were small steps, but they were steps on his own.

Using his own strength to do this surprised even Dr. Schug. "Wayne, I'm as proud of you as any doctor ever could be of his patient. You're doing wonderful."

Wayne turns to Angie, and what he saw surprised him. Tears were gently rolling down her cheeks as she watched her husband do what at one time was just a dream. There had always been the possibility of his being paralyzed from the operation or from the after effects of damage done to the brain during the operation. There had also been the possibility that he wouldn't be strong enough to survive the operation. That was how most of the patients were lost during this procedure. This operation took so long and was so hard on the entire body that there was less than a fifty percent chance of survival.

Since Wayne was in such good condition physically, the doctor felt his condition had been what saved him. The other thing, which was an intangible, is his will to live.

"This," according to Dr. Schug, "is one of the most important things over and above medicine that helps people survive traumas of all types in their lifetime. Some people just give up while others feel they have so much to live for that they will never give up until their heart stops beating. Then it will stop only after it knows it has been in one hell of a fight.

"Wayne seems to be one of those people who will never give up as long as there is a breath of air left in his body. Thank God that Wayne happens to be the kind of person who survived this operation, and now for the rest of his life, I feel that he will never go down without fighting."

Wayne had now taken several more steps as they talked and he walked.

Dr. Schug finally tells Wayne, "You've done enough for today."

With that Wayne asked, "Can I try again later this afternoon or this evening?"

Dr. Schug looks at Nurse Little, and she lookes at him.

She finally says, "I'm game if he is. We just don't want to overdo it."

It's very evident that Wayne wants to be able to dress myself and to go to the opening of the Swinging Years Club this next Saturday night."

Dr. Schug assures him, "You'll be able to go if you promise to use the wheelchair at least to do most of your motovating. Dr. Bates has already said he also wants to go to that opening and that he will be glad to keep an eye on you for the evening if it is all right with me."

Wayne looks at Angie and tells her, "I am ready to go dancing next Saturday night if you are."

I'm ready but "We will hold off for a month or so on the dancing, but we will definitely go to the opening and enjoy the music and the friends."

Wayne insisted on walking back to the bed instead of riding the wheelchair. Dr. Schug finally gave in and let him walk back across the room to the bed.

When he got to the bed, he literally flopped down on the bed, dog tired but real proud of himself.

Angie gave him a big hug and kiss and congratulated him on his first walk after the operation.

Angie got on the phone and called the hotel. She told Roxie about the walk, and after she hung up, Roxie started to telling everyone who was near about the walk, but most of us were gone. When we were finally all home, she was the happy bearer of wonderful news for us.

We were all extremely excited, but we agreed that Pug probably needed rest this evening, so we decided that we would wait until Sunday afternoon to go see him. I did, however, call his room to congratulate him on his accomplishment.

Sunday was a nice quiet day for everyone. We all seemed to be just sitting around reading the paper and watching television, which was something we seldom did. It seemed that all of our schedules were so hectic that we had very little time for TV or relaxation.

Later in the afternoon we all went to the hospital to observe for ourselves this great feat of walking with no help.

Wayne was so proud of himself that he was about to bust the buttons off his pajamas. Now all he could talk about was getting out of the hospital and back into the harness of the job that he had been hired to do.

Everyone kept telling him to just take it nice and slow and easy, but that wasn't his style.

I, personally, thought that in the short time he had been working with me, he had almost become a workaholic. He loved working with me and taking care of details for me. He said that it made him feel important, more important than he had ever felt in his life. He admitted that what we were doing for other people was truly exhilarating.

He said, "I really feel needed to help complete what we have started."

He admitted, "I was a little startled to see so many people had come to see about me and be with me through my ordeal."

He smiles that crooked smile at Angie and says, "This is something we will never have to worry about again as long as we live. And I admit that it is a very large load lifted off my mind. It seemed to always be lurking in the back of my mind before this happened.

"After I met Angie and we were married, I was afraid something would happen, and I would die and leave her alone. I wanted to look after her and take care of her for the rest of her life. I could never seem to shake this monkey off my back till today.

"Now that I am walking and feel wonderful with no more headaches, I feel that I can honestly say that I will be able to do what I wanted to do. I will be able to be a husband, father, and friend to my family and loved ones. I have thanked God every day since I had the operation, for letting me survive. Now I can thank Him for all the wonderful things this world has to offer me, and the things I can offer to others in this world who are less fortunate than I am.

"Now I can see that all of that time spent on the street was meant to teach me what life is really about. I can see life from both sides now, which should help me be a better person. I hope my wife and my family, when we have one, will realize that my ten years on the street was not for nothing. Now I know that when you love someone, you must do it deeply and with all your heart – no provisions, no exceptions.

"If you love, you should love without any stipulations. Love is love even if there are things you don't approve of and things you don't agree with. This should not change your love for someone. Hell, I sound like a preacher or a psychiatrist or something don't I? I don't mean it to sound that way, but I'm just so thankful for what has happened here in this hospital, the doctors and God giving me a new life."

The gang has gone home now and the waiting room is quiet. Angie finally tells Pug goodnight. She and Sid head for the hotel to try to get a good night's rest because tomorrow is going to be a full day.

Back at the hotel they find that everyone has already gone to their rooms to relax and watch TV for a while. Everyone hits the sack to get some rest and relaxation. Angie and Sid decide that it is time for them to do the same thing, so without bothering anyone they go to their rooms and relax for a while, then they too, hit the sack and got some rest.

At breakfast Cowboy comes into the restaurant looking for me to tell me he had received a call from a T.J. Burk. Cowboy had gotten Mr. Burk's name from a guy over at the stockyards.

Cowboy tells me, "They say that T.J. Burk raises some of the best rodeo stock in this part of the country. Mr. Burk called when I was not at the room, but he left a message with the desk clerk telling me that if I wanted to come out to his place this afternoon and look at some of his stock, I was more than welcome.

"He said he would be home after 2:00 p.m. He left instructions on how to get to his place, so I thought I would like to run out and see just what kind of stock this breeder of rodeo stock has. The guy at the stockyards says that it's some of the very best breeding ranches around here and that I should go out and look at it if I can find the time."

He also told to me, "If nothing else is going maybe I would like to run out to the ranch this afternoon. Maybe Sid, Johnny, and Art would like to go out with us."

These guys had become the four musketeers. It seemed that they went everywhere together. Right now they were going down to the stockyards to look at some stock. They would be back in time for the lunch meeting at the hotel.

The girls were out looking for more furnishings for Cowboy's house. They were really fixing him up well. The house was going to be really nice inside when they get it finished. They had even bought him a new desk for his office and a computer to go on top of it. They told him that he would have to go to classes to learn how to run it.

"A computer is a must now for people in the stock-breeding business. They keep all of their records on the computer, such as the bloodlines and their bookkeeping. There are special computer programs that handle nothing but blood lines and stock histories to give you all kinds of information that you might ever need. This is just the way of doing business these days."

Cowboy has agreed that he would go to night school and take classes on how to operate the computer.

After looking at the stock at the stockyards, they realized that they had spent most of the morning there, and that it is going to be time for the lunch meeting before long, so we had better get back to the meeting at the hotel.

The meeting at the Lariat Room at the hotel brought no surprises. It was just a general meeting, letting everyone know that the clinic and the club would both be opening this weekend.

"Well, not this weekend for the clinic," I added. "It will open on Monday."

We were all assured that Pug would be back with us very shortly and that he would be at the opening of the club this Saturday night.

I let them know that "Everyone is expected to be there. We want a good crowd."

Everyone agreed that they would be there.

Doc lets all of us know that he finally has all of the equipment he had ordered and that several of the pharmaceutical companies have donated medicine of different types, as well as supplies such as gauze, tape, disinfectants etc etc.

It seemed that everyone was really into the projects.

Bing tells everyon that "The band and the dancers are ready to put on a show for everyone and to give dance lessons to those who are interested in learning to swing dance." They have been rehearsing and they are very very good.

Mabel and Amber tell us that, "Shawn has the kitchen set up to handle a big crowd. We're hoping we have enough customers to eat all of the food we have ordered and are preparing."

After the financial picture was given, everyone is ready to go back to his or her work.

I enocourage all of you go ahead and head back and we will all meet Saturday night at the club."

With that Cowboy turned to Johnny, Sid, and Art and asked them if they are ready to take a ride up toward the ranch.

It turned out that T.J. Burk's place was only a couple of miles south of Cowboy's place. On the way up to the ranch, they are all wondering just what this guy raises that makes his stock so special.

Love for Cowboy

They had heard that T.J. had some of the best bucking stock around. As they drive up to the house, they noticed the drive goes on around the house to a barn and corral at the rear of the property. As they drive around, they see that someone is in the corral giving a horse a workout. They park and walk up to the fence to get a better look.

Cowboy says, "Oh, my God, guys, do you see what I see?"

Sid looks at him and knowingly says, "Cowboy, I have seen quite a few horses that looked a whole lot better than that one."

"Horses hell. I'm talking about the rider dummy. Look at the rider. It's a she, not a he. She sets that horse like someone born in the saddle. Not only that but look at that beautiful woman. I don't think I have ever seen anyone that beautiful."

As she rode the horse around the corral, they could see the beautiful wavy, raven-black hair float softly on her shoulders as the horse changed his gates from a trot, to a fox trot, to a pace. With each gate, she just seemed to float in the saddle, hardly touching it as she rode around the corral.

When she finally notices them she comes riding over to where they are standing and asks, "Can I help you?"

Cowboy was so busy looking at her that he forgets to speak, so Johnny speaks up and tells her, "We are looking for T.J. Burk."

"Well, you found her; I'm T.J. Burk."

Cowboy's lower jaw was really loose and hanging with his mouth wide open.

Johnny introduced himself along with Sid and Art, then he turns to Cowboy and tells her, "This young man is Larry Steele, better known as Cowboy to his friends." He nudges Cowboy. Say hello to the Lovely Lady cowboy.

He finally comes out of his trance and embarassingly says, "I'm sorry Miss, but I was expecting a man, not a beautiful lady."

Those dark eyes, that dark hair, and that olive complexion along with her ability to ride a horse the way she did had completely mesmerized him.

She smiled and held her hand out for him to shake it. The only thing he could think of now was how those beautiful dark eyes reminded him of a girl he had fallen in love with when he had been in the fifth grade. She also had beautiful dark eyes that had shined and sparkled when she was happy. He hadn't thought of her in twenty years. He took her hand and stood there holding it, looking at her.

She finally took it from him and asked, "What can I do for you?"

Cowboy finally came out of his daze and explained that one of the boys down at the stockyards told him that she raised bucking stock for rodeos.

"Yes, I do. I raise rodeo stock since my father passed away about three years ago. He left me the ranch and stock. I have no brothers or sisters, so I just happened to be the one who inherited the place and the stock. My mother died when I was very young, and I hardly knew her.

"One of the guys from the stockyards called and told me that he gave a guy my name the other day, and he thought you would be getting in touch with me about some stock.

"Cowboy, are you a rider?"

"Well, I used to be when I was a few years younger. I got hurt real bad just before the National Finals Rodeo about seven years ago. I never got back into the saddle for competition after that."

"Too bad that you had to have something like that happen just when you were about to hit the big time."

"Yeah I agree, but I'm doing fine now. I have a place just a couple of miles up the road near the river. I bought the old Carpenter spread."

"Oh, yeah, I know that place. They have a nice little house, good barn and corral, with some good grazing, real good water from the spring. What do you plan on doing with it?"

"Well, I'm hoping to raise some rodeo stock like you're doing if I can find some good breeding stock."

When she looked back at him, he saw those beautiful dark eyes smiling even when she had a frown on her face. He had just never seen anyone so beautiful in his life. She would, as a horse breeder would say, stand about fifteen hands high, and she had the body of a show horse: straight back, good shoulders, fine hind quarters, great chest, and it was easy to see that she had good breeding.

Cowboy followed her around the barn and stock pens as she showed off some of her breeding stock, plus she had a few more out behind the barn. She had some real good-looking bulls and mother cows as well as some nice fillies and a couple of studs that she said she could be talked into selling if the right price could be agreed upon.

They visit for a while just talking and getting to know each other without even mentioning the animals.

Sid, Art, and Johnny just start looking around for themselves, while T.J. and Cowboy got better acquainted.

After a while Cowboy told her about himself, and he told her about the opening of the club on Saturday night. He asked, "Would you be interested in going to the opening with me? I know we have just met, but I promise to be a good boy, and I know you will like my friends."

Surprisingly she said, "I would love to go with you. I haven't been out for an evening in a long time. Since I have to look after the cattle myself I don't go out much. My hired hand got sick and has gone to live with his sister in Oklahoma so she can look after him till he gets back on his feet. I haven't found anyone to help me out since he left."

Cowboy asked, "Would it be all right if I come over Saturday afternoon and help you with the cattle so you can be free for the evening?"

"Cowboy, that's a wonderful idea. Why don't you come over early, and we will have lunch here. After we get the work done, you can run up to your place and get dressed, and then come back by and pick me up, and we'll go to the club."

Cowboy asks her, "Before you came home to run the ranch, what kind of work did you do?"

"I hope you won't hold it against me, but I was a school teacher. I taught fourth grade children and loved every minute of it. After Dad died, I just didn't have any choice but to come home and take over this place and try to make it pay. I was raised here, and Daddy had me on a horse by the time I was two years old. I love being here with the animals.

"What is important to me is that I love children also. I had hoped to have a good hand to run the ranch. That way I could have time to get a job teaching here in either the Sherman or Denison school districts. Since my hired hand left, I haven't had much luck finding anyone I could trust to handle the stock. They have to be handled properly, or they won't be worth much as bucking stock.

"We have a good reputation for breeding good rodeo stock, and I would like to keep it that way."

"T.J., I like the way you think. After we get to know each other better, maybe I could help you find someone to help you here at the place?"

"That would be fine, Larry, or would you rather I called you Cowboy?"

He kind of blushed and says, "You call me just anything you want to call me."

She smiled and said, "I kind of like the name Larry. I used to have an uncle named Larry, and he was one of my favorites, so if it's all right with you, I'll call you Larry."

"Larry it is then, T.J. By the way, what does the T.J. stand for?"

"Well, Larry, T.J. stands for Tracy Jean, but most folks just call me T.J. because that's what my father always called me. You can call me which ever you prefer."

Cowboy laughed and said, "I kind of like T.J. if you don't mind."

She assures him. "You can call me whichever you choose."

By this time Cowboy had seen most all of her stock, which he admitted was really fine-looking stock. "The big thing will be when I see them buck. Some bulls and horses are just mean and love to buck. They are bred that way; on the other hand, some of them just don't want to buck, regardless of what you do to them."

The other guys came around the barn and asked, "Cowboy, are you about ready to head for town, it's getting late?"

He says good-bye to T.J., tells her that he will see her later and joins the others. They head back to Ft. Worth. They were no more than out of the drive when they started to hoorah Cowboy.

Johnny started with, "Boy, did you see Cowboy's eyes when he saw that lady?

"Cowboy, I'll bet that is the prettiest cowboy you have ever seen."

Sid chimed in with a bit of his own. "I'll bet you never saw a cowboy like that on a bucking bull."

Cowboy just grinns. "Well, I'll tell you guys one thing. I got a date with her for Saturday night to go to the club. Now go ahead and laugh if you really want to, but you know that you're just jealous."

Finding such a beautiful girl as a breeder of rodeo stock is totally unbelievable. Not only that, but she was found right here, right within two miles of my own home.

Back at the hotel Cowboy dropped the guys off and heads back to his ranch to see what the ladies had done to his house today.

When he arrived, he found that he had a whole house full of furniture. It was beautiful but now he was going to have to learn to use his new vacuum cleaner. He found that the girls had done a beautiful job and had gone back to the hotel before he got home.

He had his beautiful leather couch and easy chair, the desk and office furniture in his third bedroom. Cowboy had just never thought that he would ever have a home like this.

He had never told anyone where he had come from or how he had grown up. He guessed they had just always thought he had grown up on a ranch somewhere, and they had never given it much more thought than that.

The story as he finally told me was that he had grown up in a small town in Arizona. The town was called Snowflake, and they really had seen a lot of snow.

Snowflake was just north of Phoenix. When he had been just a small boy, his father and mother had been killed in an auto accident. After the accident, a rancher friend of the family had taken him home to raise.

The rancher raised Cowboy as his own son, sending him to school and making sure he got an education. Cowboy had gone to a college where they had a rodeo program. While he was there, he had become extremely adept at riding bulls and broncos.

He had been on his way to the top and to the National Finals Rodeo when he had gotten trapped in a chute by a bull that had almost killed him.

When he had gotten out of the hospital, he found that he had lost his nerve. He tried to ride a few more times, but each time he would get the shakes just before he would get into the chute with the animal. He had finally become disgusted with himself, and went on a big drunk that lasted almost seven years.

Now that he was finally sober and on his way again, he said that he would never take another drink again as long as he lived.

Back at the hospital, Pug was doing real well today. Today he went for another walk up and down the hall with the help of a nurse and Angie. Pug had made up his mind that he was going to be walking a long way before long. He was also absolutely sure that he was going to the opening of the Swinging Years Club on Saturday night.

That was the greatest news the gang has had in a long time.

Meanwhile, back at the club Shawn, Mabel, and Amber were getting the kitchen ready for the big opening. Bing and the band and the dancers were rehearsing so they would be able to give the customers a good show and a lot of real good swinging years music.

Back at the clinic, people found Doc working all day and a big part of the night with the volunteer help. He had hired some office help, and they had finally set up the computers to handle the business books and information on their supplies. They had to have that operating so they always knew just how much medicine they had on hand and all of the pertinant information on the patients.

Dr. Davis and a couple of other doctors had been there all day setting up procedures to be used. The doctors were all volunteers, and that would tell people one thing about the people in Ft. Worth.

Along with the volunteer doctors, there were several volunteer nurses such as Linda, who had been helping Doc for several weeks now. They would be ready for their opening this coming Monday.

The rest of the week everyone was doing his or her little thing to get everything off to a good start.

Now that Cowboy had found some breeding stock, he could start moving in the right direction to get his business off the group and going.

Pam and I had been talking about going back to Chicago before very long. It seemed that we had most everything set up and going. We had some wonderful people to look after everything, such as Bill Bartlett to look after the legal end of the businesses that had been started.

There was Charley Johnson who had helped so much on all of the different programs they had started. Charley was now on the Board of Directors for the clinic and also on the Board of Directors for the Swinging Years Club. Charley had decided that he was going to take retirement before too long and accept the job I had offered him.

I wanted to make one more trip to the plant over in Dallas before I go home. I wanted to find out if they had done anything about my request to start the scholarship program again.

Pam thought her mother and dad were about ready to go back home to Norfolk for a while. The big thing we were all waiting for now was to see how Pug did during the rehabilitation program for the next week or two.

Pam had been more tired lately than she had been when we had first reached Texas. She said, "I guess I need some vitamins."

I asked Johnny and Art if they would you like to go back over to the Dallas plant with me so we can visit with the manager and see just how things are going? I need to see if they have done anything about the scholarship program that I suggested they look into."

They were both interested in going with me, especially since Art had not been to the plant here in Texas. We loaded up and headed for the plant, leaving all of the rest to do their thing to get ready for

Saturday night and for the clinic opening on Monday morning.

When we arrived, the receptionist recognized us and suggested we have a seat while she called Mr. Kountz and let him know we were there. She made the call and informed Mr. Kountz that we were waiting in the reception room. She informs us, "He will be right with you."

Presently, Mr. Kountz came walking down the hall toward the reception area with his hand extended to me. We exchanged pleasantries, and I introduced him to Art, telling Art, "This is our Texas manager, Mr. Gene Kountz. He has been with the company for quite a few years, and he was well acquainted with my father.

"Gene, Art is my father-in-law."

Gene turns and greets everyone. He shakes hands with them and asked if Johnny had been able to see the Rangers play when they had been here a couple of months ago.

"Not only did I see them play, but I got to meet Pudge; I also got his autograph. I turned around from our box, and I saw Pudge and his family sitting in a box just a little way up the steps from us. I was a little hesitant, but I finally did go on up to where he was sitting and I asked him I could bother him for his autograph. He was the nicest person you ever met. We talked for a while, and just before I left, he asked me for my phone number in Chicago. I was totally floored, but I gave it to him, and he actually told me that next year when he comes to Chicago to play the Sox, he will call me. I will wait and see about that, but if he is half as nice as he seemed to be, I would bet you that he calls me. I sure hope he does."

I ask "Gene, do you have time for a cup of coffee so we can visit for a few minutes?"

He led us to the break room where a young lady had just finished making fresh coffee. We all sat down and had a cup of coffee.

Gene, "Have you had time to look into the scholarship program we talked about on my last visit?"

Yes Jim, "We took the idea up at our last meeting of the Board, and we decided to check back to where we had left off before. We found the names of the teachers and others that had been involved in the program. I contacted them myself and found that they were very interested in getting the program started again. They came over to the company and met with the new Scholarship Committee, and they now have the program ready to go.

"They have even received applications for the scholarships, which will be reviewed in time for a decision to made before the next semester resumes.

"They are looking at scholarships for four students. Each Scholarship will be worth $25,000 a year for four years if they keep their grades up. If they want Graduate school, we will help them there also just as long as they keep the grades up and their nose clean.

"I had the accountants look into the possibility of writing off a part of the cost of these scholarships, and we found that we could write them off at a hundred percent. That was the when point we decided to go from two scholarships to four. We hope you don't object to us going to four instead of two." Hell no Gene, I sure don't mind if you go to six as far as I was concerned. "I told you before how much these scholarship programs mean to me."

This made Gene feel very good. We discussed things a little more about the business. I found that they were turning a very nice profit, and they had just secured two more nice contracts from the government which would increase our overall net profit picture for the year, and that would make our stock go up. This was great news for the company.

I asked Art and Johnny if they were ready to head back to Ft. Worth. They both agreed, and we said our good-byes and headed back to the hotel.

On our way back to the hotel, I ask Johnny if Pam has mentioned feeling tired to him?"

"It's funny you should ask about that, Dad, because the other day when she and Jenny got back to the hotel from a shopping spree, she went straight to her room to lie down. It seemed that she was a little more tired than usual. What's the matter Dad? You think something is wrong with Mother?"

"No, no I don't really think there is anything wrong with her; I just feel that she ought to slow down a little bit. She isn't used to running like this."

"Dad, are you kidding? A woman who worked as a waitress in a restaurant like the Black Angus can work you and me both under the table.

"You know, Dad, I have noticed that she has changed her eating habits a little bit. She doesn't seem to be eating as much as she used to eat. I just think that all of the excitement of the things you're doing has her so hyped up that she just isn't eating properly or getting enough rest."

"Johnny, I think you're probably right. I guess I was just jumping at shadows. You know how I worry about her. I just want to be sure that nothing ever happens to her."

Dad, she is going to be just fine. Now let's get back to the hotel so we can have some lunch, I'm starved.

Art agreed with that and said, "I would like a big hearty hamburger for lunch today, with a glass of tea.

We all laughed and headed for that big Texas Burger place just up the street from the hotel.

Back at the hospital Pug was getting another walking lesson, and he was doing real fine with it. He was walking down the hall and back for the second time.

Dr. Schug came by and stopped to talk to him. "Wayne, if you don't stop walking so much we may have to send you home in a week or so. I just couldn't believe that you have been up and walking for the last couple of days. I made a quick trip to Houston, and when I got back, they told me you have been up and walking all over the place. I just couldn't believe it. I am real proud of you.

"You know that you are one of the very few who has ever survived this type of operation, let alone done as well as soon as you have. I'm very proud of you and your strong desire to get back on your feet and back to work. I have a feeling that Professor is going to be proud of you too. I'll bet that beautiful wife of yours is one happy lady. You guys will be able to go back to Chicago before long.

"As far as I'm concerned Pug, I can go back to Houston and leave you in the hands of Dr. Davis and Dr. Bates. They are two of the finest doctors I have ever worked with. I have worked with Dr. Davis for the past twenty years, and I have found him to be one of the most honest and knowledgeable physicians I have ever known and been associated with.

I'm sure you have found him to be the same way.

"I understand that he's working with a friend of yours in opening a clinic for the homeless and needy people of the community. I think you will be back doing your part within a couple of weeks. Just remember not to over do it until you have time to get your strength back.

"If you can promise me that, I can go back to Houston without worrying about you. I'm going to trust you to use good judgment. I have a feeling that your wife will help keep you on the straight and narrow." Pug walked over to Dr. Schug and put his arms around his shoulders and really hugs him real hard. "I really appreciate what you did in saving my life. Dr. Davis told me you were one of the very few doctors who had done this particular operation with success. I am just thankful that he knew you, and that you weren't too busy to come to Ft. Worth and do the operation for me. I just wish there was some way for me to pay you back for what you've done for me and my family. But, how do you repay someone who has saved your life? You know I would do anything I could for you if you ever need anything. I know that sounds a little weird, but, Dr. Schug, you know what I mean, and that my family and I will always be indebted to you. I hope you will do us the honor of calling us and coming to see us if you ever get to Chicago.

"I know it sounds a little corny, but since I had the operation, I always say a prayer before I go to sleep, and in that prayer I thank the Lord for your being here when I needed you so much. I will continue to always include you and your family in all of my prayers.

"I didn't used to be a very religious person even though I was raised in a good religious family. You have changed all of that.

"Now I believe that everyone has been put on this earth for a purpose. Now that you saved my life, I just have to find that purpose and try to fulfill that purpose because I know God saved my life with you as His instrumentfor some reason. Now it's up to me to find that reason and show Him that I was worth saving."

"Pug, I don't think anyone has ever said thanks so eloquently as you have just done, and I will never forget it.

"Young man, I can promise that you and I will be good friends as long as we live. When you come back to Texas, you be sure to call me. I am going to give you my home phone number, and I want you to use it. I would like for you to meet my family, and for them to meet you and that wonderful wife of yours.

"Now I must be leaving because I have patients in Houston who need me, and I know you wouldn't want to hold me up from taking care of them." Dr. Schug gave Pug a big hug and told him that he would never forget him and that he would be looking forward to seeing him again when he was feeling better.

"So long, Dr.Schug, and God bless you."

As Dr. Schug walked away, there were tears rolling down the cheeks of both men.

The Grand Openings

The rest of the week went by slowly even though everyone wasworking as fast as we could to be ready for the grand opening of the Swinging Years Club on Saturday night, followed by the grand opening of the clinic on Monday morning.

Bing had been working his rear end off rehearsing the band and the dancers and making sure the sound systems were just exactly the way he wanted them to be. He wanted good sound, but he was extremely picky about having any echo or reverb in any part of the building during performances. He said that it could cause problems with the vocalist, of which he would be one.

Feedback was the other thing he was very picky about. He absolutely hated to hear a microphone squeal or squeak. That was the sign of a beginner in the sound business, and he certainly wasn't that. After all of these years in the business, he had become a perfectionist and had to have everything just perfect.

Bing told us, "I wish you could hear that band. You would think it was Glenn Miller's or Artie Shaw's band. These old timers, along with the few younger musicians, really have that swinging years feel for the music they are playing.

"If you hear them and think they are great, then you should see the dancers. They are absolutely fascinating when you watch them do the New Yorker, the swing, and the jitterbugging that you would have seen in the early 1940's at the Hollywood Palladium or the Stagedoor Canteen in San Francisco.

"Another thing that makes it seem so great is that Hattie McKinney criticizes everything that doesn't seem to be just right. The band and the dancers get a big bang out of her. I think they have all formed a mutual admiration society, while all of this is going on inside the ballroom on that beautiful newly finished dance floor and on the band stage.

"Shawn Griggers, along with Mabel and Amber, are making sure their supplies are ample for a large crowd of customers tonight. They are checking and double-checking everything with the new waiters and waitress. They are having what is basically a dress rehearsal. The waiters and waitresses are all dressed up in early 1940's costumes and dress of the times. The girls look especially cute with their poodle skirts, white blouses, and beehive hairdos.

"The maître d' is dressed in an original 1940's zoot suit. The waist on the pants comes up under the armpits, while the legs on the pants are about twenty-two inches around the knees, and at the ankles they are only about seven inches wide. The coat comes down to the knees and has some of the biggest shoulder pads you ever saw on a suit. Top that off with the black and white wing-tip shoes and the hat that has a flat top with a three-and-a-half-inch brim with a big feather sticking out of the band. Topping it off is the four-foot long, heavy-duty watch chain that drops below the knees and fastens to the vest. If you think he isn't a sight to behold, you are mistaken.

"Charley Johnson has talked a couple of traffic cops into coming out and handling the parking lot tomorrow night. They will have free valet service tomorrow night, but I swear that it will be the last time they have free valet parking. But, who knows what is going to happen if the public brings pressure to bear.

"Bob Hitch put a real nice pitch in the paper yesterday and again today. He even got a friend of his from the Dallas paper to put a small spread in it. His friends came out and shot a few pictures of the dress rehearsal this afternoon, and they will run them on the five o'clock television news tonight. Apparently someone from one of the stations in Dallas didn't want to be scooped on an opening such as this, and they came over and got some pictures also.

"They wanted to get some background on the people behind this whole thing. I have a feeling they will be contacting you, Jim, since they found out there would be an opening of the People's Clinic on Monday. It's kind of like Bob said earlier, once the people find out what this is all about and how it got started, there might be a lot of people who would like to become involved in it.

"There are a lot of ways people can help in all of the work done both at the club and the clinic. Most of the help will be at the clinic because it is a nonprofit program.

"Yesterday, there was a story in Ft. Worth's paper about the club, and the phone started ringing off the walls. I bought several advertisements in the Dallas paper as well as the Ft. Worth paper, and as a result, it has become well known. I even bought spots on the radio in Dallas and Ft. Worth, which are being played several times a day.

"As a result of all of this advertising and free press, the club is totally booked up for tomorrow night. There have been a lot of calls after finding we were sold out; some folks just want to just go to the bar and have a drink and watch the dancers and listen to the band. I told them that that would be all right just as long as the fire marshal doesn't complain about us having too many people in the club. Some of the young people want to watch and see if they can maybe get a dance lesson from the dancers. They seem very interested in learning to do the jitterbugging." Bing just went on and on in his enthusiasm for the club.

The interior decorations were really something to see. Hattie McKinney and a couple of her friends who were interior decorators had helped her find the proper decorations for the club. This had really tickled Bing. He dearly loved the way the club had turned out.

The Peoples Clinic was busy with Doc and Linda and a couple of her friends working hard to get everything ready for Monday morning. They had the beds, tables, cabinets, and everything they needed for six examination rooms. They had one room that would be used primarily for emergencies such as broken bones or bad cuts and bruises that could be handled at the clinic. They didn't want to take any revenue away from the hospitals. Anyone that had Medicare or medical insurance needed to go to the hospitals because they would handle the paperwork for them. Here at the clinic, they would not be handling any kind of paperwork except the medical paperwork.

The clinic was beautiful inside. The rooms were all a beautiful soft pastel shade, and they didn't look like a normal clinic or hospital. Doc had seen the Scottish Rite Children's Orthopedic Hospital in Dallas, and that was the way it was decorated – no drab white colors for them. This would make people feel a lot better when they came into the building. The Scottish Rite Children's Hospital had been painted this way for years. They had found it put the children at ease much quicker.

There was just one thing that people couldn't understand, and that was why they were keeping the sign on the building covered.

Doc said, "It is because we don't want anyone coming in for treatment before we are open."

The rest of us thought he had another reason.

There were already two doctors from the hospital who had signed up to work on opening day Monday. There was a list of doctors from hospitals around town that had volunteered for duty for the next three weeks, at which time they would make a new schedule.

There were several nurses who had come in and/or called to offer their help and had left times when they could work. It was truly amazing what people would do to help the needy.

Doc had trouble believing all of these people were wanting to help just out of the goodness of their hearts. Doc would have to wake up and realize that there were a lot of wonderful people in this world. Many had told him that since he was donating his time and efforts to get this thing rolling, they felt that the least they could do was to help out also.

Saturday morning our entire group was having breakfast together downstairs in the restaurant, and all of the conversation was about opening the club tonight.

Pam said, "Jim, we should have gone to a costume shop and rented some forties costumes for tonight."

I looked at her and said, "I'm not about to be caught dead in one of those zoot suits."

Johnny started laughing and said, "I think you would look real cutein one of those suits, Dad."

I said, "There is no way you're going to get me into one of those monkey suits."

After breakfast we contacted Bing to see if there was anything those at the club might need a little help with before the crowd got there tonight.

Bing said, "Rest assured, everything is in good shape."

Then we contacted Doc to see if he needed any help.

He assured us that they were just about as ready as they could be, so they really didn't need any help at this time either. They just wanted everyone to be on time for the opening Monday morning at 9:00 a.m.

We promised we would be there.

Club Opening Night

Time went by slowly as usual because we were waiting for something good to come along. It was finally getting near 6:30 p.m., and we were all getting ready to go to the club.

Everyone was all dressed up in fine shape when we headed out the door. The ladies were lovely, and we men were, well, I guess you might say, we were just men all dressed up fit to kill.

It took us about twenty minutes to reach the club out on Camp Bowie Road. As we approached the area where the nightclub was, we saw spotlights flashing through the moonlit night. When we arrived, we found that Hattie had ordered two big spotlights to shine up into the beautiful moonlight to let people know just where the club was located.

Above the club was a beautiful neon sign flashing the Swinging Years Club. Below the name, it offered dinner with entertainment from the 40's and 50's. We found we were not the first ones there by any means. There must already have been ten cars in the parking lot. There were the two policemen acting as parking lot attendants, and there were a couple of young men acting as valet parking attendants.

Wow, what a way to open the club. The young men opened the doors for the ladies and helped them out, and then they gave us numbers for our cars, and they took them to the parking lot.

We all headed for the front door where a very nice young man, acting as doorman, opened the door and greeted us. He welcomed us to the opening of the club with a little momento for the ladies and the gentlemen.

There in all his glory stood Bing all dressed up in his tuxedo. Boy did he look sharp.

We glanced around the room, and several tables were already full of people who were having cocktails. The waitresses were all very pretty with their full poodle skirts and their beehive hairdos. The bar had several people sitting and visiting with the bartender and other patrons.

The maître d' approached in all his splendor with his floppy felt hat with the feather and three-and-a-half-inch brim. The zoot suit looked as though it had come directly out of a fashion magazine for the musicians of the 1940's.

Big wide shoulders on this little fellow and the waist of the pants coming up under his armpits really made him something to stare at. He took us up front near the dance floor where we wouldn't have anyone seated in front of us. Bing had told him that we were his special friends, and we were to be treated royally. There was also another table on the other side of the dance floor reserved.

After about five minutes, the waiter came to the table and took our order for drinks. We had plenty of time to just lazily sip on the drinks before ordering our dinner. We leisurely ordered dinner.

Bing had arranged a long table to accommodate all of the gang, including the people like Bill Bartlett and wife, Charley Johnson and wife, Dr. David Davis and wife, Dr. Bill Bates, Wayne Gregory and wife, along with Art, Nora, Sid, and June, and all of the rest of the people connected with the program.

After about twenty minutes, the door opened, and I heard some applause and turned to see Pug and Angie coming in the door. The applause was from all of Pug's friends at the club. Pug was in the wheelchair, and Angie was pushing him. The entire table stood and started applauding as he and Angie approached the table.

When they were about fifteen feet away, he told Angie to stop. He locked the wheels on the wheelchair, stood, and started walking toward the table on his own.

The applause really increased now. He walked straight to the chair while the maître d' took the wheelchair and placed it close by, near the wall yet out of the way, but close, in case it was needed.

Pug and Angie had a seat, and the conversation really started to fly. Everyone was wanting to know how he was feeling and how long he had been walking, and a million other questions.

They were ready to order their dinner along with the rest of our crowd. Some had already ordered theirs. We all decided to order something different just to see just how good the new chef really was. In a couple of minutes, the chef, Shawn Griggers, came out of the kitchen and over to the table and asked the group if there were any special instructions to go with our orders. He explained that they wanted everything to be exactly the way the customer wanted it tonight. "This being our opening night, I want everything to be perfect."

By now there were a lot of tables occupied. He stopped by every table to chat just a moment with all of the customers and ask questions. This seemed to really go over big with the people who had come for dinner tonight.

After he had made the rounds, we noticed that the curtain on the stage had been drawn, and we heard a little commotion behind it. At the same time, we turned to see five or six couples come in the front door and stop to talk to the maître d'.

The maître d' very politely asked them to please follow him to their table. He led them to the table on the opposite side of the dance floor that had the reserved sign on it.

As they were seated, I saw Hattie get out of her chair and head for the table. At that same instant Bill Bartlett got up from his chair and headed for the table also. They arrived simultaneously. It seemed that the new occupants of the table were the Ft. Worth mayor and wife, along with four councilmen and their wives. They visited with Hattie and Bill for a short time.

Bill turned to the table where the others and I were sitting. He motioned to me and asked me to bring Pam over as he wanted to introduce us to the mayor, his wife, and the councilmen and their wives.

Pam and I walked over to the table, and Bill introduced everyone.

When he was through, Hattie asked, "Are the mayor and the county commissioners going to make it tonight?"

"There are going to be at least two of them and their wives later in the evening," Bill said.

After the introductions, we returned to our seats, and in a few minutes Bing appeared center stage with a spotlight on him. He introduced himself as the new owner of the club and welcomed everyone this evening. He said, "I would like to ask you if you like the way the club is decorated?"

Everyone applauded loudly. When the applause had died down, he said, "I really didn't have much to do with the decorations, but a certain lady in the room did have a lot to do with the decorations with the help of some of her friends."

The spotlight then moved to a table near the back where four lovely ladies were seated. He asked them to stand so he could introduce them to the audience.

"The first lady I would like for you to meet is kind of like a silent partner in the club. She, of course, like most women, is sometimes not so silent."

The crowd loved this.

Bing then introduced Mrs. Hattie McKinney. He then introduced the other three ladies and told them how much he appreciated all they had done to help in getting the club ready to open and how lovely the interior decorating was. There was great applause for the ladies and their skills as interior decorators.

He next asked, "Would the spot operator swing the light around to the long table at the front on the west side of the dance floor?"

They swung the light around to our table, and then he asked, "Would all of you please stand while I introduce you?"

I tried to stop him from introducing us, but Bing was insistent. "Please, folks, may I have your attention? Professor Jim Dixon is the sole reason I am here tonight opening this club. Beside Jim is his wife Pam, and I guess you might say she is the brains behind the club along with people like Hattie McKinney. The remainder of the table will not be introduced because that would take too long, and I know you would rather hear some of the beautiful dinner music by the Swinging Years Club band.

"After dinner you will be the recipients of some real swinging years music and dancing, but for now let's just give a great big welcome to the dinner music of the Swinging Years Club band."

The curtain opened to the music of "Moonlight Serenade." The applause was loud and appreciative. The leader came to the microphone. "I hope you like the music this evening, and if any of you have requests for music from the Swinging Years, please stop by, and we will be glad to receive them. We know most of the tunes, but occasionally there will be one we don't know. But, if that happens, we will be glad to substitute.

"If anyone wants to dance while you are waiting on dinner, please feel free to do so."

With that they continued with "Moonlight Serenade."

When they started the second tune, I asked Pam, "Would you like to dance?"

She accepted the invitation readily. We headed for the floor, and while we were dancing, several other couples joined us.

Just before the tune was over, I glanced at the front door, and there stood Cowboy in all his splendor in a new suit, dress shirt, and tie. Boy, did he look sharp. I also saw why Cowboy looked so sharp. I nudged Pam, and she turned to see this very lovely creature holding onto Cowboy's arm as they left the door and moved toward the table where everyone was seated. By now the entire table was looking back at them.

When they reached the end of the table, various men at the table were rising and speaking to Cowboy and acknowledging the young lady.

When things kind of settled down, Cowboy said loudly, "I would like for everyone to meet Miss T.J. Burk. T.J., believe it or not, is the cattle breeder that I went to buy cattle from earlier this week. Her ranch is only a couple of miles down the road from mine. By the way," he declared, "you can either call her T.J., or her name is Tracy Jean. She will come regardless of which name you call her.

"Now, T.J., I would like to introduce you to these people." Cowboy started with Pam and me, and then he went around the table all the way to Pug and Angie.

When he saw Pug, he left T.J. for a second and said, "Excuse me, please, for just a minute."

He walked around to Pug, and when Pug stood up, he couldn't believe it. He reached over and hugged Pug, and then he patted him on the head, and said, "Well, hell, Pug, I just knew you'd be here."

He turned to T.J. who, by the way, was dressed in a white embroidered lacy dress that really made her features stand out – if you know what I mean. Her beautiful black hair and eyes could almost hypnotize you. She was certainly as beautiful as the boys had said she was.

It was kind of like Johnny had said when he said, "I never had any school teacher that looked like her."

Cowboy told her, "This is one of my closest friends and his wife, Mr. and Mrs. Wayne McKenzie, better known as Pug."

After he had introduced everyone, he helped T.J. with her chair, and as he did, Pam nudged me and said, "Don't tell me that young man doesn't have manners; his manners seem to be as good as anyone's here at the table."

I agreed.

When the band played the next tune, Johnny came over to Pam and said, "Mother, would you have this dance with me?"

This was a great and pleasant surprise to Pam. She gladly got up from her chair and danced with her new son.

I then asked, "Angie, would you do me the honor of having this dance?"

Pug said, "That will be just fine since I'm not really able to dance at this time."

Then came the big surprise when Bing went to the table where Hattie and her three friends were seated and asked her to please dance with him.

She smiled broadly and turned to the other ladies and said, "I told you he had manners." With that they headed for the dance floor.

By this time the dance floor was beginning to be just a little bit crowded because the people were really flocking in.

Our dinner was ready to be served, so all of us at the big table left the dance floor and were seated.

The waiters and waitresses served the dinners. There were about twenty people at the table, and there must have been at least fourteen different entrées ordered. The gang started to taste this and taste that from each other's plates to see just how good this new chef was.

I tasted my food and said, "Man, this guy is great."

Everything he served, from a fillet steak to a steak Dianne or Lobster, Oyster Bienville, Oyster on the half shell, to even a Mountain Trout with the eyes staring at us, was delicious. He served up a beautiful Beef Stroganoff. He even had some sort of casserole made up of several types of sea foods.

After we had tasted of each other's dishes, no one could find anything to complain about. The food was excellent, as was the dessert. The pies were out of this world, as were the ice cream desserts. They even had several different types of mocha to offer along with about a half dozen types of regular coffee. This chef must have really gotten an education while he had been working at that fancy restaurant in New Orleans.

By the time dinner was over, everyone was literally stuffed too much to feel like dancing.

Jitterbug, Anyone?

Since everyone seemed to be just about through with eating dinner, Bing went to the bandstand and took the mike.

"Ladies and gentlemen, at this time we would like to give the band a short break. Some of these gentlemen aren't as young as they used to be, and they may have weak kidneys, so why don't we give them about fifteen minutes to relax while you finish your desserts?"

With that the curtain was drawn, and the spotlight turned off.

Bing went on to say, "This is a no-smoking club, so anyone wanting to smoke will have to retire outside for their smokes."

A few of the men retired outside to smoke.

After a while they returned to the club, and by now most people had finished their desserts.

Bing looked at his watch and walked slowly toward the stage. He peeked behind the curtain, and apparently the band was coming back to the stage.

Knowing that, the spotlight was again turned on him. He says Ladies and Gentlemen, "You now have a real treat in store for you. If you have seen the young folks from the forties and fifties in the newsreels, you have seen them doing a dance called the jitterbug.

"Well, the jitterbug is a combination of several dances that, during the late 1930's and the early 1940's, the young folks rolled all into one. Jitterbug dancing has some of the New Yorker, the swing step, and other dance steps that are sometimes originated by the dancers.

"The kids who jitterbug throw a lot of their own imagination into the dance. Some even get a little wild from time to time with their dancing. Some will just show you how to do the New Yorker or the swing step.

"At this time, I would like to introduce you to the Swinging Years Club dancers doing the New Yorker first and then the swing, and then they will go right into the real old jitterbug dancing – each with a style of their own."

With that Bing turns to the leader of the band and asks, "Buddy, how about a little 'String of Pearls'?"

With that the band struck up "String of Pearls," one of the best swing dancing tunes ever written.

With that six young folks came onto the floor. They are wearing costumes reminiscent of the World War II years. They begin to dance, and the audience goes wild with their applause every time they did something fancy.

When they had gone through the New Yorker a couple of times, they go into the regular swing step, which was similar to the New Yorker with a few subtle changes. Again the audience applauds wildly. They go through this routine a couple of times, and then the band really started to swing it with "Tippin In," which was another of the very great jitterbug tunes.

With that the boys started throwing the girls over their heads, between their legs, and several other ways. They get real "loosy goosy" jitterbugging. Jitterbugging lets the dancer use a lot of his imagination in making up his steps.

The audience goes absolutely wild with this one, and they just continued to applaud. When the band concluded "Tippin In," the dancers all line up and bow to the audience who were now standing and applauding.

At this point, Bing comes to the microphone again and tells the audience, "If anyone would like to learn to do these dances, the dancers will be glad to teach you right now, right here, on this dance floor."

With that Johnny goes over to his sister Jenny, takes her hand, and says come on little sister, "Come with me so we can learn to do this kind of dancing."

They were one of the first couples on the floor.

When others saw them, they also get up and come on up to the dance floor. We look across the floor, and the mayor and his wife both walk out onto the floor.

Now these folks were no spring chickens, but they were willing to try, and they hollered at a couple of the councilmen and their wives to "Come on over and join in the fun."

Other couples decided if the mayor could do this, they would try also. Before long, there were about ten or twelve men and about that many women out on the dance floor ready to learn to jitterbug.

With that, the dancers started lining everyone up and talking to them. They went through the basics with them and answered a lot of questions. In a little while one of the boys turned to Buddy, the bandleader, and said, "Start on String of Pearls Buddy at about half time while we get the people started."

This went on for a while, and when everyone seemed to be learning what was happening, he turned to Buddy and said, "Now, how about three-quarter time?"

With that Buddy and the band picked up the tempo.

It was amazing, but most all of them were doing real fine. Of course, there were always one or two who had three left feet. In these cases, one of the girls took this guy or that lady to the side for some personal instruction.

Everyone was really getting into it now, and that was just when the television station camera crew came in and set up their cameras. They let them roll while the students were learning.

After about three or four minutes, one of the dancers turned to Buddy and called for the music to stop. He announced to the people who had come up to learn to dance that they were just about ready for the real thing. He again turned to Buddy and said, "How about full tempo this time, and let's see just how much these students have learned."

With that, Buddy and the band struck up "String of Pearls" at full tempo. The camera crew had already recognized the mayor and the councilmen and their wives. They turned the cameras on them along with the other dancers, but they spent more time on the mayor and councilmen and their wives than they did on the other dancers.

The dancers with their partners and the other dancers who had paired off were starting to really get into this swing dancing thing. Each of the dancers went to the audience and chose one of the audience to be their partners, which really worked out great. The television cameras were going full glare on them as they danced. It was amazing, but almost all of them had learned the basic steps and were doing a great job at full tempo.

The crowd started applauding, and in a little while, the crowd was actually standing and applauding as they watched the people dance. At that time, we saw the camera crew turn the cameras on the crowd, and they were catching the reaction of the crowd to this type of music and dancing.

When the tune was through, everyone was applauding, and the student dancers were going back to their seats. The leader of the dancers went to the microphone and invited others to come up and learn the dance at this time.

More of the audience joined in on the fun. All the while the TV cameras were rolling and catching all of this. What publicity! Publicity like this was hard to buy, let alone get for free.

This routine continued for the next hour or so. Finally, the dancers admitted that they were exhausted, but when they did, the leader went back up to the microphone and told everyone, "We will be here at the club five nights a week. We will not be here on Monday or Tuesday evenings. We will, however, be here every other night of the week, and we will be more than happy to give you dancing lessons.

"Now, ladies and gentlemen, if I may, I would like to call Mr. Bing Horton to the microphone and ask him if he would be kind enough to do a couple of ballads for you to kind of change the pace a little."

With that Bing came to the stage. Bing said to the audience, "I have a request from one of my friends at this big front table. He would like for me to dedicate this first tune to his wife. He feels that it is a rather fitting title for a very sophisticated lady. With that, he dedicated the song "Sophisticated Lady" to Pam.

Pam and I danced. We had the floor all to ourselves, which seemed to temporarily embarrass us.

When the tune was over, we were joined by our son and daughter and several of the other couples from the audience. This made for a great evening.

After a while the county commissioners and their wives showed up. They were really good natured about everything, and they joined in on the fun.

The evening was an overwhelming success. Sunday evening news would confirm that.

There in full view of the television audience, we saw the mayor and wife, along with some of the city councilmen and their wives learning to jitterbug. The way the TV people showed it made it look like so much fun that everyone would want to come out and be a part of it. This was shown by both the Ft. Worth and Dallas television stations.

Monday the phones started to ring off the wall. Most people were wanting to come out when the dancers were giving lessons. Wednesday through Sunday was booked up in a hurry. They booked up well on Monday and Tuesday also because of the reviews they got from the gourmet section of the newspaper. The gourmet section of the papers really played up the bit about the food and the Chef and his background.

They did have music on Monday and Tuesday, just no dance teachers.

It seemed that there had been a food critic at the opening and you know how food critics generally rate new establishmnets. He had nothing but wonderful things to say about the chef and the food he had prepared. It sure looked as though the Swinging Years Club was off to a wonderful start.

Opening Day at the Clinic

Sunday came, and we all relaxed all day long after the long Saturday night at the club. After a day and night of rest, we tried to make sure we were at the clinic long before it was supposed to open at 9:00 a.m.

We walked into the clinic to find all of the professional people ready and waiting on their first patients.

The Mayor and Councilmen and the County Commissioners all arrived just before it was time to cut the ribbon to the clinic. Bing arrived with Hattie and a couple of her lady friends just before time to cut the ribbon. They had asked Hattie to cut the ribbon for them since she had donated the property to the clinic, and since it was also named for her.

By now the television crews were at the clinic and all set up to record this big event. Charley Johnson and his wife, along with the Bartletts and several other interested parties were at the opening.

Doc asked for everyone's attention, so he could say a few words. He spoke about how much gratitude he owed to the city and to people like Hattie McKinney and Charley Johnson and especially to Pam and me, without whose help he would never have been able to accomplish this dream of his. He acknowledged that Hattie, Charley, and Bill Bartlett had helped spearhead this project and said how appreciative he was of the way the Mayor, Councilmen, County Commissioners, and all of the other people in the medical community had helped and accepted them.

The Mayor was introduced, and he said a few words about the clinic, and fortunately for everyone he made his speech short.

He turned the proceedings back to Doc who says, "May I have everyone's attention, please? It is now time for the unveiling of the sign on the front of the building, revealing the full name of the clinic."

He turns to Hattie and asks, "Hattie, will you step over and pull the string that will release the canvas that covers the name of the clinic, please?"

She steps over and pulls the string; down comes the canvas and there in all its glory is the name of the clinic: ***Hattie McKinney People's Clinic***. It looked for a minute as if Hattie was going to faint. She was so stunned that she turned ghostly white. Doc reached over and put his arm around her to help hold her up in case her knees got weak. She finally got some color back into her face and then she turned to Doc and told him that she could shoot him for not asking her about this before he did it.

"We joked about it," Hattie said, "but that's all it was, just a joke."

"Not to me it wasn't. I knew that if I asked you, you would say, 'No thanks, I don't need this kind of notoriety.'"

She reached up and hugged his neck and kissed him on the cheek, and said, "You guys beat anything I have ever seen. You are continually surprising people with your actions."

"Well, now if you're gonna get too mad, I guess we could take it back down."

Hattie looked at him and then at the sign and said, "Well, I guess we might as well leave it since you had it made out of neon and all that stuff."

With that everyone got a good laugh.

She turns and tells the mayor, "I feel it's time for you to cut the ribbon to open the doors Big Boy."

With that the mayor took the scissors and cut the ribbon and opened the door, while Doc and the staff invited everyone in for punch and cookies as well as a tour of the clinic.

"Doc, old friend," I said, "this is a red-letter day for the poor people of Tarrant County and the street people in particular. The place is full of dignitaries and newspaper people getting their stories, as well as the television crews from three of the stations."

Things were going real fine with the punch and the coffee and cookies. People were loving the pastel colors of the interior, and they were very impressed with the equipment and pharmaceuticals that had been donated by the different manufacturers of medical equipment and the drug companies who had been so free with their medicines to help the clinic get started. They had been debating about getting a small ambulance in case it was needed. They never knew when something might come up where they would need to transport someone from the clinic to a hospital when the medical aid might be more than the clinic could handle.

Roxie heard them talking about the possibility of needing something along those lines. She got Dr. Davis cornered and asked him, "What do you think about the need for an ambulance?"

He studied the idea for a while and told Roxie, "I haven't given it much thought before, but there could be cases where a heart attack or something similar might occur, and we would need to transport the person to the hospital. This would save the time of an ambulance coming from the hospital over to the clinic, and then the time of the return trip just might be the thing that could save a person's life if they only had the trip to the hospital instead of the round trip.

"You know what, Roxie? I think that would be something worth looking into, but you know how expensive those ambulances are."

"Dr. Davis, I never asked what the price would be; I just asked if it might save someone's life, and your answer seems to be that it could possibly do just that. Now, please tell me how much one would cost for this place. I know you can't tell me exactly, but you can give me a good guestamate."

"Okay, if I was guessing, I would say what you would need would cost in the neighborhood of three hundred thousand dollars completely outfitted."

"Thank you, Dr. Davis, that's just what I wanted to know."

She turned to Doc and said, "I need to talk to you."

He walked over to where she was, and she took her checkbook out of her purse and wrote a check for three hundred thousand dollars and handed it to him. On the check she made the notation that it was to be used only for the purchasing of an ambulance to be registered to the Hattie McKinney People's Clinic.

Doc looked at her and asked, "Just what brought this about?"

"Well, Doc, I just had a conversation with Dr. Davis, and I feel that you never really know when an ambulance just might save someone's life."

With check in hand Doc started hollering for everyone to please quiet down just a little because he had an announcement to make. When everyone had hushed talking, he said, "Roxie has just donated three hundred thousand for the purchasing of an ambulance to have just in case it is needed."

There was a lot of applause, which Roxie really didn't want. She just acknowledged it by saying, "If it can save a life, even one life, it will be worth a lot more than that."

I went over and hugged my mother's neck and told her how proud I was of her for doing such a nice thing. Jenny was next to hug her neck, followed by Johnny and Pam.

An ambulance pulled up in front of the clinic, and guess who got out? If you guessed Pug, you would be right. Dr. Davis and Dr. Bates had conferred this morning, and they had decided he could come over for a while if he didn't stay too long. He got out of the ambulance and walked to the door of the clinic, with

Angie just a half step behind him. Everyone moved back to let him enter.

The television crews and newspaper photographers all got some real good shots of his getting out of the ambulance and walking to the clinic. This caused quite a stir with all of the people in the clinic.

Jenny asked, "Angie and Pug, would you like to have a cup of punch and a cookie?"

"Sounds good, Jenny; we'll drink and eat as we look around."

This was the first time either Pug or Angie had seen the interior of the clinic. They loved the pastel colors. Most of all, they like most of the other people, found it hard to believe that drug manufacturers and equipment supply companies had donated so much to the clinic.

I explained some of it to them. "There are three or four of the drug company representatives or whatever you call them. I think you call them detail men; anyway they have told Doc and Dr. Davis that they will check in with them from time to time and make sure they don't run out of supplies."

Doc and Dr. Davis made sure the TV people and the newspaper people heard these remarks so the drug companies would get some publicity out of their generosity in helping the clinic.

The First Patient

Doc was busy pouring punch for one of the dignitaries when he looked up to see a man and woman coming in the front door. It wasn't hard to tell that they were indigent and needed help.

Doc walked over to greet them. "Can I help you?"

The man said, "Please, mister, we were on the way to the hospital when we ran out of gas a couple of blocks down the street. My wife is having labor pains and she is right on nine months, so we tried to make it, but we don't have money for gas. While we was walking down to the hospital we happened to see your clinic. Well, her water broke, and we really need some help."

Doc quickly led her back to the emergency room, and he called Dr. Davis. Linda saw her come in and saw Doc take her back to the room so she and another nurse followed.

They started helping the lady onto the bed. They asked the father to step outside if he didn't mind for a few minutes.

Dr. Davis started examining the lady. As he did, he told. Linda, "It's too late to call for an ambulance right now. She is dilated; I can see the head of the baby, so we don't have any time to lose."

About that time Hattie came down the hall and stopped to talk to the husband. He explained, "We just got to town yesterday and ran out of money, so we slept in the car last night.

"When my wife started having labor pains, I stopped a guy on the street and asked him where the nearest hospital was. That was when we headed for the nearest hospital. The car ran out of gas, so we thought we might be able to walk, but then her water broke about a block up the street. We were parked on the other side of the street, and we could see the word 'clinic' on the front of the building, so we decided this would be the place to go. We didn't know there was a big party going on here. We just needed help, and we figured that with all the people here, maybe we could get some help. Sure enough we are getting help, thank God."

He apologized to Hattie and told her that he was sorry that he must have forgotten his manners with worrying so much about his wife. He introduced himself to her as Johnny Martin from Borger, Texas. He told her he lost his job and hadn't been able to get one in Borger. "We thought it might be easier to get work in a larger town."

Hattie introduced herself, and she told him not to worry about something like that at a time like this.

He looked at her and asked, "Are you the Hattie McKinney whose name is on the front of the building?"

"I plead guilty, Johnny, and I can tell you that your wife is our very first patient."

Just as she said that, they heard some crying and groans from the emergency room. He looked real scared.

Hattie said, "Don't worry because your wife is in real good hands with one of the best emergency room doctors in Ft. Worth."

Things seemed to be quiet in the room now, well, for at least a short while, when all of a sudden we heard a baby crying. Johnny started for the door, but Hattie grabbed him by the arm.

"Johnny, everything is all right. The doctor will come and get you in just a few minutes. First, they have to have time to clean the baby and mother a little before you see them."

Johnny tells Hattie, "I don't know much about having babies because this is our first one."

Hattie laughs and says, "Well, Johnny, I never would have guessed." With that he realized how funny he must have sounded. He started talking to Hattie because he was so nervous he had to do something while he was waiting.

He said, "I'm really a very good painter, but the construction trade has fallen off in a town the size of Borger."

"Johnny, do you have a place to stay tonight?"

"No, ma'am, we don't, we slept in the car last night," Johnny responded politely.

"Johnny, tonight your wife will be in a hospital bed, and you will have a room in the hotel right next to the hospital."

When he protested, she let him know that if he really was a good painter, he would be able to pay her back. "Johnny, I have several rent houses that need painting real bad. I have a real pretty small one with only two small bedrooms, but it's nice, and it needs painting badly. The other problem is that I don't have anyone living in it right now.

"Do you happen to know where I could find a good tenant, maybe someone with a new baby who could use a place like that to live in? I could let them work out the rent, you know, by painting and handy work at other houses that I own. The rent isn't very high. What do you say?"

As she glanced out the window, Hattie briefly changed the subject. "I think I had better have a friend of mine move your car so it won't go to the auto pound tonight. I think I can get Charley Johnson to move it over to the address where you are going to be living when your wife gets out of the hospital."

Just as she said that, "The door to the small emergency room opened, and Linda came out with an arm full of beautiful baby girl. She showed it to Johnny and asked if he wouldn't like to hold his new daughter. He very hesitatingly reached out and took the baby as if it was a fragile piece of china.

Linda said, "She isn't going to break; you can hold her a little closer if you want to."

He pulled her closer to his body, and with his big hands he pulled back the little blanket she was wrapped in. With a great big smile on his face, he turned to Hattie and said, "Boy, she sure is pretty, isn't she? She looks just like her mother, thank God."

Hattie eased on over to get a better look at the baby.

He started in the room, but came back and handed the baby to Hattie and asked her if she would mind holding the baby while he went into the room and talked to his wife. This surprised Hattie, but she was very willing to hold a little bundle of joy like that.

Johnny was in the room about four or five minutes when he came out. "Mrs. Hattie, my wife wants to talk to you."

This surprised Hattie, but she went on into the room where Dr. Davis and Linda were cleaning things up.

The mother looked up at Hattie and introduced herself. "I am Martha Martin. I guess my husband has already told you who I am and what we are doing here in Ft. Worth."

"Well, yes, he told me about your problems, but I think we have that all worked out."

"Yes, ma'am, he told me. Now I have a question to ask you. Would you object if we named our daughter after you? We would like to name her Hattie Linda Martin after the two ladies who were so kind to us when she was born."

Linda almost dropped the instruments she was cleaning when she heard this. She turned and looked at Hattie and the mother. Linda asks, "Are you serious? You don't even know me."

"I just met you, and I feel that I know you better than you think. The two of you would make me very happy if you would agree that it would be all right if we named her after you and Mrs. Hattie."

Linda looked at Hattie and asked, "Well, what do you say, Hattie?"

Well Linda, "It would be quite an honor for both of us. I would like that very much." Hattie adds, "Hell, I've never had anyone named for me before."

"That's great; my husband and I already discussed it when he came in the room a while ago. "Dr. Davis, that's the name that we want on the birth certificate, please."

Dr. Davis thought that was a very nice gesture.

When Doc walked in, he was told the entire story. He just grinned and said, "Man, what a way to open."

Doc, Martha asks, "Is there is anything I can do for you when I am back on my feet, I will be more than glad to work and pay for the work they did today. I used to work in an office before they closed. I'm very good on the computers, and I wax a mean floor. I learned that from my mother who did housekeeping for some of the more wealthy people in Borger before she died a couple of years ago from cancer."

Martha, "I'm sure we can work something out because we need someone who knows these dogone computers, but for now, you just get some rest and take care of that little girl. We'll talk later about the future for all of your family."

The celebration continued for the next couple of hours until everyone seemed to be getting tired.

Doc looked at Linda with a large wrinkle in his brow. "Linda, are you as tired as I am?" he asks.

"Doc, I have a feeling that I'm even more tired than you are. I've been going since yesterday, and my butt is dragging. Why don't we look at the schedule and see who is going to be here tomorrow?"

"Linda, darlin', you just came up with a wonderful idea. I could kiss you for that."

"Well, don't just stand there; get busy, I can't wait all day. Either kiss me or look up the schedule, and I know which one it better be."

Doc was stunned, but he walked over and gave her a real big hug. and kiss. "Doc, I wondered how long it was going to take for you to get around to that."

Review of the Agenda

The clinic was finally open.

The club was finally open.

Pug was getting better every day.

Cowboy had his ranch, and it looked as though he might also have T.J.. He sure had taken a shine to her.

Mabel and Amber were together and working with Bing at the club. She knew that she could have her own café anytime she wanted it.

Hattie was involved in the clinic and the club.

Charley Johnson was going to work for the company over in Dallas.

Lynn and Annie were receiving the dividends from the trust fund set up for them.

The hospital had already received its new ambulance, and it was the talk of the town.

The trust fund for the Police Officers Retirement Fund and the Widows and Orphans Fund had been executed, and they were receiving funds from them.

The warehouse was just about completed for the street people to keep them out of the heat this summer. They had installed four fifty-two-inch televisions and had sixteen tables for cards and dominoes. They even had four pocket pool tables and plenty of Q Sticks and several ping pong tables. They already had the soft drink machines, and they had volunteers to run the warehouse coming out the kazoo.

Our family seemed to have grown a little tired of living in a hotel.

For the next week Johnny, Art, the rest of the guys, and I tried to tie up any loose ends that might be hanging.

The girls made one more trip to Cowboy's ranch to check and see if he needed anything more for the house.

Pam asked, "Angie and Jenny, if we should we take anything with us or should we just go out and check first?"

"Pam, I have an idea that if he needs anything else for the house, T.J. will see that he gets it."

I made a trip to the hospital this afternoon and found that Pug was doing just fine. I walked in and found Pug watching television and reading at the same time.

"Hey Jim, he hollers at me, I have an idea. How about us going back to Chicago? I want to see our new home. I'm able to work, or at least I will be in a week or so. The doctor has already told me that I will be as good as new in another week. He just told me not to ever crawl into the ring again. I let him know real quick that I have no intention of doing that. I think I've had just about all of that kind of life that a man should have. Now I have a wonderful wife, and we want to have a family when we get back to Chicago and get settled.

"Jim, I hope you know how much we love you and Pam. You have been more than just a friend to me, and I don't seem to have any way of repaying you for what you've done for us."

"The hell you don't; you just keep on being my friend and a good man for our company and I couldn't ask for more. I know that I'm not quite old enough to be your father, but you are the kind of a man that any father would be proud of. Now hush up before I start crying. You just talk to Angie and see if she is about ready to go home, and I'll talk to Pam and see if she's ready to head for home."

The next few days were quiet, thank goodness.

Saturday morning the phone rang, and it was Bob Hitch. "Jim, this is the weekend."

"What do you mean 'this is the weekend?'"

"This is the weekend that your story runs in the paper. You know, the story about you, the whole story about you and all of your friends and what has happened to you since the tornado hit Fort Worth."

"Bob, are you saying they're running the story about the club, the clinic, the ranch, and the other things that are going on? Have you talked to Pug and Angie about running the story of his operation?"

"Sure have, Jim, and they seem satisfied with it. I hope you like it because they're running the presses today, and the papers will be delivered tomorrow."

"Okay Bob, I just hope it goes well for you and the paper. Thanks for letting us know. We'll be looking forward to reading it."

"Thanks to you, Jim. Without you, there wouldn't have been a story. I'll talk to you later. Tell Pam hello for me."

"Okay Bob, I'll tell her, so long and take care of yourself."

Sunday morning came, and we ordered breakfast brought to the room with a a couple of newspapers. When the paper arrived, sure enough, there it was on the front page: pictures of Pam, Pug, Angie, and me. There was a notation under the pictures that the full story was on page four.

I read the caption under the picture that said, "From street person to entrepreneur and philanthropist." I turned to the rest of the article on page four to see what Bob had said about us. I read the remainder of the article, which took me about fifteen minutes. I guessed that Bob had outdone himself on this one and he really had done just that.

While I was reading, Pam kept asking, "What did he say?" Finally I smiled and handed the paper to Pam and said, "Honey, you've just got to read this yourself to believe it."

Pam started reading and a big smile came across her face. The more she read the more she smiled. When she finally finished the article, she started to hand the paper back to me when the phone rang.

She dropped the paper in my lap and answered the phone. Pug was on the line. Pug immediately asked, "Pam, have you read the article in the paper today?"

"Well Pug, I just finished reading it, and I think this young man is going to be a winner of the Nobel Prize for journalism one of these days."

"Pam, that young man made me sound like a hero of some kind."

"Pug, you are a hero to a lot of people. You came up off the street, and you are now a married man and soon, we hope, you will start a family so we can be grandparents."

"Pam, just wait till we get back to Chicago. Our lives are sure going to be great. I just know they will. Does Jim have a minute to talk to me?"

"Sure thing, Pug.

"Jim, Pug is on the phone and wants to talk to you," Pam said.

I got on the phone, and Pug told me the same thing he had already told Pam. "Pug, I have to agree whole heartedly. I think Bob did a great job on that article. He made us sound like some kind of supermen. We know better though, don't we?"

"Sure do, Jim. Well, Angie is about through reading the article now so I gotta run. I'll talk to you later. Maybe lunch, okay?"

"Okay, Pug, lunch it is, but let's have a late one."

Just as I hang up the phone, it rings again, and this time it is Roxie. It seemed that Johnny had gone downstairs early and had seen the paper. He had brought it back up to her room.

"We have all been reading it."

For the next couple of hours the phone kept ringing with calls from all of the rest of the gang, as well as Charley Johnson, Doc Davis, and Dr. Bill Bates. The phone continued to ring most of the morning.

By now Roxie, Jenny, Jake, June, and Sid, as well as Art and Nora, were all in our room. The chatter was so loud, we could hardly hear ourselves think.

Hattie McKinney finally called and began to really tease me about being such a big celebrity. I really didn't know what to think of that title.

The big surprise came when Gene Kountz called and told me that he had just gotten through reading about the gang and me. "Jim, that story has really impressed me and a lot of other people."

Monday and Tuesday went fast. Wednesday morning as we were having breakfast, the phone rang. I answered and the conversation that followed was mostly yes and no. I finally said, "All right, we'll be there by next Wednesday at the latest." I finally hang the phone up and I turn to Pam.

"Well, Honey, it looks like we have to go home next week. That phone call was from Frank Wells telling me that they have a group of businessmen coming in from Germany, and they want to meet me as well as all of the managers of our other Satalite plants. All of the plant managers and I must be there by Wednesday morning for a briefing on the proposals for these people. It seems if we can reach an agreement, it would run into the multi-millions in sales. I feel this is large enough for me to be there." It could be a contract almost as large as the largest Government contract we have ever received. That would be something that could carry the company for several years in the future.

Roxie says she is proud of me for agreeing so readily to go back home and take care of business.

"Mother, I think we have everything taken care of here, and if we don't, those we have left in charge can finish everything with no problem. Besides that it's only a couple of hours flight here if we are needed for something.

"Pam, can you be ready to leave on Tuesday?"

"I sure can, Hon, but it will have to be an afternoon flight. I can be ready, and I'm looking forward to getting home." "Daddy, Jenny says, I am very anxious to get home. I have enjoyed it here, but it will be nice to get home."

"How about you, Johnny? Are you ready to go home?"

"Sure am, Dad. I have plans when I get home."

"Art, are you and Nora ready to head back home? Have you had enough of Texas for now?"

"We sure have enjoyed Texas, and I have sure learned a lot about Texas and how big business works, but I think we should get home to pay a few bills and take the load off of Tommy and Jerry. I know that Louise and Ralph and the children are anxious to see their grandmother."

Pam seemed to be a little tired the last three or four weeks, and she needed to get a checkup when we got back to Chicago. She might need more rest than she had been getting. Since she had been here, she has been on a merry go round helping to get everything taken care of. Just getting the ranch house taken care for Cowboy had taken a lot out of her and Jenny, as well as Nora. She didn't seem to mind it though. In fact, I thought she had really enjoyed it even though she had really been on the run.

"Mother, what do you think? Do you think Pam needs a checkup?" I asked.

"Well, Jim, I'm afraid that I have to agree with you. She won't admit it, but I think she may need some vitamins or something else. She should go to the doctor and get a checkup because we don't want her to overdo."

"Mother, I can promise you that just as soon as we get back home, I will see that she goes in for a checkup."

We all started getting things completed in order to go back home. We made arrangements to return the leased cars back to the leasing companies Monday afternoon. We made sure all the loose ends were taken care of.

Heading Home

One of the most important things was for Pug to get a clearance from the doctors. Once he did this, he would be ready, willing, and able to head for Chicago.

As soon as Bing heard that the gang was headed back to Chicago, he called me. "Jim, we want to have a big blowout here at the club on Saturday night. We want to invite everyone that has done anything for us to be at the club as our guest for the evening. The club will reserve enough tables for all of you. You never know when we'll all have the opportunity to get together again. Hattie said she wants to pick up the tab, so the club won't lose any money. What do you say, Jim?"

"Bing, I have to say that it looks like we will be going back to Chicago on Tuesday, due to business that is very urgent."

"Hell, Jim, can't it wait just a week?"

"Sorry, old friend, but we could be talking about losing a contract worth millions of dollars, and I just couldn't in good conscience do that. I owe it to the stockholders to do what I can to make money for the company and them.

"If you don't mind, I guess we had better take a rain check on this one. We will be back before too long. We will be checking in with you, and we will be back to Ft. Worth to see how everything is going. You aren't rid of us by any means.

"If you don't mind, I will call Hattie and the others and tell them why we are leaving so suddenly. I'll talk to you later. Let us hear from you and keep up the good work, old friend."

I hang up the phone and tell everyone what Bing and Hattie wanted to do. "Pam, do you think you can take care of all your loose ends and have us packed and ready to go home on Tuesday?"

"Sure can, Hon, but I think I will let Angie do some of our calling to let folks know we are going back home so soon."

"Well, it looks like I need to get busy and stop by the hospital and the Bible Sanctuary and tell them that we are leaving. I guess I had better get in touch with Charley Johnson and finalize everything with him. He needs to go over and get together with Gene Kountz at our Dallas/Fort Worth plant. They can work out the details since I have already told Gene what I wanted him to do for Charley. Charley is going to become an employee of the company. I feel that with all of Charley's friends and local connections, he could be very valuable to the company in the Public Relations department."

"Jim, I think that is a wonderful idea. He's a natural, and he is really a good speaker. I noticed that at the meetings where he would stand and say a few words or give a report on the progress of things. That's great, but how does he feel about it?"

"Honey, I think he would start tomorrow if he didn't have a few months to go on his thirty years with the police department. If he stays till then, he will have a very good retirement to go along with his salary from Dixon Plastics,".

"Seems like you have thought everything through for Charley. How does his wife take all of this?"

"Pam, she thinks it's just great. She wants him away from the police department and the danger."

Changing the subject, I ask, "Pam, can you get Angie to make the reservations for all of us. I know that Art and Nora, Jake and June, and Sid all want to get back home to get some things taken care of. She could check on Sid's ankle and see if it is still swollen, and she could see if any of them need anything before leaving."

"I don't know what we would do without Angie," Pam commented.

"Pam, I just thought of something. Let me run it by you and see what you think. I wonder if Angie would consider taking over the job of handling travel, hotel, and business arrangements for the company when we get back to Chicago. She could set up an office in the house, and that way, if they have any children, she could be home and yet take care of travel and hotel reservations for the Chicago's company office. What do you think? That would relieve one of the people in the home office to do other duties. I would never let an employee go just to do this, so I wouldn't be hurting anyone by giving one of our friends a job. Now what do you think? I know I said that before, but is it a good idea or not? That is if she wants it."

"Jim, I love the idea. Now, when we get home, you can approach her with it and see what she thinks."

"I sure hope the doctors don't mind if Pug leaves the hospital a few days earlier than expected. We can assure them that he won't be doing any strenuous physical work. I sure hope they let him go."

Monday morning we were all running around taking care of last-minute details. The cars were turned into the leasing agency late in the afternoon. The cars that the gang had were all bought and paid for – no leasing on them.

Cowboy had met with the ladies, and it seemed they had really fixed him up well. Televisions in the living room, bedroom, and a small one in the kitchen.

I commented, "I really don't think he is that crazy about television though. He does like music. He had the tack shop swinging the other day. He bought a small CD stereo unit and put in there. He also is talking about putting one in the barn because he read somewhere that music helps calm animals. I hope he isn't intending to play hard rock."

Pam had talked to Mabel and Amber. She assured Mabel that if things didn't work out to her satisfaction at the club, she could still have her own small café.

She laughed when she was told that, because she really loved working with Shawn in the kitchen at the club, and Amber was really learning a lot. They absolutely loved living together.

Amber said that she was not going to let her mother get away again, regardless of what happened.

"I believe she meant it," Pam said.

About dinner time Roxie had all of the family meet in Pam's and my room. "Tonight we are going to have dinner downstairs for the last time on this trip. Angie said she thought she and Pug could be here. I have taken it upon myself to invite the rest of the people who have helped put these programs together. The whole gang will be there including Hattie and Bing, the Bartletts, the Johnsons, the Gregorys, the Davis family, Robert Hitch, Lynn and Annie, Pug and Angie – if the doctors okay it, Doc and Linda, Cowboy and T.J., Mabel and Amber, and Dr. Bates. I hope I haven't left anyone out.

"The hotel is arranging everything for us in the Lariat Room. They are serving prime rib with a side of baked potato and asparagus. If anyone doesn't like asparagus, he or she can order another side of whatever they want. This will be topped with their best red wine and a dessert of cherry cheesecake. If anyone complains, I just won't hear it. Does this sound all right to you?

Roxie says very explicitely, "I took it upon myself because I had an idea that Jim might not think it was necessary. I do think it's necessary, and after all, I am the matriarch of this family, and per tradition I am doing this without any help from the rest of the family."

Johnny and Jenny got a big kick out of Grandmother's attitude.

I graciously bowed to my mother. "Mother, you are one of God's greatest creations, and I just don't know how in the world I got along without you for ten long years. I can assure you it will never happen again. What time, Mother dear, is this bash supposed to take place?"

"Eight sharp, dear son, eight sharp, and don't you be late or I will chastize you severly and if that don't work, I will skin your head."

Eight o'clock came soon. Everyone seemed to be here, so Roxie taps gently on her glass to get our attention. "Friends, and you truly are the most wonderful group of friends any person has ever had the privilege of knowing, I just had to get you all together one more time before we leave this wonderful town. Jim could never have accomplished his goals if it hadn't been for you folks.

"As a wise man once said and I quote, 'Never has so much been done by so few in so little time." Well, maybe it wasn't a wise man who said that; maybe it was one old lady. Regardless of who said it, I feel that it covers all of you sitting here tonight. I feel that we are all truly family – maybe not in blood, but in our feelings and love for each other.

"With that, I have one last thing to say. Well, maybe two, but you all know how much we, meaning my family, all love each and every one of you. Second thing is a warning to you. If any of you ever get to Chicago and you don't come to see us, we will swear out a warrant for your arrest.

"Now if any of you have anything to say, this is the time, but just remember to keep it short because I'm hungry."

Several did stand and say their good-byes. They did as they had been instructed and kept their remarks short.

The dinner was a great success, and no one complained about the asparagus. The wine was overflowing. Even Pug and I had a glass in order to toast the group of friends and to say so long for now, not good-bye.

"I hate good-bye, so I won't say it. I will just say that we will all get together at least once or twice a year. How about that? Do you all agree that we can do that?"

There was a loud applause and a lot of, "You bet we can, Jim."

"All of you just remember what Mother told you because you don't want any trouble with the law."

As we all said goodnight and so long for now, we didn't hear one person say good-bye.

It took a long time for our crowd to disperse. Finally, the Dixon family and in-laws and "out-laws" were left. We agreed to adjourn till breakfast. Angie told us the times of each person's flight tomorrow, and she told us to just pick up our tickets at the ticket counter. "They will be waiting for you. I will give you your flight times at breakfast. The flights are all after 1:30 p.m. tomorrow. See ya'll at breakfast, pardners."

Johnny and Jenny were first at breakfast. It wasn't long before the rest arrived. We were all given our departure times and other travel information such as change of planes. We uncharacteristically ate breakfast hurriedly this morning.

Angie said, "Since you all have flights that leave within a half hour of each other, I have ordered two vans to take us to the airport. The vans will pick us up here at noon. I know some of us will be a little early, but this should work out best for all."

I smiled to myself and nudged Pam. "See what I mean about her taking charge of the travel and hotel accommodations for the company? She's a natural."

Pam agreed. "You're right, Honey; she is a natural, and she seems to make it look easy."

Noon came, and we were all checked out of our rooms, and we were awaiting the arrival of the vans. Sure enough, right at noon, two oversized vans pulled up to the hotel curb.

I met the drivers, and the rest of the group started to get onto the vans while the drivers took care of their luggage.

Roxie looked at Jenny's and Johnny's luggage. "That's a lot more than you arrived here with, isn't it?"

"Yes, Grandmother, it is, but we had to have a few momentos didn't we?"

"Yes, you did."

"Wait a minute, Grandmother, look at the two extra bags you have now that you didn't bring with you. What's that?"

"Momentos, Johnny, you know I just had to have something to remember Texas."

"Right, Grandmother, me too."

We all loaded onto the vans and are on our way to the airport.

Upon arrival, we found that the McKenzies' flight was first, followed by the Steele family's, then Sid's, and then our gang's for Chicago. This gave the gang time to eat something if anyone was hungry. Guess what? No one was hungry. We knew we would be fed something while we were on the plane, so we just waited.

The wait didn't really seem that long. We finally were on the plane and on our way home.

Angie came over to where Pam and I were seated. "Pam, I just can't wait to see our new home. You guys are so kind to us."

"Not at all, Angie," I said. "I have a way to get even. I will tell you all about it when we get home and get settled."

Angie went back to her seat.

This was a real smooth flight to Chicago. It seemed almost too soon, and yet the pilot was announcing that we were to arrive within the next twenty minutes. We looked out the windows, and sure enough there it was, Chicago – just as we had left it.

The plane touched down and reached the terminal very quickly. We seemed to disembark more quickly than usual. We were headed for the baggage area when we happened to think about Oscar.

I said, "I'll bet Oscar is here somewhere waiting on us, and we have apparently just walked past him."

Johnny went running back, and sure enough, there Oscar was. He was on his way, trying to follow and keep up with us.

Johnny apologized, "Oscar, we are so glad to get home that we just didn't think about you being here to meet us. I should have known you would be here.

"Wait a minute, who called you?"

"Mrs. Angie called and told me when you would be arriving and asked if I could meet you. She also instructed me to bring a van in addition to the limousine because she felt that there would be quite a bit of luggage. That Angie thinks of everything."

Home at Last

We reached our baggage and found that even Angie was so excited she had forgotten to tell Roxie and me about calling Oscar. Angie was a very embarrassed person when she saw Oscar. Everyone started to tease her, but she took it in the good way it was intended.

After a short wait, our luggage started showing up. Johnny, Oscar, and I began to gather the baggage when the driver of the van tapped Oscar on the shoulder and offered to help. It seemed that Oscar had been kind of excited also because he had forgotten the driver of the van.

We got the baggage into the van. The gang was now in the limousine and headed home. Just before we arrived, Oscar turned to me and said, "Mr. Jim, those articles you ordered were delivered this morning. I just thought you would like to know about it."

I thought for just a minute, and finally it came to me. "Oh, yes, those things. Thanks, Oscar, I was hoping they had arrived. Are they in good condition?"

"Yes, sir, they are in beautiful condition. I'm sure you will like them."

Nothing more was said about them. Just as we were entering the driveway, Roxie said, "Jim, we must have company. There are a couple of cars in the driveway. Do you know who they belong to?"

"No, Mother, I don't have any idea."

We pull to a stop behind the beautiful powder blue Lincoln Continental. We get out of the limousine and start walking to the door when I said, "Pam, there's a note on that steering wheel. See what it says; it might tell us who it belongs to."

"Jim, why don't you do that? I have my hands full," Pam said.

"Well, Sweetheart, I have to help the boys with the luggage. Why don't you put your stuff down and see what it says?"

By now, Julia had reached the front door, so Pam turns and asks her to hold the things she had in her hands. Pam went to the driver's side of the car and opened the door and picked up the note. She read it out loud.

"Dear Pam, I hope you enjoy this new car. It's a present bought for you from your husband before he went to Texas. Drive with pleasure and own it with pride." The note was signed by Jim Robertson.

There was a loud squeal as she turned and came running to me. She started to hit me, and then she reached up and hugged my neck and kissed me. "Why didn't you tell me you were going to do this? You could have at least given me a hint."

"No, I couldn't, darling, that would have ruined the surprise."

There was another one for Angie who absolutely couldn't believe it. The note said, "I couldn't get the one you ordered, so I just got Mrs. McKenzie one like Mrs. Dixon's."

My Town Car and Pug's Mercury Marquis were also in the driveway.

Sitting off to one side by itself was a new Lincoln SUV. It was a beautiful red color, and the interior matched the exterior. The note inside said, "Johnny, if this isn't satisfactory, you can exchange it for something else."

Johnny couldn't believe it. "Dad, this is beautiful. Can I really keep it?"

"You sure can, and you will earn it because tomorrow you go to work at the plant full time. I hope you like the color.

"Jenny, I wasn't sure what you would like to have, so I told Mr. R. that you would be down to pick out what you wanted after we got home. I guess I had better tell you also that you can keep the MG. Is that satisfactory?

"Mother, what do you want? Do you want a new car? Can I get you a new limousine?"

"No cars, Jim, Honey. I have you and Pam and my family. I don't need anything else."

Pug and Angie were looking over their cars. When they were through looking them over, Angie came over and gave me a big, big hug and kissed me on the cheek. "Jim," she said, "you are going to spoil all of us so bad you won't be able to stand us if this keeps up."

"Angie, just as long as you like it, that's all I want. I want you and Pug to be happy.

"Now, let's take our things inside and put things up so we can go next door and see what our neighbor's house looks like."

Angie squealed again and hugged my neck again.

Pug was doing what he had promised the doctors, but it wasn't easy with all that was happening.

Oscar and Julia helped everyone with their luggage, and soon we had everything in its place.

Soon Angie and Pug came down to the kitchen where everyone seemed to hang out in this house. They asked, "Jim, is there any chance we can get into our new home?"

Oscar spoke up and told Angie that he had the key to the house. "I have also had the power and the water turned on so you will have lights and water when you get here. If you would like, I would be more than happy to show you where I had a gate put between the two properties just the way Jim told me to do it. He wanted to make sure it was there before you got back home."

"Oscar, I could hug your neck for taking care of these things for us. I just think I will hug your neck anyway," and she did.

Oscar actually blushed which he very seldom did.

"Now," Angie said, "would you please take us to our new home?"

With that not only did Pug and Angie head out the door, but they were also followed by all of us.

As we walked out the door, Julia said, "Don't be too long. I'm preparing a special dinner for all of you tonight."

We all headed for the rear of the property and the new gate between the properties. We went through the gate and to the back door of their new home. We opened the door, and Oscar turned the lights on.

The kitchen was beautiful. We walked through the kitchen into the dining area, and we found that it had a gorgeous heavy oak wood dining room table and chairs.

Oscar stopped the group. "Angie, I have been asked to tell you that Jim and Pam did not know this, but it seems that the house is totally furnished. When the previous owner furnished it, he did an exceptional job of furnishing. Everything he bought was very expensive and exceptionally well made. The relatives did not know this. It seems that they just wanted to sell it and get the money. They asked very few questions. As a result, you have a house full of the finest antiques that money can buy. I took it upon myself to have them appraised before you came home. The appraisal came up with a value of just over $400,000. I thought you would like to know that."

"Oscar, sometimes your brilliance surpasses my highest estimation of your brilliance," I said.

"Jim, I appreciate those kind words. I learned most of what I know from your father. He was quite a businessman as you know. Since I was handling the paperwork for you while you were in Texas, I tried to think as you would think. Since you only paid about $400,000 for the property, I thought you folks would like to know that you got a bonus of about the same amount. The appraiser told me that he was sure that he could sell the furniture to an antique dealer for that amount or possibly just a little more. That would mean that the property cost you approximately zero. That's good business, Jim."

"Well, Oscar I would say that is up to Pug and Angie, wouldn't you?"

Angie and Pug were looking at each other in total surprise. "Oscar, you have done a brilliant job on this," Pug said.

"Thank you, Wayne. I try to be of as much help as I can."

"Oscar," Angie said, "I wish there was an easy way to tell you how much we appreciate your efforts."

Oscar looked at everyone and suggested we all go into the living room and parlor to see what we had there. "This will give you an idea of what you just bought."

The living room was gorgeous and very antique. Oscar suggested we go upstairs and look at the bedrooms. We climbed a beautiful walnut spiral staircase. From the landing, we entered the master bedroom. There in all its splendor was a giant four-poster bed. Angie was, by now, in total disbelief.

Pam asked, "How do you like your house so far?"

Angie was absolutely speechless.

Pug turned and asked her if she wanted to get rid of all of this old furniture and get some new modern furniture to replace it?"

"Heavens no, at least not right now. This furniture is a dream. I have never seen anything so beautiful."

We went through the rest of the house and found it was just as unbelievable.

Pam mentioned to me that she was beginning to get pretty tired. "Can we go back to the house and get a little rest? If Pug and Angie don't mind, we can look it over tomorrow when I'm not so tired."

We all thought that was a good idea. Pug and Angie would spend the night at Roxie's tonight since they didn't have any food in the pantry.

We returned to the Dixon house where dinner was waiting. Julia had outdone herself tonight. After dinner everyone was so full we were uncomfortable. We said goodnight early and headed for the bedrooms.

Tomorrow morning came early as usual. Pug and I got ready to go to the plant just as soon as we had eaten. Johnny started up the stairs when I asked, "Where are you going?"

Johnny replied, "I am going upstairs to change clothes. Dad, you did say that I was going to work on Wednesday at the plant. Well, today is Wednesday, and since you're going to the plant, I thought I might ride along."

"Right on, son, you didn't forget. We will be ready in a few minutes, and we will meet you out front. Why don't we all go in your new SUV this time?"

"That's fine with me, Dad. I wanted to drive it anyway."

We reached the plant and parked in my parking place. The three of us went inside and met with the managers of all of our branch offices including Gene Kountz from Dallas.

I said hello to Frank Wells again. I found that Frank was doing a bang-up job as the new manager of the home office and plant. After talking to some of the members of the Board of Directors, it seemed they wanted to make Frank a vice president of the company. They also felt that I should be the CEO and Chairman of the Board.

"We'll take that up later and see how they feel," I said, "but for right now, we have this deal coming up with the German company."

The men from the German Manufacturing Co. had asked that our meeting be delayed until next Monday morning. This seemed to suit everyone except those who had flown in from other plants. A meeting had been called for this afternoon to discuss the delay. In the meantime we could discuss a lot of other things like our involvement in community activities.

I said, "I want Johnny and Pug to sit in on these discussions. After all, they are going to be some of the men who will eventually lead this company in the direction it should go."

Meanwhile back at the house, Pam and Angie were looking over the house where Pug and Angie hoped to spend the next years of their lives. They had gone back and were double-checking everything in the house. It seemed that the relatives of the previous owner had not known what was in the house, and they hadn't cared. They had just wanted to sell it and get the money for the house. They hadn't wanted to be bothered with the contents.

"Pam," Angie asked reluctantly, "do you like antique furniture?"

"Honey, I love antique furniture like this, don't you?"

"Well, yes I do. I remember going to my grandmother's home when I was real young. She had some of the most beautiful old furniture in her house. I would look at it and think how wonderful it would be to have a home of my own when I grew up, and I would want it filled with furniture just like hers. Now it looks like I have that house and that furniture. If you were me, would you get rid of it or keep it?"

"Angie, this is your house. This is your furniture, so you do what you want to do. I love this old furniture, and it's better wood and better made than anything you can buy today."

"I know, Pam, and I do love it. I'm not really sure just how Wayne feels about it. Last night he just kept on saying, 'It's whatever you want. I just want you to be happy.' I just wish he had been a little more definitive in his answer."

"Angie, it sounds to me like he made the decision. He wants you to be happy, and I'm sure he will be happy with your decision. Remember, we have a lot of antiques in our house, and we love them. The other thing is if you keep it, then you don't have to go through all the trouble of selling it and replacing it with new furniture. If you replace it, just look at all the decisions you will have to make and the interior decorators you will have to put up with."

"Okay, that sold me. No interior decorators at this time. Maybe later on I will have a decorator come and help brighten up the place a little, but I know you're right. Decision made! I keep it for now!"

Surprise, Surprise, Surprise

"Pam, are you all right? You look tired this morning," Angie said.

"Well, I have been a little tired lately, but I'm sure it was just all the running around we did while we were in Texas.

"Roxie mentioned my tired look also. She has a family doctor, and maybe I'll get his name and make an appointment. I'm sure I just need some vitamins or something.

"Angie, do you have your pencil and paper so we can make a list of the groceries and staple goods you will need for the kitchen. I imagine we should just throw out the old stuff he had here in the kitchen. It may have weevils in it, or it may just be old and rancid.

"The first thing we need to do is to get you some help in cleaning out the pantry and cupboards. I'm sure Julia knows someone we can get to help. Once it's cleaned out, we can start stocking it again with fresh supplies. How does that sound?"

"Sounds fine to me, Pam. Let's go back over to your house and talk to Julia, and while we are there, you can get the name of that doctor and call him for an appointment."

Pam and Angie walked in just as Roxie was about to leave. "Roxie," Pam asked, "can you give me the name and phone number of the doctor you told me about. I think I probably need some vitamins or something, maybe some iron supplement of some kind. I thought I would call and make an appointment with him."

"That's fine, Hon; come into the study, and I'll write it down for you.

"He is a fine doctor and a good person. He has been our doctor for over twenty-five years, through thick and thin. You'll like him. He has already heard about you and Jim getting married. Just call him and tell him who you are, and I'm sure he will get you right in."

Roxie left, and Pam and Angie went to the kitchen to have another cup of that great coffee that Julia made. They also wanted to pick Julia's brain and see if she knew anyone who could help Angie get her kitchen straightened out.

They took the coffee first, and then they asked, "Julia, do you have a friend or someone who could do the job?"

"Sure do, Honey. I know just the gal for that job. I'll call her and ask her to come over and talk to you," Julia said.

After coffee, Pam decided to call the doctor and make an appointment. She dialed the number. A nice lady answered, and Pam told her who she was, and there was an instant reply.

"Oh, you must be the beautiful lady I have heard so much about from some of my friends who came to your wedding. Are you calling about an appointment?"

"Yes, I am. I would like an appointment soon. I'm feeling pretty tired most of the time now. I think it's because of the mad pace we all had while we were in Texas. We seemed to be on the run all of the time."

"Well, Mrs. Dixon, we can see you tomorrow at 2:00 p.m. How does that sound?"

"Oh, that sounds just fine, but I really didn't expect to be seen that soon."

"Don't worry, Dr. Guzick will be glad to have you come in. He's been anxious to meet you.

"Pam, we will see you tomorrow after lunch."

With that they both hung up the phones.

"Angie, they are going to see me tomorrow right after lunch. How about that? I thought I would have to wait a few days."

"Pam, you have to remember that you are the wife of Jim Dixon now, and most folks don't make Dixons wait," Angie remarked.

"Well, I don't like being treated special like this. There may be someone out there that is a lot worse than I am, and they may need a doctor a lot more than I do. I'm sure it's just a vitamin deficiency."

At dinner Pam told me that Dr. Guzick had given her an appointment for tomorrow after lunch. She was going to go in and see if he had some vitamins or something for her that would make her feel a little stronger.

Angie and Pug were also having meals with us until Angie got her kitchen in shape to cook.

Pug, Johnny, and I discussed the day's happenings at the plant.

"The out-of-state plant managers are going to stay in town till next Monday when we have the big meeting with the German people. This looks like it could be a real big order if it can be worked out. They want a lot of material in a hurry. We have to see if all of the plants are geared up to manufacture the materials they want. From what we heard today from the managers, they feel they can do the job.

"Pug, I think we are on our way to a very large contract."

After dinner we all sat around and talked about business, the McKenzie house, and antique furniture, as well as a lot of other things.

Julia came in to tell Angie that she had just talked to a friend of hers who would love to come over and help her any way she needed help. "She's real good in the kitchen, but she's also real good elsewhere. She can do just about anything you want done."

This pleased Angie and Pam a lot because there was a lot of work to be done, and it would be nice to have someone who knew what she was doing.

Jenny informed Angie and Pam that she could help. She felt slighted since they hadn't asked her to help.

"Well, young lady," Angie said, "don't feel slighted because you can sure help all you want to help."

"Angie, I can't help tomorrow afternoon because I want to drive Mother to the doctor's office."

"That's fine, but when you get back, I will be expecting you."

By now everyone was a little tired and wanted to go to bed. It didn't take long for all of us, one by one to disappear up the stairs to the bedrooms.

Morning came, and the beautiful sun was filtering through the trees in the yard, and a gentle breeze was slowly wafting in from the lake and over the countryside.

I came down the stairs, and when I saw Roxie, I grabbed her, hugged her and said, "Good morning, Mother Dear."

"Boy, you must have had a good night."

"Mother, it's just so good to be here in our own home where I can look out at that beautiful backyard. It brings back so many memories. Dad and I used to plant our fall garden about this time of the year. We had such good times together. Now maybe one day my children will get married, and I just might be able to do the same thing with my children and grandchildren. I'm really looking forward to the day when that will happen."

"Jim, did you notice yesterday evening that Oscar had a man come in and break up the garden area so you and Johnny could plant a garden. You can teach Johnny what your father taught you about growing things. He was really good at being a small-time farmer, wasn't he?"

"Yes, he was, Mother."

Johnny and Jenny came down the stairs at the same time. They saw their father and grandmother smiling, and they wanted to know why.

"Well, I will tell you, kids. Your grandmother and I were just reminiscing about your grandfather and me planting our garden about this time of the year. It was so much fun to get our hands dirty when we planted, and then to watch the plants grow. There is no feeling like being able to pick your own tomatoes right off the vine. There's just nothing like it.

"Johnny, I'll let you help me plant a fall garden. How about it?"

"Fine, Dad, I would like that."

Pam was now coming down the stairs. She looked a little tired even after a good night's sleep.

"Jenny, you be sure to take her to Dr. Guzick's office this afternoon."

"Okay, Daddy, I'll see that she gets there."

After breakfast we men all headed for the plant for another meeting.

The girls hung around and had another cup of coffee. Jenny asked Angie if she could go over and look at her antique furniture again. Jenny was totally intrigued with that beautiful old furniture. Just as soon as they finished the coffee, they were ready to leave.

They turned to ask Pam if she would like to go with them, and she said, "I really don't think so. I'm still a little tired."

Jenny and Angie left to go to look at her new house's furniture.

At noon, Pam didn't eat much. She said that she really ate too much breakfast, and she just wasn't hungry. Once she did say that her stomach felt a little queasy and that she thought she might be getting a bug.

Just before lunch Angie and Jenny came back from across the back lot laughing and discussing some of the furniture. They were surprised that Pam didn't eat lunch since as Jenny said, "Mother, you didn't eat much breakfast either."

After lunch they talked for a while before Jenny told her mother that it was about time for them to go to the doctor's office.

When they arrived at the doctor's office, she was surprised at how much the doctor knew about her.

He just laughed and said, "I read about you in the newspaper. Well, Mrs. Dixon, or can I just call you Pam? What has been your problem?"

"Dr. Guzick, I have just been feeling tired and worn out most of the time, but I feel that it's because of the pace we worked while we were in Texas. I don't have as much of an appetite as I used to have, especially in the mornings."

"Well, young lady, I suggest we do a complete workup on you, and that will give us a good place to start. We can analyze what we find and take it from there. How do you feel about that?"

"I think that would be fine."

"Pam, I want you to meet my nurse, Carla.

"Carla, would you take Pam into the examining room and prepare her for a full examination. We will also want a blood study done, and we might need a sonogram. We want to cover all bases because a young lady your age should not be feeling tired all the time."

Carla took Pam into the examining room and got her a smock that, of course, opened in the back like all of those smocks did. She weighed Pam and took her blood pressure and pulse rate before the doctor came into the room.

He listened to her heart and chest first. He examined her from her head to her toe. When he was finished with his examination, he told Carla, "Get her dressed and take her downstairs and get a blood and urine test and have them do a sonogram while she is there. It won't take that much longer."

When Pam and Carla were gone, Dr. Guzick called Jenny into the room. "Jenny, I need to ask you a few questions about Pam. How long has she been feeling this way that you have noticed?"

"I'm not sure, doctor, but I first noticed it about three months ago when we were in Texas.

"When we first got there, she was on the run all the time doing something for Daddy's pet projects that he had started. After a while she began to look tired, and she seemed to want to rest more and more. She didn't seem to eat as much as she used to eat. She never complained, but she just seemed to slow down a 'little bit each week."

"That's what I wanted to know, Jenny. By the way, you have a very lovely mother now, and I hear that you guys get along famously."

"Yes, we do doctor. I consider her my mother, and we do love each other a lot."

Carla came back and told the doctor that Pam would be back in a while. "They are about ready to start the sonogram."

After about an hour, Pam came back to the office. "Dr. Guzick, how soon will you know something? I know you will find something because you guys have gone over me with a fine-tooth comb today, and if there is anything wrong, you will find it, won't you.?"

"Don't worry, Pam. We will call you in a day or two with the results of the tests."

Dr. Guzick says, "Jenny, you can take you mother home now and let her get some rest. I'll be in touch as soon as I have the results."

When they got home, they found that Angie and the new lady that Julia had found to help her had really been working hard. They had cleaned out all of the old staple goods in the kitchen like flour and cooking oils and other things and had now made a list of all the things they wanted in the kitchen, from salt to pancake mix, and from pepper to frozen steaks for the freezer.

It seemed that the freezer had a lot of meat and other things in it. Most of it was from old to very old, so they had just thrown it away.

It was just about time for us guys to come home from the plant. While Jenny and the other ladies were having a glass of tea, they heard the car doors close in the driveway, and they knew their men were home.

We men come in with big smiles and ask, "Is dinner ready?"

It seemed that they had really been accomplishing a lot at the plant today.

"Well, let me tell you guys what we have been doing," Angie said. "We have done a lot of cleaning and stocking up on goodies for our house. Now I am looking forward to our first real dinner in our own home.

"Pug, darlin', you will finally be able to find out what a good housewife your woman is."

"Hell, I already knew that. You don't have to prove anything to me."

"I know, Honey, but I want to prove to you that I really am a good cook."

"Sounds good to me."

Julia walked in and asked, "If anyone is hungry, I have a real good dinner prepared, and I want all of it eaten or I'll be hurt."

"Don't worry, Julia," Johnny said, "I'll eat all of mine. I don't want to make you feel bad."

Pug and I agreed.

With that Julia said, "Okay, be ready in fifteen minutes."

Julia was right; she did have a wonderful dinner for us. Roxie praised her for the meal as did the rest of us. Julia topped it off with one of those cherry cheesecakes and coffee. That made it just about the best ending to a good dinner that anyone could have asked for.

Friday morning Pam got a call from the doctor's office. It was Dr. Guzick himself. "Pam, do you think you can get Jim and the rest of the family and come into the office this afternoon after lunch? I feel this is something I want to discuss with all of you. I think I know what your problem is, and I want to talk to the family about it. Can you do that for me?"

"Yes, sir, I sure can, but is there something bad wrong? You sound very concerned. Is it something you can't tell me over the phone?"

"Well, Pam, let's just say that I feel it would be better if we discuss it with the whole family, including Roxie and the children, as well as you and Jim. I will see you this afternoon after lunch."

Pam called Roxie and Jenny and Angie and told them what the doctor had said. Roxie called me and told me that Johnny and I needed to come home so we could all go to the doctor's office right after lunch.

Angie said, "Roxie, have Jim bring Wayne also because they aren't going to leave us out of this, whatever it is. We're family too, and we want to be there."

That was just fine with Pam and Roxie. Jenny had a real strange worried look on her face as did Roxie, Angie, and Julia.

Julia told Oscar to have the limousine ready to take all of us to the doctor's office right after lunch. Oscar left to get the car ready.

The boys and I got home, but nobody seemed to be hungry for lunch. We just sat around and looked at each other or fidgeted around in our chairs. We swirled the ice around in our iced tea and put it down, and then we picked it up again.

Johnny finally said, "Dad, I'm going nuts; let's go to the doctor, and maybe he can see us early."

I looked at my watch, "Okay, everybody, let's get ready to go."

It sure didn't take us long to get ready this time. We were all out the door in a hurry. Oscar even seemed to drive a little faster than he normally drove.

We arrived at the office a little after 1:00 p.m., but it seemed a lot later than that to us.

When we walked in, it was like the office had been invaded. We filled up the waiting room, but we didn't have to wait long.

Carla said, "Would you all please come back to the doctor's conference room?"

We entered the conference room and had a seat.

Carla asked, "Would anyone like a Coke or a glass of water or something?"

We all declined.

Carla started to leave, but before leaving, she turned and told us that Dr. Guzick would be with us in just a few minutes. "He is on the phone right now, but as soon as he is off the phone, he will be right in."

The tension was awful. We sat and waited. It was so quiet we could actually hear each other breathing. We could have cut the tension in the air with a knife.

I finally broke the silence by saying, "I can't take a whole lot of this. I'm going crazy, and if he doesn't come in here pretty soon I'm gonna come totally unglued.

Johnny reminded me that I had always been the cool head in this family. "Now is the time for you to be cool and just wait like the rest of us, Dad. I'm sure Dr. Guzick will be here just as soon as he is off the phone."

It was quiet again. We could actually hear the doctor walking down the hall on the carpet. The door opened, and in came Dr. Guzick.

"Well," he said, "I see that everyone is here, even a couple I don't know."

I introduced Wayne and Angie, "Angie is like a sister to Pam, and Wayne is my best friend.

"Doctor, for God's sake, tell us something before we all go nuts."

"Jim, the news isn't all bad. The truth is there is no bad news at all, in my opinion."

Johnny was holding hands with Roxie on one side and Jenny on the other side. Angie was squeezing Wayne's hand so hard it was turning white.

Dr. Guzick began. "As you know, we did just about every test we could think of on Pam yesterday to find out why she is feeling so tired and weak much of the time. I hope you are all prepared for this – because I did find the problem.

"Jim, Pam, Roxie, kids, friends, are you sure you are all ready for this?"

"Hell, doctor, don't keep us in suspense. What is it?" I asked.

"Jim, Pam, I know this is going to be a total surprise, especially after what Pam told me about her past health history. You have to be well prepared for this.

"Jim, Pam, you are going to be parents."

Roxie, that means you are going to be a grandmother.

I must have been as white as a ghost, my knees felt weak, my stomach was queasy. "Are you sure of what you are saying?" I asked incredulously.

"Jim, I'm about as sure as any doctor can be because the sonogram just doesn't lie. ***You are going to be the proud parents of twins!***"

Printed in the United States
1422300002B/23

9 781414 027326